Demeter's Child

Demeter's Child

❖

The Chronicles of Patrick Brighton

-Book 1-

By

Jeffrey N. Snyder

To order additional copies of this book, contact:
Xlibris Corporation
1-888-795-4274
www.Xlibris.com
Orders@Xlibris.com
45753

CONTENTS

PART I—The Beginning of the End

PART II—Demeter's Path

PART III—Belial's Reach

First off, I would like to thank everyone that listened to my constant rants while I wrote this beast. You are definitely an exceptional group.

I would like to thank my parents (smile) for their constant help and understanding as I rambled on and on (and still do) about this endeavor. Some people aren't fortunate enough to have two good parents. I got lucky and ended up with four.

To Mike, Thanks again! And yes, I know . . .

To my one and only—Donna. Thank you for your daily dose of love. No one else puts up with me like you. No one else understands like you.

And finally, to the real "Patrick Brighton"—my son, Patrick. This one's for you, kiddo.

PART I—
THE BEGINNING OF THE END

CHAPTER 1

The Boy That Didn't Know Who He Was

"Mom, I'm home!" the boy announced automatically as he walked through the front door. He turned and pushed the door closed with his foot, and then casually leafed through the mail that had been put on the table underneath the 'last look' mirror in the front hallway. He was hoping to find the birthday card that his grandmother had sent with a few dollars in it that would continue to support his ever growing baseball card habit, but was disappointed when he found nothing with his name addressed on it amongst the "You may be the lucky Grand Prize Winner!", the Home Décor magazines, and the glossy, grocery store inserts.

He plopped the stack back down, took a step, and gave a toss of his backpack full of schoolbooks and schoolwork, the entire assortment landing with a thud next to the steps that led upstairs to his bedroom.

"Mom!" he repeated to the house as he walked down the hallway toward the kitchen, expecting the same response he received most every day, "I'm right here, hon. How was your day?"

This time, though, he received nothing in return.

She must be over at the Myers', he thought as he walked to the back side of the kitchen to peer out the window towards their neighbors' back porch. The boy, dressed in Koolaid green, baggy cargo pants, a black "Yes, I am Einstein" t-shirt, and white Converse tennis shoes, pushed himself up on the edge of the sink to get a look out the back kitchen window towards the Myers' house. He stood on tiptoes, but all that he managed to see was their freshly cut yard and an empty back porch. He pushed his uncombed black hair back from his face, and shrugged.

Oh well, he thought, I'm starved and thanks to that pain Mr. Davis I've got enough homework to keep me inside until dark.

The boy was unusually tall for 12, a good head above most of the 500 or so classmates at Juniper Grove Middle School, and had been tagged with the nickname 'Icabod' due to his gangly thin frame.

His growling stomach took his next movements to the refrigerator in search of something to snack on until dinner.

He walked past the kitchen table glancing at the place where someone had been sitting. His mom, he guessed. A glass of iced tea in a smiling sun glass was sitting next to a pale blue plate that held some kind of sandwich with one small bite taken out of it.

He pulled the refrigerator door open, the cool air billowing out to greet his face as he turned his attention back to his left.

Something wasn't quite right.

He looked back towards the table, past the unfinished food and drink, and then past the far end of the table to the back side of the kitchen.

There on the floor were the toaster, the marble rolling pin, and a loaf of Martins Blue Label sandwich bread, scattered and smashed over the hardwood floor. The slices of bread were tossed like someone had decided to play 52 card pick up. Small speckles of something that resembled jelly dotted the floor and had splattered against the white cabinets behind.

His hand and attention left the refrigerator as he walked towards the damaged area. He flicked on the overhead fluorescent light, a nervous kind of warmness coming over him with each small, silent step.

"Mom?" this time with concern and unanswered questions.

"Mom?!" he shouted as he looked down the connecting hallway, just off the back half of the kitchen that led into his parents bedroom. He ran over to the window to make sure that his mom's car was in the driveway. The emerald green Nissan Altima stood silent, just as it had when he passed it coming in.

He turned and quickly walked toward the bedroom, half expecting her to come around the corner laughing at his growing concern.

He cautiously entered his parent's bedroom due to the many times he had been scolded to "knock before entering" so he wouldn't see something he was sure he didn't want to see anyway.

"Hey, anyone there?" he asked, and then continued on into the room.

The bedroom seemed undisturbed with most everything arranged as it should be. He walked straight on through the bedroom to his parent's bathroom, with each step that he took his stomach churning as he half expected to find his mothers body in some stage of development that his mind wouldn't allow him to picture.

As he approached the bathroom he could feel the warm, humid air as if someone had just taken a hot shower. As he expected, towels hung in perfect lines from the towel bar. Nothing was amiss.

Where is she?

He turned and made his way back to the front of the house and towards the living room.

This is stupid, he thought, nothing is wrong. She's probably over the Myers'.

He gave one more, "Hey, anyone home?!" shout as he crossed back to the kitchen, and then exited out the back door that led across to the Myers' house.

After knocking and pounding on the Myers' back door, and then going around to the front and trying the same, he came to realize that no one was home. The boy jogged back over to the same door he had departed his house and pulled it closed behind him.

Upon seeing the unnerving scene in the kitchen again only one thought came to his mind.

Call dad.

That was the easiest thing—and the right thing—to do.

He walked over to where the phone hung from the wall and reached to pluck the ivory colored receiver when he heard a slight giggle come from the room on the other side of the wall he was facing.

He turned, took a step and asked quickly, "Mom? Is that you? Where are you?"

The giggle rose into a hoarse, throaty chuckle.

A queer, mocking voice came from the dining room just down the hall from the kitchen.

"Mommy! Oh, help me, Mommy! Where are you?"

"Who's there?" the boy asked timidly, shocked that someone else was in the house. He wanted to see, wanted to know who was over there, but his feet wouldn't move him from the kitchen.

Curiosity always killed that cat, he could hear his grandfather saying in the back of his mind.

His body screamed for him to flee like a deer sensing the danger of a nearby human, but his mind couldn't get the wheels in motion.

"Who are you? What do you want?" the boy forced the words forward, but wasn't sure he wanted an answer. "Where's my mom?"

Silence.

Or was that footsteps he heard.

The boy's head was just behind the edge of the doorway, sure that he couldn't be seen by whoever was in that direction. And he didn't want to look either. The brightness of the cheerful yellow paint in the kitchen reflected his, and all shadows, giving no cover. He had to force himself to breathe quietly as he felt his face and chest began to tighten with fear.

He tried to take a few carefully placed steps backwards to reposition himself closer to the back door, when he bumped hard up against the refrigerator door he had left open causing the rattling of pickle jars and ketchup bottles.

"I—hear—you," the intruder's venomous tone rang down the hall like a child's game declaration.

It wasn't a man's voice. It was a monsters voice—from lips and teeth that bite. The boy's fear was conjuring up images in his head from childhood nightmares and X-files episodes that his mother had told him not to watch. He could imagine an inviting, sharp toothed grin of a vampire as those words came forward from its lips.

There were two ways to get to the kitchen from inside the house. One was the way in which the boy had come, to move directly down the main hall from the front door that connected most rooms on the lower level. The other, was to circle back under the stairs in the front of the house and come through his dad's study, then into the hallway that led to his parent's bedroom. The same hallway he had went before to check for his mother.

His heart was thumping hard in his chest and his face tingled as if tiny needles were trying to break through. He ran a hand over his forehead, wiping the sweat as he braved the consequences and looked down the main hallway. He peered around the corner, feeling totally exposed, unsure of what to do even if he did see something.

Nothing. The hallway was empty.

He was about to take a step to bring himself into the hallway, when to his left he caught a shadow that was growing on the wall opposite his dad's study.

The boy turned and looked towards the back porch door, gauging the distance. He silently took a step into the main hallway, trying to hide himself from view if someone was coming through his father's study. The opposite of the kitchen, the muddy, dark walls of the hallway seemed to swallow the shadows.

He pressed his back firmly against the closest wall still giving him a view in three directions. He splayed his fingers out flat against the stringy fabric of the wallpaper, wishing he could be absorbed into its cover. It made him feel a little safer, a little more hidden from view.

He listened, but only heard the sound of his own small panting breaths, and his heart pounding in his head. He slowly brought his hand up to cover his nose and mouth to try and silence his noise.

He knew that he had only a moment to make the decision.

The back door, or the front?

"There you are!" the squirmy voice proclaimed as the boy saw a bony, discolored hand reach for him. He turned and instantly made a run for the front door, slapping the hand reaching for him as he bolted. He headed down the hallway at his fastest, sure that something was right behind him. Chasing him. Reaching for him. Going to grab him.

His hand extended for the door knob, his fingers wide for its grasp.

A sudden laugh came from his left, then a thumping on his chest as someone slipped their arm under his, wrapping itself around him, and then jerking him up and back away from his intended destination.

"No! Get away from me," the boy yelped as a soft, forceful hand then collapsed over his mouth restraining any more noise. The coils that the boy were in quickly tightened to a quite painful measure. The boy started to kick and thrash, trying to loosen himself from the unwelding grasp.

"Now, now, that's quite enough, young master!" the voice from behind said in a strong yet soothing manner. "I could snap your bones like brittle twigs, if allowed."

The man continued to tighten his grip around the boy's chest and mouth, pushing the boy to the point of almost loosing consciousness. The smell of the man's breath was putrid and unnatural, reminding the boy of rotting fish. They stood, locked in an embrace, with the weight of the man forcing the boy to reluctantly ease his struggling and allow himself to be dragged back into the kitchen.

The boy's view was brought around to see his capture. A man, not a vampire, was before him. He was tall and spindly, with an unshaven face, and small piercing gray eyes. His nose, unusually long and thin, was pierced and bent hard to the right, giving the impression of a bad beating in his life at one time or another. The man was not old, but seemed worn, as though his best days were already behind him.

The man's strength was not in question though, as he picked the boy up and tossed him like a toy across the kitchen floor, sending him sliding back against the cabinets just below the sink.

Sensing this might be an opportunity to once again make a break for it, the boy started to right himself and make another dash for the door.

The man, who was surprisingly quick in nature, already had deduced this, and raised his leg high in the air as if squashing a bug, firmly planting his booted foot into the chest of the boy.

The boy's head thumped back against the cabinet, and he gave an "Ow!" as his bony hip was pinched hard against the floor.

The man, his foot still on the boy's chest, grinned down at the boy and nodded, "Now stay put, won't you? I'd hate for us not to be friends. You seem like such a decent fellow.

"The name's Tye in case you're curious. But that won't do you any good to worry over for the moment, seeing that you're not going to be able to speak it to anyone any time soon."

The boy looked up at the man and wondered who he was. Should he know him?

"Why are you doing this?" the boy asked, stunned and confused. "And where's my mom? Because if you've hurt her . . ." his voice trailed off in weak display of bravado.

He reached up and grabbed Tye by the ankle, trying to push it off his chest. "And can you please get your foot off me!? It hurts!"

Tye seemed amused. "About the second part—no, I don't think so. You're right where I want you, my little toad. As for the first part . . . Oh, she's fine. Alive," he said as he seemed to wonder aloud to himself, "At least, I think she is. I threw her down the basement steps. Would you like to go see?" And he waved his arm towards the basement door as would a game show host, directing your gaze to the winning prize.

The boy became enraged. "I'm going to kill you!" he lurched forward and screamed, his tearing eyes wild and unfocused. He scratched and punched at the man's leg hoping for any release.

With whip like quickness Tye snatched the liquid dishwashing soap from the kitchen sink, reached down and jammed the dispenser into the boy's mouth, squirting in a mouthful.

"I think that will be enough of that, eh?" Tye said through yellowed, Grinch-like teeth.

The boy turned and tried to spit most of it out, but the ferocity with which the soap had been driven into him caused him to swallow most, making him gag and cough with repulsion.

As the boy writhed and gasped under his foot, Tye calmly washed his hands in the sink above, acting as though he was completely unaware of what was taking place with the boy below. He reached for a dish towel to dry his hands, dripping water down that landed with stark coldness into the boy's open eyes and mouth.

"Ok, ok, enough with the show. You're going to live," Tye replied as though he was bored.

The boy, trying to rinse his mouth with his own saliva (and still spitting) brought his lips together to form a repulsive word, thought better of it, and let his head come down to rest on the hardwood floor.

"Very good, then. You're a quick learner."

The boy stared up at Tye, noticing the peculiar way in which the man was dressed. It was more than just odd, the boy thought, thinking that he had seen something similar before, but he just couldn't place it. The man wore an old, lime green jacket with a dirty, pink turtleneck underneath. His hair was pulled up and back away from his face, held in place with some sort of glistening gel. The jacket was decorated not with a real flower, but rather with a picture of a sunflower taped to the jacket's lapel.

The boy's mind cleared for a moment, and his eyes widened.

"You look like the Joker," the boy said directly.

This seemed to anger the man to an unexpected degree.

"What?! I do not look like anything other than what I look like, understand?!" the man said through pursed lips. "The 'Joker'? What is the 'Joker'? Do you mean that I look like a clown? A Jokester? Is that what you're saying, my little reptile?"

He bent down and flicked the boy's forehead hard with his finger.

"Hey, that hurt!" the boy exclaimed as he brought his hands up to his head.

Tye picked up a pot from the sink and peered into it, looking at his reflection.

He shook his head quickly, "Frankly, I just don't see it. My hair is not red. My skin does not possess the color of glue. My facial expressions are not locked in a perpetual look of amusement. Just because my features are askew in a rigid sort of way, and I prefer, shall we say a more colorful blend of attire? Please."

The man then smiled at himself in the reflecting pot, "Though I must say, I am quite a catch." He then dropped the pot onto the boy below with a 'clang.'

"Ok, then," Tye began as he reached down and quickly snatched the boy up by the front of his shirt, slamming him down in one of the wooden kitchen chairs.

"You and me, we're going to have a little chat. You tell me what I want to hear and I won't break any of your teeth. You lie—and I have a gift for knowing when little boys lie—then I start breaking little pieces off with these." From his right front jacket pocket he pulled out a pair of red handled pliers.

Tye moved in real close to the boy and grinned, "And I'm not joking."

The boy's eyes locked onto the pliers as if they were alive, watching their every move.

Tye pulled up another chair and sat down.

"I'm not telling you anything," the boy said defiantly, his eyes meeting Tye's.

"Now you see," Tye pointed a finger, "that wouldn't be in your—or your mothers—best interest. Since I've already put her down there in that nasty position, it would take nothing for me to go back down there and finish the job."

Tye leaned back in the chair.

"But, it's your call."

The boy turned and looked towards the basement door. His mind screamed at him to do something—anything to help his mom—but there was just nothing he could do. He had become so paralyzed with fear at what this mad man in front of him would really do if he became outraged, that he couldn't think clearly enough to put any cohesive thoughts together of escape. All the advice and lessons that he was given when he was younger as to what to do when confronted by a stranger, all lay silently in some vacant back corner of his mind.

"Is my mom ok?" he asked, his voice breaking with worry.

"She's fine. Stop worrying about her. Start worrying about yourself. You're the reason I was sent here."

What?!

"Me? Why me? What did I do?"

"It's not what you did, kid. It's what they think you're going to do."

"Who?"

"Hmmm, I think I'll just snap off that sparkling white tooth right there in front."

With that, the boy pulled his head back and sucked in his lips, remembering the man's instructions.

"Speak when spoken to and we'll get along fine."

The boy held still. And silent.

"Ok then, first, there are some things I've just got to know right off, you follow?"

A somewhat defeated, small nod come forward from the boy.

Tye leaned back, eyeing the boy from head to toe.

"You don't look like something anyone should be making so much fuss over," he sighed as he shook his head, "but, then what do I know? I'm just doing what I was told. And remember, any more funny business and my little companion here is going to be put to work," he said as he snapped the pliers twice in front of the boy's nose.

The man leaned in close to the boy, his head cocked to the side.

"Ok, first question. You ready?"

The boy barely nodded his head in the affirmative.

"Have you had any bad dreams lately? Anything disturbing? Or unusual?" the man's eyes adjusting to tiny slits of blackness as he asked.

The boy methodically shook his head from side to side. He wanted to jump up and start throwing punches at the man, but was terrified of the response if he did.

"You notice anyone in the neighborhood out of the ordinary?" Tye's eyebrows arched as he asked.

The boy stared at the small, green, crusty specks of "sleepy-ness"—as his dad would call it—that had nestled into the corners of Tye's eyes. At the white, caulk-like spittle in the corner of Tye's mouth.

Again, he shook his head.

"Make any new friends lately?" Tye asked absently.

Again, no.

"You are Patrick Brighton, correct?"

This time the boy nodded slowly, purposefully.

The man sighed, stood up, and then started to frisk him as would a cop patting down a suspect.

"I don't get it," Tye uttered with a twinge of disgust. "They're making all this fuss over you?! For what reason?" he asked as he shook his head. "You're really kind of pathetic."

Suddenly, Patrick noticed something fluttering outside of the smallish widow next to the cupboard to the right of the sink causing a shadow to dance helter-skelter about the brightly lit room. Tye caught the image as well out of the corner of his eye, and jumped back as if he was frightened.

"Oh, hell, what do you want?" Tye said to something unseen by Patrick.

A soft bell-like response came from just outside the glass. Patrick couldn't tell if it was a man or a woman's voice as it spoke. He crooned his head and neck to see, but remained seated for fear of Tye's swift response.

"You must be quick. The time to go is at hand," the voice said from outside. Patrick noticed that the voice, though soft, was commanding in its tone. "Your personal interest is of no need at this time. You are to do as you are told. Take the boy and go."

Tye rolled his eyes and threw his arms up in disgust.

"Good Grief! Don't you get it! I don't understand you, you twit! I don't know what you're saying! I NEVER know what you're saying!"

Patrick's attention quickly went from the window to Tye and then back. He was bewildered at Tye's response.

Huh?! How could you not understand what they just said? You're the twit!

"Go away! Leave! Be gone!" Tye shouted at whatever it was outside the window. Annoyed, Tye angrily shook his head, turned and picked up the drinking cup from the table and flung it at the window. The ice from the cup cracked like marbles against the glass, startling Patrick greatly.

What is going on?! Patrick's mind screamed at him. Please! I just want my mom! Where's my dad?! He bit down on his lip to keep from screaming.

Tye removed the water sprayer from its position at the back of the sink, turned the water on, and began spraying the window. Water spit and spattered in all directions.

"Go AWAY!" Tye barked irritatingly.

Due to the lunatic's behavior, Patrick began to seriously question the man's sanity. It was as if Tye was teetering on the brink of a full scale meltdown. On one hand he talked with the cunning of a cat, making Patrick believe that the man was even more dangerous than he let on. But on the other hand, he was now acting like the old madman down at the park who yelled and threw bottles at the squirrels. Patrick began to seriously fear for his life, and he had no idea what he should do to calm the man down.

Finally, perplexed, Patrick could stand no more.

"What are you doing?! What don't you understand?" Patrick interjected, wide eyed as he looked queerly at Tye. "All that they said was that it was time to go, I think. Or something like that."

Tye's animated behavior of just a few seconds ago turned to stony, frozen silence as he took a careful step backwards—and then stopped.

"You heard what it said?" he asked, cocking his head in the direction of the boy.

Patrick gave an unsure nod, hoping that he had answered correctly.

Tye smiled proudly and danced a quick little jig, finally coming to a graceful kneeling position at Patrick's feet.

He lowered his eyes toward Patrick with a menacing, wicked glare, resembling a cat just before it was to pounce on a fat, juicy mouse, and hissed, "I am honored, my dear sir. You are the indeed the lad I have come for after all."

What did I do?!

Tye, quick as a snake, got down to his business as he placed one knee into Patrick's chest to keep him in place, and swiftly brought out two plastic wire like objects from his pocket. "Ty-wraps" Patrick's father had called them. Patrick had seen his father use them to secure wiring in the basement, and for bundling objects that he didn't want to get loose.

Tye then stood and went around behind Patrick, reaching and pulling the boy's arms back. He secured the plastic bands around his wrists with a small grunt that made Patrick lose his breath for a moment at the pain they caused. He could feel his skin tear as the abrasive plastic was pulled quick and taunt.

For bundling objects that he didn't want to get loose.

"What did I do? Tell me! What is it that I'm going to do?" Patrick pleaded, hoping for any morsel of information—trying to focus his thoughts. If he was going to get out of this he was going to have to start thinking his way out of the situation. Due to the advantage Tye had over him strength wise, he definitely wasn't going to out muscle the man.

"Sorry lad, question and answer time is now over. We've got to move."

Tye grabbed Patrick by the hair, jerked him up and out of his seat, and shoved him towards the back door. "Let's go."

Patrick turned sharply to look back towards the window to catch a glimpse of who was out there, but saw nothing but the robust, leaf filled trees gently flowing in the breeze. His mind went back towards the basement door, awash with a sickening helplessness in fear for his mother.

Tye led him outside with his left hand tightly around the back of Patrick's neck, and in his right hand holding the remote to Patrick's mother's car. As Tye pushed the button on the remote for the trunk it automatically popped open with a small 'thunk.' Before Patrick was even aware what was taking place, Tye hurriedly lifted him up and then firmly stuffed him down and into the trunk. Tye uttered a final "Ta-ta!" and slammed the trunk shut.

That's when Patrick had enough and started to thrash about, screaming "NO!" over and over, hoping that someone, anyone, would hear him.

He could feel Tye quickly getting into the drivers side as the car rocked from his movement. The Altima was started, a silent thud was felt as it settled into gear, and then the car started going backwards out of the driveway.

Though in complete darkness and total distress, Patrick tried hard to think how he could get out. He remembered that the middle section of the back seat folded down, so he twisted his body around and started to kick hard against the thick, black cloth and metal frame. He knew that once out of his neighborhood, since they lived so far out in 'farm country,' that no one would ever hear his screams for help if someone didn't hear him by the time the car passed through the brick columned entrance of his subdivision.

But it was of no use. Patrick could feel the car slowing as it approached the entrance, and then turning right as it merged onto Kimbletown Road.

Patrick turned on his side, and with a painful effort, looped his bound hands under his feet, bringing them around to his front to free himself to some degree.

He continued kicking the rear backseat frame as the car sped up faster and faster, listening as the tires hummed against the road. The car traveled another ten seconds, the Altima constantly accelerating, when Tye slammed on the brakes sending both of Patrick's knees crashing into the backseat frame, and his face into his knees. Patrick's chin felt like it had been cracked in two. His top left, front tooth popped from its spot, and neatly found a place on his tongue. He started to groan from the pain, coughing hoarsely as he cupped his hands together as he spit the tooth out, wondering how he would ever be able to put it back in it's place.

Patrick listened as Tye got out of the car, walked around, and opened the trunk.

"Listen you little crapper, if you don't stop it I'll crack a rib or tear a tendon on you that'll hurt so bad—and will never leave a mark. I'll have you in so much pain that you'll whimper with every breath. And believe me when I tell you that I am an expert at distributing pain. Is that what you're after, eh?"

Patrick wiped his mouth with his palm, his tearing eyes looking up at his captor. Upon seeing the red on his hand, Patrick puckered his lips and spit a mouthful of blood-tinged saliva that landed on the front of Tye's jacket just below the flower.

"My dad's going to kill you," Patrick said coldly, his fears now slowly burning to anger.

But Tye didn't move, instead staring blankly down at the boy in the trunk as the boy smiled a bloody, vengeful smile back up at him. Patrick sensed that Tye was keeping his distance, now unsure of just what he might try and do.

"Alrighty then," Tye said somberly, looking down at the boy's red stained grin.

He shook his head slowly, pulled a handkerchief from his pocket, and began wiping the thick, red spittle off of his jacket.

"You have no idea what's coming down the track for you, Master Brighton," Tye smiled nervously. "I can wash my jacket. Sure. No problem. But you, little man, are you going to be able to wash away the pain and suffering that you're about to endure? Because you have no idea what true pain really is—but you're about to. Now think about that for the next two hundred miles." And with those final, dangerous words still sitting on the air Tye slowly closed the trunk until it locked again

Patrick started crying and slamming his fists against the carpeted interior even more ferociously than he had before, feeling as if the lid of his coffin had just been shut.

The words came back to him like a knife in the dark.

"It's not what you did, kid. It's what they think you're going to do."

CHAPTER 2

Exposure

Dan Brighton sat silently in his driveway behind the steering wheel of his Black Ford F150, stunned by what he was hearing. He sat, listening to the radio as he had done all the way home from work, consumed by what the news reporters were telling him. A few times, as he sat at an intersection waiting for the light to change, he'd put his window down, asking the person in the vehicle next to him if they were listening to the same news that he was. Most acknowledged that they were, either uttering a, "I can't believe it," or "What the hell is going on?" and then would quickly put their windows back up due to simple paranoia. Others wouldn't even look in his direction, Dan noting that they must already have heard, and out of fear were not going to expose themselves any more than they had too.

Not from Dan Brighton.

But from what the news was relaying to them over the airwaves.

Dan looked up from the digital face on the radio, focusing on his house before him. He wondered if his wife Pam, or his son Patrick, had been listening to the news and were already up on the story, or was he going to have to break it to them? That wasn't going to be easy. Surely Pam's mother or father had called to talk to them about what was taking place. Someone must of told them by now. Becky, next door, perhaps.

Dan shook his head, and then shut off the engine. He got out of the truck and looked skyward, wondering exactly what he might be breathing, and then moved purposely up the walk to the front door.

From a distance, Dan Brighton looked like a man of some size. He was tall, but not particularly large, carrying himself in a way that quickly made anyone who came upon him forget that he was six foot five. He was thin, but not frail, and had always been disappointed in his looks. His hair, a ridiculously premature color of gray (an almost white) was pulled back tight from his head in a short, curling pony tail. His teenage years had left his face with numerous scars that no prescription creams, or magic ointments, had seemed to clear up. Over the past few years though, he had learned to release some of the unease he felt about himself, and learned not to believe everything you see in the mirror.

"Pam?" he called out as he went through the door, hoping she wasn't already fixated in front of CNN. He went to the living room and found the television turned off. He put his hand on the screen, finding it cold to the touch.

"Pam?" he tried again. "Patrick?"

He left the room, noticing his son's scarlet and black backpack at the foot of the steps in front of him. Dan frowned, shaking his head at the little black and white skull and crossbones sticker plastered to its side. He turned down the hall and headed towards the kitchen.

"Hey, where are you guys at? Anyone home?"

He was trying to remember if there was some place that they told them they were going to be after school, wondering if he was wasting his breath looking for them, when the scene in the kitchen exploded into view.

"What the hell happened?" he asked to no one as he made his way into the ruptured kitchen.

The overturned chairs, the scattered objects on the floor, the shattered window—all giving him pause.

"Pam? Patrick?" this time louder as his body started in the direction of his bedroom, his eyes still locked onto the scene in the kitchen.

Finding the bedroom and bath untouched Dan moved back down the hallway. He dashed through his study and raced over the steps to the upstairs, repeatedly calling his wife's and his son's names, hoping for any response.

The upstairs—two spare bedrooms, a bonus room, and Patrick's bedroom—were cold and silent, mocking him as if they knew what had taken place, but weren't about to tell.

He went back downstairs, snapping his cell phone off the clip on his hip as he walked to the garage to see if his wife's car was there. The Altima was gone, and he knew that he hadn't seen it when he pulled in, so he quickly punched in her cell number to find her. His concern was growing, and if someone didn't tell him what had happened pretty soon he was going to have to assume the worst and call the police.

He jumped, startled when he heard her cell phone start ringing from behind him. He turned and located his wife's purse and phone sitting on the desk in the corner of the kitchen. His worst thoughts began to come to the surface. Pam never left without her cell phone—or her purse. She was a real estate agent, and her cell phone was one of her most important points of contact. To hear it ringing, and see it vibrating in front of him like an excited toy, left Dan at a complete loss.

What in God's name happened here?

Dan knelt and delicately touched the still wet redness dotted over the cabinets with the fingertips. He rubbed it between his fingers and then tasted it to be sure. It definitely was blood.

But who's? Either his wife, or his son—and neither was part of the equation he wanted to consider.

He dialed 911, but to his surprise found it was busy.

He pulled the phone away from his ear like it had bit him. He stared at it, shocked.

How can that be? 911 is never supposed to be busy.

He tried it again, but got the same result.

He stood, but didn't know what to do. He slowly looked around the room and then made his way over to the refrigerator to push the door closed. He picked up the chairs and settled them back underneath the table, then absently walked over to the basement door, noticing that it was slightly ajar. He reached to push the door closed, only touching the doorknob lightly, when a feeling of dread fell over him. His shoulders sagged.

No.

He clutched the knob, threw the door open, and saw what he hoped he wouldn't. There was Pam, still dressed as when he left her that morning—white t-shirt and gray sweatpants, lying at the bottom of the steps like an unused doll tossed in a heap.

Dan took the steps three at a time getting down to her, holding his breath, wondering if she was even alive.

Her unpleasant position made Dan feel outraged—and helpless.

One arm was awkwardly pinned back under her body, her shoulder surely separated. The other was bruised, a brutal purple and black spider web that extended along her forearm and elbow. Her legs and hips twisted, like she had been corkscrewed down to the basement floor, her bare feet resting against the bottom two steps. No sign of blood was evident other than the slight bleeding that was coming from her left temple.

"Pam?" he spoke barely above a whisper.

She attempted to say his name, but it came out low and guttural, as if her tongue was stuck to the roof of her mouth.

"Oh, thank God," he said as he cradled her head softly.

Her eyes fluttered, and then closed again, wincing from the pain.

"No, don't move. I don't know exactly what's happened to you, Pam, but you're not looking too good," a little, anxiety filled chuckle escaped from him. "I don't want you to move till someone takes a look at you."

Her lips curled slightly into a faint smile, and then surprisingly, said, "I hurt."

"I know. I know. Just lay still, please."

Dan looked down upon his now broken wife, his heart breaking. He knew that if she was in pain, then it was bad. Pam had been an endurance runner most of her adult life. He could see her tiny body suiting up every morning for her daily runs, covering hills and terrain that made others squeamish at the thought of the toll that it would take on their body. With the rigid and intense training that she had put herself through the years to achieve her goals, it had made her able to withstand a lot more pain than the average Joe. Blisters, sunburn, and snake bites—she had gone through them all. Always commenting that she wasn't good enough yet, continuing to push herself harder.

"I'm still me, until I'm better than me," was her mantra.

She was as tough as piano wire.

That caused Dan to be even more weary at the state she was in now.

Dan grabbed his cell phone and hit redial again, almost throwing it across the room when he heard the busy signal come across.

"What is going on!" he screamed.

Pam coughed, and then asked slowly, "What's wrong? I . . . I mean besides me."

"911 is busy. I didn't even know that they could be busy. I thought there was a law or something."

And then it dawned on him. But that couldn't be true. Not yet. Not now. It was only supposed to be spreading as far as the upper Midwest.

Not here. Not yet.

"What happened, Pam? How did you fall down the steps? Did you slip or something?"

Her tongue parted her lips for moisture, her speech coming in low rasps.

"I didn't fall. I was pushed."

"What? Who pushed you?"

"Someone came into the house," she began to sob. "A man. He beat me up, Dan. He threw me down the steps."

"Who? Do you know who it was?"

She shook her head and mouthed the word, "No."

Pam turned her head towards Dan, her face contorting into panic.

"Oh, God," she could barely get the words out of her mouth, "where's Patrick?"

"I don't know. I just assumed that he'd be with you. And, when I saw you . . ."

He hit redial again, but this time the busy signal didn't sound. Instead, a low, slow aural tone, one that Dan didn't recognize, came over the speaker. There was a hard 'click,' and then a woman's voice answered.

"Marion County Sheriff's Department."

"Hello, is this 911? I'm trying to call 911. I have an emergency."

"This is the Marion County Sheriff's Department, sir. They're having some technical difficulties over at the other dispatch. A 'system overload' is what they're telling me. Your call was redirected to us. Now, how can I help you? What is your emergency?"

System overload?

"Dan," Pam desperately clutched his arm, "where's Patrick? You've got to find him! I think the man wanted Patrick!"

Dan turned his attention back to the dispatcher. "Yes, it's an emergency! Someone has broken into our house. They beat up my wife. She looks bad. She's in a good deal of pain. Can you please send an ambulance? She needs one as soon as possible!"

"Yes, sir. Sir, I see you're at 263 Timberlake Trail, just west of Mt Jackson, correct?"

"Yes, that's right. Please, hurry."

"Yes, sir," she paused. "Give me a moment."

Dan reached over and began smoothing back the hair from his wife's face.

"Sir?" the dispatcher came back on the line.

"What? Oh, yes . . . you're sending paramedics?"

"No, sir. I'm sending a patrolman at this time. We are having . . ."

"What?! She doesn't need a patrolman. What's wrong with you? She needs medical attention, she needs a paramedic."

"Sir, as I was saying, we are having difficulty locating an available paramedic unit at this time. They all seem to be dispatched. I am sending a patrolman who will be in constant communication with us as to when an available EMT can be sent your way."

"What?! But that's insane, there's got to be . . . ," but Dan's voice drifted away with his swift realization.

There aren't any available paramedics at this time.

But then, where could they all be?

Dan knew the answer, but he just couldn't accept it.

"Ok," was all that Dan could reply to the dispatcher, his head now swimming with all sorts of scenarios that he didn't dare share with Pam. He lowered the phone from his ear, the dispatcher at the Sheriff's Department still talking on the other end.

Dan's focus now shifted.

He knew that the Altima was gone. He knew that Patrick had come home. He now knew that someone had come into the house and beat up his wife. And now Patrick was gone.

"Babe, let me go upstairs and see if I can find him. He's got to be here somewhere. Maybe he's just out playing, and didn't realize what had happened to you," Dan lied. "Stay still a minute. Don't move. I'll be right back."

"Dan," she started to sob, not letting go of his arm.

"There's no one else here Pam, I promise. Whoever it was is gone."

She seemed to calm at his words.

"Are you going to be ok while I go look? I'll be right back, I promise. You're going to be ok."

Dan made his way back to the front door, trying to gather his thoughts, awaiting the arrival of the patrolman.

He knew that Patrick was either hurt somewhere just as Pam was, or that the man had taken Patrick. The last thought wouldn't register.

Don't let it be that. Please, God, no.

Dan began to randomly scout through the house again, then the backyard and surrounding areas, hoping to find Patrick no matter what condition he might find him in. He had to be quiet for fear of alarming Pam. As he looked his mind began playing the scenarios.

If Patrick had been taken, he was a pretty tough kid. He had some fight in him. He was pretty mature for his age, and handled himself well in most situations. But this? This was totally out of the context to expect anyone to handle. Hopefully he wasn't drugged, or beaten unconscious. Maybe he got a few good shots in on whoever took him.

And where would they go?

Dan remembered the Altima—and the Randomguard feature. It was an anti-theft device. A GPS—Global Positioning System—that was used to track the car in case it was stolen, or if you had gotten lost and needed to know directions from where your position was by satellite. And no one would know that the car had it installed except for him and Pam.

He uttered a silent "Thank God" at remembering his purchase—and at his remembering that he even had it. He scrolled down the list of numbers on his phone, finally locating the Randomguard number.

Much to his relief he didn't hear a busy signal, but instead was instantly connected to a cheery, youthful sounding woman named Michele.

"Thank you for calling Randomguard—where your car is under complete . . ."

"Uh, thanks. Michele, is it?" Dan cut her off.

"Yes, how can I help you," she replied, still sounding like a cheerleader during pep week.

"I have an emergency," Dan began calmly, trying to control his fears. "I need to locate my car. It may have been stolen."

"Oh, no," she sounded truly concerned. "Ok, let me get the last four digits of your vehicle identification number and your password, and we'll see what we come up with."

A silver and dark blue patrol car had just turned the corner and was coming down the street towards their house. Dan put a hand up to make sure he knew where to stop.

"Sir?" Michele was still waiting for his information.

"Oh, yes. 5481. And, my pin is . . ." but he couldn't remember. He agonized a moment as he tried to remember the number, fumbling for his wallet to see if he had written it down and placed it in there.

"Give me a moment, Michele. The sheriff's department just showed up."

The patrolman got out of his car, his hand automatically going to rest on his sidearm. He was an older man, his glasses sitting on the bridge of his nose like Santa looking at his Christmas list. Dan had expected someone younger for some reason, and he was surprised to see this plump little fellow moving his way.

Dan extended his hand, with the officer accepting his hello.

"I understand there's an injured woman inside," the deputy began.

"Yes, my wife. Through the front door, down the hall and to the right. The basement—she's down there."

"Sir, you should probably come with me," he said, his arm extended, implying for Dan to take the call another time.

Dan shook his head, trying to stay calm. "I'm trying to track my car. I think it was stolen. My son may have been kidnapped with it."

The deputy's complexion instantly changed from one of suspicion, to a now truer sense of concern. He reached for his walkie talkie and immediately called in to the dispatcher.

Dan watched as Deputy Barnes (he got that off of the man's name plate) explained to his dispatch that the situation had drastically changed, and that he was now going to need some help.

"Sir, any luck with that password?" Michele responded, still sounding patient.

"Uh, give me a moment, there's too much going on right now. I'm sorry—just give me a second to think."

The deputy turned back towards Dan.

"Sir, do you know what the tag number is for the missing car? Also, the make, model, and color of the car? I'm going to need a description of your son as well. A picture would help."

Dan quickly gave him the information requested, pulling a recent picture of his son from his wallet.

Deputy Barnes forwarded the information on to the dispatcher. After a few moments of back and forth communication with his dispatch, Dan watched as the deputy suddenly became silent, staring down at his feet as if he had just lost something.

Dan wasn't all that great at reading body language, but what he was picking up now from the deputy made him wonder as to what was going wrong.

The deputy sighed as he made his way back over to where Dan was standing.

"Unfortunately, at the moment, I seem to be the only available patrol in the area. Maybe the entire county. Things are starting to get out of control. I'm sure you're aware of what's going on? Have you watched the news?"

Dan looked towards the light clouds that were moving lazily across the sky.

"Yeah, I've heard. But I didn't think that it was here already."

"I don't believe that it is, sir. Unfortunately, it seems most people aren't realizing that, and they aren't acting as you would hope in a situation like this."

Dan could only imagine the message that the deputy was trying to get across. If they couldn't send a paramedic, if they couldn't send any other deputies to help, then total chaos must be ensuing in the other parts of the county.

"Well . . ." Dan started to the deputy, "hold on . . ."

"Michele?"

"Yes?"

"It's chocolate."

"Ok, chocolate. Thank you. Just give me a moment to put a track in place."

"Well," Dan continued, "what do we do? I'm starting to feel sick. My son is gone. Oh, God, what is going on? My wife . . . my wife is a mess in our house. She doesn't even know about our son. I need someone to help me."

The deputy nodded in a sympathetic manner. "First, know that we're going to try and contact every available patrolman from state and local municipalities to help look for your son. But I'm not going to lie to you. I don't know who they've got available. Things are not going well out there." The deputy gave a slight motion with his head, as if he was motioning to the rest of the world.

That's when Dan first noticed it. He looked up and down the street, amazed that there wasn't anyone else outside besides himself and the deputy. Not a single soul. With a Sheriff's department vehicle sitting in the driveway, surely one of his neighbors would be curious enough to come out and inquire as to what was taking place.

In fact, the more he began to notice, he couldn't even see any animals as well. No dogs. No cats. He couldn't even hear any birds chirping. There seemed not to be any noises at all. It was if he was living in a vacuum. It gave Dan an eerie, creepy feeling as he felt incredibly alone and isolated.

Some of his neighbors had to be in their houses, of that he was pretty sure, but they were either tied to their televisions trying to keep up with news that was breaking, or peering out of their windows, not wanting to leave the safe confines of their homes.

Dan jumped as Deputy Barnes put a hand on his shoulder.

"Let's go take a look at your wife. Let's try to make her as comfortable as possible. That's all we can do for the moment."

Dan let out a sigh, then nodded in agreement, his heart dying for his son.

They began to head towards the house when the sound of an approaching vehicle caused them to turn and see a red and white Conner's Ambulatory Care van pull up along the curb.

"Thank God," Dan sighed as the paramedics got out and began to approach him.

He led the paramedics and the deputy into the house, down to where Pam was located, and watched as they began to examine her, their gentle hands trying to alleviate her discomfort as best they could.

The deputy stepped back into the kitchen, talking on his walkie talkie about something Dan couldn't make out.

"How you doing, babe?" Dan asked, feeling as if he should be doing something other than just standing around. He wanted to tell her about Patrick. He wanted someone to share his awful feeling with. But he couldn't do it to her now.

Pam nodded slightly; her pain seemed to be overwhelming her.

Just then Dan realized that his cell phone was still connected to Randomguard, and dangling by his side. He quickly raised it to his ear.

"Hello? Michele? You still there?"

"Yes, Mr. Brighton, I'm still here. I can hear what's been going on. The microphone picks up quite a bit. I just want to say that I'm sorry for what's happening to you."

"Did you find the car?"

"Yes. I was trying to get your attention, but understandably you were preoccupied. The car is moving North, Northwest from your address, approximately a hundred or so miles away. It's nearing a small town called Reedy, West Virginia, just off state highway fourteen."

"That's not that far away," Dan said, surprised.

"Ok," Michele replied. "We're in Atlanta, but I've alerted the West Virginia state patrol, and they should be pursuing the vehicle very shortly."

"If they have anyone to do the pursuing," Dan uttered under his breath.

"Yes, sir," Michele said. "Actually there's quite a few people missing from work today, even down here. I don't know. I just can't believe it's as bad as they're reporting. Some people are saying that it's the end of the world."

"You know what is going on then? Sure you would," Dan said, answering his own question. "It's not like it's a government secret anymore. It's the only thing anyone is talking about."

Deputy Barnes called down to Dan, asking him to come up to the kitchen.

"Thanks, Michele. I've got to go. You've been a great help."

"Good luck, and God Bless, Mr. Brighton. You'll get your son back. He'll be ok."

Dan closed his phone and quickly went up to see what the deputy wanted, hoping that they might have found his son.

"You hear something?"

"No, sir. But, since the paramedics are here, I'm being sent to another area."

"You're leaving? Isn't anyone going to check out the area? This is a crime scene for God's sake! You can't just leave."

"I realize that, but the situation is getting worse at some of the more populated areas. They're calling for all available bodies. I have to go. Your wife is being attended to. As soon as someone has been freed up, we're going to return and address the situation—if we can. My dispatch has informed me that your car has been tracked into West Virginia, and that they have two state patrolmen heading in that direction."

The paramedics where coming up the steps with Pam strapped onto a stretcher, the wheels clacking against the steps as they went. Dan and the deputy moved to the far end of the kitchen.

"Sir," the deputy began, his voice barely above a whisper. "Your wife is in capable hands. There is nothing more you can do here."

The deputy began to rub his hand along his chin, his eyes dancing like he was contemplating his next choice of words.

"What's wrong?" Dan asked. "Something's bothering you."

Deputy Barnes took a deep breath.

"Well, sir, ordinarily I'm not one to go telling other people how to handle their affairs. But if it were my son, forgetting that I work for law enforcement and all, and I knew that he was only a relatively short distance away . . . well, I'd go after him. With what is taking place, and that none of us knows what's really going on, I'm not so sure I could just sit around and wait for a phone call from someone in hopes that he might be found. If you know where he is heading—if you have a way of tracking him—I'd go get him. You might be his only hope. I'd hate to think that I didn't do everything I could to get my son back." He nodded. "I'm not telling you what to do, you understand, but I think that you still have some time."

Dan returned his nod, but not feeling totally comfortable with what had just been exchanged between the two of them.

"I know that they've quarantined a good bit of the upper Midwest," the deputy finished, "but you should be able to make your way through to most of the areas you need. And, I'd make sure I took along one of these," the deputy added as laid his hand gently on his gun.

Dan began to feel a sickness rise up inside, pounding at him with a fear and confusion like he never had before. This wasn't something that an officer of the law was supposed to be telling someone. Not anyone. Not like this. He was supposed to assure you that the sheriff, the police, or whoever, were doing all that they could, and for you to rest easy. That they would get back to you with word as soon as something developed. They were supposed to be the heroes. They weren't supposed to tell you that it was up to you now. That there might not be anyone else out there that could help to try and save your son.

Dan began to realize that the deputy was probably only telling him this because he most likely couldn't be sure himself. How did he—how did anyone—truly know if there was actually someone going after Patrick. Was there anyone left to go after Patrick?

The deputy stepped aside and held the door open for the paramedics as they wheeled Dan's wife out of the house and towards the rescue van.

Dan walked behind them, quickly catching up with Pam, taking her hand.

"Dan?"

"Relax, I'm right here."

"Did . . . you find Patrick?" she asked, the medicine they had given her for the pain was causing her words to come out slow and slurred.

"Yes, hon. Try not to talk."

He watched as they loaded her into the back of the van. The older paramedic, before he closed the door, turned to Dan and asked if he wanted to ride along with her.

Dan Brighton looked over at the deputy as he was getting into his patrol car.

"No," he said hazily. "I'll follow in my truck."

Dan hadn't realized that he had made the decision until he had spoken the words, but the decision was made. He watched as both vehicles turned around, both applying their sirens and lights as they sped away.

Dan tried to swallow, but no spit would form in his mouth.

God help me, what am I doing? he thought.

He got into his truck and tried to remember what roads he needed to seek out in order to get him into West Virginia, wishing he had a map, thinking that he'd get one along the way.

He started the vehicle, the radio instantly coming on, the same news reporters still droning on and on about the crisis. He turned it off.

If he was going to do this, he didn't need any distractions. He had to focus on one thing—and only one thing.

Where was Patrick—and was he still alive?

CHAPTER 3

Something Scratching and Digging

Patrick blinked twice as he woke, allowing the darkness to once again settle over him.

He felt foolish for allowing himself to grow in comfort with his surroundings to the point that he had fallen asleep so easily, but as the car lurched from side to side it instantly brought him back in a stark reminder of where he was and the predicament he was now in.

"Ow!" Patrick said as the car shifted on the winding and bumpy road, finding that he was now bouncing sideways. It was as if gravity had become his sudden dancing partner—and gravity couldn't dance very well. It swung him in one direction, then back in another, picking him up by its large, soft hands, and then none to pleasantly dropping him by the same. He smacked the back of his head into something sharp and unforgiving, immediately reaching to rub the screaming area. But as he reached, his hands struck the abrasive and hard dried carpet lining of his prison, twisting his fingers back as if stubbing a toe.

"OW!" again, and "Darn it!" as he rubbed his fingers briskly trying to push away the pain. His hands, still bound by the tugging plastic ties, made it nearly impossible to gain any sense of relief.

He pulled his head back slowly and to the left, positioning himself to peek through the tiny cracks around the rear taillight compartment where he had earlier managed to tear away the carpet.

As the pain in his fingers started to subside, clarity started to again assume control of Patrick Brighton's fatigued mind. The churning knots in his stomach took over, and his breathing slowed.

I'm still here, he thought, as he slowly raised both hands to touch the now growing lump on his head. The air had become warm and stale, carrying the rank odor of his own breath. And as he pushed the hair back away from his face the realization of where he was, and what had taken placed, splashed over him like jumping into a pool in the middle of January.

Where are we?

Though he could see nothing of distinction through the tiny openings of the tail light compartment during the daylight hours, due to the suffocating darkness he was now in it became obvious that he had slept well into the hours after sunset. And, either the tail light on that side of the car had burned out, or Tye had turned the lights off for some unknown reason, because the red glow of the tail lights was nowhere to be found as Patrick had expected.

Maybe he didn't want anyone to see us.

The car was definitely slowing, and the notorious sound of crunching gravel implied that they had moved off the main highways and were now on a side road or long driveway. Due to the extensive time in the trunk, Patrick's orientation had become skewed to the point where he couldn't tell whether they were going left or right, up or down.

But the speed, now that he could tell was changing, and changing fast. They were stopping.

What was he doing? And what was he thinking?

Tye.

Patrick's mind and body froze at the sound of his captor shutting off the engine, the door opening and then closing, and the sound of his footsteps moving over the gravel coming to get him. Patrick couldn't shake the mental picture of his captor. The image of Tye, like a snarling, grotesquely painted carousel horse pounded over and over in his head.

Patrick could hear him stop just outside of the trunk and pause, Tye's fingers beginning to strum (out of rhythm) on one of the fiberglass panels on the rear of the car. This made Patrick so uncomfortable that he didn't even realize that he was holding his breath.

Tye paused again—the strumming stopped—and then he began walking away.

Patrick took one very sharp, deep breath and then held it tightly as to not allow his wheezing gasps to interfere with his attempt to listen to what Tye was—or was not—doing.

He then heard the sound of Tye faintly stomp stomp stomping up three wooden steps, a squeaky screen door being opened, and Tye going into some building.

Patrick closed his eyes, gave one good swift kick to the lid of the trunk, and screamed, "Open the trunk, you deranged, stupid, idiot!"

As quickly as he had uttered the volley, though, he wished that he could have taken it back. His outburst of anger might be well served if he was back at school and facing confrontation from someone his own grade level and age. But with Tye, Patrick had no idea what he might come back with in exchange for the confronting tone. Especially after the liquid soap.

Patrick's tongue darted in and out of the newly made gap on his upper row of teeth, licking the shrill, sensitive area of his gum line where his front tooth should have been. He moved his hands to his pants pocket to find the small, marble like lump where he had placed his tooth for safe keeping. He didn't want to lose it. If he could hang on to it and somehow get it back to his mom and dad, surely they'd have a way to put it back in its place.

His mom and dad. It had only been a few hours, though it might have been a few months, but Oh god, how he missed them. They could do anything. Take care of any problem. Especially dad. If only they could take care of this . . . Oh, please.

And then his mind went into that hole. That deep, wet, dark, nasty place where nightmares are born.

Is mom ok? He could imagine her lying at the bottom of the basement steps, her body twisted and deformed. From underneath her came a growing pool of red. Is she dying . . . or dead? And dad? I WANT MY DAD! I didn't even get a chance to call him. They probably don't even know where I'm at! And maybe will never know. Can I just see them one more time . . . please!? Please!

As Patrick lay in the dark with tears falling away down the sides of face, he had forgotten all about Tye who had stomp stomp stomped back outside and was now walking fiercely back towards the car. The trunk popped open with a smooth 'thunk', and then was fully opened. Patrick tried to turn up and look out, but was momentarily blinded by a light from the flashlight that Tye had pointed at him.

"Alright sunshine, out of the trunk . . . slowly," Tye said with a certain degree of uneasiness in his voice.

Patrick brought his hands up to shield his face from the penetrating light. His body, cranky and uncooperative, would not move as quickly as he wanted, feeling like the Tinman who needed a squirt of oil to soothe his frozen and creaky joints.

"C'mon, move," Tye said briskly. "A young man such as yourself should be hopping mad to get out of there."

"I'm trying!" Patrick answered through gritting teeth.

As he climbed out of the trunk Patrick's vision was rapidly trying to adjust to the conflict between the intensity of the flashlight being streamed into his eyes and the solid dark surrounding him. His attention was abruptly brought around to what Tye was now pointing at him besides the flashlight. It was a shotgun. Tye leveled it at his waist with the barrel aimed at Patrick. He was beginning to be aware that Tye was not completely comfortable with the arrangement that was being established between the two. Why? Patrick couldn't understand. Tye was bigger, stronger, and now had a gun. A shotgun at that.

Why was he worried about me?

As Patrick climbed out of the trunk, and had taken a few unbalanced steps to gain his footing, he noticed that Tye was moving in step with him, taking a few carefully placed steps backwards as well, as if to keep a certain amount of distance between the two of them.

Patrick wanted to test his theory, to jump at Tye and utter a "Boo!" just to gauge his reaction, but with the shotgun as the marshaling point between the two, he didn't want to test Tye's scare factor. Or end up with a hole blasted in his chest at the unsureness of Tye's trigger finger.

The air was thick with the smell of rotting, dead leaves, and cow manure in a nearby pasture.

"Where are we?" Patrick asked with trepidation, unsure if he really wanted the answer.

"Welcome to your new home—'The middle of nowhere, West Virginia!'" Tye replied like a cheesy salesman. He pointed with the end of the shotgun, "Ok, towards the house—get going."

Patrick turned around and now saw the structure he had heard Tye going into earlier. It was an old, dilapidated farmhouse. Anyone with any sense surely had long abandoned this place a good time ago. It certainly didn't hold any farmers anymore. As Patrick approached, Tye's flashlight cast a light on the building, and he could easily make out the outline of the terribly forlorn place. Time and tide had not been kind.

The porch overhang slanted, lurching to the left, with one pillar that had completely given up hope and had jumped off the edge of the porch, now supporting itself on the ground as if it had tried to run away. The darkened shingles, from what Patrick could make out, were lacking any of their gritty sand, and hung, drooping and sagging, like water logged cardboard. The paint that had remained on the building, a kind of dirty-snow color of white, was chipped, and curled away in miniature 'C's, just barely hanging on before one last, great gust of wind would take them scurrying away.

"C'mon, c'mon," Tye barked as he jammed the gun into Patrick's lower back, "Inside with your skinny self."

Patrick grabbed the door handle, pulled it open, and went inside. He quickly wiped his hand on his pant leg trying to remove whatever sticky substance that had transferred to his hand from the handle. It was as if Tye had brought Patrick to his own personnel haunted house.

The flashlight was strong and quickly gave radiance to the rooms and their contents. Not that there was much of either. Patrick couldn't see the end of the house, but it did seem, either because of the shadows or just an odd guess, that the house extended a lot farther back. As for the front, he could make out only three rooms. Two of which didn't contain any furniture, unless you counted spiders, brittle leaves, and dust as furniture. He wondered for the moment how so many leaves had made it into the house. He looked up quickly to see if there was a hole somewhere in the ceiling, but Tye gave him a sudden push towards the kitchen, and he never got a solid chance to look.

The two headed to the left and into the kitchen where an old, yellow table and two faded green chairs seemed to await their arrival. Patrick walked up to one of the chairs and reached his still tethered hands out to pull a chair aside, assuming he was going to sit, when Tye gave a quick, "Uh, uh. This way," and continued to walk him deeper into the crypt-like place. As they passed through the house, the rooms and their shadows seemed to recoil, as if being exposed to a light for the first time.

They came to a door that had already been partially opened, when Tye reached the gun barrel over Patrick's head and pushed it the remainder of the way. The door creaked and snapped as it begrudgingly gave way, giving the unobstructed view of steps. Basement steps.

"Is this where you're going to kill me?" Patrick stopped and turned to ask, trying to be calm, wanting to know exactly what Tye's intentions were going to be. If he was going to die, he was to at least go out fighting and biting, kicking and clawing.

The light from the flashlight lit up Tye's face in a scary, kind of campfire story telling way, which only added to the fear that Patrick had already held.

"No, I'm not going to kill you," he said as if he was growing tiresome of this game. "Not unless you force me to. I'm here only to make sure that you don't do anything stupid. Or go anywhere. That's all she wants for me to do for right now."

Tye smiled slyly. "And if I were you, I wouldn't be afraid of what I might do," his eyes widened as if Tye seemed afraid himself, "I'd be a little more concerned of what's down there."

The word "she" had just started to register, when Patrick turned to look down into the darkness. His face went cold as all his childhood fears and nightmares rushed to the surface of his imagination, pushing their way into his present reality. He quickly turned towards Tye and did what he thought he'd never find himself doing—reaching out to grab and hang onto the evil man.

"No!" he begged to Tye, as he tried to clutch onto his arms and jacket. But the man with the dancing eyes and the rotten eggs smile just gave him a great push and shoved Patrick tumbling and crashing down the wooden, splintering steps.

When he finally came to a stop on the dirt floor below, he found that the fall wasn't as far as he thought it would've been. He had taken the last three steps going backwards, bouncing on his rump, taking each step one at a time. And now, as he righted himself to a sitting position, he checked to see if anything was broken.

On his body, no. As far as that went, he seemed to have taken the fall quite well. But as he looked back up at Tye, who was at the top of the steps with the flashlight still beaming, Patrick could see that the termite eaten, rotted basement steps had carried their last passenger. What was left of the steps hung in tatters. They must have been damaged long before he had ever come across them. And still Tye had just thrown him down without any regard as to what may happen.

Patrick wanted to scream and rant. He wanted to make Tye feel like he now did—full of rage, and without hope. But the only thing he could do was to force himself to stand up and brush the dirt and splintered wood from his hands and clothes. He couldn't even reach his hands around to brush off his backside due to the restraints that were still in place.

"Can I please have something to take these off with?" he asked as he held up his hands, "I can't go anywhere. They hurt. Please?" Patrick explained with a resigned monotone that signified defeat.

"Uh . . . no, I don't think so. Frankly, I just don't care. You're going to have to learn to deal with things that sometimes you don't have any control over, lad. It could be worse. A lot worse. We all have our own leashes, my friend. And mine, right now, is a lot shorter than the one I'm allowing you. Try not to hurt yourself down there," he said as he slowly closed the door, chuckling, "and don't let the boogey man get you."

With the click of the door latch Patrick Brighton was instantly surrounded in more darkness than when he had laid in the trunk. He listened as he heard Tye walking across the floor, his heavy, booted footsteps heading towards the front of the house. The footsteps then slightly began to fade as they seemed to skip off the front porch steps. And then nothing. Hearing no sounds, he lost Tye's movements for a few moments. Patrick stood on his toes, straining to listen for anything distinguishable. Finally he heard the Altima start up, which frightened and enraged him even more.

"You're leaving me!?" he said aloud, incredulously. All air seemed to leave his body in one, long, exhaustive breath. He turned and leaned his back against the wall, his head turning towards the heavens, or at least towards the floor above him as he slowly shook his head.

"Why is this happening to me? What did I do?" he asked as if he expected a response from the dreary house. He blinked quickly, trying to adjust to any light that he might find bleeding into his damp confines.

Patrick, like any twelve year old, did not like being in the dark. Especially a basement in the dark. His mind danced back to the few times his dad, after they had finished playing in their basement, would beat him to the top of the stairs, turning off the light and closing the door on Patrick to put a good scare into him. Patrick would then race up the steps, his heart beating wildly, screaming at his father not to do that. The two of them would then spend the rest of the day chasing each other through the house, laughing, and generally play-fighting over the incident.

But no matter how light hearted those events had been, it had always continued to bother Patrick. The thought of when that switch went to the off position that he was still left alone down there. It had frightened him terribly because, after all, it was still the dark.

Those feelings were there at the moment, but just below the surface of what was now going on. He wouldn't allow himself to feel the touch of the dark's cold embrace as it surrounded him. He had to push it away. He didn't have time to be afraid—even though he was. Things were moving along too fast, and he needed to figure out a way to get out of there. Or at least prepare for Tye before he came back.

He reached his hands out to his right, trying to feel for the wall to gain some sense of balance in the room. His fingers were met with what Patrick could only think were slimy, mold covered bricks. He took a step closer and then started to finger his way around (hugging close, but not too close) to the damp, direction giving wall. As he shuffled his feet for progress, he could feel the dark slime sliding under his fingernails as his fingers guided his movements.

After a few minutes of timid progress his attention was drawn to a sound that seemed to come from his left. He stopped for a moment as he thought he heard something digging, or burrowing, but he couldn't quite place it.

He remained quiet for a moment, trying to locate its source, but heard nothing more. He knew he had heard something, but what it was he couldn't tell.

If it was anything it was probably just a mouse or chipmunk, his mind told him in an attempt to soothe his apprehension.

He turned slowly and once again resumed his blind exploration. But after a few minutes passed the noise began again.

This time he was sure.

He turned and searched the wall for anything that he could focus upon; anywhere close to where the sound was coming from. He stood, none to sure that he really wanted to see what was making the noise, but somehow thinking that if something was tunneling towards him, to him, that maybe he could follow the tract back out. Even if it was something as small as a rat, if it had found a way in, then perhaps he could find a way out. He raised his hands and felt along the upper ridge of the brick, just below the wooden supports of the floor above. He started to move to his left, pausing occasionally to wipe the thick spiders' webs off his hands, trying to center himself with the digging.

Surprisingly, he soon found more than he expected.

A window. A window that had been painted over, glass and frame.

"YES!" he screamed at his excited discovery. But his joy was soon tarnished as he ran his hands over to gauge the size of the window. It was small. Very small. Patrick guessed that maybe it was a foot high, by maybe two feet wide. He didn't care. It was the smell of hope. He quickly tried scratching the brittle paint off the window, his fingernails trying to dig in and peel back the layers, but was having little luck. It must have been painted over multiple times, for it had the feel of leather, and was not responding to his probing attempts at all.

Patrick, swift as a thought, brought his left foot up and removed his shoe. He hurriedly fit it over his right hand, the laces dangling and tickling his forearms, and then snuggled in his left hand together with his right and attempted to smash the glass. His first thrust surprisingly cracked the glass. The sound, the crunch, was distinct. But it didn't shatter. It still held its place inside the window frame. Patrick punched again. No crashing, tinkling sound of glass falling to the floor.

What?

He pulled his hands from his shoe and reached up and felt the fractured window. He could feel the tiny fissure cracks exploding from the point where he had struck, but the aged paint, even though it was starting to pull away from the frame at the edges, held the glass firmly in place. When he pushed on the glass to experiment as to why it was not breaking loose he could feel the push back from the other side like a hard pillow, gently holding its position and not giving ground. He began to whack at the glass with his tennis shoe again, but still nothing broke free.

What could be outside of this window holding the glass?

He soon began to realize that the reason the glass was in place was because it had been buried. He was underground—and so was the window. Someone, however long ago, had decided that the window was of no use and had pushed dirt up and over it on the outside. It didn't matter though. Patrick scrambled down to his hands and knees and turned back in the direction of the broken steps. Though they were of no use to him in climbing, perhaps he could use some of the ruptured pieces to smash the glass, and then start to pry some of the soil that had plugged up the hole. He began to move across the floor, hoping that he was headed in the right direction, his hands out in front of him like a blind man's cane.

During all of this time, Patrick would occasionally pause to listen, becoming painstakingly aware that whatever it was that was digging from outside of this wall was now moving towards him faster and faster. And, whatever it was, was not small. At about the time when Patrick had reached the center of basement floor was the same time when whatever had been digging reached the outside of the broken window.

Patrick turned around when he heard the growling, heavy pant coming from just the other side of the glass.

This was definitely not a rat.

His fear of whatever was out there made him realize that he was going to need the broken wood from the steps sooner than he may have expected, and he began to move faster, his adrenaline moving him forward without regard to what he may run into.

Whatever creature was out there began to thump relentlessly against the window. Now broken pieces did start to crash to the floor in rapid succession. Each piece seemingly larger than the last.

Patrick turned and could only listen in terror as the determined creature rammed its body hard against the window, blow after blow. He winced as the glass gave away piece by piece. Now sitting, Patrick pushed with his feet, his hands clawing, trying to drag himself backwards. He finally came upon the fractured steps and quickly found a piece of wood with which to defend himself.

With a smash the animal fell through the window's opening and landed with a thud on the ground in front of Patrick, its legs kicking and thrashing wildly.

Patrick pulled the stick back as if he were waiting for a ball to be thrown and spoke, his voice breaking, "G-go away! Get out of here! Go!" he finished in a near whisper.

Though it was still somewhere in the middle of the night, the hole that the animal created brought in a faint, trailing light, giving the room a hesitant glow. Patrick watched as the animal picked itself up and shook its body fiercely, throwing off the remnants of earth and glass. It began to pant, shook itself again, and then began looking around the room.

Patrick still couldn't see all that clearly, and he was hoping that what he was seeing was true, for before him stood a dog. A golden retriever to be exact. Once the dog located Patrick across the room the animal started to make his way over to him. Patrick thought that maybe it was a trick of the shadows in the dark, or maybe it was due to his mental state at the time, but he swore it looked as if the dog was smiling at him.

And then it spoke.

"Come! Now!" The dog said in an urgent tone. It turned and bounded back to a point below the window.

WHAT?!! Patrick thought, bewildered. That can't be!

The dog, displaying a sense of aggravation, turned back to Patrick and spoke again.

"Boy. Human. You. Come. Now." The language and speech were broken, but quite understandable. The dog's head bobbed, trying to convey his meaning.

Patrick's mouth hung open in disbelief. His chest felt restricted. It was as if his old classmate, pork chop faced Olsen Myers, was now sitting on his chest. He couldn't breathe.

The dog lowered his head in a show of disgust, and then trotted back over to where Patrick was sitting.

"No, get away" was all that Patrick could muster from the little air he had left in his lungs. But the dog persisted in coming closer, finally coming face to face with the boy.

The dog looked down at Patrick's bindings and sniffed his hands. He licked Patrick's fingers a few times and then began to gently gnaw at the plastic wraps binding his wrists. The dog worked meticulously, careful at from what points he was to attack the job.

Patrick watched in complete awe. He was dreaming, surely. This couldn't be happening. But as he allowed the animal to continue he gradually found a sense of calm, and his breathing began to resume at an even pace.

The dog chewed and snarled, working with a persistence that amazed Patrick. Finally the dog pulled back from his task, shook his head vigorously, and spoke.

"Pull," it said.

Due to the minimal light, Patrick had to put his hands close to his face to examine the plastic ties. They had almost been entirely chewed through. Patrick did not look up at the dog, but it spoke again.

"Pull."

He flexed his wrists and gave a quick snap with his arms as the wraps came apart, flying away to the floor.

Respect, as well as the still ringing awe that he felt, now flooded over Patrick as he looked at the dog.

"Thank you," he said timidly, sensing an almost pleased expression on the dog.

"You. Now. Go. Yes?" the dog said. "I. Dig. Hole. For. You.

"Uh . . . yeah. Let's go." Patrick found himself answering to the animal as he rubbed some circulation back into his aching wrists.

I just talked to a dog. I *am* talking to a dog!

Patrick was stunned by what was taking place.

"How can you talk?" Patrick asked hurriedly as he brushed the dirt from his pants and hands. "There's no way you should be able to do that!"

"I. No. Talk," his brown eyes blinked twice, "You. Understand."

"I understand? What do you mean? You're talking now. I hear you."

"No," the dog sat as he tried to explain, "You. Just. Understand."

Patrick's face wrinkled like he was learning Algebra from the Gym teacher.

"You. Understand," the dog tried again, "Just. You. No. Other. Man."

Patrick slowly began to grasp what the dog was trying to convey.

"You mean, I understand you . . . but no one else does?"

"Yes."

"How come? I mean, why me? Why is all of this happening to me?!"

If the dog had been able to shrug at any point in his life this would have been the most opportune time to do it.

"I. Don't. Know," was all that it could reply. "Enough. Talk. You. Go!"

Patrick moved over to where the dog was positioned, just below the recently opened window. He surveyed the height he was going to need to get himself to the level of the window with which to push himself through, but he was just too small. He looked around the basement hoping to find a box (or anything with which to stand on) but the place was barren.

"What's. Wrong?" the dog asked.

"The window's too high. I need something to stand on to get up into the hole," Patrick responded, shaking his head, "I still can't believe I'm talking to you!"

The dog look puzzled for a moment, almost deep in thought, then said, "On. Me."

It quickly positioned itself, nudging in front of Patrick, forming a furry step against the wall.

"How's. This?"

"No! I can't stand on you! I think I'm too heavy. I'd break your back."

The dog shook his head. "No. You. Skinny. Weigh. Like. Feather."

Patrick cocked his head slightly, totally unsure if this would work or not. Finally he tentatively placed a foot onto the animal's shaggy backbone and gave a great push to propel himself into the hole where the glass had been. It was a tight squeeze, but Patrick was determined to pull himself through.

The dog had dug a clean path down to the window. Patrick easily hauled himself up and then out of the soft, dirt hole, quickly finding himself in the light of a full moon. He was on the side of the house that was closest to the forest. His only thought was sprinting away as fast as he could, to get as far away from Tye as possible. He entered the forest in a dash as low hanging branches, and high growing, thorny bushes whipped and tore at his arms and face as he ran. He could feel blood flowing freely from his skin, but he didn't care—his only thought was to put as much distance between him and Tye as fast as he could.

After the boy had pushed on the dog to lift himself up, the dog turned and watched as the boy's shoes vanished straightaway into the hole. This brought joy to his heart. Although he didn't know the boy, his job, his mission, was to free the boy and to bring him to a special place on the other side of the forest as he was told. And although he wasn't going to be able to bring the boy as instructed, he still was able to get the boy away from harm's immediate way—the evil man.

The dog moved away from the wall and knew at once that he had been wrong about the boy—he did weigh a lot. He dipped his back low to stretch, trying to free the wee bit of pain he was feeling where the boy had pushed off.

"He. No. Feather," he said aloud, "More. Like. Rock."

He lazily walked around the room, sniffing and trying to find a feel for his present surroundings. He sneezed twice at a smell that he didn't recognize, and began licking at an old, dried, piece of some fruit that was in the corner of the room. After walking about for a few minutes he soon found himself back at the corner where he had started, and he plopped himself down with a sigh.

"When. Bad. Man. Come. I. Get. Out. How. He. Get. In." he said to himself, his panting slowing to a comfortable pace.

That's when the boy poked his head back in through the window.

"Yes?" the dog responded, surprised to see the boy again.

"Come on, I've got to help you get out."

"No. I. Fine."

"No way. I'm not leaving you. You saved my life."

This time Patrick could clearly see the dog smile. "My. Job."

"Well, I don't care what your job is. Come on. I'm not leaving without you."

"Bad. Man. Back. Soon," the dog rose up, now angry at the boys' sudden return.

"Then you'd better get over here you dumb dog," Patrick said quickly.

The dog jerked back as if swatted on the nose.

It was obvious to Patrick that he had just stung the dog's feelings with the hurtful remark.

"Sorry about that. I didn't mean it," Patrick said with remorse. "Please, just come on. We've got to move!"

"How?"

"Just come over here. If you can jump high enough against the wall I should be able to grab your front legs. I'm not that strong, but I should be able to pull you up."

Patrick wasn't sure if he could actually pull this off due to the angle of his body as he leaned down the hole. He was more likely to just slide right back into the basement with the weight of the dog pulling on him.

The dog did as it was instructed, and although it took three tries, it worked out better than Patrick had imagined, though it took a lot longer than he thought. They worked together, inching their way upward, with the dog's hind legs kicking and pushing all the way.

Finally the two made it to the top of the hole. The dog looked towards the front of the house, and said, "The. Bad. Man. Not. Here. Now. We. Must. Go. Quickly."

"Ok, this way," Patrick said as he started in the direction he had taken before.

"No," the dog insisted as he started around the back side of the house, "This. Way. Is. Best."

Patrick didn't question, and promptly followed the dog as it ran. If this dog could talk, Patrick figured, then it must know where it was going.

The two streaked around to the back and soon came to another entrance into the thick forest. They entered without hesitation and began putting distance between themselves and the edge of the woods.

After they had covered almost a mile they were stunned to hear a shotgun blast coming from behind them. The dog ducked down hard as if a large bird was swooping in at him, his tail immediately curling under his legs. Patrick moved over to kneel beside the frightened animal, trying to calm him down with a few simple strokes of its fur.

"It'll be ok," Patrick replied in a soothing voice trying to convince the dog. Trying to convince himself.

It was Tye. It had to be him.

But he wasn't close. He couldn't be. The blast from the gun seemed too distant. Patrick figured that it must have been a signal shot into the air to alarm him that Tye knew that he had escaped, and that he was on the run. It was a shot of frustration.

"Let's keep going," Patrick insisted. "Don't look back."

Patrick ran faster than he had ever run in his life, desperately trying to keep pace with the dog. They both ran hard, covering almost the same amount of ground as they had from the start in little more than half the time. Patrick ran until he could run no further, so out of breath that he couldn't even shout to the dog to tell it that he had stopped. His head was swimming.

The dog, though, was quick to discover that his companion was not with him anymore. He slowed, turned back and trotted over to his new friend. Patrick was bent over, his hands on his knees, gasping for breath, when he swallowed hard and said, "I'm . . . I'm so tired. Just give me a moment."

"It's. Ok," the dog said as it sniffed the air, trying to catch any scent of Tye. "He. Not. Close. He. Not. Catch. Us."

"How much farther?" Patrick asked, his breathing ragged.

"Not. Much. We. Find. Help. Soon."

Patrick took one long, deep breath, then another.

"Ok, let's go. I'll be alright."

"This. Way. For. Help," the dog said with urgency.

Patrick didn't respond, but kept close contact with the animal as they ventured further into the forest. Help—that meant only one thing to him. His mom and dad. If the dog was truly taking him to find help, then possibly he was taking him home. In that, Patrick could only hope.

They soon faded into the forest's misty cover, like two forgotten ghosts running into the black.

CHAPTER 4

Flies in the Ointment

Aster Tye, with his small and unfocused mind, had actually found the boy to be quite captivating.

No, he thought for a moment, that wasn't quite right. Not captivating. He put a hand to the side of his head as he searched for the proper word.

Intriguing! Yes, that was it—intriguing.

Yes, the boy was definitely intriguing.

How they were so afraid of the Brighton child. So thin and frail, yet they talked of the boy as if he were some power this world had not yet seen.

Tye chuckled to himself at the thought.

When they had first learned of him they were absolutely beside themselves with fear. Tye remembered the ten cloaked women, all sitting around an enormous, oaken table in the dark, cackling like hens with a fox in the pen at the thought that a small twelve year old boy could somehow disarm their plans. They had been given a sign that one would be sent that would oppose their quest. They had known that there would be ones that would emerge from the far reaches that would try to hinder their life's work. Their calling. But they had expected, and prepared for, a more charismatic leader of men, a shaman, or a disciple of another teaching. Not some small boy from Northwest Virginia. It was almost laughable. This was who was to be called to do Man's bidding?

But as the days grew shorter Tye remembered their slight, unsettling thoughts of the Brighton boy simmering until they had reached a point of near rage at what possibilities this child may possess.

"If he is truly what is to be believed, then we must not postpone our responsibilities any longer—the boy must be dealt with at once," one spoke aloud.

"Yes, we should take some form of action, now, before it moves too far along," added another.

"He's just a child," another spoke in dissention, "he can do nothing to us. The book was brought to us for a reason. Because all of us—and only us—are committed to restoring this hallowed earth to its rightful state. We were willing to evoke the words that had never been spoken to bring us our savior. And now, with her guiding hand, the boy will become an insignificant factor to our goals. I believe we are wasting too much of our energies worrying about nothing."

"But he's far too dangerous for the thought of him to be just set aside," came another voice from across the room.

One woman stood, slammed her hand on the table and growled, "The boy should be killed. Or at least crippled in such a way that he can serve no purpose against us!"

"And, if he is killed, they will just send another!" a fourth spoke as she shook her head. "We've all sacrificed our lives, and in some instances our families, to follow our commitment. We've come too far to allow any one, let alone this boy, to prevent our restoration."

They had tried hard to mask their growing fears with their purposeful talk, but Tye knew all along that nothing would be settled unless She spoke of it first.

From the far end of the room the woman entered, her presence alone silenced the others. She was cloaked in a dark, hooded tunic that only hinted at her physical form.

"No," She spoke, her voice calm and assuring, "we do not need to kill the Brighton child at this time. His death would only cause undo alarm and provide complications that I have seen that do not yet need arise.

"Yes, there will be others," She gently bowed her head in the direction of the one who had broached the subject. "As a matter of fact they are already on their way here."

Barely audible gasps began to encircle the room.

"But, I can assure you, they will be dealt with in an appropriate manner.

"My dear sisters, you have come too far to allow thoughts of any missionary to break the bonds of this inner domain. You have summoned me to provide you with the chosen direction with which to take to accomplish our goals. Our time is here, my children, let no man try and take it away from us.

"The Brighton child shall not be killed—for now. Just placed out of the way, like a fine piece of china set up on a shelf. The others that will come—they are of no mind to me, do with them as you all wish."

Tye remembered glancing over at her as she uttered these final words, barely catching a faint smile piercing her shadowy face.

He had been permitted to reside in a far corner of the room while all of this took place. No one had really seemed to be interested in him as he sat quietly listening to their plans as he was joyfully bathed in the true evil of their words. Tye had wanted desperately to be able to join them. He wished that he could partake in their lively discussions about how they would accomplish their goals. But they would never allow it. A few would come and sit next to him, holding him, trying to make him understand that as he was he could never hold a place at the holy table. Others would bring him food and water, and talk with him at length about their past lives away from the coven. But it wasn't until She turned towards him and offered him a small bone for his patience that he became truly alive.

"You," she pointed at Tye, "you will take care of the Brighton child for me, yes?"

It had been presented to him in the form of a question, but Tye knew all to well that this was not a request. This was a proclamation from the highest being he had ever encountered. And, after hearing the awful screams from behind hidden walls that had come from the four who had been chosen for other duties earlier that evening, he could not say that he didn't have a moment of pause before accepting.

He remembered bowing, and uttering a thoroughly delicious, "As you wish, your majesty." She, extending her hand for him to kiss, as the others in the room smiled their approvals and gratitude.

And he was off, traveling faster than he could remember, taking him to the very doorstep of the Brighton boy's home.

The boy's mother was so completely unawares, so truly trusting as she allowed him inside for a drink, that when it came time for him to take her it had been surprisingly easy. So small, so helpless, she was easily dispatched. This had allowed Tye to be able to turn all of his attention on how he was to ensnare the boy.

The boy, Patrick.

Could it be that he doesn't know? Hadn't any one told him what he might be? Tye had wondered about this many times. The boy displayed such innocence, an almost unsuspecting nature as to what was taking place. Surely his parents would have told him at the proper time.

Or would they? And did they even know?

Tye chuckled lightly, shaking his head while he ate.

Then he had a sobering thought—Perhaps the boy was merely keeping his hand in check? Toying with me?

No. He quickly dismissed that thought. The Brighton child didn't seem to be one to possess that sort of awareness.

Perhaps the coven didn't have the correct information about him? No, that couldn't be true either. They had been accurate about everything else so far without exception. They had even frightened him a bit about things that had not yet come to pass; things Tye wished that he hadn't been told once he had been given the prophecy.

No, it must simply be that the boy was in the dark about what was taking place.

Tye laughed out loud, spitting small amounts of food on the steering wheel in front of him at the joke he had made to himself.

In the dark . . . the boy was in the dark.

"Yes," Tye chuckled, "He most certainly is."

Tye's thoughts drifted to what the boy must be going through down in the dark of the basement.

Again he laughed. This time he snorted.

The boy did have some fight in him, Tye allowed. He wasn't some little prissy boy. No, Tye thought that in a few years—not that the boy's going to be around in a few years—but just the same, he would be a tough little monster to deal with. Tye was glad that he had gotten to him when he did. The boy struggled some, and had put up a little bit of a contest, but Tye knew that as with most of his prey, the coils that he created were very hard, if indeed impossible, for any to break.

Tye then turned his attention back to his meal. He was ravenous. He could not remember the last time he had eaten. He knew that it must have been days. That seemed to be the pattern of his feasting. He would eat, gorging himself on the meal that was before him, and then not be bothered by thirst or hunger for days on end. He came to realize that his eating habits were to an extreme as compared to the others, but he could not alter the habit he had set for himself. Though he could not remember how far back it started, this was just how it always had been.

After he had finished his banquet, Tye started up the car and began heading back to the farm. He was beginning to feel quite proud of what he had accomplished in such a short amount of time. Surely he would be rewarded in such a way as to allow him to hold a place of honor somewhere within their order. As well he should. Their minds, although curious and cunning, could never hold a candle to the wickedness that he possessed in his beating heart and clever mind. He thought that if they would just allow him a few moments to present his thoughts, they would welcome him to the table with open arms. And once he had taken a place at the table, then his march to stand next to Her at the head of the table would be thorough and swift, allowing him to rule as he knew would someday be his right.

The lights from the Altima lit up the dreary house as he pulled in, and were quickly extinguished. He sat in the car, knowing that the boy could hear him pull up, taunting him with his patience as he sat behind the wheel.

"I have all the time in the world," he said aloud to himself. "And, you, my dear boy, are running out of sand in the hourglass."

He got out of the car and walked into the house. The moon, now out and full, had emerged from beneath the early evening clouds and gave enough clarification of the things before him so that he didn't need to bother with the flashlight that he had stuffed in his back pocket. He walked straight to the kitchen and purposefully stomped on the wooden floor to alert the boy that he was indeed back from his errand.

But he didn't hear a peep from below his feet. Not even a whimper.

The boy couldn't be asleep, he thought. It wasn't that late. It couldn't be more than a little past midnight. And, with the state he had left the young man in, Tye couldn't imagine anyone finding a cozy spot down there to lay their head.

Nevertheless, Tye walked past the basement door, down the hallway, and took a right into a large back bedroom that was equipped with a small, tattered bed with which to lie upon.

He laid there for the better part of fifteen minutes, trying to find some peace with his erratic mind, but finding he was unable to get the quietness of his downstairs companion out of his thoughts. He leaned over the edge of the bed and yelled down to the boy. "I imagine you are finding yourself quite hungry at this point, eh?"

He listened for the scorching remark that was sure to come back to him, but all that he got in return was silence.

"Fine, if you don't want to talk, I can understand. But if you're going to get any of the food I've brought back for you," he lied, "you're going to have to ask me for it. I can wait."

Again, nothing.

"Y'know, I can make you talk, my little mouse, if that's your aim! And it won't be pleasant either."

Silence.

This infuriated Tye greatly. When he spoke, he wanted—no, demanded—an answer in return.

"No little pissy boy is going to bugger me off," he said under his breath as he jumped to his feet and headed back towards the kitchen.

He found the shotgun where had left it, on top of the cabinets just before the hallway, and checked to make sure that it had still shells still in it. He unlatched the door to the basement and yelled down to boy one last time.

"If I have to come down there, all bets are off. Maybe you should start saying some prayers, if you have a mind too."

Tye had no true intentions of trying to climb down the broken steps to see the boy. He was just playing the game, trying to get the boys attention. Reminding him who was calling the shots.

As he stood at the top of the stairs, waiting for any response from the boy, a new thought entered his mind.

What if the boy wasn't just holding his tongue.

What if the boy was seriously hurt? Or, worse—dead?

That would not be good.

"Oh, hell!" he said aloud at his sudden realization.

He pulled out the flashlight, turned it on, and scanned the darkness below. His fears of what retribution he might receive from the others were dancing in his head like an out of tune symphony. He began to have a sickening feeling in the pit of his stomach as he could not spot the boy no matter how far out he leaned and shined the light.

That's when he saw the plastic bindings laying on the floor.

What?! That can't be!

Tye wanted to jump down immediately, but reason told him that once he went down, due to the condition of the steps, he might not be able to get back up.

"How in the hell did he get those things off?"

At that moment, as if a giant bell had begun to chime in the distance, another realization swiftly followed.

The boy is not down there.

"OH NO!" he screamed, and not concerning himself with reason, threw himself down into the basement.

He landed hard, but recovered quickly, scanning the light frantically searching for something that . . .

The window.

"HE GOT OUT THROUGH THE WINDOW!"

Tye ran forward in a frenzy, throwing the shotgun and the flashlight to the floor. He started to rip and tear at the window's frame, his fingernails splitting and cracking until his bloodied, and splinter-laced hands finally pried the thing out with a great roar.

Soft dirt began falling in towards him as he tried to haul himself up out of the hole. He pulled most of it down and away from him, directing it to the sides. He grabbed the flashlight and shotgun, thrust himself upwards, and clawed his way to the surface.

He stood, examining the surroundings for any sign of where the boy might have gone, but it was too dark. Even with the full moon overhead it would be impossible to locate where the boy might have headed. And Tye was not very familiar with the area. He hadn't picked out the house at this location, but had only been given directions on where to take the Brighton child. He didn't know how deep the woods were that surrounded the farmland. He didn't know how close the next set of neighbors were. He didn't know.

"No no no no no no no no no no no no!" he repeated as he closed his eyes and gritted his teeth. The once sickening feeling that he felt in his stomach now had spread to every pore on his body.

He fired the shotgun into the air, and began to rant and scream into the dark, threatening Patrick with every possible thing he could think of if, hoping the boy was still within earshot of his frustrated tirade.

He slumped forward, exhausted, using the shotgun as a lean to, feeling as if he had just fallen into a deep dark well.

"What are they going to do to me?" he said as he began to fear for his life. "What is She going to do to me?!"

He walked back towards the car, stopping short, realizing that he didn't know where he would go.

He headed back towards the house, fumbling his way into the kitchen, and slumping down into one of the wooden chairs.

His life was over.

Maybe I could just say that he died. That he died while trying to escape.

Tye slowly shook his head, realizing that they had ways of knowing things, and finding out things, that he couldn't comprehend. They would know. They might already know. Tye put his face in his hands and tried to think of a way out of this.

He stood again, thinking that he needed to be doing something, anything, to get the boy back. But shortly he began to realize, as he slowly sat back down, that until the morning light came he would have no idea in what direction the boy would have gone. And by that time he could be miles and miles away.

He grabbed the flashlight and went back to the basement doorway and shined the light on floor again. Something was not quite right. How could the boy dig his way through all of that dirt? How would he even know in which direction to dig? How did he get his bindings off? He began to look for something, anything, as the light moved slowly from one end of the basement to the other, though he was not quite sure what he was looking for.

Not seeing anything particularly out of place, and about to give up, he spotted the animal tracks along side the human footprints dotted around on some of the loose dirt areas.

Something else had been down there with him.

Something that had come to get him out.

Tye knew who it had been, and it wasn't the boogeyman.

"I'm going to kill him," Tye seethed. "They must of knew he was going to be down there the entire time."

He threw the flashlight in disgust at the back wall of the basement, the instrument exploding into pieces.

Tired of his fearful thoughts, Tye realized that he wasn't going to be able to track anybody, or anything, until first light. The best thing to do was to get some rest and then make an estimated guess, based on the tracks in which direction they had gone, and then follow. He grabbed the shotgun and went back to the bed. Amazingly he soon began to doze, his body twitching back and forth, as bad dream after bad dream filled his head the entire night through.

It was the next morning at daybreak when Tye started to pull himself awake. Though he had a fitful nights rest, he woke with one purpose consuming his mind.

The boy.

His mind trumpeted at him that he didn't deserve to have any kind of comfort, any kind of peace, until he had the boy back in his grasp. His intense anger would carry him from here on out.

He knew that it was just a matter of time, that if he didn't find the boy soon, the witches would be on him like sharks to blood. The thought of what they might do to him caused him to shudder.

He sat on the edge of the bed trying to gather his plan and focus his thoughts, when a buzzing, irritating fly zipped by his left ear. He absently swatted at it and headed to the kitchen with the shotgun, leaving the fly behind him.

Or so he thought.

As he grabbed the extra box of shotgun shells from the top of the refrigerator and began to make his way towards the door, the buzzing fly suddenly returned, zipping madly around his head, infuriating Tye further as he tried to swat at it even harder.

"Get away!" he ordered.

Very quickly, a second and third fly appeared. Their buzzing and flittering causing Tye to pause. He watched as they played and danced in front of him, giving him even more reason to become incensed. A fourth, fifth, and sixth then joined the fray.

"What the heck? Leave me alone, you stupid flies," he said as headed for the door, now completely frustrated by the insects.

Before he could take two strides the flies started to come at him in a rhythmic, work like pattern, first darting for his eyes, then diving towards his ears. He wanted to get to the front door, but the flies persisted in buzzing and attacking him, and would not let him pass. Finally the flies irritated him to the point where he grabbed the shotgun, stood and fired in the direction of the smallish insects, blasting a hole in the wall adjacent to the spot where a refrigerator used to stand.

Like an exploded bag of flour, the air was instantly thick with a white chalky fog. The smell of gunpowder, and blasted plaster, crept into his nostrils.

"Damn bugs, you're supposed to be on my side," he said under his breath.

And then it slowly dawned on him as to what was taking place. His eyes widened. He knew.

The flies.

His mind, so focused on finding the Brighton boy, had pushed all other reasonable thoughts aside.

How could I have not remembered?

He turned and looked over his shoulder to the window above the sink. Like fungus, the flies were mushrooming on the window, starting to siphon the light that was coming through. Hundreds began to form on the outside of the two other kitchen windows. He could hear more of them coming down the chimney in the adjoining room. More in the basement, probably coming through the ripped out window. And in the bedrooms. And at the front door.

Thousands.

Tens of thousands.

No No No . . .

Tye now realized what was taking place. He remembered the last time the flies had come at him like this. They had sent them because they knew what had happened. And now they were going to punish him for his mistake. Just like the last time.

He fell, knocking over the chair, and staggering backwards into the corner of the kitchen, crumpling to the floor like an infant. He began to cry as he raised his hands to fend off the horde that was forming before him, and shaking his head "NO!" again and again.

The flies were coming.

And they were not happy.

CHAPTER 5

The Gathering of Beasts

During the night Patrick and the dog traveled many miles, taking Patrick as far as the remainder of his body's strength would allow. The dog was insistent on the direction that they take, pausing for only a few seconds every now and then so that he could sniff the air to ensure the direction they were taking was correct. At first they ran, their legs pounding through the forest until they emerged on the other side of the heavy woods miles away from the farmhouse, the basement, and hopefully Tye. Then they settled into a light jog, going over a few large lazy hills that were teeming with tall grasses and wild flowers that appeared golden in the dark. The grasses and flowers were so tall and thick that Patrick had to hold his hands up as if he was wading through water. The plants had completely engulfed the dog. Patrick could barely follow its course, except that he would occasionally catch the animal's fluffy tail bobbing to and fro as it progressed.

They crossed two small creeks that were situated only a few hundred yards apart, trying hard not to splash too much water for fear of the noise that it would create, then scrambled across a silent, two lane road. Other than themselves, the only other noises they heard were the far off sounds of crickets chirping and of bullfrogs croaking, trying to outdo each other for attention in the cool midnight air. They made it over another rocky hill before Patrick had to rest again. The lack of food and his exhaustion were overtaking him rapidly.

Lastly, they walked. Strolled, actually. They did not talk much other than the random times when the dog would ask Patrick if he was ok, the boy continually assuring him that he was fine. Patrick's unshakeable fear that Tye would show up just over the next ridge, jumping out and snatching him up, kept pushing him forward. As the hours passed they had slowed to the point where they were not making much progress at all. Finally, at the end of their night's journey, as Patrick began stumbling, his feet barely lifting off the ground with each step, the dog informed him that they were at their stopping point until morning. They had come to an old barn that was nestled back into a crook between another forest, this one of tall pines, and a large hill that Patrick could have easily mistaken for a mountain.

Patrick lifted the bolts to the latch, pulled the door open, and went inside. It smelled of wet hay and poop. Whose poop it was, he didn't care. He just wanted to put his body on the ground at any spot and go to sleep. The dog followed him only to the edge of the open door and then stopped.

"I just wish that I knew why all of this was happening to me. What was going on?" Patrick asked, exhausted.

"Most. Answers. Will. Come. When. It. Is. Time," the dog assured.

"What does that mean? You sound like my dad. I'm too tired to figure out riddles right now."

Patrick hesitated for a moment while he was trying to make himself comfortable, his thoughts flashing back over the nights events.

"Hey, how did you know where I was at, anyway? How did you know when to come and get me?"

"I. Will. Try. To. Answer. In. Morning. You. Need. Sleep. Now."

"You must know something. Why can't you just tell me now?"

The dog walked over to where Patrick stood and began to push into his leg.

"You. Need. Rest. Now. All. Answers. Given. In. Morning."

"You're really being annoying. You do realize that, don't you?"

"Yes," the dog smiled.

"But what about my mom and dad? Are they ok? If you know, can you at least tell me that?"

The dog sighed. "I. Think. They. Are. Ok. But. I. Can. Not. Promise."

Patrick stared at the ground. It wasn't exactly what he wanted to hear, but at least the response was something he could hold to for the time being.

As his vision began to adjust to the dark framework of the barn, Patrick quickly found a vacant spot to rest. The dog, walking in miniature circles as he inspected the layout of the barn, turned and announced his plans for the night.

"You. Sleep. And. I. Will. Watch," he said firmly, confidently, acting as if he was in charge.

Patrick turned towards him and smiled. "What about you? I know you're just as tired as I am."

"No. I. Have. Lots. Of. Strength. Left."

"Liar."

"No. No. I. Have. Strength."

"If I said 'sleep' to you three times in a row you'd be out before I would."

"No."

"Oh, yes you would. Watch," and Patrick proceeded to do his best imitation of a hypnotist's voice, like the corny, cartoon-ish men he had watched on television. He kept repeating "you are getting sleepy" over and over to the dog.

After the third chant the dog fell over on its side and began to make horrible pretend snoring noises as if the trick had worked. This made Patrick chuckle lightly at the dog's attempt at humor, responding with a slight, "Oh, brother."

It wasn't that the dog was so funny, but that he looked so ridiculous as he was attempting the comic routine. The animal's flopping hears flipping up and over his head, his tongue dangling out the corner of his mouth.

The animal opened his eyes at the boy's laughter, righted himself to all fours, and laughed himself.

"You. Sleep. Now. No. One. Bad. Come. This. Way."

The dog turned and began pushing the barn door closed with his nose, allowing Patrick the chance for sleep.

Patrick stopped him short with one more question. "Hey, I don't even know your name. What do I call you?"

"Dog," the animal responded. He seemed surprised by the question.

"No, what's your name. Not what kind of animal you are."

"I. Am. Just. Dog," he answered, taking a step back inside, "We. Do. Not. Have. Names. Like. Others."

"You just call each other 'dog'? How do you know who you're talking to? How do you tell each other apart?"

"Oh," the animal began to smile, "We. Tell. Each. Other. By. Smell."

"When. We. Talk. To. Others. We. Know. Who. We. Talking. To."

"By smell, huh? You guys must create a lot of stink with so many different dogs running around."

The dog seemed amused at the conversation, it's tail dancing back and forth.

"Everyone. Has. Smell. Even. You," Dog said as it wrinkled its nose.

"Hey, I don't stink," Patrick said, but quickly took a whiff of his underarms. "Well, ok, but I haven't had a chance for a bath. And we had gym yesterday."

Dog turned to leave.

Patrick then remembered seeing the collar and name tag around the dog's neck.

"Didn't you have an owner at one time or another? What did they call you?"

The animal looked back over it's shoulder.

"Yes. I. Had. Owner. Master. But. I. Did. Not. Like. What. They. Call. Me. They. Not. Kind. Man."

"Why was that? What did they call you?"

Dog paused as if remembering something unpleasant from it's past, and then flatly said, "Dumb."

With that, the animal turned and went back out, finishing the job he had started and closed the door.

Like a stake through the heart Patrick remembered the word that he had used earlier in referring to the animal. "Oh geez, how could I have been so stupid? I didn't know."

He jumped up and ran back out to find the animal to again apologize for his careless remark. He caught the dog just as it was about to begin to patrol the area in the closest proximity around the barn. Patrick expressed his sorrow at the slight, and promised it wouldn't happen again. He knelt and read the name tag attached to the collar.

It read, 'DUMB,' in big silver lettering.

"Nice," Patrick said sarcastically, wondering what kind of blockhead would name their dog 'Dumb.'

He undid the little metal wire that was holding the nametag in place, freeing the unflattering trinket, and tossed it into the woods.

Patrick instinctively started to stroke the dog's head, his fingers finding their way to scratch the soothing area behind the animal's ears. The dog looked at him, letting Patrick know that it was a mistake made without intention for harm.

"Do. Not. Worry. Bright. One. I. See. In. Your. Eyes. That. You. Not. Bad. Man. The. Eyes. Do. Not. Lie."

The dog nudged him back towards the door to the barn.

"Now. Go. Sleep."

But it did trouble Patrick as he made his way back into the barn, that he could wound something so quickly, and easily, with just a simple word.

He would think more on it in the morning, he decided, for he was just too tired to punish himself now. He returned to his sleeping spot, curling up into a tight ball to help keep himself warm, and closed his eyes, waiting for the overdue sleep that was to claim him.

But just before he did sleep, in that gray, hazy place where he wasn't quite awake, and yet not fully asleep, he thought he heard what sounded like the dog talking in a hushed, secretive voice to someone outside. Patrick lazily dismissed it from his mind. Who could the dog be talking to? They hadn't seen anyone the entire nights journey. How could there be anyone out there now? His thoughts whispering to him that he must already be dreaming. He smiled to himself, yawned long and deep, and took those thoughts with him as he eventually drifted off to sleep.

The next morning, shortly after sunrise, Patrick rolled over to his side on the hard ground of the barn, wishing he had a blanket because he was freezing. His mind drifted back to his house, his bedroom, his bed. The thought of the soft, thick comforter that would cover him at night made him feel like a man walking in the desert who would give anything for a drink.

How I wish this was a nightmare. I just want to go home.

He was still thoroughly exhausted, the unforgiving ground not making much of a suitable mattress. The thought of nothing more than falling back asleep began to caress his mind when he heard the sound of a woman's voice. Well, at least he thought he did.

He wrinkled his brow and yawned, knowing that he had dreamed it. He pulled his arms into his shirt for warmth, and began to return to sleep.

But then he heard it again.

"Mom?!" he said excitedly as he bolted upright, turning himself towards the barn doors.

That was no dream.

Then he heard two women's voices.

What?

Then a third.

And then other voices started to come into his now clearing perception. Both male and female.

What is going on, he wondered? It sounded like the auditorium back at his school during morning assembly.

There must be a hundred people out there. Maybe more.

Patrick cautiously approached the door of the barn, holding his hand up to block the sun as it ran streaks through the wooden slats of the structure.

The voices grew louder as he approached, and he could now hear a definite conversation taking place, but with everyone talking at the same time, each trying to talk over, and louder, than the person next to them. Some were agreeing. Others were disagreeing. But about what, he had couldn't quite make out. He didn't care, though. If there were that many people outside, then they could surely keep him safe from Tye.

He took two long strides, pushed open the barn door, and went out to meet his potential saviors.

The old, wooden door swung open with a slow creak, and Patrick rushed through the doorway to greet all of the people who . . .

Except there wasn't any people to greet.

Huh?

Patrick stopped, his mouth hanging open in disbelief. This was too much for his twelve year old mind to take in.

The barnyard was full of animals.

Hundreds of animals. With even more pouring over the hills, and coming through the trees. They looked like ants marching to a picnic.

Animals that were talking like humans.

Talking about him.

"There he is . . . oh my . . . that's the human that's supposed to save us," a rather large, uncomfortable looking skunk was saying to a chubby little raccoon that was nearby. "He's not very big, is he?"

Patrick turned to his left, watching as an anxious puma began to pace back and forth along the far corner of the barn (his eyes never leaving Patrick) as he carried along a conversation with an intelligent looking black bear (if bears can look intelligent) that was stroking his right ear and looking totally displeased with what he was seeing. "This? This is what's going to save us? You've got to be kidding. He's just a cub. How's he going to do anything? As far as I'm concerned we're doomed before we start."

"He's not what I expected at all" the wolverine from the far side spoke. "I thought he'd be a little taller, a little more aggressive looking."

"What is his special gift?" an angry gaggle of geese asked from the rear.

"Yes, what can he do anyway?" an assorted group of cows and goats demanded. Patrick was amazed as they seemed to be holding their own little separate debate off to the side, concerning whose milk was better tasting and why.

"We've already failed if we're relying on 'that' to save us," a slightly aloof sounding bull moose spoke as he pushed his way to the front, motioning towards Patrick with his magnificent set of antlers. "And if you ask me, I think we'd be better off if we would just cease and desist with all of this silly arguing and just let mankind die off. Take the planet over ourselves, I say. Why are we waiting around for him to save us anyway?"

"But nobody asked you," a small, irritatingly high pitched voice came from Patrick's right, "now did they?" An auburn colored fox raised her pointed head, looking directly at the moose, not backing down from her comment.

"Yeah, give the kid a chance. Those who've had the dream envisioned him. Not some overly ripe, long haired know it all from the north," a mother kangaroo put forward, trying to maintain control of her children who were bouncing around, and over, a group of irritated chimpanzees sitting next to them.

"Are you implying that I stink?" the moose asked, indignant.

"You haven't noticed the ten foot radius everyone's been giving you. Catch a clue, pal."

"Hey, that's enough already! Let's stick to the plan," an angry hippopotamus appealed to the bickering mob. "There is a plan, right?"

The murmuring questions and resentments began to trickle through the crowd.

"I haven't heard of a plan," said one.

"News to me," answered another.

And so forth.

The angry, conflicting debate began once again to rise up, stifling the original intention for the gathering.

Deer, Panda, Squirrel, and Zebra began quarreling with Elk, Beaver, Gorilla, and Wolverine. Rabbits with Rats, Porcupine with Lion.

It was all a bit too confusing to tell who was actually making an argumentative case that was worth listening to due to the many different opinions that seemed to grow louder and angrier with each passing breath.

To watch the animals converse with each other was amazing to Patrick. He had watched enough National Geographic and Animal Planet to know the different movements and various gestures the creatures before him would make as they would interact with each other. But to see their actual movements with genuine words being spoken instead of the squeaks, and squawks, and growling noises he had come to expect, gave him an unexpected feeling of exhilaration. It was as if he was Columbus and had just discovered the New World.

And all the Patrick Brighton could think to ask, in his most astonished, and bewildered way, was, "Where did you all come from?" as he overlooked the great throng of arguing beasts.

"Why, from the good earth, of course" a quaint little voice spoke.

Patrick looked around to see from which animal the voice had originated, unable to clearly pick out from which direction it had been spoken. Most of the animals that he could see had turned their focus away from him, still caught up in their own petty discussions about things that Patrick could not comprehend. The feelings he had garnered as he has walked from the barn a few minutes ago had quickly vanished as he again began to feel small and unprotected. These creatures did not seem to be interested in safeguarding him from anyone.

Patrick watched as a small, unconventional looking penguin poked his head from around the backside of a mountain goat that was standing several feet away. The goat, whose attention was so caught up in the furious debate he was having with a tiny gray squirrel, did not seem to mind as the smallish penguin slowly pushed past him. The penguin smiled, walked up to the boy, and extended a wing.

"Hello. My name is Bing."

"Huh? Oh . . . hello," Patrick hesitantly reached down and shook the small birds wing. If anyone would have told him twenty four hours earlier that he would be shaking the wing of a penguin, a talking penguin at that, he would have thought that the person making the suggestion might be in need of some serious medical attention. But, if one of these creatures was going to extend the courtesy of a friendly gesture, he was surely going to return it—no matter how strange it seemed.

"But where did they come from?" Patrick asked again.

"There are quite a few of them, aren't there?" the penguin answered in return.

"Yes," Patrick said, gazing out at the masses.

"Well," Bing began, "I believe most, like myself, have come here from a few nearby city zoos, or nature preserves. The others, probably from some of the more out lying wooded areas, the mountains, or other natural surroundings that are close by."

Bing turned and smiled at Patrick, "You'd be amazed at what lives right out your own back door."

"They came from zoos? How'd they get loose?"

"I suppose that when no one is watching, all that it would take is one smart chimpanzee, a set of keys, and the know how to shut off the main power grid to the gates and cages." Bing paused for a moment, and then explained further. "Well, he doesn't actually know how to shut off a power grid; he just sort of learned that by watching the keepers do it."

In his bewildered state all that Patrick could utter was a quiet, "Oh."

"Some of these animals have traveled more than two days just to be here. Just to see you."

"Me? Why did they want to come see me? What is it that they want to see?"

"Well, I believe that both questions ask the same thing, really. The creatures that you see before you . . . well, they didn't have much of a choice. They were compelled; driven to be here."

Bing smiled and looked out towards all of the animals, and then back to Patrick.

"Please don't let all of the excited discussion by all of these silly creatures alarm you in any way. I assure you, they are, or will be, of one mind when it comes down to the matter that needs attended to. They just need assurance."

Patrick shook his head, not sure that he understood what the penguin was implying.

"They need to know that you're going to be the one to set things right," the penguin continued. "That you are the 'difference maker.'"

"Huh? I'm the what?" Patrick looked down at the small bird as if it was speaking Portuguese.

"It is rather confusing, I realize, but all will be explained in proper time."

"They're all just so loud," Patrick said, "I didn't realize that there were so many animals mad at me—and I don't even know what I did to make them that way. I just wish somebody would please tell me what I did to make everyone hate me so?"

Bing smiled compassionately, and poked Patrick in the leg with his wing.

"You did nothing wrong my friend. It's just that with what is taking place in the world at the moment, the animals are finding themselves without anyone's guidance for the first time in their lives. Man's guidance. And I'm afraid that they are not taking the news very well. Though they would never readily acknowledge it, they are experiencing a wee bit of fear of being on their own."

Though Patrick could hear and understand the words that the smallish penguin was saying to him, he just could not quite grasp their intended meaning. It was as if he was looking an incomplete puzzle—he just didn't have all the pieces needed to give him the picture.

"I don't know what is going on, and I don't quite understand what you're trying to tell me, but I do know this—if they don't lower their voices, somebody nearby is going to hear all of them and come down and find all of you here. And I wouldn't even know where to begin to have to explain all of this . . ."

Bing looked up at him sharply.

"Someone . . . to find us?" Bing asked, startled, realizing what the boy did not.

Suddenly, as if a signal had been given that Patrick was not aware of, the animals, and all of their noisy discussions, suddenly quieted to an eerie, whispering stillness that instantly unnerved Patrick, though he didn't know why.

"He doesn't know," a growling voice came from the crowd.

"Nobody's told him yet?" a rooster barked from overhead.

"Hasn't he seen?" came yet another voice from the out reaching audience.

A sickening, lightheaded feeling came over Patrick as the ranting and raving of the ever growing mob came to a complete silent stop.

Bing turned to the crowd, and then back to Patrick. His face seemed apprehensive and tired, as if he were balancing the entire weight of the world on his shoulders at that particular moment. He began looking around the crowd for someone to help him; silently pleading, but finding no takers. Bing's mouth opened as if he was about to speak, but no words came out.

A light breeze blew a few small strands of his black hair into Patrick's face, his hand reaching absently up to push it away.

"Something bad has happened, hasn't it?" Patrick's shoulders sagged, his focus dropping to the ground at his feet. "Has something happened to my mom and dad? They're dead, aren't they?"

Bing smiled sympathetically and shook his head.

"Lift your head, young one. No. As far as I know at this moment, they are both still alive," Bing finished his sentence, but had the look of someone who had volumes yet to speak.

"But?" Patrick pushed forward.

"It's not your parents that are the ones you should be concerned for at this present time; it is the rest of your kind that is in trouble. Mankind is facing a crisis of proportions never seen before. They are being destroyed, exterminated, by as deadly a plague that has ever been seen by this world."

"What . . . What are you saying . . . everyone in the world is dead? That can't be true," Patrick said, disbelieving.

"No, not everyone. The entire race of mankind hasn't been exposed to the virus as of yet. It has only reached a small part of the northern world. But millions have died so far, unnaturally, and millions more are dying every day."

"A plague? Are you sure?"

"If what I am being told is to be believed, I'm afraid so."

Millions are dead?

Patrick felt like he had been kicked in the stomach. If it was true what he was now being told then his everyone in his entire school might have died. His neighbors. His friends.

"No, no. This can't be true. When did all of this start?"

"Only a few days ago. And it is moving rapidly, growing with each hour that passes."

"What about you? Aren't the animals being affected?"

"No, not so far. I believe her plans are to spare us."

Her?

"You said 'Unnaturally.'"

"Yes."

"What do you mean by that?"

An older, gray bearded Gelada baboon stepped forward, the crowd giving him a wide berth. He was an imposing creature with his large white mane, yellowed fangs, and powerful arms. Patrick took a careful step backward, away from the massive animal.

"It is the witches from the north, of this we are sure. They have caused this wickedness on your kind," the baboon spoke.

"Witches? What are you talking about? Is this the "Her" everyone keeps mentioning?"

The world began to spin, Patrick's balance coming into question. He was beginning to see two of everything as his head began to feel as light as a balloon. His hunger and exhaustion were catching up with him.

"I don't understand any of this," he said weakly. "Why is this all happening? Who is this lady that everyone keeps referring to? Can somebody please tell me what the heck is going on?"

Someone from the crowd shouted out, "Uh, oh. You better watch him. He's gonna blow. I know that look."

Bing sighed, and gave an off handed glance to whoever was speaking.

"Please sit down, young one. Do you feel ill? You're not looking so well."

"No. I'm ok . . . I guess. I think I need to eat. I'm just feeling incredibly tired."

Bing took Patrick's hand, guiding him over to a small pile of spider web covered bricks that were stacked against the side of the barn.

A brown and white Palomino horse trotted over and plopped two red apples down onto the ground at Patrick's feet.

"Maybe this will help you my friend," the horse said as it slightly bowed its head.

"Oh . . . thank you," Patrick gratefully replied, returning the simple gesture to the horse. He then snatched the apples up and began wiping the horse's spittle off of their peel. He devoured the first apple in several large bites, and began crunching on the other when Bing and some of the other animals gathered in close around him.

"I will try to explain all I know," Bing paused, motioning to the animals now gathered that seemed to number well into the hundreds, "or I should say, all we know.

"You had better stay seated for what we are about to tell you. The story is not pleasant, but from the few, small fragments that we have gathered, we now have a better understanding of what is taking place. The birds have relayed most of the information to us, amassing what once was a few burdensome pieces of an unrealized puzzle that now has come together to form a web of desperation and death. We are very thankful to our friends from above."

Bing, along with most of the other animals, turned their attention to the treetops around them, slightly bowing in gratitude. The assortment of multi-colored birds that inhabited the trees nodded their approval in return.

Bing motioned to the baboon for help.

"Syrian, if you could give me a hand up. Thank you."

The baboon, Syrian, lifted the flightless bird and set him down next to Patrick.

Bing filled his lungs with an extremely long breath, exhaled slowly, and then began.

"It seems there is this book. A rather old book . . ."

CHAPTER 6

The Snake's Trail

It was a horror movie. It had to be.

There wasn't any possible way that the scene that was unfolding in front of Dan Brighton was real.

He slowed his truck to barely a crawl as he maneuvered through the obstacle course of overwhelming wreckage that was scattered across the four lane highway. Cars, trucks, and eighteen wheelers were tossed in uneven piles that resembled a child's sandbox collection of toys.

And the damage didn't seem to be isolated to just a certain stretch of the road. As he continued down the highway he could look out over one long continuance of twisted metal and plastic as far as he could see. At some points he had to drive off the road to either the right, or into the center median, to avoid the devastation.

There didn't seem to be any type of rescue units on the scene either. No police. No ambulances. No mobile rescue units or paramedics of any kind. Nothing.

Just silence.

The one sheriff's department cruiser that he did manage to see was buried beneath a Marion's Trucking Company tractor trailer that was tilted on its side, pinning the brown and gold car to the ground.

Dan kept replaying the same question over and over in his mind—How did he escape from being infected, and not the other drivers that had once occupied the seemingly abandoned vehicles that were scattered around him?

When he first left the house he'd made sure that all the windows to the truck were up and tight, and that he had closed and secured the vents, knowing full well that it probably wasn't going to matter. If the virus, plague, disease, or whatever it was that was destroying the human landscape was as destructive as the reports were saying, short of locking himself into an air tight vault, it wasn't going to make much of a difference as to what precautions he decided to try.

He finally concluded (for the time being anyway) that perhaps he was one of the few fortunate people that possibly had some sort of built in tolerance to the disease. That it wouldn't (or couldn't) affect him for whatever odd reason. Of this, he was thankful.

But his mind kept drifting back to his wife, and to her ambulance drivers; to the people waiting for her at the hospital. And it wasn't a question of what was going to happen to them? Rather it was when was it going to happen to them? Just how fast was this thing spreading? That was the question.

The first hour that he was on the road he'd only come across three other vehicles, none going in the direction that he was. The few people that he did see were heading in the direction that he'd just came from, frantically yelling at him to turn back, informing him that he was going the wrong way. As he would pass he would mouth a silent "I know, I know" and then step on the accelerator a little bit harder, trying to push his way past them as fast as he could.

After Dan had merged onto the main interstate he quickly became overwhelmed with the feeling that no one could possible be alive in some of the more rural areas that he was traveling through. The suffocating stillness that engulfed him as he drove gave him an eerie feeling that not only was he the only one on the road, but that he was the only one within fifty miles in any direction of his present location.

While he drove, he vigilantly made an effort to keep an eye out for a certain green Nissan Altima. His heart was high in his chest with anticipation of finding the car. Part of him was hoping to spot the car straightaway, hoping that he'd find Patrick inside. The other part of him wasn't sure he wanted to find it, knowing that if he was out there, he might have been taken with the virus. Or worse, he might have been killed in any one of the assortment of crashes in front of him.

As he started to navigate through some of the more populated areas of wreckage he began to be aware that from his position he couldn't see anyone in their cars. It was as if all the people had either abandoned their automobiles, or every person in every crash had decided to slump over in their seats with their one last gasp of air. That seemed a bit too comical for Dan to believe. But the fact still remained that no one seemed to have been left sitting upright in their seats.

Dan pulled up behind a white Honda Accord that had its rear end lifted high into the air by a blue Mercedes that had plowed directly into the Accords back side.

As he stepped out of the truck and had taken a few steps, he chuckled as he caught himself holding his breath. He felt like one of those astronauts in the old science fiction movies he had watched as a kid. The ones where when the spaceship first lands on the new planet, and as they open the hatch one brave soul would stick his head out to breathe the air making sure it was ok for the rest of the crew. He had expected an overwhelming smell of death and decay to hit him in the face as he emerged from the cab of his truck, but to his surprise the only smell that seemed to be prevalent was of spilled gasoline and burning oil.

He walked cautiously over to the tilted Accord. It was almost like he was expecting somebody to jump out and shout "BOO!" as he made his way. His mind began teasing him with all sorts of random thoughts of zombies, and body snatchers, causing his thoughts to teeter back and forth from the saneness of reality, to the incredibleness of what was actually taking place.

As he approached the driver's side door he tried to peer in through the shattered windows, but he quickly discovered that the spider web pattern of damage to the glass wouldn't allow him to see anything clearly inside. He braced himself as to what he might expect to see, grabbed the door handle and gave a quick pull, finding that the door slid open effortlessly.

But to his surprise there wasn't anybody inside. At least not in the form he expected to see.

Dan's attention was immediately drawn to the slimy red and tan colored goo that was splashed over the driver's side seat and the floor below. It looked as though the body had been melted down like candle wax.

Dan quickly took two steps back in panic, removing his hand from the door.

No way! That can't be what's happening to them!

There was nothing remaining in the front seat of the car that resembled anything that once was human.

He quickly walked back to the Mercedes and looked inside. It was the same as what he had seen in the first car. Only this time there were two thick, gooey puddles inside. One in the driver's seat, the other dripping from the purple Barney car seat in the back. He stood, staring at the unbelievable sight, unable to move. He looked at his arms, and lightly began to rub his skin to see if any tissue might be starting to pull away. To see if anything was beginning to dissolve.

This wasn't a virus. This was no plague.

With the way in which the bodies remained gave the impression that they had been melted, or dissolved, leaving Dan to believe that this could only be caused by some form of biological attack.

But who could do something like this? Who would create something so lethal, something so potentially devastating, that it could destroy human tissue as soon as a person would come in contact with it? He wondered who had manufactured the stuff. The military? But for what purpose? And how did it get unleashed on the world? His first reaction wanted to believe that it was terrorists. But surely the safeguards that would be maintained to control a substance such as this would be tremendous. No terrorists could get their hands on something of this kind. And then, if they did, who in their right mind would want to unleash it? Knowing that they could wipe man off the face of the world. Maybe they didn't know what it was? Or worse still, maybe they didn't care?

He wanted to reach down and touch the gooey looking mess of tans and reds and grays that was left on the driver's side seat, curious as to what the mass might feel like. It had an almost gelatin look about it. But he didn't dare.

He then noticed that some of it had leaked down and was now dripping onto the road at his feet. He stepped back, alarmed that he was stepping in something that was once a heart-thumping, breathing, human body.

He staggered backwards, and then turned towards the front of the car, bracing himself on the hood as he vomited up the Oreo cookies he had eaten when he had first set out.

He wiped his mouth with his shirt sleeve, took a deep breath, and leaned back against the car.

He needed to let someone know about this.

He needed to hear another person's voice.

Dan reached to his hip and pulled out his cell phone. Unbelievably he still had four bars of reception showing on the screen. He dialed the Randomguard number and waited for an answer. But all that he got was a prerecorded message announcing that all circuits were busy, and to try his call again later. He tried the number three more times, each time receiving the same message.

The sun was starting to set to his left, giving long irregular shadows of the empty vehicles surrounding him. He felt as if he was standing in a great automobile graveyard. Only what he truly was in, was in a graveyard of what was left of yesterday's humans. He began to feel like he was the last man on earth.

He got back into his truck with a concentrated effort, still overwhelmed by the display in front of him, and began navigating back down the road. It was slow going in stretches, the combination of the oncoming darkness, mixed with the light from his headlights, created deceptive and confusing shadows that gave him fits of anxiety.

Dan drove for another four hours, covering the distance that it would normally have taken him to make it in one, still able to continue in the direction that the Altima had been tracked earlier. He soon found himself on the same highway that was the last known spot where the Altima had been traced. He wanted to keep going—no, he needed to keep going—but the fuel gauge was approaching empty. He needed gas, and he figured now was as good a time as any to stop.

The green and yellow BP station was lit up like it normally should have been at that time of night, except that it was empty of all human life except his. As he pulled up he instantly noticed the many distinctive spots of bodily liquids that were deposited around the station grounds like giant spilled slurpies.

He slid his credit card into the reader to pay (amazed that it still took his information like nothing had changed) and kicked the pumps on.

Automation. Just how long would parts of the world continue to stay powered with only machines at the controls?

As he pumped his gas, he tried to push his thoughts away from the liquid human remains that called out for his attention, instead trying to concentrate his efforts back to finding where Patrick and his captor might have gone. But no matter how hard he tried, his gaze was continuously brought back around to the various spots of death.

He finally couldn't stand it anymore and walked over and knelt beside one of the spots of human residue.

As he stared at the sticky substance, he quickly began to realize that if it wasn't for the clothing and the various items such as wallets or purses or rings that were intermixed with the fluids on the ground, short of bringing in the best CSI teams, there didn't seem to be a way to figure out who each of the fluids belonged to. Even the bone and teeth had been dissolved. He could be standing right next to Patrick's remains at the moment and wouldn't even know it was him. He was both sickened and awestruck at the same time.

Before he left the gas station he glanced over the map again, hoping he would spot something that would give him a clue as to where he might start looking. Some sort of off the beaten path motel, or road. He tried to put himself in the position of the kidnapper, hoping that he could think like the kidnapper would think and decipher an area that the person might head towards that might seem abandoned and a good place to hide. But he soon concluded that it would be useless. For all Dan knew the two of them might already be half way to Minnesota by now, or worse, somewhere along the highway, dead.

He left the gas station feeling empty and worried, because he really wasn't sure in what direction he was supposed to go. He knew that he was on the correct highway, but after that, he didn't know what to do. He was lost.

Dan turned the radio on, not really wanting to hear about all the horror that was taking place, but hoping that maybe something would catch his ear that would give him some information as to what was taking place locally. Possibly leading him to finding his son. But when he heard nothing but static coming across the wide range of radio bandwidths, he knew he was in trouble.

He pulled the truck under an overpass and turned off the ignition. He sat in the dark and wanted to cry, something he hadn't done in twenty years, but wouldn't allow himself the luxury now. Crying meant you felt sorry for yourself. That you had reached your limit and you couldn't go on. But Dan didn't actually feel that way. He wanted to go on; he just didn't have a clue as to what to do, or where to go.

He was trying to come to grips with the realization that it may take him days, or weeks, or months to ever find Patrick.

Or possibly never.

He leaned his head back against the window and closed his eyes to think. And though he hadn't planned on it, he soon fell asleep.

Ring! Ring!

Huh?

Ring! Ring!

Dan instantly sat upright.

"I got it," he said to an imaginary someone as he woke up.

He blinked twice, then reached to his hip and plucked off the cell phone and flipped it open.

It was Randomguard.

"Yes! Yes, I'm here!" he answered frantically.

The woman at the other end was sniffling as if she was crying.

"Mr. Brighton?"

Dan immediately recognized that it was Michele.

"Yes. God, yes. How are you doing? I've been trying and trying to get a hold of you guys all night. Can you tell me anything? Do you know where my son is?"

"That's why I'm calling, sir. You're going to end up being my last call. They're shutting the place down, Mr. Brighton. They're sending us all home. I'm so scared."

Dan tried to think of something to say to calm the young lady, but all that he could do was to sit quietly in the dark and stare blankly at his steering wheel, waiting for any morsel of information that she may have to give him.

She quickly took a deep breath and went on.

"Everyone's running around in a panic. I didn't know what to do. I taped a note up on my screen after our last conversation reminding myself to keep tabs on what was happening with your son, but with what is taking place, I . . . I don't even know if my mom and dad . . . I can't get a hold of them . . . I just couldn't . . ." She began to sob. "But I wanted to call you back for one last piece of information concerning your son."

"It's ok, Michele. It'll be ok. Just tell me, do you know where he is?"

"Yes," she sniffled. "The last known fix we have on the car seems to be off Highway Fourteen, someplace on Markers Run road. They're still in West Virginia, Mr. Brighton, but they're pulling the plug on everything here, and that's the last best fix I could get on him. I don't know if the police got to him or not."

She was getting frantic.

Dan immediately started the truck up and put it in gear to move towards where she had just given him directions.

"It's ok, Michele. Calm down. God, I thank you. It's a miracle you got through to me. I was lost out here in the dark. I had no idea where to go."

Silence.

"Michele?"

He pulled the phone from his ear and looked at the screen. She was gone.

He stared at the screen, wondering if the loss of power was the reason he had lost contact with Michele, or . . .

He didn't want to think about it.

Dan wasn't sure how Michele had finally gotten a hold of him though, but he still looked towards the heavens and thought, Thank you, God!

He pulled the map out and began tracing out the area with his finger where he needed to go.

He could see to his right that the sun was in the early stages of coming up over the ridge as the pinks and reds gave a magnificent display against some of the low lying clouds. At least this would give him a little bit of light to maybe make out where he needed to be.

Dan drove up and down Highway Fourteen several times before he finally saw the tiny, bent over backwards sign signifying that he had found the spot.

Dan was surprised that the road was even registered on a map. It was an old gravel road that led back into continuing darkness between some low reaching trees that scratched and squeaked against his truck as he drove down the lane. Every hundred yards or so he would see a wayward driveway that would lead back into the distance. He imagined that he was going to have to drive back and check every single driveway until he hopefully came across the Altima. But after traveling a little more than a mile down the bumpy road, and at about the time when he figured it was time to turn around and begin his methodical search, was when good fortune intervened.

He spotted the car.

He had to squint and lower his head, looking back and to his left about a hundred yards or so, but there it was, sitting in front of an old farmhouse just as pretty as you please.

His first instinct was to whip the car into the drive way and race down to the house and rescue his son. But after what Deputy Barnes had said to him, and being that he didn't bring along a gun, he decided that using caution might be his best course of action. So he silently parked the car and made his approach on foot.

Dan decided that if at any moment he heard any screams, or anything disturbing coming from inside, then he would just make a run for the house and the rest be damned. But otherwise, he was going to keep to the cover of the various trees in the front yard and approach the house from the side.

The house was dark except for the one pale light that came from a side window. It seemed to be taunting him as he approached, as if it was inviting him inside. It's dark and silent form starting to creak and groan from the mornings first burst of sun.

Come and see! Have we got something planned for you!

As he crept by the car he quickly glanced into the windows to see if anyone or anything was still in there.

Nothing.

Disappointed, but somehow glad, he moved on.

Dan continued slowly around the side of the building, just out of reach of the porch supports. He began peeking into the windows to see if he could spot Patrick, or anyone that might be moving around inside, raising his head just far enough to peak over the window sill.

Again, nothing.

The only two things that he was sure of at that particular moment were that if anything had happened to Patrick, whoever the someone was that had committed the grievous deed was going to suffer twice over in punishment for whatever may have happened to him.

Secondly, he was scared out of his mind.

He began to move around to the back of the house when he found something odd. There was a rather large hole beside the house that someone had recently dug. The dirt was still moist, and still had that granular look about it like it had been freshly shoveled. Footprints that were way too big for Patrick moved over the dirt and away towards the darkened woods behind the house. Dan mentally shrugged and continued on.

The sun was now starting to peek just above the horizon and Dan was rapidly beginning to lose his cover of darkness.

He was just starting to believe that there wasn't anyone home, when he heard someone uttering something like, "get away," or something like that, from inside. He couldn't be sure.

He instantly ducked down, trying not to be seen by whoever had made the noise.

Dan was trying hard to listen to the other words that were now being spoken, words he couldn't quite make out, when something strange began to happen.

He heard a humming. Or buzzing.

A loud buzzing. Like the world's biggest electric razor was coming over his head.

He was already on his knees but he ducked even lower, hugging the ground, feeling like something was swooping down at him.

And it was.

Flies. Lots of flies. More flies than he had ever seen in his life.

But they didn't seem to notice Dan as he flattened out on the grass, covering his head. Most pelted the windows with a sound like cracking ice on a winter's pond, while others began flying down the freshly dug hole, with the rest going around to the front of the house.

He now heard the distinct sound of someone crying inside. An adult man crying. Screaming.

Dan picked himself up, and couldn't help but slide back over to a window and look back inside. He wanted to run away, but even more he wanted to see what was happening in the house.

And, as his eyes widened in disbelief at the sight that was now taking place in front of him, he began to wish that he had run away.

Tye was on his hands and knees, his body convulsing involuntarily as the flies worked inside him. Most had already exited his body, but the last few were still trying to make their way up to his mouth for their release. He could feel them coming up the back of his throat like tiny pieces of undigested food, and he hacked and coughed them the rest of the way up, spitting them out onto the floor.

Tens of thousands of flies were in front of him, buzzing and swarming in one gigantic mass.

Tye couldn't lift his head just yet to look up at them, but if he could have he would have seen them begin to take shape. To take a human like form. The figure they made was cold and black, like a shadow in winter.

Tye's mind couldn't even begin to acknowledge the pain he was going through. He was too far past that point. His only concern at the moment was determining whether his body was still in one piece. Or had the flies removed anything from him?

"W . . . What did you do to me?" he asked in a near whisper.

To his shock and surprise he received an answer.

"wE HAvE cOrrEcTEd YoUR foRm," the rasping, hideous voice came from the swarming mass.

Tye's tearing eyes lifted to take in the thing that was now speaking to him.

"STAnD, FLeSh eAteR," it instructed.

"I . . . I don't think I can," he said as he grimaced from the pain.

"sTAnD!" the form commanded.

Tye pulled one leg underneath his body to support his weight and to try and push himself upwards. His body tingled and itched madly just underneath his skin, and he wondered if there were any flies still inside him. He lifted his hands in front of his face and watched as several small muscle seizures continued like ripples on a pond along his skin lines. He pushed himself upwards, his strength rapidly returning as the pain he was feeling continued on in its unrelenting rush.

As he stood, and began to steady himself, he began to comprehend what the flies had meant when they told him that they had "corrected his form."

"What did you do to me? I feel different," he said as strings of saliva dripped from his lips. "Larger."

"yOU arE WhAT yOU wERe, ONly mORe sO."

He blinked slowly, trying to find his bearings through the pain haze he was still experiencing.

"More so?"

"tHe COnfiGuRAtiOn oF tHe FOrm tHaT yOU inhABiT NeEDed mOdiFIcaTion."

His realization of the situation came quickly.

"You changed me? Into what?"

"a bETteR CoNfigURatIOn."

Tye closed his eyes tight and bit down on his lip. The wrath that was building within him was immense.

"How dare you," he seethed as he opened his eyes. "You don't have the right! She doesn't have the right!"

Before the mass could react, Tye reached out like a snake and snatched a great handful of the flies in front of him, squishing them in his hand until their bodies turned to jelly, dripping to the ground.

The flies quickly scattered and then began to reform to his left. Tye lunged again for their form, but once again they scattered and reformed, this time behind him.

"THE fOlly Of yOUr IntENt iS eVidENt. AcCEpt yoUr pRESenT StatE aNd cOntINue wiTh yOur TaSk. We kNOw WheRe thE BOy is goiNG."

"You changed me? How could She do that to me? To hell with the boy. You go find him."

"noN-aCCeptAnce oN yoUR bEhaLF WiLL oNly bE deALT WitH By ouR REadmiSSion inTO yoUR fORm foR FurTHer ModiFicaTion. AcCEpt yoUR pRESent STate."

Tye snapped his head back.

Further modification?!

"There will be no "further modification," Tye said as he took a threatening step towards the fly thing, while the fly thing took a cautious step backwards away from Tye. "Do you understand?"

He began to examine his form, trying to take stock of what changes the flies had spoke of.

"So this is what She would do to me?" he asked bitterly as he straightened himself. "This is my punishment, then?

"Well, one thing is clear," he said as his eyes lowered to blackened slits, his voice sounding as if doom was on the horizon. "When you go back to report to your masters, please make sure that you extend to them my eternal appreciation. And be sure to let them know that I will be paying them a visit when I am finished here. I believe that they and I have some matters to attend to that require attention. It may come that they soon regret that they only modified my being instead of taking me down for good."

Though Tye was still wary of the fly thing in front of him, it did seem that the two were now at an uneasy truce.

"You may have altered my form, my little friends, but I believe you may have also altered my mind set on a few matters as well."

Tye turned to look at his ghostly reflection in one of the windows of the kitchen.

"So, where is the Brighton child?" he asked.

"hE HAs PlaCEd hImsELf wITH tHe ANimAls."

"That I know. Tell me something I don't know."

"HE iS mOVinG UNdeR tHEir GuIDAncE. thEy aRE MovIng HiM tO The nORth. bECauSE OF YoUR mODifiCaTIOn yOU sHOULd Be Able to SmELL in WhICH dIrEcTiON tHEy ARe hEAdIng."

Smell them?

At first Tye seemed unsure of what they might be telling him.

Was he really able to smell them? The idea seemed preposterous to him.

But he wrinkled his nose, and lifted his head slightly, trying to identify any scent that might be off in the distance. Not the nearby odors of the house, or the yard, or the forest right out back, but further on. It took a few seconds, but to his delight he soon discovered that he could sense and smell things a good ways off. He concentrated hard, pushing his mind to discover any scent that might be farther and further away.

Tye began to smile. The flies were right—he could smell the boy. He could smell the animals, too. Their scent was faint at best, but due to the distance that existed between where they were, and where he was, as he breathed in their bodily oils and sweat it was almost like they were standing right there next to him in the room.

"Amazing," he said as he shook his head. "I do believe that I may grow to like this new form. But where exactly are they. It could take me a week to track them just by following the smell that exists on the wind. It would go a lot faster if I knew the exact point where I can snatch the little toad. I need to teach him, and his little traveling companions, a few lessons about what happens when you take someone else's property."

The fly thing began to explain to Tye the exact location of where the animals had gathered. If there is one thing that a fly will definitely know, it's the location of where a horse, or horses, might be. And at the great gathering that the animals had assembled, there were plenty of horses to go around.

Dan watched as the events in the kitchen of the old farmhouse unfolded. He was shocked at first. His mind having a hard time dealing with the reality of what was taking place. But soon, just as he had with the plague, his mind began to adjust to the sight that was before him and he quickly found a place in his head that would allow him to continue on without losing his sanity. Though he felt like crying and giggling at the same time, he bit down hard on the inside of his lip to remind him to hold his thoughts together.

Dan was determined that nothing was going to surprise him anymore. He regained his focus and concentrated his thoughts on what he needed to do. He was here to do one thing—bring back his son alive—and he was intent on accomplishing that goal.

And, as he had listened to the monstrous conversation that was taking place in the house, the one thing that was continually ringing through again and again—the one thing that he now clinged to—was that Patrick was still alive.

It may have been that a Stephen King novel full of freaks might be going after him, to reclaim him for whatever awful purpose they may have had, but the fact still remained that he was definitely alive.

And Dan wanted to keep him that way.

But even as he watched the display of devilry that was taking place in front of him, Dan's mind slowly crept away as he pondered continuing questions that kept coming up about Patrick.

Why were they seeking him so desperately? And what is it that they want from him? Did he do something to this man? Surely he doesn't have any part in what's happening with the state of the world, does he? And who were the others that the man in the house kept referring to?

So he listened carefully as the fly thing told the peculiar looking man where his boy was located.

As Dan Brighton listened to the talking flies, his attention danced back and forth from the fly thing and to the man that it was talking to. Dan wasn't sure if the strange man even knew what was happening to him or not, but the stranger's features were definitely starting to change. To grow. To elongate. Whatever the fly thing had meant by "the modification," it was undeniably beginning to take place.

Dan stepped back from the window, paying particular attention not to raise his head for fear of being seen. He had heard enough for him to get moving in the direction that was given to begin looking for Patrick, and he believed that now might be his best chance for escape.

He turned and began creeping away, his eyes going towards his path of escape, when to his misfortune his foot caught an old clay flower pot that was perched up against the side of the house. He kicked it at first, the pot tumbling madly in front of him, finally coming to a rest sitting upside down. As he tried to regain his balance, he stumbled a bit more and then stepped directly on the pot. It cracked in two with a 'pop!' and finally exploded into pieces.

He cringed as he put his hand down to the ground to maintain his balance, and quickly turned his head back towards the window to see if anyone had come to catch his spying. When he didn't see anyone at the windows, he turned and bolted for the truck.

A loud whack and then a thump came from just outside one of the kitchen windows causing both Tye and the fly thing to turn their heads in that direction.

"IT aPPearS yOU HaVe a VisiTOr," the fly thing hissed.

Tye moved instantly towards the window, grabbing the kitchen table and tossing it out of his way like it was made of paper. For a moment he saw what looked like a figure of a man dashing away from the house. Tye smiled to himself and then headed for the front door, the mass of flies following closely behind him. He opened the front door and stood, watching as the white haired intruder ran from the house. The man was already at the end of the lane when Tye quickly surmised that this was not the opportunity to pursue the spy. If he had wanted, he could have easily captured the man straightaway. But he let the man go, figuring that sometimes it was best to let the prey get away to be caught another day.

"So, I see daddy wants to play as well," he said wickedly.

He smiled a wide and toothy grin as he watched from the shadows as the man got into his truck and hurriedly drove down the lane.

And although Tye hadn't sensed it, nor felt it, but a small forked tongue slid effortlessly from inside his mouth, slipping gently between his lips before sliding back inside.

CHAPTER 7

All That Had The Dream

"It seems there is a book. A rather old book," Bing began somberly. "A book that we believe no longer serves any purpose for the betterment of man or beast. One that long ago should have had each of its pages ripped from their bindings and burned until the ashes no longer resembled anything more than the feathery dust from whence they came.

"It is said that the book was originally created and intended as a guide; a written example of what life should be like on this Garden of Eden. That it had been given to a group of human men and women thought to be preservers of the earth. They, along with the union of the other creatures of this world, were to shepherd the book, and the world, taking care not to have any one sect abuse the privileges of the others. And though they had good hearts, and their intentions were of a just and noble way, sometimes the ways of men can become . . . misguided. Through treachery and treason, through greed and misfortune, the book went exchanged from hand to hand as it was never meant to be, until there came such a time when no one truly knew where the book had fallen to, and who exactly had it in their grasp.

"So, through time and tide, and man's foolish error, the book had become lost.

"No one is really sure who created the book. Some believe that the book was conceived, or dictated, by the 'Creator' as a way to serve man, helping him to guide and rule the world as it was intended from the beginning.

"Others believe that the book may have come from a more subterranean level of thinking. That it was created as a method of deceit. To fracture man's thinking into questioning whether or not there truly is a Creator.

"Either way, the book is believed to have language in it that can bring forward certain beings that can either aid, or admonish, the caretaker of the book as to whether the way of the world is traveling in the direction as it was intended."

"Is the book you're talking about the Bible?" Patrick asked quietly.

"No. I know of the book of which you speak. That book is a document created by man, for man. This book, the one I refer to now, is something that deals only with the planet and it's wealth and resources. It is an ancient book that deals with all creatures and how they are meant to live, and with instructions on how the planet should continue to flourish."

"And nothing on how it should be governed. One has nothing to do with the other," Syrian added firmly.

"But that doesn't sound so bad. Why do you wish that it was destroyed?"

"Because, like most things, it comes down to a matter of interpretation. If the book were to fall into the wrong hands then whoever possesses the book could interpret the meanings of its passages for ill ways. Make no mistake, it is a very powerful book. And it was given with the understanding that it was a book to help, not hinder, the ways of the world. It has become a matter for debate now that it has resurfaced."

"So where is the book?" Patrick asked.

"I'm just getting to that," Bing nodded in Patrick's direction. "One of the many different factions that congregate on this world believes that there is not a Creator, but carries a belief that there is only the earth, and that man is the descendant of the earth itself, rather than that of the Creator. These beings are the ones who have come across the book. They have it in their possession as we speak.

"They are a group of Wicca, or Earth witches, that have splintered away from the very core ideals of their own original following and beliefs. The animals have watched and observed the Wicca throughout the world for many centuries. For the most part they are a harmless group, devoted to the good earth and all that it has to offer. In some ways we have grown quite fond of their interesting ways. They do not seem intent on bringing harm or foulness to any form or group that belongs to the earth.

"The assemblage we now speak of though, a group that has become corrupted it's own beliefs, has come across the book of ages and has somehow deciphered it's contents in such a way as to bring forth a temptress that has seduced their minds into believing that they have been given the keys to the kingdom of earth, and that it is their duty, and theirs alone, to rule over the land.

"But their beliefs are wrong. Even though man was set upon this planet with the Creator's blessing, and given the gift to rule over it, and even though he has made ghastly errors in judgment in how to manage the earth, there is still an intricate balance, an invisible web that exists between you and me and all life around us, that the animals and plant life know exists like the air we breathe."

"Unfortunately, man does not sense this link the binds us together," Syrian spoke aloud. A small swell of agreement began to ripple throughout the great crowd.

"Though the debate rages," Bing began again, "—as you have plainly witnessed for yourself—as to whether or not man should continue in guardianship of the planet, it is not up to us to make this decision. Though mankind has done many evil and perverted things that we in the animal kingdom do not easily understand, it is still not one group, or one single being's decision, outside of the Creator, to decide man's fate. This decision was made long ago by the Creator and his decisions are not to be amended. If he should judge that it is time for mankind to give up its rule over the earth, then it will be his decision to make. Rather than this group of humans who have taken it upon themselves to make the decision for the Creator. This is wrong.

"The evil one, a woman of such evil and wickedness, has spoiled her summoner's minds. She has taken over their very beings—and souls—twisting them into perverted creatures that should never have been born onto the land.

"She, the one who has no name, but is the witch queen, has taken several of the humans that have summoned her and created from them four abominable destroyers of men.

"'Pestilence', the carrier of the plague. With her every breath the death she exhales floats on the air bringing man kind closer to his end.

"'War', the deliverer of carnage and destruction. She comes in many guises. She is whispering into the many ears of man as we speak, filling him with her many destructive deceits. At this very moment she is playing man against man, friend against friend, country against country. She is being used to deceive man into believing that the plague of death that is spreading rapidly around this world was brought about by men in foreign lands. The men, in turn, are gathering for war as tensions build across many continents as one group accuses the other of this atrocity. Fighting has already begun to break out throughout based on this assumption, much to War's pleasure.

"'Famine', the end result of both pestilence and war, has been unleashed upon man to destroy his food source and suppliers—the things that are not being affected by the plague.

"And finally, 'Death.' It is told that she rides across many lands of the Earth on a fiery horse of death, claiming her countless prizes as human bodies are torn asunder by War's weapons of death, and by the very plague itself. She is very busy these days—and reported to be very pleased. At present, she sits at the right hand of the witch queen.

Bing's eyes began to water with his passionate plea.

"The earth witches do not realize exactly what they have done. They have summoned something so horrific, and calamitous, that the very world is cracking at its core. With the abominable decision that they have made in delivering the earth into her loathsome hands, She has decided that she will now rule unopposed.

"They have corrupted the very existence of all who walk and crawl and grow over the land. And they must be stopped."

The air was heavy with the final words that Bing had spoken. Not a breath could be heard.

Patrick's mouth hung open, un-chewed apple still resting in the corner of his cheek. He pulled himself away from Bing's intent gaze and surveyed the faces of the many animals now watching him, waiting to see how he was going to react. It was painfully obvious as to why they were looking at him. They believed that he was somehow going to give them the answer as to how to put things right. An answer he knew he didn't have to give.

He turned back to Bing.

"Why are they doing this? Why do they want to kill off men? Aren't they men also?"

"True. But this is a group of men and women who are of a belief that man has wasted his time on this earth. That he has spoiled a good part of the world for the rest of creation with his own filth and greed. These are the beings that have summoned forth the out-worldly creature to aid in wiping out the race of man. They have brought her into the world. She has brought forth the plague to accomplish their request."

Patrick swallowed hard, his mind not believing what he was hearing.

"And, you want me to do . . . what?" Patrick asked, knowing before he had even finished the question that he didn't want to know the answer to it.

The baboon smiled lightly, "We were hoping you could tell us."

The small penguin then sighed. "You see, some of us are here by choice, the rest of us are here because of something that came to us all while we slept. It has come to us in our dreams. There were a select few of us throughout the kingdom of the animals that had a night vision, a dream, about a man, a human boy, who would be able to stop the wickedness that was coming. It was a dream about you.

"All of the animals that have traveled here, as far as we know, have had a dream that showed them the way to this spot. Some couldn't make the journey, others didn't want to, or ignored the dream. And, of all the animals that have made it to this very spot, there are only four animals that had the specific dream about you—of us going with you—on this journey."

"And where did it show you . . . us . . . going?"

"I think you already know the answer to that question, my young friend."

No . . . oh no no no!

Patrick's reaction was frantic.

"But what am I supposed to do against a witch? I don't have any magic powers. I can't do anything special. I can't even run very fast."

A few groans, along with a few chuckles, floated forward from the crowd.

"Well, being that we don't know why the four of us were selected for this either, it kind of makes it even, don't you think?"

"No. No I don't" Patrick said as he shook his head. "Why do you need me? Why can't I just go back to my home? Why can't I just go back to my mom and my dad?"

Bing was torn with sympathy, as were many other animals, at Patrick's reaction. They had previously discussed amongst themselves the concern with sending out one so young to accomplish such a daunting task. They tried to imagine if they had to send out one of their own, one of their young, to go out on this chosen chore. And many did not take kindly to the thought of it. They came to understand the reservations that Patrick was now displaying through the eyes of their own young. They talked with their children and tried to find the mental positioning that one so young, even if it was a child of man, would have to comprehend in burdening themselves with the given assignment. Even if it did mean that the entire fate of man possibly rested in his hands.

Patrick tugged at his fingers nervously as he looked around the many different faces of the animals. He could sense that the decision was already moving past the discussion stage, as if they weren't even going to ask him if he would go. Patrick could see that as far as they were concerned he was going and he didn't need to be asked.

"Why do you need me? Why don't you all just attack them? You should be able to take them out with just the overwhelming amount of animals that you have," Patrick offered, pleading his case for his dismissal.

Uneasy whispering promptly broke out among the different groups at his inquiry.

"It has already been tried, I'm afraid," Syrian spoke, "and the results were very sad. Horrible, in fact. Most of the animals were laid to waste the moment they began their attack. All were slaughtered, save for a few. We tried attacking them with sheer force, brought by the superior number and dominate size of the creatures, hoping to overpower her. We tried to match her with our own cunning and deceit, but she was wise to our plans, torturing the animals that were left alive. Their minds were hollow when we found them later.

"It seems there has been a great alignment of all beings that live and breathe on this Earth. Each taking a side in this situation. The kingdom of animals—that we have spoke of—has joined itself with the side of man, hoping to preserve, or better, the present state of the planet.

"But the reptile and insect worlds have decided to give their allegiance to Her, the summoned one. They are the warriors in which we came to battle with as we approached. She has issued to them a great promise of unimaginable wealth and growth on the planet subject to man's dismissal. With greater freedom, and less prejudice, the reptile and insect worlds would then dominate our world as well. This we cannot allow to happen."

Bugs and snakes. Patrick hated bugs and snakes.

"So over the last two night's fall," Bing began again, "we have decided that to risk any more embattlement with her mercenaries would not be prudent. As we felt that we should have from the very beginning, we have decided to follow our thoughts, and to trust our feelings about the dreams we have had, to take us to the task of vanquishing this nemesis. If our dreams are telling us to follow man into battle against this evilness, then we should do so without further delay.

"We came to believe, through many discussions, and interpretations, being that only four held the dream of seeing you, of seeing your face, then it must be that we have been chosen; destined to carry out this task along side you. Perhaps this is what the Creator wants. We cannot hope to know. But it has been decided that this is what will be. We are honored to be going with you."

Patrick looked out again at the great beasts before him. He felt as if his soul was being split in two. Part of him still so badly wanted to turn and run away—run back to his home, run back to his mom and dad. Not to believe that any of what the animals were telling him was true. To go back to his life. The other part now thrusting itself more to the forefront, felt a sense of honor at being chosen by such a great number of creatures—though he still didn't understand why.

"So who are the four animals that are going with me? You keep referring to yourself as one of the ones who've had this dream you keep telling me about—so I guess that means you're one of the four?"

"You are correct, young one. I will be honored to accompany you on this journey."

"Ok . . . but what can you do? I mean, you're just a penguin? I expected someone like him," Patrick said as he pointed to Syrian, "to be one of the ones going. Someone who looks like they can kick some butt."

A good many of the animals erupted in laughter.

"Sorry. I didn't mean anything insulting by that," Patrick quickly interjected.

Bing puffed out his chest and thrust out his beak. "Yes, I realize that I am not the expected companion one would like on a mission of this nature. But, I too, had the dream. I cannot refute this."

Syrian then stepped forward. "I believe then that you have gotten your wish, Patrick Brighton of the men. I, too, have had the dream."

"Good."

"But be forewarned, Patrick Brighton, brute strength is not going to be the way in which this battle will be won. Of this, we have already seen."

Patrick nodded his agreement.

"Well, that's two," Patrick said, "Who are the other two? You said there were four."

Bing turned to his right, looking back to the far edge of the barn. He then turned back, looking out over a group of animals to his left. "Are they here yet? I don't think I see them," he asked to no one in particular.

"Yes, we are here," a stern response came as three razorback boars walked to the front of the crowd. "We have brought him as it was requested."

Patrick was instantly surprised to see what was in front of him. Not because of the type of animal that they were, but at the smallish boar in the middle of the three. It was solid white in color. An almost blinding white. Not even his whiskers, or his hooves were of a different color. Even his eyes were white. It was frightening, yet mesmerizing, at the same time. Patrick could not pull his gaze away from it.

"Has he agreed to go, then?" Bing seemed to ask of the two older, larger boars.

"Yes," the one to the left answered.

"And what of his parents?" Bing asked as he arched his brow. "Are they in agreement with this decision?"

The elder boars only stared back at Bing with anger. "You are well aware that he is an orphan."

"Yes, I suppose," Bing said slyly. "It's just the way in which he became one that bothers me." Bing shook his head. "I'm not so sure I agree with the way your kind handles its problems. It seems a bit harsh, if you ask me."

"But the decision is ours to make," the larger boar answered in return. "The elders in our tribe have made their determination based on the ways in which we have practiced our culture for many years. It cannot be altered now. You will either take him, based on the dreams of the entire tribe, or he will be cast out."

"Well then, I guess it's pretty convenient that your entire tribe had the dream, since we may never know whether the lad actually had one himself." The small penguin then looked to the ground. "Nevertheless we will gladly take him with us. If of nothing more than to get him away from the wonderful people who have raised him," Bing added sarcastically.

The larger boar on the left snorted gruffly, and began to take a step forward. "Be careful with your words wise little bird. Any more of that disrespectful tone and we may have to educate you in the ways of respect."

As a few of the other animals stepped away in fear of some retribution at the remark, Syrian quickly stepped between the angry, insulted boar and Bing.

"I believe that any further advance on your part would be an unwise mistake," Syrian spoke slowly, casually, as if this type of conflict was nothing knew to the baboon.

"It is how it is," the boar spoke defiantly. He then turned and began walking silently away. The other boar that was to the right of the small white boar then turned to leave as well.

"Excuse me," Bing asked quickly of him, "but before you go, could you please do us the courtesy and at least tell us the lad's name?"

The boar that was second to leave looked back over his shoulder and spoke with contempt the name of the white animal.

"He is called, 'Sin.'"

Bing rolled his eyes at the words.

"Well, that fits," he said disgustedly, "How nice."

"What did he do?" Patrick asked in a near whisper to Bing, his eyes continually glancing in the direction of the white boar. "Did he do something wrong?"

"No," Bing said without taking his eyes off of the boar, "his parents did."

"So, why is he in trouble?"

"Exactly the question, Patrick. Why is he in trouble?"

"I don't understand."

"Sometimes the ways of man are not so unlike the ways of the animal world."

Patrick pulled his head back, looking queerly at Bing once again.

"I know, I know," Bing said as he shook his head, "you don't understand. I will try to explain later. We must move this along before it becomes too late in the day. We are wasting precious time."

Bing directed his attention to the small animal.

"Young boar—Sin, is it—we welcome you to our gathering. Do not worry over words that may have been said in the past. Your past stays where it belongs—back with your tribe. It does not alter our appreciation of your presence here today."

The young boar surprisingly bowed deeply.

Bing returned the gesture.

"Well, who is the last to be going with us, then?" Patrick asked.

"That is a good question. I never did find out who was to be the final partner in this. Syrian, do you know who the final animal is that will travel with us?"

The baboon shook his head at the inquiry.

Bing looked out at the gathered beasts and asked for the last of the animals who've had the dream of the boy to come forward.

But no animal advanced.

"Surely, the fourth animal is here. Who is it? Please come forward."

Slowly, a fidgety, black weasel stepped into view.

"Um . . . here I am. I . . . I'm the one who had the dream," he said as his head pivoted from side to side in some sort of nervous twitch.

Bing smiled to reassure the small creature.

"Please come over and join with the rest of us. Do not be afraid. Your dream is the same as our dream. We are linked together in this as brothers. Do not be in fear of us."

The weasel began to nod in agreement as he shuffled his way towards Bing and Patrick.

"Uh . . . ok. Yeah. Yeah. Sure. I'm not afraid. I'll go with ya. Sure."

"What is your name, small one."

"Uh . . . Malard."

Patrick started to giggle at the sight of the timid weasel.

"Do not laugh at him, young one. We should all be as nervous as he is as we set off on the road we are about to travel."

"Sorry."

But if Bing could see into Patrick's head he would have seen that he was not giggling at the excitable little creatures nervous habits. Rather, he was giggling because of the situation as it was beginning to lay itself out in front of him. He was afraid. Deathly afraid. And he was in fear for his life.

What am I doing? I'm going off to fight a witch with a penguin, a hog, a baboon, and a scared little weasel? This can't be happening.

As the little weasel began to make his way over next to Patrick, Bing began to address the crowd for what seemed like the final time.

"Well, we have given our explanations. We have given our debates. And the conclusions drawn are still the same. We must continue to pursue this to find an end. I do not see any reason not to begin at once and embark on this undertaking. If there is any animal that wishes to join us, please feel free to come and stand beside us. If not, then we will be off."

Bing did not intend on making the final plea for any animal that may want to offer their services, but he himself was feeling a bit overwhelmed at the daunting task he was about to partake in. He was hoping that he could possibly find others that would make the decision to join up with the group. Hoping to make it easier on the burden that they were about to carry.

A heavy silence drifted over the shamed animals as not one other beast would step forward.

Bing nodded.

"Then it begins. We trust the birds will send along any word of our going, and of any word of anything coming to us. Wish us well."

"Wait a minute," a growling, agitated voice came from the very rear of the masses.

All heads turned to see who had uttered the unnerving volley.

Slowly the animals began to move aside as something large began to navigate towards the front of the assemblage. A slow rumble of distress began to echo through the crowd at the recognition of who was now making its way forward. Even Syrian's face held a look of dread as he caught sight of the advancing creature.

Bing was the first to speak her name, trying to curb the anxiety that was sweeping the crowd.

"Kirsdona, what a pleasant surprise it is to see you. And to what do we owe the honor of this meeting," he said as he swallowed.

"Save it, Bing," The great tiger, Kirsdona, spoke with a voice like fire blackened rock.

As the creature walked out of the crowd the sight of her caused Patrick to lose his breath.

The tiger, Kirsdona, was a legend within the kingdom of animals. An animal so large that she was almost twice the size of any normal Bengal tiger. Each of her alternating orange and black stripes was easily five fingers in width. Some didn't believe in her, referring to her only as a myth as they would talk about the supposed great cat of Indonesia.

But she was indeed real.

Reportedly she had been captured by zoologists and brought to North America for study at a local zoo. But her appearance here—now—was quite a shock to the many beasts that had heard of, but never seen, the magnificent cat.

Bing, though, seemed to already be well acquainted with the lady.

"We do not have time to spend on the trivial things that you may want to bring about, Kirsdona. As I'm sure you have heard, we need to go at once."

But the great cat ignored the penguin and continued right on through, her tail flicking the penguin in the beak as she walked by, moving to position herself in front of the boy. She leaned in her massive head, coming to a stop just close enough so that she could lick the boy's face if she had been inclined to take a taste of him.

Patrick was having a moment of shear panic worse than at any time since when he had first encountered Tye. If Patrick had held any urine in his bladder it would have surely come running out and down his leg at that moment. His back was hard up against the barn, the wood creaking as he pushed all his weight against it trying to move away.

"This is the boy, then?" she asked, not expecting a return to her inquiry. She let out a great "Humph", the warm air and tiny specks of moisture from her nostrils blasting out on to Patrick's face. "I'm not impressed."

Patrick's eyes burned from the putrid stench, and he quickly pulled his head back and away from the tiger.

"Ugh! You need a breath mint," Patrick said without thinking as he waved his hand. But immediately afterward an alarming look of regret came over his face at his realized error.

"Um . . . sorry about that. I didn't mean it."

"Of course you did. You are only speaking the truth that is on your mind," Kirsdona spoke. "Don't worry; I'm not so easily insulted. You are merely inhaling the remnants of this morning's breakfast—freshly slaughtered Elk," she finished as she licked the remnants from her lips.

"Enough, Kirsdona. What is it that you want?" Bing asked impatiently.

"What everyone else here came to do. I wanted to see the boy."

"Well, now you've seen him. You've wasted enough of our time. We have got to go."

Kirsdona began to look over the boy's features, as if he was examining the boy for something, but she would not look directly into his eyes. This disturbed Patrick greatly.

"What is it that . . ." Bing began again, but was cut off as Kirsdona pressed forward.

"Do you really believe that you are going to do anything to save your kind, boy?" Kirsdona asked in a disruptive manner as she took a step back, her tail flipping like a snake slowly from side to side. "I mean truly believe? Believe that not only are you going to even make it to your final destination, a journey that could consume thousands of miles, but to then have enough strength left to do battle with the kind of evil that would just as soon kill you as it would take a breath of air? Hmm? Because I know those kinds of creatures. I am one of those kinds of creatures.

"And you're going to do it with these paltry animals as your guides? And what will you do when you get there? What is it that you are capable of doing anyway, boy?"

Patrick was white as a sheet, his jaws clamped up tight with fear from the confrontation that Kirsdona was inducing, scaring Patrick out of his wits.

Bing jumped from his stoop, landing down in front Kirsdona.

"That's enough!" he cried. "Do not attempt any more of your foul and unwanted words trying to confuse and suffocate the poor boy with unwelcome thoughts. He has no choice. We have no choice. Do you understand?"

The corners of Kirsdona's mouth curled up into a neat little grin.

"Calm yourself little bird. Of course I understand. I just wanted to see what was deep within the heart of this human," Kirsdona looked away as if disinterested. "I'm afraid I didn't see much at all," she said as she yawned.

"Then move away, please."

"I know. I know. It's time for you to go," a disgusted look covering Kirsdona's face. The great cat let out a long sigh, and then turned away from the boy.

"Malard?"

"Y . . . Yes?"

"You are free to go."

"What?!" Bing said.

"W . . . what?" Malard repeated, caught completely by surprise, "But . . . but you said . . ."

"You heard me. You are free to leave. I've changed my mind. You won't have to go," Kirsdona said as she walked over and began rubbing her backside against the grainy, rough wood of the barn.

"Now wait a moment!" Bing protested. "You cannot intervene in the decision that . . ."

"Well it seems that I can—and I am. I've decided that I'm going to be your fourth companion on this little escapade."

Upon hearing the words coming from Kirsdona, the little weasel began edging away towards the far side of the barn.

"Does this mean I can go? She did say I could go, right? You're not going to eat me or anything, right?" Malard asked, his nervous eyes twitching from side to side as he began to make his escape.

"Um hmm," Kirsdona purred as she continued her vigorous rubbing.

"What is going on?!" Bing asked, his little body beginning to quake with anger.

"I had the dream, Bing. Not Malard. Not anyone else. Me. Get it? I just needed someone to take my place temporarily because I didn't think I was going to be able to make the trip. But things have changed."

"You had the dream?" Bing repeated, now completely in shock.

He seemed to echo the sentiments of the other animals as they felt insulted by Kirsdona's revelation. They instantly began to comment and inquire as to her integrity and placement among the group. Words came forward that were not kind at all.

Kirsdona turned towards the animals, her body tensing to a threatening posture.

"I'd temper your responses, my friends. I'd hate to use one of you as an example."

Bing was outraged.

"What?! You forced another animal to go in your place because you didn't think you could make it? Why would you do such a thing?"

"I have my reasons."

"And what reasons could those be that would supercede something that may have come from your Creator? Or do you just have night dreams all the time?"

"Like I said, I have my reasons. Get over yourself, would you?"

"I don't get you," Bing went on, "You were just going to allow us to journey away from here and not even say a word to us about 'your reasons?' Allow us to take an innocent creature that would have had no business going along with us in the first place?"

"Hey, didn't you say something about us getting a move on?" The great cat had moved away from the barn and was now stretching her enormous body. "Are you going to drone on all day like this, or are you going to wrap this thing up?"

Bing was furious.

"Please tell me that this is not how your attitude is going to be while . . ."

But Kirsdona just rolled her eyes, "Blah. Blah. Blah. I do believe we've spent enough time debating this. Next subject, please."

As all of this silly talking was taking place, Patrick began to notice a few crows circling overhead, slowly descending down to the crowd below. They continued their descent until they were low enough to speak to the group.

"We have spotted the trickster, the thing called Tye. He is getting close. He is traveling fast and should reach this spot within hours."

The crowd of animals went into an uproar upon hearing the news from the crows.

"Then we must make haste," Bing said as turned and motioned to the group. "We need to leave as soon as possible."

"Wait a minute, shouldn't you guys be able to stop him? I mean, look at all of you, there must be a thousand animals here. I see lions, and bears, and all kinds of things. Shouldn't you guys be able to stop him? To kill him?"

Bing, already upset at the confrontation with Kirsdona, tried to be kind to the boy's impatient pleas. "First of all, most animals—though there are of course a few exceptions—believe that killing is only to be done when there is no other way out of a situation, or in hunting food for survival. But even though neither are the case as it comes before us now, I must say that I don't believe any one of us here wants anything to do with the Tye creature at the moment."

Patrick's frustration with Bing was obvious. "C'mon. He's a bit scary, but look around; you guys should be able to take him easily. Just look at her!" Patrick said as he pointed towards Kirsdona.

"It's a matter of choice. We'd rather pick our chance to do battle with Tye at a later time. When we have no other choice. It is said, that there are times when it is best to run to fight another day."

"Why?" Patrick pleaded. He couldn't believe what he was hearing. "Why are you so afraid of him? What can he do against all of you? He's just a man."

Bing whipped back towards Patrick, his voice sharp and cautioning.

"Is he?" Bing paused for moment. "You know this 'man' well, do you?"

"I know that he came to my house and kidnapped me. I know he wasn't going to kill me, but I'm pretty sure he's going to do it now. Why? What's the matter with him?"

Bing looked out over the dispersing group; animals were making paths into the underbrush, and through the trees with a momentous surge.

"We shall talk more on this later. The time to go is at hand. I don't think Kirsdona is of the patient kind."

Patrick looked over at the great cat, her hind legs nearly reaching his chest. He glanced back up at the circling crows, his mind a mess of unanswered questions, of riddles, and now of an unnerving new fear of Tye.

Patrick looked out on the now emptying landscape, amazed at how quickly the animals were dispersing upon hearing about Tye's progress.

Why would all of the animals be so afraid of him? he wondered.

As they began to gather themselves and started to move away, Patrick noticed that Sin wasn't following them, but rather was still standing exactly at the point where he had been left in the beginning.

"Bing, the boar is not coming with us."

Bing turned back and took a step towards the young boar.

"Sin, you are coming with us, correct?"

The boar nodded slightly.

"Well, come along, then. We are making our start."

Bing turned and returned to Patrick's side when he glanced back over his shoulder and watched as the boar began moving in the direction of the barn.

"What is he doing?" Bing asked as he shook his head.

The boar continued straight until he collided with the side of the barn, bouncing off of it slightly, as if he hadn't known it was there.

"Sin, we're over here," Patrick yelled out to the animal.

The boar steadied himself, and then began to walk in the direction that the rest had taken. But as he started to get closer to the group he began to drift off to the left, heading towards the hillside.

"Oh, no," Bing said as he watched the little boar begin to veer away.

"He looks like he's drunk," Patrick remarked.

And that's when Bing realized what was taking place.

"Patrick, run over and catch him," Bing ordered. "I can't believe this. I can't believe that they would send him in this condition. They should be ashamed of themselves."

"Is he drunk?" Patrick asked, amazed that he might be correct in his assumption. Wondering how a boar would get alcohol.

"No. He's blind," Bing replied in anger.

Patrick went as instructed and guided the white boar back over to the others.

Syrian knelt in front of the boar, waving his hand in front of the boars face, trying to gauge if there was any reaction, any movement in the animals eyes. He stood after a few moments.

"Not a thing. He's totally without sight."

"So, he's blind and mute? Nice combination," Kirsdona said matter of factly.

"Enough, Kirsdona. The poor creature can still hear."

"But what do we do with him? Syrian asked. "He can't go with us in this condition."

"Well, we can't leave him here," Bing said quickly. "Most of the animals have left. There'd be no one to look after him. And we can't take him back to his tribe. You heard what they said they'd do with him if we didn't take him. Besides, we're running out of time. With Tye just a short distance away, we've got to get moving."

"I could always just eat him," Kirsdona added slyly.

"Now that's not even funny," Bing scolded. "I'd appreciate it if we'd limit any attempt at joking right now."

"Who was joking?" the great cat said as she arched one eyebrow.

"Hold on," Patrick spoke. "I thought I saw some old rope in the barn. We could always loop it around him and make a leash out of it."

Kirsdona slowly turned in his direction, still not making any eye contact.

"An animal on a leash—how original. Isn't that so typically 'human.'"

"Do you have any better ideas?" Patrick said, beginning to realize that he was going to have problems with the big cat. She definitely did not like humans, and it was becoming more and more apparent that she did not like him in particular.

Kirsdona approached the boar, moving directly in front of the small creature.

"Can you hear me little one?" she began in a surprisingly motherly tone. Patrick shot a look of amazement to Bing and Syrian at her change in attitude.

The boar nodded.

"Ok. So, how about smell? Can you smell me?"

Again the animal nodded.

"So, do you think that you could follow me, and follow my scent if I went at a slow enough pace for you to keep up? At least for a short ways until we can find a place for you?"

Sin moved towards the tiger, his nose sniffing as he went, taking in Kirsdona's scent. The animal smiled hesitantly, and then nodded.

"Gentle creatures, I believe we have found a solution to your problem," she said as she started to walk on with the boar in tow.

Patrick looked at Syrian and Bing and shrugged.

"I guess that'd work."

"Alright then, Kirsdona," Bing spoke, "we'll make Sin your responsibility until we can find a proper place in which to leave him."

Bing pointed his wing at the cat.

"But, he had better not turn up missing."

Kirsdona could hardly contain her mischievous grin.

"Bing, I'm highly disappointed. How could you ever entertain such thoughts?"

The penguin did not remove his authoritative stare at the cat.

So after a little past noon on the fourth day before fall would break, with the sun at its highest point in the afternoon sky, the group began its trek north. They quickened their pace and vanished through some small low lying brush, making towards the tall trees in the distance. The group moved forward silently, each consumed with their own private thoughts. Wondering what foul torment could possibly be ahead.

CHAPTER 8

Into the Wild

He truly hated to admit it, but Patrick was already starting to get tired.

Patrick and his four animal companions had been walking for what had seemed like an eternity to him, but in the unimaginable reality that he was living it unfortunately had only been several miles. The bottoms of his feet felt like broken glass had been sprinkled in his shoes, and his legs ached and cramped, feeling as if sacks of potatoes were handcuffed to his ankles. But he made sure he didn't dare say a word about it to his escorts. No, that he would never do.

He already had an underlying feeling that they thought that he was nothing more than a weak little human boy, not nearly as powerful, or as swift as the animals that surrounded him. And though they might not come forward and readily admit this to him, he still made the assumption just the same.

Patrick thought this true of the others, but not of Bing.

The smallish penguin had never uttered a discouraging thought, or negative word to Patrick, even though he had known that he was trying Bing's patience at times. Though they were facing a task (something that Patrick tried not to think about) that was completely overwhelming, Bing never despaired. When Patrick had asked a few questions of the little bird that may have annoyed some, Bing had always come back to him with helpful, insightful answers, allowing Patrick to feel a little more at ease with the situation that was laid out before them.

Patrick was amazed at the pace the little penguin was able to keep up as well. From time to time the little bird would ask Patrick to pick him up and carry him for a ways while he rested, but he was always pleasant enough when Patrick had put him back down on the ground to continue the journey.

Though he had only known the little penguin for a few short hours, and though Kirsdona and Syrian might disagree, Patrick was already beginning to realize who the leader of this little group really was.

Patrick watched Bing carefully. His dad often referred to people (though Bing was only a penguin) as either optimists or pessimists. And Bing was definitely an optimist. *His glass is definitely half full,* his dad would always say referring to people like that. Bing just didn't seem to get upset. Even when he was relaying the information as he had earlier at the barn, though he had moments of anger and frustration at what he was describing, he never seemed to lose his cool. He was steady in his thinking.

Bing reminded Patrick of his father, and Patrick wanted to be like that.

The problem at the present—at least in Patrick's mind—besides the fact of his growing hunger and fatigue, was that he was confused as to what was actually taking place. He seemed to be placing all of his trust with the animals that had addressed him earlier with their mounting concerns. Yes, he could now somehow talk, or at least understand the animals as they were conversing.

And that was definitely something.

But besides that one thing, (although it was an interesting thing to say the least) it just didn't add up that he would be someone that the animals would give so much thought and so much importance too. They had pulled him from harm's way, sure, and had spoken of him in such high reverence. But as to what they were basing it on, Patrick didn't have a clue. If they were placing all of their trust on the dream that each of them had, then what did the dream mean? And what exactly did it spell out? When Patrick had asked the animals as they walked what had been in their dreams, they each had a problem with actually remembering exactly what their dreams had foretold. Syrian had described it not so much as a dream, but likened it more to an awake vision. A daydream. It was like a tug, or pull from inside their minds that each of them had felt, stronger than anything else they had experienced in their lives.

It was unexplainable.

They were thoroughly convinced that they each had seen Patrick's face in their dreams, determined that he was someone that they were compelled to seek out no matter the cost. The animals had quickly explained that things like this just didn't happen all the time. That they had each spoken on it within each of their tribes, or councils, and had come to the only conclusion that they believed was possible to make.

But in Patrick's mind, the certainty that they brought forward with their way of thinking only brought confusion that clouded his thoughts.

How exactly did they know that what they believed about him was coming from a good place, this thing that they were pretending to understand? How did they know that it wasn't coming from someplace darker? From some completely foreign place? Maybe from the place that had supposedly started the plague?

How did they know?

He was also having serious doubts about his ability to handle the situations that lay ahead of him—the ones that the animals were going to be counting on him for.

The one thing that he did know more than anything else—was that he knew himself. He knew what he was, and what he wasn't. And he was afraid that the animals would soon figure out what he wasn't. That when the moment would come for him to somehow perform whatever great and wondrous deed that the animals were going to expect, that he was probably going to mess it up; sure that he was going to let everyone down.

And what exactly was it that he was supposed to do anyway?

He had come to realize over time that there were just some things about him that he wasn't capable of. He could play sports, sure, but he wasn't very good. He could play baseball, but couldn't make the team. He could catch a football, but wasn't fast enough to outrun anybody. He could think on his own, but he wasn't on the debate team or anything like that.

Besides a dream, what gave these animals any idea that he was going to have the ability to save them, let alone save mankind?

A small mocking voice giggled at him in the back of his mind. A voice that toyed with his perceptions, creating the one thought that continually wobbled in his mind like a spinning top that was coming to an end.

Maybe the animals had made a mistake.

That maybe they had made a horrible mistake. That maybe even though that they had thought that it was him, and that they had thought that he was the right person, but maybe, just possibly, it was supposed to be some other boy from some other place in the world that was to lead them?

That he wasn't even supposed to be there.

This thought, and this thought alone, gave him a sickly, coppery taste in the back of his mouth that would not go away.

Patrick looked around at the faces of the animals. He didn't know what he was going to do, but he did not want to let them down.

He began to say a silent prayer asking that when the time came he be given the chance to muster whatever strength he possessed to help them accomplish their goal.

As time moved on the group began to be more purposeful in its progress.

Patrick walked on silently, as did most of the other animals. The only exception was Syrian, who walked beside the others humming a low, rhythmic marching song of some nature that Patrick couldn't quite decipher. It was definitely nothing he had ever heard before. He listened, wondering what the words were that went with the song. The tune found a soothing place in his thoughts, and he soon began to make up his own words in his head as he walked. And although he didn't realize it, he began to recite them out loud:

> I am walking to the north
> And I don't know where I'm going
> I am walking to the north
> That's where they are taking me
> I am walking to the north
> Walking with these animals
> Wishing I had some food to eat

Syrian turned his head toward Patrick and stopped his humming.

"You are mocking one of my kind's most sacred hymns. Please stop."

The group quickly came to a halt.

"Sorry. I didn't know. I was just putting words to the beat," Patrick said, embarrassed.

Syrian nodded his understanding, allowing the mistake.

Bing moved over next to Syrian. "So, what are the words that go with the humming, Syrian?" he asked. "What is this hymn?"

Syrian turned his attention from the others and began walking again. "You would not understand their meaning."

"Oh, yes," Kirsdona interjected, "Your kind is so much more advanced than any of us. We could never comprehend the meaning of your clever little song."

The baboon glanced sideways towards Kirsdona, "Are you always this sarcastic, tiger? Or does that extremely large body of yours come only equipped with a moderately sized brain?"

Kirsdona smiled knowingly. "You know, I once ate a baboon. It tasted a good bit like skunk. Only it was a lot chewier."

"Be careful, tiger. I am a Gelada. We are not as easily amused, or as easily frightened, as some of the others you may have encountered."

Kirsdona glanced away from Syrian as they walked, turning her focus out over the high grasses to the group's left.

"Yes," Kirsdona turned respectful, "I will give you your due. I have come across a few Gelada in my past, and they are not the most pleasant of creatures."

Syrian lowered his eyes. "Yes, some of my kind are even hateful of the term 'baboon.' Wishing that they could distance themselves from our brethren apes.

"But I do not believe in that path. We have all fallen from the same tree. The tree that our creator has blessed us with. We are apes. Nothing more, nothing less. I believe that my kind should strive to continue on the path for the betterment of all my kind. Not just one tribe."

"Well," Bing added, "Between you and the gorillas, you definitely do have a superiority complex."

Syrian smiled, amused. "That is because we are."

"Well, I don't know about all that," Kirsdona said in a somewhat coarse manner, "but, maybe we ought to shift our attention for the moment. You all might want to make yourselves aware that there is something tracking us in the thick grass to our left."

Patrick and the others stopped, quickly focusing their attention to the point that Kirsdona spoke of.

"I don't see anything," Patrick said.

"Of course you don't, because it has stopped, just as we have. It's pacing us."

"You're sure something's out there, Kirsdona?" Bing asked.

Kirsdona turned harshly towards the penguin, "If there is one thing that I will not be questioned on, it's on the subject of the hunt. It's what I do, and what I do best."

The great cat turned back towards the area of suspect. She lifted her massive head and began sniffing the air. "And something is definitely tracking us, possibly hunting us, at this present time."

Patrick took a step backwards, positioning himself behind the tiger.

Bing made his way next to Kirsdona. "Maybe you should go investigate what is out there, Kirsdona. Though I'm sure that Syrian is quite capable of taking care of himself, I do believe that any assistance you could provide him with would be appreciated."

Kirsdona turned back to discover that the baboon was gone.

"What? Great. Now where did he make off to?"

The tiger took her first step, then turned towards Patrick.

"Boy, keep a watch on the pig until I get back," Kirsdona instructed. "Anything happens to the little guy, and I'm coming for you."

She smiled unpleasantly.

Patrick moved next to Sin and watched as Kirsdona covered the distance to the edge of the high grasses in three enormous bounds. Patrick was alarmed at how much noise she created as she moved forward, and wondered if that was possibly her intent. Maybe there was a time for hunting, when she operated in a way where she could barely be heard. Being as quiet as a mouse before she would pounce. Then he imagined, there were times like this, when possibly causing as much noise as possible might in turn flush out the intruder by causing it to panic, and giving her the advantage.

Patrick followed Kirsdona's path as long as he could until she became lost in the overgrown weeds and dry grass. He listened as she shuffled and moved about.

Then there was silence. A long and annoying silence.

"What's happening?" Patrick whispered as he leaned down towards Bing.

"Patience, my friend. Let the creatures of the land do what they do best. Watch and learn."

But Patrick was a nervous as he ever could be. He didn't know what was going on out there, and he urgently wanted to know. He wasn't particularly fond of the tiger, but he sure didn't want to see any harm come to Kirsdona. He imagined that Syrian was out there somewhere, possibly tracking the other creature as well, but he couldn't know for sure.

Patrick stared out into the distance, his eyes wide for any hint of the progress they were making. He began to realize that he was glad to have the great tiger on his side. To make an enemy of that nature would defiantly be a fool's errand.

His mind began imagining what would happen if Kirsdona did catch something, and what she would possibly do to it. Patrick was sure that he would have to look away at the moment that any animal would begin to scream, not wanting to have to acknowledge the gruesome details. His mind already creating images of what Kirsdona could do to most other creatures.

Including himself.

Kirsdona moved through the grass silently, lowering her body as her massive limbs pushed her through the grass as silent as a snake. She raised her head only once when she caught Syrian out of the corner of her eye clinging to a splintered oak tree that appeared to have been damaged by lightening. Syrian gave her a nod of acknowledgement, and then moved further off to Kirsdona's left, circling around to come up behind their prey. Kirsdona was now a good 50 yards or so from the remainder of the group.

She smiled to herself as she caught herself doing what she always did when she was about to finish the hunt. She began to talk to her prey in her mind.

Come now, little one. I only want to get a little closer. I promise that I won't hurt you. I would never do anything like that. Just keep ignoring me. I am a breeze. I am the grass. Nothing over this way to hurt you. You won't even know when I'm coming. I just want to smell you. Just to get a little closer.

From the hesitant movement of the grass in front of her she knew that her prey was just off to her left, a few short yards away.

Kirsdona jerked ever so slightly as she caught the first scent of the animal, but it was not what she expected.

What?!

She rose up, abandoning the role of hunter.

"You have got to be kidding," she said aloud.

Kirsdona took two steps forward and then leaped to her right coming down in front of, and surprising, the creature that was tracking them.

Patrick heard an animal yelp loudly, and then saw Syrian in the distance move at an unbelievable speed past two trees, heading in the direction from where the sound had come.

The animal's cry had given Patrick and Bing a noticeable jump.

"What was that?" Patrick asked.

"I can't make out the tone. But I pray that Kirsdona has enough sense to bring whatever it is back alive so that we can question it as to why it was following us."

The next few seconds were particularly trying to Patrick's patience. He wanted to run out and discover what had taken place, but he had been entrusted with the defenseless hog's care, and he dare not abandon that for fear of Kirsdona's wrath.

Soon the grasses in front of them parted and Syrian stepped out. His expression was not of death and regret, but rather he had a look of relief.

Kirsdona soon followed him out shaking her head, with a surprising creature behind her.

It was Dog.

Patrick's eyes widened in disbelief, his heart racing with joy. "You?" he said as a smile broke out on his face. "That was you out there following us? Why?"

"I. Wanted. To. Come. To. Help," the animal responded, his tail wagging wildly.

Patrick moved over and began to pet the dog freely.

"But why didn't you just volunteer your services when I asked the crowd at the farm?" Bing asked.

"I. Did. Not. Hear. You. Ask. I. Was. Busy. Taking. Care. Of. My. Business."

"'Taking care of your business?'" Patrick asked, confused.

"I believe he is referring to the process of passing away his bodily wastes,'" Bing said matter-of-factly.

"Oh, I get it."

"And. Since. I. Did. Not. Have. The. Dream. I. Was. Unsure. If. I. Was. Welcome. Or. Not."

Bing smiled. "Well, of course you're welcome. We can always use another friend. But I don't understand as to why you didn't just come up and introduce yourself to us? Why did you sneak around behind us?"

Dog looked over at Kirsdona, his tail quickly lowering to between his legs. "I. Was. Afraid. Of. Her."

"As well you should be," said Kirsdona, licking her lips.

"Kirsdona, is there ever a moment where you are a pleasant thing to be around?" Bing asked disgustedly.

"Excuse me, but I don't remember anyone ever telling me that it was my job to be pleasant."

Bing turned back to Dog. "Don't worry about her. She's ok once you get to know her."

Kirsdona walked up and began to sniff at the dog. The animal quickly backed away, still unsure of his welcome.

"So mutt, what's your name?" Kirsdona asked.

"Dog," the animal responded timidly.

"No, not what kind of animal you are," Kirsdona returned, "What's your name?"

"We've already been through this. His name is Dog," Patrick interjected.

"You've got to be kidding? The dog's name is Dog?"

"Yes. Really. My. Name. Is. Dog," the animal answered back. "All. Dogs. Are. Named. Dog."

"Oh, brother," the tiger said as she rolled her eyes. "Are we sure we want to take along another passenger. I mean, he is a bit lame."

"There. Is. Nothing. Wrong. With. My. Walking," the dog said defiantly.

"I mean that you're a bit useless," Kirsdona said tersely as she shot him a sideways glance. "And if I have to take all of my time maintaining care for the pig . . ."

"It's a boar," Bing interjected.

". . . whatever . . . then I'm going to have to expect that the dog takes care of himself. Ok?"

Patrick was growing tired of the useless whining.

"Look, I'll take care of Dog, and of Sin, if that will make you happy. But quit acting like such a baby. You're the biggest and meanest of all of us, by far. Why are you always trying to intimidate everyone?"

Patrick surprised himself with his display of unexpected anger, and after he had said it, he did not feel the same regret that he had earlier after his outburst towards Kirsdona. He knew that she could rip him to shreds with just one swipe of her claw, but he knew that she would never do that to him, no matter what he said. And though he wouldn't abuse the alliance that was established between the animals and himself, he still wasn't going to be continually pushed around by the big cat any longer.

Kirsdona approached the boy, her eyes narrowing, but Bing put himself between the two, trying not to allow any conflict to generate.

"Patrick's right, Kirsdona. Though I have never met you directly before today, I have known of your reputation for some time. You are a great and wondrous creature, one that will likely never be duplicated again, but you have got to stop acting like you are the most superior being that ever walked the face of this earth. You had the dream. We need your help. We have got to keep moving forward. And by moving forward, I mean that we have got to stop with all of this pettiness. That's all I ask."

Kirsdona looked around at the other animals looking back at her. Her uneasy embarrassment was evident as she smiled unpleasantly and let out a great sigh, then turned and began to move on.

"Fine. I didn't realize that I was acting like such a "baby." I'll try to do better," she added sarcastically.

"Well, you were," Patrick added.

Kirsdona snapped back around to the boy, but Bing quickly headed her off.

"Patrick, that's enough! The situation is resolved. Put an end to it, now."

"Sorry."

Bing sighed, and uttered a silent "Kids" under his breath hoping that no one, and everyone, was listening.

The slightly disgruntled group began moving once more in the direction that they had first set out. Patrick and the dog moved to the front, talking amongst themselves like they had known each other for years, with the razorback Sin (after readjusting his scent processes to now follow Patrick's smell) trailing just behind them. The rest moved silently forward, with Syrian once again humming his enchanting tune.

They soon covered another four miles, purposefully staying away from any of the main roads or highways, and continuing to distance themselves from any housing settlements that were suspect.

The sun was beginning to get low in the western sky, and Patrick began to wonder just how far they had actually traveled, his exhaustion catching up with him. They moved on further, still moving in and out of small uninhabited forests and wide grassy patches with no luck of finding any places that they could investigate for something to satisfy their hunger.

Before too long they came to an area that looked like a ghostly wall of fog that had settled down into the low lying region of trees in front of them.

"I. Smell. Man's. Fire," Dog spoke first, jerking to a halt.

"I smell it too," Kirsdona added.

"Smoke? But I don't see any fire," Patrick said.

"It. Is. Off. In. The. Distance."

They moved over the hilltop and directed their course into the smoky haze.

Bing soon stopped the group's movement and turned to Patrick. "Being that an animal would not create, nor would go near any a thing of that nature, it can only mean one thing—a man is out there and he has created the fire. I am not so sure we should continue any further in this direction."

Patrick's heart jumped at the thought. That could only mean that another person was near. He could sense that his reaction was not as positive as the others.

"I thought you said that everyone was dead?"

"I said that most of the humans in the northern regions were dead. There are a few that have survived, I imagine."

"Well, then we've got to go see who's out there," Patrick said. He turned and started moving in a light jog, quickly moving ahead of the group, his anticipation propelling him forward.

"Wait!" Bing called out to him.

Patrick stopped and turned back towards the penguin.

"Why? There might be someone over there that can help us. Someone that can help me."

"I realize this, but you have to move ahead with caution. The times as they are at present are not without trepidation. As far as you know these people are strangers. And they might not be as eager to see you, as you might be to see them."

"That's ridiculous. If there are only a few of us left, then they surely would be looking for survivors. I'm a survivor!"

With that he took off in a run down over the remaining part of the hill, quickly being swallowed by the smoke and trees.

"I'll be right back," was the last thing he shouted before he disappeared.

Bing shook his head slowly.

Sin started after the boy, but was quickly restrained by Kirsdona.

"Syrian, follow him," Bing instructed. "Make sure that nothing bad comes about because of this."

CHAPTER 9

Fire Bugs

Patrick moved through the thick smoke, his eyes beginning to burn as he got nearer to the flames. The animals were right, he could hear the crackling roar of the fire ahead of him but wasn't quite to the spot where the flames came about. A slight breeze was pulling the smoke from his right to his left, and he coughed a few times as he tried to side step through the areas where the smoke was thickest.

After a few more moments of walking he began to hear a man's voice giving instructions to someone ahead. He ran forward, now feeling the searing heat billowing out towards him. He skin was beginning to feel like it was blistering as beads of sweat rolled down his face, dripping off his chin.

The roar from the flames was tremendous. And as he rounded the top of the next small hill he began to see the orange glow of the fire just ahead.

It was a magnificent blaze, the fiery charge dancing and leaping from the grasses and trees along the edge of a great forest to his right. The fire, both thick and dense, pulled the air like a vacuum all around him tickling the hairs on his arms.

He took a few more unsure steps forward when someone came like a shot from the shallow trees to his left and thumped him hard in his chest knocking him down.

"Hey! What'd you do that for?" he asked as he found himself lying on his backside.

As he looked up, Patrick found himself staring into the soot covered face of a girl that didn't look much older than he was. She held a small rifle in her hands, the butt end raised high and ready to whack him again.

"Stop! Don't hit me!" he said as he threw his hands up to protect himself.

The girl froze, her stringy blond hair hanging in front of her face.

"Rebecca, get back over here!" a voice barked from behind her. "You don't know if he is a carrier or not! Get back behind the fire line."

The face of the young girl quickly turned to fear as she did as instructed and ran back in the direction that she had came.

A bald, somewhat cartoonish looking man with owl like glasses stepped into Patrick's view. He seemed to be the one barking out the instructions. The man was covered in soot like the girl, and he managed to stay about twenty yards or so away from Patrick. He had a rifle as well, and it was most definitely pointed at Patrick.

"What do you want, young man?" the man shouted over the roar of the fire in a thundering, most unwelcome tone.

"I don't want anything. I'm lost, and I'm only trying to find my way. I'm just glad to see someone else. I thought that everyone was dead," Patrick said, relieved.

"Don't believe him, Mathew," another man said who was standing to the left of the first, the fire behind him masking him in shadow, making it difficult for Patrick to see his face. "He's probably a carrier like the others."

Patrick jumped uneasily as the fire heated the timber to his right, the sap from the trees snapping and popping as it burst from the burning wood.

"A 'carrier?' What's that?" Patrick asked.

"Do you have the disease, boy?"

"The disease? No, I don't have the disease. And if I did, don't you think I'd be dead by now?"

"That's not the way it works. You could be infected and not even know it."

"How do you know?"

"Don't try fooling us with your trickery, son. We've seen this from the others. That's why we have the fire. We've been safe as long as we keep the fire burning to keep the unholy plague away from us."

"How is the fire keeping you safe?" Patrick asked, confused.

"The fire kills the disease. It is the fire of our Lord. It is the fire that keeps the plague from us, giving us the gift of life. We are his chosen ones, for he has allowed us to live so that others may die. He has chosen us to live within this holy ring of pureness."

Patrick was beginning to become aware that these people might not necessarily be the kind of people he wanted to associate with after all.

From behind Patrick, purposefully hidden from anyone else's view, Syrian tried to get Patrick's attention.

"Patrick, you need to leave this place. These men are not what you think. I believe this to be a place of evil. I think that they may be murderers."

Patrick turned back towards to where Syrian's voice was coming from.

"How do you know?" he asked, a bit startled by the revelation. The intense heat from the destruction was beginning to make Patrick feel lightheaded.

"I have seen their dealings."

Patrick was alarmed at Syrian's last statement.

What exactly were their "dealings?"

The bald man took two steps toward Patrick. "Who are you talking to? Are there others out there with you?"

"He's just one of my friends. He's not here to harm anyone, either. We're just looking for help."

"Why can't we see him then? Is he hiding something from us?"

"He could have the wickedness also, Mathew," the man that was hidden by the fire spoke. "We are allowing our minds to be clouded by these impure beings if we converse with them any longer. I say we burn them the same as the others—for the purification."

"No!" Patrick said, shocked by the conversation that was taking place. He had ventured here only hoping to find help, but now his hopeful journey was beginning to take a tragic turn.

"Nobody has the disease," Patrick implored. "You don't know what you're talking about. This is a plague brought about but something you don't understand. Nobody carries it. It's carried on the wind."

"Do not listen to him, Mathew. How could he possibly know. His mind could be corrupted, giving us false testimony."

The bald man remained in his spot, a grim look on face. "Then if it is carried by the air, then our righteous pyres must be burning the evil from the wind, keeping us safe, because we are still alive. And if it is carried by the wind, then you could have it scattered all over your person. You could be a deliverer of death to us all."

"Then why am I still alive. Shouldn't I be dead as well?"

"Spoken like a true devil," a female voice spoke to Patrick's right.

Now Patrick became aware that there were more than fifteen people making their way from behind the roaring fire, each holding either a pistol or a rifle pointed at him. Most were teenagers; some looked like about the same age he was.

Patrick watched in disbelief as they moved through the fire without any regard for themselves, stepping through the flames as if they weren't affected by it. He waited to hear them cry out in anguish as the fire licked at them, but they seemed immune to the torrid blaze.

A rapid thought crossed his mind—If he could speak to animals, then perhaps these people couldn't be burned by the fires.

He knew now that he did not want to be around these people after all. But he had to pose one final inquiry before he turned and took his leave.

"Look, I'm not after any trouble. I am just looking for some food. I'm starving . . ."

The shadowy man stepped forward, raising his rifle.

"We don't have any food for you. We only have enough for us, not for anyone who harbors the plague of death. I'm sorry, but you are not welcome here. You had better take your leave of this place and move on in another direction."

"But, I . . ."

"I don't want to harm you son, but if I am forced to choose between you and my people . . ."

The bald man that was referred to as Mathew raised his rifle as if he was intent on fulfilling his goal. "Now go."

Patrick was stunned by the turn of events. This was something he had never expected to find.

"Patrick, we must leave this place—NOW!" Syrian implored.

Patrick could hear one of the teens that was standing just behind the fire line, turn to another and ask, "Did you just hear a monkey?"

Patrick took a few steps backward, then turned and began moving away, back in the direction where he had left Bing and the others. After Patrick had made his way clear of the people of the fire, Syrian soon found his side.

"We are best to leave this place as soon as possible. We should take a wide berth away from this land. Those humans are not the kind I believe you were looking for."

"No," Patrick said. "I guess they are having a hard time dealing with what is happening in the world."

He stopped and turned back towards the billowing smoke.

"I wonder how much they will burn to keep that ring going?" he asked aloud. "And they don't even realize that they're doing it all for nothing."

"I do not know," Syrian said as he grabbed Patrick by the arm and continued him away from fire people. "But in my tribe we have a term for what I believe they are experiencing. We call it hircata."

"What's that mean?"

"It is a phrase that we use when we are describing a creature that will not accept his fate, or his present being. In that his judgment is clouded."

"Well, they are definitely having one big hircata over there."

Patrick and Syrian quickly joined up with the others and relayed their brief story. Bing cautioned them all on venturing away from the group at any point further, and it was decided that no one would journey away from the group, especially Patrick, without another animal as a safeguard.

After a few more cautionary words, they soon resumed their journey. Only now they took a path that routed their travels a good mile or so away from the people of fire, circling them in a wide pass away to their left, and then reconnecting with the course that they had started from the beginning. As they climbed a steep ridge that brought them to an area where the smoke was beginning to thin, they turned and looked back down towards the burning area behind them. It was indeed a ring of fire. The black smoke rising from the blistering earth, climbing high into the cloudless sky. It looked to Patrick like it was a mile or so across. A massive, almost perfect ring of protection, Patrick thought. If that was what they truly believed.

They weren't very far from the ring, but now were on the other side and were starting to move away. Dog took the lead and had set a pace that was a good deal in front of the rest, moving with purpose. He was setting a tempo to get them away from the bad people behind them, and he wasn't about to slow down. Patrick and the others tried their best to keep time with the determined creature, but they were beginning to fall behind.

"What is with that stupid dog," Kirsdona moaned. "What is he trying to prove?"

"I believe that you're correct," Bing agreed. "If we are to keep up this pace, by the time we would run into trouble, we could quickly be overrun."

Just then Dog stopped, his tail going to a straight line behind him.

"I wonder what's up?" Patrick asked, curious as to the reasoning for the dog to stop so suddenly.

"Who knows? He probably has to take care of "his business" again," Kirsdona said under her breath.

The group moved to within twenty yards of Dog when he turned to them with an alarmed look on his face.

"Bees!" he said, his legs starting to backpedal away from what was in front of them on the soft dirt road.

"What? Where?" Bing asked, concerned.

"Listen," Dog instructed.

The six of them stood silent. Patrick listened intently, trying to catch any unnatural sound that he could pick up, hoping that the animal was mistaken. With the way in which the dog was reacting, Patrick guessed that there must be a horde of them just around the next corner.

They stood like frozen statues, all barely breathing, trying to understand what was taking place.

"No. No. Not. Bees," Dog said finally, his head dropping, his voice lowering to a hush. This time his voice was missing the alarming tone.

Kirsdona and Syrian's shoulders drooped, their reaction drifting to a sense of calm.

"You idiot," Kirsdona cursed. "The next time you . . .

"No. No. Not. Bees," Dog said again.

"Yeah, we heard . . ."

"Dog," Bing interjected, "the next time you sense something of this nature, we all need a little more time to digest the situation. A little advance warning would be nice."

But the animal didn't seem to be listening to the others. His focus was still out ahead of them, somewhere in the distance.

Patrick walked up to the animal and knelt beside him. He stroked its back, his hand running through its warm fur, hoping to calm the animal down. Dog's head was moving from side to side and his face was puzzled, as if he was searching for something but was unable to find it.

"What's the matter, Dog? Something got you spooked?" Patrick asked, his concern masking his undeniable fears.

"Shhh," Dog whispered quietly, his attention still drawn elsewhere.

But after Patrick had made a few strokes along the animals back, the dog suddenly went rigid, his head snapping forward.

Patrick turned and looked back towards the others, hoping to find some understanding to the animal's reaction. But when he saw all of them looking back over his shoulder as if something was behind him, he began to feel a terrible sense of dread wash over him.

And then he saw the look on Kirsdona's face.

He would have never, ever believed that she could possibly be in fear of anything on this planet. Nothing he could think of anyway. But at that moment, the look in her eyes alone was enough to cause his skin to crawl.

Patrick turned back to look in the direction that Kirsdona's sightline (as well as the others') seemed to be focused.

He stood and noticed that there was a dark cloud to the north of them, away in the distance, just above the tree line. From Patrick's perspective it seemed to be a good ways off, and at first he didn't think much of it. He knew he didn't possess the eyesight that the animals did, but the cloud didn't appear to be anything of a suspicious nature.

"It is the witches," Bing said to the others. "I believe they are sending us a greeting."

"And not a very welcome one at that," Kirsdona added.

"The witches? What do you mean?" Patrick asked as he stared at the dark cloud.

"I believe that they are attempting to finish this before we even get started. That cloud has death written all over it."

"What do you mean? What is that?" Patrick asked innocently.

That's when he began to hear it. It was low at first, like the grind of a far off airplane. The humming.

The air slowly began to become electric with the immense sound of it.

"This is not good," Syrian uttered.

This time Dog turned towards the others, his face full of terror.

"Not. Bees," he screamed, "HORNETS!"

It was like a dream to Patrick. One of those dreams where you know that you should do something. Anything. That you should run, run for your life. But for some strange reason your legs don't want to work correctly. That they become rubbery and just won't move. That all the sounds becomes muffled, and the air gets thick like water.

Patrick knew about hornets. They were the one thing his father had always, always, told him to stay away from. A bee sting was a light prick. A wasp felt like a shot at the doctor's office.

But a hornet. A hornet's sting was like getting hit with the crack of a whip.

Syrian screamed "RUN!!" at the top of his voice, and the animals scattered.

Patrick remained frozen in his place, though. He was mesmerized by the sound that was getting louder by the second.

What could make a noise like that?!

He knew that he should go, but he just couldn't.

He wanted to see.

But Kirsdona had been paying attention. She had taken a few long strikes in the opposite direction, beginning to make her break for cover, when she realized that the boy had not moved. She instinctively turned back and ran for the human. She opened her great mouth and grabbed him at the waist, picking him up and then returning to her task of getting the heck out of there.

"Oww!!" Patrick screamed, "You're crushing my hip! Put me down!"

The great cat stopped immediately, her paws grabbing into the dirt road creating a cloud of dust around them. She spit him down onto the ground and then jumped over him, continuing her rush.

"Come on, you fool!" she growled back at him without missing a beat of her gallop. "Those things aren't going to come up to you and politely introduce themselves."

Patrick turned to look back at the black cloud of hornets moving closer as he got back on his feet. The cloud didn't seem to be coming at them at any great speed, but instead seemed to be swirling about, moving slowly as if it still hadn't found its target. But Patrick knew that once they found what they were looking for (and he rightfully assumed that it would be him) that the speed at which the hornets would move would be something that he, nor the animals, could possibly outrun.

He started running as fast as he could, his feet pumping hard across the gravel and hard dirt road, trying his best to keep up with the tiger. But it was no use. The animal was ten times as fast as Patrick ever thought about being and was quickly out of his sight in no time at all.

He kept running, though, pure adrenaline and fear pushing him onward. His mind entertained the thoughts of the others only briefly, his head darting from side to side trying to find them, but he quickly figured that they had made their own escape and were probably way ahead of him by now.

And, as his lungs burned at the pace he was attempting to keep up, the real dagger of fear soon struck into his heart. For he realized as soon as he started to once again smell the smoke from the burning underbrush that he was heading back in the direction that he had tried so hard to move away from before.

He was heading directly back towards the fire people.

Patrick started to slow up, aware that he was going back into territory where he was not wanted. But the humming was getting closer, of this he was sure, and whether or not the hornets had finally zeroed in on him he couldn't tell. But by this time he realized that it didn't matter. With the other humans waiting ahead there might be a chance that he could rationalize with them, to make them understand his dilemma. But with the hornets, he didn't believe that they would be in an understanding mood. Particularly since they were probably coming to kill him.

So, realizing that he had no other choice, he quickly resumed his haste and broke for the ring of fire.

As he approached the wall of flames in front of him, he didn't give a moments thought as to what it would feel like as he ran through. He just lowered his head and brought his arms up to shield his face from the searing heat and leapt through to the other side. Unfortunately the width of the fire wall was a lot greater than he imagined, and he found himself moving through a blinding heat that continued on until he collapsed on the other side, a good twenty yards from where he had first jumped. He was just about to bring himself up to one knee when he discovered that his shirt was on fire, and with a shriek that he didn't even comprehend had erupted from his own lungs, turned and threw himself onto the ground, rolling back and forth trying to extinguish himself.

He quickly put out his burning shirt, still continuing to tamp out the smoking areas with his hands to ensure that nothing would start back again. He reached up and felt his hair, or what was left of it. The sticky mess left on the side of his head was alarming to say the least, and from the pungent smell that now flowed around him he knew that half his hair must be gone.

But he quickly discovered that his hair was the least of his worries. He began to notice several shadowy figures moving towards him from inside the fire line. His heart nearly froze as he jumped to his feet.

"I believe you were told to leave," a feminine sounding boy barked out at him. Patrick looked at the redheaded teen that Patrick would guess was no more than the age of fourteen. The youth stepped plainly into his view, his rifle leveled at his shoulder in a shooting formation.

"I'm . . . I'm not here because I want to be," Patrick tried his best to explain, all the while taking small awkward steps to distance himself from the others; moving farther and farther away from the fire line and towards the center of the ring. "There's something coming. Something bad. We all need to run. Now!"

Two other young men stepped forward, each with his weapon pointed at Patrick.

"Before it was food that was what you wanted—now something is coming to get you? A liar who cannot keep track of his lies is what you are!"

"Please!" Patrick pleaded. He turned and looked back in the direction he had just came. "They're going to be here any moment! Can't you hear it?!"

And for that moment, just for a second, he could sense that the young men in front of him did hear something off in the distance. Their eyes moved away, and their heads turned ever so slightly to the west. It's just that they didn't have any idea as to what it might be.

Just then a familiar voice came from off to Patrick's right. A voice that he wished he would have never heard again. It was the voice of Mathew.

"I warned you, young one!" he yelled as he pointed an accusing finger at Patrick.

Mathew then turned towards the others of his group. "He is a liar, and is a bringer of death. Kill him and burn his body with the others."

"No," Patrick said silently, and closed his eyes. "You don't understand."

Patrick's body went stiff with the expected execution. He held his breath expecting it to be his last.

The boy that was farthest to Patrick's left was the one who aimed his rifle first, and was about to fire the initial shot.

But the exact instant that the young man pulled on the trigger to send the killing shot on its way, was the same exact time when Kirsdona burst through the underbrush much to everyone's shock and amazement, her orange and black hairs still smoldering from the heat. She threw herself at Patrick with her head catching Patrick squarely in the chest knocking him high into the air, his body landing with a thud about ten yards away.

Unfortunately the bullet had already been sent, and although it didn't find the intended target that the shooter desired, it did find a target just the same.

It found its way into Kirsdona's right rear end, just above and behind her massive hind leg muscle.

She tumbled slightly along the high grass, her face grimacing from the penetrating shot. But she quickly righted her massive body and then lowered herself for an attack. She growled low, building slowly to a roar that sounded like a demon had possessed her. Patrick jumped at the unnerving fury that she brought forward.

"You will pay for that, human!" she snarled.

Patrick, for the first time completely realizing that he could understand her while the others could not, wished that they could have heard her last words, for they were spoken with such venom that Patrick truly felt sorry for the people in front of him.

The people of Mathew's group were in complete awe at the enormous tiger that had somehow materialized before them, but they quickly composed themselves and once again aimed their weapons. Some at Patrick, with the others switching around towards the great tiger.

Patrick, still rubbing his chest from the thump that the Kirsdona had given to save his life, yelled out to the great animal.

"Kirsdona . . . NO!" he screamed, "They'll kill you for sure!"

But his call was too late.

Not for Kirsdona, because unknowingly to Patrick, she had already deduced what was about to take place. And it had nothing to do with the people from the fire.

The hornets had arrived, and their arrival was like a thundercrack. They came with such a fierceness that Kirsdona even jerked a little at the incredible display.

Kirsdona had already known that the insects were poised for their attack, and she had merely bought enough time to lure them into the position she had wanted. The humans didn't stand a chance. The cloud of bugs that enveloped them was as thick as paste, and no matter how much thrashing and screaming and kicking that they tried it would not deter the hornets from their deadly chore.

Patrick watched in awe as the hornets arrived. They burst through the fire like a blackened hand, reaching out its grasp through the wall of flames. Most of the insects made it through unharmed, but a few of the bugs snapped and popped, their bodies bursting like popcorn from the intense heat as they traveled through.

Patrick imagined that the hornets' instructions were simple—seek out and kill the human boy without hesitation. But when they launched into their attack, and not expecting the amount of smoke and fire that they encountered, their confusion led them to do the next best thing—they sought out the nearest human and proceeded to inflict as much lethal damage as possible.

Kirsdona once again ran at Patrick and grabbed him again in her mouth, this time gumming him with her lips as she proceeded to tear away from the onslaught behind her.

The great cat ran as fast as she ever did, with Patrick reaching up and grabbing a hold of one of her ears for support.

Patrick could tell that she was hobbling slightly from the bullet she had just received, but he didn't dare ask for her to stop. He looked behind the tiger's tail and watched in horror as the hornets began tearing the people to shreds that remained behind them. The destruction was over in mere seconds, the humans no match for the small killing machines. Patrick watched silently from his increasing distance as the insects began making a regroup and were now storming in their direction.

"Kirsdona, they're coming," was all Patrick could say, his throat so dry from fear that he could barely get out the words.

But the great cat did not hesitate. In fact, Patrick believed that she actually went faster, if that was possible.

The wind whipped and stung at his eyes as she tore over a shallow hill, the speed at which she traveled reminded him of when he had went riding on his dad's motorcycle, how the air had come at him at such a rush. She was moving so fast, that when they first hit the water, it took Patrick a good two seconds to even realize that they had splashed into a large pond.

"What?!" he bellowed at his disorientation, wondering where the cold water was coming from as it splashed up his nose and into his eyes.

But Kirsdona didn't waste time.

"Under!" she yelled as she reached a great paw up and grabbed him by the head. "Get under!!"

Patrick barely had enough time to get a breath of air as the strength of the tiger pushed him completely to the bottom of the pond.

Patrick turned, his eyes wide as he looked back up into the murky green water. And then a sight came to Patrick that he could have never possibly imagined.

The hornets came at him, diving into the water with such a force, and in such a tremendous flood of insect bodies, that Patrick lost some of his air in an audible gasp.

Patrick was a good eight feet below the waters surface, but still the bugs came at him like streaking needles down into the water seeking to inflict their damage.

Patrick's fingers dug deep into the soft silt on the bottom of the pond trying to pull himself even lower. Kirsdona thrashed and kicked above him, trying to keep herself from the surface as well, but wasn't having as much luck at it as Patrick.

Patrick did the only thing he could think of to help the tiger—he reached up and grabbed the cat by her underbelly. He took a great handful of her white skin and with all his strength he tried to pull the cat down to him. The roar that the tiger made, even in the water, caused Patrick to loosen his grasp ever so slightly, but he still continued to pull her down, trying to get her away from the persistent insects.

The evening's light was faint at best already, but with the massive amount of bugs that were impelling themselves into the water, they caused a swift blackness to overcome anything below the water's surface.

Patrick clung with one hand to a buried rock underneath the sludge on the bottom, and with the other desperately hung on to Kirsdona.

He wasn't sure how long the attack could go on, but the pulsating water above him let him know that the hornets had not yet given up on their mission.

It seemed like at least ten minutes had gone by when Kirsdona finally kicked at him several times for him to loosen his grasp so that she could surface.

Patrick watched as an opening of light trickled down to him as the tiger made her way through the insect bodies and onto the edge of the pond. He let go of the rock and pushed himself up from the bottom. As he cautiously broke the water's surface he was quickly hauled up and out of the pond by Syrian's powerful arms.

"He is alive, thank goodness," Bing said as though he was surprised to find him in that state.

Patrick pushed his wet hair back from his face and wrinkled his nose. He noticed that every one of the animals was staring at him in some form of disbelief.

"Of course I'm alive. She saved my life," Patrick nodded in Kirsdona's direction, "though I don't know why. Thank you, Kirsdona."

Kirsdona trotted away, barely acknowledging him, and began rolling in the grass away from the others, trying to dry herself off.

"That's not what I meant," Bing continued. "You were underneath the water for quite a long time. We didn't know that humans could stay underneath the water like that. Are you sure you're ok?"

"I'm fine," he said as he waved his hand. "But Kirsdona's been shot. I don't know how bad she is."

"What?!" the others snapped around towards the tiger.

Kirsdona finished her rolling and tussling on the grass, finally coming to a graceful position as she laid her head on her paws.

"What's everyone looking at?" she asked.

"Patrick said you'd been shot. Where did the bullet hit you? Is it bad?"

"Oh, the human's making a big deal out of nothing. I think it just grazed me," she said nonchalantly.

Patrick walked directly over to the tiger's backside and surveyed the damaged area.

"It's no "graze." It's in there," he said as he pointed to the entrance wound.

The others quickly came up and examined the tiger's backside.

"Ok, ok. Get away. Visiting hours are over. Get back," she shooed the animals and Patrick away with her paw. "I'm fine. I barely even feel it."

Bing looked at her sideways.

"It's your backside, Kirsdona. I believe we would all understand if you decided that you could no longer accompany us. The wound looks painful."

The tiger rolled her eyes and then lifted her body back on all fours with a grunt.

"I'm fine," she said, trying to sound believable.

She walked over to Patrick and proceeded to look him up one side and down the other.

"So tell me, kid. How did you keep your air all the time that you were down there? Even I snuck my nose up every now and then to catch a breath of air. Is there something going on that you're not telling us?"

Patrick was surprised by the question. He hadn't even paid attention to the amount of time that he was under the water. He knew that it had been a good while, but he never gave a thought (until now) as to how he stayed under there holding his breath all that long.

"I . . . I don't know. I didn't even think about it. How long was I under?"

"Longer than any creature that I can think of—besides a fish."

The others nodded their agreement.

Patrick again found himself disturbed by the animals as they stared at him.

The extended silence was broken by the sound of someone, or something, making a slurping, crunching noise behind them.

The animals and Patrick turned to look behind them in the direction of the pond. There they saw the little boar, Sin, up to his knees in the water, eating the remains of all the dead insects as they rested on the top of the water.

"We had better get that lad some decent food," Bing said to the group. "This place is not one where we should stay any longer than necessary. I'm not sure if there are any more humans nearby or not. If they would come across this scene with us still in their presence, then we would be held accountable for the crime. We need to move on."

A few of the hornets were still buzzing about, the dog snapping at them as they passed.

"Well, this seems only to have been a test," Bing spoke. "Our first. I believe that if She had been truly trying to eliminate us, we would not be here having this conversation. I'm sure that with what they have at their disposal that the next encounter we have with their force we might not be as fortunate in our survival."

"But we are such a long way from there," Syrian said, "why is she bothering with us at this point?"

Kirsdona strolled up beside Syrian.

"Are you really that dense to believe that she is going to allow us to just waltz right on up to where she is hiding? Don't kid yourself. She's doing this to entertain herself. She's letting us know that she knows that we're coming. It's not a test. It's a warning."

"And," Bing continued, "if she knows where we are at, and where we are going, then she can pretty much pinpoint our every move."

"Then we must move at night," Syrian began. "The cover of darkness should allow us to have some vantage in this little game."

"They can still track us at night, though."

"Yes, but not as well. I believe you are correct in your thinking, Syrian. We should try to sleep during the day, and continue our movements at dusk."

"Then I guess we won't be resting anytime soon, seeing that the light is quickly fading at our surroundings. This would be our time to move on, then."

Bing sighed. He knew the group was exhausted, but they had to keep moving to pick up the pace of their advancement.

"Yes, but we must find food soon. It would definitely pick up our spirits to have something in our stomachs as we continue on."

The conversation and the planning that the animals discussed began to bore Patrick slightly, and he started to explore his surroundings. Specifically, he made his way away from pond and back to where the other people had been left. He had never experienced death this close up, and even though he was sure it would make him feel ill at the sight, he still wanted to see.

It wasn't as bad as he had expected. He stood about ten yards away from the first body, still cautious of just the thought of death, and of seeing a dead person, but the body wasn't in any sort of gruesome state as his imagination had led him to believe.

He approached the body slowly, noticing first the many punctures that the hornets had inflicted. They must be in the thousands, he thought. It was incredible. The young man's face in front of him was swollen horribly, his eyes bulging from their sockets. He knelt beside the person and lifted his arm, examining the incredible amount of tiny little holes that had been drilled into his skin. He set the arm back down, somehow thinking that he shouldn't be touching the body. That he was doing something wrong.

And then he saw the gun.

Patrick, knowing nothing about guns, couldn't even begin to guess what kind that it was. He picked the pistol up and turned it over in his hands. It was much heavier than he imagined. It felt about as heavy as a book, and the metal was cold. He began to wonder what it would be like to carry it, to have it with him the next time something was to happen. To have something of this nature, he imagined, might give him an advantage whenever the next confrontation might take place. Since he couldn't do anything to help and protect the others, such as Kirsdona, or Syrian, then he thought maybe this would be an aid.

He stood up, and was just about to put it in his pocket when a sound came from behind him that made him jump through his skin.

"PATRICK! NO!" came the bellowing screech from Bing. "Put it down! Now!"

Patrick dropped the gun as if it had become heated by a furnace. And a furnace was the way in which Bing's next words arrived.

"How dare you even touch such a thing!" Bing scolded. "I don't know why you humans believe that having one of those things is the answer to everything, but if you are to travel with us, then you will not ever entertain the thought of having one of those in our company. Do you understand?"

Bing was furious. And even though Patrick had opened his mouth to argue his reasoning for even picking it up, he quickly shut it understanding the tone that was coming from the penguin would not be something that would be discussed.

"Especially after what has just happened to Kirsdona," Bing said as he stared at Patrick with a look that Patrick had only seen come from one other being before in his life.

His father.

Patrick looked over as the other animals who had now moved into sight of what was taking place. He felt like he wanted to be anywhere other than where he was standing right now. All he could think of to reply was a silent, "I'm sorry."

Bing stared at him a few minutes longer, with Patrick expecting a few more scolding words to come forward from the little bird, or maybe from one of the others. But Bing turned around and shouted for the others that it was time to continue on. He started to move next to Patrick, looking over at the body as it lay in the thick grass.

"Patrick, I do not mean to be so cross with you, but I am not a creature of this world that brings harm to others. I am not Kirsdona. I am not Syrian. My kind is of a peaceful nature that shuns the workings of the other beasts of this world and their violent ways. Man has always been a subject that brings incredible debate to our kind, and to the wicked ways in which he rules over the land. I realize that man uses those things for his protection from the ravages of the world. But I have also seen what can happen when one of man's weapons are used for the wrong purpose. But strictly dealing with of what I know so far about our journey, I believe that in the circumstances that have be put out before us, we will not need such a weapon. Please rest easy on this, Patrick."

Bing grabbed him by the hand, the small bird's slight wing cupping his grasp, and began walking.

"Because we have you."

Patrick so badly wanted to explain to the bird, and to the rest of the animals, his reasoning for wanting the gun. His feelings for feeling so inferior. For feeling like he didn't belong.

The flood of thoughts and emotions that traveled through Patrick's head at that moment made him both sad and very afraid at the same time. In a little over twenty four hours he felt that he had traveled so very far, and yet so very little.

"I feel badly for what has happened to your kind, Patrick. Such a waste. Is there anything that we should do for them? I am not familiar with your ways of dealing with the remains."

Patrick surveyed the landscape with the dead scattered amongst the high grass, and he sighed.

"They should be buried, but we don't have the time. You're right. We need to get moving. This isn't a good place to be."

"If you are sure."

Bing looked into Patrick's eyes to make sure he was clear in his decision.

"Alright then, let us continue."

In the distance Patrick heard Dog shout out a quick, "This. Way," with the rest following without hesitation.

"What a pleasant trip this is becoming. I want to thank you all for inviting me," Kirsdona spoke to everyone in her most sarcastic tone.

This caused a few of the others, including Sin surprisingly, to giggle at the tiger's light attempt at humor.

Patrick barely acknowledged the tiger as she carried on her conversation with the others as the group moved away. With the way that his head was now swimming with so many different emotions and confusing thoughts, he was only vaguely aware that Kirsdona was walking directly in front of him. Patrick feeling like she was a million miles away.

CHAPTER 10

292 Degrees

Dan Brighton was no fool.

He may have been half scared out of his mind at the moment, but he definitely was no fool.

He knew of the instructions that had been given to the freakish, changing man back at the farmhouse by the flies. But he also knew that the changing man didn't have Patrick. So even though he gave the impression that he was running away, what he actually was doing was making time to find his son.

Now that he knew that Patrick was being sought after by someone (or something?) other than himself, the question kept coming to the surface as to how he was actually going to win the race in finding his son. The horrified reality that faced him was even worse than when he had first set out. Now he wasn't just hoping to find Patrick, he was in a life and death contest with a madman who was trying to do the same.

The flies were the kicker. Exactly what they were, and under whose (or what's) control they came under, Dan didn't have a clue. They were even scarier than the man himself. If they had somehow (however unbelievable it seemed) actually changed that man's bodily form, then he didn't want to go anywhere near the miserable insects. If that's even what they were. If the man had something like that on his side assisting him in his search for Patrick, then Dan had to wonder how he was ever going to beat him to the goal.

Dan kept checking his rearview mirror; his nervous glances expecting to see the madman at any moment come flying up behind him in the Altima, his ghastly face laughing at him as he went.

He also kept a constant eye on the digital compass that was displayed in the overhead console. The flies had specifically said that Patrick was situated on an abandoned farm in the woods due north from their position at the farmhouse, approximately a days walking distance for a man. So Dan kept the truck moving in the direction that kept the digital blue N continually displayed.

The flies had said that you would know the woods by "the humming lines that ran in the sky." It had taken Dan a few moments to think over what they had meant before it came to him.

The overhead power lines.

Dan scanned the treetops on both sides of the highway for a line of the giant erector set structures that held the thick cables. He drove for another four miles before he finally he spotted a line of them ahead of him in the distance.

He was fast running out of the road that would take him in the direction he needed, the blacktop of the highway beginning to veer off to his left. But it didn't take much thought. He immediately shifted the F150 into four wheel drive and started moving off the pavement, taking the hard course down through the cable support pathways.

The truck bounced and lurched over the rough terrain as he tried to keep his speed up in hopes of getting to Patrick first. He wasn't exactly sure of the path that the changing man was going to take to get to the farm, but Dan was doing everything in his power to shorten his own distance—and his time.

He continued down a steep gorge, the truck bouncing so bad that his head kept thumping off the roof of the cab, and as the wheels tracked through the muddy, deep trenches, the steering wheel kept wanting to whip to the left or the right making it hard for his hands to maintain their control.

He was just making his way over the crest of the first hill when he was surprised as something passed in front of him like a child running across the street. He instantly slammed on the brakes showering rocks and dirt into the path in front of him, the truck starting to spin and go sideways. He finally came to a stop just inches from plowing head on into something he never thought he'd see. Well, not see out here, anyway.

It was a giraffe.

No. Make that two giraffes.

Dan couldn't believe what he was seeing.

And it wasn't just giraffes, but other animals as well.

Lots of other animals. And it seemed like they were in quite a big hurry.

Some of the animals paused to stop and stare at Dan as he looked out at them in astonishment. And (if anyone would ever have questioned him about this he would have denied it to his grave) he swore that it looked as though the animals were talking to each other in some sort of odd exchange. Almost like a head-bobbing, sign-language type of communication.

But as soon as the animals had gotten over the near miss with the truck, they resumed their hurried trek across his path. There were so many creatures that Dan thought for a minute about blowing his horn to startle the innocent things, but with so many of them traveling in front of him he didn't think it would help.

"Come on, come on," he mumbled aloud as he tried to be patient with the parade.

Then it hit him like a snap.

The animals. Of course. The animals were coming from the farm.

Dan reached his hand to open the door, but quickly pulled it back due to his uncertainty that if he went out the door that some of the more ferocious looking creatures might decide that he was going to become their instant breakfast.

His mind giggled at the thought of the conversation he imagined.

"Why yes, I had a delicious tasting human just the other day. He walked right out in front of me."

So he waited.

It seemed like it took almost a quarter of an hour, but he waited until the last animal (however small) was out of his sight and long since gone before he finally emerged from the truck.

The air was thick with the smell of sweet pine as he walked into the short underbrush and found his way through the forest ahead of him. The trees continued on down the steep hill for a mile until at last they began to clear, and he soon found he was looking out over a vacant field. He guessed that the size of the cleared grounds was about a hundred yards across in both directions. A small weathered barn, much too small in serving any real purpose as far as holding hay or horses would go, sat across from him on the other side of the shortened valley. He started towards the barn, suspecting that if Patrick were to be found any where in the vicinity, then that was probably the best place to begin his search.

He made his way up to the barn, opened the door and peered in. He immediately caught the scent of something that must have relieved itself back into the far corners of the deserted place, his nose to wrinkling at the putrid smell. As his eyes adjusted to the darkened interior, he gave a quick once over to see if he spotted anything that may give him an idea as to Patrick's whereabouts. There were a few items scattered about the place—several coils of rope, a small piece of farm machinery, some rotten ears of corn—but there was nothing that could give him any clues to the location of his son.

He yelled "Patrick!" just once to ease his curiosity—but only once—for fear of what reprisals it might bring if the shout fell on preying ears that could bring him harm.

Finding nothing, Dan walked out and followed the barns exterior till it brought him to a small pile of bricks wedged up against the barn's near side.

The animals, and he guess that there was quite a few of them, had definitely been here. The sandy soil was covered with so many paw and hoof and claw prints that Dan had to wonder exactly what had taken place.

Dan thought back to the conversation the flies had with the changing man. He was so astonished at the time that the fly thing had could actually speak, that he didn't pay attention as well as he should have as to what had actually been passed between the two.

Did they (it) say that the animals had aligned themselves with Patrick? That they were taking him along with them?

If that were so then there must have been two groups of animals, because the one that he encountered a little while ago definitely did not have Patrick.

Dan began scanning the nearby areas wondering where exactly would they go?

And what were they doing with Patrick?

It wasn't long before he began to hear a distinctive low buzzing sound coming from beyond the hills to his left. It was a sound that he was already quite familiar.

The flies were coming, and that would only mean one thing—the changing man was coming as well.

Dan had a moment of shear panic as he debated as to where he should hide. He couldn't cover the distance across the wide open space that had brought him to the barn, there wasn't enough time. And it was obvious that the barn would be the first place the man would look.

Dan looked around the corner of the building and instantly took three hurried steps to its rear, finding space behind a small group of spruce trees that were tucked away behind the rear wall. It wasn't much, but at least in wasn't in a very obvious place, and someone would have to really look just to find him.

Dan couldn't see the front side of the barn from where he stood, so he couldn't exactly tell from what direction the changing man had entered the open grounds, but he knew that he had arrived. The air around him seemed to crackle with the strange man's approach.

Dan peered around the side of the barn, watching as the man walked slowly, purposefully, as if he was contemplating something of a serious nature. But as Dan watched, the strange man stayed clear of the barn, instead making his way towards the middle of the open area that extended away from the front of the barn. He continued on, walking in small semi-circles before he briefly stopped, crouched low like a baseball catcher, and looked thoughtfully at the ground before him. Dan imagined that the man was examining the same animal tracks that he had just viewed a few minutes earlier.

Then the man brought his head down low to the ground and sniffed, his head moving in small arcing movements back and forth like a pendulum. He smiled and stood, and then turned and looked directly at Dan.

But how was that possible? Dan thought. How could he know? I haven't made a sound!

"Why Mr. Brighton, is that you hiding back there in the bushes?" the man asked, seeming quite amused with himself as he peered from the distance around the corner of the barn.

But Dan didn't answer. He just stared at the ground to his left, holding his breath, and trying not to make any kind of movement.

"Come now, I know you're back there. Don't act so surprised. You'd be amazed at the things I know."

Again, Dan didn't utter a sound. He only closed his eyes and prayed that this would only end soon.

"Allow me to introduce myself. My name's Tye. And I just want you to know that I have become well acquainted with your son. A very fine lad you have there. I could tell right away he was raised by fine parents. You should be proud."

Dan didn't respond to the man's tease, still choosing to remain silent.

"I don't know what you may have seen back at the farmhouse, Mr. Brighton, but I can assure you that what you saw there is nothing compared to the possibilities that now exist within my world. Endless possibilities. Things that would make your eyes spin and your mouth water. Things that could be happening to you now if you only allowed them to happen. I am becoming quite special myself, as you can so plainly see."

Dan watched as the changing man turned around like a debutant showing off a new dress. He was repulsed, yet mesmerized as he viewed the man's state of progression. The man who called himself Tye was still a man, but just barely. His ears had formed back, recoiling into the sides of his head, and his nose was beginning to flatten out and compress. The man's hair was falling out in large clumps leaving long open patches of bare, oozing skin. And he was shaking. Not a constant rumbling shake, but every few seconds his eyes would roll back in his head and his entire body would convulse like a tremor from a small earthquake.

"I believe I know where he is going. Your son, that is. We both know that's who we're looking for. And truth be told, you might actually be a help to me in finding the boy. A boy like that always listens to his father. Otherwise . . . well, it's a long, wide open country to have to start scouting around in, and he's one tiny needle to look for in a giant haystack that could be just about anywhere. Personally, I believe you'd be better off working with me. I have many options to aid me in my search."

Dan couldn't believe what the man was saying—what he was asking. He wanted to answer him with anger, but he held his tongue just the same.

"You probably don't even realize what a special boy you have there, Mr. Brighton. Truly remarkable, he is. One of a kind special. He is yours, isn't he? I mean, by birth?"

"Yes, of course he's mine!" Dan finally shouted, surprised as the words flew from him.

"Well, then perhaps you know just how talented he is?"

Dan didn't say a word.

"You do know what he can do, don't you?"

What he can do? Dan was startled by the question.

"Yes, oh yes, he is one talented young lad."

Dan now realized that the voice had gotten closer, and as he peered out around the edge of the tree he was surprised to see the man was now no more than fifty feet away.

Too close. Far too close for Dan's comfort.

And at that moment, Dan became aware of something that he hadn't before. The flies were gone. Dan's eyes darted all around the changing man, the farmyard and along the tree lines, but darn if he could spot them.

Where were they?

The 'not knowing' gave Dan the creeps.

He knew that he'd definitely heard them coming this way earlier, but he never did actually see them.

"Well, Mr. Brighton, I believe that the animals have gotten a several hour jump on us. And it seems that they are moving to the north—northwest. I'm not exactly sure where they are headed, but I have a good idea."

"And where might that be?" Dan couldn't resist asking.

"Ah, no, now that would be cheating. You're going to have to just trust me on this one. I won't be that hard of a person to follow. But you'll need to stay close. You're welcome to ride along with me if you'd like. We both know that I am going to kill you at some point anyhow, so you might as well come along with me now."

An icy finger ran up Dan's spine as he watched Tye sneer as he pronounced the last sentence.

"If you're going to kill me, then why not just get on with it?" Dan asked.

"Well, for one thing, I'm not quite so sure that I'm not going to need you at one point or another. I hadn't figured on your son escaping my grasp, so I never entered you into the picture. But now, with what has recently transpired, I am not going to be so quick to dismiss anything that may be a needed tool in reacquiring the boy. At one point or another you may actually turn out to be useful. Sort of like the carrot on the end of the stick, so to speak."

Dan contemplated the words carefully that the man was speaking. He obviously didn't like the tone or the words that were being spoken concerning his likely death, or the thought of him being used as bait with which to lure his son into this thing's clutches. But if it meant that it was going to make it possible to find Patrick, then perhaps he could deal with the later consequences as they arose.

"Just one question," Dan asked. "Why are you after him? What did he do to you?"

Tye giggled slightly.

"Well, that was two questions, actually. But they ask the same thing, so I'll give you your answer."

Tye shrugged his shoulders slightly and laughed, his eyes going wide.

"The boy hasn't done anything, actually. Not one thing. Yet.

"And, you see, the people that have employed me want to keep it that way. They have requested that I do nothing more than to just store your son away for safe keeping until the plan that they have put into motion comes to completion. I'm not exactly sure of the timetable that they have established for this to finish up, but they have made it very clear to me that if I do not retrieve your son in the immediate, then they may do to me more than just make the simple rearrangements to my person that have already taken place. Understand?"

Dan stood quiet, stunned by Tye's revelation.

"Your son has done nothing. But it is the fear in which they hold towards your son for what he could do. That is the driving force behind all of this."

"What can he do?" Dan asked, bewildered.

Tye's lips pressed firmly together in a tight little grin.

"You truly don't know, then?"

"No."

Tye took a deep breath and sighed.

"It's a pity. Because they haven't told me yet, either. But from what they have alluded to, your son is something quite extraordinary."

"Quite extraordinary?!" What does he mean by that?

Those words chilled Dan to the bone. If this man in front of him, someone who was turning into something that could not possibly be from this world as it was, wasn't the pure definition of the term "quite extraordinary" then what in the world could possibly be happening to Patrick?

Dan thought on the idea presented to him by the strange freakish man, but he knew that he could never, ever accept the favor. He would be riding with death.

"I won't go with you, but I'm not going to lie and tell you that I won't follow you. I want me son back. If you get to him first then you will have to kill me, because I'm sure as hell going to try and kill you. Of that you can be sure."

Tye continued his sly smile, all the while his expression never flinching. "Don't go getting so overly melodramatic. There isn't going to be any 'scene' when it finally gets down to it. I could kill you with two words right here, right now, and you wouldn't even have taken a step in my direction."

Tye started to walk away to the left of the hill from which Dan had first entered, but he stopped and turned back towards Dan, laughing as he spoke.

"When you finally begin to see the big picture, believe me, you won't carry yourself with such bravado. When you finally do begin to put the whole thing together, you'll be lucky if you don't wet your pants!"

Dan heard something snap behind him just as Tye began his laugh. He instantly turned around, but he couldn't see anything behind him—if there ever was anything there to begin with. Dan quickly turned back towards Tye, but the devil was gone. Vanished.

Huh? How did he move so fast?

Dan emerged from behind the spruce slowly, cautiously, almost expecting an attack just the same even though the man said he wouldn't hurt him.

His courage quickly gathered strength, and he headed for the front of the barn.

Tye couldn't have moved a hundred yards that fast! No way.

But no matter how hard Dan surveyed the surrounding area, the man was nowhere to be found.

He was gone.

Just then Dan realized something else. Something that caused his chest to grow tight, and his breathing to slow.

Where was he going to go now to look for Patrick? If he didn't keep up with Tye, then how was he ever going to find out where Patrick was heading?

Oh no.

Dan ran as fast as he could back across the grassy area, his heart thumping hard in his chest; a slick, nervous sweat starting to flow over his body.

He sprinted up the hill and through the woods to his truck. He didn't know how he was ever going to find Tye again, but the man did say that he was heading north-northwest.

Dan got in, fired up the truck, and then positioned it so that the compass was now giving him that direction.

As the truck rumbled, ready to take off, Dan pulled out the map and laid it across his lap. He ran his finger along blue and red vein-like lines that marked the path he needed to pursue, and then took off.

The initial path he traveled was rough going due to the uneven terrain, but soon enough he found his way back onto the main highway. Once on smooth pavement again, he accelerated the truck, pushing the red needle on the speedometer till it was pegged at its maximum. Luckily, the amount of wreckage on the road was minimal, allowing his attention to be focused from the highway to the map and to the overhead compass.

After only a few minutes he spotted something that he thought he would never see again.

The Altima.

It was just ahead of him, the car now beginning to accelerate away.

He knew that it was wrong to allow this man to continue on with his plans, but he felt helpless to try and stop him. He also knew that he didn't have any control over the situation as it was. Even though he trailed behind, he still felt as though he was the one being pursued in the situation.

Dan followed the highway for more than a hundred miles with the hilly, vacant scenery never changing much as he traveled. It seemed like hours (with the Altima still in view) before street signs and houses began to dot the landscape once again. They were finally approaching a small town, and for that Dan was thankful.

Dan had continued to give himself a much needed cushion of space between his truck and the Altima. He guessed he was giving two hundred yards or so, maybe more, maybe less, though it was still the cushion Dan needed to feel a sense of comfort about the situation.

The highway was winding in front of him like a snake, with wide patches of road where Dan lost sight of Tye from time to time.

He soon found himself on a long straight stretch of highway, the road narrowing from a four lane down to a two, and although he had a good viewing distance ahead of him for a mile or so, he quickly took notice that he seemed to have lost sight of the Altima.

Dan could see up ahead the multiple, multi-colored store signs that populated the downtown area, the three fast food restaurants, and the speed limit signs now registering that he go thirty-five.

But where was Tye?

Dan slowed to almost a crawl as he made his way through the tiny haven. The town seemed to be divided straight down the highway, almost an East/West type of division. His eyes darted from one side of the street to the other in hoping to spot the green automobile, but he couldn't spot the slippery bugger now matter how hard he looked.

The problem for the moment was that Dan wasn't sure if Tye had actually stopped here, or continued on through the town.

How would he know?

And what if he had been lied to? What if, instead of the direction being North-Northwest, the course that his son had taken was South-Southwest? How would he know?

Dan pulled his cell phone out and tried the RandomGuard number, but of course it was of no use; all circuits were dead.

He was stuck.

The only direction he could even think of to go was to move on straight as he was, but he decided he wasn't going to make any movements in haste. He put the truck back into drive and continued on, continuing to spy down dimly lit alleyways, and darkened back areas that Tye might have found to hole up in.

He had traveled a few hundred feet further before he finally spotted the car. His heart settled high in his chest at the sight of it. At least it looked like his car. He had to get close enough to it to make sure. It was one street over pulled up next to (of all places) a public library.

Dan was baffled.

A library?! What was Tye doing now?

He felt exposed, an almost nakedness as he exited the truck, but he knew that he had to see what this character was up to. If he was walking into some kind of trap, then so be it.

Perhaps this was where Patrick was being held? But he knew that would be too easy.

The Cochran-Lee Library was obviously an old building. The exterior was a weathered yellow brick and mortar, with large cracks running like twisting vines from its foundation, zig zagging all the way to the top. Some of the letters across the face of the building had fallen off leaving only a shadowy reminder of where the O and one of the E's had once been.

As he moved towards the building, his attention came around to the gelatin-like, human puddles still drying in the sun in front of him. He almost wished a hard rain would come just so he didn't have to continually smell or view the remains. It wasn't that he was being cruel, its just that as they dried the scent that came forward from the puddles was steely and harsh, much like rotted tomatoes. A continual reminder of his desperation.

Dan stopped only for a moment as he listened to a clicking or clacking sound that seemed to be echoing all around him. It sounded a lot like the locusts or cicadas in the summer, but he knew that they all had to be long gone by now. He glanced around to locate the source of the sound, but it seemed to be coming from everywhere, and nowhere, at the same time. He briefly wondered if it was someone's PDA or iPod that had run amok with no human around to keep it maintained, but he didn't have time to worry about that now.

Dan moved to the doorway cautiously, looking in through the glass doors first before opening them up and proceeding in.

The structure inside was surprisingly modern compared to the decaying exterior. From the outside the building looked as though it was built all on one level, but in reality there were actually two floors. The one that he had entered on, the upper floor, and then another that was sunk down and away to the rear.

He wound his way around the upper floor, moving past the thick wooden shelves that held row after row, and aisle after aisle of multiple categories of books, at each opening peering in to the hidden corridors hoping to locate Tye amongst the shadows.

As he completed the top circle he finally found himself situated at the main librarian's desk, with the steps that led to the lower level beginning off to his right. There were several areas of human remains splattered on the desk (and some sliding over the side) as if the plague had struck a great many people as they were attempting to check out a book. He glanced briefly at the books that were scattered on the desk. Gardening, Dr. Seuss, and mystery novels seemed to be the featured attraction that day.

Dan quickly turned away, side stepped a small puddle on the carpet in front of him, and then made his way to the lower level. He grabbed the brass handrail as he made his way down, but hurriedly pulled his hand away when he realized that it still had human remains dripping from it.

On the final few steps at the bottom he came to realize that the lower level was not as evenly lit as the upper area was, and Dan had to strain to see back into the more remote areas.

That's when he heard a shuffling sound, as if someone was dragging their feet. Dan turned and saw Tye sitting at a table that was tucked back underneath the upper level overhang.

"I was wondering if you were ever going to make it," the strange man spoke without looking up from the book he was reading.

Dan was beside himself with rage at seeing Tye so comfortable. "What are we doing here? I thought we were looking for my son?"

"Well, things have changed over the last little bit of time. I have received some news that should benefit us both."

Tye's head tick-tocked back and forth as he flipped through page after page with a speed that Dan could barely comprehend.

"What's that?" Dan asked of the book Tye was looking in.

"Oh, nothing. I was just curious about something."

"Curious about what? What's the news?"

Dan stood silent, patiently waiting for the man to give whatever news he had to give.

"Well?"

Tye looked up quickly.

"Oh, yes," he said hurriedly. "The good news is that you won't have to come with me after all. During our travel I received news that I now know exactly where your son is located, and what direction he is heading. I'm afraid that it could turn out to be quite a long journey and I simply don't see the usefulness in bringing you along as I had originally thought."

Dan's eyes darted away as he began to hear the clicking/clacking sound he had heard outside. It now sounded as if it was coming from inside the building's walls.

"But you said . . ." Dan started.

"I am quite aware of what I said. But unfortunately for you I have been sent some assistance with which to accomplish my task in, shall we say, a more expedient manner. And I just don't have the time to play this little game any longer."

That's when Dan saw the tongue. It startled him as he watched it slither out between the man's lips, dancing in the air for a second, and then quickly darting back inside to find its resting place.

Dan wanted to ask someone—anyone—if they had just witnessed that. He was now beginning to feel ill at the sight in front of him. Dan didn't normally have a weak stomach, so whether it was his lack of food, or just the overwhelming amount of sensory overload he was experiencing, but he was beginning to feel nauseous.

The noise was now growing louder, and Dan began to look around to see if he could locate where it was coming from.

That's when Dan felt the first spider drop onto his shoulder. It felt like an acorn falling off a tree. He quickly brushed it aside and then looked up. He immediately knew then what the man had meant by 'assistance.'

Thousands upon thousands of spiders were descending from the ceiling above him. Spiders of different colors and shapes and sizes dropped down at him like slowly falling petals. They came at him on their thread like webs, some clicking their mouths, or pincers, creating the menacing, awful racket.

"Oh, God!" was all that Dan could say as he started to back away.

"Yes," the strange man began, "they are quite beautiful, aren't they? I was thinking that since the plague did no harm to you, that I would need something that I could ensure would take care of both killing and securing you at the same time. And voila! These little beauties arrived just in time."

Dan was dancing back and forth trying to find some cover from the avalanche of spiders that began to fall. It was as if a thousand marionette strings descended from above. He backed up against the furthest wall away from the steps and urgently looked around for something to use as protection.

Dan's rage took his attention to Tye, who was now using a pencil to hurriedly draw a line on something in the book that he had been so engrossed in. He watched as Tye tore the page from the book, and then quickly made his way up the steps as the spiders gave him passage.

As he reached the top step he turned back to Dan and uttered his final volley.

"Do be a dear and just die quickly and quietly. I would surely hate to tell your son how you screamed like an infant before you made your final peace."

Dan was beginning to panic as he looked around the room. He was hoping that he could spy something that he could use as either a weapon, or at least something to fend off the growing horde that were now making their way not only from the ceiling, but from the floor areas and vents as well.

Where could they have all come from?

This was not what he had expected at all. Even though he had entered the building knowing that he did not trust the man in the least, he still held some small reason to believe that this madman was going to get him to his son. But as he stood, trying to reason in which direction would be the best method to try his escape, he realized that everything the man was about was one big lie.

'You don't make deals with the devil,' he could hear his grandfather telling him. And the devil, this man certainly was.

Most of the spiders moved silently, their padded feet making no sound. Some hissed at him, while others danced back and forth like they were doing a jig. Each spider preparing in its own way to make an attack.

Click clack. Clickity clack.

Dan slid along the wall, figuring that if he could make his way down behind one of the larger bookshelves, then perhaps he could push one of the giant units over and use it as a bridge to make his escape. But it was as if the spiders had already deduced this, and immediately cut off his point of entry.

Dan grabbed a large flat book off one of the shelves and started swinging it wildly over his head, trying his best to keep as many spiders at bay as he could. A few of the larger spiders hissed and angrily jumped at him as he slapped at them as they inched their way closer.

As he slid along the wall he bumped up against something hard that dug into his lower back. It was a small silver handle of some nature that stuck out from a smallish door, but he dismissed it immediately because the spiders were almost on him.

He turned back to refocus his attention on what the spiders were about to do, when finally it began to dawn on him—he was up against the door to the fire extinguisher. He took one last long swooping arc with the flat book, throwing it at the largest mass of the spiders, and then whipped around and threw open the small metal door. With one motion he grabbed the extinguisher and yanked it out of its holder, turned and pulled the pin, squeezed the handle, and unleashed the frothy white foam at anything that moved.

He sprayed it over his head and from side to side, blasting everything and anything in his way, covering a 20 foot arc around him causing the room to look as if it was snowing.

Dan then moved forward.

The little beasts wouldn't back down so easily, and when one of the spiders would manage to overcome the thick foam and continue towards him, Dan then proceeded to kill it the old fashioned way—he stepped on it.

A quick glance to his right made him aware that some of the spiders had overcome their initial fear of the extinguisher's foam, and were now making a renewed advance.

Dan was just about to reach the bottom of the steps, the extinguisher still holding the spiders at bay, when out of the corner of his eye he caught sight of the book that Tye had been so engrossed in earlier. The spiders were still coming, but if that book was so important as to cause Tye to stop off to find it, then Dan wanted to know what it was. He stopped his spraying for an instant, and dashed over to the table where Tye had been sitting. He didn't bother to look at what the book was, but rather just scooped it up, stuffed the book down the back of his pants, and then tried to make his way back to the steps.

He kicked the extinguisher back into high gear and thought that he might actually make his way out of the place without many more problems, when a yellow and black spider, no more than the size of a quarter, landed on his left hand and bit down hard causing Dan to scream in pain. He instantly let go of the fire extinguisher, and reached with his other hand to kill the determined creature, the extinguisher clanging and banging its way back down to the floor.

But the spider that had seized his hand would not let go. Even after he had smashed it several times with the palm of his other hand, Dan had to dig his fingernails underneath the wicked creature just to pry it loose.

The clicking and clacking was now resuming its full fury, and Dan quickly realized that he had but a few seconds to get up to the top.

Spiders now began to throw themselves over the upper railing in order to stop his advance. He turned and saw a group of black, furry spiders that were as big as his hand now making their way behind him, each speeding towards him like a small electric car.

Dan rubbed the back of his hand where the spider had bitten him. It was beginning to turn red and swell. He wasn't sure what kind of poison the thing had injected into him, but he figured that he didn't need anything else to bite him, or things could go from bad to worse.

He scooped up the extinguisher again, and began spraying the spiders with even more determination. But almost immediately the fire extinguisher started to spit and cough as it began to lose its charge.

It was now worse.

Dan threw the empty extinguisher at the largest of the spiders and began to run up the steps. To his relief he spotted another fire extinguisher just behind the librarian's desk, and instantly made his way to it. As he began to pull the extinguisher from it's retainer he felt something heavy land on his back. He knew it had to be one of the furry, hand sized spiders.

He instantly turned his back to the wall and slammed his body against the brick. He felt the spider flatten, but Dan couldn't be sure or not if he had killed it. So he slammed his body back again and again. When he felt something burst like a soft boiled egg, he knew that he had killed the determined beast. Dan turned and saw the brown and red remains sliding down the wall, and could only shake his head.

He turned around and put the new fire extinguisher into action just as the little hellions made another advance, the foam blasting them over the edge and back down to the lower level.

He ran for the front doors, the thick, gooey remains of the spiders making it feel like he was running through sludge as he trampled the spiders along the floor.

Once outside, he threw himself on the ground, rolling over and over, hoping to kill any of the monsters that were still attached to him.

Dan leapt to his feet and ran back around to the side of the building until he came to his truck.

He swung himself behind the wheel and instantly felt something dig into his back. Thinking that another spider had him, he jerked forward at once.

Then he remembered the book.

What was it that Tye would want to look at so badly?

Dan pulled the book around to the front of him, surprised to see what it was.

It was an atlas. An atlas of the world.

Dan's face wrinkled up into a knot.

What would he want this for?

But before he could fully try and understand the book's significance he saw that his hand was now swelling to a serious degree. It tingled and felt warm from the spider venom that was now in his system. He knew that he needed medical attention soon, but assuming that anyone with any medical abilities was either dead or many miles from here, his next best thought was that he needed a drugstore.

Dan took off down the road (and though it took him the better part of an hour) he found a Walgreen's drug store just off the main highway.

He entered the store and went straight for the pharmacy section, searching for Benadryl and a steroid pack, hoping that at least for the interim the mild drugs would get him through. He found the Benadryl easily enough, and downed a dose of the liquid in two large gulps. He had no idea what dosage amount he should have been taking—but he didn't care.

After a few moments he made his way back out to the truck—and the atlas.

As he held it in front of him, he fingered the large, flat book as if he had discovered a valuable item. He remembered seeing Tye tearing a page from the book, and he was extremely curious as to what Tye had been examining. Dan started to leaf through the dog-eared pages, counting the numbers until finally coming to the missing page.

It was the map of the United States.

Dan ran his hand along the page that was underneath, feeling the indentation that Tye had left from his marking. He couldn't tell in which way the page had been positioned, and wondered how the mark would make its way across the U.S.

As he sat with the atlas on his lap, he pulled out a blank piece of paper and laid it over the indented page. He then took a pencil and began to lightly rub the pencil across the blank page, tracing the desired mark. Once he had completely covered the entire page, and had come to the two ends of the straight line, he pulled the page up and then looked back at the book.

If the page that was missing had been situated long ways with the state of Florida to his left, closest to the spine, then the line that Tye had made would have taken a path that would have started or ended in the Atlantic Ocean.

That couldn't be right.

He then turned the book around and then laid the page over it again. This time Florida would be situated to his right, but away from the book's spine. He turned the book towards him with the imaginary map of the United States sitting straight in front of him.

Dan's eyes grew wide. The point that was to his right would have started in West Virginia. He quickly flipped through a few of the pages to adopt a scale for about how big the map might have been compared to others in the book. He then flipped back to stare at the blank piece of paper. It was then that he came to a stunning revelation.

If the ending point that Tye had stopped was to be believed, and Dan's perceptions were correct, then Patrick was on a journey that would take him further than the boundaries of the lower forty eight states.

No way.

Question after question continued to pile on top of one another as they raced through Dan's mind, making it hard for him to focus.

Dan raced back into the drugstore, searching for something in the school supply aisle that he needed to aid in his search. Once he found it, he held the little clear plastic protractor in his hand, and smiled.

He laid the instrument across the line of the page that sat square to the edges of the book. He made sure that everything was perfectly aligned, and then read the degree indication that it produced.

Two hundred and ninety two degrees.

North by northwest.

Where on God's green earth were they going?

Dan closed his eyes and sighed. It was becoming obvious that Patrick was into something that was totally beyond Dan's scope and abilities. And he had to wonder at how he ever going to save Patrick, when in the end Dan was probably going to need someone just to save him?

Dan had never been in any kind of scrap like this before. He had always hated confrontation. For most of his life he had been sheltered from most of the threats that the outside world had to bring. But now, as he stood face to face with something that he could never have prepared for, the answers weren't coming to him like he would've hoped. He didn't know what to do.

As he stared at the desolate highway ahead of him, every thought in his head told him that the conclusion to this wasn't going to end in the Walt Disney-esque, fairy tale, happy kind of way no matter how hard he wished it to be so.

And he was scared.

CHAPTER 11

All the Money in the World

Throughout the night the strange little group marched on, their feet and paws tromping through the damp and wide hay field that they now found themselves, a fiery red moon rising in front of them. At first the animals were reluctant to search for any kind of human establishment, their fears of what may be lurking around and in such a place gave them more reservations than that of running into more 'messengers' that the witches may send. But now, with their hunger reaching deep, their fears began to lesson. It had gotten to the point where they now thought that they would welcome just about anyone or anything as long as it brought along something to eat.

Patrick walked without taking his eyes off of the sky in front of him. The look of the moon made him feel uncomfortable, giving him an ominous feeling as he watched it slowly creep into the night sky. He had heard of moons such as this but he had never actually seen one. He tried to remember the saying—How did it go?

Red skies at night, sailor delight
Red skies at morning, sailor take warning

"Do you see that," he asked Syrian as he pointed ahead.

"I am trying not to," the baboon replied, his voice unable to hide his misgivings. "It's definitely weird. I've never seen one like that before."

"I'm not taking it as a good sign. It could possibly be an omen."

"I don't know about any "omens," Bing replied, "but I will say that I've never seen such a moon as this before either."

Patrick tried to dismiss it from his thoughts, but it was like they were walking right up to it, feeling as if he could almost reach out and touch it, the man on the moon's face now a devil's face.

It may be an omen.

They didn't need any more omens, Patrick thought, his eyes trying to look away from the always following orb. As far as he was concerned they were living an omen right now.

Luckily, as they continued, it wasn't long until they came upon a small cabin that was tucked away against a crop of pines. They approached cautiously, trying not to come across anyone else who might deem them unwelcome.

This time Patrick was made to wait as Dog, who was believed to be the most ordinary looking of the group, made his way towards the house to see if the dwelling was occupied or not. The small band watched as the golden dog trotted up the driveway, past the white truck that was parked in front, and then up to the front porch. He scratched at the front door, hoping to cause some attention, but was quickly alerted to the fact that no one was home.

As Patrick watched Dog move up to the house, he became aware that Syrian had now moved next to him.

"How did you do that, back there at the pond?" Syrian whispered to Patrick referring to his extended time he had spent under the water, expecting Patrick to share some uncommon secret with the baboon.

"I don't know," Patrick said sincerely; now beginning to question himself as to what had truly happened as well. "I really don't know."

Syrian seemed to accept the explanation, nodded and then looked away.

They watched as Dog moved to his right, then suddenly jumped back, staring at something on the porch floor. He turned to look back at the group, his expression now one of concern, and yelled out for the rest of them to come forward.

"Well, let's go see what the hairball has discovered," Kirsdona said reluctantly.

As they met at the porch entrance they found Dog sitting beside a t-shirt, a pair of jeans, and a puddle of multicolored goo that way lying on the floor. It looked to Patrick like someone was in a hurry and had quickly abandoned their clothes.

"Yuck," Patrick said to no one in particular. "What's that?"

"That's. Why. I. Called. You."

"Did someone throw up?"

"I. Do. Not. Believe. That. Is. What. It. Is."

The dog moved in and sniffed at the clothes and liquids.

"I. Think. That. It. Is. A. Human."

"What?!" Patrick said incredulously.

"A. Human. Woman. I. Think."

The dog leaned forward and started to lick at the gooey remains.

Patrick immediately kicked out towards the dog. "Stop that! That's gross!"

The dog backed away instantly, it's tail between it's legs.

"You didn't need to do that!" Kirsdona yelled in return.

"Sorry. But if that's really a person . . ." Patrick looked stunned. "I guess I didn't think. I'm . . . I'm just not used to . . ."

"To what? Realizing that animals have feelings? How would you like it if I kicked at you? Hmmm?"

"Yeah. I know. I mean, knowing that you guys can talk and all . . . it kind of makes it different."

"How? That we're not just some objects that you can call and dismiss at your own pleasure? That you can feed us, or give us attention whenever you want? Oh, I feel sorry for the human. He's realizing he has feelings. Oh my."

Patrick looked towards Bing and Syrian, hoping for any kind of rescue from Kirsdona's sharp tongue, but they only smirked at him as he endured the tiger's outburst.

"I said I was sorry. It won't happen again. It's just that . . . Is that really a person?" Patrick was bewildered at the sight in front of him.

Bing walked up beside him to examine the human residue. "Well, you could have handled that one better, young one."

"I know."

"So what do we have here? It is quite nasty looking, whatever it is."

Kirsdona moved to the other end of the porch and laid down. "The dog's right. It's human. I'd know that stench anywhere."

"Ok. But what happened to him . . . er, her?"

Patrick took a silent step backwards and began to shake his head. "This isn't from the witches, is it? They can't do this to me, can they?"

"Rest easy, Patrick. To answer your question, I would have to say both yes and no."

Syrian squatted next to Bing.

"I have not seen it for myself, but if this is what the birds were describing to us yesterday, then I would have to say that it is from the plague."

Patrick turned and stepped off the porch, walking over to the truck parked in the driveway. He noticed that the passenger side door was open and his curiosity took him around to the side to have a look. There he saw another puddle intermixed with another set of clothing.

"Oh, god. Here's another one," he called out to the animals.

"Well," Kirsdona said matter-of-factly, "at least we now know what the plague does. I'm sure glad that She's not perturbed at the animals."

Patrick's face twisted up in a knot. "Not funny, Kirsdona."

"But to continue," Bing said, "I would have to say that it has already been proven that you are immune to whatever the witches have sent this way."

Patrick relaxed slightly at the answer, but not by much.

"Yes," Syrian added, "And now that she is eliminating the entire human population in the areas that we travel, it will be much easier for her spies to watch our progress."

"The bugs and things?" Patrick asked.

"And the reptiles."

"And the birds."

"The birds? I thought the birds were on our side."

"Some birds are good. Some birds are bad," Syrian said.

"And. Some. Birds. Poop. On. Your. Head," Dog added from a distance, as if he was having a bad memory.

"It's hard to tell with our flying friends sometimes. They're a very elitist group."

Patrick moved in closer to inspect the remains beside the truck. "That is nasty. I can't believe that this was a person. It's like they were melted."

"I don't know," Bing began, "I know what it looks like, but I'm not so sure that they were melted. It might be that the plague may have just removed the stabilizing compound that keeps things solid in their bodies."

The animals and Patrick all turned towards Bing at once.

"Huh? How did you come up with that one?"

"It's just a guess. But if their bodies had been melted I would think that either it would have come from some sort of heat, which there isn't any sign of. Or, if it was by the use of some outside substance, then I'm guessing that it would have thoroughly melted them down into nothing. But as you can see, most of their elemental state has been left intact. Like I said, it's just a guess."

Kirsdona wrinkled up her nose like she was about to sneeze at the explanation.

"Compound? Substance? What the heck are you talking about? Where on earth did you come from, bird? What goes on down there in the Antarctic?"

"I understand your confusion, Kirsdona. I realize that some of our ideas and behaviors have become slightly askew. But haven't you sensed that we have become more than we are? Your thoughts? Your ideas? Your emotions? Haven't you noticed that the way in which we have been thinking and behaving is slightly outside the normal realm in which we go about our daily lives?"

"I've noticed," Syrian spoke. "But I just accepted it as nothing more than our minds enhancing ourselves to deal with the situation that is before us. I think I know where you are going with this, Bing. And I agree. I believe that the Creator has enlightened us with such 'extra illumination', if you will."

"So someone is messing around with my mind? Is that what you're saying?" asked Kirsdona.

Bing smiled reassuringly. "No. But you do realize that we are some of the same creatures that go around eating our own bodily waste? And to be conversing as we are, this is not a common thing. You know this to be true, Kirsdona, if you truly think about it."

"You mean you guys don't always act like this?" Patrick asked, his mind trying to juggle the concept of the conversation.

"We do. It's just done in a much more primitive way, I believe. I agree with Syrian's assessment. We may have been blessed with some sort of 'extra illumination.'"

"Even. Me?" Dog asked innocently.

"No," Kirsdona added. "You're still the way you've always been, I'm sure."

Bing turned his attention to the dog.

"Yes. Of course, even you."

He then turned to Patrick.

"I imagine that even our young human friend here has been enhanced to a certain degree also. Two days ago he couldn't understand us. Today he can."

Patrick didn't say it, but what he was thinking was a quick, "Why me?"

"But, whatever it is—it is acting in us, with us, and around us. And what it is, I cannot say."

The animals, and Patrick, silently began looking around at each other in a slightly different light.

"Now," Bing continued, "back to our current problem. What are we to do with the human remains, if anything?"

"And," Syrian spoke up, "I realize from the boy's perspective that this might not be a good time to bring it up, but we did come here with the intention of finding food. We still need to look inside for something to eat."

"Patrick, would you like us to leave you alone with these humans, to pay your respects? I realize that we didn't do so well with the others we left back at the area of fire."

Patrick, still standing next to the puddle on the ground, took a step back and began walking towards the house. A sudden rush of anger came to the surface of his mind, his face feeling flush with heat. He felt outraged at the display of human remains as they appeared.

How could anyone come up with something as disturbing as this. And why? Why dissolve their bodies down to nothing? Not letting them die with at least the dignity that they came into the world with?

And then Patrick remembered Bing's words back at the barn. She didn't just want mankind to be killed off, She wanted them eradicated, completely wiped off the face of the earth. As if they had never been. And once a good hard rain would come, then they would be washed down the drain forever. Never to be thought of again.

He looked up, staring into the bright starry sky. There wasn't a cloud to be seen. He began to wonder what the view would be like back at his house. Would he have the same perspective, or would it be from a different angle.

He lowered his eyes and thought that how the same way of thinking could be applied to what was now taking place all around him. How different the perception was of the world in his back yard, compared to the spot he was in now.

If this is what She wanted to do, then she was going to have a fight on her hands.

"No. I don't need to pay my respects," the bitterness obvious in his tone. "But we need to find food to get back our strength. We've got a long ways to get to wherever this witch person lives—wherever that is. I don't want to be tired and hungry when we show up." He swung the front door open and started to go inside. "I want to make sure that when we do get there that we're ready for her."

Patrick was ten steps into the house when Kirsdona stood up, her expression meeting with the rest of the surprised animals.

"Hmm. It seems our boy is developing a little attitude. This could be interesting after all."

Syrian trailed the rest as they entered the house. "Yes. This could get interesting, indeed."

Unfortunately, and much to their dismay, the cabin was empty of any food. Patrick tried his best to explain that he believed that the cabin, since it was so secluded, may have been used only as base of sorts for hunters, and not as a main housing place for anyone to remain long term.

"In fact, the two that died probably came here hoping to seclude themselves from the plague. Maybe they thought that the plague was passed from human to human. Maybe they were hoping that they'd escape it by hiding up here."

Syrian moved past Patrick and started to make his way outside. "Well, we'd better find something to eat soon, or I think we are going to have a bigger problem than worrying about the witches."

"Ok. Ok. Just a little further. There's has to be a store or something somewhere around here."

And he was right. Shortly after they had set out again, as they had moved down into the bottom of the ridge that they were crossing, they could see the twinkling lights in the distance of what Patrick believed to be a small town.

"Finally," Patrick said as he directed everyone's attention to the far off lights.

They soon came upon a darkened four lane highway which Patrick began to walk straight down the middle of, using the yellow lines as a guide to take them into the hopeful town. The animals closely followed him, but only hesitantly.

"How's your backside holding up, Kirsdona?" Syrian asked. "Does it hurt?"

"Only when I walk," she snorted.

"Oh."

"Anything I can do?" Patrick asked.

"You could carry me."

Patrick just stared blankly back at her in return.

"Then don't ask silly questions," Kirsdona responded as she looked away and smiled.

"Uh, do you think that's it's wise that we walk so out in the open, Patrick?" Bing asked quickly. "I would think that we may be a little too exposed."

"There can't be anyone around here, I'm sure. It's too quiet."

"And how can you be so sure?" Syrian asked. "Is this the same sureness with which you said that the people back at the burning field would be glad to greet you?"

Patrick stopped, took a deep breath and rolled his eyes.

"Ok. Ok. Let's move off into the woods. But can we at least walk along the side of the highway. It's probably going to take us right into town."

And it did. The road twisted and snaked its way downward, advancing the group closer to the beckoning lights. As they approached they could see the glow just around the next bend even though they were still some several hundred yards away.

A fluorescent road sign sat motionless to their left. It was like a silent sentry that was there to alert the town of anyone that was advancing, still standing sharp in the darkness.

"Holly, Ohio, population 1680," Patrick read the sign on road marker as they passed. "I hope there's not going to be sixteen hundred and eighty puddles of goo ahead of us. That would be disgusting."

As they moved along the side of the road they began to notice the various automobiles that had run off on both sides of the highway. There were only three, two cars and a truck, each quiet and unmoving like a sleeping animal. Patrick almost felt a sense of sorrow for the motionless hunks of metal and plastic, wondering if anyone would ever use them again. The cars were almost calling for him to come over and run his hand along their smooth exterior, hoping to entice him over to take them away from their frameless prison. But Patrick didn't dare, for he knew what would be inside the dormant vehicles. He wanted to go over and look inside, to see the melted bodies. He knew they were in there, but he felt a heavy sense of respect. As if he should leave the bodies as they were and not disturb them.

The forest soon dropped away as the clearing entrance to the town became clearer. Small, unlit houses dotted the landscape off in the distance to either side of them. They looked to Patrick like the tiny houses that were used in the game of Monopoly, each small and uninhabited. Plastic houses.

Patrick became aware that the animals were slowly dropping their pace behind him, their building anxieties of what may come of them in the town.

"Come on," Patrick tried to reassure, "it'll be ok."

Though he wasn't as sure as he led on, he still wasn't going to be deterred by any useless fears that were going to keep him from finding something to eat.

They ended up coming upon the small town of Holly by way of the highway after all, being that it was the only way in.

They passed two gas stations, each lit up as if it were business as usual, an Allstate insurance office, and a Wee Ones daycare center.

The animals and the boy moved cautiously at first before Patrick began running forward, his eyes fixated on something ahead of him on the ground.

The animals were startled to see the boy running and they immediately began to look for cover, figuring that whatever it was that must have spooked Patrick was something that they didn't need to see.

But what the animals couldn't possibly know, or understand, was that Patrick had spotted something that he had been chasing his entire twelve year old life. Something that he believed could control the world.

It was money.

Lots of money. Hundreds, possibly thousands of dollar bills were lying scattered all over the highway and parking areas on both sides of the road as they entered the town. Some of it was in clumps, still wrapped up in plastic wrapping, with the majority of the rest strewn out in odd patterns across the dark roadway.

Patrick began scooping up the various bills, each either a ten, or a twenty.

"Oh my god, we're rich!" he exclaimed. "Try and pick up as much as you can! Get it all!"

The animals didn't move, each looking at one another with inquisitive, puzzled expressions.

Patrick was in a frenzy trying to stuff the money into his pockets as he darted from spot to spot grabbing handfuls of the green paper.

"Is this going to help us get food?" Bing asked.

"Yeah, what's this stuff got to do with me getting fed?" Kirsdona asked as she watched Patrick move with maddening motion. The boy resembled a humming bird, darting back and forth from plant to plant collecting nectar.

"Don't you get it, this is what we buy the food with," Patrick exclaimed, his voice expressing a sense of anger at the reluctance of the animals to help him. "This is the stuff that gets us the food!"

"Buy the food? What does that mean?"

"You know, we give them this stuff, and then they give us food. It's like a trade. We trade them this paper, and they give us food."

"You have got to be kidding," Kirsdona said as she looked at him pitifully. "You humans are truly a sorry bunch. So someone controls all the food? You have to get it from someone else? You just don't go get it for yourself. Nonsense. Sheer nonsense."

"Well, it's not just food, its other things as well. It's how we get things. When we work we get paid this stuff. Then we can take it to the store and give them this money and then they give us stuff. Cars. Clothes. Lots of stuff. Even food."

"And the Creator put you guys in charge of this place. Oh, brother."

"I know it all sounds crazy to you, but believe me we won't ever have to worry about anything again."

Patrick pulled out all the money he had collected and set it in a pile in front of the animals. He quickly turned and began scurrying around again collecting more, his excited voice chirping on and on.

"I don't know why all of this money is out here . . . maybe it was a robbery or something . . . I don't know, but whatever, there must be thousands and thousands of dollars here."

Bing stepped away from the group and began walking slowly towards Patrick. "But if there is no one to give the money to, then what is the worth of that paper you are collecting? I mean, I hate to be the bearer of bad news, but exactly who are you going to trade this paper with? If I am not mistaken, we seem to be the only ones here."

Patrick was bent over, still picking up the dollar bills, when the realization of what Bing was trying to tell him slowly began to sink in. He straightened himself out, and then stood staring off into the distance.

Oh, no.

How could he have been so stupid.

He blinked slowly.

How could he have been so blind.

Money just lying there in the street? Oh, yeah, happens all the time.

His hands opened slowly and the few bills remaining began drifting back down to the street like leaves falling from a tree.

There is no one else alive. Everyone else here is dead.

And I'm all alone.

Patrick's breathing started to come at him in short, hard bursts. Like he couldn't catch his breath.

He ran over to the Allstate storefront and grabbed at the door handle. "Hello! Is anyone here?!" he screamed frantically.

The store remained dark, silent, and unresponsive.

He then ran to the next building, the children's clothing store. There were two little stick figure children holding hands on the door, just above the name, each painted blue and red and yellow.

Again Patrick grabbed at the door handle and began jerking and pulling on it with all his might, trying to get someone to answer him.

"Please!" he screamed, "Anyone!"

Tears began falling from his eyes as he ran across the street to the Exxon gas station, all the time screaming "Hello!! Is anyone here?!!" to loudest extent that his lungs could push forth the words.

The animals watched, each feeling pity for the boy as they figured he was finally realizing that he was truly alone. They had talked about this behind his back, but now as they watched the display, they didn't know what to do.

Dog ran over next to Patrick, trying to get his attention.

"Patrick. Patrick. It. Will. Be. Ok."

"No! No!" Patrick cried out, he turned and screamed at the dog. "Get out of here! All of you! Get out! Go away!"

He grabbed the door handle to the gas station and pulled it open. He stood, staring in at the empty store. He finally slumped down to the ground and pulled his knees up to his chest as he sobbed.

"I just want my mom and dad," were the only words the animals could understand through all the tears that came forth.

The animals, except for Kirsdona, began moving over next to where the boy laid.

Dog laid his head on Patrick's lap and tried to nuzzle up next to him to let him know that he wasn't alone.

"What should we do?" Syrian asked.

"I do not know," Bing responded. "Perhaps he just needs some time."

Patrick cried silently for a few moments, and then sat upright, his hands pushing the tears from his eyes. He sniffled twice, and then leaned his head back against the cold glass of the door.

"I'm ok," he began as he wiped his nose on his shirt sleeve. "I . . . I just didn't really think . . . really think that everyone would be gone. That I'm really doing this. That this is really happening. I'm the only one left, aren't I?"

"Well," Bing looked down at the ground, looking for answers. "You're not the only human left in the world, of that I'm sure. There's still time."

"But I'm probably the only one that's within a hundred miles from here."

"I realize that it must be a great blow to your sense of human camaraderie."

Patrick stared at the small bird, his face wrinkling up into a slight chuckle.

"What? 'Human camaraderie.' What's that mean? You do say some of the most off the wall stuff, Bing."

"Are you quite finished?" Kirsdona asked from behind the huddled group. Her eyes never coming in contact with anyone in front of her.

Patrick could sense that the tiger was not expressing any sympathy for his predicament in the least. Though his heart and head were throbbing with incredible feelings of helplessness and loneliness, he pushed himself back to his feet and began wiping the dirt off his behind. He stared at the animal, trying to make eye contact with her, something that had bothered Patrick ever since he first met the tiger—how she refused to look at him directly.

"I'm ok. And you can forget about the money," he sighed, "I guess I'm not going to be rich after all."

Bing looked around the brightly lit haven, and then back to Patrick.

"Well, if it is wealth that you wish to possess, I believe that since you are the only one here, then you are now the king of this settlement. You should be able to have anything that you want, and you don't even need the trading paper."

"It's called money."

"Ok. You don't need the money. You can have anything that you see, if that will make you happy."

Just then, Patrick looked towards Syrian, and then past the baboon's right shoulder. The faintly illuminated sign down the block caused Patrick's heart to skip. Finally, something good was in front of him.

"Alright!" Patrick yelled, startling the animals.

"What. Is. It?" Dog asked.

"It's a Giant Eagle! Yes!"

The animals all snapped their attention in the direction Patrick was now looking.

"A giant eagle? Where?"

"Right there!" he said as he pointed.

"How big is it? I don't see it?"

"Is it coming at us?"

The animals started to scurry around looking for cover.

"Right there! C'mon, let's go!"

"Are you sure that it's not looking for something to eat? A normal eagle is worry enough, but a 'giant' eagle could be extremely dangerous."

Patrick had taken a few steps when he stopped and turned back towards the worried animals.

"What? What are you talking about?"

That's when he realized that he and the animals were talking about two different things altogether.

"Oh, I get it," Patrick said as he smiled. "It's not an 'eagle' eagle. It's a food store!"

"Humans call the places they store food, 'eagles?'"

Patrick rocked his head from side to side.

"Well, it's just a name. It's a grocery store. A food store."

"But, why eagle? Is there some significance in the use of the name?"

"Would you guys stop! Who cares why they call it a 'Giant Eagle?' Let's just go! There's probably more food in there than you guys have ever seen in your lives."

With the furious explanation given, the animals made for the store that Patrick had pointed out, each moving at its fastest to get to the food source.

With the power still on the automatic doors opened as soon as Kirsdona, who was the first to get there, arrived. She was hesitant at first, but Patrick yelled from behind her to just go on in.

Patrick watched the expressions on each of the animals faces (even Sin, whose keen sense of smell had put a polite little smile across the boar's face) as they entered into the brightly lit food warehouse. He chuckled as they took timid steps across the white tile flooring, their heads drifting back and forth as they eyed the multicolored boxes and displays.

Syrian was the first to take part in the exercise of eating, having quickly found the produce section he squealed with joy at the wide range of assorted fruits and vegetables that were stacked in huge piles.

Dog, who was sniffing furiously at everything he came in contact with, turned back towards Patrick and seemed confused.

"How. Do. We. Get. To. The. Food?" he asked.

"Like this," Patrick replied, and grabbed a box of cornflakes off one of the shelves. He ripped the box open, showing the bounty that was to be found inside, and then laid the opened box at the dog's feet.

"How's that?"

"Perfect!" the dog answered as he buried his face into the box.

Patrick looked around for Kirsdona, Bing, and Sin, but couldn't find them anywhere. He then heard some rustling coming from the back of the store. He quickly made his way down the sugar and flour aisle, and then followed his ears to the meat and fish section. He began laughing when he saw Kirsdona lying in the meat case, eating packets of raw steaks and hamburger without removing the plastic wrappings. To her left was Bing, plucking thumb sized pieces of shrimp out of the fish display with his beak, hurriedly tilting his head back allowing the tiny creatures to be devoured. Sin, having discovered the nut section and its open baskets of nuts, was consuming as many pecans as his little belly could hold.

Patrick, satisfied that the animals were now taken care of, went off in search for what he could only think of in a pinch—Lunchables. He ran over to the lunchmeat section and began tearing open the little yellow cardboard boxes, stuffing the cheese, meat, and crackers mounds into his mouth faster than he could chew.

They ate and ate and ate some more. Each acting as though they hadn't eaten in almost two days—which they hadn't.

Finally the eating frenzy came to a conclusion, with each of the animals making their way to the front of the store where they carefully plopped their full belly's down on the cool tile floor just behind the checkout area.

"I love Giant Eagles," Kirsdona said as she roundly yawned, her lazy tongue flopping to each side of her mouth. "I think I could live here."

"Yes, as long as there aren't any humans around," Syrian said, nodding.

Patrick stretched out on the floor with his hands folded under his head for a pillow.

"Well, someone has to restock this place. And I don't think the cows are going to volunteer their services by just dropping by."

Bing scuttled down next to Patrick and Sin, his protruding belly giving him a hard time in maneuvering. His turned his attention to the boy, his eyes meeting with Patrick's,

"Are you ok?" he asked of the weary boy. "I mean, are you alright? I just want you to know that you may feel like you are alone, but I promise you that we will do everything in our power to try and fill the void that you are discovering. We will never be able to be human, but that does not mean that we aren't able to comfort. The burden that you will carry on your young shoulders is something that we will never understand, and we have long discussed the implications of this happening to one so young as yourself. But things happen to every creature on this earth every day for reasons that can't be easily explained. Sadly, sometimes a creature dies without ever knowing why a thing has happened to them. Sometimes a simple gesture will extend another creature's life without them even realizing that it has happened. Some good. Some bad. But things happen. I don't know why this has happened to you, and to you alone, I have not been blessed with this knowledge. But before your days are over, you will find the answers to your confusion and fears. Of this, Patrick Brighton, I am sure."

A soft smile came across Patrick's face, and then he slowly closed his eyes and nodded.

"I know. It's just hard."

Bing took a deep breath and sighed.

"Unfortunately, I do not think that it is going to get any easier."

Early morning streaks of sunlight began to make their way through the store windows.

"I think we all need some rest. If we are to stick with the plan, we need to sleep until dusk, and then begin again. I believe we have found our safe haven for the day, the sun is just starting to come up over the horizon. We need to take turns in keeping watch, just in case the witches should send out scouts to look for us, or in case a human or two decided to drop by to replenish their food supply. I'll take the first turn."

"No argument from me."

"Me neither."

"Thanks, Bing."

"Well, Kirsdona, I'll wake you when the sun starts to approach the mid morning sky. You can pick who you will after that."

But Kirsdona was already fast asleep, her tail twitching ever so slightly as if she were dreaming.

And that's how they spent the day. No intruders came looking for them. No spies, and no humans. They slept through the day uninterrupted, each sleeping the sleep of the most restful kind.

PART II—
DEMETER'S PATH

CHAPTER 12

Talk of War

"Alaska?! We've got to go to Alaska?! You're nuts!"

"But that's where they are hiding."

"You act like we can be there in two days. We couldn't make it in two years!"

"Be patient, my young friend. Things have a way of presenting themselves that you cannot foresee at this particular moment in time."

Patrick and the animals had finally awoke from their day long sleep, with Patrick asking innocently enough the first thing that had popped into his head—Where exactly were they going anyway?

"But . . . Alaska?! Good grief! Do you realize just how far away that is?"

"Nevertheless, we have got to continue forward. Standing here debating this is not getting us any closer to our goal."

"How did you come up with Alaska, by the way? I'm going to guess that's where the witches are at, right?"

Bing cocked an eye at Patrick. "Well, then I suppose it's even obvious to you.

"Yes, a little while ago we received some news from a group of sparrows. The witches are still holed up in the southern mountainous regions of the placed called Alaska. Why they picked that particular part of the world to inhabit I do not know. But I am sure that it holds some significance to them, and for that we should prepare ourselves."

Patrick looked at the ground and sighed. "The great battle that you spoke of the other day, Syrian, the battle that involved the animals, where did that take place?"

"On the great western plains to the north. The birds referred to the land as Canada. It is believed that some of their legions were only traveling through that area, making their way to the west, when the animals caught up with them."

"But Alaska? That's going to take forever. Do we have enough time?"

"Not if we continue to stand here and debate this."

The animals and Patrick awoke with tired, lazy expressions that seemed to indicate that they were not quite ready to begin their travels again. But with Bing's insistence the group quickly gathered themselves and prepared for their immediate departure.

The first order of business was to once again replenish their bellies with enough food to carry them throughout the night. They knew that this next stage of their journey was going to be a march. No strolling allowed.

As the others began to eat to once again fortify themselves, Patrick decided that he was in need of something else, something he was sure he was going to need for the long trip ahead. He set out to another part of the store that didn't house food surpluses, but rather carried various school supplies that included paper and pencils and things of that sort. It was really a miscellaneous aisle that most stores had set up for those last second things that someone may need in a pinch. But Patrick wasn't looking for paper and pens and pencils, he was looking for something he knew that he had seen at other grocery stores closer to home. It was something that he never would have ever given a second thought to at any other time. In fact he probably would have laughed over it on most occasions, mocking it as he looked, but at this particular moment he hoped that his memory was correct.

When he came upon the aisle his eyes darted over the various shelves and hooks displaying the different coloring books and protractors and different colored pens and markers, hoping that he could find what he had in mind.

And then he spied it.

It wasn't exactly what he was looking for, and as he picked it up from the shelf he groaned a little as he held it in his hands. He even looked around for a second just in case anyone else would see him with it.

It was a back pack.

He knew that this would be the best thing he could come up with for the moment in which to carry supplies on the trip. More than likely they would probably come across some food or convenience stores in the more populated areas that they would travel, but with what they had discussed earlier about avoiding such areas for fear of the spies of the Witch Queen, he wanted to make sure that he had something on hand to put in his stomach when his hunger had reached the proportions that he had just experienced.

The problem he was having at that moment was that the backpack was pink. And it had something on it that truly gave Patrick reservations as to whether he actually wanted to carry it or not.

It was a Barbie backpack. Her little blonde head smiling out with a little gold crown stuck on top of it. The words "Barbie!" scrolled across the top of it in sparkling gold letters. It even smelled pink. Pink, with that new fresh vinyl smell. Like a new car.

He held it out in front of him and then carefully looked over the other shelves to see if any other back pack was available. Of course there wasn't. He sighed and then frowned as he finally unzipped the pack and looked inside. It was plenty big enough to carry everything he would want, and as he started to go through the store and gather various items to take with him, he surely hoped that no one that they may possibly run into would know what the back pack symbolized.

He walked back to the front of the store and greeted the others as they assembled for their departure.

"What. Have. You. Got. There?" Dog asked as he tilted his head inquisitively.

"Uh, it's a supply bag," he said as he pulled the backpack in front of him and opened for all to examine. "Hopefully this will keep us from getting too hungry before we find our next place to stop."

"That's a good idea! Have you something in there for all of us?" Syrian asked.

"Yeah. I tried to get a little something for all of us."

Patrick zipped the backpack up and then threw the bag around behind him. He had to loosen the straps to their most expanded length just to get it around his shoulders.

In his mind Patrick was grateful that the animals didn't understand human culture much, and didn't have a clue about the Barbie symbol. That was, until Kirsdona spoke as they began to move from the store.

"Uh, nice bag. Colorful. I'm sure the other girls would just love seeing you with it."

Patrick drew a deep breath and exhaled.

"Can we just go please," he said as he tried to move past the agitating tiger.

Kirsdona's smile was wide when Bing walked up beside her and thumped her in the leg.

"I sure hope that whatever he has inside there for you to eat doesn't mysteriously end up missing as we go, eh?"

Kirsdona chuckled slightly at the comment.

"Well, if that happens I'm sure I can always find a somewhat dry, probably uneventful tasting, flightless bird to munch upon. What do you think?"

Bing had to smile at the retort.

"Yes, I suppose you probably could."

As they moved from the store Patrick glanced up to the sky to look at the stars, but found that they were covered by clouds.

"Which way?" he asked to the group.

"Up behind those tall structures to start," Bing said as he pointed past the buildings to their west. "Those hills should take us in the needed direction."

And so they began again. The rain that the clouds had carried finally came down a little more than an hour after they had set out. It came hard in short bursts, but for the most part was steady in its purpose. Even thought it was early Fall, the temperatures stayed well high enough for the rain to feel warm, almost refreshing.

As he walked Patrick wondered if the rain was hard enough to wash away all of the dead, his mind imagining all the small puddles floating down into the sewers and drains. He tried to push it from his thoughts, but at times it seemed to stick like glue to the forefront of his thinking, not easily being put aside.

The small group walked on, trying their best to avoid any human populations, continuing on through the night until they decided to take their rest under a thick group of Poplar trees as the morning began to break.

They continued this routine for several days, sleeping through the day with each of them taking a turn to watch for intruders or spies, and then continuing on with their journey during the night. They were lucky enough to find several convenience stores from time to time to restock the backpack and keep their spirits somewhat high with the continuing influx of food.

As they traveled the conversations were mostly carried along by Bing, Syrian, Dog, and Patrick. Sin of course could not speak, but seemed to follow along to the discussions as his little head would move from side to side as each party would add their turn to the talk. Kirsdona stayed out of most of the conversations, choosing instead to walk ahead of the group, her enormous stride allowing her to stay several yards in front of the others. But every so often she would over hear something that someone would say that she found amusing and could not help herself but to add a sullied insult, or sarcastic remark to the words that had just been spoke.

They each talked about their homelands and the various customs and ways that the different parts of the world had to offer. They talked about their friends and their families.

Syrian talked the most. He seemed to take great pride in his native land of Ethiopia and all that it had to offer.

They each asked questions that caused chuckles by some, and intense follow up questions to others.

Much of the conversations were just a way of passing time, keeping their minds away from the intent and purpose of their travels, but every so often a question was asked that would cause a heavy silence that seemed to settle over the group like thick fog.

On their forth night out, a stranger to the group asked such a question.

Bing had just finished telling about one of his brothers and how he had tried to get an extra fish during feeding time at the zoo, the group chuckling at the retelling of the story, when they heard a startling 'boom!' out in the distance to the north.

They stopped, each wondering aloud as to what could have made such a loud explosion.

And then they heard it again, the ground rumbling beneath their feet.

They each stood, holding their collective breath for silence sake, each hoping that they didn't hear the noise again.

"That sounds like a bomb or something," Patrick said in a near whisper.

From high in the trees above them came a small whistle-like voice.

"It is not a bomb. It is a human place out in the hills beyond the river," a small black bird spoke. "Because there are no more humans around, save for yourself I believe, the machinery that man has made is starting to die and give itself up."

"Machinery?" Patrick asked. "What kind of machinery?"

"Large buildings with large long singing wires coming from them."

The only thing Patrick could think of was that an electrical station must be close by. Possibly, he thought, that since they were left unattended that they may have overheated and caught fire.

"Thank you, friend," Bing spoke to the small bird. "What is your name, if I may ask?"

"My name is Twither."

"Well, Twither, can you tell us if there is any danger for us to continue traveling in the direction we are taking? Is there any danger of the fire?"

"None," the bird replied. He fluttered his wings quickly and then asked a question.

"Are you the group that is shepherding the human boy? Is he the one that is being spoken of in hushed circles?"

"We are," came Bing's cautious reply, "and he is."

The smallish bird fluttered his feathers again, seemingly in an attempt to gain comfort. "Are you truly taking the boy all the way? That you will not be passing him off to another group of humans?"

The animals looked stunned by the question.

"What do you mean? Why would we do that? If you don't know, if you have not heard, we have been charged with the care and safekeeping of this human," Bing responded.

"But what of the danger that lies ahead? You are very brave souls indeed to be risking your lives for a human."

"We do realize this," Syrian spoke, "But we have accepted this task. We know of the daunting position this places us in."

"But what of the terrors that lie in wait for you? What will you do when you come upon the human war? I shutter to think what it must be like!"

That was when the silence fell.

The animals lost their voices at that moment, no one knowing exactly what to say.

"The human war?" Patrick repeated, questioning the words that were spoke. "What war?"

Bing looked around at the others, realizing quickly that they were now all looking back at him. He sighed heavily and spoke with a sorrowful tone. "Don't you remember when I spoke of this back at the barn, when we first met? I mentioned of the wars that have broken out."

Pat nodded. "I remember you saying something about a being that was creating hatred amongst men. You said something about man against man. And country against country . . ."

Patrick's voice trailed away at his quick realization.

"What's happening? Is there really a war going on?" he asked with alarm.

"It seems that each division of men, each country, is blaming the others for the outbreak of death that is sweeping the world. I believe that the men that have yet to be affected by the plague are only accomplishing what the plague will do in time. They are killing each other off with warring authority."

Patrick looked stunned. "How bad is it?"

The blackbird spoke from on high. "Oh it is terrible, this death that man brings. I have heard tales of lands in far off places where great machines run over the land causing great calamitous explosions. Of sticks that burn and explode. Of man's great bird machines that drop death on the humans below. It is terrible and sorrowful. Most of my kind have fled those places and have brought word back here."

The tiny bird lowered its head.

"Save for the vultures. They fly to those places with great lust and joy. I have not seen this for myself, but it is said that they can whisper into a man's ear and cause him to bring death to himself and to others."

Kirsdona, who had mainly stayed distant from the conversation, strolled over and asked a question herself, her voice holding a commanding tone. "Is this war close? Is there any of man's war going on in the direction we are taking?"

The bird looked away off into the distance. "If I am to understand the direction you are taking is true, then you are still a long ways off from coming into contact with the destruction. But you will encounter it if you stay your present course."

"How soon?" Syrian asked.

The little bird paused. "I do not know of the exactness with which you ask. I fly to places that take mere moments in the span of my life. For you, since I do not travel in the same method that you do, I cannot hope to guess."

Syrian turned towards Bing. "We have not prepared for man's war. I have not given it any thought since it seemed so distant. And, I am not sure of the others here, but I did not have a dream of seeing war, either. I know what the bird has just told us, but I cannot help to think that he may be mistaken."

Patrick continued to look up at the bird as it perched on the high off branch. The bird's gaze seemed fixated on something in the distance.

"I am not sure what we should do once we encounter such a thing," Syrian continued.

"Perhaps," the bird began again, "the human boy should ask his kind what he should do."

The group almost jumped at the response.

"What?! There are humans around here? Where?" Bing hurriedly asked.

Patrick could feel the tension around them build like paste. Especially after their last encounter with his kind. He was even having reservations about the subject.

"There is a large grouping of them over the next hill, inside the wire gates."

"Wire gates?" Bing asked.

"The place where man places his dead," the bird responded.

"A cemetery?" Patrick asked. "There's a bunch of humans at the cemetery? Where?"

"To the west. Just beyond the giant oak that sits alone."

The bird jumped from its perch and flew in the direction they needed, giving them a quick "In this direction," before it turned and flew back into the tree.

"Well, then we know where we need to avoid," Kirsdona spoke assuredly.

"Yes. We don't need another encounter like we had before," Syrian added.

"Now wait a minute. Can't I at least go have a . . ." Patrick began.

"No!" they all spoke in unison.

But Patrick was persistent. "I won't go up to them this time. I just want to see what they are doing."

Kirsdona flicked her long tail and smacked Patrick in the head with it. "Are you just being dense for the moment, or are you completely stupid?"

"I mean, really," Bing began. "What would possess you to want to chance another horror like the last one."

"All humans aren't like that, Bing. You know it, too."

"I do know. But things in the world are not like they were before. A lot has changed, and that goes along with human behavior. At this moment in time I just do not trust it."

The bird was becoming fidgety with all the distress being exhibited below.

"Why are you all alarmed at the thought of the humans? They are in the wire gates. I believe they have been placed in there. They cannot get out, for whatever reason. I do not understand your degree of alarm. They are only human spirits, after all."

All at once the bickering and discussion that was taking place below the lowest tree branch came to a rapid stop. Kirsdona's face twitched slightly as she glanced back up into the tree.

"What did you say?"

"The humans. The ones in the wire gates are only spirits. They can talk and move just like living humans, but they cannot leave the grounds that they occupy. I have sat in the nearby trees and listened to them as they moan and cry. I cannot hope to gain an understanding as to what they are saying, but they seem to be agonizing over their current predicament."

"Ghosts?" Patrick asked, his eyes growing wide.

"I believe that he is referring to spirits," Bing responded. "There is a difference."

"I don't care what they are; I've got to go see that!"

"This can not serve any purpose for us. If they truly are spirits then they cannot help us in our decisions in the real world. They can't possibly know of anything more than what has happened to them, and what has put them in the position that they are in at the present."

"Patrick," Syrian responded as well, "I believe that this could only complicate things. We need to continue on in our present course. Time is wasting. I am beginning to think that we should not have gotten into this conversation with our friend from on high. He has done nothing but to alarm us."

The small bird looked away, indignant.

But Patrick wanted to see. No, he needed to see.

His mind danced round and round with the thoughts of seeing a ghost. Or spirit. Or whatever. The idea that he could actually see something that was only ever thought of in terms of spooky stories and made up tales was giving him a rush that would not be denied.

"I'm going. You guys can come if you want to or not. You can wait here for all I care. But I'm going over there to see the ghosts, or whatever is over there. Just for a quick peek anyhow."

Kirsdona had silently moved around behind the boy and had placed herself between where he was standing and the desired direction he intended to go.

"And what if I were to say that you are not," she purred aggressively.

The hairs on the back of Patrick's neck stood on end at the sound of her voice. But as he turned towards her his determination seemed to override his beckoning and rightful fears.

"You can say anything you want. I don't care. You all are making this into something that isn't. It may turn out to be nothing at all, but can't we just go over and have a look. I promise I'll stay to the rear and one of you can go forward first."

The animals exchanged glances between each other, readily acknowledging without words that they hoped that someone would speak up and volunteer for the front line position, being that none of them actually wanted the job.

"I. Guess. That. I. Will. Go. Then," Dog finally spoke up softly.

"No," Bing responded by walking up beside the hairy animal and stroking its side. "I appreciate your courage, my friend, but I will go and have a look. If there is going to be any blame placed for a situation that arises out of our control, then I would rather that I was the one to shoulder it."

And with those words still sitting heavy on the air, and not allowing anyone else time for rebuttal, Bing took off with a start up and over the hill.

The minutes passed by unbearably as they waited on word from the little penguin. Patrick watched as Kirsdona paced like an expectant mother, while Syrian climbed the nearby trees and used them like the 'monkey bars' on the playgrounds back near his home.

Finally, with the minutes seeming to hang on the air like hours, Kirsdona could not stand it any longer.

"That's long enough, I'm going to see what's delaying that silly bird's return."

"But it's only been a few minutes," Syrian tried to reason.

"I don't care. You stay here and keep an eye on the group, I'll be back as quickly as I can."

"No way!" Patrick shouted. "If you go, we're all going."

The tiger turned back to him and growled, "I said stay!"

Patrick closed his eyes and tried to let his fears subside, but he spoke anyway, no matter what retribution may come.

"No. We're all in this together. We all need to go, Kirsdona."

The great tiger looked to the ground and then from side to side, glancing at the faces of the others.

"Alright. But just stay behind me then," she allowed as she turned and bounded away up the hill.

Patrick went over and alerted Sin as to what was taking place, with the small boar quickly getting into position to move himself behind Patrick.

Dog and Syrian each started in the same direction once Patrick began his movements.

They each ran hard. And it was only moments before they spotted the enormous oak tree ahead of them. Its large, flowing limbs seemed to extend to the sky. It's reach an almost limitless shadow in the pitch black night.

Kirsdona was like a knife through the dark, slicing her way closer and closer to the huge and ancient tree. Patrick ran hard, trying his best to keep up, but was of course no match for the speed of the tiger. But soon, as he spotted the great tiger coming to a rapid stop ahead of him, he realized that he didn't need any speed to catch up to her as she pulled back on her haunches like she had hit an invisible fence.

Patrick, Syrian, and the others made their way beside her, each looking down into the shallow valley below them. The sight in front of them gave them each a moment of pause. They all continued to stare, disbelieving what their eyes and their thoughts were trying to convey.

Patrick's hearing finally caught up with the rest of his senses as he began to hear exactly what the small black bird had told to them earlier.

It was the moaning, their voices, that carried softly on the air up to his ears.

He heard sorrow. And fear.

He could hear everything.

And worse, he could see everything.

"All that I see is lights. Twinkling lights," Syrian responded in a low, unsure way.

"Yes, me as well," Kirsdona replied. "But the sounds. The voices. Those things I can hear quite well. Those are the sounds of humans who are in pain. I know that sound. Those lights must be their spirits."

Patrick, bewildered, turned and looked at the others, "What lights? What are you talking about? I don't see any lights."

Syrian turned towards Patrick, "You cannot see the twinkling lights that seem to dance and move all around?"

"No," Patrick shook his head, "but I can see people. You guys don't see the people?"

"No," Syrian said as he shook his head.

"Where are these people? There isn't any one down there, none that I can see," responded Kirsdona.

"Me. Neither," came a low response from Dog.

"Neither do I," Syrian replied as well.

"Right there!" Patrick said as he pointed.

That was when the realization was delivered to them as to what was going on.

"It is because he can see what we cannot," Bing said as he came up to them from their left.

The animals turned and looked at Bing, acknowledging that they were glad to see him safe, then they all turned and looked back at Patrick.

Patrick felt them staring at him now with the same eyes that they had used when they had first caught sight of him after he had emerged from the water days earlier.

"So, I see our young friend managed to get you all to bring him over anyway," Bing said in a parental tone of disapproval.

"So you guys can't see the people?" Patrick asked innocently.

"It appears not," Bing replied. "But if you can see the people, then perhaps that is something that can benefit us to some degree. At this moment in time, though, I cannot see it. But all things happen for a reason."

Patrick stood for a moment, lost in time. He knew that he had to go down there. He knew that he had to see what had happened to those people, and to find out where they had come from. His head ached at the thoughts that washed over him as he watched all of them moving about. Some seemed to be in agony, while others seemed to be wandering about in a certain depression.

Like a magnetic pull, Patrick felt himself take a step past the oak tree, and then another past the breach that marked the descent down towards the graveyard. He absently slipped the Barbie backpack from his shoulders and set it on the ground.

"Patrick, wait," Bing said as he reached out to him. "Are you sure about this? Our discovery here could mark us in a bad way. Please try and be judicious in your approach."

Patrick took another step and then turned back towards Bing.

"What does that mean?" he asked.

Bing gave him a thoughtful, knowing look.

"Don't do anything you're going to regret."

Patrick glanced around at the faces of the other animals, nodded silently, and then continued on down towards the dead.

CHAPTER 13

Dead Travel

As Patrick approached the graveyard, the people, or spirits in front of him began to come into view more clearly than from the view that he had up on the sloping hill where the animals still held their position. Patrick noticed right off that the spirits seemed an almost faint alabaster in color, and were unmistakably transparent in their form. On several of the people he could see only the top half of their being, and on others only seeing extremely faint images of anything at all to their structure.

As he broke the veil of his darkened cover and began to expose himself to the spirits, the voices from the dead were unmistakable as they seemed to drop away and become distant. They could now see Patrick approaching, and their shouts and moans and crying voices were quickly silenced and replaced by whispers that sounded ominous and suspicious to him.

Patrick guessed that the fencing that surrounded the gravesite was only about five feet high, and was made of a thick black metal that had been bent and twisted to form a very intricate and sophisticated weave that wound itself through and through like ivy. The enclosure seemed time-worn, most of it having been built in long sections with some of the pieces broken and bent inward like crooked teeth.

He couldn't locate the gate right off, for the gravesite seemed to expand back into the far off tree line to his left, but after he had made a few more unsteady steps he located it off in the distance to his right. It was positioned behind the far aft corner that rounded back around a large loping mound where the more momentous and stoic monuments were displayed.

It seemed like everyone in the area was holding their breath as Patrick moved in closer with each step, the silence being broken only by the sounds of Patrick's feet crunching along in the dried weeds. He turned and looked back towards his friends, their positions never wavering from where he had left them. As the distance between he and the graveyard grew shorter the crowds of spirits quietly began making their way to the edge of the fence line that marked the graveyard's boundary.

Patrick noticed right off that the bird Twither had been correct, for the spirits did seem to be held by some unseen attachment that would not let them come past the fence line even though there were large patches of metal railing that lay in ruins that they easily could have passed over. And he laughed at himself for thinking this—because they were spirits after all—but what could possibly be holding them at bay? Couldn't they just walk on out to him? Weren't spirits supposed to be able to walk through walls and come and go unobstructed like he had seen on Casper and Ghostbusters?

A woman and man spirit stepped closest to the gate as Patrick approached. They appeared to be clothed in common everyday attire—jeans, a light shirt, and possibly shoes (thought he couldn't really see their feet.) Things that Patrick assumed that they must have been wearing when they died. The man's shirt had something written on it that appeared to say Ohio State University, but with the way it shifted and moved as the man walked it was hard to tell. Patrick noticed that the woman seemed on the verge of a breakdown, her hands tumbling together in nervous fits, and her front teeth gnawing at her lower lip. She looked like she was more in fear of Patrick as he approached, than he was of her.

The man was the first to speak, which startled Patrick a bit as his attention was continually drawn to the frightened woman.

"Are you the boy?" the man asked, his tone and his words seemed heavy in the dark night.

The question alarmed Patrick. He knew what the man was asking—was saying—but he was surprised that this man, this spirit, would be so direct with his revelation.

"How do you know who I am?" Patrick asked reluctantly.

At his response the voices of the spirits began to chatter at their own surprise.

"He can hear us!"

"He can see us!"

"How can this be happening? How can he know that we're even here?"

The spirit of the man in front of Patrick turned back and waited for the gathering to calm so that he could continue his conversation.

"You'll have to excuse our reaction. Even as we were in life, none of us has ever known of anyone that can communicate with the dead. That you can see us and hear us is quite a shock. You'll have to forgive our bit of hysteria. With what has happened and brought us to this point, our anxiety seems to have gotten the best of us."

Patrick's mouth hung open as he watched the various spirits flow in and out of view.

"Who are you?" Patrick got up enough courage to ask, "Why are you here?"

From behind the man Patrick noticed more and more spirits pushing their way closer to the forefront trying to catch a glimpse of him, trying to listen to the conversation.

"My name is John Gulledge. And this is my wife Denise," the man said as he motioned to the spirit of the nervous woman who was standing to his right.

"Nice to meet you," Patrick heard himself saying; half wondering what the appropriate response was when someone was introducing himself to a ghost.

"And who are you?" the man asked.

"My name is Patrick Brighton. Me and my friends," Patrick motioned back up to the hillside towards the animals, (and as he did this each of the animals comically took a step backward trying to remain hidden from view), "are trying to make our way north."

"How come you're not dead like the rest of us?" a voice asked, clearly perplexed at Patrick's position.

"I don't know," he said as he shook his head.

"Are you the only one that's alive?" a voice from the back of the crowd asked quietly. "Is there anyone else alive that is with you?"

"No. I seem to be the only one I know of right now. There were others," Patrick said as he remembered the people of the fire, "but they didn't make it."

"Is he the one that the others have been talking about, John?" the spirit woman said as she looked to her husband. "Maybe they were right? Maybe there really is someone that can't be killed by the witches."

"You know of the witches?" Patrick asked.

"Yes," the man spoke, "we know of them. We know what they've done to us. We know what they're trying to do to all of mankind."

"Is that why you're in there? You were all killed by the plague?" Patrick asked, directing the questions to the man and his wife, but throwing out the question to all the other faces of the spirits as his eyes danced around to meet their own.

Most simply nodded in the affirmative, with a few "Yes" responses coming from various sections of the growing mass.

"Yes," the man responded, now speaking as the group's representative. "I believe that's why we are all here, stuck in this prison."

"What do you mean? Why are you stuck here?" Patrick asked simply.

"Whatever is out there that is trying to kill us off has turned a nasty trick. The natural law of death has been broken. Whoever is doing this has destroyed the very fabric that establishes mankind as who we are—spiritual beings. They have figured out a way to kill us without allowing us to find our way home, to go back to where we came from."

"Back?"

"We can't find our way to move on, to pass over into the next life. It's bad enough that this plague, this death has taken all of our lives, but now this thing that has fallen on us will not allow us to leave the earth's confines. It has perverted our deaths. We seem to be stuck here in limbo."

"You mean stuck on earth?"

"Yes and no. Yes, we're stuck on earth, but we are also stuck here in this graveyard. For whatever reason, as each of us was destroyed by the plague our spiritual forms were taken up and transplanted to places like this one. And we can't move beyond the boundaries that are set by the gated walls."

"You mean all the graveyards? All of them are like this? With more of you stuck there?"

"That's right."

"Whoa."

"It's almost like that whoever is doing this wants to torment us with this, to punish us. It's bad enough that they murdered our bodies, but now they won't allow our souls to leave and rest in peace. And to make things worse, we are all being kept imprisoned at all the gravesites that are scattered about."

Patrick looked around at all the various faces and could see their pain. Most of them were adults, but there were a few children and teenagers scattered throughout. He didn't believe it was a pain that was coming from a hurt or wound that was causing their expressions to be filled with so much angst, but rather from a feeling of helplessness and hopelessness that was tied to their spirits. It seemed to Patrick like it was a feeling of betrayal.

"You're trying to find the witches, aren't you?" the man asked bluntly, surprising Patrick with his knowing remark.

"Uh . . . yes sir," Patrick responded, unsure at how much information he should dispense.

The man looked towards the ground; his face held an expression that was both grave and concerned. He looked like someone who had given up hope.

He slowly raised his eyes to meet Patrick's.

"Son, I'm afraid you can't stop this thing if that's your aim. From what we have heard and are led to understand, this thing isn't something that can be stopped.

"I have never given much thought to witches and their like, but if this is what kind of power they possess, then I don't see any point of trying to find them. In fact, as we communicate with the other burial grounds close by, we hear tell of someone that is walking the earth doing the witches' bidding. Someone that is doing the devil's work. We hear that it is a man, but not a man."

The spirit paused.

"You haven't come across anyone like that, have you?"

Patrick stared at the man's face, and then looked around at the others as they drifted in and out of his view, and he knew.

Tye.

It had to be Tye.

"Yeah, I think I know who he is," Patrick answered reluctantly.

The man nodded back in return, and then took a deep breath.

"I'm afraid you won't succeed. I don't think anyone can."

Patrick's breath hung on the man's last few words.

I don't think anyone can.

And he believed the man to be right.

Just then the spirit of John Gulledge's wife, Denise, lunged forward and reached out for Patrick.

"Please help us!" she exclaimed. "Can't you do something for us?"

Patrick jumped back instantly, alarmed at the outburst as John Gulledge slowly reached for his wife to try and comfort her. And then the rest of the spirits leaned forward and began to question and beg at Patrick with the same type of outburst.

"Please! Help us!"

"Do something for us!"

"Help me!"

The outpouring came over and over again as Patrick felt his heart break in pity for their predicament. Patrick watched as John put his arm around his wife and tried to ease her agony.

"Hon, it will be alright. We'll make it through this. Someone will put this right."

Then Patrick watched in horror as the spirits pushed forward against the invisible barrier, the graveyard's boundaries holding them in check.

"I . . . I'm sorry, but I can't do anything," Patrick responded, "I don't know what I can do to help you."

The spirits then began to cry and wail again, their misery overwhelming them.

The realization that the spirits were nothing to be afraid of began to come easily for Patrick. After all, they were only people that had died, Patrick reasoned. And with the state that they were in at the moment it was hard for him to feel anything more than simple pity towards them. His friends or his family could be going through the very same ordeal at this moment, with the assumption that most (or all) of them were dead. And he wouldn't hold any fear towards them.

No, as Patrick watched the frustrated spirits in front of him, he began to get mad.

It wasn't fair.

If the Witch Queen wanted to do away with mankind, then that should have been enough. But to torture their spirits by binding them to the earth was another matter all together.

"Everyone, please listen!" he spoke up, trying to calm the mass of hysteria.

He took a step closer to the fence to be heard, but no one seemed to be paying attention.

"Everyone, please!" this time he shouted, and again he took another step.

Patrick didn't know exactly what kind of comforting statement he was going to make to the spirits, but just the same he wanted to let them know that he could do something. What it was, well, he wasn't exactly sure as of yet, but if there was anything that he could do, then he would try and get it done.

A piece of fence line in front of him had fallen over and lay in ruin, and the edge of the cemetery was now only two steps away. He positioned himself to step over the broken pieces of metal and into the graveyard as he made his way forward, when he began to hear Bing shouting at him from up on the hill. He turned and looked back at his friends, but couldn't make out what Bing was trying to say to him. It sounded like he was saying "No! Stop!" but Patrick couldn't be sure with all of the ruckus that the spirits were making all around him.

And he didn't care.

The animals didn't understand what had happened to all of these people—these humans—and his heart tugged at him as he felt a duty to try and help them any way he could. He was going to have to deal with this whether the animals approved or not, and he didn't need them giving him instructions on what he could and could not do.

Patrick heard Bing shouting again, but he dismissed it for the moment and turned his attention in trying to get the spirits to quiet down and listen to him.

After a few beleaguered moments (and with the help of John Gulledge) the spirits finally began to settle, and Patrick quickly found that he was once again gaining their attention. He opened his mouth to speak, trying to find the words that would comfort as many as he could until he and his friends could figure out something that might give them hope.

As his mind finally cleared, and the words began to come forward, he lifted his left foot and began to step over the broken fence line and enter the graveyard. At the same time Bing moved forward and again shouted for Patrick to stop.

But Patrick didn't hear him.

And it wouldn't have made any difference anyhow, because once his foot had crossed the threshold to the cemetery it was already too late. For as soon as Patrick's foot came into contact with the faded and withered straw grass inside the boundaries of the old cemetery, something truly unexpected and extraordinary happened.

Patrick fell down.

Not down, like falling down some steps and skinning your knees. Or tripping over a gopher hole or something.

No, when Patrick fell, he fell all the way down—into the earth.

He fell, and continued to fall, tumbling over and over into the blackness.

And he didn't stop falling until he ended up in Nebraska.

"Oh, no," Bing uttered softly.

As the animals had watched the approach by Patrick to the gravesite, nary a word was exchanged between them. They were too worried.

Patrick's continual faith that humans were going to help him in his travels whether they were alive—or dead—continued to be a sore spot amongst the group. And as it went, with Patrick taking steps that were moving him closer and closer to the twinkling lights below, it gave each one of them a hard moment where they had to make themselves breathe to overcome the anxiety that each was experiencing.

They had watched as he talked.

They had watched as he moved backwards, frightened as the lights came toward him.

Then they watched as his shoulders seem to slump in some form of relief.

And then they watched as he began making movements to go into the graveyard. To go in with the lights.

This had startled Bing to no end, and he began to shout his disapproval again and again to the boy.

And then they watched as he disappeared.

"Huh?" uttered Syrian, as his head jerked backwards in disbelief at what he was seeing. "Where did he go? What did the lights do to him?"

"Oh. No," Dog words echoed Bing's, his voice sounding as if he were in shock.

A look of astonishment fell over all their faces.

Initially they hesitated to move, their continual fears of discovery overwhelming them, but then they threw reason and fear aside and bolted down the hillside into the valley with Dog leading their way.

As they approached they could hear the commotion arise from the human spirits at Patrick's disappearance even though they could not understand the words from the discussions that were being spoken.

At first the lights were like fireflies, staying in small groups twinkling along the edge of graveyard's boundaries. But as the animals grew nearer, the lights of the spirits scattered like someone had swatted a bee's hive, their shrieks and outrages adding to the pandemonium.

"I knew it! I knew it! I knew something bad would come of this! Why did you ever bring him here?"

Bing had now turned and was directing his rage at Kirsdona.

"Me?! It wasn't me, you little bird! Don't go getting all high and mighty with me! You know how he is. You know how those humans are. Always so pushy! Thinking they own the world!"

"But you allowed him to come! I told you all to stay back at the tree."

"Ok. That's fine and all that, but I believe you were the one that let him go on down to the graves, you little bug."

Bing took a deep breath.

"Are you quite done?"

"Are you?"

"I suppose," Bing replied as he looked away and sighed.

"So what do you think happened?" Syrian asked loudly as he nudged up next to Bing, his eyes never leaving the agitated lights.

"I'm not sure. But I believe that whatever has happened has also caught the human world off guard, as well, due to the reaction that is taking place."

"How did you know that he shouldn't have gone in there?"

"I didn't know anything, really. It was just a hunch. I just figured that if the humans couldn't get out from inside there, then maybe it wasn't such a good idea for Patrick to go in.

"If we could only understand what they were saying. It sure is convenient to have someone like the boy around. Having him understand us, and we him, sure makes it a lot easier to understand what is taking place sometimes."

"Yes," Syrian nodded. "And I believe this is one of those times where we could surely use him."

Bing paused, and then looked about.

"Well, spirits or no spirits, we've got to go in there and look around. It doesn't seem to be that big of an area. Perhaps he is behind one of those grave markers."

Syrian nodded in agreement.

"We all need to go in and look, even Sin. His sense of smell is just as good as ours, and with the way he has attached himself to Patrick I believe that he just might be able to sniff him out of there."

"That's going with the thought that he's even in there," Kirsdona interjected.

"Well, where else could he have gone? I'm going with the impression that he either disappeared from our sight somehow, or he has been hurt and is hidden from our view and needs our attention. Either way, standing here is not doing any good."

And so they went in.

Dog, who wasn't necessarily the bravest of the group was the first to enter, his tail tucked neatly in under his rear haunches displaying his fear. His growing devotion to Patrick made it a must in his mind to find the boy no matter the cost. So if he needed to enter this dreadful place first, then he would not hesitate.

Kirsdona was the next to enter, with the rest slowly fanning out behind her as they went.

The continual shrieks and cries from the humans only compounded their own fears as they moved about, the lights moving to and fro before them in reckless abandon.

Bing, who was probably the least afraid of the group, made his way behind the different ornamental displays that the humans created to mark the remains of their dead, searching for the boy. His mind wondered aloud at how the human spirits seemed so afraid of their presence, yet they could not do a thing to any one of their kind. Being that they were spirits and all didn't make much sense that they would be so upset and worried.

Each member of the group spread out and searched for the boy, with each (except for Sin) calling his name over and over in hopes of a response.

But none ever came.

In a short amount of time, and having their search come to no avail, they soon regrouped and moved back outside the metal fencing of the cemetery. This seemed to ease the voices of the spirits to a certain degree—but not by much.

The animals each turned their attention towards Bing for guidance, the small penguin pacing back and forth and was now just staring at the ground.

"Now. What. Do. We. Do?" Dog asked, his voice begging for a quick answer as he looked around at the others.

But the answer that came was not the one that any of them really wanted to hear at that moment.

Only two words would form in Bing's mind for his response.

"We wait."

It was as if he was on a roller coaster.

But no metal bar placed across his lap held him place, and no seatbelt strapped him in.

He was in a lazy kind of freefall.

But he wasn't.

At first, as Patrick fell forward, the initial sensation he experienced was like he had splashed into a swimming pool, the air thick, like it was slowing him down and yet moving him ahead. As he progressed forward it pushed his hair back from his face like the wind.

But in this place there didn't seem to be a wind of any kind.

His body was continually being propelled forward faster and further through a weightless black veil that had substance—but not anything that he could reach out and touch.

What is this place? his mind continued to ask, What have I fallen into?

He tried to turn quickly, to head back from where he just came, but the underlying current here in this place seemed to move him along faster than he could think.

He was vaguely aware that he was definitely not in the graveyard any longer, but as to where he was now, he could only guess. It took a few moments for his perceptions to tell him that he was traveling, but as to the ability to tell where and when this was taking place he didn't have a clue. His senses told him that he was still amongst the dead in some way, but he could no longer see or hear them speaking to him as they were.

But there was whispering. Silent, almost unconceivable, off in the distance whispering. As soon as he would try to locate from which direction the silent words were coming, he had already moved past that location and was heading off in another.

That part was disturbing.

Patrick was scared and surprised. What place was this that he had fallen into?

It certainly didn't seem like Heaven. At least not in any form he had come to believe and understand.

Could this be Hell? That, too, seemed completely unreasonable.

At first the blackness around him was not unwelcome. It wasn't like the basement in the dark. No, there was a kindness here, lingering off out of his reach. Like a mothers hug. It wrapped itself around him and protected him and carried him on his way.

But soon the comfort he felt slid away and was replaced by something else.

He began to get cold. Very, very cold. The veil around him began to change into a hard and dense cold. It began to eat into his skin and soak into his bones. Pretty soon he began to shiver.

And then he saw them.

The dead.

Their bodies twisted and deformed, it was like a Halloween parade gone mad. Monstrous, yet only mildly so, Patrick watched as they moved around him as he passed through. Their arms and legs moving in contortions, and bending in places that Patrick thought impossible.

What was this place? Patrick's mind asked again and again.

Why were all of the dead here? Could he only be seeing a different form of the beings back at the graveyard where he had just left? Was this place where the remnants of their bodies remained?

As he traveled past them they reached out for him, some of their decaying fingertips barely contacting him as he went by, their touch feeling like dried burlap as it scraped his skin.

He wanted to leave this place—and leave it now.

As his eyes adjusted even more to this dark place he began to see out past the remains of the dead, further on to outlying lands that were rocky and menacing. Long, huge cliff walls that seemed to drop forever populated these areas. Mountains, cast in purples and blacks, towered above him, their peaks beyond his perception. Dim lights seemed to protrude from the interior regions of these lands, beckoning for Patrick to come nearer.

Then, after what seemed like more than a few minutes, but in a reality that was probably only a few seconds, he began to sense that he did have some degree of control to his direction. It was as if his mind was guiding him through this place without giving it much thought. But when he would begin to think directly about which way he wanted to go his course seemed to adjust in that direction.

As he got nearer to the massive cliff wall to his left he began to see what looked like long lighted tunnels with faintly lit openings at the end of each one. And as he would look to each opening he began to notice that he would then begin to drift off towards the connecting tunnel to that particular spot.

Like he had been caught up in the undertow of a river, he seemed to flow towards the exit that he selected, continuing straight ahead until the opening seemed to disappear before him. As he felt himself beginning to drop, he positioned his body to take a step, the same step he had begun to make back at the graveyard where he had left his friends, and he found that as he emerged from the opening he seemed to walk right out onto another patch of grass at the doorstep of yet another graveyard. One that he wasn't familiar with at all. Not that he was familiar with any other graveyards, but just the same this wasn't the one he had just left. He took two steps on the grass, and then tumbled to his knees with an unexplainable exhaustion. He turned quickly and came face to face with several spirits he didn't recognize. Spirits that stared back at him with faces full of awe.

Patrick began to panic, quickly crawling backwards to move himself away from the unfamiliar faces. In fact, he moved so fast that he ended up whacking his head against an old poplar tree that he didn't see coming up behind him.

"Ow!" he said as he reached his hand up to rub the spot. He continued to stare at the faces of the spirits across from him that were still looking back at him in amazement.

His hand continued to try and rub away the pain on his head, when he began to hear someone giggling from above him in the tree.

"My, you'd think that an experienced traveler such as yourself would be a little more careful scurrying around on the ground as you were. But, then again, maybe you're not so experienced," the voice teased.

Patrick turned and cocked his head skyward trying to locate the voice. He had to scout over the branches several times before he spotted the little gray squirrel that was perched high on the side of the trunk several yards up.

Patrick opened his mouth to launch into his own little rebuttal to the squirrel when he began to experience a crippling pain that was so overwhelming it caused him to lose his voice. His ribs felt like they were beginning to contract in his chest, and his legs cramped so horribly that his toes began to curl under his feet. He fell over on his side gripping his chest, his face wincing with agony.

He tried to cry out, but all that he could do was make funny little movements with his mouth like a fish would when it was placed out of water.

"Funny little human boy. Are you in a great deal of pain?" the squirrel asked with a mischievious smile.

But Patrick barely heard the squirrel speak. He writhed in agony, rolling back and forth on the ground trying to catch his breath, wondering how to make the pain stop.

What is happening?! This hurts so bad!

"Why, I thought that everyone knew that when you travel with the dead that they always try and steal your life. I take it that you didn't know that?"

The squirrel scampered down the tree and nosed up to Patrick's face like he was a doctor assessing the situation.

"Or I should say that most animals know this, but it's hard to tell with humans. I wonder how many years they got from you, eh? One? Two? It seems that they definitely got a little piece of you, though, since you're in so much pain. But who knows?"

The squirrel moved back a few steps when Patrick opened his eyes and began to growl at the small animal.

"Get away from me," he said through gritted teeth.

"Relax. You'll be fine. But the next time you go through, you'd better be quick about it. You spend a long time in there and they take a lot of your days."

"You . . . you," Patrick was trying to talk through the pain as it was starting to subside slightly, "mean that . . . the dead took . . . my life?"

"Well, that's what we're told is what happens. I don't think I've ever met anyone that has actually gone through and then come back. But I've heard tell that when you travel with the dead they want so badly to be alive again that they have ways of stealing the life from you that causes you to feel the loss shortly after they've stolen it."

"What?! Is that what's happened to me?" Patrick asked, now shocked by the explanation. "You've go to be joking."

The squirrel made a face and then shook his head from side to side.

"No. In fact that stuff coming off your body might just be your life leaving you now."

Patrick quickly glanced down to his arms and saw the few spider web-like wisps that looked like steam rising from his skin.

Oh no.

It took a good while before he was able to fully move again, but once he was able, he took a deep breath and then slowly raised himself till he could stand. He turned and then inched his way closer to the graveyard, keeping a safe distance between himself and the spirits.

"Who are you?" one of the spirits asked.

"Never mind that, what did you do to me?" Patrick responded, his breathing still coming in shallow gasps.

"We haven't done anything to you," one of them responded, "It was the 'others.'"

"The 'others?'" Patrick asked, his head still full of cobwebs that he just couldn't quite shake. "What 'others?' What are you talking about?"

The spirits looked back and forth amongst each other with glances of mistrust, as if they knew a secret that they weren't exactly ready to share. Finally the spirit who had posed the initial question spoke again.

"You traveled amongst the dead and the undead. You found a gateway through our world. We didn't know that any of the living could do such a thing."

Patrick was still feeling pretty rotten, his breathing coming in short quick bursts, and he kept staring at his arms as the ghostly mists began to fade. But he made himself keep up with the conversation that was being presented to him.

"The place we speak of is the world of the 'undead.' A place that is not spoken of very often. It is a place where all creatures, both human and animal alike, go when they do not want to give up their life here on this earth and pass on to the next. It is a terrible place. A place where bitterness and deceit and unhappiness reign. It is not a place for the timid. This is the place that you have just passed through."

"How did you do that?" another spirit asked quickly, her voice fearful yet demanding in its tone.

"I . . . I don't know," Patrick answered hesitantly. "I didn't know that was what I just did. Did I break a spirit law or something? Am I in trouble? If I did, I'm sorry. I just didn't know . . . it happened so fast. I was back at another graveyard with my friends and I was asking for help when . . ."

The spirit in front of him raised his hand for Patrick to stop, and then closed his eyes and smiled.

"We know how you came here. We've already had communications with the area that you left. It's just that we have never seen any of the living do what you just did."

"Did the 'undead' really take some of my life? Am I going to die?"

The spirit looked as they he did not want to dispel the unpleasant truth.

"Yes, I am afraid that you are going to die. That is a fact that is shared by all that are born onto this earth. That is inevitable. But I don't foresee it in your immediate future if you are careful with your steps, my young friend.

"But, as far as when you passed through the gateway, if you came in contact with any of the foul creatures that reside there, then they in turn may have taken away some of your youth. No one can truly tell.

"But know that they linger in those dark places in the land of the living as well. Always hoping to snare some careless person who is willing to give up a few years for the turn of an easy trick. It is something that most do not see happening to them as they go, but be assured that it is happening all the same."

Patrick stood and stared, trying to absorb what was being told. It chilled him deeply.

"Where am I?" Patrick asked, astonished at all that he was hearing.

"You are a long way from where you left. Quite a long ways, indeed."

"Where am I now? Which way do I need to start heading to get back to where I just came from?"

"No, I'm afraid that is not going to happen so easily," the man said as he shook his head. "You have traveled quite a ways, my friend. You have made it all the way to the great state of Nebraska. And if I am to understand correctly where you have left your friends, then you would have a heck of a lot of walking to do to get back to them from here. I think that you're going to have to go back the way you came, like it or not."

Patrick was stunned. "What?! No way! I don't want to go back in there. It does something to me when I go through. It hurts."

Patrick took a deep breath to try and ease his anxieties. "I can't. I can't do that again."

"Take your time and think it through. There is no rush. I'm sure that given time you'll figure out what is best for yourself.

"I must say though that you are keeping some unusual company. Your friends, the animals, they are very worried about you and are keeping a vigil at the site as we speak. You are a very unusual little man. Like I said, we have never seen anything like that take place before. Do you know how you did that?"

"No," Patrick responded, and then looked to the ground as if he were searching for an answer, "I don't know how anything is happening. It just does. And it keeps happening. I don't know why, but it just does."

The spirit smiled wide at Patrick's response, and extended a hand that he laid on Patrick's shoulder.

"Do not be so alarmed at certain gifts that may befall upon you, my friend. It seems that perhaps you are on this journey of yours for a reason. It has been communicated in our world, the world of the dead, that you are seeking out the cause of all this destruction and death, and perhaps this is a needed tool that you can take with you to use at another time. I do not know. But for now, you must use it to get back to your friends, for they're patiently waiting for your return."

Patrick shook his head and turned, making his way back over to the tree and the squirrel, and sat down. He definitely did not want to go back into the graveyard any time soon—if ever again.

The land of the 'undead?'

That was something that he could do without. But did he have a choice?

In the end he knew that he didn't. He knew that Nebraska was a lot further away from Ohio than he could travel on his own compared to the time it would take him to go back the way he came.

He rubbed his legs. They were still aching from the cramping he had experienced.

The squirrel came up beside him carrying several acorns and politely offered one to Patrick. Patrick declined, and then thought of the food in the backpack he left with his friends.

That's when he knew that he had to go back.

"Can one of you tell me first how I am to get back to where I left?" he asked as he walked back over to the cemetery. "It isn't like I know my way around in there, and I'm not sure from which direction I even came from."

The spirit smiled and then nodded slightly realizing the decision that had been made.

"Just follow the path that your intuition tells you. Trust your instincts. You'll recognize the place as soon as you see it. You'll sense it. You'll know."

And with those few words of encouragement Patrick found himself in the same position that he been in just a few short moments ago.

"But remember, do not stop, do not hesitate, and do not talk to anyone in there, ok?"

Patrick nodded quickly. He raised his foot, took a deep breath (why? he didn't know) and took an unsteady step forward.

In the blink of an eye Patrick emerged from the point at the graveyard he had first left.

Bing, who had been pacing back and forth uncontrollably, first caught sight of the boy and instantly made his way to him. His initial fears of maybe never seeing Patrick again dropped away and soon were replaced with new ones, for as soon as he had gotten within a few feet of the boy, Bing watched as Patrick gave a quick smile, uttered a "Hey guys," and then collapsed face forward onto the grass next to Dog.

The animals quickly gathered around Patrick, but kept a wee bit of distance as they watched the ghostly mists flowing from him as if tiny spirits were leaving his body.

Patrick laid unconscious for almost two hours while the animals kept guard on him. Even the twinkling spirits stayed close to the gates watching in earnest for his safe recovery. No one spoke much after Syrian assured everyone that he was alive, but had just fainted from some sort of exhaustion.

It was a little before daybreak when Patrick finally started to come around, his eyes opening slowly at first, and then he rolled over and coughed. And then coughed again.

"What's the matter? Can't you breathe?" Bing asked in an alarmed state.

Patrick sat upright, his eyes lolling around in his head, trying to focus. He slowly shook his head. "No, it just feels like I'm going to throw up. I feel sick."

Sin moved in close to Patrick and began licking at his left ear.

"Hey, stop that, will you," Patrick said as he giggled and then pulled away.

"What. Happened. To. You. Back. There?" Dog asked.

Bing then moved in front of Patrick's view. "Yes, where did you go? We were all terribly frightened at your disappearance. What happened to you?"

Patrick smiled the best he could, and then gave them the explanation they wanted.

He told them of how he traveled and what it was like as he went.

He told them of where his 'trip' took him and who he talked to and what was said.

And he told them of how it made him feel inside after he had went through and then came back.

"I know you guys don't know what it is, but it was like going through a 'black hole,'" he said

"A 'black hole?'" Bing asked.

"It's a hole in space. A hole in time. We learned about it in science class."

"Ok, what's 'space?'" Kirsdona asked, her left eyebrow rising in question.

"And. What's. 'Sigh-ince?'" Dog followed as well.

"Never mind, it's not important. I just don't ever want to do it again."

Kirsdona continued to stare in the direction of Patrick. "Who are you anyway? I mean—What are you? I've never known or heard of any creature that can do that."

"I'm still me, you dumb tiger," Patrick said as he shook his head. "Nothing has changed. I'm still me."

At least I think so, his mind teased at him.

"What. Else. Can. You. Do?" Dog asked innocently.

Patrick sighed. "I hope nothing else."

How Patrick was able do the things that he could caused the animals a great deal of frustration. It was a feeling of dread that as each of these things crept up on them some new and awful predicament was about to take place.

"I'm beginning to think I know why the witches want you stopped," Bing said with some unease in his voice. "If we are only beginning to learn of some of the things that you can do, what I would like to know is—and I'm quite sure the witches want to know as well—are what some of the things are that we haven't learned about you yet?"

And then came the look again. The look that the animals gave Patrick every time something funny came up that was not easily explained.

In short order Patrick announced that he was feeling better, and that they needed to continue their journey. He made his announcement to the spirit community as well, and they in turn gave him some advice as to what areas to avoid as he continued on his journey. And even though they could do nothing to help him in his purpose, they still told him that they would help him if there ever came a time that he needed an ear to bend. They just didn't have much more to offer.

They retrieved the forgotten backpack and distributed a little food to each, (Patrick not taking anything for the moment due to the discomfort in his stomach) and then set out to the northwest again, trying to find a place to stay hidden and settle down for their days rest.

After they had covered several miles, and just as daylight was beginning to break, Patrick turned and looked to his left, spotting another cemetery off in the distance. It was an extremely large area for a graveyard, one that was perched high on a hillside next to a large ornamental church. His steps hesitated for a moment, and he found himself looking over to the spirits as they gathered at the edge. Their forlorn faces made him pause as he pondered the promises he made in helping the spirits to move on. Wondering just how he was going to help them, when he wasn't exactly sure how he was going to help himself.

CHAPTER 14

Just Under the Skin

The dark amber colored bug scurried across the floor, stopping every now and again to investigate the cracks in the floorboards for forgotten crumbs. Its tiny antenna danced around in front of it like a blind man with a cane checking the area as it went. Every so often it would find a piece of dried something or other that had dropped to the floor, and it would hurriedly devour the discovered treasure.

Tye watched the bug as it zigzagged its way from one end of the room to the other, finally coming to a stop just in front of him at his feet. He bent down and gently gathered the bug into his hand, cradling it in his palm as if he was holding a small precious thing.

"And where might you be going, my little friend, hmm? You should be careful as you expose yourself in the light. Stick to the shadows and the corners and the creases, I say. If you venture out from the shadows something bad could come along and pluck you up and squash you into so many little pieces."

Tye began to stroke along the back of the little bug, and then running his fingertips along the entire length of its antenna.

"Yes, you should be careful where you tread."

Tye listened to himself as he said the words to the bug, casually thinking that he could almost be having the same conversation with the boy.

Stick to the shadows, my friend, or something could come along and squash you as well.

He had been traveling for almost three days straight trying to locate the boy without taking a break for rest, tearing his body to the point of near exhaustion. The change that his body was undertaking was still in work beneath his skin and seemed to be consuming his energy as well. He needed rest, and he either stopped now or he wouldn't be able to continue later.

Food and rest.

Finding a place to rest was the easier of the two. Any secluded house or bungalow would do. Finding food would be another issue altogether.

It wasn't that there wasn't an ample supply of various things to eat in the cupboards and refrigerator of the house he'd found. But it was just that Tye's tastes were beginning to change. To mutate. He no longer desired the simple prepackaged thoroughfare that was in abundance at just about everywhere he looked. No, his hunger now seemed to crave something that had a little more juice to it, a little more substance.

He wanted something that scurried behind the walls. Something hair covered that lived in the cracks and crevices. Something that was alive.

He wanted flesh and bone.

As he was contemplating what he was going to do to satisfy his hunger he heard a noise that came from his left that was quick and sharp.

"Yes my little friend, you should really be careful where you next find your way," he said soothingly just before his long tongue reached out and plucked the bug from his hand and pulled it into his mouth to be devoured.

Tye knew that the flies were back.

"What do you know?" he asked without turning to greet the flies, his mouth gently chewing his morsel.

"wE hAVe TraCkEd tHe Boy hEAdinG in thE DiReCTiOn yOu HaVe suRmISed," the flies hissed, "anD WE wEre weLL oN oUr WAy to cAtcHIng hIM uNAwaRes, onLy a FEw sHOrt milES AwAy we WEre, wHen hE seEMs tO HavE dISappEAred."

"Disappeared?"

"YEs. wE fiNd thIS inCreDUlouS ouRselVes, BuT thE bOy is NOt wHerE hE is sUPpoSed tO be. wE hAve otHErs ouT aSsAUlting THe fAr oFF LAndS fOr hiM as wE sPEAk. HOPefuLly we WilL HeAr of HIm sHorTly."

Tye, who was sitting in an overstuffed lounge chair at the center of the room, neatly folded his hands in a relaxed posture across his chest and sighed.

"So the boy has learned tricks, has he?" Tye asked as he closed his eyes.

"Is ThiS sOmEThinG tHAt yOu HavE fOReseEn?"

"Yes and no. I am not privileged to know exactly what all the boy can do, but I am aware that he possesses something that frightens our masters greatly. And it must be something so horrific as to cause them to chill at his very name."

The flies dispersed and then reformed in their shadowy figure next to Tye.

"dOEs it BoTher yoU thAt tHE boY caN ManIPuLAte coNseQueNces LIke he hAS? DOeS it cHilL yOu aT tHe MenTIon oF hiS nAMe as It doEs thE oTHers?"

Tye gave an exasperated look.

"Please! You have got to be joking," he said in disgust. "No, I am not afraid of the Brighton child, but I would greatly like to have an understanding as to what power it is that he perhaps possesses. Power my dear friends comes in many guises and understandings, some of which take a great deal of strength with which to control. I am sure that our masters have their reasons for only wanting to recapture, and not kill, our fine little friend, but it is after I have come to repossess him is when I shall have a little more say as to how this game will be played."

The flies buzzing began to sound a lot more like screeching at his words. Their shape began to become darker and more dense. Their words sharper and more clear.

"Be cAreful your toNgue, Tye, foR our allegianCe will always be With our maSter. She would Not take kiNdly to the tone with whiCh you speak. ReMember—our ears are her eArs."

Tye's face curled up into a tiny sarcastic smirk as he turned towards the fly thing, his eyes forming to darkened slits.

"Oh, I know. Believe me, I know. I am well aware from what depths you have traveled my friends. I am quite aware at whose right hand you sit. Do not tempt me to further perjure myself, for you know as well as I that questions have begun to not only come up about myself, but also about our fair lady as well. Birthright does not necessitate competence."

The fly thing stood silent for a moment, the screeching sound it was producing now subsiding to a normal humming as it became more relaxed.

"As long as we stay aware of where the boy is traveling we will eventually come across him. He is not capable of doing anything that could do harm to any of her plans in his present state of hiding. So I figure that he is moving in a position that is the equal of having him in hand. Your master wanted him out of the way—and he is—in a manner of speaking. Our job, as I see it now, is to ensure that he stays out of the way."

The fly thing again dispersed and then reformed to Tye's left.

"I sEe wHere yOU arE gOIng With tHIs TyE. BUT, if YoUr pLaNs do Not prOCeed aS yoU diCTate, anD thE boY is LEft to SliP thRoUgh unAbateD, thEn YOu coULd finD yOUrseLf in A loT WoRse pOSition THan tHe boY coULd."

"Allow me the privilege of worrying about myself. I believe that I have managed to bring this thing along to the point where we are now close to the end. As far as I am concerned you need to see to it that all efforts are stepped up in shepherding the boy in the course we desire. Once he is driven in that direction we only have to sit by, for it will be only a matter of time before he falls right into our lap."

The fly thing paused for the moment, giving the impression that it was thinking over what Tye had just said.

"YEs. YeS yOU aRe corRecT iN yoUR tHInkIng. BUt if THe QueEN bEgiNs to aSK quEStioNs, iF shE beGIns to Get suSPiciouS as To wHEre thE bOy is LOcateD, thEN thiS wILL aLL FAll oN yOUr heAd. aND YouRs AlOne."

"Tell me something I don't know."

But Tye did know. Oh how he knew.

He would never let on that he was in fear of the Queen and her minions. It was a position that he tried very hard to present.

But he was worried.

The flies were one thing. Since his re-modification had begun to take place he knew (as well the flies, he suspected) that they were not as threatening to him as they once were.

But the Queen, well that was another matter altogether.

Just the sound of her voice was enough to make Tye almost lose his fluids. He didn't even like to be in the same room with her if he could help it.

When she had first ordered the initial modification to his body by the flies he was caught completely by surprise as to what she had in mind for him. When the flies had finished their pain giving process, and he was allowed to view himself for the first time in a mirror, he was amazed at what power she possessed that could transform him as he was.

He then began to look on her with awe.

Who was this person that could do this to him? Where could someone like this have come from?

But he knew. Somewhere deep deep down inside him, a tiny voice spoke to him announcing who she was, even if he didn't want to believe it. This woman, this thing was not someone who should be trifled with.

And when the flies had showed up to administer the second modification to him, it was confirmed to him in such a way as to not allow any sort of argument to come forth.

He knew.

No, Tye was all too aware of what fate might hold for him if he did not keep the boy from making any progress in the pursuit he desired. The flies did not need to remind him of his position in the matter.

So, for the moment Tye dismissed the flies to accomplish their given task, and he went back to his latest pursuit—his hunger.

His sense of smell had grown tremendously since he had been changed, and he was now trying to catch wind of what might be hiding just around the corner, or someplace close nearby, perhaps in the backyard.

Hours drifted by as Tye sat in his chair with his eyes closed, concentrating and using his heightened senses to scan the local areas for something to eat. But the frustrated thought that every creature around the area must have vanished tested his patience.

And then the sweetness of the pungent form came to him.

Food.

He began to stalk the small creature as soon as he had stepped from the house. His reforming body allowed him to move in such a way as to bring no notice of himself as he went. Looping and curving he glided effortlessly closer and closer to his unknowing meal. The aroma of the animal drifted back to him and gave him the oddest sense of comfort. Its oily fur and heavy breath drifted up and into Tye's nostrils making his eyes roll back into his head with heightened pleasure.

He watched as the unknowing raccoon moved closer and closer to its now stationary stalker, sniffing the ground itself for want of some small food to store for winter.

Tye waited as the gray and brown animal moved closer and nearer to him.

Six feet, and the animal still had no idea what was in front of it.

Four feet, and Tye almost giggled with pleasure at how easy this was going to be.

Two feet, and Tye tensed his body, readying himself for the attack.

And then he sprang. The raccoon had no idea what was happening and before it could move it was over.

Tye cradled his prize to him and began to consume the beast when he heard something nearby.

The buzzing that Tye was hearing in his ears was at first thought to be the overwhelming sense of excitement he was experiencing for the kill, but he quickly came to understand that it was just the flies returning sooner than he imagined they would.

"We hAvE LOcaTed thE boY," they announced with a sickly, excitable air.

The flies then noticed what had taken place and hurriedly spied what they also desired.

"FooooD," it said in one long low rasp.

But Tye paid little attention to the fly thing and its words. He knew that he would have to react, that he would have to once again drive himself to reclaiming the boy once and for all. He knew where the boy would eventually end up if he continued on the path as he was, and Tye had already set in motion a means for his capture. Deals had been struck with vermin that were grateful for the opportunity to serve, and for the rewards that would come thereafter once the boy was back in hand.

But for now all of that would have to wait, for he was eating and the rest of the world would have to remain in motion without him as he finished his meal.

Dan Brighton awoke from his dreamless sleep, his eyes fluttering lazily at the dark that surrounded him. He tried to guess whether or not it was early morning or just after sunset, the pinkish hue of the horizon off to his left leaving him unsure. But a quick glance at his watch told him that the sky was about to get bright, and morning was about to set in.

Dan had stopped multiple times along the rode since his encounter with Tye and the spiders, the bite on his hand still giving his entire arm fits of itching and pain. The frequent stops were only necessary due to the medication that he was taking caused him to become drowsy and in need of sleep. But as he flexed his arm this time the pain and swelling seemed to be finally subsiding, allowing him to forgo his next dose of the medications.

It was clear that he had long ago lost any hope of relocating Tye, and the overwhelming sense that he was the last man on earth was taking its toll on his sanity. He picked up the map that he had since acquired and stared at it wondering how he was ever going to be able to find Patrick. A long straight line on a piece of paper was not going to produce any quick results in being able to pinpoint where he may be heading.

Dan gave up the ridiculous thought of somehow tracking Patrick down and finding him along his path. No, the plan that he now came to see as his only hope rested in the idea that if he could find a junction point, a place where Patrick would be sure to cross, then perhaps Dan could beat him to it and be there in waiting.

But where that point would be . . . well, that was the problem.

Knowing his son as he did he figured that Patrick was more than likely to stay close to the roads. His son was never the kind of kid who was much of an outdoorsman. Oh, Patrick loved to play sports and spend time outside when he could, as was the case with most of the other friends he had. But it was just that Patrick had never really been camping, or spent much time hiking or exploring in the woods. No, Patrick was more the kind of kid from the new generation of youth coming up that was raised on subdivisions and neatly arranged soccer fields and play areas. The days of unattended exploration and imagination were replaced by organized events.

Dan knew his son, and as he looked at the map he quickly surmised that if he was ever going to find a spot to locate Patrick, it was going to have to be on a main road leading into a main area or town.

The wildcard in all of this was the animals. How much did they control Patrick's movements? And would they even allow him to come close to moving along a highway or road for fear of running into another human?

So many questions then began to jump back into Dan's thoughts that he had to push them aside and focus his thoughts back on the task at hand. Once he found Patrick then hopefully all of his other questions would soon be answered.

As he looked over the map, as it stood without having a clue as to how far the animals had taken him, Dan believed that if he could cover the distance to the next greatest point on the map that Patrick might move towards then he would surely have a chance.

And the next greatest point he could find was Chicago.

It sat so dead on the drawn line on the paper it was like a beacon. It was so obvious to him he was surprised that he hadn't seen it sooner.

It was spaced far enough ahead that even if the animals and Patrick had charged ahead far faster than he could have imagined, then Chicago would still be a good ways off in the distance of their travels.

But there were other reasons as well.

Chicago was a city. A major city at that. And even at his age Patrick was still awed by cities, his face always perched up against the window as they would travel through a major metropolitan area as he scanned their immense skylines and structures.

And Chicago had trains. Lots of trains.

Not that Dan thought that Patrick could somehow commandeer a train and high tail it out of there. No. It was just that Patrick loved trains. He had collected trains and train sets ever since he was three, the growing collection so great that they had to set aside an area of the basement just for his displays.

So Dan reasoned that if Patrick was to somehow catch any glimpse of the high towering buildings in the distance, or to realize that he was within any distance to coming in contact with the Windy City, then the boy would assuredly make a beeline straight for it. In fact, the more he thought about it the more he liked the idea he had come up with.

Dan figured that if the railroad tracks coming from this direction ran along side any one of a number of major highways then that's where he would stake his place and wait.

If—and this was a big 'if'—the animals would even allow Patrick to travel there.

Dan sighed at this thought, his chest exhaling the air slowly from his lungs. He just had no way of knowing for sure. But sitting here thinking about it was not going to get it done. His hand reached out and turned the key to start up the truck and get moving, when an alarming event took place.

The truck wouldn't start.

Dan turned the ignition again and again with the same results—nothing. The engine wouldn't even make a sound like it was attempting to start.

And that's when Dan realized what had happened. He reached down and turned off the headlight switch. He had left it on all night and now the battery was dead.

"No no no," he said aloud in frustration.

Dan sat behind the wheel, mentally admonishing himself for his careless act.

He got out of the truck and looked back and forth along the area in hope of locating another vehicle with which to use. But along the particular stretch of roadway that he was standing there wasn't anything to be found.

He reached back into the truck cab and grabbed the only thing he believed that he would need to take with him—the map—and began walking.

Dan walked for miles, the unrelenting countryside offering nothing for him to use, and no residential areas with which to search for one in either.

He walked for the remainder of that day and well into the next before he finally came across an abandoned mail truck that was sitting along side the road. After wiping the remains of the driver from the front seat Dan slowly got in and tried to start the truck, but quickly found that it was of no use. The mail truck behaved just as his truck had earlier—Dan realizing that the battery was dead as well.

Disgusted and tired he walked on until dark, sleeping the night through on the warmth of the asphalt road.

The next day, after walking the entire morning through and now making it halfway into the afternoon, he finally came upon a horse farm that expanded back and away several miles to his right.

A sign hung high over the fence line, "Coronado Horse and Buggy," in wide red and green letters, and the overwhelming smell of hay and horse droppings reinforced the thought.

Dan stared at the horses in the distance. He counted 9 that moved back towards the far off trees and pond at the sight of him. Most were of a rich solid chocolate color while the others were a mix of white spots intertwined with browns and blacks.

He spotted the barn right off closer to the trees, but there didn't seem to be a house located on the property to go with it.

He jumped the fence (which spooked the horses greatly) and then proceeded to see if there was any kind of vehicle that he could use in the barn. After finding nothing inside except a few saddles, riding gear, and three bags of horse pellets he exited back out into the midday sun.

Dan stared at the horses, wondering if he could possibly ride one of them to make his way. He quickly dismissed the thought, thinking that if he had never even petted a horse before, how could he possibly even think about riding one now.

Dan watched as the horses, still spooked by the stranger, kept their distance down by the pond.

He walked back to the fence and leaned up against it as he caught his breath from his walking. He gazed out into the tree line across the road as his thoughts turned to Tye and Patrick and his next course of action.

When he heard the noise coming up behind him he quickly turned and was surprised to see three horses slowly making their way in his direction. This time he was the one who was spooked as he hurriedly made his way back over the fence to keep a barrier between himself and the horses.

The horses stopped about thirty yards away, their round, full eyes fixed directly on Dan.

What was going on? he wondered. What is going on with all of the animals?

It became a staring match of sorts as Dan looked at the horses and the horses looking back at him. Dan didn't know what to do. Was this a threatening posture? Did they want him to go? Surely the creatures were obviously used to humans caring for them—so is that what they wanted? For him to help them in some way? He was at a complete loss to explain what was taking place.

And then five words came from Dan's mouth that he never expected to say. It was as if someone had slapped him on the back popping the words from his lips.

"My son is Patrick Brighton."

And then to Dan's shock and amazement the horses whinnied and bowed their heads at the words.

Dan took two steps back, more to steady himself from what had just taken place than out of fear.

No. Way.

No way! They couldn't have understood what I said!

"Do you understand me?" he asked, surprised that he was actually entertaining the idea that he was going to receive a response.

But the horses just stood there staring blankly back at him.

Huh?

"Do you know my son?" he asked, not sure if he should be moving his hands in some kind of symbolic gesture or not. Even more so, feeling foolish for even thinking it.

But again the horses remained unmoved by his words.

And then Dan tried something else.

"Patrick Brighton," he said in a clear perfect tone.

This got the reaction he wanted, for the horses jumped slightly as he said his son's name again, and once again they bowed their heads in an awkward sign of reverence.

"You know my son," he said.

And even though he knew that they probably didn't understand what he was saying he still had to follow through with his next question.

"Do you know where he is?"

The horses turned and looked at one another as if some unspoken communication was taking place. They then turned and galloped back to the company of the other horses down by the pond.

Dan watched from a distance as it appeared as though they were having a discussion—about what, he couldn't possibly imagine. Something was going on, he just didn't know what it was yet.

He waited and waited, still perched up against the fence hoping for the horses' return.

Soon, the three horses that had initially come to greet him turned and trotted back in his direction. The larger of the three, a brown and white spotted horse with a great white mane, began to break from the pack and started moving faster and faster in Dan's direction. The horse was moving with tremendous speed and was heading directly for Dan.

Uh oh. This can't be good.

Dan took two steps backwards, realizing that the horse was not going to stop, and through his hands up and over his head as he ducked.

The horse leapt high and long clearing the fence in a magnificent leap that brought it out of the confines of the enclosed pasture.

"Uh . . . good boy. Nice horse," was all that he could think of to say as the horse now stood only twenty feet from him.

He started backing away from the now freed horse, and continued to move until he bumped up against the fence.

The other two horses then came up behind Dan and nudged him away from the fence with their noses.

"What?! Hey, don't do that!" he said alarmed.

Dan then realized what was taking place as he watched the horse outside the fence kneel in a posture that would allow him to get on its back.

Dan turned and looked at the two remaining horses.

"I've never done this before. I'm not sure that I can," he said, forgetting that they didn't understand him.

But the determined horses just walked up to him and gave him another shove in the direction of the kneeling horse.

"Ok. Ok, I get it. Just give me a moment here."

Dan walked over to the welcoming animal. He knew his hesitation was ridiculous due to the thought that these animals might very well know where his son was located. And based on the reaction they gave him at the very mention of Patrick's name they knew something, and it didn't seem to be in a negative or bad way.

Dan nervously slid his leg up and over the creatures back, and before he could say 'boo' the animal had risen and was steadying itself to go. He didn't know exactly where to place his hands so he did the only thing he could think of and grabbed hold of the horse's white mane.

The horse turned and paused for a moment, allowing Dan the time to look over at the other remaining horses as they moved along the fence.

Dan could only think of one thing to do.

"Thank you," he said, and bowed his head deeply in a return sign of gratitude.

And then in a blink of an eye the horse he was riding took off like a shot across the roadway, galloping hard and steady into the tree littered hills on the other side.

"I hope you know where you're going," Dan said silently as he held on for dear life. "Because you're the only hope that I've got."

CHAPTER 15

The Wages of Sin

The rainstorm pounded on Patrick and his companions as they trudged their way through the night, the heavy drops completely soaking through the animals' fur as well as Patrick's clothing. It was a sudden thunderstorm that had come up from the plains to their west, catching the group totally unprepared as they scrambled forward to find cover, and showed no signs of letting up any time soon. It had begun shortly after they had left their daily resting spot, the dark of night hiding the swollen clouds as they approached, the only clue coming in the random streaks of lightning that had flashed the sky.

Patrick's shoes squished with water with every step, his annoyance with the situation growing more intense with every hundred yards or so that they covered.

"Can't we stop somewhere? I'm so wet I feel like a sponge," he announced to his friends, water dripping from the end of his nose.

"We must continue, Patrick," Bing, who was a little ways ahead, turned and said without stopping. "This weather is not hindering our advance. We have lost a good deal of time over the last few days, and I feel that our best chances of gaining ground is slipping away if we do not move forward with more determination. Besides, the water feels kind of refreshing, if I must say so."

Patrick grunted.

"Yeah, I'd agree if I was a duck," he said testily.

Kirsdona laughed aloud at Patrick's remark.

"I always wondered what sort of ill mannered bird you really were, Bing. I believe the boy has figured you out. You're a duck. A quacking, squawking, annoying little duck. Everything about you now makes sense."

Patrick chuckled a little at Kirsdona's decree.

"Quack quack," he said quickly.

"Quack quack," Kirsdona barked out as well.

And then Syrian followed along with the quacking, as well as Dog. Before long they were all quacking in unison as they walked.

Bing could do nothing else but laugh.

"Ok, my little ducklings, please follow along behind . . ."

Just then a crack of lightning split the sky so fiercely that it caused them to all gasp in unison. It arced and zigzagged it's way down to a tree no more than fifty feet from where they were standing, the ground rumbling so hard beneath their feet that it caused Patrick, Syrian and Bing to collapse to the ground. The bolt exploded the tree as it hit, sending sparks flying in all directions resembling a Fourth of July fireworks display.

"Gosh," Dog said, his eyes wide with terror.

"Now can we maybe find some cover?" Patrick asked angrily as he picked himself up off the ground.

Another bolt streaked high above them, the lightning dancing from one cloud to the next, the air vibrating with its intensity.

"Yes," Syrian nodded. "Rain is one thing. Lightning is something else."

"Unfortunately," Bing agreed, "such a place seems to be in short supply at the moment. We need to move on, but keep an eye peeled for anything that would afford us shelter that may be in front of us."

With all in agreement, they once again began their push forward. But as their luck and misfortune held true, they found nothing to suit their needs as they continued their march on through the night.

Finally, just before daybreak as they crossed another puddle ridden, dirt road, they came across a small group of houses that were tucked away neatly at the edge of the woods.

The rain had slowed from the fierce storm that had taken them through most of the night to an annoying drizzle that would not seem to let up. They were completely soaked to the bone, and they desperately wanted a dry place to gather their thoughts. So, any fears that each of them may have held towards entering another human dwelling were easily cast aside.

In the house Patrick quickly found towels for himself and the animals to dry off with, and they found plenty of food in the pantry for each to ease their hunger. Patrick stripped from his wet clothes and hung them over the kitchen chairs to dry, wrapping himself in a quilt for warmth he found in the den.

Before long the warm air that circulated through the house put them in drowsy mood. Though the house was big enough to garner each their own private accommodations for sleeping, they seemed to want to stay in close proximity with each other rather than to separate for their day's rest. So, as Patrick curled up on the couch, and the rest nestled in around him on the floor, they let their fears and anxieties drop aside for the day and they all quickly fell asleep.

Early next evening before any of the animals awoke, Patrick got up from his restless sleep and decided to do a little exploring. Nothing major, just a quick glance around the back of the house and into the garage was all that he was hoping to do. He'd never been in another family's house before free to explore as he wished.

At first he felt a little awkward going through someone else's stuff, but just the same he knew that whoever had lived here wasn't going to need their possessions any longer. And he reasoned, that if they were alive and had known of the predicament that he was currently in, that they probably wouldn't mind a bit if he borrowed something that he might come across to make his journey a tad easier.

Patrick first made his way down the main hallway, coming to the area of the house where the bedrooms and baths were located. As he stood in the hall and looked around he found the two smaller back bedrooms in various states of distress. This made him smile. From the clothes that were piled in the corners of the rooms sitting ridiculously close to the empty clothes hampers, to the unmade beds, and to the posters that hung on the walls, let Patrick know right off that there were teenagers that lived here. He walked amongst their belongings, trying to get an understanding as to who they were, but didn't touch or take anything, thinking that he wouldn't want anyone to touch or take his stuff—dead or alive.

He then made his way to the master bed and bath, finding the dried remains of one of the owners of the house in the doorway. He turned and went back the way he came, not wanting to step over the remains of the dead person. He wondered for a moment at which graveyard the spirits of the family of this house had been placed; wondering what kind of torment that they might be going through. Patrick shook his head and lowered his eyes. It was thoughts like those that made the hairs stand on end.

He turned and moved on through the rest of the house, making his morning stop in the bathroom, and then ending up in the kitchen. He grabbed a box of Honeycomb out of one of the cabinets to satisfy his hunger. He dipped his arm into the yellow box, eating the cereal dry as he made his way to the door on the opposite side of the room. He found the light switch, flipped it on, and then moved into the oversized garage.

Patrick quickly discovered that this garage was no ordinary garage. It was a mechanics dream garage. Row after row of every type of tool imaginable hung from hooks extending from perforated board covering just about every square inch of wall space that existed. He walked along fingering the glistening chrome tools, marveling at the exactness with how each was placed. A long wooden work bench ran along an entire wall length to his right. And to his left, in the far corners, were air compressors and other, larger tools that he didn't recognize. This place seemed to have everything you could want.

The shiny red truck in the middle of the room did not go unnoticed. Patrick walked up to it with caution. He didn't expect anybody (or any thing) to be in there, but just the same he approached it slowly.

The door opened like it had just come from the dealer, smooth and solid. It was a Ford F-150 just like his fathers, only this one was new. It still had 'that new car smell' his dad would always comment about. Patrick didn't think much of the smell other than it smelled kind of stinky.

Before he had even realized it he had slid himself in to the front seat and was placing his hands on the steering wheel. Patrick checked for the keys in the ignition, but found the spot empty.

And then a silly little thought came to him. He wondered why he hadn't thought of it before. At first he dismissed it as foolish, smiling and shaking his head to himself, realizing that he could never pull it off. But then after he had thought about it for a few more moments, rolling it over and over in his mind, the idea sort of settled in to an agreeable place in his head.

That's when he went to find the keys.

After a few minutes of looking he found them sitting in a bowl on the kitchen counter just inside the doorway to the house. He snatched them up and walked back out to the truck.

After he had placed them in the ignition and gave a quick flick of the wrist, the truck started right up with a low rumble. He smiled at the sound.

This was definitely going to make traveling a lot more enjoyable.

"What is that noise?" Kirsdona asked as she yawned.

"I don't know," Syrian said as he stretched his long arms, "but I don't think it's coming from in here, is it?"

The animals looked around at each other as their wits began to return to them from their sleep. The obvious question soon penetrated the room.

"Where's the boy?" Kirsdona asked loudly.

The noise from outside was growing and then would fade. Growing and then fade.

Bing rose from his sleep and looked around. "He's not here?"

"No. It seems he's been gone for a while now."

"Great. We're supposed to be his guardians and we can't even keep track of him. No wonder he's the human."

Bing's head went from side to side as if he was searching for something. "And what is that annoying racket?"

Syrian had already started making his way out the door. "I'm assuming that the answer to both of your questions lies in finding our way outside. I'm sure Patrick has found something out there that we'll find interesting enough."

The animals quickly filed their way outside following Syrian's lead, nearly bumping into one another as they rounded the corner and caught sight of what was in front of them.

"Hey guys! How do you like it?" Patrick asked enthusiastically from the front seat of the truck, the rumble of the truck cutting into his speech. Patrick had backed the truck carefully from the garage and now had it positioned out in the driveway.

His friends only blankly in return, each astounded and speechless at his proclamation.

"You have got to be kidding," Syrian spoke with trepidation. "I'm not getting in that thing. It could kill us."

Patrick shook his head, turning the ignition to off.

"No! This is a good thing. It'll help us move along faster. Plus it'll keep us safe from anything that may come at us."

"I don't know . . ." Bing's voice trailed away as he looked quite nervous at the idea the boy presented.

But Kirsdona stepped forward with mild excitement, surprising the others.

"I have to agree with him. I have ridden in several of these things. I believe they call them 'Vee-hick-calls.' They are quite enjoyable to travel in. Mind you, I was locked in a cage in the back of the one I traveled in, but it was quite the experience. For once, I think the boy may be right."

She turned her attention up to Patrick.

"Do you know how to operate this 'vee-hick-call?'

Patrick gave a look that did not give great assurance.

"Uh . . . sure. At least I think I can. My dad used to let me drive around the school parking lot on weekends for practice. He used to say that I drove better than my mom."

"Where did you find it?" Syrian asked.

"It was in the garage. In that building over there," he said as he pointed. "There wasn't any one left in it . . . I mean there wasn't any of the remains in the thing, so I just jumped up in it"

The animals started to move closer to the red contraption, each harboring their own idea on Patrick's proposal.

"I've. Never. Been. In. One. Of. Those. Before. But. I. Have. Seen. Other. Dogs. Moving. In. Such. A. Thing," Dog responded as he moved up beside Kirsdona. "It. Did. Look. Kind. Of. Interesting."

Patrick could see that Bing and Syrian were still having doubts about allowing this 'thing' to transport them around.

"Look, if you don't like it after we try it for a while, then we can all get out and leave it alone. But you've got to at least try it first."

Bing walked around the red piece of machinery surveying and scrutinizing it like he was intending to purchase it. Sin sniffed at the wheels and then backed away quickly.

"Just because I don't understand it," Bing said straightaway, "doesn't mean that it isn't something that we can't put to good use. If you think that you can maneuver it around, then I guess we should give it a try. How does it work?"

Patrick tried his best to explain all he knew about the truck and how it operated, but he quickly gave up as the questions (questions he couldn't answer) began to mount and he began to get frustrated. Finally he told them that it would be far easier if he just showed them how it worked rather than to explain.

Since the truck was only a single cab it was decided that Sin, Kirsdona, and Dog would be the ones to travel in the back, with Bing and Syrian riding up front with Patrick.

Loading the passengers was far easier than it sounded. Strapping Bing into his seat was easy enough, as was loading Dog into the bed of the truck. Neither Patrick nor Syrian wanted anything to do with trying to load Kirsdona, so she took it upon herself to get in, making one gigantic leap into the back end, cleanly covering the tailgate and landing with a thud next to Dog.

Lastly came Sin. The once little boar was now noticeably larger than when they had first set out, surprising both Syrian and Patrick with his girth.

"How the heck has he grown so much? Do boars always grow this fast? What's he been eating anyway?"

"I do not know," Syrian responded, "but I don't think we can use the term 'little guy' any longer."

They grunted and struggled but finally wrestled the growing boar in to the back end of the truck as well.

As soon as they had all settled in, and Patrick started up the truck, Patrick paused for a moment as he was about to put the truck into gear.

"Well here goes nothing," he said with excitement, his hand shaking slightly as he fingered the shift select.

Bing and Syrian both turned towards the boy.

"That does not sound very encouraging. Are you sure you know what you're doing?"

At that moment Patrick jammed the truck into drive, gave it too much acceleration, and bounced everyone back against their seats.

"No," was all that he could say as he floored the gas pedal again, hit a deep puddle in the driveway, and sent them bouncing around the cab as they took off down the road.

After the initial 'break in' period was established, the truck ride went better than expected—at least by Patrick's estimation. He kept it pretty steady on the road, never going faster than 45 miles an hour, and had to slow only the few times when they would come upon a snarled traffic situation that the plague had caused. Otherwise, the animals all seemed to enjoy it. Their initial unease turned to excitement as they realized that were moving as fast as (or faster) than the birds could travel. Pretty soon they all seemed content to relax and allow Patrick his triumph.

As the hours passed the driving (as are most long periods spent on the road) soon began to get boring, and Patrick thought it was about time to ask something that he had wanted to ask for a long time. As he stared into the mirror at the white boar in the back, he turned and finally asked Bing the question that had nagged him ever since they had left the barn. It was something that had continued to bother him again and again.

Who was Sin—and what was he all about?

". . . and when we loaded him into the back was when I knew something was wrong. There is no way he could have grown as fast as he has in such a short time. It's just not possible. With everything else that has taken place, this is something that just can't be normal." Patrick had a pleading look on his face. "Please tell me what's going on."

Patrick paused and took a deep breath. He had finished his questioning, laying out his entire point of reasoning of why his suspicious nature was getting the best of him. It wasn't just a point of curiosity anymore, it was now beginning to make Patrick edgy just at the sight of the white creature.

And he needed Bing to explain.

After listening to Patrick's questions and reasoning's, Bing sat quiet for a long time. The silence was so long and overwhelming that Patrick was beginning to get embarrassed for even mentioning his suspicions and how he felt. He wasn't sure if Bing was formulating what he was about to say, if he didn't know what to say, or if he just didn't want to talk about it.

"Uh . . . I'm sorry," Patrick began again, breaking the uncomfortable silence. "Maybe I'm making a big deal about nothing. I . . ."

Bing turned to Patrick, laid a wing on his arm, and gently smiled.

"I'm sorry, Patrick. It is not you. It's me. It's just that you have awakened an anger and an apprehension in me that I thought that I had put aside.

"I was trying to collect my thoughts on how to discuss this, trying to think of the proper overview in how to share this with you. I do not want you to think that this is how all animals of our kingdom behave, nor do I want you to come quick to judge on how others should or should not behave."

Bing paused.

"The world of the boars is not one that many other creatures of the world have ever had the privilege of taking part in. They are a secluded, secretive race that values its rights and rituals as something, at times, more sacred than the rules we believe were set down by the Creator.

"Do not let their exterior demeanor and coarse behavior distract from how they conduct themselves within their tribe. They are a proud group. One that I have not had the privilege of meeting first hand, but have come to understand by the retelling of their dealings I have heard from others.

"They believe, above all else, in the sanctity of obedience, the following of their truths, and of obeying the strict doctrine of their ways within their commune. You cannot be 'a little' wrong, or make 'a little' mistake in their view. There is no point of allowance when a wrong deed has been done. All mistakes are punishable.

"They are harsh and cruel and unforgiving when you fall outside of their beliefs. To cast one from a tribe is nothing to them. Many a boar who has been cast out will roam the wild country for weeks, or months, until they may join up with an outcast band that will take them in. Some will roam until they pass, never rejoining another tribe and finding acceptance."

"Did Sin do something wrong?" Patrick asked. "What could he have done that was so bad?"

Bing took a heavy breath, his head bobbing back and forth. "It wasn't what he did. It was what his parents did."

"His parents? Why is he being punished for something his parents did?"

"That is the point of why I am relaying all of this preliminary guidance to you.

"Sin was born into a world where just having two loving, caring parents is not enough. He was born to a female boar and male boar that were not joined together by the rites and rituals of their tribe. It the world of the boar, males and females are adjoined by an agreement brought forth by the council elders. They are the ones that decide who will be joined and with whom. They make their decisions not based on politics or favors, but based on what will work best for their system within their group, for the whole of the tribe. Theirs is a system based on economics. But it is within their divine beliefs that are what they base their guiding decisions.

"So, when Sin was brought into this world, he was brought into it with a predestined shame that he had nothing to do with. The problems his parents brought about by having a child not arranged and blessed by the council elders were only complicated by his appearance at birth. They were outraged when he first appeared. Surely, they thought, his color, his unfortunate loss of eyesight, as well as the inability of speech was a byproduct of an unholy joining. There could not be any other explanation. There would not be any other explanation.

"So, being that the child was brought into this world with the beliefs that followed with the tribe, the child was given the name Sin for the act that it was believed was committed."

Patrick's heart sank. "I'm glad that I don't live there. Isn't there something that you can do to them to make them stop?"

"Like I explained, this is their culture. In the animal kingdom it is a law that others do not interfere across cultural boundaries."

Bing paused again, his face contorting in an awkward posture.

"But there's something more, something that has been bothering me ever since I've heard about all the goings on about the young boar."

"What's that?"

"It's a little known part of the story, one that many haven't heard, or don't particularly care to hear. Two things, really. It concerns the parents and the family that briefly raised Sin.

"It seems that when they were questioned concerning his birth the parents never actually explained where and when they birthed him. The story that they told to the council, a story I'm sure the council easily dismissed, was that they couldn't remember having the child. I know that sounds a bit ridiculous to believe. They believed that the mother was carrying the child, but they were never completely sure. Being that they were trying to keep not only the fact of their feelings for each other a secret, but the fact that possibly they were going to bring a child into the world because of those feelings, made any disclosure of such impossible.

"The story they told was that while they were out supposedly collecting food for the tribe they found their way to an outer grassy knoll that seemed secluded enough for them to rest a while and talk. They began to get tired and soon fell asleep. Their sleep was long and unnaturally deep and took them terribly past the time that they had been allotted. When others were sent out to find them, they not only discovered the two boars sleeping, but found the infant boar nestled between them as well."

Syrian jumped into the conversation.

"But that doesn't necessarily mean it was their child. It could have come from another couple. Possibly someone who felt shame at seeing the tiny babe as it appeared. Perhaps they stumbled across the two of them sleeping and then deposited the child."

Bing nodded.

"True, but the fact that the tribe was such a closely guarded group made it near impossible for any others to have been with child and no one knowing about it. And second, the mother's appearance after the arrival of the child was now different than even earlier that day. Thinner. From what I am to understand—remarkably thinner.

"So, the three were brought before the council and questioned, their shame discovered, and the punishment was administered."

"What was that?" Syrian asked in horror.

"Well, it's not that they were killed or anything like that. But it wasn't a happy welcoming either.

"First, the male boar was cast out of the tribe and banished to never re-enter their territory—upon punishment of death. The female's punishment was that she was to be used as a drone only, a worker, never to be allowed to marry or bare children again.

"Of course, the worst of all was the treatment of the infant. It had to be cared for by a foster family in the mean time. It was decided upon that he was to be raised on the outskirts of their territory by a family that was known to be very harsh and disciplined in the ways of the council. A very wicked and unforgiving family. It was to be raised by this family until at the earliest possible age and time that the animal could then be banished, set free away from the tribe."

Bing laughed in sort of a cruel, mocking way, motioning to Patrick.

"It's kind of funny how it came about that the entire tribe had the dream of the little boar and you. It was as if they were overwhelmed with the situation as it was, and then they were given an easy situation to hand him off to. They didn't have to share in any of the guilt at having to ban someone so small from the tribe. All that they had to do was to let him go with us. Their situation was then resolved for them."

The three of them sat in the truck for a few moments in silence, digesting what Bing had just told them.

"But, you said that there were two things that bothered you. One was about the birth of Sin. What was the other?"

Bing turned his attention out the window to his right. Patrick watched as Bing's left wing twitched ever so slightly, as if something was indeed bothering him.

"It was about the family that took Sin in. You see, the council never sent a representative out to check on the little boar after he was placed in foster care. It was assumed that since the family that they placed him with had children of their own that the boar would be looked after as they looked after their own. The council had given their instructions to the family to 'care' for the infant until he came of age. It was then that they would be compensated for their 'generosity.' So as the shortened time passed, at no time had anyone even bothered to go and check on the creature. It wasn't until one morning just a few weeks ago that Sin came strolling through the main regions of their territory unattended that the outrages began all over again. Several emissaries were sent out to contact the family that was charged with Sin's welfare, to bring them back for their explanations as to why the boar was allowed to roam free. But the emissaries returned empty handed. They could find nothing of the family back at their place of living. From what I am to understand, it appeared as though they had just up and left. It was as if they had never been there. Moved on. Vanished. They were never seen again."

"You don't think that Sin had anything to do with . . ." Syrian began to ask.

Bing gave him a look of disgust.

"No, of course not. I don't see how. You've been around him. He seems kind of sweet. Affectionate. No, I can't see how he could have done anything to them. Besides, he would have been too small."

"What did the council finally conclude?"

"Well, you know that they brought the young boar to us. That's as far as that end of the story goes.

"But later it was discovered that some of the council elders had gone missing from that particular tribe as well. Just as the foster family for Sin had. No trace of them could be found. That's why the tribe has imposed a sort of 'martial law' in keeping all outsiders out, and keeping all that remain within their territory under strict obedience. As far as what happened to the parents, it seems that they too have vanished. And now from what I have heard, a good many of the tribe cannot even remember who they were or what they looked like."

"That sounds kind of spooky," Patrick said.

Bing erupted in laughter. "Yes, I guess you could say that it is kind of 'spooky.'"

Syrian, who did not share in the point of humor Bing was making, began to ask another question.

"So, if they decided to—Look out!"

Patrick turned quickly towards the baboon.

"What?"

That's when he heard both Bing and Syrian scream "LOOK OUT!!"

Patrick turned his attention back to his driving just in time to see the back end of the eighteen wheeler that they were rapidly approaching. He quickly jammed on the brakes just before they smashed head on into the rear end of the huge truck. Their truck then skidded, turning slowly sideways, and came to a stop just after the left front end had smashed into the rear end of another truck. The air bags deployed causing all three up front to be 'ballooned' up against the back of their seats.

Patrick became hysterical.

"Is everyone ok? I'm so sorry! I wasn't paying attention! I'm sorry! I'm sorry . . ."

"It's ok, Patrick," Bing said as he pushed the airbag away from his body. "Calm down. I don't think that any of us are hurt."

Bing got up from his seat and turned back to see how the occupants were doing in the back end of the truck. Just as he turned he got a face full of Kirsdona looking awfully unhappy as she stared at the back of Patrick's head.

"Though, I'm not so sure our friends in the back are as relaxed with the situation as we may be."

"I'm sorry, again. It's just that with the story you were telling, and that there wasn't any other cars or trucks on the highway. I was just cruising along. It's dark and I just didn't see up ahead. Where did all of the cars and trucks come from all of sudden?

"I don't know, but I think that we will be walking from here on out for a while."

"Yes," Syrian agreed. "I think that we have more than made up the amount of time needed for the time being. I need to put my feet back on the ground for a bit."

As they exited the truck, and after Kirsdona gave Patrick a deserved earful about his lack of paying attention, the animals assembled a few yards away, ready to set out on foot again—much to Patrick's displeasure.

They decided as a group that it might be easier for a time if they continued traveling on the highway, given the point that it was taking them in the direction they desired, as well as it made Patrick feel like he could have another chance at getting back behind the wheel of another 'vee-hick-call.'

Patrick lingered in the truck cab a moment longer, deciding that before they left he was going to give the inside a quick search in case he missed anything that could prove useful, something he had neglected to do earlier.

"Come on," the animals shouted to him, now irritated that he was holding up their progress.

"Yeah, yeah," he mumbled to himself. "Just a minute."

He was just lowering himself out of the truck, satisfied that his search had produced nothing beneficial, when he ran his hand under the driver's seat in front of him for one last check. He was surprised when he felt something heavy and cold just beneath the touch of his fingertips. He grabbed it firmly, and pulled it out to reveal something that made his heart jump.

It was a small gun. A pistol.

Patrick turned in panic and looked at his friends through the window, marking the distance that now stood between them and himself, his mind struggling with what he should do with his new found discovery.

Even though there was a cool northern breeze circulating about, Patrick began to sweat, his fear of his finding the gun now rising to every pore on his body.

He knew instantly that he should put it right back where he had found it. He didn't want to upset Bing the way he had earlier, but in his head he kept replaying instance after instance where he could have used such a thing to help with his survival.

He stood looking at it for several seconds before he heard the others now coming back to see what was taking him so long. He just didn't have enough time to think it through clearly. So he made an impulsive decision and stuffed the gun down the back side of his pants, figuring that if he decided that he wanted to get rid of it later then all he had to do was to throw it away when no one was watching.

"What're you doing?" Syrian asked from behind him. Patrick jumped at the question, startled to realize that the baboon was so close.

"Nothing. Nothing. I just thought that I found something to eat. I'm done. Let's go."

"What'd you find?" Syrian asked as he looked over Patrick's shoulder, pressing the conversation further and in a direction that Patrick wanted to avoid.

Patrick just shook his head and closed the truck door.

"Nothing. Let's go," he replied, his voice straining a little to convey his annoyance. He hitched his pants up a little and continued on his way as if nothing had happened.

Patrick then asked a question of the others to quickly change the subject with Syrian, already knowing the answer before he even asked.

"If you guys still want to ride in this thing, we can. We could make up a lot of . . ."

An instant, growling "No!" came from most of the interested parties. They each added other small commentaries such as "Are you crazy?" or "I'm never getting in one of those things again!" Enough negative conversation on the subject to allow Patrick to realize that he had sufficiently changed the subject with Syrian so as not to cause any unusual state of alarm.

But Patrick cautiously watched his friend as they moved along just the same. It's not that he didn't trust the baboon (of course he did, implicitly) it's just that he wanted to avoid the confrontation—and the embarrassment—at all costs.

If Syrian had suspected anything, surely he would have said something by now.

Patrick continued to wonder if Syrian had seen what had just taken place, but decided to hold his tongue until a later time. Patrick watched him over the next few hundred yards and hoped that no further questions would come forward.

And soon, as they began to move away and distanced themselves from the truck, Patrick felt assured enough to realize that Syrian had seen nothing, allowing Patrick to slowly breathe a little easier for the time being.

It was still a few hours before day break, Patrick calculating that they had probably traveled a few hundred miles in the truck, though he continually looked for a highway marker or sign that might show them just how far they were from the next major city or town to be sure. When Patrick saw the sign announcing that they were only twelve miles from the city of Chicago his eyes lit up with excitement.

The thought of seeing Chicago made the walking far easier to accomplish, and since it was only twelve miles he figured that they could possibly make the trek in the next several hours.

As they walked the group noticed the odd differences in how some areas were lighted and others were not. Patrick figured (as they had seen before) that most of the power systems had either shut down completely since they had gone unmanned for so long, or they were in the process of shutting down. It was only a matter of time, he figured.

After they had traveled enough to warrant a point of stoppage for rest, they crested a small uphill curve in the highway and were surprised to see in the distance the darkened outline of the city. From their distance, with only a few lights illuminated, the city looked like it was asleep, a huge castle of darkness with only a few restless lanterns lit from within.

They made their way closer and closer, the animals not saying much as their own sense of wonder and awe overtook them.

"How. Many. Humans. Live. There?" Dog asked, his eyes never leaving the darkened mass of concrete and glass.

"Well," Patrick answered, "at one time I suppose there were millions. But now I couldn't say whether there is anyone alive in there or not."

"Did you say 'millions?'" Syrian asked, astonished at what they approached.

"Yeah. But that's really not a lot of people. Besides, there are a lot bigger cities in the world than this one."

"Wait a minute," Kirsdona said as the rest of the group gradually came to a stop. "You mean to tell me that there are bigger cities than this one? Where? How much bigger? I can't believe that man can build such massive structures such as this, yet walk around with such stupidity that he carries with him daily."

Patrick laughed slightly.

"I know what you're trying to say, but I can't give you the answer. I'm only twelve . . . well, almost thirteen, but still, I don't understand a lot of what goes on in the world. I don't have the answers."

Patrick looked around at the face of the animals and wished that he could somehow share with them all he knew about being human. But there wasn't enough time. It had taken him twelve years just to get to this point, and he knew that it would take him another twelve years just to try and explain all the little points of interest that make up a human life.

The group moved on, their next steps more cautious than the ones before. The amount of cars and trucks that were wrecked and overturned was astonishing. They had to continually move around, through, and under debris that boggled Patrick's mind.

As they made their way to a point just inside the boundary of the city, Patrick yelled out a "Hello!" just to hear the echo return back to him.

"That's pretty cool," he said as he grinned.

"Yeah. I'm sure that's an momentous stepping stone in the advancement of human socialization," Kirsdona added as she moved past him.

Patrick opened his mouth to respond to the tiger when he thought he heard someone or something whispering his name. It almost sounded like several voices at once.

"Did you guys hear that?"

The animals, with their keen sense of hearing were already way ahead of him, and were surveying the landscape from where the voices may have come.

"Of course we did," Kirsdona whispered, "who couldn't hear that?"

"Do not forget, Kirsdona, that he does not have our quality of hearing," Bing added.

"Yeah, yeah," she rebutted softly. Kirsdona took a few more steps and then nodded ahead. "I think that it was coming from . . ."

And then the whispering voices began again, this time causing all of the animals to jerk towards the city in unison as they tried to pinpoint from which direction it came.

Dog moved close to Kirsdona, the two forming a mismatched pair of hunters.

"Do you have any idea where it is coming from?" Bing said in a low, almost secretive voice.

"I. Think. That. It. Is. Coming. From. Below. The. Road. Level," Dog said firmly.

Kirsdona nodded slightly. "Yeah, the echo is what gives it away. I'm not sure how far away it is, though. It could be further ahead of us, or it could be coming from right below our feet."

The tiger moved forward with a few more cautious steps.

"And the smells in this place," she wrinkled her nose, "there are just so many that makes it hard to distinguish what is what."

"Yes," Bing agreed as he looked around, "The filth and the death here are overwhelming my senses as well."

Patrick turned back to make sure that Sin and Syrian were still behind him. They were so quiet that he had almost forgotten that they were still there. And, with the story that Bing had told him just a little while ago, he was now going to make sure that Sin was not out of his sight.

"How do they know who we are, anyway? Or who I am?"

"Word travels fast, my friend."

"Do you have any acquaintances in this place that you may have forgotten about, boy?" Kirsdona asked sarcastically. "Someone who has taken up residence underground?"

Patrick could only shake his head as he listened to the voices as they once again called out to him, causing his skin to crawl.

Then, like a streak, Dog took off up the street to their left, screaming, "I. See. It. I. See. It!"

Kirsdona then took off in the same direction.

"Well, here we go," Patrick said as he was about run after them.

But Bing put up his wing and firmly planted it in Patrick's chest.

"You are not going anywhere!" he said sternly. "Kirsdona and Dog will take care of this matter."

Patrick, realizing that Bing was right, stayed in his spot.

Within a few seconds, both the dog and the tiger returned. They were out of breath, but delivered their discovery to the group.

"It's a bunch of rats!" Kirsdona said, looking as though she had a hairball stuck in her throat.

"We. Saw. Them. Move. Quickly. Away. But. We. Saw. Them. Go. Down. Under. The. Street."

"Rats? I wonder what they would want with us? Or him?" Bing asked as he motioned towards Patrick.

"Perhaps. They. Are. Just. Playing. A. Game. With. Us?"

"That could be. They aren't the most trustworthy of fellows, that's for sure."

"Do you think that they could want something from us?"

"What could they possibly want? What could we have to give them?"

The group stayed silent for a few moments, each trying to understand the situation.

"I wonder if this has something to do with Tye?" Patrick wondered aloud.

"Tye? Why would you bring him up?" Bing asked. "We haven't seen nor heard of him in quite some time."

"That's what I mean. I haven't forgotten about him, and I'm sure he hasn't forgotten about me."

"Do you think that he would employ the aid of vermin like this?" Syrian asked.

Bing sighed and scanned the surrounding area. "I really don't know. From what I have heard of that slithering devil I would not put it past him."

From the shadows of a drain hole to their left came a voice. "You should listen to the boy. He is far more wise than I believe you give him credit for."

The animals all turned towards it at once.

Two small, yellowed eyes peered back out to them from the darkness of its retreat.

"Rats," Kirsdona said with a look of revulsion, "I hate rats."

As she finished her words a silent, almost inaudible squealing (from what sounded like a great many ill-tempered rats) seemed to come from all around them.

"Be careful what you say, tiger. There are many more of us down here than there are of you up there."

And then another set of eyes appeared next to the first in the drain.

"Do you want me to go bite him in the leg, M? I will. I'll bite his legs right off."

"Calm yourself, Beagel. That won't be necessary for the moment."

Bing uneasily took a step forward, bending low to look into the drain.

"What is it that you want, friend rat? Is there something that we can help you with? Or is it that you are merely stalling us for some other purpose? A purpose that would not serve us well. We do not have time for games."

The rat's eyes narrowed. "No, there are no games that are being played. At least not by us. We are simply trying to lend assistance."

"Assistance? In what form?"

"Beagel, please go above and show these fine animals the way down to our home," the rat referred to as 'M' spoke to the other rat beside it. "This conversation would much more be suitable if it were carried on down here."

Kirsdona pulled herself back in a reaction that was not unexpected.

"Down there!? I'm not going down there!"

"Wait a second, Kirsdona," Bing said in a calming tone. "We have to take this one step at a time. Let's hear what they have to say first before we do anything, ok?"

"'Wait a second?' Are you insane? Or has everyone here just temporary dipped their big toes in the pool of insanity? I've dealt with rats before, and they're not the type of individuals that give a lot of credence to the term 'believable.'"

"This commotion is going to get you all killed if you do not lower your voices and do as I say," M said with persistence.

"Why is there such urgency in your voice?" Syrian asked as he leaned in, "What is going on that we don't know about?"

"There are enemies around that are planning to ensnare your little group and put an end to your journey. There are eyes and ears all around us. We are all being watched now, even as we speak."

Just then, a gray rat the size of a shoe box appeared from behind several large dumpsters that were situated on a side street just off to the groups right.

"You should follow my brother, Beagel. He will guide you down here safely."

Patrick and the others held their place for the moment, each looking at Bing for some sort of guidance in the situation. Bing then turned back to the rat in the drain.

"And how do we know that you are not the 'enemy' of which you speak?"

The rat hesitated only for a moment, his nose twitching slightly.

"You don't."

CHAPTER 16

Melanbach and Beagel

As Patrick entered the first tunnel all that he saw were rats, rats, and more rats. The place was dripping with them.

"The price on your heads is high," said the rat who guided them, Beagel, with a glint of a smile.

Kirsdona turned and glared at the plump fellow, a low guttural growl coming deep from inside her.

"Don't try and intimidate me, you overgrown fur ball," the rat hissed back, "I'll rip your throat out."

Syrian hurriedly made his way beside the tiger.

"Antagonizing them is not going to make our way through this any more enjoyable," he said, trying to sound as pleasant as possible as he looked around at the thousands of rats that aligned the walls as they were led through the tunnels. "I'm not in the mood to end up as the main course in their dinner arrangements for the evening."

The rat, Beagel, had led them through a succession of torn wire fences, battered plaster walls, and endless mildew stained steps that had brought them down to a doorway (that was missing the door), finally allowing them to crawl along a narrow ledge and into an open sewer line.

Kirsdona had grunted and growled her displeasure the entire time, but silenced herself when they had finally emerged into the open space.

"God, it smells," Patrick said as he pulled the collar of his shirt up over his nose.

He had no idea what was actually below the streets in such cities, but as his eyes made their way around the filth and decay in the oversized tunnel he was amazed to see all the things that were scattered and left about. Old tires, multiple pairs of shoes, shopping carts, old lamps, mattresses, and even the front end of an old car, all lying in different states of deterioration.

A few of the rats giggled with pleasure at the group's uncomfortable state.

"You've never had is so good, you street walker!"

"Once you live like a rat you'll never go back, kitty cat!"

"Look at the beak on that one, willya, oh brother!"

The animals were getting more nervous and apprehensive, their heads darting from side to side.

"Must we have to put up with all the self gratifying comments?" Bing asked, announcing his displeasure with the heckling to Beagel.

"They'll knock it off soon enough," he replied. "They haven't had many visitors, so their manners aren't maybe what they should be, y'know."

"Yes, I believe you state the obvious."

"So what is this nonsense you were saying?" Syrian asked from the rear. "Something about a price on our heads?"

The rat shrugged. "Yeah. You guys must have made someone real mad, cause the word on the street is that if someone points you out and you get made, then whoever that individual might be would then get some kind of big reward. Something special."

The animals exchanged nervous glances with each other as they walked. Beagel casually observed as they did this.

"Then it's true," he said as he shook his head. "Here I thought that all you were was just another lost group of 'upsiders.' M was right."

"And exactly where is this 'M'?" Bing asked.

"Uh . . . we're just about there. Around the next corner and then up another couple of blocks."

The silence drifted behind them (as did the larger groups of the rats) as the animals and Patrick found themselves working deeper and deeper into a much narrower tunnel. The lights that hung that were once numerous in the outer, larger tunnel, were now becoming more and more sparse as they went. Patrick had to squint just to see a few feet in front him.

"I don't like this. I don't like this one bit," Kirsdona uttered as her paws sloshed through the slimy water below them.

"I realize your discomfort, Kirsdona, but our guide assures us that we are almost there."

"And where might that be, Hades?"

Beagel turned back towards Bing.

"Your friend there has got a big mouth, for a broad. Either she learns to keep it closed or I might just let her have her wish and we'll let the 'bugs' have her."

Patrick leaned in close to Syrian.

"What is he talking about? I haven't seen any bugs? Have you?"

"No. But from the sound of it they must have some really nasty ones if he's threatening her with them. I just wish she would shut up."

Kirsdona let out a low little laugh.

"You know, I'm not deaf. I can hear you back there."

"We're in a tunnel, the sound echoes a bit," Bing said matter-of-factly. "Why don't we all just stay quiet until we get to where we're going, hmm? We don't need anymore trouble."

As Beagel led them over a small jagged cut in the cement wall between two connecting tunnels the light became a little brighter, and they could see a small gathering of rats just ahead of them. The rats were having a silent conversation of some nature and hurriedly ended their discussion as soon as Patrick and his group approached. All of the rats then scurried away, except for the largest, which remained where he was sitting.

"Here they are M. What do you want me to do with them?"

"Well, introductions would be in order," the larger of all the rats explained simply.

"Well . . . uh . . . I don't know who they are, really," Beagel said awkwardly.

Bing then stepped forward and extended a wing.

"Hello. My name is Bing," he said, and then quickly introduced the remaining members in his party as he pointed to each as he introduced them.

The rat rose up to his hind quarters and then bowed.

"I am Melanbach. I am honored to meet with you."

"Are you the one in charge," Kirsdona asked gruffly.

"Hey, cat, I told you to watch your tongue," Beagel jumped forward and said angrily. "You don't talk to Melanbach that way, you understand? He deserves respect."

Beagel turned to Melanbach, his hind leg scratching his side.

"You want me to bite 'em, M? I will, y'know. I'll bite 'em right where it hurts the most."

Melanbach, an embarrassed look coming over his face, shook his head and turned to his brother.

"Please, Beagel, you can tone it down a bit. I don't think that our guests mean any disrespect."

He then turned his attention back to the animals.

"Yes," Melanbach smiled, "I would like to say that I am only the caretaker of this underworld, but for the practicality of our conversation I guess I am the one in charge."

"So why are we here? Why did you insist on bringing us down here?"

"It is because I did not wish to witness your deaths. You are being stalked by something rather unpleasant, and it has been discussed by our group that it is in all of our best interests to keep you alive."

"Who is stalking us?

Melanbach turned to his brother.

"The 'bugs,'" Beagel snarled.

The group looked around from one to another.

"'Bugs?' What 'bugs?'" Syrian asked. "We encountered a legion of hornets a few days back, but with the way you speak of these insects they must be significantly more dangerous."

Melanbach shook his head.

"Not insects. Mice."

Everyone from Patrick's group let out a relaxed sigh, and it was obvious that they didn't share with the two rats who were entertaining them the same degree of alarm.

"Mice? Well, that's sort of a relief," Patrick said.

Kirsdona chuckled lightly. "You mean the little soft furry creatures that are about as big as my toe? You're worried about them?" she asked sarcastically.

But the two rats did not alter their expressions.

In fact, the longer that the two held their silence as the animals chuckled around them began to give the group a very uncomfortable feeling. It was as if they were becoming aware that the two rats knew something else, but hadn't gotten around to sharing it with them as of yet.

"Please excuse our rudeness," Bing extended, "It is just that we have come a long ways and perhaps our weariness has caused us to forget our manners."

"Your apologies are not needed. I believe that you just do not understand what is taking place."

"But I think we do," offered Bing. "Mice are a part of the animal kingdom, and they are not involved in the dealings that we have so far fought against. We have found that the insect and reptile world are waging war against human kind. Not the animals."

Melanbach waved his hand.

"For the most part, what you say is true. But the ones who wish you put aside have made a bargain with the mice. They have now been included in the deal."

"But that's absurd. You're the same breed, how . . ."

"Just a minute, pal," Beagel snarled, "we are nothing like those stinkin' 'bugs!' I can't help it if they fell from the same tree as we did. But I'll bite the legs off of anyone who says that we're like 'em again."

"I don't understand," Patrick began, "How are they so different from you? I'm not trying to get my 'legs bit off,' but a mouse and a rat are the same thing, aren't they? That's what I was taught in school."

"And. Why. Do. You. Keep. Calling. Them. Bugs?" Dog asked again.

"That's because that is what they are, you morons. They think like bugs. They act like bugs. They move like bugs. If it walks like a duck, etc., y'know."

"Please, please, let me explain," Melanbach through his arms up into the air to try and calm things down. "Beagel, please try and control yourself for the time being." Melanbach then turned back to Bing. "Please excuse my brother, it would seem that he has received the greater degree of anger in our family, and I would like to believe that I have acquired the greater degree of intelligence."

The large rat then turned to the rest of the group. "Yes, my human friend, you have been taught well in the ways of human belief and understanding. But let me assure you that you do not know. And from the attitudes of the others in your group I assume that they also are falling under the same misconception that has been passed along that is quite the opposite from what is true.

"You see, much to our kind's displeasure, we must acknowledge that we are from the same bloodlines as that of the mice. But other than the fact that we share the same likeness, that we scamper on all fours, and that we have a hairless tail, we have more in common with a squirrel than we do with our white skinned cousins."

"And that's not saying much," Beagel interjected.

"It's just that the way in which they think and conduct themselves is the biggest differential between the two of us. Whereas we are your common, everyday street vermin, they are much more calculating in how they think and conduct themselves."

It was becoming noticeable to most that Beagel was becoming agitated at what Melanbach was saying.

"Ah, pooh," he said abruptly. "You use all those fancy terms and words. What I said is true. And it's easier to understand, M. They're bugs.

"When I say that they think like bugs, it's because they do. They don't carry on with their own personal selves, like the rest of us, like you would think. It's always about what's best for the group. Heck, you could almost substitute the word 'hive' for 'group.' They think like bugs and they move like bugs. Always as one. They don't even try to think like we do. They won't talk. They won't eat. Everything's done together, just like bugs. You watch a group of ants. If you go near the hill the ants will go berserk and try and rip you to shreds. Always working for the anthill and the queen. That's the way they operate. Like ants."

"I didn't know that the mice have a queen," Syrian asked, confused.

"That's just it—they don't. They think of themselves as the queen. The entire unit as one. If one of them dies, then another moves up to take its spot. There's no feelings involved. And if you're not pulling your weight then you'll get killed off as well."

Patrick was looking overwhelmed.

"I had no idea . . ."

Melanbach then took back over the instruction.

"Have you ever held one of them in your hand, human?"

"Yeah, in school. In science class we would use them in experiments. Checking to see how they reacted to different things. You know, cold, heat, water. We would put them in a maze to see if they could make it through."

"Yes," Melanbach continued, "and did you know that the entire time that you thought that you were studying them, that they were actually studying you?"

"What?!"

"They allow themselves in certain situations to be taken and placed in confinement in the human world. They believe that this is for the greater good. That if a few hundred of them die while living within the space of a human, then they can study and carefully begin to manipulate how they can arrive at a plan to better work their world."

"But that's crazy! Then how come they haven't taken over the earth or something? There can't be that many of them."

"Do you know how many mice actually exist? I'm afraid that I don't know the exact number, but if you knew what it was then it would definitely cause you to rethink your approach to them."

Patrick's mind drifted back to his time in school when he used to hold a little mouse that was named 'Harry', after 'Harry Potter,' in class. He would curl his fingers around it's soft white haired body, watching as its little red eyes would look up at him.

He used to think that it would be kind of cool to have a pet mouse that he could keep in his room. But now he began to wonder, thinking of all the times he would look over during class at the little glass enclosed case where Harry was kept, watching as the little mouse was looking back at him. Patrick thought that it was just that the little mouse recognized and liked him for who he was, but now wondered what little Harry was actually thinking as he stared back at him.

A cold chill ran down Patrick's spine as he continued to listen to Bing's questioning of Melanbach.

"So how have you come across this information?"

"It is becoming widely known throughout our world that there is a group of animals that is escorting a human to confront a wicked force to the north. We, like the rest of the kingdom, are in agreement with the need and continuing belief that the humans should remain, not only alive, but in control. Because if not, then our world down here would surely perish as well.

"We know what we are for the most part. Bottom feeders. Scoundrels. Pirates. Thieves. But we know what we are, and we take great pride in it. Without the humans to provide us with our meals, or our water, we would never survive for very long.

"I know that it seems sad, that unlike our brothers who live in the outlying areas outside of the city, who can live without the need of human refuge, that we must submit ourselves to the gravity of waste. But it is just that we have lived for so long down here that to undertake a journey alone to another land would be a great burden in itself, let alone to learn survival skills that we do not understand. We would surely perish in a shortened amount of time.

"I do not know exactly who you are, or why you are traveling with a human," Melanbach cocked an eye towards Patrick, "or even how it can be that he can understand us, or we him. But from the words that has traveled down here from the animals that we have good relations with outside of here, I am to understand that the less we know perhaps is for the better."

Patrick watched as Bing took a deep breath, wondering if he was going to spill the beans about who they were. And more directly to the point, who he was.

"So what do you want us to do? What is your plan, Melanbach?" Bing asked.

Melanbach rubbed his chin, and then stroked his whiskers.

"I would say that the best course of action for now is to do nothing. I can see it in your eyes that you all are in need of sleep. And perhaps food, though I am not sure you would be so inclined to accept what we may have to offer."

Patrick knew that the last sentence was intended for Kirsdona. He had watched as Melanbach had turned to the tiger as he spoke.

"But whatever you may want to do, it would be best to travel through the city during the night and emerge during the day. The mice do not like the bright of day directly on them. Nor do we, for that matter, unless we know that it is coming."

"And how are we going to get through the city? And how long will it take?"

"From where we are sitting now it should take no more than a day to travel through the underground system that we have. We dare not take you above ground until we have found our way to the other end of the city. Then it will be easy enough for you to make your way back into the wild on the other side."

"The mice won't follow us there?"

Melanbach smiled. "No. Fortunately they are like us. Once you are born into the city, you become a part of the city. They cannot survive in the wild either."

Bing turned to the group and nodded. "Then it is settled. We will rest and enjoy the hospitality that our hosts provide us with until it is time that they find it clear for us to continue."

"One question, though," Syrian asked. "Why don't the mice just come down here? Is there some reason that they won't?"

Melanbach and Beagel both chuckled at Syrian's questions.

"You of all people, my friend baboon, should know the answer to that one. When was the last time you ventured into the land of your enemies?"

Patrick watched as a knowing expression overcame Syrian's face. The baboon smiled faintly and nodded.

"Please follow us, then. We will show you to a place where you can rest. If you desire food, we will do our best to bring you what we have."

And as they all began again down another tunnel together, Patrick wondered silently to himself about the mice.

What deals had been made? And exactly who had they struck them with?

The laughing image of Tye then danced around in Patrick's head. He knew now more than ever that he was probably on collision course with that monster sooner, rather than later.

And what the outcome of that meeting would be, he didn't even want to think about.

CHAPTER 17

Under the City

When Patrick awoke all that he heard and saw was chaos and confusion.

"Let's go, pretty boy, time to wake up," Kirsdona growled as she shoved him from his sleep. "We've got to move."

It had only been a few hours after the group had made their way down into the underground world of the rats. Patrick and the others had decided to pass on the few scraps of food that had been provided, deciding instead that they were more in need of sleep. The rats had instructed that they would allow the group a few hours of uninterrupted rest unless something of a more serious nature would come about.

"What's the matter?"

"I don't know, but the rats are in all kinds of turmoil. Something isn't right."

Patrick watched as Syrian and the others were scurrying about.

"Where's Bing?" Patrick asked.

"He was meeting with Melanbach. Here he comes now."

Bing hurried over to the small group, a look of astonishment across his face.

"What's going on?" Syrian asked.

"Well, it seems that something is taking place that Melanbach didn't expect. The mice could be planning to do exactly what he said they wouldn't—make an advance down here."

"Wonderful," Kirsdona added sarcastically. "So what are we going to do?"

"Melanbach is making arrangements to disperse separate divisions of rats to shore up the different entranceways into their domain. I've never seen so many rats before in my life.

"He wants us to hold up here for the moment. He and Beagel are going to bring another group of rats with them that will begin our escort to the far end of the city."

Patrick could hear the constant pattering of what sounded like were thousands of tiny paws urgently making their way through the underground passages.

"So how did they figure this out? Did someone see some of the mice entering their domain?" Syrian asked.

The group heard someone shouting from behind to "Get out of the way!" just as a large collection of angry rats came storming past them.

"It seems that overnight in some of the more outlying areas of their underground a great many of their guard rats have turned up dead. As it was explained to me, it is not uncommon for a guard or two to fall at times when battling a stray cat or dog, or other intruders that may wander into their territory. But it seems that a lot more than just a few guards have been killed this time. I overheard one of their messengers reporting that entire quadrants in certain areas of the tunnels had been breached. They're sending out all available bodies to check out the situation and report back as soon as possible."

"And that leaves us where?" Kirsdona asked abruptly.

"That leaves us right here for the moment," Bing said directly. "What would you have us do, Kirsdona? We don't know their territory. We'd be fools to go off on our own through these tunnels."

"It's just that I don't like being confined down here. If I have to fight, even if it is against a bunch of mice, I like to have as much room as possible. In case you haven't noticed, I'm not exactly what you would call 'petite.'"

"Then we should leave at once," Melanbach said from off to the group's left. Every one of them jumped at his words, each startled by his quiet approach.

"I wish you wouldn't do that," Syrian said as he gathered himself.

"I apologize, but I have learned that the term 'quiet as a mouse' does apply, even if I am not so easily amused by the use of the word 'mouse.'"

"Are you the only one going with us?" Patrick asked.

"No. The others are waiting for us in the adjoining tunnel. We do not have any more time for delays."

Melanbach started to turn in the direction to lead them, but then stopped for a moment and turned back to the group.

"But I will give you a few words of warning. Do not underestimate anything that we may encounter. No matter what you may think you know, down here, sometimes your mind can deceive you. The shadows can play nasty tricks with your thoughts. Surprises can jump out at you from just about anywhere. There are tunnels and passages down here that are many and great, and have monstrous creatures in them that even we do not attempt to disturb. Do not become lost. Stay with the group whatever you do. Because if you do become lost, it could be weeks before we may find you again—if we ever would.

"As we pass through these tunnels, trust what I say. If I, or one of the other rats should say stop, you should stop instantly. Is that understood?"

They all nodded in agreement.

"Good. Then follow me."

Melanbach brought the group forward until they came to a split in the tunnel, half of it going to the left, the other going to the right. As they took the tunnel to the left they soon found Beagel and an assortment of rats. Patrick guessed that there were about fifty or so.

"Have you seen anything, Beagel?" Melanbach asked as he continued on, not stopping to assemble the groups together.

"Nothing yet, M. But word has come down through the tunnels that it's definitely the bugs."

"How do you know?"

"A couple of guards spotted them coming through a hole in the wall next to the sewage collection point to the east. They were shimmying along the electric lines, trying to go unnoticed." Beagel shook his head. "Mice coming through the sewage point, who would have ever thunk it."

"Indeed," Melanbach responded, clearly unsettled by the report.

"What's so surprising about that?" Bing asked.

"Well, mice are not very fond of finding their way into filth. They will normally avoid it at all cost. For them to come down that particular path tells me that they are indeed in a desperate circumstance. Whatever it is that is driving them to commit these acts, deeds that go against their very nature, is in itself alarming. We should all be on guard. Do not trust anything, even if it seems the least bit unusual."

Patrick was just behind Melanbach and Beagel, the group intermixed with a few rats and animals, with the majority of the rats protecting from their rear. Other than Melanbach or Beagel, the rats that traveled with them did not talk. Their attention keenly focused on the job at hand.

Patrick was so nervous as he walked that his stomach was shaking uncontrollably. It was bad enough that the tunnel that they were walking in was barely lit, but with the smell and the shadows, it was playing havoc with his imagination, causing most everything that came by him to give him some sort of imaginary horror waiting to pounce.

"Calm down, boy," Kirsdona said without looking at him. "It'll be ok. We'll get through this."

"I'm fine. I'm not scared," Patrick responded, trying to allay his fears.

Kirsdona smiled.

"And neither are the rest of us."

Patrick slowly turned his head to look at the tiger. It was about the nicest thing that she had ever said to him. It was an awkward way of thinking, but he knew that she intended it to be kind. And for that moment, he actually forgot about where he was and just looked, really looked, at the great animal as she walked beside him.

She wasn't as bad as she had portrayed herself, he thought. Without a doubt she was one of the more vicious, mean spirited creatures he had ever met. But there was something else there, something deeper, but what it was he really couldn't put his finger on it at the moment.

Patrick again heard a large number of rats scrambling in an adjacent tunnel, heading off in an unknown direction, but with no squeals or cries announcing their approach.

They traveled this way, silent, moving purposefully forward through the first hour that they walked. They would hear distant screams and cries echoing from far off hollowed places, but would never stop to question or wonder if they should lend a hand.

There was a war going on somewhere out there, at least in Patrick's mind. He imagined the rats battling hordes of white mice, their bloodied whiskers and gnashing teeth grinding into each others necks and backsides causing great amounts of pain and death. But they only heard the sounds, never witnessing the battles.

Patrick wondered about the course in which Melanbach was taking them. He brought them in such a way that the group never came close to actually encountering any of the fighting. Rather, they pretty much skirted most of the hostilities. And it must be causing great anguish to Melanbach's dignity, Patrick thought. He sensed that Melanbach was a creature with great sense of pride and appreciation for the appointment of which he held. To only be involved in the escort of the group, and not actually taking place in the planning and fighting to protect his people must be bothering him greatly. But he never said a word.

That's when Patrick thought of something that he had thought of many times before, but hadn't spoken aloud. If Melanbach was here protecting this little group of animals, rather than working and fighting with his own kind, then just how important was the job he had undertaken. If keeping a human and all of these strange animals alive was more important than protecting his own people, Patrick had to wonder what it was that made himself so important.

So important that all of these rats would risk their lives to protect.

He had heard Kirsdona pose the question earlier, seemingly in jest. But then again . . .

Who am I? He wondered. What am I?

That's when the lights in the tunnel shuttered and blinked a few times—the electricity trying its best to stay on—and then went out.

Patrick stumbled forward slightly in the sloshing water, stepping on the tails of quite a few rats with all the shouts of, "Hey! Get off!" and "Watch it, Bigfoot!" that began to gush from below him.

"Quiet!" Melanbach barked instantly.

The silence came immediately, and was frightening.

Patrick tried as best he could to peer into the darkness to try and make out any shapes that he could, but he found that it was of no use. It was as dark as the basement Tye had kept him in before, and that dark was impenetrable. He wanted to ask if anyone could see anything. He wanted to ask if everyone was still there. He wanted to ask anything, but didn't for fear of what Melanbach had instructed earlier.

That's when he heard a new sound. A sound that didn't seem quite as heavy as the padded footsteps that the rat's little feet would make as they would scamper along. It was lighter, almost like the beating of a moth's wings.

And it was coming from above his head.

Patrick looked up, moving his hand above him, thinking that he was going to hit a bird or a bat.

But that was absurd, his mind told him. A bat maybe, but a bird? Down here?

When the first mouse dropped on top of him it quickly scrambled down to his shoulder and bit him hard. Patrick screamed with agony and quickly pushed the creature off.

But when a second and third mouse fell on him, that's when Patrick lost it. He began to thrash about and took off running.

"Patrick! Stop!" he heard Dog yelling behind him.

But the thought of what might be happening to him was too much for Patrick to bear. His imagination began to kick in and he was sure that there was at least twenty other mice on him, crawling under his clothes and running through his hair. This was not what he had expected at all.

After he had run a good fifty yards or so he slowly began to regain control of his fears, and he stopped. He reached up to his shoulder, grabbed one of the mice and flung it hard against the wall. The second one he had to reach around to his back, plucked it off by its tail, and threw it as far as he could down the tunnel.

Behind him he began to hear the others thrashing about as well. The mice had finally showed themselves, and now the others began to battle with the little monsters.

Patrick slowly backed up, trying to feel his way and find a wall that he could steady himself against.

He used his ears for sight, listening to the battle taking place from where he had just came. The growling and snarling that echoed all around him made him fearful, but also mad. He realized that his friends and the rats were back at the spot he had run from, fighting their way through, doing their best to defend and safeguard his life.

Patrick swallowed hard. He didn't know what he was going to do, but when he heard the definitive sound of Dog yelping in pain he could stand no more. He was going back to fight.

And that's when he began to glow.

It wasn't a brilliant glow, not like the sun or anything, but a very dim, low light. He held out his hands in front of him and yelped a little himself at the sight he was experiencing.

What's the heck's going on?!

Upon seeing the slight radiance coming from his arms, and realizing that his entire body was now producing light, he began to back up again, afraid that this would surely give the mice a good target to shoot for. The initial growth of anger that had swelled in him a few seconds ago was now beginning to wane.

Patrick turned and frantically began to hunt for a hiding spot. He noticed that the glow that was coming from him was slowly beginning to fade, but it gave him enough light and time to find an abandoned tunnel just ahead of him.

Then, as quickly as the glow had come forward, it just as quickly extinguished.

"What was that all about?!" he said aloud as he stopped. He held his arms in front of him to see if any of the light remained.

"What was what all about?" came a gruff response ahead of him that he didn't expect.

Patrick jumped at the voice, turning at once to see three pairs of crimson colored eyes sitting just above the waterline.

"Uh . . . who's there?" he said nervously.

One of the pairs of eyes turned to the others like a set of spinning marbles.

"I believe we have found lunch," it said decisively.

The first set of eyes then began to move slowly towards Patrick.

"Wait a minute, who are you?" Patrick asked, a bit of anger in his voice. He wasn't as afraid as he thought he should be, and with his friends back there fighting for their lives, he wasn't all that ready to start running away blindly.

The eyes stopped.

"Who wants to know?" it responded.

"I do," Patrick said with some authority.

"And who might you be?"

"I'm the one who can make you regret your decision if you come any closer," he said, surprised at himself as the words came forward.

The center pair of eyes looked back and forth to the other two.

"He's bluffing."

Then for some reason, Patrick got mad. Really mad. In the back of his mind he knew that he shouldn't, that he should be afraid, but he wasn't. It was if the boy that he had always wanted to be finally took a tiny step forward from inside him.

"Try me," he said.

He reached his hand around to his back, slightly fingering the small gun that was still wedged between the waistband of his jeans and his back side. He didn't know what was approaching him, but if it was something that he could shoot then this was as good a time as any to finally use the weapon.

But a strange thing started to happen that he didn't expect—he began to glow again.

Patrick heard something moving, sloshing in the water behind him, and he turned in time to see Sin making his way past the entrance to the tunnel he was now in. The boar sniffed the air and then stopped, finding his direction towards Patrick.

"Sin, go back," Patrick ordered. But the little boar trotted on into the tunnel, finally coming to a stop beside him.

Patrick turned back towards the eyes that were questioning him, realizing now with the light that was coming from him illuminating the darkness, that he was facing three alligators perched on the rocks just ahead of him.

But even though he was the alligators main attention of just a few seconds ago, not only because he was glowing—but because he was going to be their lunch—the alligators now seemed to have lost their focus on him. The alligators had turned all their attention to the white boar standing next to him.

"Did he say 'Sin?'" one asked, alarmed at the appearance of the boar.

"No. That's not possible," the other responded. "It can't be him. Not here."

"I thought he was just a myth," said the last.

At the alligator's words, Sin's attention instantly snapped forward and he began to do something that Patrick found astounding, and never thought he'd hear.

Sin growled.

And then as Patrick watched, Sin began to change. The sweet little boar that had accompanied them so far on this journey was slowly being replaced by a monster. Patrick couldn't be sure if his eyes were playing tricks with him or not, but what he thought he was witnessing made him take two steps backward, his hand dropping away from his backside and the gun.

The light illuminating from him was starting to fade again as Patrick lost focus with his anger. It was quickly being replaced with as sense of bewilderment as his attention was now focused on Sin.

At first, (and as he would tell this part of the story over and over again, he still wasn't quite sure what he was seeing) it looked like Sin disappeared. Patrick thought that maybe it was a trick of the light. When Patrick blinked again, there was Sin, still standing in the spot that he had occupied no more than a second ago.

But now there was only two alligators remaining in the tunnel.

What?

"It is him," said the alligator on the left. Things began to happen so fast that Patrick had a hard time keeping up. The alligator that had initially spoke made a low guttural sound and then launched itself at Sin like a crack of lightning. It's jaws opened with a snap and seemed ready to devour Patrick's friend in an instant.

But then it too disappeared, almost in mid air as it was lunging forward.

Patrick's head snapped toward Sin who seemed to materialize as if he had vanished again. This time he was slowly licking his lips. And though the light was low in the area, Patrick swore he could see a few small drops of red liquid sitting on the edge of Sin's whiskers.

Patrick turned in time to see the others, including Melanbach and Beagel, just beginning to enter the tunnel's entrance.

The remaining alligator then spoke for the last time, using words that Patrick had never heard before, but never ever forgot.

"En meterto sun 'e rezer loucot."

And then the light coming from Patrick's body went out again. Though it was infuriating to Patrick that he once again lost his ability to see what was taking place, he could still hear. And what he heard made him a little bit glad that maybe he couldn't see.

Patrick heard a noise that sounded like the snap of the wind, a splash, and then a sickly squeal of some kind coming from a creature that he didn't recognize.

A short silence followed, and then Patrick felt the thick bristle-like hair of Sin's back brush up against his hand as he walked by him. It was an alarming thing to feel, and Patrick quickly snatched his hand away.

The lights overhead flickered once, twice, then came on again, causing all to squint as their eyes adjusted to the reborn light.

"What just happened?" was all that Patrick could ask.

Dog made his way over to Patrick, his joy at seeing him unharmed was evident in the wagging of his tail. "I. Am. Happy. That. You. Are. Not. Hurt."

Patrick smiled slightly. "I'm fine. But what just happened? There were three alligators right over there that were getting ready to have me for dinner. But now they're gone."

Bing stood behind the rest and watched, following Sin's path as the boar made his way to the back of the group and then stood silent.

"Look at him. He's already growing," Bing said with concern.

"Yes," Syrian agreed. "You might be right about him."

"What's that?" Kirsdona asked. "What are you thinking, Bing? What's wrong with him?"

"I don't know," Bing said as he let out his breath. "It's just a feeling. But I don't believe it's anything we need to concern ourselves with now."

And then Patrick did look, and wished that he hadn't. Sin was noticeably larger, now coming up to Patrick's waist. It was if he was growing even as they watched him.

"Ok, so what happened to the alligators?" Kirsdona asked as she looked from Bing, to the boar, and then back to Bing.

"Yeah. What happened anyway?" Patrick asked. "What did that alligator say there at the end?"

Melanbach turned and looked at the boar, his expression one of uncertainty.

"'I have met who I have become,'" Melanbach said to Patrick. "That is what that creature said before he died."

"What did he mean by that?" Patrick asked silently.

"It is a saying that I have heard only a few times before in my life. It was told to me in a story that my descendants used to tell us when we were young. It was told to keep us in line. To scare us into behaving.

"En meterto sun 'e rezer loucot. That if you become what you should not, then what you have become will one day come for you."

The entire group, plus the remainder of the rats that had now caught up with them, all turned and stared at the white creature.

"Ok, so is someone going to tell me what happened to the alligators?" Kirsdona asked in a more demanding tone this time.

"What is he?" Beagel asked quietly.

"I'm not sure," Bing responded as he walked over and began to stroke the boar's face.

"I'm sure glad he's on our side," Patrick said.

A faint smile creased Melanbach's face. "That is, if he is truly on anyone's side."

Patrick walked over and knelt in front of the boar, the animal not looking anything like the monster Patrick imagined he'd seen a little while ago.

"I suppose he did save my life."

Melanbach moved over beside Patrick and Sin, lifting himself up onto his hind legs. He took a moment, looking deeply into the face of the white animal as if he was remembering something from his past.

"Did he, my friend?" Melanbach asked. "Or did he just take theirs?"

Patrick was about to ask a question, but couldn't form the words to fit. He stood and turned, surveying the group in its entirety.

"Hey, how did you guys get away from the mice? It doesn't look like anyone even got hurt."

Beagel turned to him and smiled wickedly, Patrick's eyes meeting with the wiry rat.

"We were lucky. They were just an early patrol. If we'd come across an entire legion of the bugs we wouldn't be having this conversation."

"And assuredly," Melanbach interjected, "they have sent word back to their leaders. Now that they have a general idea as to where we are they will soon send out the bulk of their army to hunt us down and kill us. We had better get moving. We don't have much further to go."

Kirsdona was now fit to be tied, her questions going unanswered.

"You don't mean to tell me that he ate them, do you? Because that's just not possible."

"Calm down, Kirsdona," Bing said as he walked by her. "Now is not the time for this. I believe the reasoning behind the questions you ask is going to be hard to fathom for all of us."

Kirsdona turned and watched as the boar began to position itself again behind Patrick.

"And to think you had me protecting that thing, when it should have been the other way around."

Melanbach hurriedly reassembled both rats and animals, and the entire group began to move on in their initial direction.

Patrick soon found himself once again next to Kirsdona as they walked. The great cat inching her way closer and closer to him, so close that her shoulder rubbed up against his.

"Don't think I didn't see you back there, either," she purred in his ear.

"What?"

"The light."

"What light? What are you talking about?"

"Don't play dumb with me, kid. I know what I saw. And I think that quite a few others saw as well."

Patrick walked along in silence for a bit, pondering what his next words would be.

"I don't know, Kirsdona. It was just another one of those 'things.' I don't know what they are, or why they keep happening."

"Well, keep it under your tongue. The rats are already suspicious as to why you are here. I don't think they would take kindly knowing that you have some sort of 'gift.' It might really spook them. And we need them to keep their wits and get us through."

Patrick nodded, and then followed her movements as she quickened her pace and distanced herself from him.

They made their way deeper and deeper under the city, Beagel and Melanbach each explaining how far they had traveled and how much further they had to go.

Many hours later, when they had reached a point where a giant number 18 was painted black on the wall next to a rusted door, Melanbach turned to the animals and looked relieved.

"Well, we have made it. Once you go through that door you should follow the stairs that lead up to the street level exit. There is an old human school across the roadway. Go through the main entrance of the school and then follow the green flooring that will lead you out the back. You should be free and clear from that point on. About a hundred yards behind the school is where the forest begins. You won't have any trouble once you get to that point."

"We thank you," Bing said as he extended his wing to Melanbach. "I hope we didn't cause you too much trouble. I am fearful, though, that you will have troubles with the mice on your way back once they discover that we have made it through safely."

"Do not worry," Melanbach said, raising an eyebrow. "I had most of my kind making their way to this point anyhow. We'll have ample support on our return trip."

"That's good. We wish you well, then."

"And you the same," Melanbach said as he bowed. He then turned to Patrick.

"I do not know what keys you hold in your possession, human, that will prevent the catastrophe that is taking place all around us. But I dearly hope that you use whatever you have at your disposal to help you live long and to triumph in your pursuits. Farewell."

And with that the animals said their goodbyes and proceeded up the abandoned stairwell.

The door at the top opened with a rusty squeal, the morning sun coming at them in such a way that it disoriented their vision as they emerged.

"Well, there's the school," Patrick said as he pointed to the brick building across the way.

"Yes," Bing nodded. "And let's move quickly. I do not like the fact that we are not clear yet of the dangers that this place holds. Once we are in the cover of the forest, I will feel a good deal better."

Patrick readily agreed. He felt exposed, an almost nakedness running across the street. His initial reaction at first seeing the city yesterday had made him want to wander in and out of the gigantic metropolis, exploring as he wished. It had given him that feeling of wonder and excitement inside like he was a little kid again.

But now, with everything that had taken place in the last twenty four hours, all that he wanted to do was to get as far away from this place as possible, his head continuing to turn behind him, hoping he wasn't going to see anything that had followed him from below.

The group moved hurriedly across the street and soon found themselves moving up the long concrete steps leading up to the school's entrance. Two ornamental concrete lions stood on either side of the steps. As the animals passed by them Patrick watched as each give a wary eye in that direction.

Two sets of double doors, with all four doors fully open, stood before them. It was as if the school had been expecting them and eagerly awaited their arrival.

As Patrick moved through the open doors he figured that a quick jaunt through the school and then out the back would put everything behind them. But as they made their way through the entrance they immediately came to a halt as a large metal device blocked any further advancement.

"What is that thing?" Bing asked.

It took a few seconds to register, but Patrick soon enough figured it out. He had seen them at airports before, but never in a school. He'd heard that some schools had them installed, but he'd never seen one first hand.

"It's a metal detector," he said as he reached over and touched it, the green painted metal feeling cold and isolated. "It looks like it's still on."

"So what's it do?" several of them asked at once.

"It's to make sure that none of the kids that come to school are able to bring a gun or knife in with them. Guns and knives are made of metal. So this machine can tell if someone tries to bring one with them."

Patrick heard his own words and froze with the realization of what this meant. If he walked through the machine with the gun then he would surely be discovered. His fears of what the animals—especially Bing—would say quickly came to the surface, and he slyly took a casual step backward.

"How does it work?"

"It sort of takes a picture of their body," Patrick said as he took a deep breath. "It can see all the way through you."

As he was explaining this, Patrick watched as Kirsdona was taking several steps away from the machine herself.

"It's not dangerous. It's safe. People go through them all the time," Patrick said, trying to reassure them.

But Kirsdona did not seem as confident as Patrick did in his explanation, and she continued to remain in her spot.

Syrian sighed loudly and pushed his way to the front.

"If the boy says that it's safe, then that's enough for me. Let's move on with it. We don't have much time for debate. I'll be the first to go."

Syrian walked right up to the machine, passed under the overhang, and then on through to the other side. It looked as if he was holding his breath as he did so, but once he was through he turned and readily encouraged the rest to follow.

"See, it's fine. Nothing happened."

Sin walked up to the machine and bumped into the side of it. He righted himself, sniffed the air, and then followed Syrian's scent through the opening to the other side as well.

"Well, this seems simple enough," Bing said as he began his way through.

He was followed quickly followed by Dog, the golden dog's tail tucked underneath it as he went.

They all turned and looked at Kirsdona.

"There's really nothing to it, Kirsdona," Bing explained. "Patrick is right. I didn't feel a thing."

"Me neither," Syrian said.

Kirsdona took a few steps closer, but continued to stay clear of entering the detector in front of her.

"Are you sure this won't hurt my body?" she asked as she continued to look over the machine.

"It's fine. Please, come on. We have to go," Bing said impatiently.

"You're sure? I mean absolutely sure?"

Patrick could sense Kirsdona's overwhelming fear, but couldn't understand it.

"You are one freaky cat, you know that," Patrick said as he moved over next to her. "Here, I'll walk through it with you. There's really nothing to it."

Patrick knew that the alarm would go off once he entered the machine, but he decided that once he had gotten everyone through then perhaps he could best explain it away as the machine experiencing a glitch or mechanical failure of some nature. But he needed to get Kirsdona through first.

Kirsdona let out a long sigh. "It's just that you said that this machine can see into my body, right?"

"Yeah, so what?"

"It's just that I have to make sure that it can't hurt anything in my body."

"You haven't got anything in your body that's different than ours," Bing said, exhausted. "And each of us went through it ok. What's the point of all of this?"

Kirsdona began to pace back and forth. "Well . . . yeah, I kind of do have something different. I'm carrying a cub."

The shock of the revelation penetrated the room like an explosion.

"WHAT?!" was all that Patrick could say, his mouth hanging open in shock.

"Oh, no," came from both Syrian and Bing.

Only Dog seemed the least surprised, his tail wagging wildly as he pronounced forward, "That's. Great. News!"

Kirsdona smiled meekly at the golden retriever, "Thanks."

Bing rushed back through the machine.

"When did you find this out?" he asked.

"I've known since before we first set out. Remember I said that I had some business to attend to before I arrived at the barn. Well, that business was me trying to figure out if I should go on this little excursion or not. I finally came to the conclusion that

I'm so early in my pregnancy that I don't think that it will matter one way or another. And so far I haven't had any problems with it. But that was before I knew that I had to walk through this human machine. That's where my reservations are coming from. Now do you understand?"

Patrick's expression of shock slowly slid from his face as his understanding became evident.

"That's not a problem, Kirsdona," he said as he shook his head. "Pregnant humans walk through the machines all the time. It won't hurt your baby."

"You're sure?"

"Absolutely."

With Patrick and Bing beside her, and Sin, Dog and Syrian on the other side of the detector, Kirsdona finally made her decision, took one deep breath, and began her advance through the machine.

"And you won't feel . . ."

And then the metal detector alarm went off, a large red warning light flashing overhead.

BEEP! BEEP! BEEP! BEEP!

"What the . . . ?!" Patrick said as he was startled by the alarm, his head zig zagging all about, trying to look over the machine to determine what was happening.

Kirsdona, startled so badly by the explosion of noise from the machine (and only half way through) leapt the remainder of the way in such a rush that she knocked Syrian to the floor.

"What happened?" Bing asked as he looked to Patrick.

"I don't know? She can't have any metal on her. The machine must be nuts!"

"Can't you shut that blasted racket off?" Syrian screamed over the beeping.

"I don't know how."

Kirsdona rushed back to the exit point of the machine.

"You said that it wouldn't hurt me!"

"It didn't, did it?"

"Well . . . no," she thought for a moment, "But what the heck is going on?"

"Patrick, please shut that noise off!" Bing demanded. "If anyone should hear that racket they'll know we're here for sure!"

"I'm trying! I'm trying! I just don't know how it went off. There's no way that she has . . ."

And then it came to him. He closed his eyes and remembered the bullet. The bullet that Kirsdona took back at the place where the people were burning the fields. She had dived in front of the shot and saved his life. That's what the detector must have seen.

Patrick furiously searched and searched for how to shut the metal detector off when he finally came to the simplest of solutions. He found the electric cord and with a great pull, yanked the plug out from the wall.

The last BEEP! echoed down the halls—and then silence.

"Thank goodness," Syrian said with a gasp.

Patrick threw the cord to the floor and rejoined the group.

"I know what it is," Patrick said as he pointed to the tiger. "The bullet in her butt. Remember? That's got to be what set the detector off."

"You're kidding?" the tiger said as a scowl came over her face. "Just great. How nice. The gift that keeps on giving. I want to thank you humans for inventing such a wonderful device. It's really serving us quite well."

Bing made his way over to the great cat. "But you're ok, that's the important thing. You should have told us about this from the beginning, Kirsdona. There's no way you're going to continue."

"Oh brother, here it comes," Kirsdona said as she rolled her eyes. "Blah. Blah. Blah."

"He's right," Syrian added.

"Not you, too!"

"In your condition, there is no way that you can see this through to the end. The risks are too great. We could all die at any moment, and you now have much more important things to attend to. You need to go back for the sake of your cub."

Patrick watched and listened to the back and forth argument that was taking place, but all the while becoming more and more aware that to his left Dog was once again doing his "No wait, not bees" routine. The animal's tail sticking straight out behind it, his head erect and listening to something that no one else was. Patrick began to have a sick feeling rise up in his gut.

Oh no.

"Hey, guys! Guys!" Patrick interrupted loudly and pointed at Dog.

The conversations ended suddenly, and a heavy silence fell as all eyes were directed to the animal.

"What is it, boy," Patrick whispered, trying to get the dog's attention.

But the animal didn't have to respond, for before he could even turn to make a gesture as to what he knew, they all heard it together.

It was the sound they thought they would never have to hear. A sound they thought they had evaded.

The sound was a million mice.

And it was coming from inside the school house walls.

Chapter 18

Mouse Traps

The horse had ridden hard for more than half the day without breaking stride, and the inside of Dan's legs were chapped and bruised from the exhausting ride. He thought for sure that the horse was going to tire sooner or later and allow him—and the horse—a much needed break. But no, the horse seemed to be determined to keep up its pace and would not be deterred from its task, continuing its hard ride until the sun had set low in the evening sky.

Finally, without warning, when Dan had just about reached his breaking point, the horse pulled up and stopped next to a small group of trees that were standing alone in a vacant field. Dan noticed right away that the trees seemed distant and out of place in the wide grassy plain. Another horse was there, a large black stallion that stood at least a head taller than the horse Dan was on. The dark horse was leisurely munching on the underbrush and wild grasses that were nearby. The horse that Dan was on then whinnied loudly and shook its head.

"What? What's the matter?"

The horse then kicked a little and shook his head once more.

The realization came quick to Dan.

"Oh, ok. You want me off."

Dan swung his legs over the horses' back, stumbled as his feet hit the ground, and then landed with a thud on his backside. It became painfully obvious to him that his legs had become so numb from the riding that they couldn't support his weight.

As Dan laid there trying to catch his breath, the horse that had been grazing underneath the trees casually walked over and seemed to laugh.

"Oh, I know. Laugh at the human who can't stand. Yeah, I guess it's pretty funny," he said with a scowl. Dan stretched, and then began rubbing up and down the length of his legs trying to get back some circulation.

The horse that delivered him then walked over, nudged the horse that was beside Dan, and took off, returning in the direction that they had just came.

"Don't you guys ever take a break?" he asked, surprised by the horse's actions.

The new horse then whinnied as the first had, and bucked.

Dan pulled himself up slowly, his legs feeling as if he was trying to steady himself on toothpicks. He leaned against the horse for a moment, waiting for the great beast to lower itself for him to get on. The horse turned and looked at Dan, a small suggestion of a smile crossing its long face.

"If you think for a moment that I can jump high enough to get on your back, then you're going to be standing there for a long time, friend," Dan explained frankly.

But then the horse seemed to sense the meaning of Dan's words and lowered itself as the other horse had done earlier.

Once Dan was seated, the black horse rose and began to move at once.

Dan noticed right away that this horse was definitely different. For one, it was much faster than the first horse, its stride much longer and more powerful. And second, it didn't stay on the course that the first had taken at all. Unlike the first, who had steered clear from anything man made, this horse soon found a highway, turned on it, and began making its way up the road. The horse drove hard over the terrain for endless hours as Dan lost track of time, the wind whipping his face so fiercely in that his eyes seemed to water on end.

It wasn't long until Dan became aware of the direction they were traveling. He just caught sight of the sign as the horse soared past it, the speed with which the stallion was traveling making everything go by in a blink. But it was definitely a sign that brought joy to his heart. It was the signpost that read Chicago was only fifteen miles ahead.

Dan had wanted to stick to his initial plan of trying to find a train track along the way, but as to how he was going to communicate that to the horse, he had no clue. It didn't matter though. With the speed in which they were making time, surely he would have the jump on Patrick and the animals anyhow.

It was just about time for morning to break, a small half moon still hanging over the horizon to his left, when Dan and the horse first entered the outskirts of the city. The early morning air was surprisingly warm so late into the year, the mosquitoes and moths still out in abundance. Dan was stunned to see that there were still spurts of electricity running through the city, thinking that with so much time having passed since the plague began that surely the unmanned power plants would have shut down by now. Most of the shops and office buildings were dark, but every now and then, dotted along the sidewalks a hesitant glow, or overhead neon sign, would sparkle. Dan caught the Starbucks off to his left and wondered just how long had it been since he'd had one of those. His fragile mind teased his senses and whispered to him that he could almost smell the aroma coming from inside.

But what snapped Dan's attention back to reality was a smell that he knew was all too real. It was the overwhelming smell of death that hung over the city like the underside of a rotting pumpkin. He put the back of his hand up to his nose to try and block the rankness from reaching inside, but there just wasn't a place where he could find relief.

The horse's cloppity-clop steps echoed loudly in the noiseless streets that they traveled, the feeling of isolation growing fiercer with every advancing step.

The horse was moving in a direction that only it was aware. Dan had tried to pull on the horse's mane in one direction or another to see if he could steer the beast, but it ignored the hard tugs and continually moved in the same direction.

The horse traveled slowly along its path, making its way through the expansive city street by street as if looking for something it knew was here, but wasn't quite sure where it could find it. Dan guessed that the horse was looking for Patrick. He could feel the anticipation rising inside of him as he felt he was getting closer and closer to finding his son.

Then the horses' pace began to quicken, the animal snorting several times.

"What is it boy? What's wrong?" Dan asked as he rubbed the side of the animal's neck.

But the horse definitely seemed spooked, and no amount of consoling seemed to calm it down.

The horse would gallop and then slow, repeating the order several times before finally coming to a complete stop.

Dan felt an overwhelming sense that made him wish that he could speak the horses language, for as they stood there, the horse and him both silent, he could tell that something was wrong, but as to what it was he hadn't a clue.

And then he saw something that surprised him, it looked so out of place. He wasn't sure if it was just the way the dawn was approaching, the light somehow playing tricks with his focus, or if he had truly lost his mind. Because it looked like a wave was coming down the street towards him. A white foamy wave of water like you would see at the beach, coming in his direction. Only as it got closer this wave never seemed to collapse on itself the way water will as it makes its way across the sand. In fact, this wave seemed to be picking up speed.

The black stallion didn't hesitate, for it knew what Dan did not. It bolted from its spot and escaped down a side street to their right. Dan hung on for dear life as the horse moved like a shot. He could barely turn around to look behind him with the horse's momentum so great, but when he did he immediately realized his error in believing that what was coming at them was water. His face folded into horror as the horse quickly outdistanced them from the astounding sight that was coming down the street behind them.

It was mice.

Lots of mice.

Patrick reacted on instinct.

He instantly grabbed up Bing in his arms and rushed out one of the doors to his right.

He turned in time to see the others moving frantically behind him, not waiting for any instructions to be given.

The sound that came from inside the school was death. Patrick's ears filled with the noise as the deafening roar of mice tore from their places of hiding inside the walls and surged outward. They spilled out in a mass of teeth and hatred and moved in only one direction—towards him.

Patrick ran as fast as he could, only looking down for the time it took for him to make it over the steps below so that he wouldn't stumble to his death. When he did lift his eyes he was terrified to see thousands and thousands of rats moving to form a line in front of him.

For a moment Patrick thought that the rats had double crossed the group, that they were now going to prevent Patrick and his friends from running away. But that notion was quickly dispelled as he spotted Melanbach and Beagel's grim faces along the front lines. The rats immediately opened up a path for him and the animals to escape through, and then instantly collapsed the gap to protect their backs.

Patrick continued to run, only slowing for a moment as he and Bing turned around to watch in horror as the rats and mice finally collided with one another.

In Patrick's mind the magnitude of the battle could only be thought of exactly as Beagel had described it earlier.

They were like bugs.

It was as if two separate ant colonies were waging war against each other, the mass of bodies pulsating together making it difficult to differentiate who was who.

Patrick remembered how he had kicked over many an ant hill in his day, and had watched as the mass of swarming insects would come out of their holes in a fury, trying to find the destroyer who had breached their domain. And now, as he looked out upon the battle that was taking place, the mice did indeed resemble that same swarming mass.

"What happened?" Bing yelled out to Melanbach who quickly made his way over to where the group now stood, hiding themselves around the corner of a building.

"As soon as we gathered our forces to make our way back, we compared notes and it soon became evident that none of us had encountered any of the mice in the proportions we expected to find. They had baited us, and laid a trap. Before we could get back to you we heard the siren go off and knew that you were in danger."

"What do we do?" Bing asked urgently.

"I'm afraid you are on your own. I have a responsibility to defend my kind. But it is obvious that they have cut off most routes of escape."

"We've got to get out of here, and not by our legs!" Syrian screamed to Patrick over the squealing death match that was going on behind them. "Can you operate another one of those machines? The vee-hick-calls?"

"Yeah, I think so," Patrick said as he turned and looked at the smallish cars that were nearby. "But we need something big, not one of these. Something that we can all fit into."

Even though the rat reinforcements were still filing out of the drains and side streets (and numbering in the thousands) the mice were just too many in number. They were overwhelming the rats just in sheer volume and were now starting to push through the front lines that the rats had established.

"I'm not going to stand here and watch this massacre," Kirsdona growled, her attention focused on the battle at hand. "They helped us. The least we can do is lend a hand."

"Yes," Dog snarled. "I. Have. Eaten. Many. Mice. In. My. Time."

"No!" Melanbach railed at them. "If you engage these creatures you will be making a mistake that will cost you your lives. They will overwhelm you, and then they will consume you. There are just too many. We are making the sacrifice so that you can continue. Now go!"

With his words still lingering in the air, Melanbach turned and launched himself into the battle. Patrick watched as Melanbach, Beagel, and the other, much larger rats would break the backs of the smaller mice with just once bite. Their fury and size a daunting mixture that kept a good majority of the mice at bay, but even Patrick he could see that they were just no match for the amount of mice that kept flooding from the school. As soon as Melanbach would kill five of the mice, seven would then take the place of the five that had fallen.

"Patrick, we've got to move!" Bing shrieked at him.

Patrick pulled his attention away from the battle and knew what he had to do.

He began running from car to truck to car, trying to find any vehicle that had human remains still sitting in the driver's seat. If there were remains, then there was a good chance that the keys would still be there as well.

After hurriedly checking more than ten cars, he finally found one with the keys still inside. He opened the door, tried to scrape as much human residue and clothing that he could from the vinyl seat, and seated himself behind the wheel. But he quickly realized that there were going to be two problems. One, it was a Ford Escort. It was four doors, but it appeared way too small to fit all of them inside. And second, it was a stick shift, not an automatic. In all the times that he and his father had practiced driving, Patrick had never attempted to drive a car that you had to shift and drive at the same time. Push the gas pedal and go was all that he knew.

The animals were jumping up onto Patrick's lap, pushing their way into the Escort in a frenetic mass of arms and legs, when he realized why they were all in such a frantic state—the mice had already broken through the lines set by the rats.

Patrick rose from inside the car, his heart sinking as he searched the battle lines for any sign of Melanbach or Beagel, but finding none.

"Get back in! What are you doing? Get back in!" Syrian yelled to Patrick from inside the car.

Patrick looked around and found that somehow, miraculously, all of his friends had managed to find a place inside. All except for one.

"Where's Sin?" Patrick asked frantically.

"I don't know," Bing replied, now realizing that the razorback wasn't with them. "He was right behind us!"

From where he stood Patrick hurriedly searched the streets for the boar, but was hard pressed to locate anything with the place now so completely saturated with the warring mice and rats.

"There. He. Is!" Dog responded, pointing with his nose.

And then they all saw him. Or what was left of him. He was covered in a mountain of mice. It was so hard to pick him out because of the blending of his fur with that of the mice that they were lucky to see him at all.

They all watched, a feeling of anguish pouring over them, as the boar tried his best to move underneath the weight of the horde on top of him.

"Oh, God! What do we do?" Patrick asked without taking his eyes from his friend.

"Get in, Patrick! If you want to help him, then get in the car now!" Bing ordered.

Kirsdona, with her enormous size, had taken the entire back seat to herself, with the rest somehow crammed into the front. The only problem now was that there wasn't much room for Patrick to fit. And, as he turned one last time to look towards the battlefront, he came to realize something he wished that he hadn't. The mice now knew where he was. It was like watching a dam break forward, the onslaught of mice that came at him caused him to lose his breath.

That's when he felt the pull of someone behind him, tugging him into the car.

"Patrick, get inside now!" they all screamed at him.

He jammed himself in up against Syrian, but half of his body still hung outside of the car. He tried and tried to pull the door closed, but his hip kept preventing him from getting it fully shut.

The mice were only fifty feet away at best, Patrick's fears of being eaten alive by the 'bugs' growing with each passing second, when Syrian reached out one of his long, massive arms across Patrick's chest, grabbed a hold of the door handle and pulled it hard with a grunt. The door panel collapsed around Patrick's hip with a crack, and finally closed.

It was like a hailstorm the way the mice came at the car.

Whap whap whap whap whapwhapwhapwhapwhapwhapwhap!

Patrick was horrified to find that the car was actually teetering from side to side with the colossal way in which the mice threw themselves at the car.

"Let's go!" Kirsdona yelled from behind him.

Patrick fumbled a moment trying to locate the ignition, then turned the keys. The Escort bucked at his efforts, but would not start. He tried to start it again, but only got the same results.

"What's wrong?" someone asked inside the car, but at this point Patrick hadn't a clue who was talking.

Then he remembered to push in the clutch. His left foot mashed the pedal down with a thud and he turned the key again. This time the car whirred into life. But he let out the clutch too soon and the car sputtered, coughed, and then died on the spot. The momentum with which it kicked threw all the occupants forward and launched most of the mice from the car. It felt like a broken amusement park ride.

Patrick's sweaty face turned to look at the animals that were squeezed in around him.

"Sorry! I'm doing the best I can!"

"Then do better!" came a reply. There was no mistake as to who's voice that remark belonged.

He went again with the clutch and then the keys, the car coming alive once more. This time he pushed on the gas pedal, the engine revving loud. He let out the clutch slowly and the car finally began to move . . .

. . . backwards.

In fact, with the way the Escort was positioned, the group was now actually going towards the advancing mice horde.

Patrick reactively took his feet off both pedals at once and the car again bucked and then died.

Patrick swallowed hard and initiated the process over again. This time he put the stick shift into the 'one' position to get it to go forward.

The car's engine screamed as Patrick would not allow his foot to ease off of the gas pedal in any way, and they began to move forward.

Then they noticed something else that gave them all a moment of great panic. They could see that some of the mice had made it part of the way into the car, sitting just behind the plastic air vents, trying to rip and bite their way through.

Dog began to bark and snap as the tiny white creatures made their immediate presence known.

And then the engine began to cough and sputter again, Patrick imagining that the mice were now throwing their bodies into the engine's machinery of belts and pulleys.

"How do we go faster?" Bing asked from somewhere to Patrick's right.

Being that Patrick had never driven a stick shift before he had forgotten to change gears, the car still moving in first gear. The attempt was more difficult than the actual deed as Patrick feared that he was going to stall the car again, so he never removed his foot from the gas pedal. The car kicked like a wild mule each time that he did this, but the car finally started to speed up. Just when they started to get rolling a little faster with each change of gears was about the same time when all hell broke loose.

The first mouse made it into the car.

The horse swerved and twisted its way from street to street, trying to steer clear of the mice.

Dan wasn't sure what was going on with the little creatures, but with the way they had come at him moments ago, he wasn't so sure he wanted to stop and ask them for directions.

He turned behind and tried to see if anything had been able to follow, but with the speed in which the horse was moving he felt hard pressed to believe that anything could keep up with them.

Anything, except maybe a car.

As Dan tried to listen to what was going on all around him he began to notice that he heard some sort of engine in the distance. Well, something motorized anyway. He chuckled to himself, wondering if his hearing was now playing tricks with him in his isolation.

But the horse seemed to be running parallel to the awkward sound, whatever it might be coming from, and not moving towards it.

Every so often Dan would catch a glimpse of something down the long running streets, his sight stretching as far as he could see in hopes of spotting what the horse was tracking.

And then the horse took off again, this time running as hard as it had before. Dan clung to the horse with all his strength as the horse lowered its head and propelled itself even faster still. When Dan raised his eyes he could see what the horse was moving towards.

It was the mice.

But why? he wondered with a gasp.

The horse was closing the gap between themselves and mice with heartbreaking speed.

And then he realized the why. The mice had entrapped them. The horse had tried to move cautiously street by street trying to avoid coming in contact with the mice, but somehow the mice must have slowly closed down each point of escape. Dan could see that the tiny creatures were now pouring from every side street and shop in all directions.

But why was the horse storming head on to greet them?

But before Dan could entertain another thought something in his gut told him to hold on, and at that moment he began to grasp exactly what the horse was going to try and do—it was going to try and leap over them at their weakest point.

And that's just what it did.

At the center point where it seemed that all the mice where converging, the horse launched itself over the smallest point of the blockade. The animal's might carried it far past the convergence point, and up and over a great many mice.

As it landed the great beast stumbled slightly as it squished a large amount of mice under it hooves, their remains causing the animal to slip as if it were on ice.

The mice seemed to have no answer for what had just taken place, but instantly regrouped and began their pursuit. A few mice actually attached themselves to the horse, their teeth sinking deep into its hide. But with the sheer force of the horse's gallop they were easily cast aside.

The horse took a hard left and stormed down a vacant street. Dan watched as basketball hoops and clothes drying on wires zipped past his ears. And then the horse took another left and Dan could see the back of a school in the distance. But as they approached it was clear that they could not make any progress in that direction. Dan was bewildered as he watched what appeared to be a fight between thousands of large gray rats and some of the same horde of white mice that were attacking him.

And then he saw the car. It looked amusing at first, the thousands of mice all clinging to it as it moved. But then Dan felt horrified, wondering what the person in the car must be going through with such an onslaught taking place.

The horse was continuing to charge in that direction when Dan thought that the person in that car needed help. If someone was alive then Dan wanted to try and keep them that way as best he could.

"We need to get the mice away from that car," he spoke into the horse's ear, not sure if anything more than the compassion in his voice was getting through. "If you can ride past them then perhaps they'll have an easier go of it with the mice chasing after us."

Dan knew that with the speed that this horse possessed there wasn't much that was man made or otherwise that could keep up with it.

It began subtlety, the horse seeming to nod as it ran. But then the two of them became as one in their purpose. The horse charging even harder at the mice, veering at the last possible moment away from their death.

The first mouse came through the air vent, its mouth bloodied from the biting it had to complete to get past the plastic louvers. But it made no mistake about its intentions—it went straight for Patrick's throat.

All the animals lunged for it, causing Patrick to swerve as they threw themselves in his direction. But Syrian grabbed the mouse and broke it's neck without a thought. Then other mice began to enter, launching themselves through the broken vent, this time with Dog snapping them up in his powerful jaws, crushing the life out of them as they came.

Syrian found the floor mats and quickly stuffed them into the air vents temporarily blocking the passage way of the mice.

"Patrick, can you see Sin?" Bing asked quickly.

It was almost impossible to see out of the front windows with the mice covering the windshield like a furry white rug, but Patrick turned on the windshield wipers and plowed the tiny beasts from their places. But, just as Beagel had forecast, when one mouse went down several more were there to take its place. As soon as one swipe of the wiper blade came across to clear his view the glass would cloud over again as hundreds, possibly thousands more were there to clog his vision. The tiny beasts began gnawing and biting at the window desperately trying to get through to their prey.

"I see him! He's over to our right."

"Then go towards him if you can."

"But how are we going to get him in the car?" Syrian asked. "We can't open the vee-hick-call back up, can we? At least not without letting the mice inside!"

Bing pushed himself up next to the windshield, his little wings leaning against the dashboard. He was trying hard to get a glimpse through the mass of small bodies, his little head moving back and forth for a view of Sin.

"Keep moving as you're going, Patrick. I see him. He's just ahead of us."

Bing glanced over at Patrick.

"Can you go any faster?"

"I'm trying," Patrick responded, his head shaking back and forth, "but it's like were driving through paste."

"Why do you need him to go faster?" Syrian asked. "How are we going to stop and get Sin if we're going faster?"

Bing swallowed hard.

"Because I want Patrick to run into him."

Everyone, including Patrick, turned to look at Bing as if he had lost his mind.

"I'm not going to hit him!" Patrick said, alarmed. The car was now just circling around, making an arc back to the spot where Sin remained. "I'll kill him!"

"No you won't. I don't think that you could if you wanted too. We've got to get those mice off of him. Once he's shaken most of the mice from himself, he'll be ok. He's just completely consumed with them at the moment. I believe he's trying to eat his way through, and it looks like its just too much, even for him."

The words that Bing was saying just didn't make any sense to Patrick.

Drive into Sin?! And it wouldn't kill him?

Whatever Bing was trying to communicate was getting lost in the translation.

"Please, Patrick, just do as I say! Hurry! If I'm correct about what I suspect, then you won't even put a scratch on him."

"'If'? That's the best you got?" Kirsdona growled from the backseat.

But Patrick trusted Bing, more so than he trusted just about anyone else in his life. With his teeth clenched together he aimed the car and proceeded to do as instructed. The Escort began building up speed, the speedometer almost at forty five, when Patrick gripped the steering wheel as if his life depended on it. The windshield wipers made another slow, choppy pass just giving him enough time to see the mound that was Sin get thumped by the front end of the car.

The hood of the car crumpled slightly at the impact as the Escort slowly skidded to the right, Patrick doing his best to maintain control.

Sin skidded away and to their left, and looked unharmed, with the mice showering off to their right. As the mice were blasted from Sin the scene reminded Patrick of a snow globe. It was as if he had just shaken the little ball of water and now the tiny little mice that had once covered Sin were falling all around, resembling snowflakes as they fell.

The delivery of the car hitting Sin had a two fold affect.

First, most of the mice that were still attached to the car were jolted from the areas that they tried to cling to. And second, it appeared that Bing was right. They could see that Sin was now up and moving towards them, sniffing the air with that strange little smile that always seemed to be on his face.

"How can that be? I know I plastered him pretty good. He shouldn't be able to get up that quickly."

But Bing only shook his head. "I think that the mice took the brunt of the hit for the most part. But I think anyone would be hard pressed to cause harm to that creature."

"How are we going to get him in the car?"

"We aren't. We need to go now. He'll be ok."

"We're just going to leave him?"

"Yes. But please don't worry about him. I have a feeling he'll manage to catch up with us. And I trust it won't be too long, either. Now go, before those blasted creatures begin their assault again!"

Kirsdona looked out of the rear window, a strange look of amusement across her face.

"He isn't like any boar that I've ever come across," she said as she smiled mysteriously.

Bing turned and glanced at her with the same expression.

"And you likely will never see again."

The mice that Dan believed they had left behind them in the side street had taken a short cut and were now filing out of the street just in front of them. Dan knew that the horse would beat them to the point of entry, and then make its way down to the fields just back behind the school. He had no way of knowing how far the open spaces in that part of the land would stretch, but he figured that once they made it out of the confines of the city there wasn't any way that the mice could keep up. No matter how many they had on their side.

But as Dan looked over his shoulder for the one last look at the Escort, he saw something that made him feel both ill and exhilarated at the same time.

It was the black and orange stripes of an enormous tiger in the back seat of the car. He was shocked at first, wondering if he had imagined it. But then he looked again and knew what he saw was true.

Dan instantly knew that the tiger couldn't possibly be driving the car. In fact, he knew of no animal that could. And that left only one thing remaining in the vicinity (associating themselves with animals) that he knew of that could drive.

And that would be Patrick. His realization came at him like a hammer.

Dan screamed aloud, "No, we've got to go back! My son is back there!" But the horse was still doing its best to avoid being taken down by the mice, and didn't seem to be paying attention to the concerns of the human on his back.

The horse galloped on, continuing past a parking lot and then circling back, just skimming the edge of the school yard before heading into the woods.

Dan turned back again, but by the time that he did the car was out of sight.

"No! No! No!" he screamed in frustration.

His eyes began to water, not from the wind stinging his eyes this time, but rather from the torment he felt at being so close and yet losing his son once more.

As Patrick began to steer the car down the highway, and away from the horror behind them, he wondered aloud as to the fate of Melanbach and Beagel.

Everyone remained silent at the query, each lost in their own private thoughts as to what they imagined happened to the brave and valiant rats.

And just as they were making their way clear of the city limits, Patrick was startled as he caught a brief glimpse of a shadowy figure in his side view mirror. It was hard to tell if he was really seeing something, or if it was just a trick of the light and shadows. But just for the moment it did look like a man on a horse riding in the opposite direction from their current path.

Patrick wondered silently if it was Tye. He smiled to himself with the thought that if it indeed was him, then they again had bested the lunatic's plans. And if they could take nothing else away from what had just happened, then at least Patrick could hold onto that.

CHAPTER 19

The Devil's Tongue

They ran out of gas before an hour had even passed, the car sputtering and coughing, finally coming to a jerking halt in the middle of the highway.

The animals were totally relieved. The cramped confines of the car, plus the fact that Patrick would not allow anyone to open the windows or vents for fear that a few of the mice might be still clinging to the outside of the car, made conditions quite uncomfortable, to say the least.

Their exit was immediate, but their feelings of sadness and exhaustion allowed for no casual conversation as they moved from the car. Bing pointed in the direction they needed to begin, and they readily set off again without a word being spoken.

They walked as they had before, their grueling exercise continuing in the direction that they always seemed to find themselves following—North by Northwest.

They didn't talk very much as they walked either, their journey now consumed with so much death and commotion that they each seemed to enjoy the silence.

And they were tired. The hills that they climbed seemed steeper. The gravel that they walked over seemed sharper and more jagged. The length of the time that they walked without taking time for a break seemed more exhausting.

They found themselves in a quandary of trying to limit their approach to any more places that humans may dwell simply for the fact that it always seemed to bring them continuing problems. They needed food, and that was about the only reason that any of them could come up with that would cause them to venture into places where men used to live. But for the most part they kept to the original plan and made the most of their journey through the woods and hills and forests.

It wasn't long before the silence that they were carrying along began to weigh on their mood. It was as if they needed something to say to break the doldrums that they now found themselves, but the gloominess that was all around them made it difficult to offer anything worthy to say. It wasn't until they had traveled well into the afternoon, and were crossing an old, forgotten dirt road, that Dog brought up something that they all seemed to have forgotten.

"You. Haven't. Said. Anything. More. About. Your. Impending. Motherhood," he said, bright eyed and happy to once again bring up the subject.

Kirsdona glanced over at him with disdain, her expression speaking volumes as to the question that was asked of her.

"I was hoping that the point had been forgotten," she said coarsely. "What's to say, I'm going to be a mom. It happens."

"You don't seem so overjoyed about it," Syrian interjected.

"It's just that I wish it could have happened at a better time. Don't misunderstand, I'm happy, but it's just that with what's been going on . . ."

Bing nodded, "Yes, it does put a damper on things."

"To say the least."

"Have you thought anymore on what we briefly discussed?"

"What? The part about me leaving? Forget it. You're not getting rid of me that easily."

"But you're sure that you won't hurt the baby?" Patrick asked.

"It's called a cub," she responded, her voice tilting towards agitation. "Humans have babies, alright?"

"Sorry. So you're sure your cub won't get hurt?"

"It's still early. I'll be fine."

"Thought of any names?"

Kirsdona took a deep breath.

"No. Change the subject."

They walked a little ways further in silence, but Dog once again pierced the lull.

"Does. The. Father. Know?"

"Ok, now we're getting a little too personal. Can we just move on?"

Patrick began to laugh. It started small at first, like it was something just off in the distance. But then it began to build, slowly causing a contagious affect that went from Bing to Syrian to Dog. They all were trying to hold back a bad case of the giggles.

"What's so funny?" Kirsdona demanded.

"I'm just imagining who the father is," Patrick said as he busted out in laughter.

Syrian laughed so hard he snorted.

"Oh, the poor guy. He's probably at home preparing the nest even as we speak."

"Isn't that the female's job?"

"Exactly!"

And they all began laughing again. Everyone except Kirsdona.

"Alright, alright, enough with the jokes at my expense."

But Syrian motioned over to Patrick.

"I was thinking that it was that weasel . . . what was his name? The one at the barn . . ."

"Malard?"

"Yes! He's who I'm imagining the father is."

Even Kirsdona giggled slightly at that suggestion.

"Oh yes, my dear, dear Malard," Kirsdona smiled as she shook her head. "Yep, you guys have figured it out."

Patrick was laughing so hard he could barely stand.

"Yeah, and then when it's born you can name the cub 'Maldona.'"

They all laughed . . .

"Or 'Kirsdonalard.'"

. . . and laughed even louder.

They carried that laughter through the rest of the day until they found their nights rest. They were all still on edge, but the mood had been broken, and their nights sleep came a lot easier indeed.

On the second day after they had left Chicago and the mice, Patrick and the animals found themselves in a better mood than they had experienced in several days. They soon were caught up in relaxing talk, and they even played a game of tag with each other as they moved through the autumn like day. The leaves that clung to the trees were now brilliant yellows and oranges, with a few escaping the trees' grasp and lazily drifting down to the group as they traveled through the great forests.

As they walked on they soon found their way across a barren highway, littered only with a stationary van that had crashed against a guardrail. Bing and the others wanted to continue on around it without stopping, but Patrick's curiosity got the better of him.

"Come on," Kirsdona barked. "Whatever might be in there we don't need. Let's go."

"Just a minute," Patrick responded, agitated at her voice. "It'll only take a minute. I just want to see what's in here."

It was a white panel van with no lettering or markings on it that would cause it to stand out. The animals stood away from the van while Patrick approached. He swung the back doors open, half hopeful that he might find something to eat, the other half cautious at anything that could be potentially dangerous.

The doors opened with a groan due to the age of the van, Patrick finding only small cardboard boxes stacked from floor to ceiling inside, not even a square inch of breathing room separating each.

"What'd you find? Anything we can use?" Bing asked from ten feet away.

"Yeah, anything to eat?" Kirsdona asked as she began sniffing at something that was flattened and dead in the middle of the road.

The labels on the boxes were easy enough to read, Patrick relaxing his shoulders at his discovery, wishing that it had been something else.

"It's only hairspray," he said absently as he began to pull a few of the boxes out to see if that was all that the van held.

"Hairspray?" Dog asked as he moved up beside Patrick. "What. Is. Hairspray?"

Patrick only shook his head and laughed as he put the boxes back inside.

"It's nothing we can use. It's this stuff that my mom uses to keep her hair stiff. It's like spraying glue on your hair. The only thing I've ever used the stuff for is to blow up things."

Syrian walked over and watched as Patrick closed both of the doors.

"Blow things up? What do you mean? You don't blow up your hair do you?"

"No!" Patrick said as he giggled. "The spray comes in these cans. And the cans are under pressure. If you shoot them with a BB gun then they explode. It's pretty cool."

The animals acted as if they understood, but Patrick was pretty sure that they didn't have a clue as to what he was talking about.

"Does. It. Hurt. When. It. Explodes?"

Patrick laughed again, now making his way around to the front of the van.

"No. We'd stay pretty far away. My friends and I used to steal the old cans that were almost empty from our moms, and take them into the woods and shoot them off of old tree stumps. They'd make a pretty loud noise, that's for sure."

Patrick opened the cab door and began looking inside. Meanwhile, the animals had now moved past the truck, crossing into the grassy areas on the other side. Patrick was careful not to touch the now dried remains that were on the driver's side seat. He arched his body up and over to see if there was anything remaining in the glove compartment or in the pocket between the seats, but found nothing.

"Not even a lousy bag of peanuts," he said in disgust.

"Can we go now?" Kirsdona asked impatiently. "I'm starved. Because unless you've found a nice juicy lamb in there for me to dine upon, I suggest we continue in any direction that has food waiting for us at the end of it. Each and every one of you is starting to look mighty tasty at this point in time."

Patrick smiled as he closed the van door and began to move over with the others.

"Yeah, I was thinking the same thing," he said. "I was wondering what roasted tiger might taste like."

Dog and Bing each smiled as they began to make their way.

"Hey, now that's not even funny," Kirsdona said in surprise, slowly bringing up the rear.

"Yes it is," Patrick responded, laughing slightly.

"No. It's not."

"Yeah, it is."

"No."

Just past mid afternoon on that second day, as they made their way up a barren, stony hill—just as the journey had once again resumed its tedious and monotonous ways—they began to hear a whistling.

It was surprising at first, the group quickly dismissing it as the wind rifling through the trees to their west. But as they advanced higher and higher up the hill, they found that the sound became more distinct, and definitely carried a tune.

It was a pleasant sound, more flute-like and high pitched, and their steps were quickened as each was eager to find from where the sound was coming. But as they reached the summit of the trek upward, they found the one thing that they had never expected to see. The vision in front of them froze their hearts, and took all the wind from their lungs.

It was Tye.

The odd toad was sitting on a collection of rocks that formed a queer looking triangle, his lips perched together blowing out the tune that had brought them to this spot like an evil pied piper. The whistling stopped, and his head cocked to one side as he smiled.

"Well, well, well. Look what the cat has dragged in," he said in an unpleasant way. "No disrespect intended, dear lady."

Patrick was so surprised to see the man in front of him that he stood dumbstruck for the moment, his irrational fears getting the best of him. He couldn't speak, his tongue feeling as if it had swelled in his mouth. And he couldn't move, his limbs tingling as if they were rubbery and numb.

"Should I eat him now," the tiger asked as she stepped forward, "or should I just wound him so that he dies slowly and painfully?"

"Hold your line, Kirsdona. Do not advance on him," Bing said in warning.

A slow, methodical smile crept over his Tye's face.

"Always the pleasant kitty, aren't you, my dear. It is always such an honor to be in your presence. And I'm surprised that I don't hear anything more from the rest of you. What's the matter, mouse got your tongues?" Tye asked as he chuckled at his remark.

"Shut up," the venomous words flew past Patrick's lips before he even knew what he was saying.

"Oh, I see that your manners haven't improved from the last time that we spoke, master Brighton. But I don't believe I hear that many unpleasant squeaks or squawks coming from your friends. My dear boy, you do seem the sourpuss."

"Just shut up," Patrick replied, his voice low and unwavering. "You have nothing to say to any of us. There's nothing you can do here. There's nothing that you can do to me now."

"Oh," Tye's eyes brightened, "is that so?"

Patrick took a step back, now becoming alarmed at the sight in front of him.

"And what's happened to you anyway? You look really, really bad."

Tye seemed insulted.

"It's a mild transformation that is almost at its completion. You should be so lucky to experience what I am about to participate in."

As the animals looked on they realized that Patrick was right, for Tye's appearance had indeed gotten worse. His head had elongated and grown back, not a stitch of hair remaining. His legs looked shriveled and weak, as if they had never been used. His ears were now completely gone. And the five fingers he had on each hand had grown together to form three.

Patrick's mind raced back to an earlier time, a question tickling his brain.

"Hey, how can you talk to the animals? I didn't think you could understand them."

Tye smiled slyly, "I've learned."

Bing moved over to Patrick, his eyes never leaving Tye.

"Patrick, beware of engaging conversation with that being. And be careful what you say. He is merely playing a game with us. His is a great deceiver—a fox—and his words are aligned in deception."

"Yes," Syrian agreed. "He's trying to bait us. He wouldn't be here, and acting so calm, if he didn't already have the upper hand in some way."

"But I must say that you all are one remarkable assemblage," Tye continued. "To overcome what you have so far is amazing. I surely would have turned and ran home to my mommy and daddy a long time ago. But not you. No, you just keep moving onward and upward. And it is really quite annoying to my masters. You see, they are thoroughly upset with the situation as it stands. Well, I should say that they're quite upset at me. Being that I was the one that was supposed to insure that you didn't become the pain in the rump that you have become. And so, I have been instructed that I personally will handle the matter at hand . . . which is, that you are mine. You were placed in my possession, and these creatures stole you from me. And I want you back."

"You don't own me."

"Oh, but I do. You see, in the world of treachery and thieves, ownership consists of whichever scoundrel possessed the merchandise last. And seeing that I was the one who last . . ."

"Are you insane?" Patrick spit forward. "My father and mother . . . ."

And then Tye's complexion changed from one of a prankster, to that of a person on the edge of becoming a monster.

"My dear boy, do not take that tone with me any longer," he hissed, the Tye that Patrick knew all too well coming forward, "or I'll rip out that cute little tongue of yours and feed it to your pets."

Tye then closed his eyes, appearing as if he was trying to collect himself.

"And about your father and mother, well, I wouldn't worry about them for the time being. I shouldn't speak on the subject much longer, for it would be rude of me to speak ill of the dead."

"What?!" Patrick said, shocked at Tye's words. "No! I don't believe you."

Bing grabbed Patrick by his arm.

"Remember what I said. Do not listen to his treachery, for it will cause you to lose sight of the problem at hand."

Kirsdona turned back to the group, her anger near the point of rage.

"Why are we even having this conversation?! He's all alone. I could cut him down before his next breath."

"But to continue as I was," Tye began again, dismissing the cat with a yawn, "being that I was the last to possess ownership of the boy, then he belongs to me. The ways of trade in the world have changed."

"You talk about me like I was a thing. I'm still human in case you hadn't noticed. Not like you."

Bing stepped forward, trying to place himself between Patrick and Tye.

"Well then," the penguin began, "if ownership is what you're going by, then I guess that would make us the ones who are in possession of the property."

Tye thought for a moment.

"Well, yes, I can see your point, but I don't believe that any of you will be alive long enough to make the claim that you infer.

"You see, I have assembled a large amount of serpents just over the next ridge," he said as he pointed. "A rather large group, indeed. I will give you till the dawn of tomorrow's sun for you to surrender the boy to me, or I will use everything in my master's power to ensure that you won't see another dawn in this lifetime—or any other."

Patrick stood silent, still stunned by the revelation that Tye brought forward about his parents.

Could it be true? That they were both dead?

Patrick didn't want to believe any of what was being said. The only thing that had made this journey even the least bit bearable was the continuing thought of seeing his parents alive again.

"You do realize that isn't going to happen," Kirsdona snarled.

But Tye dismissed the venomous talk from the tiger and directed his gaze to Bing.

"I believe you, of all the creatures, know that I speak the truth on this subject, my friend penguin."

Bing stood silent as all the others turned towards him.

"What does he mean, Bing?"

But Bing lowered his eyes as if he was being tormented, then looked back up at Tye.

"I do not know how you possess the knowledge that you do, but be warned that sometimes the perception of knowledge is only that—what you perceive."

Tye smiled.

"I know what I know what I know. How I come across this knowledge is for my understanding alone, and to use as I deem necessary."

"I don't get it Bing," Patrick said, bewildered. "What is it that he's talking about?"

Tye laughed again.

"Tell them. Go ahead. I think they'll get a kick out of it."

Kirsdona turned and now took a step towards the penguin.

"Bing? What's going on?"

Bing's gaze did not leave Tye's. The two stood locked in some sort of complication that the others could not comprehend.

"It's my dreams," Bing began, his voice distant and unassuming. "It seems that every time that I sleep I seem to be having dreams about where our next day's travels are heading. At first I thought that it was just an odd coincidence. And that all it was, was just that—a dream. But then I came to understand that even though I was given the gift of some sort of ability to see ourselves in the not too distant future, it was given at a price. At the end of each of these dreams our friend here has managed to find a way to pluck those images from my mind. That is how he has been so keen in his ability to track us."

The animals and Patrick looked dumbfounded.

"How can he see into your dreams?" Patrick asked. "Is he dreaming the same thing as you?"

"I don't know how he does it," Bing replied in disgust.

"Perhaps it is witchcraft," Syrian answered. "The allegiance he is keeping is tipped in that direction. But why didn't you tell us this before? We shouldn't have to hear it from that creature."

Tye raised his eyebrows and giggled at the discussion. "Perhaps he's a witch? I've never really been too sure about penguins, you know."

Bing took his gaze from Tye and slowly turned to the group.

"I have only just become aware of it myself. Most of the time your dreams disappear and vanish once you awake, just as mine usually do. But lately, the dreams have been staying with me well into the morning, haunting me until the day has passed and I am sure that he hasn't crossed our path. I didn't tell any of you because I didn't want to cause alarm for something that I wasn't even sure was happening."

"Well, why is this happening?" Kirsdona asked. "Is there something we don't know about? I mean, why you?"

"It is because of who I am. I am my council's high priest. I am the one that the council elders' come to for their guidance. It is something that I'm sure that I should be more proud of, but I look on it more as a burden. It is not that I am blessed with any special direction or knowledge. I am just blessed with the ability to 'see.' I had no idea that my gift would come into play in this journey. At least not in the method that it has been used."

"Well, that doesn't seem so bad," Patrick responded.

"It is when someone else can tap into your thoughts," Tye giggled.

"What he's saying, Patrick, is that I may be jeopardizing all of your lives. I should probably relinquish myself from the group. If this should continue then not only might they find the ability to see where we are going, but they might also be able to tell the where and when."

"Is there anything that we can do to prevent this?" Syrian asked.

"Nothing that I know of."

Patrick was stunned by the news. In his mind he believed the others now looked at Bing as if he had become some sort of traitor, giving away their whereabouts to the enemy. And the bad part was, he wasn't even doing it consciously. It was all taking part while he was unconscious.

"Well, it doesn't matter to me," Patrick initiated. "He's still my friend, and he belongs with us. I don't think he needs to go anywhere."

Tye laughed at the response.

"Ah, bravo! What a marvelous friend you are," he said sarcastically.

"Boy," Kirsdona began, "are you sure about this. I realize the attachment that you and Bing have formed, but this thing he's talking about could truly put us in dire straits."

"I know. I'm not stupid. But there's got to be some way to get past this. Even if it means that he just won't sleep. But he's not leaving the group. Because if he doesn't go, then I'm not going either. And since I'm the only human that can take care of the witch . . ."

"What?!" Tye yelled in surprise as he clamored from his perch. "The only human? What are you talking about? You're not that special, kid. Please. You're just the only one that's still alive."

Patrick reacted as if he had been struck, the words Tye spoke stinging him readily.

"What are you talking about? Is this another one of your lies?"

Tye slid down from his roost, his arms folding across his chest.

"You mean to tell me that you truly believe that you're the only human that has undertaken this path?" Tye about fell over in a fit of laughter. "Oh, brother! You mean that your dear, dear friends here have led you to believe that you are the only human in the world that is attempting to put an end to what is taking place?"

But the question went unanswered. Patrick stood still, not knowing what was happening. He turned to look at the animals, but they seemed to have lost their focus, their gazes reluctant to meet his own.

"Bing?" Patrick asked, confused by the turn of Tye's words.

"Oh no, don't look for him to help you now. And he calls me the 'trickster'? My dear boy, there have been countless others that have attempted the same folly that you are in the middle of. You are merely one in a long line of humans that has taken this path."

Tye was clearly pleased with himself, his animated tale now dominating the conversation. The air became more foul with every word that he uttered.

"Well, well, well. Just when you think you know your friends . . . up jumps the devil! That's pretty funny. So, how did they do it? Did they tell you that you were the only one in the world that could save the planet? That you have all sorts of special abilities that can save mankind? That they had a dream about you?"

"Bing?" Patrick looked for any words from his friend, but the only thing Bing could do was to stand silent.

"Do not listen to his words, boy," Syrian spoke with anger. "He's only twisting his lies."

Patrick was in the eye of a hurricane, his head feeling light, his eyesight starting to blur. The storm that was Tye was raging all around him, spouting off sentence after sentence that caused Patrick to begin questioning everything about not only himself, but about all of the animals as well.

"And just a few moments ago, Bing, the boy was willing to forget about all the problems you may have brought about with your 'sight', all the while thinking that he could trust the animals that were escorting him. And here, all that time, it was a lie."

Kirsdona forgot all about the instructions she had been given and immediately turned and pounced on Tye.

"That's enough!" She snarled as she leapt across and dug her claws deep into the man's chest, her ferocity driving him to the ground. But to her surprise Tye immediately grabbed her paws and threw her to the side.

"You are making a grave error in judgment, little kitten, if you are to attempt something as foolhardy as that again."

Kirsdona righted herself to all fours, a look of amazement across her face.

Syrian then placed himself between Tye and the others, his face dark and grim.

"Creature, I do not know what it is that you have become, but it is not natural, or of this earth. But you should go, now, while you still have the chance. I do not think that you want to interact with all of us in this instance."

Tye stood up, and smiled lightly.

"I believe that I will not have to, wise monkey. I have given you my instructions. If they are not honored by the time given, then it will be my pleasure to watch as you and your friends are eaten alive. The boy is mine. Do not make the mistake in believing otherwise."

Kirsdona, though, was definitely not finished with Tye, and she threw herself at him once again.

But then Tye did the amazing. Large, leathery, bat-like wings spread from his back and he lifted himself off the ground, just out of reach of Kirsdona's murderous jaws.

The animals stared in disbelief as Tye took flight, dust and dirt swirling into the air beneath Tye's wings.

"My. Word. What. Is. He?" Dog asked, the fear in his voice evident.

"Whatever he has become, he is no longer to be considered a man," Syrian said to all as they watched Tye leave the area.

"Patrick," Bing began, his head shaking in dismay at the sight before him, "now you know what I meant when I asked you earlier if you truly knew what sort of creature Tye was."

Bing's outrage at the situation caused him to turn to see if Patrick was listening to his words, but when he turned to locate the boy he found that he was no longer there.

"Patrick!" Bing called after him, but Patrick would not acknowledge that he had even been addressed. Rather, he quickened his pace and started to run back down over the hill.

"Oh, no. What have I done?" Bing said aloud.

Syrian took out after Patrick without a moments thought, and began a strong advance down the hill in pursuit. "I'll go after the boy. Don't do anything foolish until we return," he yelled to the others.

Kirsdona nodded, and then approached the penguin, her sight still following the now winged Tye.

"You should have let me finish this before it even began, Bing. All of this could have been avoided. Now you see why I do not like talk. It's just words being used as poison."

Bing looked heartbroken.

"I fear that I've crushed the very trust we've established, Kirsdona. He'll never believe me again."

Kirsdona stared at the bird, her expression shifting as she shook her head.

"Don't worry too much about this, Bing," Kirsdona spoke. "We all made the decision that it was the best thing to do. I was never in favor of lying to the boy, but not telling him the truth was probably just as bad."

Syrian finally caught up with Patrick near the bottom of the hill, just as the ravine was beginning to level out.

"Patrick, wait!"

But Patrick's mind was not in the mood to listen to any more talk. He was near tears, the betrayal he felt consuming his thoughts.

Finally Syrian landed in front of him with a thud, his face full of regret.

"Patrick . . ."

"No! I'm not listening. I don't want to hear any more lies. Not from you. Not from Tye. I just want to go home. Don't you understand? I just want to go home!"

Syrian lowered his head in resignation.

"I can understand how you feel, young one. You feel as if we betrayed a trust that we have spent so many days trying to establish. But I can offer to you nothing more than an apology. Although, a tempered one. You see, we may have not told you all the truths that exist to all the complexities that are in play, but we have not lied to you, either. Of that, I can promise."

"But you did lie! You said that you all had a dream about me. That I was the only one."

"Do not listen to the words that the creature has spoken. He can twist a mighty oak and make you believe that it is a rose. His tongue is split, for it speaks from both sides of his mouth. We did have the dream about you. Nothing he can say can take away the facts as they are.

"And do not dismiss the wondrous and amazing things that you can do. Things that we probably haven't even discovered yet. Things that Tye has no way of knowing about. Tye is taking the limited knowledge that he has and is using it to confuse any subject that has possibilities for him to pervert.

"Patrick, you have to understand that we are older than you. In terms of mere human days and hours you may have spent more time on this world, but we have lived much longer in terms of growth and experience. When we discovered the undertaking that was going to take place, and with whom we would have to escort, we were each alarmed at how young you really were. We questioned as to why you, someone who is so young, would be chosen for this challenge. We didn't undertake this lightly, and we had to formulate from what perspective we would approach the situation. Sometimes, giving all the truth all at once is not the best path to take. And, given as to who you were, and taking in consideration your age and maturity, we thought it best to deal strictly with the problems that arise, as they arise.

"I promise that we didn't lie to you. You have endeared yourself to us in too many ways for us to treat you like that. We have all formed a bond." Syrian found himself smiling. "Even the tiger. She has begun to realize that you are not so typical as she had originally thought. There is something here, something going on that I cannot explain, but it is something that has formed that I hope you will not take lightly.

"We just didn't think that you would be able to handle the knowledge that other humans had already attempted to avenge this dreadful situation, and that all had failed. They all perished from their different regions that they each had set out from. Yes, most had an animal escort just as you have, but there was a difference—they could not communicate with us as you do.

"You see, as word traveled to the far reaches that we, the animals, were having a dream about a human that was going to be the 'difference maker', someone who was going to make peace and bring things back to order, the wickedness to the north must have caught wind of what was taking place. For no one had any other dream than the one we had of you. No other. We believe that the queen must have placed false thoughts in the minds of many creatures, casting a belief that other humans were to also make the trek as you have. It was a deception that caused the deaths of both the humans and animals. That is why the other animals are so uncertain about you. The witch queen has created exactly what she had hoped—a state of chaos and confusion.

"Patrick, do not dismiss all that we have accomplished. And remember all the creatures that have put lives in jeopardy. Some already giving up their lives so that you can continue."

Patrick sat down on the ground, pulling his knees up to his chest.

"I'm just so tired, Syrian. I just want to forget about all of this and go home."

"I know, young one. But you cannot give up now. If they are so desperate to prevent you from achieving the goal of approaching their hallowed grounds, then there must be something about you that they are dearly afraid of. And I must admit, there is a little part of me that wants to know exactly what that is, as well. Why is it that they are so afraid of you? It can only be that there is something that you can do, or that you have some knowledge that you possess, that can do them harm. Or both."

"And now Tye wants me back. He scares me, Syrian. Did you see him fly away? He wasn't like that back at my house."

"Yes," Syrian said as he looked skyward. "I do not know the why and how as to what he has become, but he is a being that possesses an evil that I fear without question.

"But you have to ask yourself a question, Patrick. One I'm surprised that you haven't asked yourself already. Why do they continue on as they do and not just finish the job by killing you? Why didn't Tye just take you now? I have continued to wonder about this for quite some time. I know that this will not make your mind sit any easier, but I don't believe that they can. And I wonder if Tye isn't just a little bit afraid of you."

Patrick wrinkled his nose.

"Of me? Why—because I can hold my breath under water? Because I can somehow move through the land of the dead? That doesn't sound like something that I'd be afraid of."

"That is not it, though, young one. It is the fear of the unknown. You are something that they are very uncertain about. I believe that is what is driving this entire charade. Because the unknown, in this instance, is a very uncomfortable and considerable thing."

Syrian reached a hand down to Patrick.

"But enough about this, I think it is time for us to return. The others, especially Bing, are probably feeling terrible about what has taken place. Do not be too hard on us for our decisions."

"I know. But I just want to sit here for a while. Is that ok? I don't want to go back up there just yet."

Syrian nodded, and then positioned himself on the ground next to Patrick. He stretched his long arms behind his head and leaned back. "Then I will sit with you."

"No," Patrick said, shaking his head. "You don't have to."

Syrian closed his eyes and breathed deeply. "But I want to."

And that's how the next hour passed, the two of them just lying there amongst the rocks and weeds, not a word being spoken.

Patrick appreciated the baboon's efforts. He didn't want to talk, and he didn't want to face all the questions and apologies that he knew would come once they crested the hill again. Patrick knew that his friends could not keep him clear of Tye. He wasn't even sure if they had ever encountered the man before, but with the way they behaved it was obvious that they held a great fear of him. That's the point where Patrick worried the most. What did the animals know about Tye that he didn't?

Time passed slowly before Patrick decided that enough was enough and he needed to let the others know that he was safe. The two of them made their way back up the hill with the remaining animals waiting for them at the top. Bing made an attempt at another apology, but Patrick assured him that he was ok, and that he would continue as he had with the group.

"But if there is anything else that needs to be said, please give it to me now. I can handle it. No more secrets."

Bing nodded.

"Of that you have our promise. But please know that we are a bit ashamed. We should have realized early on that you are not like the other humans. Of that we now have a clear understanding."

Patrick nodded and took a deep breathe; he still had to address the business at hand.

"So what do we do about Tye?" Patrick asked, trying to sound as upbeat as he possibly could considering the situation. "He's never going to let me leave. At least not alive."

Bing sighed and nodded in agreement.

"I know. The problem is complex. Tye will surely be aware of all avenues of escape. To run would be futile. There may be only one option, and that is to confront him. And perhaps that is what he wants. That is not the course of action that I want to see take place, but I cannot foresee any other response to his demands, and we only have until morning to come up with a solution. But be sure of one thing, Patrick, we are not going to turn you over to him."

"And now there's another question we need to ask," Kirsdona intervened, taking a deep breath before she continued. "What do we do about you?"

"About my sight?"

"Yes," Dog approached from behind. "Is. There. A. Way. To. Use. Your. Ability. To. Help. Us? Or. Is. This. Only. Going. To. Be. Problem?"

"Or," Kirsdona finished, "are we going to have to insure that you don't dream?"

The question was then raised as to Bing's ability to 'see', with all wondering if he could somehow tell them what was going to take place the next morning? Or if he could even 'see' past that moment in time?

"I'm afraid it doesn't work that way," he said, visibly uncomfortable with questions. "It comes to me at random. I really have no control. I suppose that I am nothing more than a 'receiver', if you can understand that. Like I alluded to earlier, sometimes it is more of a burden than a gift."

Kirsdona still pressed the issue. "Well, we have to find a way to control it, or it is going to make things go a lot rougher from here on out."

Bing took a few steps away, his back to the group.

Patrick could see that it was hard on the little bird, his not being in control of the situation. For the most part, Patrick reasoned, Bing's thought processes could find his way through most things within his control. But with this, it definitely was not something he had a firm grasp on.

"For now," the penguin began, "we need to concentrate on the problem at hand—and that would be Tye. After that I'll try and find a way to deal with my part of the problem we're facing. Since I don't think that any of us will be sleeping this evening, I can say with confidence that I won't be having any more dreams."

The group's discussion lasted well into the early part of the night, with every possible way of approaching their predicament examined. The longer it went, the more the talk became awkward and burdensome. They seemed unable to come to any conclusion that would be satisfactory to the problem at hand. It was hard for each animal to put aside their natural instincts and arrive at an agreeable position, with the more aggressive creatures (of course) wanting to fight their way through, and the more passive trying to come to a conclusion that may divert the prospect of fighting. But in every conclusion the fear of death hung over them like a spectre.

Patrick began to get tired and excused himself from the meeting. All the talk that was going on was getting them nowhere, and his fears were only growing with every moment that passed, the constant agitation at not coming to a conclusion weighing heavily on his mind.

He began to stroll a short ways away from where the group was sitting, silently brushing past the thick spruce and pines that occupied the area they were in. He wanted to ease his mind, trying to drive away the feeling that this could possibly be his last night he would spend with his friends.

A cool breeze was forming on the night air, and Patrick wished that he had a jacket to keep him warm. The late summer air was definitely moving out, and Fall was taking a firm hold on the weather.

As he walked away from the group's little area he watched the stars overhead, the feeling of loneliness creeping under his skin. He tried to shake the feelings of sorrow he felt, trying to convince himself that things might turn out alright, but he could not get rid of the feeling that he was probably only fooling himself.

He moved on a little further still, not sure exactly how far he had wandered, and now noticing that he could no longer hear the others as they talked. He turned and looked back, but shrugged absently and continued on.

He walked another few minutes until he came to a clearing. The only thing in the immediate area that he found was a tiny little graveyard settled underneath a large maple tree. With only four headstones in the small area, and only four spirits moving quietly underneath the tree's low branches, Patrick imagined that this was probably an isolated family owned plot.

As he moved in closer, Patrick uttered a calming "Hello" to the inhabitants, alerting them of his approach so that they wouldn't be alarmed at his arrival. From what Patrick could tell of the four, their forms seemed to indicate that there was a mother, father, and two little girls.

In an odd way Patrick was grateful to come across them. The animals and he had become fast friends, but their animations and emotions could never replace the simple return of a human gesture or emotional outreach that any kind of human contact could provide. Even if it was from the dead.

Patrick thought that perhaps he could work up an even trade. He'd tell them all he knew with what was going on in the world, and what he was attempting to do. And he was hoping that they in turn could calm his fears with some polite conversation.

But to Patrick's surprise they didn't seem as startled at his appearance as he would have thought they would have been. In fact, they sort of looked like he wasn't unexpected. They nodded in acknowledgement of his presence, but it was the way their eyes danced back and forth between himself and the trees just off to his right that gave him concern.

"What's the matter?" he asked, his head turning in the direction that they continued to give their attention.

And then the spirits began to back up, the four of them not saying a word as they moved as far back against their boundary as it would allow, the father pulling his family in close to him. Patrick instantly began to fear that Tye was close by.

Patrick realized then that he had strayed too far away from his friends and their safety, and wondered still, why hadn't someone come looking for him by now?

When he first saw the movement through the trees it was like an apparition, the form as it presented itself. It was something that he had only ever believed was present in myths or fairytales.

As it approached, the steps that it took seemed graceful and haunting, not crooked or painful like he would have imagined. He could see the hands extending from beneath its black robe, the skin draped over bone in torn and broken patches. Patrick tried to look at its face, but the hooded shadows held their mistress's features behind blackness and imagination. Patrick wanted to see . . . but his mind deflected his eyes away in fear that he would.

"Patrick Brighton?" she whispered seductively, sounding almost as if a smile was gracing her face.

"Yes," he answered with the little air he had left in his lungs.

Patrick knew who it was, but his sanity wouldn't allow him believe it.

It was Death.

CHAPTER 20

Death

"Are you here for me? To kill me?" Patrick managed to squeak out, his throat dry and sticky.

"No," she said, Patrick imagining a skeleton-like smile behind the blackness. "Of course not. I have simply come to speak with you."

"Who are you?"

The being in front of him laughed at his inquiry. "You mean to tell me that you don't know who I am?"

"No, it's not that. I . . . I mean that's not what I meant. You're a woman. I always thought you were a man."

Again the laughter. "You are quite a charming little person. No, I come in all forms and guises."

And then in a blink she changed to the figure of a police officer. The man that appeared before Patrick was short and squat, with bushels of salt and pepper colored hair curling from beneath his hat. He was dressed in a navy blue uniform, a wide and toothy grin dancing on his face.

"Is this better?" she asked.

"No," Patrick replied instantly, his mouth agape. The mere ability to transform herself would have caused Patrick to say no to any form that she had picked.

She then appeared before him as a smartly dressed woman in a business suit.

"And this?"

Patrick couldn't respond, his fear not allowing his mouth to move.

"Then how about this?"

And then the being appeared as a girl, one that Patrick knew well.

"Abby Greendale," Patrick responded, his voice distant and hollow. "She lives down our street."

The little girl in front of him sighed. "I'm afraid not anymore."

Patrick met the little girl's eyes with his own. "She's dead?"

The girl nodded uncomfortably. "Just like the others."

Patrick took a step back, "I don't like this. This isn't right. You're mocking the dead."

"My dear child, how can one 'mock' the dead? I am merely paying homage to their forms."

The being continued to change shapes. Patrick's aunt. His uncle. One of his teachers. A girl. A boy.

"Death comes in many shapes and sizes."

The being then formed into Patrick's grandfather, someone that Patrick hadn't seen in well over three years.

"Papaw Frank?"

"No, still me," the image of his grandfather said. "I thought that maybe this form would make it easier for us to converse."

Patrick took a deep breath, allowing it to slowly exhale from his lungs.

"I guess that's ok. But you still sound like a girl."

His grandfather's face smiled at him.

Patrick was astounded. It was the same wrinkly face, the same drooping eyes, the same bald head.

"Is this better?"

And then the voice was his Papaw Frank's.

"Yeah. I guess."

"Wonderful."

Patrick looked up into his grandfather's eyes.

"Then you are Death?"

"Well, I am the embodiment of that being, but the term you use is so coarse. For I am known to many people as many things.

"For I am Azrael. I am Mictlantecuhtli. I am Yama, and I am Ankou. I am both the Destroyer, and the Angel of Mercy. I am everything that you think you may have heard, and probably a little bit more.

"To some, I am as sudden as a cold winter's snap. To others, I am as welcome as a warm embracing kiss, or welcome prayer. I can be your friend when you least expect it, or enemy so fierce that many fight with their last breaths trying to hold me at bay.

"But in the light that you seem to want to place me, then yes, I am indeed the being of which you speak. But I am known by so much more. From the far reaches of the world so many beings utter my name with such bitter contempt, and call out to me with their last breaths in exalted praise."

His grandfather's appearance did make it a little easier to deal with even if he was only Death in disguise. Patrick swallowed once, trying to free some saliva in his mouth to bring his words forward.

"And why do you want to talk to me?"

"Curiosity, mainly. I wanted to see what my sister was so in fear of."

"Your sister?"

"But I also wanted to find out why you feel so compelled to continue this journey of yours. What is it that you hope to accomplish?"

Patrick stood quiet for a moment, the rich smell of nearby wild apples filling his senses. If he answered her as she wanted, he wondered if that would somehow jeopardize their position.

"Come now," his grandfather spoke, "there must be some reason."

"No," Patrick said as he looked at him queerly, his nose wrinkling at his grandfather's questions. "Nothing that you'd understand."

"So where do you think you'll be going on this little trip of yours? And who do think you might find when you get there?"

Patrick's eyes darted back to connect with his grandfathers'.

"The witch queen," he replied, none too sure of himself.

"A witch?"

"Yeah," Patrick replied, his eyes narrowing with caution. "If your sister is who I think she is, then she's the one I'm trying to find."

"Oh," his grandfather said as he folded his arms behind his back. "So you just woke up one morning and decided that you were going to find yourself a witch?"

"No, that's not it and you know it."

"Oh, and what is it that I know?"

"Well, for one thing, why your sister would be afraid of me?"

His grandfather shrugged.

"I would think that would be obvious."

"Obvious for you, maybe."

"And why would that be? Is there something that I would know that you do not?"

"You probably know everything."

"Not as much as you might think."

"I just don't understand why she would be afraid of me? What is it that she said that I could do to her?"

His grandfather chuckled and pointed a finger.

"Ah, now, that would be cheating. You're trying to disguise the nature of this talk. I am beginning to believe the rumors that have been whispered are true—you don't quite know who you are."

"I know who I am," Patrick bluffed.

But his grandfather only shook his head slowly.

"No. I don't believe you do. If you did, you would have already taken care of the problem as it exists. At least as far as you could."

Patrick stood silent, staring back with eyes of mistrust at the being in front of him.

His grandfather walked a short ways away from him, almost as if he was leaving, but quietly turned and plucked a still green leaf from a branch overhead. Patrick watched as the leaf sat in his palm for a moment, then immediately turned black, shriveled, and became dust.

"Come now, it is because of who you are, my child. I would think that would be clear enough."

Patrick looked at the ground.

"You'd think," he mumbled.

"But I wonder," the old man replied, completely disregarding Patrick's questions, "When you find this witch that you seek, what will you do then? Are you prepared for what a witch can do?"

Again Patrick stood silent, but this time his eyes belayed his true feelings.

His grandfather smiled.

"You haven't a clue. You don't have any idea what you are going to do even if you do meet her. Am I correct? Or have the tens of thousands of years in reading the faces of men still left me a little short when it comes to reading yours?"

Patrick tried to hold his gaze with the being in front of him, but he slowly let his eyes drop to the ground.

"No. I don't know what I'm going to do. I'm afraid I don't know what I can do."

His grandfather came in close to Patrick, so close that he could smell the foulness and decay on his breath.

"My little man, I will give you a word of warning, then. Be careful. Because if you are to continue as you are, I see death blowing you a cold kiss at every stop you make. You see it really doesn't matter to me the how and the when that each being comes to their end. I pay a visit to all at one time or another, without exception. My appetite is insatiable. But at the rate things are progressing it could get kind of boring if my sister would win this struggle she is presenting.

"Actually, I'm kind of torn about the whole ordeal. I mean, if my sister has her way then mankind would be wiped off the face of the earth. And yes, it is nice to have a booming business. And sure, I'd still be left with all the other living things that inhabit the world. But it wouldn't be the same. I don't know if I'd state this to her directly, but in a way I'm hoping that maybe you might actually, shall we say, slow down the progress she's making."

Patrick found the trunk of a maple tree and leaned back against it, his feet together as he stood. Whether it was because Death had taken on the appearance of his grandfather or not, but Patrick was definitely becoming a lot more relaxed with the conversation as it carried on.

"I realize that you are being guided by trust and by feelings. Two horrible ways of allowing yourself to be taken up in a situation where you are made to feel that you need to prove something. I would think that maybe it should be more? Hmm? That maybe it should come from inside you. Something that compels you forward without regard to how you feel. Because if you are mainly 'going along for the ride' in this instance, then you are going to be in for quite a shock when you arrive at your destination."

"What do you mean?"

"I mean, that if you are merely doing this to appease someone else's appetite, then perhaps you had better rethink your reasoning behind all of this. This had better be something that you want to accomplish. Something that you feel compelled to see through till the end. Because I'm here to tell you, from where I sit it's going to get a lot worse before it gets any better.

"I have found that in my many days on this planet that the beings who are the ones who change the paths in front of them are the ones who risk complicating not only their lives, but the lives of all those around them. They choose to change because they felt compelled to change the direction they are taking themselves, not because someone else told them to do it, but because they knew it was the right thing to do. It should come from your heart. If you're going to accept your destiny, then you're going to have to assume the risks that go along with it.

"I'm not telling you that it would be best for you to run as far from here as you can, and never look back. And I'm not telling you to stay and finish your quest. It's just that as I sit, watching and observing as I do, I realize that the one being on this entire world that can make more of difference than any other is the one being who doesn't even know why he's here. Or, even why he's doing what he's doing. It's almost like you're the ghost, and not them." His grandfather pointed to the spirits still huddled in the tiny gravesite. "You've got to feel it in your heart, as well as your head, if you are going to persevere in this endeavor."

Patrick began to feel the cold knife of responsibility twist in his gut.

"I know. I understand what I have to do," he responded, his voice quivering with doubt. "It's just that I'm worried about so many things. And I'm worried about my mom and dad."

Patrick's papaw Frank began to leisurely walk along a natural fence line of holly and wild shrubs, his facial features becoming hidden by the night's shadows.

"About your mom and dad, well, I think they must be doing alright because I don't have their names on any of my lists to be collected."

Patrick lifted his head, his eyes brightened with the words that were spoken.

"Do they know where I'm at? Do they know what's happening to me?"

"Sorry, that's not my department. But I will tell you this, I don't see our paths coming to a crossroads. As far as your friends go, well, that's a different story."

"What? My friends? Are they going to be killed? Are they going to die?"

Even though he could see that his grandfather was looking to something off in the distance, Patrick could still see enough through the shadows to see his grandfather smile that same warm and happy kind of smile that Patrick remembered seeing all those Christmas mornings when he was younger.

"Of course they are. They will all meet their ends at one point or another. Everything born onto this land eventually does."

"But you make it sound like . . ."

"Yes. I did. And that's because out of all the possible scenarios that exists for you and your friends, no one, not even I, knows what path they may choose to go down. If they so happen to choose the path that I might be waiting on, then I will have my say. But if they don't, then they will continue on as they are to pursue their existence for another day."

Patrick watched as something in the shadows was moving closer to his papaw. It was a large figure with blood red eyes that slowly bobbed up and down as it made its way to him. His papaw raised a hand and began rubbing along the creature's body. That's when Patrick recognized that it was a horse. The animal was so black that even as it shifted and moved in the shadows it was hard to tell the size and nature of the beast. And then Patrick's heart begin to sink as the voice and body of his papaw began to melt away and the initial figure of Death that he had first seen began to re-emerge.

"But know that I do see their paths crossing with mine. And soon. In fact, that's why I am here; I see my path and a lot of other creatures' paths crossing at first light."

"Then we're going to fight Tye? You've already seen this?"

"See? No. I can't 'see' anything. I can smell it, though. Lots of death. Enough to complete my day."

The female figure emerged from the shadows. Tall, yet stooped, she made her way back over to Patrick, the horse following closely behind.

"But the one thing I will leave you with that you should always remember and never forget—is that you are human. Made from the same clay and dirt and water that created the very first man that stood upon this wide earth, many many miles from where you stand right now." The hooded being stood very tall above Patrick, the words coming from deep within her, and were all consuming. "And you can die. Never forget that. Don't listen to others as they may fill your head with nonsense. You can be killed. But as I said, even though I do not see our paths crossing at present, know that you are the one who can change that path. But Patrick Brighton, I dearly hope we will not meet again for a long, long time."

The giant black horse stared down at him, it's heavy breath falling over Patrick as the specter of Death mounted the great beast.

"I greatly enjoyed our talk, little man. Do not forget my words."

Death pulled hard on the reigns of the sinister looking horse, turning it back in the direction from where they had first emerged.

"And remember, Patrick Brighton—that all the creatures in the world can escort you to the ballroom, but in the end it is you who will have to ask the lady to dance."

The horse then began to move. Slowly at first, it's pace slowly progressing to a sprint as they moved down a darkened path until Patrick could see them no more.

Patrick stood stunned by the encounter he had just experienced. The figure of Death, as she rode away, made Patrick feel more isolated and alone than at any other time in his life. Her words still buzzed in his head, his mind trying to catch them and place them in a position so that he could understand all that was said.

He hurriedly turned, ignoring the spirits in the graveyard next to him, and ran back to the landing where he hoped his friends were still waiting. The tree limbs and high grasses stung his face and arms as he passed, but he ran with the speed as if something was chasing him.

After a few minutes he found his way back, emerging into the clearing, and finding the animals just as he had left them, still debating the crisis as it approached.

"I can't believe you guys didn't even come looking for me!" he bellowed. "Didn't you even notice that I was gone?! I could have been lying dead somewhere! Or worse, Tye could have caught me!" he railed at them further.

The animals turned to look at him, but not in the way Patrick imagined they would.

"What are you talking about?" Bing asked, his reaction only one of mild concern. "You just left a minute ago."

"Yeah," Kirsdona agreed. "Get over yourself. I know you're afraid of just about everything around here, but I didn't realize that you were that big of a girl. You just stepped through the trees."

Patrick's eyes widened in shock.

"What are you talking about? I was gone over an hour! And you guys didn't even wonder where I was at?"

Syrian smiled slightly as if he was embarrassed for the boy.

"Patrick, I was watching you. You only just walked through the ivy and wild flowers a short time ago. If you had been gone any more than a few moments then I would have been the first to know, and the first to go looking for you. Now please, stop with the silliness, this is not the time to be fooling around."

All the animals turned away, once again beginning to decipher on how to handle the situation before them.

"But . . ." Patrick began, but stopped short of finishing his sentence.

I know I was gone. At least an hour!

He stood, his mind replaying what had just taken place, when he began to wonder if it had all been a dream. That possibly he had imagined the entire thing.

Patrick turned and looked back over his shoulder into the dark of the woods.

Or had Death merely stepped into that moment in time and stopped everything while she had her say?

Patrick started to walk over to the group. Dream or no dream, he was still going to have to tell them what had just taken place. They needed to know what she had just told him.

That's when he saw something emerge from the woods that he feared he would never see again.

It was Sin.

The boar came waltzing through the trees to their east, the same pleasant little smile that they had all gotten used to still attached to his bushy face.

"Hey! Look who it is," Syrian said as he quickly stood and greeted the animal.

Patrick and the others were then given another shock as they drew nearer to the beast, their jaws falling open as they then saw who was sitting on Sin's back.

"Melanbach!" Bing said as he caught sight of the rat. "I don't believe my eyes!"

The others then moved over, greeting the boar and rat with rounds of hearty thanks, and pleasurable pats on the back.

"But. What. Are. You. Doing. Here?" Dog asked.

"Yes," Syrian added, "We feared for your lives. I thought that you were never going to leave the city."

Before Melanbach could answer, the group then spied several hundred other rats making their way into the clearing.

"I know," he said, his voice sounding tired, yet relieved. "I find it hard myself to believe that we have traveled as far as we have. But when you left, and after we had survived the mice, we found another creature who was searching for your little group. Only this individual was seeking you out to offer help and advice. He was desperate to find you, and we couldn't just let him go on blindly. We finally concluded that given enough time the boar would lead us right to your doorstep."

Melanbach turned just as a small brown mongoose entered after the last of the rats.

"Allow me to introduce, Gurd," Melanbach began. "He is the fellow of which I speak."

The mongoose nodded in acknowledgement, a hearty smile across his face. "G'day, mates."

"Hello," Bing returned.

The others then followed suit and offered their own simple greetings to the mongoose.

"But who is he? And why is he seeking us?" Patrick asked.

Melanbach turned his attention to Patrick.

"Because he has been following something unusual that the rest of us were concerned might be wanting to bring you harm."

The mongoose stepped forward.

"Yes," he added with a nod. "Bloody snakes, are what they are. We've been tracking 'em for almost four days from beyond the Black Stump. A whole blooming pack of 'em. We hear you've got problems with a bunyip."

Patrick wrinkled his brow.

"A bunyip?"

"Yeah. I realize it's not a common term you folks use in these parts. It's a creature my kind speaks of back home. Real sneaky devils, they are. Some say they're not real, but I'm here to tell ya that after you hear one of 'em scream at you in the middle of the night, ya won't make the mistake into believing that. Not many have actually seen one, but to gaze upon the beast is said to cause a few kangaroos to go loose in the top paddock, if you know what I mean."

Patrick watched as the mongoose twirled his finger around his temple like he was describing someone who was nuts.

"How do you know of these things? The bunyip?"

"I used to be a tracker. Me and my brothers were of a kind that were used to hunt the bloody beasts."

"And what do they look like?"

"Well, mate, it's said that they look like a lot of different things. I suppose it depends on your point of view. But from what I am to understand, it mostly resembles something that is a cross between a man and a snake."

Patrick knew at once who he must be talking about. And as the others slowly turned to look at him he knew that it was the same conclusion that they had drawn as well.

"His name is Tye," Patrick said to Gurd.

The mongoose seemed surprised. "He has a name, does he? That's the first I've heard of that one."

Syrian stepped from behind the rest of the group. "I'm sorry for sounding so rude, but we already know about the snakes," he said flatly. "I don't understand why you came all this way to tell us this. Unless there's something going on that I don't understand, you're just one creature. How can you help us?"

Patrick watched as the mongoose smiled an evil little smile, something that instantly unnerved him.

"Ah," Gurd said as he stood and put one of his paws on his hips and looked around. "Yes. I see what you mean."

The mongoose then put the other paw to his mouth and began whistling long and low, and before Patrick could even believe it more than a thousand sets of eyes began to peer back to him from the dark of the woods.

Patrick and the others found that they were surrounded by mongoose.

"Then I guess you had better meet my friends."

And then Patrick heard a tremendous fluttering overhead, as if a thousand birds beat the air with a thousand wings, filling the trees above them. Though Patrick couldn't see the birds through the darkness, the hairs on the back of his neck stood on end at the image that formed in his mind.

"How did you get them all together?" Bing asked, surprised.

Gurd motioned to Patrick.

"You'd be amazed at how just the simple mention of your friend's name will rally the troops."

"But I didn't think that birds would fly during the night. That they were leery of traveling in the dark."

"Yes, you're right about that. But with the urgency that is fast approaching, it didn't take more than a couple of shakes on the fanny to get them rolling in this direction."

Patrick took a moment to digest what was taking place, but he instantly began to realize what kind of position this now put them in.

"Boy is Tye in for a surprise," he said with a smile.

"Yes, young one," Syrian said, a mischievous look in his eye as he turned to the boy. "And that is exactly what we've wanted to talk to you about."

The baboon smiled wide, his bare fangs glistening in the moonlight. It was a villainous smile, one that Patrick didn't care for at all.

The animals that arrived late for the most part stayed hidden on the suggestion from Bing, just in case Tye would want to come to meet with them again, face to face. The morning was just approaching, the orange hue filling the eastern sky. Most of the animals found places of rest, not really sleeping, but merely keeping to themselves awaiting the trying time that lay ahead.

It had been several hours since Syrian had spoke, Patrick finishing what Syrian and the others had asked of him, their plan now taking on a complexity that Patrick found exhilarating. All that they had to do now was to wait and hope that Tye took their bait.

It was the waiting that Patrick had the hardest time dealing with. While he was completing the chores he was given his thoughts were focused and completely on the task at hand, allowing no outside interference to creep in. But as soon as he completed those tasks his anxieties slowly began to fill the void again.

He replayed the words that Death had spoken to him over and over in his mind, the haunting quality in which she had delivered them made him struggle with the misgivings they brought forth.

She was right, and Patrick knew it. He didn't want the animals to have to keep shepherding him through this ordeal. He needed to step up and find himself, and find out what he was capable of.

It was just that with the continuing fears that kept thrumming in his twelve year old mind, it made it hard to just conjure up bravery like you were performing a magic act. It wasn't something that came easy like pulling a rabbit out of the hat. Patrick knew that there was something in the hat, he was just afraid to put his hand inside.

As Patrick moved through the tiny compound he spied Melanbach slumped against a swollen tree trunk. The questions that he had for the rat were many, and he figured that now was as good as any to ask, hoping that the distraction he would receive with the answers would ease his heavy thoughts.

"Where's Beagel?" Patrick began, startling the slightly dozing rat. "I don't think I see him."

The large rat opened a lazy eye as he took in the boy. "Ah, poor Beagel. I'm afraid he didn't survive the mice," Melanbach said as he slowly opened the other eye, his voice drifting away with sorrow. "I didn't see him fall, but we found his body a short time after the mice began to retreat."

Melanbach then smiled in remembrance. "My brother may have been a little brash, but he was a great hero to all of our kind."

"And to us, as well," Bing added, suddenly appearing from the underbrush nearby.

The others acknowledged Melanbach's loss with silent nods, and issued soft words of praise for his fallen brother.

"But how did you ever beat the mice back. The last time we looked you were being overrun."

Melanbach turned and looked in the direction of Sin.

"Your little friend over there. He began devouring the little monsters in great quantities. They soon sensed that they were no match for him and ran for their lives."

Patrick looked over at the sleeping boar as he found a seat next to the large rat. He knew his next words should be cautious, for he didn't want alarm or agitate anyone by their meaning.

"Melanbach, what is it that you meant back in the tunnels. It almost sounded as if you know that Sin is something more than what he appears to be. It's as if everyone around here has been let in on a secret except me." Patrick pulled his knees up to his chest. "Is he a monster or something?"

Melanbach smiled slightly, and then shifted his way around to face Patrick.

"I don't know if this is the right time or place for this, friend human."

"But you know something, I can hear it in your voice. Please, tell me the truth."

Melanbach looked as if he was struggling with the decision, his face tired and forlorn, but he continued on with the discussion anyway.

"Well, all that I can tell you is what I believe to be the truth. It may cause some here to think twice at my words, but I have formed a theory that I have believed to be true ever since I first encountered the creature.

"It is hard to explain, what I am about to say, for it forces you to think about things from a perspective that is outside the normal way of observing the world."

The large rat then took a deep breath and sat back on his haunches.

"Don't be too quick in passing judgment here, but rather listen and then examine all the facts. You might just find yourself believing more than you thought you were capable of.

"The boar, I believe, is a composite of the very nature of the name he holds—sin. That is not to say that I believe he is sin, only that his being may possibly be the essence of sin as we have come to understand."

"You mean, like when I tell a lie or do something wrong on purpose—that kind of sin?"

Melanbach smiled.

"Yes. But it's not quite as simple as that. To understand what the creature that walks amongst us is really all about, you have to fully understand sin, for it is pure in its availability.

"The sin that I refer to has no boundaries that it inhabits. It is always within reach, and it is plentiful in all the forms that it can be found. It sees no color, and holds no colors of its own. For sin to be true, it cannot see at all. And it is blind to the ways that one will use the very nature of its being."

"Well," Kirsdona began, "if that doesn't describe him, then I don't know what does."

Melanbach winced at the tiger's grated words.

"You see, since the beginning of the time when life was first breathed on this planet, there has been sin—the simple prospect of sin as you have just mentioned. Sin in all its vast forms, and simple ways of distress. It lives and breaths in all creatures, partly because most of us are all so full of torment and destructive properties.

"So, yes, you do understand sin from a simple enough perspective. But I believe that the sin we speak of is taken from a moral perspective. To commit sin you have to be aware of the consequences involved with your act. A plant, of course, cannot commit sin. Nor can a rock, or water. But a thinking, illuminated being can. It is a choice in most instances. And in most instances it is a decision made to commit an evil act."

Though Patrick's attention was keenly fixed on Melanbach and his words, he still was very aware at just how many of the others were now paying attention to the captivating conversation. Melanbach was now not only talking to him, but to everyone else that was inhabiting the small encampment.

"But, the complexity that I," Melanbach then nodded towards Bing, "and others have observed, is that the boar before us has somehow been melded together to form a ferocious being that not only exemplifies sin, but seems to be some twisted personification of the very nature in the power of sin."

Melanbach paused for a moment, and arched an eyebrow as he continued on, his little head turning and watching the white boar sleep.

"But the act that we have all witnessed concerning the consuming of the sin-committing creatures is something that I am still having a hard time dealing with. It is as if he is the prevailing substance of sin, and yet he seems to claim back the very users of his being in some kind of strange, distorted form of vengeance. The alligators recognized this almost immediately. If you remember their words, they knew that what had come to find them was the very nature—personified by the creature—by which they lived—in sin."

Patrick stood and moved over next to the boar. He knelt and began rubbing his hand along Sin's coarse hide. Sin woke almost immediately, and smiled.

Melanbach shimmied over close to Patrick, his breath warm against Patrick's arm.

"Why he is with you, and what his purpose amongst your group may be, is one for speculation. But I do believe, being that you are on such a righteous path, that you will not be harmed by him. And perhaps only be protected, for I believe he is a guardian of some nature."

Patrick stared into the white, blind eyes of the now larger boar. He continued to stroke its fur, and rubbed its head kindly.

"I don't know," Patrick shrugged. "It's just that he's so nice. I understand what you're saying, and for the most part it does seem to be true in some weird way. But when I sit here with him, he just seems like he's another one of the group."

Melanbach did not say another word until Patrick turned and looked at him again. The large rat blinked twice and then settled back against the stump he had found for his earlier rest.

"Yes, he does. But I would sure hate to be paid a visit by an angry version of what you now have at your fingertips."

CHAPTER 21

War

A short time after the conversation with Melanbach the time came for Patrick and the others to find their way to a point near the opening where Tye had said he would be waiting.

The talk for most of the night had centered on just having the mongoose and birds fight while Patrick, Bing, and the others tried to make their escape. But Patrick and his friends would have nothing to do with that idea. They reasoned that if they had made it this far together then they needed to show Tye that from here on out they weren't going to back down so easily.

That's when they were presented with the plan.

It was just before sunrise, the light drifting lazily over the hills giving just enough illumination for them to secretly make their way to the clearing. The area just past the threshold of the forest was still silent and unmoving, much to their relief. They moved as quiet as they could to an area just east of where Syrian had instructed Patrick to park the van.

Patrick could still hear Syrian from earlier that morning, questioning him again and again on his absolute certainty that the hairspray cans would explode once they were punctured.

"Yeah, I guess they will," Patrick said, bewildered. "Why?"

"Because I believe I remember a story from my youth that we may be able to put into play to give our friend a little surprise. Do you still have the instrument that you found in the truck?"

Patrick instantly went flush with fear, his stomach twisting into knots.

No! How did he know?!

His eyes immediately went to Bing, the knowledge that his secret was out was surely going to bring immediate and swift consternation from the penguin.

But Bing merely cocked and eye, and smiled ever so slightly.

"Well, do you?"

"I . . . what do you mean? What instrument?" he lied.

Syrian gave him a scolding look. "I'm not going to reach for it, if you think I'm so inclined. I'd never touch one of those things. But you do still have it, don't you? The thing lodged in your backside."

Patrick now realized what his friend Ronnie Koontz must have felt like the time Patrick was with him, and Ronnie had tried to shoplift a candy bar from the local five and dime. The store manager had hurriedly blocked Ronnie's exit from the store, demanding the candy bar returned, and exacting a tongue lashing that caused Patrick such embarrassment that he quickly made his way over and stood in the milk aisle, waiting for Ronnie to leave, not wanting to acknowledge that they even knew each other.

Patrick listened to Kirsdona as she circled behind him, sounding much like an older sister now scolding her younger brother, "You are in so much trouble. I'm sure glad I'm not you."

"Shut up," was all that Patrick could say as he reached behind his back and produced the weapon.

"I'm sorry," he said as he held it in front of him. He leaned forward and began to hand it over to one of the animals, but all that they did was back away in fear.

"Uh . . . no," Syrian said, a bit alarmed at the sight of the pistol. "We don't want anything to do with it. But we do have an idea where you can use it to help us with Tye."

Patrick froze with surprise at the remark.

"You want me to shoot him?" he asked, thinking that his friends had totally lost their minds, bewildered at what he thought they were saying to him.

"No, no. Nothing like that. I don't believe in using such a thing against another living being, even if it is Tye."

"But," Bing interjected, "we can use it to give them a taste of their own medicine."

Patrick was shocked by their attitudes.

"I can't believe this. I thought you'd never forgive me if you ever found out. How did you know?"

Bing took a deep breath. "We saw it one night while you were sleeping. It was a point of great discussion, believe me. But we came to understand that if you needed something like that to allow you to feel more comfortable until you came to believe in yourself, then we came to the conclusion that we'd have to make this one concession."

Patrick smiled hesitantly. If Bing and the others had made this allowance within themselves, then he knew that he then would have to hold up his end of the bargain, no matter what it was that they wanted.

"Ok. What is it that you want me to do?"

And that's when they laid out their plans to him.

It was simple enough. Patrick was to navigate his way back down to the road—with Dog's protection and assistance—and acquire the white panel van that they had passed earlier. Then he was to bring it back to the spot where Tye said that he would be the next morning.

The terrain that Patrick needed to maneuver over and around wasn't all that crowded or steep, and he made the trek in under an hour. That part of the plan worked easily enough because Tye was nowhere in the vicinity once they brought the van into the hills. Scouts had been placed at various locations trying to make sure that Tye and his forces where on the other side of the hill, completely unawares of the situation as it was unfolding.

Patrick would then take a position in a tree that was earmarked for him to hide as Tye and his group (hopefully) would make their way in close proximity to the van. The position that Patrick was to take in the tree was such that his back would be to the brilliant morning light, allowing a natural camouflage of sunlight to take affect for anyone that would be facing him or trying to spot him in the tree. Once he was in place, then the animals would all take their positions strategically placed in a semi circle around the area, all hidden from plain sight.

As the plan went, with gun in hand, a simple shot by Patrick into the belly of the van should puncture several of the hairspray cans, thus causing numerous explosions that would in turn cause all the remaining cans to then explode. The van should remain in one piece, but with all the racket and potential damage occurring within the van it should surprise Tye and his group greatly. With Tye and his group in chaos, this should allow Gurd and his band of mongoose, as well as the birds, to begin an attack in earnest.

All they had to do was wait.

And now, with Patrick at the base of the tree he was to mount (and the rest of the assemblage hopefully assuming their positions) he turned to the others that had accompanied him to this spot and wished them well on their return.

"Oh, we're not going anywhere," Melanbach said flatly. "We're staying right here with you."

"But this is too close," Patrick replied, alarmed. "I thought that I was to stay here alone until I took the shot. Then I was supposed to backtrack to the rear again."

"You are. But we are not going to just leave you by yourself. If something should go wrong you may need our help."

"You're kidding."

"No. We're not leaving."

"And don't let our size fool you, either," another of the rats chimed in. "We are quite capable of handling more than a few snakes."

"Yeah, but don't snakes eat rats?"

The rats all smiled and glanced to one another.

"My, you do have a lot to learn about the animal world, my friend. Believe me, that is not always the case."

Patrick rolled his eyes.

"Ok, climb on."

The rats scampered up Patrick's arms as he reached down to them, their tiny paws tickling him as they went. As he began to climb the tree Patrick looked down upon who his potential saviors could be—three rats—and shook his head.

"This is just great," he mumbled to himself sarcastically, moving upwards tree limb after tree limb. "I hope nothing goes wrong. 'Cause if it does I wonder who'll be saving who."

Minutes passed slowly as Patrick sat up in the tree, his attention never leaving the entire width of the potential battlefield. In time, though, he spotted two beings that he wished he hadn't.

The first was Death. She sat on her horse at the far west end of the field, solitary and seemingly unobserved. Patrick suddenly remembered that he had forgotten to tell his friends of his encounter with the dark figure earlier that morning, wondering if it was even worth bringing up at this point being that it was so late in the hour.

The other, of course, was Tye. He was across the field, a good one hundred yards or more away, perched on the side of a small grassy knoll, his arms folded in front of him like an overseeing general. It wasn't long before he and his group made their way to the top of the far hill.

Patrick was quickly surprised to find just how many reptiles Tye had at his disposal. The field in front of them began to become ripe with alligators, Gila monsters, and lizards. But what was truly amazing from Patrick's perspective was the amount of snakes that now streamed into the area. They wrapped themselves around each other, twisting and turning and hissing with such magnitude that Patrick forgot to breathe for a moment. Black, red, and gold banded serpents moved along the grass, some as small as a foot in length, while others that were completely immeasurable from Patrick's point of view, stretched out in layer after layer of writhing coils.

"How are we supposed to fight that?" he whispered, quite alarmed by what he saw.

Melanbach and the others settled in below him.

"I see what you mean," the rat replied. The others said nothing, their shock at seeing what was displayed before them much too overwhelming for words. "I sure hope Syrian's plan works."

Patrick watched as Tye made his way into the clearing, the scoundrel's attention becoming more and more focused on the van.

Patrick heard Tye yell for all to stop as he made his way over to the white vehicle. He lifted himself off the ground with his massive wings, landing on top of it with a thud.

"What's this?" he asked aloud. "Don't tell me they tried to make their escape in this thing? I was going to give them a little more credit than that."

Tye scanned the surrounding hillside, his head darting from side to side looking for anything that moved, but found nothing.

Patrick watched as Tye tilted his head back and began sniffing the air. A broad smile then filled Tye's face.

"Ah, I may not be able to see you, my little piggies, but I can most definitely smell you!"

He crouched down low towards the van, sniffing as he went.

"There's something here all around us. I can smell their sweat and fear," he said as he sneered. "I think that the fools may actually be right under my feet!"

And then as Patrick watched, he could see a revelation take place in Tye. His eyes went wide and he lifted himself high into the air with his newfound wings.

"I know this story! I know it well," he said as a look of condescendence overcame him. "Please. They're trying to steal an old tale from the history books. Do you really think that you can fool me this easily?"

He then turned to the reptiles as they waited his instructions.

"They're in the van. At least a few of them are," he said as he spread his arms. "Dig them out and bring to them to me."

Patrick turned as he caught some movement out of the corner of his eye. It was Kirsdona and Bing, just as planned. They moved to the top of the other hill, the one to Patrick's far left.

Tye spotted them as well. Patrick watched as Tye lifted himself off from the top of the van and made his way to the center of the battlefield, hovering just long enough to utter a few venom filled words to the animals before him.

"I see you have chosen death this morning," Tye began with a mocking smile. "It's such a shame too. Such a nice day to have to slaughter so many, when all you have to do is to give up one."

Kirsdona could not contain herself.

"I didn't quite hear you. Why don't you come over here and say that again?"

But Tye only smiled bitterly.

"Perhaps when you grow a pair of wings we can discuss this a little further, eh, pussy cat?"

But Kirsdona didn't flinch.

"I won't have to after I gnaw off yours," she growled in return.

Tye only stared back with blank, soulless eyes.

"Be sure to ask yourselves," Tye began again, "that as the day progresses, if one small boy is really worth the effort you are about to make. All this can be stopped with four simple words. Just say to me that the boy is mine, and I, and all my companions will leave you to live out the rest of your days in peace. My master has no quarrel with the animals of this world, she only wants the boy."

Bing made his way to the front slowly, his head hanging low. He stopped when he reached a spot just in front of Kirsdona, slowly finding a voice in which to deliver his reply. It was obvious he was tired from lack of sleep, but his voice was so calm and reassuring—and filled with such majesty—that Patrick had to peer around several branches to locate the small penguin to make sure that he hadn't just tripled in size.

"I know that you believe that what you are doing is the right thing in your head, Tye, but it is your heart where you have to search. I ask you the same question as you just posed to us, 'Is the boy really worth the effort you are making?' If you let us pass, I assure you that we will protect you as we would any other from the harm that your master may bring. She is a deceiver, and is making you perform acts that only consist of foolish trickery. Do not make the mistake in believing that she considers you an equal. For at the end of the day, is ending your life, and the lives of all of your companions really worth the risk?"

Patrick watched Tye the entire time that Bing was delivering his speech. And though it was extremely difficult to tell, Patrick swore that a small part of Tye, somewhere deep deep inside him, was actually contemplating what Bing was saying.

But then the evilness and wickedness that was still so overwhelmingly prevalent in Tye began to reemerge, the laughter that came forth from him speaking volumes. He quickly turned to his army and sent out his brief instructions.

"Bring me the boy, my pretties. Fresh meat is now being served," he screamed aloud.

Patrick and the others watched as Tye began to fly back towards the van.

Patrick then began to hear the birds coming from overhead. He turned just in time to see the southern sky completely darken with hawks, eagles, falcons, osprey, and owls as they made their assault to the trees all around him. Patrick watched as the various birds of prey mounted the branches as they awaited their instructions, their eyes keenly fixed on their quarry before them. The birds were visibly upset at seeing the creature Tye had become, presumably because they had never witnessed such a thing before. Their shrieking and shrill squawking was completely disturbing, causing such a racket that it made it difficult for anyone to hear.

Patrick knew that there was no better time than the present. With the lizards and snakes beginning their examination of the van, and Tye now within an eyelash of stepping on top of the vehicle, Patrick raised the pistol and took aim.

"Boy, did you just mess up," Patrick said aloud, his words setting the tone for the entire event.

Patrick pulled the trigger, the pistol jerking hard in his hands, and awaited the expected results.

But just like all things that are planned and scrutinized and thought out for great lengths of time, sometimes it's the smallest of miscalculations that can cause things to go astray.

Patrick's shot did indeed puncture the side of the van as intended. The shot surprised Tye to such a degree that he momentarily lost control of his flying and dropped ten feet in the air before he caught himself.

But the true shock came when after the bullet passed through the side of the van and then punctured and ruptured the various cans of hairspray. What Patrick didn't know was how a bullet can sometimes react after it interacts with another object. The trajectory doesn't always stay straight and true. For as the bullet instantaneously traveled through the cans of hairspray its course took an unexpected turn downward, ramming through the floorboard, and then piercing the gas tank below.

The explosion that came forward from the van was nothing that anyone had expected at all. It was as if a bomb had gone off. The force from the explosion was so fierce that it knocked Patrick and the rats out of the tree and onto the ground below, instantly knocking the wind from all of them.

Tye was propelled twenty feet away, tumbling over and over before he too finally came to a stop on the ground below him. The snakes and other reptiles that had overtaken the van were instantly incinerated. Even the birds and the other animals that were to begin their attack once the hairspray cans exploded, paused at the unexpected sight before them.

Tye slowly picked himself off the ground, his left wing still smoldering from the explosion. He stumbled slightly, the concussion from the blast still lingering.

"So this is how you want to play, then?" he asked vehemently. "Kill them all," he directed to his forces, "I want nothing left that is breathing. Nothing!"

Kirsdona then turned to the creatures that were nearby.

"Let's end this now," she ordered.

The group of animals emerged from their places of hiding, throwing themselves at the reptiles with such a rapid assault that the snakes were caught completely off guard. The animals screamed as they tore head on into the pulsing mass of reptiles—ripping, tearing and biting anything they could get their hands on.

Dog moved to the front of the line next to Kirsdona, his teeth bared, and growling savagely.

Kirsdona glanced over at him in surprise, her dismay at the position he had taken becoming obvious.

"You don't belong here, Dog! Move to the rear!"

But the animal would not budge.

"No. This. Is. Not. About. You! This. Is. About. The. Boy," Dog growled low and fierce, baring his fangs for the onslaught. "You. Are. Not. The. Only. One. With. Teeth. And. A. Temper."

Kirsdona opened her mouth to reply, but slowly brought it to a close. It was evident that she had just gained a little more respect for the animal.

"Ok, then. But hang close to me. Don't let them get at your hind quarters. That's where they're most likely to try and strike first."

Dog nodded in return. "I. Have. Been. In. Fights. Before. And. Though. I. Do. Not. Believe. That. Any. Good. Will. Come. Of. This. I. Will. Not. Let. Them. Have. The. Boy."

The war was on, and nothing was a certainty except that death would be the obvious result.

Patrick watched in awe as Kirsdona began, going from reptile to reptile no matter the size or quantity, and destroying each of them in a fit of rage that was unmatched by any other. Her bite and claws so lethal that even the alligators and crocodiles backed up at her approach.

The birds became aerial dive bombers, launching themselves in groups of twenty or more, each picking out a patch of real estate they would direct themselves towards and then scoop up unsuspecting reptiles in their talons and beaks, carrying them off to their deaths to points unknown.

Dog was slow in his pursuit, but he still held his own as he progressed, sure not to allow anything behind him as Kirsdona had instructed.

The mongooses were the slowest, but the most sure handed when it came to the snakes. Their dance of death was artful and dutiful as they would firmly catch the snakes by their necks, holding on for dear life until death quickly overtook its victim.

The others held no weapons of choice, other than their teeth, claws, and their wits, but Syrian held a huge tree branch that he had fashioned into a club, swinging it back and forth in front of him like a baseball bat.

It seemed to Patrick as though Kirsdona and her group were driving a huge hole into the landscape the reptiles had created. It was almost too easy.

That's when the ground beneath the front few rows of mongoose and animals began to vibrate and fall apart, the sandy soil tumbling away revealing a trap.

It became obvious that some of the snakes had buried themselves earlier, and were now emerging from under the very ground where Kirsdona, Dog and the rest now held their position.

"Oh, hell," was all that Kirsdona could say as she began pushing her way backwards, realizing what was taking place.

The snakes came up through the ground, snapping and spitting at anything that moved.

For a moment it looked as though everything was going to go wrong with the snakes moving through the ground at their feet, and the animals in total disarray with the sudden and unexpected attack. The snakes wrapped themselves around several of the unsuspecting mongoose, pulling them down into the freshly dug pits where they had been hiding. Lizards of all sizes then jumped into the holes to fight the entrapped animals.

But Syrian acted instinctively, grabbing one large snake by its tail and began swinging it like a whip, cracking every snake and lizard that he could with a blow so mighty that it instantly killed all that came in contact with the snap. In his other hand he still held the branch, raining blow after blow down upon anything else in his path.

Watching Syrian react as he did caused the others to pull their ranks together and reengage their attack in earnest.

After Patrick regained himself after his fall, he did as he was told. It had already been discussed that he would be of no use in trying to stop the slithering beasts. He didn't possess the quickness, fortitude, or have the experience in dealing with such a lethal adversary.

Patrick moved up the grade a little, with Melanbach and the other rats at his side, finally finding Bing underneath an old elm tree. A few of the other animals moved forward to form a protective line in front of them.

"I don't like this," Patrick said low. "It looks like we have about as many as they do, but something isn't right. I would have expected the witch queen to send along more than this to help Tye."

Bing nodded knowingly at his remark.

"I understand that the battlefield to the north was an overwhelming massacre. Either she is allowing Tye to stand or fall on his own, or she is busy with thoughts that are placed elsewhere."

Patrick watched as Tye retook the position that he had held across the field, a silent chess match in progress.

Patrick then began to wonder where Sin had made his way to, his eyes searching the immediate area but not finding the white animal. Patrick finally spotted him; the animal was just making his way from where they had spent the night, lazily walking towards him as he stood by the tree.

"That's strange," Patrick said aloud as he motioned to the boar. "I thought he would have been the first one out to fight."

But Bing only shook his head. "You have not been threatened as of yet. I believe he will do nothing more than to stand by until such a time as your life comes into danger. Then you will see him react."

Melanbach nodded. "He is your guardian, Patrick. I feel sorry for the creature that finally gets their hands on you."

Bing turned his attention back to the battle front. "Let's hope that we never have to see that happen."

They all watched as wave after wave of reptiles was slowly but surely beaten back, their position now half of what it had been but a short time ago.

Patrick looked across the field, gauging Tye's reaction. He expected to see Tye fuming at the display in front of him, but the devil was doing nothing but standing there, his attitude alarming to Patrick considering the circumstances.

"Something's not right," Patrick said, his voice barely audible. "This is going too easy, and Tye's not even concerned."

"I've noticed that as well," Melanbach began. "It's as though . . ."

And then they all watched as Tye turned and looked behind him. His sight seemed to be trained on something beyond the hill he was standing, something that hadn't come into Patrick's view as of yet.

They watched and watched; minutes passing by with Tye doing nothing more than looking behind him as if he was expecting something sudden. With the peculiar way in which Tye was behaving, Bing, Patrick and Melanbach gave all their attention to finding out what Tye was concerning himself with.

Finally they saw him turn back to the battlefield—and he was smiling. A small, dark figure then appeared to Tye's right from out of nowhere.

"Who's that?" Patrick asked aloud. He squinted hard to make out the figure, but whoever (or whatever) it was, was dark and formless.

Melanbach, Bing, and Patrick all watched as Tye and his sudden companion began to converse. Their ease of conversation at this moment in time made Patrick feel helpless, his thoughts only consumed with the many terrible things that Tye could possibly be conjuring.

That's when Patrick saw what it was that Tye had been expecting.

It appeared from just behind the hill, appearing at first like a shimmering veil, then growing larger and more dense.

"I know that cloud," Bing said ominously.

Patrick's heart sank. He, too, recognized what Bing was observing.

"Oh, no."

Melanbach looked doubtful at the two, his understanding of what was taking place in question.

"I don't understand. What is it that you see?"

"You see the sky behind Tye. The dark cloud forming in the distance?"

"Yes."

"It's insects. Lots of insects. Killing insects. Patrick, we have got to leave! We've got to tell the others. We've got to leave at once!"

But just as the words left Bing's mouth, from the east came a great wave of reptiles that had been hidden from the initial gathering. They stormed the area to their west, attacking Kirsdona and the others that were caught unawares.

"Oh, no," Bing said as he closed his eyes. "We've been such fools! How could we have expected something such as Tye to fight a straight on battle! We've got to get everyone out of here! Now!"

But just as Bing was about to shout the order for everyone to begin retreating, Patrick reached out and stopped short the penguin from his frantic instructions.

"Bing, look. I don't think it's what you think it is. It only looks like butterflies."

Bing looked again in the direction of the dark cloud. And sure enough, Patrick was correct. It was only butterflies.

"Butterflies?" Melanbach asked aloud. "Has he lost his mind? What madness is this? What can he hope to gain by sending in butterflies? The birds will surely . . ."

But Bing had already deduced the intent of the harmless insects.

"He's sending them in to blind us. He's using them to get at our sight. With the overwhelming number of those things sprayed across the field, our attention will be hard pressed to stay on the beasts at our feet."

"But the birds will surely snatch them out of the air, won't they?"

"Yes. But I don't think that Tye's sending in just a few hundred of the bugs. He's better prepared than that. I imagine they'll come at us like fog."

And as the three stood together, it was as if Bing was a prophet, for that is exactly what happened.

Butterflies and moths of every species and color came in a drifting cloud that settled over the battlefield, bringing disorientation and chaos to the animals as they tried to see through the mass of softly fluttering wings.

The larger birds began to divert their attack, now trying to skim just above the fray, hoping to take out as many of the irritating insects that they could.

The animals tried to swat at the butterflies that danced and looped in front of their eyes restricting their sight, becoming totally distracted from the danger that they were initially engaged with on the ground. This allowed the reptiles to become a little bolder in their attempts of assault.

But then something happened that not even Bing or Patrick expected. For just behind the cloud of butterflies came another cloud, this one the type that Bing had initially feared. Dragonflies and locusts could now be heard coming from behind the hill that Tye stood on. They stormed the skirmish bringing a devastating blow to the animal's progress.

The birds that had been flying low to rip asunder the butterflies and moths were now being pelted by the larger, faster insects, causing many of the birds to become disoriented. With their sight impaired it allowed some of the larger lizards to now leap up with their poisonous bite and snag the blinded birds, pulling them to the ground to be devoured.

Patrick, Melanbach and Bing all stood with their mouths open, awestruck by the sudden turn of events.

"We've got to go—now!" Bing shouted, running forward to try and gather as many as he could for their retreat.

Patrick tried to help as well, his fears of engaging the snakes only intensified by the butterflies and moths that now blinded his view as he made his way forward. He swatted back and forth, trying his best to clear a way to get the word to everyone to evacuate immediately.

But then a thought occurred to him that caused him to hesitate for a split second.

Where were they all going to go? In which direction were they to make their escape? And to what end?

Patrick instantly tried to find Bing, calling his name as best he could while trying to keep the moths from entering his mouth, all the while expecting to peer into the sky and find Tye to be hovering just above him.

It was chaos at its extreme.

And, if he was ever going to be the "difference maker" that the others had talked about, then this was the moment he was going to have to push it through.

It was now or never.

For the past few hours he had been toying with the idea that there could possibly be a means by which they could make their escape. One that although gave Patrick great cause for concern, still seemed to be a way that could be used as a last ditch effort. And, whether or not they had now reached that point, he was not wise enough to know whether he wanted to question it or not.

Patrick looked around and spotted Bing as he was trying his best to alert the others that things were so out of control that it was time to fall back and regroup. He fought his way through the mass of confusion, stumbling every now and again over a fallen creature, suddenly finding himself next to the small bird.

Patrick didn't even ask, but instantly grabbed up Bing and made a beeline for the small graveyard he had spotted the night before.

"Patrick, what are you doing?! Put me down! Where are you taking me?"

"We're getting out of here. I'm taking you to the graveyard."

"But what do you expect to find . . ."

A look of fear came over Bing as he began to realize what Patrick was attempting to do.

"Oh, no! Not that way, Patrick! That can't be the answer."

"It's the only way I know out of here, Bing!"

"But how do you know that we'll be able to travel through that place the way you did?"

"I don't. But it's worth a try."

Patrick ran hard, leaving the battle behind. He came upon the small site in seconds.

"You better close your eyes," he instructed Bing.

"Why? What is it that I might see?" Bing asked in terror.

"Things you don't want to," Patrick replied with a knowing voice. "And whatever you do, don't open them till we're through."

"But I'm not sure about this! Can't we . . ."

"No."

And Patrick stepped in . . .

. . . and in a blink emerged with Bing a short ways away from where the fighting was taking place.

"You can open your eyes now," Patrick said as he looked down on Bing who was tightly holding his eyes shut.

Bing opened his eyes and looked around in wonder. "Where are we?"

"I'm guessing, but I think we're just a few miles away from where the fighting is going on."

Bing was visibly disturbed. "Patrick, what were those things I heard in there? They sounded . . ."

But Patrick only shook his head. He was beginning to feel the slight discomfort of his travel, but not as bad as it had been before. He imagined that because of the close proximity, and due to the short jaunt, that the undead didn't have much time to steal away his life as they had before.

"I have to go back and get the others. I should be back pretty quick."

Bing, still astounded by what was taking place, merely nodded.

"But what about Tye? If he sees what you are attempting . . ."

"I'm hoping he won't. With all the bugs flying around that place I'd be amazed if anyone can see more than a few yards in front of their face. I'm guessing he doesn't know that I can do this. So, if he does see us leaving to the rear, he's probably only going to think that we're just running away."

And then Patrick was gone again, throwing himself back through the only way he knew to help save his friends.

He emerged at the same spot he had first left with Bing. The pain was building in his chest, causing his breath to feel restricted, but he ran on anyway. He knew he had little time to get to Syrian, Dog and the others.

He found Syrian next. It was hard for him to make out the baboon amongst the chaos, but he distracted his friend long enough to relay what his plans were and what was taking place.

Syrian expressed the same reservations as Bing, but once Patrick convinced him that it was the only way, the baboon followed without haste.

They soon found Kirsdona and Dog making their way around the far edge of the war front, trying their best to help the mongooses and the birds from becoming overrun.

Patrick relayed his plans as well to his friends, with Kirsdona being the only one with reservations that Patrick feared he may not be able to overcome.

"Well, your coming whether you want to or not," Patrick ordered.

"Do what you have to do to get the others away," she demanded. "Don't worry about me."

"I'm coming back for you, Kirsdona. So you had better get used to it, because no one is going to be left behind."

They watched as the tiger grunted and then took off again to join the fray.

"Dog, you're not going to give me any trouble, are you?"

The animal looked afraid, but quickly stuck his head high.

"I. Do. Not. Want. To. Go. But. If. You. Say. It. Is. Safe. Then. That. Is. The. Way. To. Go."

Patrick grabbed Syrian by the arm and once again began to make their way.

Patrick had enough sense to know that although the bugs were fighting the others, their primary concern was still him. He knew that his comings and goings were not going to go unnoticed forever, and probably were going to be passed along soon enough to Tye. Patrick knew that time was slipping by, and soon the element of surprise in the way that they were making their escape would become evident to all.

But he still had to find one more creature.

Luckily, as they made their way, Patrick spotted Sin and called for the animal to follow him. Patrick had to wait until the boar got close enough to relay what he intended to do, but the animal nodded slowly, and instantly began to follow his trail. Within seconds Patrick and the other two were making good time back to the graveyard.

The same instructions were given to Syrian as they had been to Bing, and once Syrian's eyes were closed Patrick grabbed his hand and made his way through.

"Unbelievable," was all that Bing could say as Patrick and Syrian emerged in a blink from the graveyard.

"Just a couple more to go and we should be safe," Patrick said as he heard the penguin and baboon share their total disbelief at what was taking place as Patrick once again headed back into the void.

Sin was waiting just where Patrick had left him. He knelt in front of the boar and coaxed him forward as Patrick kept a hand firmly grasp into its thick hairs. No further instructions were needed for Sin. Being blind, and being of the nature of a beast that he was suspected of, Patrick figured that if anyone was to be aware of what they were traveling through then it would probably be Sin.

They went in . . . then came out.

After delivering the boar, Patrick began to feel the pain emerging like a drumbeat.

Bing and Syrian were aware of the consequences of Patrick's continual jaunts, but could do nothing to stop or deter Patrick from his ways. They realized that he was too far along with this madness to stop now. He only had to rescue a few others before he could rest.

Patrick, his hands resting on his knees, his voice full of exhaustion, stated the obvious. "After I finish with this I think I'm going to be sick for quite a little while."

And he smiled. It was weak, but it definitely gave Syrian and Bing some cause for hope in Patrick's wellbeing.

And then he went back again.

This time, though, something unexpected happened.

Before he could emerge back at the point of fighting, some thing grabbed Patrick by the foot and began to pull him down into the dark material that he was traveling through. He twisted and turned, trying to get whatever it was to release him from its grasp. He kicked with his other foot, furiously trying to free himself from whatever was holding him back.

"Not so quickly," the thing that had him hissed. "There is a price to be paid for traveling through as you do."

Patrick tried to peer into the inky void to see what it was that was talking to him, but whatever it was that had him was too black to be seen.

Patrick looped his other foot behind the one that was snagged and flicked off the shoe that the creature had a hold of.

"I hope that counts for something," he said, and turned his attention back to making his way to return to collect his remaining friends.

Patrick heard the creature roar its anger behind him. It made him shiver with fear of what might be out there, but he quickly found the opening to the graveyard he needed, and made his way again.

Only this time, when he emerged, the sight in front of him made him lose his breath—and almost his mind.

Patrick had only taken three steps from the graveyard when he saw what he hoped he would never have to see.

The war was still taking place past the immediate trees that surrounded him, the animals and serpents each inflicting great deals of torture and death to one another. It was a slow and agonizing type of battle that showed no real victor at this point in the outcome.

Patrick knew that there was going to be victims. Death had told him that these things would come to be, but his twelve year old mind would not allow himself to believe that they were real possibilities.

As he stood, with the butterflies swirling all around him, with the sounds of creatures fighting and killing each other pounding in his head, he looked down and found Dog collapsed on the ground before him.

"Oh, no," he whispered as he knelt. His shock was overpowering.

No no no!

Kirsdona came up beside him.

Patrick looked into her face for an answer, but again found something that he never thought he'd see.

She had been crying.

"It's my fault," she said as she slowly shook her head. "I should have looked after him better. I should have never let him fight with me."

"How . . . ?" was all that Patrick managed to bring out.

But as he turned to once again examine the golden haired animal he could see a few of the smaller sized snakes, along with one larger one, their fangs still buried deep into the animal's skin.

Patrick slowly reached and plucked one of them off of Dog's hind leg.

Kirsdona reacted immediately, "Patrick, don't!"

But it was too late. The snake reared back its tiny head and struck at Patrick's bare wrist. The venomous fangs drove deep into Patrick's skin, the poisons released still plentiful.

That's when Patrick's color began to change. The golden color that had come forth at earlier times when Patrick found himself becoming enraged was now emerging.

"Patrick, what are you doing?" Kirsdona asked, her mouth falling open in fear.

It was then that something began to happen that no one could have expected—the gold turned to orange.

"Patrick?!" the tiger yelled, trying to get his attention.

And then the orange turned to scarlet.

Patrick held the snake in his hand, the serpent's fangs still sitting in his wrist. He watched as the snake began to twist and shake, its tiny eyes ballooning out of its head. The snake started to smoke as if it was beginning to get hot, and then all of a sudden popped like a piece of bacon sizzling on a griddle.

Patrick stood and directed his sight towards a path that went through the trees and over the battlefield to the other side.

Kirsdona knew that something bad was beginning. But as to what it was she had no idea.

"He did this," Patrick said low, his brow wrinkling downward.

Kirsdona heard a tremendous crack coming from overhead, thinking that something had made its way into the trees. But when she looked up she could see that the blue sky that had been in abundance for most of the morning was now blacked out by ferocious looking thunderclouds. It wasn't that they were moving in slowly, like a front was pushing into the area. No. The storms that were appearing above them were happening instantaneously. Rain and wind then began to whip madly from all directions. A monsoon was taking place.

Kirsdona glanced at Patrick as he began to move, knowing that he was somehow causing this to take place.

Patrick's first steps were slow and unsteady, but with each progressing step Kirsdona watched his skin begin to take on a darker color.

He was now red.

Kirsdona felt rumbles like small earthquakes coming from underneath her paws, watching as small fissure cracks began to run along the ground at the mere touch of Patrick's steps. The ground then began to split and yaw with great groans as he marched towards the battlefield. Trees began to burst into flames, and flowers melted straightaway. Tremendous lightning streaks were raining down on all sides of the battle front causing all parties involved to stop and take notice.

Patrick emerged at the tree line, his eyes fixed on only one possible thing—Tye.

"You did this," Patrick spat forward, his rage now consuming him.

For the briefest of moments his attention was drawn to a group of serpents and mongoose that had not ceased their fighting. Patrick cocked his head to the side in disgust, knelt, and laid a hand on the ground that caused fire to erupt from the grasses, engulfing everything across the battlefield. The bugs that were flying overhead were blasted with such intense heat that they evaporated in an instant.

The animals and serpents shrieked at the acknowledgement of what was taking place. Most fled without concern for their safety from their assailants, now merely fleeing for their lives from something worse. Far worse.

A field of fire now stood between Patrick and Tye.

As Patrick looked upon the winged, man-creature, a streak of lightening cracked down to the tree just behind where Tye stood, exploding it into a thousand pieces.

But Tye didn't move. He only stared back at Patrick with the same wicked and soulless eyes that Patrick had first encountered at his house.

Patrick looked to his left, watching the specter of Death still mounted on her horse, the beast now taking slow but purposeful steps in his direction.

Patrick was barely aware of what was taking place all around him, or even with what was taking place within himself. He knew only one thing—that Tye was going to pay for the death of Dog, even if it meant that he himself was going to die this day as well.

Death had covered half the distance between herself and Patrick. Tye still stood on the hilltop, possibly awaiting Patrick's next move. Possibly waiting for Death to intervene and alleviate his problem.

Patrick raised his hand, a small smile on his face. He was going to finally see what kind of powers he did possess. He was now going to see just what he could really do.

But before he could advance his thoughts, he heard a voice come from behind him speaking his name. It was a woman's voice, soft and caring.

It was his mother's.

Patrick turned instantly, abandoning all thoughts of destruction in that instant.

"Mom?!" he cried out in hope. He dearly needed someone at this, his most bewildered and confused moment.

But as he turned he didn't see his mother—it was only Kirsdona who stood behind him on top of the hill.

"Patrick," she spoke to him, her voice and posture coming from inside her at a place that only could come from a mother. Her speech wasn't loud, in fact it was as soft as a kiss on the wind. But to Patrick's ears it filled them like a symphony.

"Please don't be afraid," she said in assurance. "You have come too far to turn your life over to them. This isn't what you want. This isn't the time. They are not worth the risk of losing yourself. Your place lies elsewhere."

Patrick stood, his arms limp at his side. It wasn't his mother who he cast his vision to, but it might as well have been. The words soothed him like honey, for they were the words he needed to hear. They were the words of truth.

"But look what they did," he cried.

Kirsdona nodded.

"I know. And it is on their heads that this will have to rest. But there is nothing that you can do that will make this go away or change. There are others who have placed their faith and trust in you to see that this does not happen again. They have placed their trust in you to see this through to the end. Do not abandon their prayers with just a moments thought."

Patrick turned and looked up at Tye.

"The boy seems to have made his path, don't you think?" he offered with a shout.

Patrick only stared at him with contempt.

Kirsdona took a step towards Patrick from the top of the hill.

"My son, do not listen. Your place is elsewhere. You have to accept what you are and what you have been given. It is a gift." Kirsdona looked across the field. "Not like the disease that has been allowed to fester in others."

Patrick looked down to the ground all around him. The fire was still raging out of control, burning the fields and trees without prejudice. He raised his arms, and then slowly let them fall to his sides. The fire instantly extinguished.

"It's time for us to go," Kirsdona said finally.

Patrick felt the words from Kirsdona go through him and leave their mark, and in some strange way he felt refreshed. His mind and his thoughts returned to him, and he knew that she was right. It was a momentary peace, but he let it overtake him.

He turned and began running up the hill towards Kirsdona, and towards the graveyard, his eyes still clouded with tears. He was crying both from anger and frustration, as well as from a sense of loneliness and confusion. He ran as fast as he could, brushing past snake and serpent and mongoose that were watching from the shadows.

"NO!" Tye shouted from behind, now finally realizing what was taking place. "You are not leaving like this! If I have to rip the very limbs from your body you are not leaving here!"

But Patrick did not hesitate. Kirsdona turned and started towards the graveyard as well, her speed and length of stride bringing her to the spot just ahead of Patrick.

As Patrick ran he looked at nothing more than the ground in front of him, his eyes not wanting to look elsewhere. But he did stop for just an instant as he was distracted by something small and gray to his left.

It was Melanbach.

Patrick quickly altered his direction and leapt at the large rat, gathering him in his hands before he began his assault again.

"What are you doing? Put me down! Put me down this instant!" the rat bellowed.

"No," Patrick said as he saw Kirsdona just ahead of him. "I'm not leaving anyone behind."

"But I don't want to go with you! That wasn't my intent!"

Though Patrick couldn't see him just yet, he was sure that Tye was just behind him, surely racing at him to end this once and for all.

Patrick saw Kirsdona in the distance standing just before the graveyard. He ran as fast as he could, and although he didn't want to turn around and take a look, he could tell that Tye was quickly closing the gap.

Patrick pumped his legs as hard as could, the white noise of fear rushing in his ears.

"Patrick! Run! Run as fast as you can!" Kirsdona screamed at him.

Patrick turned around just in time to see Tye lunge at him with those three fingered hands. Both Melanbach and Patrick screamed as he reached for them. But as Patrick turned back his feet became entangled causing him to stumble and fall, landing at the base of a tree just a few feet from Kirsdona.

Without a thought he instantly picked himself up, Melanbach still in hand, and watched as Tye stopped himself in mid air like a perverted humming bird, the creature turning and repositioning himself to make another attack.

Tye, now only a few feet off the ground, arched his body and threw himself in the direction of Patrick and Melanbach.

Kirsdona was crouched low, bracing her body to throw herself at Tye as best she could, when to her surprise from above them all came a shout as Gurd and three other mongoose launched themselves from the trees onto Tye's back.

Tye screamed in rage at his attackers as they forced him to deal with them for the moment, their bites and claws digging deep into his skin allowing Patrick his opportunity for escape.

Patrick and Kirsdona's eyes locked onto one another as he ran at her, the moment for their escape now evident.

Tye shook off the final mongoose just in time to see Patrick just a few feet from the tiger. With one final lunge he propelled himself at the boy.

But Patrick was too fast. He closed his eyes and leapt at Kirsdona, the tiger raising up and catching the boy as all three of them tumbled backwards into the graveyard just as Tye reached out to them with a roar of denial and hatred.

But they were gone.

Tye's final grasp snagged a tiny piece of Patrick's shirt, but nothing more.

PART III— BELIAL'S REACH

CHAPTER 22

The Darker Way

He was lost.

Dog was dead and Patrick was lost.

This wasn't how it was supposed to be. Up till now this had always been a fairy tale. This journey—and all the things that had taken place in the world—was as if he had been taken up and placed in a land and time that was make-believe. And in make—believe stories everyone lived and only the evil ones died.

Not the good ones.

Not like Dog.

Patrick cried like he never had before. His entire body ached horribly from his travel through the land of the dead. But his only thought, his only focus, was on the remaining vision of Dog laying at his feet, twitching with so many poisons running through his small frame, his body finally giving up the fight and dying.

And Patrick could do nothing.

He had no magic powers to save this life as it stood before him. He could do nothing but stand and stare.

So Patrick cried.

The others stood silent around him, each consumed with the overwhelming grief that they each carried at losing one of their own.

"I couldn't do anything," Patrick sobbed, a look of shock on his face. "This isn't fair. He didn't do anything to deserve this."

"Patrick, it's not your fault," Bing said, trying to offer comfort.

But Patrick only looked at him with anger through tear filled eyes.

"Don't you get it? He volunteered to come. He was the only one that didn't have the dream. He was actually braver than any one of you. You all had to come. But he volunteered."

Patrick began to cry again. And as he did he heard the words drift to him from somewhere in the back of his mind.

"If you are to accept your destiny, then you have to accept the consequences that go along with it."

It was the words that Death had spoken to him. The haunting, crippling words that now were standing in front of him like gnashing teeth. Words that in their context were just, yet so painfully hard to accept.

". . . the consequences that go along with it."

Patrick swallowed hard.

This was one big consequence.

His bones and muscles ached hard with pain from the life that had been torn from him, but he was not going to be deterred from the passion that was building inside.

He shook his head back and forth to no one.

"Well, I'll tell you this," the bitterness of his words filling the air, "this isn't going to happen again. No one else dies."

Syrian raised his head from his own grieving.

"Patrick, you cannot make promises like that. It will only make the reality of when another of us falls that much harder."

But Patrick gave him a look that caused Syrian to pull back, the surprise evident on the baboon's face at Patrick's furious response.

"No," he said firmly. "As long as I am alive none of you will die like Dog. I won't let it happen."

Again Patrick shook his head.

"But, Patrick . . ." Bing began, his words filled with pity.

"If the witch queen wants me, then I am going to give her exactly what she wants. Because if she thinks that a frightened little twelve year old boy is going to show up to deal with her, she's going to be the one who is going to be in for a surprise. I'm going to treat her exactly like she did Dog."

Patrick now noticed that the others were looking at him, their eyes wide with awe and fear. But it wasn't because of the words being spoken. As he held his hands up in front of his face he began to realize that he again was starting to glow a brilliant sunlit gold. He knew that they were afraid that he would again make the ground split and the sky crack.

Patrick blinked twice and then closed his eyes. He swallowed hard and turned his thoughts to something else, thinking of his mother and father and what they must be going through at this moment. His emotions finally began to shift and release. He opened his eyes again and saw that the light was now subsiding, barely making any kind of visible statement that it had even come forth.

"I . . . I'm sorry," he said absently. "If I think of something else besides my anger I think I can control it somewhat."

Patrick struggled hard with what was happening. "But Bing, these creatures, these friends are dying . . . for me. I don't want this to happen."

"Yes. Yes they are," Bing nodded. "I believe it's that they understand the importance with which we carry out our task and deliver you safely across to your destination."

Patrick sniffed another tear away. "But look at me, Bing. Look at me. Do I look like someone who people should die for? I'm just some dumb kid."

Syrian smiled briefly. "Well, I think it is evident by your recent outbursts that you are a little more than just that."

But it was Melanbach who made his way over to Patrick, carefully pulling himself up onto the boy's lap. Patrick had never truly looked at Melanbach before, now seeing just how old the rat really was. The white and gray hairs that clouded his face gave a true indication of his time on this earth, the wisdom of his age ringing through in his words.

"When I look at you my friend I see much more than what you perceive, believe me. We all do. The flesh that you carry over your bones houses much more than muscle and blood and heart and lungs. It houses your very being. It houses your soul. We all come across so much as beings who are made up as our appearance presents. But you should know better than others just what it takes to carry yourself forward. It is something that we all bring to our daily lives. Each one of us has our role to play; each of us carries our own importance. Don't ever belittle the significance of any being, no matter how little or how big. And do not be deceived by your own eyes. For each of us—and perhaps all of us—has a mighty role to play in this to see it to the end. From what you have now seen, you should know this better than most.

"Dog's death, however painful it may be, was still part of the forceful steps that you will need to take with you as you are to continue on. Do not let his death become something that takes on a tone for remorse, but rather let it carry on as a light to guide you through to complete your purpose."

Patrick nodded silently to the rat.

And then something hit him like a thunderbolt.

As he lifted his head, with the noble words that Melanbach had just spoke still ringing in his ears, Patrick looked around at the creatures that were all so close to him.

"I know who you guys are," he said, his eyes growing wide with revelation. "You're the rulers of each of your own kinds, aren't you?"

Each creature seemed startled to hear the words coming from the boy. They looked around from side to side, each trying to beg off from the title given.

But Patrick continued on, nodding in his own reaffirmation.

"You are, aren't you? You've been keeping another secret from me, haven't you? And don't lie about it."

Bing stood and moved in front of Patrick, his eyes clear and filled with purpose—and he nodded.

"We are as you have figured out. We didn't share this with you because we believed that there wasn't any reason to heighten your alarm any more than it already was. Make no mistake that we still had the dream, only now perhaps you understand as to why it was given only to us."

Kirsdona moved into Patrick's view.

"You know, for a human, you're not as dumb as I thought. But I've got to ask—how did you figure it out?"

Patrick smiled, his understanding of the truth making it a little easier coming to terms with the situations as they have taken place.

"I don't know," he said hesitantly, a puzzled look on his face, "It just came to me."

The animals glanced around from one to another, unspoken thoughts being passed between them.

Patrick looked down at the ground.

"And what about Dog?" Patrick asked quietly.

Bing shook his head. "Unfortunately, he was just a noble being who decided to step forward to help us achieve our goal."

"But make no mistake," Syrian added quickly, "that he was one held in high reverence just for his decision to join us. The other creatures of the world have already recognized this. They've acknowledged what he has done."

"And him?" Patrick motioned towards the boar. "Surely he isn't . . ."

"No," Bing interjected. "He is still an enigma, even to us."

Patrick took a deep breath and stood. He turned and watched as the spirits in the graveyard kept their distance. They weren't as fidgety as the other spirits he'd encountered, and they didn't seem to want to engage in conversation as the others had before. Perhaps, he wondered, that word had traveled forward about him and his friends and what had taken place. He then looked down at his shoeless foot and wiggled his toes.

"What happened to your foot covering?" Syrian asked.

"It's called a shoe," Patrick said as he looked back over his shoulder towards the graveyard. "I lost it in there. One of those 'things' took it."

"What are those creatures?" Bing asked, alarmed.

The others responded in kind asking the same question.

"It's like I explained before, they're just creatures that will not allow themselves to pass on to the next life. They're in some kind of weird limbo—like they're being punished or something. I don't know."

Patrick stretched his arms wide and yawned.

"Well, I don't feel as bad as I thought I would. Maybe they didn't get as much life from me as they did last time. I guess I was moving pretty fast."

"And they sounded horrible," Syrian added.

All of the others, except for Kirsdona, began to chime in their brief recollections of what they heard as they traveled through.

But then, too, the tiger added her say. "Believe me, they look worse."

The others were shocked by her statement.

Patrick turned and eyed the lounging cat. "Then you saw? You didn't close your eyes?"

Kirsdona began licking at something unseen in the grass, her long tongue sounding like sandpaper as it went. She turned her attention to the group, her expression now showing the true side of the jungle cat. It was a look that struck fear deep into Patrick's soul.

"I have learned that to survive in this world you should never close your eyes—except maybe to sleep—if you want to stay alive. Believe me, I have seen many things in this world that maybe I had no right in seeing. Horrible, nasty things. Things done by both man and beast. But I will tell you that what I saw in there was something that I do not choose to see again. Those creatures are an abomination."

Patrick once again took a deep breath.

"Then your not going to like what I have to say," he said as he looked at the ground, unwilling to meet her gaze.

"Oh? And why would that be?"

Patrick's eyes briefly flicked up to meet hers, his mouth trying to find the air to push the words forward.

"Because we have to go back in," he said firmly.

Now Patrick expected at that moment to be besieged with outbursts of dismay and anger and extreme combativeness at his suggestion. He had gone over his reasoning in his head and had conquered the many questions that would come forth based on his suggestion. But what he didn't expect to hear was laughter.

Lots of laughter.

"You have got to be joking?" Syrian said aloud. "Why would we want to do that?"

Bing chuckled heartily.

"No, young one. We are definitely not going back in there. Your youth has clouded your judgment."

While the others chuckled, it was only Melanbach, still sitting in Patrick's lap, who now looked up at the boy, his eyes never leaving Patrick's.

"How have you come to this conclusion, human? You know the perils of traveling through that place. Even my own kind have heard tales of beings that have traveled through that land, with many never making their way back out. So far, I believe that you have been fortunate in your travels."

Patrick reached out and gently cradled Melanbach in his hand, setting him on the ground as Patrick rose. He began to slowly pace in a small patch of high grass just away from the group, his eyes never leaving the graveyard behind them. The earlier laughter that had come forth at Patrick's traveling suggestion now quieted to silence.

"You all need to listen to me for a moment. If you don't like what I have to say then I'm open to any other suggestions. But I truly believe this is the only way we can go.

"We've been moving, for what, a better part of a week, and we're still probably more than halfway to where we need to be. Traveling in a car or truck isn't getting us anywhere very fast, and most of the time seems to actually be slowing us down.

"Believe me, I don't want to go back in there either. But I'm guessing that if we decide to do this, and that we each hold on to one another—and not let go!—that I can get us to a place that might be just a stones throw from where the witch queen is hiding.

"I don't think that we'll be in there all that long once we start through. I know it's not something that is going to be pleasant, but you all just need to trust me on this one."

Patrick finally turned his attention back to the animals' expressions. He had hoped that his short explanation would do the trick and get them all onboard with his idea. But what he found as he turned back towards them was that everyone still held true to their original thought—that each was totally convinced that they were not going to go back in.

Everyone that is, except for Kirsdona.

"Sounds like a plan to me," the tiger purred softly.

Kirsdona pushed herself up from her lounging position and began to stretch once again.

Patrick could tell that with him laying out the suggestion was one thing, but with Kirsdona's approval backing up his plan, well that was something that all the others were more inclined to listen to.

"Are you ladies really going to let the idea of something that lives in the dark scare you this badly," her voice harsh and mocking. "You heard what the boy said. Those things aren't going to be able to get at you. If we all stay linked to one another then I guess this is about the best shot we've got. Because if you all are so blind to see things as they are, then let me share a few thoughts with you.

"First, the boy—as are the rest of us even if you're too stubborn to admit it—is exhausted.

"Second, we're moving at a snails pace. From what I've been told this entire time is that the purpose of this thing has been to get the boy to the witch so that he can put a stop to this madness. So I would think that we'd want to speed this thing along.

"And last, Bing, if you think that you can continue on without sleep as you have so that you won't have any more dreams; so that Tye and whatever nasty creature the witch sends at us the next time can't see where we're going to end up, then you're a bigger fool than I thought.

"If this is what it's going to take to get us a giant step closer to finally putting an end to this ridiculousness, then what are we waiting for? Just close your eyes, gentlemen. The journey will be over in a blink."

The silence filled the air with their reservations.

Patrick looked around to each of the others, watching their faces as they searched inside themselves to see if they had the strength to follow through on what he had proposed.

And it didn't take but a moment.

Bing was the first to move. He walked over and stood next to Patrick, taking his wing and placing it in Patrick's hand.

"The only thing I could think of while Kirsdona spoke was that if Dog were here he wouldn't have hesitated in the least. He would have been the first to agree. He was extremely faithful to you, just as we all need to be at this moment in time."

Sin moved over and nudged up against Bing, the penguin reaching out and taking a handful of the boar's coarse, dense hair.

"Well, that's two of us," Bing said aloud.

Melanbach scrambled over and scampered up Sin's leg, pulling himself up with a grunt to the boar's backside.

"Make that three," the rat said proudly.

Kirsdona walked over to Patrick's left and stood beside him. Patrick reached out and laid his hand on Kirsdona neck.

"Don't let go kid," the tiger said firmly. "It's up to you now."

As they stood there, each trying to muster their own courage as to what was about to take place, they noticed that Syrian was the only one that had not moved as of yet.

"You don't want to go?" Patrick spoke up, surprised at the reluctance of his friend.

"Of course I don't," Syrian said with a smile. "But don't let my hesitation belay my actions. I was just saying a final prayer to see our way through."

"I hope you included all of us in your prayer," Bing said somberly.

Syrian walked over and finally joined the others. He reached out and grabbed hold of Sin's right ear.

"Yes," he said with a smile. "Even the tiger."

Patrick took a deep breath and turned to face the graveyard.

"But Patrick," Syrian added, "you have to understand something. If those creatures in there are really stealing your life, then this has to be the last time you go through."

"Syrian's right," Bing nodded in agreement. "Who knows how much they've stolen from you already."

Patrick nodded silently and took a deep breath.

"Yeah, I know. I've already been thinking about that."

Patrick then closed his eyes and uttered a final volley. "Alright then, here goes nothing."

Kirsdona's head instantly snapped towards the boy.

"Hey, I've heard you say that before. And if I remember correctly the results were not all that welcome."

Patrick wrinkled his nose, his mind trying to recollect what the tiger was talking about, when the memory came forward of when he first used those very words when he was learning to drive the truck.

"Oh, yeah," he said as he cleared his throat nervously. "It's just a saying. It doesn't mean anything."

"How about," Bing began quietly, "let's get this show on the road."

Melanbach and Syrian each chuckled.

"Yeah, I guess that'll work."

Patrick and the others made their way to the edge of the gravesite, pausing only momentarily as Patrick uttered a brief, "Excuse us," to the spirits as they waited for them to part, and then they each took the fateful steps into the beyond.

Tye stood amongst the still smoldering fields, staring at the van as it continued to burn, imagining that he was witnessing his life as it now stood.

The flies reformed next to him.

"YOu dO rEaLIze WHaT wE HaVE To rEpORt?" it said, unsure of Tye's reaction.

Tye turned slowly towards the flies.

"Yes. I'm well aware of my failings. And I'm quite sure that She already knows what has taken place."

Tye noticed that the flies remained in a looser formation than at earlier times. He wondered if they stood there, unsure of what kind of reaction he might bring forth, bracing itself for any sort of rage that he might deliver.

"ShE HaS AskED fOR YoUr pERsoNal aPpeARanCe. THiS wiLL bE sOMethIng tHAt shE wiLL ExPeCt in THe imMEdiAte. ANy diSObeDienCe oN YoUr paRt wiLL bE sOMetHinG She wiLL NoT tAKe liGHtly."

"I know," Tye replied, his voice low as he began to move away.

Tye looked across the charred and blackened field of both earth and bodies—and he smiled. It was not a smile of evilness or desire. Rather it was a smile of recognition in how far the boy had come along. Tye had known that the boy was going to give him—and the others—fits as they tried to contain him. But he hadn't quite known just how much the boy had progressed since he had last encountered him.

Tye now realized that there was a streak in the boy of something that he could relate to. Something that was just this side of clear thinking and purpose.

It was the impulse for revenge.

In Tye's mind it was a simple enough way of thinking that was just a hair's breath away from the side that Tye now stood on. Just a cautious stones throw as to where you begin to see things from a different perspective. Because once you allow yourself to succumb to the sweet taste of revenge, then it was only a matter of time before you begin to think more on how close you found yourself to that dark, ugly place that resides in everyone.

You find yourself feeling a little scared, yet remarkably bold for being able to walk the line—but not crossing it—that separates sanity from the other way of thinking.

The way of thinking that opens immeasurable doors of opportunity. The way of thinking that allows someone to think that they possibly were immune to the trappings of what was right and what was wrong.

Tye looked over the field as the flies followed him waiting his response, overlooking the remains of the charred and misshapen bodies.

The boy had even burned some of his own in the fit of rage that had befallen him. Total disregard had overtaken him in his pursuit of his revenge.

Was the boy even aware of it? And did he care?

Or had he already decided that it didn't matter anymore?

That he would allow circumstances to materialize as he saw fit.

That he would not allow another being to control him any longer.

That he was above it all.

Tye pondered these things about the Brighton boy, noticing the strange parallels that were now shaping between himself and the boy.

The flies drifted slowly with Tye as he made his progress through the field.

"wiLL We mAKe oUR wAy To HeR tHRone noW, oR Do yOu stiLL neEd tiMe to eVaLUAte wHAt haS tAKen plACe anD HoW yOu wiLL apPRoACh heR?" it hissed cautiously.

Tye shook his head slowly.

"I don't believe I'll be making that journey, thank you very much. I still have one last trick up my sleeve that I believe will win back my existence. Something that I once had in my grasp before I foolishly let it depart."

"buT tHe qUEen DemANds yOUr pReseNCe. If yOu Do nOT hEed HeR wORds wE hAve beEN InStruCted tO foLLow tHRouGh oN a MorE aDVanCed FoRm oF mODifiCAtioN tO yoUr fORm. SOmeThiNg wE BeliEVe ThaT wiLL cAuSe yOu tHE moSt imMEnse PaiN—aNd tOTal diSSatiSfacTion."

Tye turned towards the fly thing and smiled.

"By all means, come on in," he said unpleasantly, and opened his mouth wide.

The flies hesitated at his request, Tye realizing that they were now holding back, wondering if he had some unknown knowledge that gave them a moment of pause. They vibrated loud and long with a most unpleasant noise, unsure of what to do.

"YoU aRE a DeviOUs aNd mOSt irRESponSible CreAture, TyE. ThERe arE mAnY in ThESe lANds THat aRE nOt tO Be tRUsteD, bUt yOU aRe By FaR tHE mOSt deCEItful."

Tye smiled.

"Why thank you. I'll take that as a compliment."

"WhAT iS It tHat YoU hAVe iN yoUr PLans iF yOu aRe Not gOIng tO mAkE yoUr WAy tO tHe qUEen?"

"If I were to make my way to the queen, both you and I know that she will either end my life, or see to it that I spend the rest of my days in some repentant form of punishment. If I am still able to ensure that the boy is placed out of the way and unable to bring any harm to her plans then I may be able to bargain my way back into her good graces."

Tye nodded in the direction of Death.

"As it stand now I believe I am going to have her follow me around in the interim."

The lady still sat at the far edge of the battlefield overseeing the death toll as it rose with each last passing gasp of the dying.

Tye began to walk once more, his thoughts coming together on what his next course of action would be.

"Now that the boy is beginning to have some realization as to what power he possesses this is going to become far more elusive a trick to pull off."

"whAT dO yOu MeAn?" the flies asked, confused.

"Well, that next course of action is to ensnare the boy's father. This should be a simple enough gesture on my part. Once I have him in my grasp I should be able to send word to the boy that I have his father, which in turn should have the boy paying a call to my doorstep. It will be much easier to deal with the situation in barter, rather than having to trek around to who knows where to begin our search again for the boy. The boy, nor the father, is a fool—they'll suspect the trap. But if this time we're careful with our alignments, then the boy will have to surrender himself to me if he wishes his father freed.

"The trick in all of this is whether or not the boy has a full mastery of his abilities. Though the boy does puzzle me a bit, the display he put on earlier does present a bit of a problem. If he's fully aware of who he is then we have a dilemma, because then I'm not even sure that the queen herself can handle the boy. But if he is still in his infancy regarding his awareness, then I can easily control the situation."

"dO yOu KnOw WhERe tHe fAtHEr Is?"

"I've received word that he's traveling to the north of us. He's heading in the right direction, he's just a bit off course. I'm going to handle that part of it personally. Mr. Brighton will be as easy to dispatch as was his wife. Once I have him then I will call on you to alert the boy of my proposal."

"YeS, wE uNDeRStand. WItH thE fATher iN hAnd tHEn SureLy tHe Boy wiLL gIVe uP His qUEst."

"If he's got a brain in his little head, he will. This will work only if the bond that is between them is as strong as they indicate."

"tHEn yOu wiLL LeAve aT oNCe?"

Tye replied "Absolutely" as his wings lifted him off of the ground.

"But wait on my word. Once I have the father in hand then you or one of your legions must find the boy."

"dO yOu HaVe aNY iDeA wHEre thE BOy iS aT?"

"I don't know at the moment, but the penguin has to sleep sometime. When he does then I will gather his thoughts like a spider plucks the fly."

Tye moved a bit further into the bright sky before he turned and posed a quick question to the flies.

"Up till now I've been rather happy with the transformations as they have taken place. I don't quite understand what you could have meant when you said that I would have "total dissatisfaction" with the next one."

The flies then flew apart in a giant cloud of blackness before returning to form a strange shape as Tye watched from above. Once the flies had made the shape, Tye's mouth parted slowly in amazement.

"Yes," Tye said as he turned to move away, his face forming a painful expression. "I suppose I would have to agree with you on that one. That wouldn't have been fun at all."

CHAPTER 23

Bargains Offered, Bargains Made

Patrick tumbled from the graveyard onto the snow covered ground, falling face first into a high snow bank in front of him. The rest spilled out as well, collapsing in the deep snow beside him.

Bing righted himself and instantly began brushing the white flakes from his arms. "Well, that was something that I never want to do again," he said as he shook his head slowly.

"Were we flying?" Melanbach asked, unsure of what had just taken place.

"I don't know, but that was one crazy trip," Kirsdona said as she looked around, her expression adjusting to the landscape. "Where are we?"

"I'm not quite sure," Melanbach said, his tiny eyes peering into the dark that engulfed them.

"Did you hear those things in there," Bing asked quietly.

"I know," Melanbach said as he arched an eyebrow. "There are not many things in this world that bring fear to my heart, but for the life of me I just couldn't open my eyes to look."

Kirsdona was moving behind the penguin and the rat as they talked, her nose pushing the snow on the ground.

"What kind of hell did the kid bring us to, anyhow?" the tiger said as she shook the snow from her body. "It's freezing!"

Snow flakes danced and skittered all around them, the cold wind biting and snapping at their backsides.

"Finally," Bing said with a somewhat bewildered smile on his face, "It's about time we came into my kind of climate. I believe we've found heaven!"

Melanbach rubbed his tiny hands together, "If you say so. But I could really do without this stuff. I see it way too often."

The animals walked about sniffing and pawing at the snow covered grounds, each preoccupied with their own outlook as to where they were now located.

Patrick never rose from his horizontal position in the snow—he was in too much pain. The animals, so surprised to find where they had ended up, had forgotten all about the toll the journey had taken on the boy.

Bing finally turned to see Patrick still laying in the snow, the boy's eyes rolling back into his head.

"Oh no!" Bing yelled as he ran back to Patrick's side. "Kirsdona! Syrian! Come here now!"

Kirsdona moved at once to the penguin's side, her attention now focused on the boy.

"I knew that it was probably going to be bad for him," Bing started, "But I hoped that the outcome wouldn't be as painful as it had been before."

"Is he ok?" Kirsdona asked.

Patrick mumbled a barely intelligible, "No," as he pulled his arms tightly across his chest. He rolled to his side, doubling over in pain.

"What do we do?" the tiger asked.

"I don't think there's anything we can do," Bing began as he glanced around at all their concerned faces. "His body has got to adjust to the shock of whatever those things in there do to him as he passes through. If they are stealing his life, then . . ."

But then Bing stopped in mid sentence. His tiny head turned from side to side in an inquisitive motion.

Kirsdona nudged the small bird with her paw.

"So finish what you were saying. If they're stealing his life then . . . what?"

But Bing barely heard what the great cat was saying, for his mind was now focused in on something worse. A lot worse.

"Where's Syrian?" the penguin asked sharply.

"What?" Kirsdona replied, her attention turning behind her. "Why, he's right . . ."

". . . where? I don't see him anyplace!" Bing replied, alarmed at his discovery.

"Oh no," Melanbach said, the realization dawning on his face. "You mean he's still in . . ."

And they all turned to look back at the graveyard they had just exited. All of them except Patrick, who was still rolling around on the snow in great fits of agony. Sin stood silent just at the edge of the graveyard, the small smile that always seemed to be on his face now gone. It was as if the little boar was aware of what had happened.

"How did this happen?" Bing asked, knowing that no one had the answer he so desperately wanted.

"Are you sure he's not out here?" Melanbach asked, his tiny head turning from side to side looking for the baboon. "That maybe he's hasn't just ventured away for a moment?"

"I don't see him anywhere," Bing said as he began looking to the areas close by.

"And I don't smell him, either," added Kirsdona.

"He must have let go!"

"But everyone was instructed to hold on! Why would he have let go?"

Kirsdona and Melanbach acted on instinct; without a word being spoken they moved over to line of bushes marking the boundary to the graveyard. The yelping, startled array of sparkling lights that the animals recognized as spirits scattered instantly at the oncoming tiger. Kirsdona swallowed hard, braced herself, and then threw herself across the line.

But nothing happened.

Bing, still standing next to Patrick, shook his head at her attempt.

"We can't travel through on our own, Kirsdona! It's Patrick. He's the key to going through."

"I know, but I had to try!" the tiger yelled as she hurriedly made her way back to Bing's side. "We can't just leave Syrian in there! What are we going to do?"

But Bing just stared at the boy who was now in fits of pain and desperation.

"How do we ask him to go back in? Look at him."

They all stared at Patrick as he tossed from side to side, a deep guttural moan coming from inside him.

"He doesn't have any other choice!" Kirsdona insisted. "If he doesn't go back in then Syrian is surely dead—if he isn't already."

Melanbach moved next to Patrick, the rat putting his small paw on the boy's forehead. The rat's attention went from the boy, back to the graveyard, and then back again.

"I'm not sure," Melanbach began, "but I think that as long as the boy is in that place he doesn't seem to feel any of the pain. I mean, I didn't see him having any of this trouble while he was in there. I think that he only experiences the pain once he comes back out."

A swift realization came over Bing's face. "You're right. How could I have been so blind. I would have never thought of it before if the situation hadn't presented itself as it has." Bing took a deep breath. "I don't like this. I don't like this at all. But he has to go back in and find Syrian. The only good part about it is that he won't be in the pain he's in now once he crosses over."

"Now all we have to do is to tell him," the tiger said softly.

But Patrick was already aware of their discussions. Before they were even aware that he knew what had taken place, Patrick gritted his teeth and slowly rolled his body to the point where he could raise himself to all fours. With a tremendous effort he began to crawl, pulling his body closer and closer to the graveyard.

"We've got to help him," Bing barked out the instruction. "Kirsdona, see if you can move him close enough to where he can pull himself into the site."

Patrick had collapsed after moving only a few feet. Kirsdona moved swiftly, lifting the boy by the seat of his pants with her great jaws and then laying him just inches from the graveyards boundary, careful not to stay in contact with the boy for fear that he'd take her back with him to that awful place.

Patrick didn't move for more than a minute, the animals wondering if he was even still conscious. But then he finally raised his head and yelled out in pain as he reached out a hand, his fingertips gently touching the hallowed ground of the dead.

And then he was gone . . .

. . . and then so was the pain.

Patrick found himself once again in the place where he didn't want to be, his eyes blinking their adjustment to the dark. He poked at his sides making sure that the pain he was experiencing just a second ago was gone; thinking how funny it was that something like that could come and go so easily. But then he pushed aside any thoughts of his own well being and began concentrating on the problem at hand.

He was moving through the black veil again, but this time instead of following his instincts on where he needed to go Patrick used his sight to search for his missing friend.

It was obvious that no sun ever rose in this place. It was a land of constant nightfall, where random lighting streaks illuminated the far off clouds, creating bizarre faces in the fractured darkness. The place was desolate and dim, a foreboding land where anyone that might want to make their way through had better keep their wits about them or risk the chance of losing their sanity.

The valley of darkness he was traveling over was much deeper than he had anticipated; the lights on the far off cliff walls falling below him like endless dots. As he glided over the cavern it once again tickled his belly like he was sitting at the high end of a roller coaster.

He had learned from his earlier travels that he needed to stay high enough above the rocky, unnatural terrain below so that the beings that inhabited this land could not get at him. Though some (he found out later) were gifted (as he was) with the ability to fly in this place. Those creatures were the ones that had stolen some of his life as he had carried Bing and the others through a short while ago. They had come from above him, unseen, diving down and running their touch across his skin as his life was lifted from him.

As Patrick made his way the various lights beckoned to him to enter their portals. The tug to each was enticing as they called to him to enter and exit this unwanted place. He did not want to be here, and he desperately wanted to escape this land and return to his friends, but he was determined that he could not leave until he found Syrian—or at least found what had happened to his friend.

He traveled back along the same course they had taken when they had initially escaped Tye, but as he moved through this time the path he took seemed barren. Not only was he unable to spot Syrian, he was hard pressed to spy anything else along the way—dead or alive.

Before too long Patrick began to notice that as he traveled deeper and deeper into this land that the air around him was beginning to turn cold, and held a bitter stench that hung on the air like garbage in the summer sun. The snow covered area where his friends awaited his return seemed a lot warmer and more rewarding than this forsaken place.

Patrick continued on, diving and looping around black hills and darkened, bottomless valleys, scanning for any sign of the baboon. In his desperation he finally began to venture away from his intended path, starting to search in areas that were disconnected and away from his normal route of travel.

Quite a while later, as he ventured further and farther towards the jagged hills and blackened, far off mountains, he felt the air surprisingly begin to warm and he finally began to notice below him the disfigured creatures that ruled this land. It was a curious sight as he watched them moving in small groups of five or less, all traveling with purpose in the same direction that he was.

As Patrick pulled himself up and over what appeared to be a crude rock bridge, he began to realize where the beings were headed. As he floated above, unnoticed, he watched as thousands of the creatures poured into an enormous crater just ahead of him, each finding their way towards a lighted area at the far end. It looked to Patrick as though the undead were having some sort of gathering, or assembly.

Patrick traveled further, carefully hiding himself next to the mountainous areas to his right, hoping to keep himself hidden from the monstrous eyes below.

As he found his way to the pinnacle of the crater he finally began to realize what the gathering was all about.

They had found Syrian.

It was easy enough to spot the baboon; his friend was secured to a rocky stake in the ground at the center of the crater, bound with what appeared to be a disturbing assortment of bones and rotted skin.

Patrick was alarmed as he watched the creatures as they passed by his friend, each monster reaching out and touching the baboon, then licking their fingers with the taste of Syrian's life still fresh on their skin.

At the head of the ceremony stood a creature that was taller than the others, his arms bent back to awkward positions, the creature's head resting on his shoulder as if his neck was broken and unable to support its weight. He made his way to stand on a strange rectangular rock that rested only a few yards from where Syrian was fastened, motioning to all to direct their attention to him.

"Rise and assemble, dead walkers!" the tall, misshapen creature spoke loudly. "We have a great thing before us! We have captured one of the living, and he will be the one that will supply us with our feast to help us regain our rightful way back to the land of life!"

Patrick watched in horror as a tremendous roar went up from the crowd.

"Dead walkers, we have come to learn that we are not bound by the limits set before us. We are only bound by the limits set by ourselves. Before you we have an example as to how we will all regain our lives. The juice of life from this being will dissolve the boundaries that have placed around us and will allow our forms to pass on to the land we so greatly desire to return—to the land of the living!"

The crowd erupted again with shouts and cheers.

The tall dead walker began to make his way towards Syrian. From his back he produced a sharp looking object that resembled bone.

"If the mere touch by our kind can pull forth the elixir of life from the living, imagine what will happen if we break the skin of their kind."

The dead walker raised the knife-like object high above Syrian's head.

A heavy silence came over the crowd as all eyes were fixed on what was about to take place.

Patrick could only imagine the deed that was coming next. With a shout he stormed the crater, zipping passed the startled creatures before they even realized he was among them. Like a football player he lowered his shoulder and planted it into the chest of the tallest dead walker just as he about to bring down the knife. The dead walker fell backwards, the sound of his snapping bones echoing in the crater's chamber.

A roar of anger erupted from the growing mass of dead as Patrick quickly settled on the ground next to Syrian.

"Patrick! You shouldn't be here!" Syrian said as he shook his head.

"What are you talking about? I had to come back and get you."

"That's not what I mean. You shouldn't have come back."

"I'm not going to leave you in here. I'm not losing another friend."

"Patrick, this has nothing to do with that. These creatures want you, Patrick. That's all they've been talking about ever since they captured me; about how they missed their chance at you."

"What are you talking about?"

"When we were traveling through I saw that there was a group of these creatures positioning themselves above you. I tried to shout, but I couldn't get the words from my mouth in time. So I did the only thing I could and threw myself at them, knocking them to the side and allowing the rest of you to escape.

"Ever since then they've been hoping that you'd come back for me. You're giving them exactly what they want. Patrick, this is not a place for you, you've got to leave at once!"

Patrick could here the crowd now rumbling behind him, a thrum of eagerness and surprise rising from their masses.

Patrick's dismissed the words that Syrian was saying, his anger at seeing his friend held as he was overtaking his thoughts, and he immediately began to pull at the bone and skin bindings that held Syrian in place. But as he did, as if they were alive, the fixtures that bound the baboon began to tighten to an even greater degree around his friend.

"Patrick," Syrian continued, his eyes growing wide, his body trembling, "you're not listening! They want you, not me!"

Just then a large hand fell on Patrick's shoulder pulling his attention around to see the dead walker that he had initially taken down.

"Your friend is right. You shouldn't have come back, bright one," he said in a booming voice. "But I'm certainly glad that you did." The teeth that emerged in his smile were oily and black with tiny worms moving between them.

Patrick pulled away from the grasp of the dead man, placing himself in a defensive position in front of Syrian.

"Get away from me," Patrick barked at the dead walker.

But the dead walker only smiled. "Ah, I see you've got a bit of a temper to you. A lot of good life left in that body of yours, eh?"

Patrick could hear Syrian still whispering behind him, pleading with him to leave. But Patrick was experiencing something that he had rarely felt before. And whether or not it was brought on due to his overwhelming feelings of exhaustion and anger—or because he was twelve and his own immaturity and stubbornness were getting the best of him—but Patrick was beginning to feel a sense of boldness rising inside him.

"Let my friend go," he said in a direct and menacing manner.

The dead walker turned to his kind and feigned surprise.

"My, he does have a bit of brass to him, doesn't he?" the dead walker volleyed to his audience.

"A good deal of anger in him as well!" came a distant reply as the crowd laughed and hollered their enthusiasm. He turned back to Patrick and shook his head as best he could (being that it was still resting on his shoulder.)

"No, I don't think I need to ascend to your request, young one. I sort of like him where's he at, if you don't mind."

But Patrick already knew what the dead walker's response was going to be, and had already given thought to his own response.

"If you don't let him go," Patrick said as he straightened himself to his tallest point, assuming a threatening posture. "I promise you that I will flatten this land and melt everything that I see in it."

Now Patrick knew what he was expecting to see even if the dead did not. He was expecting his anger to spill over into the might that he believed he now had at his disposal, ready to weld a power he was certain existed in him. But as to how he was to control it at this point he wasn't quite sure.

Patrick also sensed that they were aware of who he was, or at least had heard of what he could do. At first the dead walkers watched him like he was a carnival act, expecting him to change or mutate into something that would surely give them great fear. But as Patrick held his hands up in front of his face and saw that he was not changing colors, that no glow was coming forth from his body, he was the one who now looked on in surprise.

The tall dead walker began to smile again, a throaty laugh coming from inside him. "I see you do not have the powers here that you do in the land of the living, little man. The land of the undead is not necessarily a place where the rules of the living apply."

"Patrick," Syrian said in a hushed voice just behind him, "leave while you have the chance. These beings are not to be trifled with."

The tall dead walker looked amused as he overheard Syrian's words.

"'Trifled?' That's a mighty fancy word for such a humble creature such as myself. I believe you are mistaken. Perhaps you meant to say that we are a noble band only seeking our way back to our true selves. Or maybe you meant to say that we are an honorable group that deserves to be set free after suffering as we have for most of eternity. Either way, using the tone that you have puts us in such a bad light. You almost make us out to be something . . . scary."

The dead walkers burst into laughter at their leaders' words.

This only angered Patrick further.

"Why are you doing this?" Patrick asked. "This isn't our fault. We didn't put you in this place."

"No. No you didn't. I supposed most of the blame for that falls to ourselves. And by that I mean only that we allowed ourselves to be judged by someone who has a rather dim view of what constitutes a complete life."

Patrick shook his head. "I don't understand."

The dead walker narrowed his eyes. "What I mean, boy, is that we were not ready to give up what we had. We were still in the middle of the enjoyment that comes with being a living, breathing member of the above world, when it was snatched away from us without our consent. We weren't ready to give it up. No one told us what was coming. I, for one, still have some living I'd like to finish."

Patrick looked perplexed.

"But this is crazy! How can you be alive and dead at the same time?"

Patrick looked out on the throng of misshapen and monstrous souls. He could sense their agony and frustration building as their passion was being relayed.

"It is our will that keeps us from passing on. Our desire is extremely strong to remain true to our goal. We are not ready to give up the few remaining drops of life that still animates us."

"But you can't just say when you want to die. No one can. And believe me, I've met the person who controls all that."

The dead walker nodded slightly. "So you've met the dark mistress of death, have you?"

"Yes. I've spoken to her."

"Interesting. I was under the impression that she only made her presence known to those she was about to collect."

As the dead walker and Patrick were talking, a small, wet piece of skin fell from just under the dead walker's left arm, landing on the ground between them with a dull plop. It sat there a few moments, and then to Patrick's amazement began to drag itself towards Patrick, moving like a snail across the black soil. He watched in horror as the tiny piece moved closer and closer, inching its way towards his own feet.

The dead walker looked down upon the small piece of material and grunted loudly. The piece of skin then stopped and flung itself back to a position on the dead walker's leg, molding itself into a new position just below the bone that protruded from his knee.

"You'll have to excuse the eagerness that some of us extends. Every piece of us wants to once again experience the taste of the living so shamefully that they'll do just about anything to get it."

Patrick tried to regain his composure, but he couldn't help but stare at the piece of skin as it squirmed in place on the dead walkers' leg. He finally gathered himself and refocused his attention back to words that had just been spoken.

"But you can't get the life that you want from Syrian. I won't let you."

"You? And how can you stop us?" the dead walker threw his arms wide. "I believe as it stands we have the advantage in this matter."

Patrick was unsure at that moment if he was ready or not to do what he had contemplated and pull the rabbit out of the hat. But he knew he needed to do something in the immediate or things may take a turn for the worse to the point where he wouldn't get the chance to save himself or Syrian.

Patrick began to think his way through it, thinking that if this was the land of the undead (or mostly dead), then there must be at least a little of some kind of life left in this place that he could tap into. The tall dead walker had even said that they had a few remaining drops of life that still existed in and around the area. And after all, they had been taking his own life from time to time.

Patrick knew what he needed as he looked at the ground—the vision forming in his mind—and before he even realized what was taking place, several black, snarling vines raced from under his feet, springing from the ground just below where the several of the dead walkers stood at the front of the gathering. The vines snaked their way up, wrapping themselves around the undead bodies, the dead walkers screaming as the vines pulled the creatures down in to the earth, finally swallowing them up as if they'd never existed.

Patrick was shocked as he watched the event take place. And after observing the expressions that hung on the dead walkers' faces, Patrick gathered that they were just as surprised as he was.

What the heck just happened? Did I just do that?!

Patrick continued to watch as the mass of dead became frantic at the possibilities that now began to manifest in their minds at exactly what power Patrick did possess. They began to shout and scream their disapproval while each took several steps away.

"So you are the being of which we've heard so much about," the tall dead walker snarled above the unsettling roar. "That was a little unneeded showboating if you ask me. But I believe you've made your point.

"You know, you began your travels through our land without ever asking for our permission. You came on your own, venturing into this place uninvited. In quite a few circles trespassing like that might be constituted as an act of criminal behavior. And in our land criminal acts do not go unpunished. We are the judge and jury. There is a cost when you trespass through here without caution. And it seems that in this instance your friend there is going to be the one that pays your toll, regardless of what talents you may possess.

"Where you are standing is the Dividing Way. For us, this is the place where you either make your way back to the land of the living or find your eternal unrest among the land of the dead. The spilling of your friends' life is going to allow us to travel back through the way we came."

Patrick threw up his hands, annoyed at the attempts to explain the dead walker's lunacy. "But that's crazy. Being dead isn't the end of your life. I thought that all creatures have a soul. That you pass on to the next life, a place where your soul goes to live for all time."

"Yes, my living friend. But it is a place where you can no longer enjoy the fruits of living pleasure. The touch, the smell, the taste of the living are gone. Once you pass over then you give up all rights to these joys."

"How do you know that? How do you know that everything you just described isn't better?"

The dead walker lifted his eyes. "We know. There are many that have made their way forward only to find frustration as to what lays behind the veil."

Patrick couldn't find any response to the dead walker's statement. He knew that the creature was wrong, but he also knew that he was running out of time and that he needed to get Syrian and himself out of there as soon as he could.

He needed to do something—and the idea came at him like a thunderbolt.

He needed to strike a deal.

"What do you want for the baboon?" he asked, totally unsure of the response he was going to receive. "Is there something I can bring you from the outside that I can use to trade? Something that will make your lives better? I can go and bring back whatever you want. But you've got to let him go."

The dead walkers chuckled at his statement.

"Why? We have everything we need right here," he said as he pointed to Syrian. "We have a living being that should provide us with everything we need to propel us back to the world we desire. What can you give us that would make it worth our time?"

Patrick looked around at the forsaken land that these creatures inhabited. If it was up to him then they could use just about anything and everything to make their lives better. But Patrick understood the question as it was posed; he knew that they wanted nothing more than to be again amongst the living. And if that meant that they needed to steal the life (or lives) of others to accomplish their goals, then so be it. If only he knew of something that he could use as a bargaining chip.

The words that came from his mouth were not exactly what he thought he'd use for barter, but it worked out to the same degree as he intended.

"Then how about if I give you some of my life. I'm guessing that I'm a lot more valuable that he is, correct?"

Syrian was beside himself as he watched Patrick bargaining as he was.

"Patrick, do not do this! I am ready to sacrifice myself. I have already made my peace with my maker. Do not let these creatures, or this situation, dictate how you are to respond!"

The tall dead walker stepped close to Patrick, glaring down at him with suspicious eyes, purposely blocking any view that Patrick had of Syrian.

"What did you have in mind, young one? As it stands, we already have a complete life now in front of us. What makes you think your life is any more valuable to us than his?"

Patrick could feel the wave of unseen momentum shifting back and forth between the two of them as the conversation turned; his head reeling as he tried his best to keep up his end of the negotiations. He knew that if the dead walker suspected any weakness from him then he would assuredly spring on Patrick like a snake, seizing the opportunity to take advantage.

"Come on, I'm not stupid. I can see how you all are looking at me. I must be worth quite a lot if you're even willing to talk a deal with me."

Patrick could feel the murmurs moving through the crowd with a wave of excitement, but he remained calm.

Patrick had been in situations like this before. Not where circumstances had a life hanging in the balance, but rather he was quite adept at the heart of negotiations. He was an avid baseball card enthusiast, and as a trader of the small rectangular cards, there was none his age more keen or shrewd at brokering a deal.

"You might have a point," the dead walker began as he paced several steps to his right. "You may possibly possess a little more value than what your average monkey might bring."

At the term 'monkey' Syrian's head snapped in the direction of the dead walker, his eyes glaring his disgust for the term that the dead walker had just used.

"But I have to make one thing clear, you can't have the life just yet," Patrick offered quickly, the dead walker reacting with contempt at the words Patrick had just spoke. "You'll have to wait until after I finish something that I've already started."

With the monstrous creatures behind him once again hollering their disapprovals, the tall dead walker approached Patrick with a sly grin.

"It's the business with the witch, isn't it? You'll want us to wait to complete the transaction until after you've had your say with her, is that it?"

Patrick nodded, hoping the dead would succumb to his request, thinking that they would surely say no.

But the dead walker surprised him. "That shouldn't be a problem. As I see it you're just a hair's breath away from her as it is, so you shouldn't cause us to wait much longer."

Patrick lowered his eyes and nodded again, wondering just how much this creature really knew of what was taking place on the outside.

"So what are you willing to offer?" the dead walker continued. "How much of your life are you willing to give? We are going to need a great deal to satisfy all."

Patrick stared down a his hands as they knitted into sweaty knots in front of him, half expecting to find the answer he needed resting in his palms.

"Five years," Patrick said as he lifted his head and spoke aloud. It was his first offer, and an offer he immediately thought was fair.

But the dead walkers only laughed as if they had been told a wildly funny joke.

"No no no. You're going to have to do much better than that if you want to free your friend over there. And besides, we deal in percentage. I say you should offer up at least eighty percent of your time left if you are to offer anything."

But Patrick only shook his head and laughed as well.

"Eighty percent? You're nuts. Maybe more like ten percent."

"Ten?!" the dead walker wailed in anger. He stomped and waved his arms like a lunatic. "You insult my mother for ever having bore me as a child with an offer like that! Seventy five."

But Patrick only shrugged.

"If I give you twelve I'm already giving up way too much."

All eyes (or what was left of them) followed the two as if they were watching a tennis match. Back and forth the debate volleyed between the two.

"Twelve? If you'll only go to twelve then you're friend is going to wilt like a dying grape on a vine. Sixty five."

"Fifteen."

"Fifty five."

"Eighteen."

The dead walker's eyes glazed over and he leaned in close to Patrick.

"I seem to be the one doing most of the moving here, lad. I think you should rethink your negotiating skills. Forty five. And I move no further."

"Well," Patrick said as he glanced around at the faces of the dead, "if you'll go to forty five then you'll surely go to thirty five to make the deal stick."

The dead walker had turned and now had his back to Patrick as he was offered the final bargain. Patrick was unsure if the dead walker had heard what his final offer was, or if he was merely thinking it over. Either way it was unnerving to Patrick as he stood there, suspended between panic and determination in finding a way to end this.

The dead walker turned slowly and extended his deformed hand.

"Forty it is, my hard hearted friend, and we'll have us a deal."

And before Patrick even realized it he was placing his hand into the dead walkers and agreeing to the deal. But before he let go he outlined one final proposal that had been bugging him since his re-entry in to this wretched land.

"But I need one more thing. Before I leave I want you to give back the life that you have been taking from me." Patrick looked to the ground and shook his head. "For some reason whenever I leave this place the pain that runs through me is terrible. I know it's because you've stolen some of my life. And I need it back so that I won't hurt so bad when I get out."

The dead walkers chuckled at Patrick's request.

"Now that's just too bad for you," the dead walker said as he pointed a long crooked finger. "We don't know how to give life back, but we certainly do know how to take it. Whatever has happened, has happened. It is in the past. There's nothing I can do about it now."

"Surely there must be a way . . ." Patrick pleaded.

But the dead walker only shook his head.

Patrick reluctantly nodded, his eyes dropping away in resignation.

"But remember," the dead walker spoke. "When the time calls for you to give us what we have bargained for, you will not hesitate in the least. Is that understood?"

Patrick glanced at Syrian.

"Patrick, I beg you, don't do this! My life is not as valuable as yours. They know something more than they are letting on and are bargaining from an unfair advantage."

But Patrick's mind was already made up. He was not leaving Syrian in this place. He had made a pledge that no more of his friends were going to perish on the journey, and he was determined to see his promise through no matter the cost.

"It's a deal," Patrick said with a weary eye towards the dead walker. "Now let him go."

And in a blink the bones and skin that had ensnarled Syrian dropped to the ground, reforming back into another dead walker, much to Patrick's surprise.

The baboon collapsed in pain to the ground at Patrick's feet. Patrick immediately reached down and helped his friend to regain his balance.

"Patrick, you do not realize the position you have put yourself in," Syrian uttered as he tried to catch his breath.

"I know what I'm doing, Syrian," Patrick whispered. "Trust me."

The dead walker reached out and plucked a piece of Patrick's hair from his head.

"Ow!" Patrick exclaimed as he reached to the place on his head that the hair had been taken.

"This is your agreement. As long as I have this piece of you I can hold you to our bargain. You are now free to go."

The tall dead walker then moved to join with the rest of his kind, their murmuring talk unnerving Patrick as he listened to it from the distance.

"Patrick," Syrian said sternly, demanding Patrick's attention. "Do you know what you have done? Do you realize the jeopardy you've placed yourself in?"

But Patrick smiled slightly and shook his head.

"That's not what happened," Patrick said in hushed tones. "It'll be fine."

Syrian's eyes widened.

"FINE?! How can it be fine? They're going to take away your life!"

"No they're not. Not if they can't find me, they won't. Besides, it was nothing more than talk. And I wasn't really truthful with them."

"You lied?! You don't lie to creatures such as these!"

But Patrick only shrugged. "So what, I lied. I'm not worried about it, Syrian. Once we're gone from here I don't ever plan on coming back. And if I never come back then the deal I made means nothing. Once we're out of here it isn't like they can come and get me. They're stuck here."

But Syrian was adamant in his scolding. It was as if he knew something more.

"But how do you know that? Why else would they let you go? Patrick, sometimes you have to look a little farther than just the end of your nose to find your way. They know something." Syrian briskly began rubbing the areas where the bones had tightly held him. "They know that they must have you in one way or another, but as to when or where they may try to put their plan into action I can't say."

Patrick's eyes widened at the prospect that Syrian was now speculating about. The baboon's unfaltering conviction at the premise that Patrick had been deceived wormed its way to the center of his thinking.

What if they had indeed tricked him into something he hadn't thought of . . .

Syrian pushed Patrick away, trying to distance themselves from the growing horde of dead.

"They must have some alternate reason for allowing us to leave, but as to what it is at this moment, I can't imagine. Nevertheless, they have granted permission for us to make our way out of this place—and I intend on doing just that. Patrick, get us out of here now, please!"

Patrick hesitated for a moment as he turned and looked back at the growing mass of dead walkers as they stood, startled to find that they were all still looking back at him. Patrick looked into their eyes, and at their all knowing grins. Patrick felt the prospect of dread rising in him at the thought that they knew something he did not, that he had indeed been tricked. The thought that he had just swapped a priceless, extremely rare baseball card for a worthless piece of paper gripped him hard.

"Patrick," Syrian insisted, "we've got to go!"

Patrick looked back at Syrian and nodded. He reached out and grabbed the baboon's hand and began to lift the two of them off the black soil below their feet.

They moved with haste in the direction that Patrick's instincts told him to go, moving past mountains and cliff walls that he remembered from before, finally coming to the lighted hallway that his inner self told him that he needed to enter.

It was through that portal he was sure were where his friends would be waiting for him on the other side . . .

. . . But then so would the pain.

Patrick took a deep breath and began to think hard on what Syrian had said, now believing that what he had told him was more than likely true—that he had been tricked to some immeasurable degree. But as they made their way closer and closer to the light that marked their exit, Patrick turned and looked back over his shoulder at the blackened void he was leaving behind him, his mind trying to ease his fears by telling him that this was surely the last time he was ever going to be coming this way again. Sure that he had seen the last of the dead walkers. Sure that he was going to be ok.

Or so he hoped.

Chapter 24

The Greenhouse Effect

Dan Brighton's exhaustion was getting the better of him.

His backside had become so raw and so sore from the riding that he could imagine the blisters that had developed without actually seeing them. He had been without food and water for such a time that he couldn't even remember the last time he ate. And his body begged for him to find someplace warm where he could possibly wash away the stink and sticky sweat that now hung on him like morning dew.

Dan needed to stop (a least for the moment) to rest.

For someone that had never ridden before, he hadn't been granted much of a 'break in' period. He had ridden hard for two straight days, the horse carrying him ahead on an unrelenting pace that seemed to have no end. When the horse had finally veered from the side of the main highway about an hour ago, and slowed to a substantial degree, Dan began to breathe a sigh of relief. The horse had brought them into some low underlying land that was thick with fall foliage, the surrounding atmosphere quiet and uninhabited. Dan had kept up with the direction they were going by keeping an eye towards the sun, knowing that the horse was trying to keep him (as much as was possible) in the direction that Patrick was probably headed.

Dan imagined that the horse was also feeling the effects of having someone ride on it for the length of time that they had ridden, gently pulling back on the horse's mane and calmly talking to the horse, trying to convince it that they needed to stop.

But the horse would not give in as easily as Dan had expected, the horse whinnying and bucking its disapproval, only allowing as much as to slow its pace to a trot as the great beast continued on in its march.

They moved this way for another thirty minutes or so, the horse finally reaching its point of exhaustion just after dark. The horse slowed to a stop, positioning itself underneath a leafless oak tree at the edge of a colorless forest, the heavy breath from its nostrils billowing out in front of it like steam from a kettle.

Dan gratefully slid off the horse's backside, collapsing (as he had every time he got off a horse) to a heap on the hard ground below.

This time, as the horse turned and looked back, it didn't laugh at Dan as he lay sprawled out on the ground. Dan reasoned the horse was in need of the same basic necessities as he was—food, water and rest—and he knew that if the horse could collapse as he just had it would rightfully do the same.

Dan grimaced slightly from the pain as the blood rushed to areas where no blood had been allowed as he tried to pull himself up, the pain stinging and searing his legs as he began to make his way on foot.

There were no reigns for him to pull to move the horse along, and there was no need, the horse trotting steadily behind him as Dan made his way through the black forest, searching the immediate area for any signs of relief.

Together they moved silently, keeping to a time worn path that the creatures of the forest had made from their constant travels before them. Dan pulled his collar of his jacket up around his neck, the chill he felt not coming from the cold night air but rather from the unknowing surroundings that they both now traveled.

Dan was not entirely comfortable with the path they were on, his attention continuously drawn to the trees around him that seemed to menacingly lean in towards him, their long knurled branches bending and reaching at him like deformed hands, each trying to ensnare him in their grasp to prevent any further progress. He knew that his imagination was getting the better of him, but he still couldn't shake the feeling that he was being watched by something that was just out of arms reach.

From time to time he would stop and listen to the dark, finding the quiet to be disturbing. Whether it was because they seemed to be so far out in the country where the distant sounds echoed and seemed harsh, or that Dan was having one of those surreal moments where he realized that he was the only one (probably in the state) that was alive at that moment, the atmosphere that surrounded him put Dan in a melancholy mood that sat him right next to sadness.

As he stood, trying to catch his breath and gather his thoughts, Dan remembered back to the previous days' events and how close he had come to finding his son.

Initially, after he was convinced that his son was in the car that they'd encountered at the school, he had tried to get the horse to circle back to the highway that he was sure that Patrick had taken. But no matter what he did he just couldn't get the horse to agree and to move in the direction he wanted. He was aware that the horse was undoubtedly running with his (and his son's) best interests in mind, but it was hard to come to grips with that reasoning as the horse took him in one direction when he thought they should be traveling in another.

After a while Dan came to realize that the horse was (after all) moving him in the direction he had first wanted, only the beast was circling wide, moving past unneeded obstacles at a clever pace, finally arriving back along side the highway at a spot that Dan imagined was to be an intersection point.

The horse seemed to be surprised (just as Dan was) to find there was no sign of the car they had seen—or his son. The horses' head turned back and forth as if he had expected to find something at the spot he had brought them, and seemed confused when he didn't.

Finally, after the horse had stood in the area for several minutes, and with no sign that anything was going to change, the great beast snorted and began moving again with a speed that Dan thought was impossible. They moved ahead with the horse never letting up, Dan reasoning that the horse had sensed that something had gone wrong and had to move them to a point further down the line. It wasn't until the horse could travel no further that Dan began to conclude that they had become lost.

It was long after sunset before Dan and his companion finally came across a place that they could use for shelter for the night.

"I don't know if we're going to find anything to eat in there," Dan said as he motioned across to the vaguely lit greenhouse that they had stumbled upon. He turned and looked back at the horse. "Well, on second thought, I probably won't find anything in there to eat. You on the other hand will probably do quite well."

As they approached, Dan noticed that the door was large enough to accommodate the horse as well as himself, and he held the gate open for the large beast to follow, but the horse snorted slightly and backed away.

"What's the matter, boy? Hmm? Come on in. It'll help if you eat and drink a little. There's nothing in there to hurt us."

But the horse would not budge.

"Ok, I understand, you must be an 'outside' horse," Dan nodded, although he didn't really understand the horses' reaction. "But as soon as I find some water you'll be the first to drink. I promise."

The building was warm, but not overly so. It was a pleasant departure from the biting cold that was now taking hold outside.

As Dan began to make his way through the building he was quietly impressed at how the nursery was structured.

Someone had taken great pains to build this, he thought.

From the outside the greenhouse looked simple and unassuming. But once you entered and began to make your way through the depth and layout of the structure, it was spectacularly eye catching.

Exotic plants and flowers of unnatural colors grew from various angles that gave the impression that this wasn't necessarily something that was set up for the casual gardener. This seemed to be someone's own personal retreat.

The sides were not made of thick plastic, but rather were built with glass and steel frame, something much sturdier that was made to withstand more than the run of the mill storm. Great lamps hung from overhead, the light from each still radiating down to keep the room (and the plants) comfortable. And he could hear the soft trickle of flowing water coming from somewhere off in the distance.

Dan continued his way through, stopping every few steps to notice another plant or flower's beauty, his head shaking at how wondrous (and large) the plants were that adorned this place.

Soon, at the far end of the building, he found what he was looking for; a water spigot and hose that he unraveled to its fullest so that he could walk it outside for the horse to drink.

He made his way back outside and went out for the horse, the chilly night greeting him once again as he pulled his jacket tightly around him. But as he stood there, trying to adjust his eyes to the dark, he was surprised to find that the horse was no longer there. Dan listened, hoping he could hear the beast moving off in the distance, but heard only silence in the cool night air.

He tried whistling a quick high pitched call to see if the horse responded, but again all that he received in return was quiet.

Now that's weird. Why would he just leave me here?

Dan stood silent, hoping to catch the horse's movements, when he heard a hard sound coming from overhead. It flew so close to him that it made the hairs on the back of his neck stand on end, and he instinctively ducked.

. . . Or had the horse just been spooked to such a degree that he took off . . .

The noise moved above him, seemingly hovering just out of reach, and then moved over the roof to the other side of the greenhouse. The way the sound chopped at the air was much too harsh for something mechanical; it almost sounded like wings.

Dan had seen too much in the past several days, more than most men see in many lifetimes combined, and he was not about to allow anything else take him by surprise.

He dropped the hose and made his way back inside, sure that something (or someone) would be waiting.

He closed the door solidly behind him as he entered, preparing himself for anything sudden, scanning the area through the thick plant foliage for a presence that he knew would be watching him.

But he saw nothing.

He moved forward, drawing a deep breath as his mind continued to push him to keep up his guard.

He moved deeper through the maze of plants and shrubbery, beginning to notice a smell of rot that seemed to be getting stronger with every step.

What the hell is going on?

He looked to his feet to see if he had stepped in something, but his boots were clean. It was then that he began to look around the room for something that he felt was surely in the final stages of death.

But the smell hadn't been there when I came in before . . . or had it?

And that's when he knew. It was like a trigger that snapped closed in his mind.

There was only one thing that could possibly fit all the pieces of the simple puzzle that had taken place over the last few moments. The horse getting spooked, the noise above him, the smell of decay.

There was only one thing that he could think of that tied all of those things together.

Tye.

And without giving it another thought, Dan was positive he was right.

"I know you're here," Dan said with assurance. "Jumping out and trying to put a good scare into me at this point would be silly, don't you think?"

But if the creature was in the building, then he was keeping that secret to himself.

Dan stood silent for the moment, unsure as to what his next point of progress should be. He was disturbed that he had to encounter the being again, especially since the last time he had met with Tye he'd foolishly allowed himself to be tricked into believing he could trust him. In the end, Tye had only left him to die with the spiders.

A sound came from above him again and he jumped, startled as a heavy pounding beat at the glass roof overhead. It wasn't as harsh a sound this time, but rather it came at him from multiple directions. It was again the beating of wings, only this time it sounded as if there were more than just one.

He squinted past the dim overhead lights, trying to see past the reflective qualities of the inside of the glass to view what was outside.

It was bats. And there seemed to be a good many.

Friends of Tye's, I'm sure.

With Dan's attention focused on the bats above and outside, he wasn't aware of the lizard skinned hand as it began to position itself around his own throat.

As he was jerked up and back, his body being thrown hard up against the far wall, he barely caught a glimpse of exactly who he'd expected.

"Mr. Brighton, how nice it is to see you again," Tye sneered as he made his way forward.

Dan tried to shake the cobwebs from the assault, his focus shifting and unclear from the crack on the head he'd just taken.

"Yeah, it's nice . . ." he began sarcastically as he tried to pull himself up, but before he could finish Tye picked him up and threw him across several tables of flowers, his momentum finally landing him in several tubs of prickly bushes on the other side of the building.

"Let's have a clear understanding of how this is going to work, shall we?" Tye snarled as he marched his way towards Dan again, throwing enormous wooden tables and heavy potted plants to the side as he plowed his way through. "You are going to say nothing, understand? And on my end of the bargain I will try not to kill you before I bring you to your son, ok?"

As Tye made his way to him, Dan was again awash with the sickening disgust as he viewed the altered version of the monster that was Tye. He watched as Tye staggered, walking as if his legs were barely functioning. His body had slimmed, giving an almost serpent like appearance as he moved. Thin, spiny columns made their way up his spine coming to an apex on the top of his head.

And his face . . .

"My god, what's happened to you?!" Dan blurted out.

Tye's face had elongated and grown outward, with sharp, glistening teeth that protruded along oozing gum lines.

"Do I scare you, Mr. Brighton?" Tye said as he stopped, chuckling as he posed the question.

But Dan had no reply. All that he could do was to stare.

Tye reached for him, pulling him up and holding him in the air as he breathed his disgustingly wretched breath forward.

Dan's eyes grew wide as he watched something moving from under the skin on different parts of Tye's body, the ripples acting as if there was something new and alive just underneath the thin layer that held whatever it was inside.

"A new entity is about to be born on this planet, my good man. I am about to be a first. Something that has only been talked about as myth or legend. And since there isn't going to be many left on this planet to witness this new awakening, I suppose you'll have to be the one who gets to have all the fun."

Dan looked away from the mesmerizing gaze of Tye and all that he had become (or was becoming); now aware that the bats that flew above were beginning to become agitated by what was taking place below them. Some had actually taken to throwing themselves at the windows in an attempt to get in.

"Once I am finished with you and your son, I have a bit of unfinished business with my masters who I'm sure will be altogether surprised by my new progression. I believe that I have reached unspoken heights of advancement of which they had no idea could be attained."

Tye threw Dan across the room again, this time he landed with a splash in a large, black garden pool at the center of the greenhouse.

"I am tired of playing games, Mr. Brighton. I am sincerely sick of your son constantly making my life harder than it needs to be. This was supposed to be such a simple little task. But, no . . . you and those filthy animals decided that you were going to make it difficult for me. And look what has happened! Look what they've turned me into! Look! How lucky am I?!"

Dan could scarcely hear the words as Tye spoke them. He was barely aware of his surroundings as he tried to stay afloat in the shallow end of the pool, doing his best not to lose consciousness.

"So now I am going to use you as a bargaining tool to help regain my respect in all of this mess. It's something that never should have come to be, but then sometimes things happen that you don't expect, eh Mr. Brighton?"

Tye was now making his way towards Dan again, Dan trying to pull himself to the far end of the pool as best he could to get away from the beast. But Tye was too quick. Just as he made his way out of the water Tye was standing there waiting.

Tye reached his hand down and placed it slowly around Dan's neck once more, lifting him from the water. This time he began to squeeze, cutting off all chance for Dan to breathe.

"You will do as I say, won't you? I mean, I really don't want to hurt you. You can see that, can't you?"

Dan pulled as hard as he could at Tye's arm, trying to get him to free his grasp. But as Dan pushed and clawed at Tye, a remarkable, yet disgusting occurrence began. Dan pushed so hard at Tye's arm that all the human skin was stripped aside and a new skin came through from underneath. A scaly, green and gold, serpent-like skin emerged.

"See, it's beginning already," Tye said proudly as he viewed his own transformation taking place.

Dan was fast loosing consciousness. His face was hot and he was becoming light headed. His eyes rolled to the side and he wondered if he was hallucinating as he looked outside and found the entire greenhouse had become engulfed by bats. It was just like the flies at the earlier house. Dan wondered if he was dreaming or not, and if Tye was even aware as to what was going on outside.

The bats began to throw themselves at every imaginable point on the greenhouse trying desperately to get in. Dan knew that they had been summoned by Tye. They were surely there to end his life.

There was a crash somewhere, distant and out of reach. Dan could barely see now, his body blacking out from the pain.

And there was screaming. The bats were screaming.

Tye dropped Dan back into the water just before he had completely blacked out, the cold water reviving his senses for the moment. And a single rational thought hammered through in his mind—stay alive!

For Patrick's sake, just stay alive.

Dan reached forward and felt the thin, thread-like roots of the water-growing plants that were seated throughout the pond. His eyes closed, he reached out and grabbed hold of the roots and pulled himself away. He could feel the bottom of the pond as his feet kicked to push his way forward.

He finally reached the surface of the water and pulled himself to the opposite edge of the pool.

The screaming was everywhere!

Dan turned, wiping away the water from his eyes as he tried to see what was happening.

The bats had broken through. Thousands of them circled the roofline like angry bees after someone had swatted their hive.

Tye stood laughing as he looked on at the spectacle of the bats. "Now you see what power my master possesses, Mr. Brighton! Now you can see what you are truly up against."

Dan had never seen so many bats in his life. Their screaming was seeping into every pore on his body as they shrieked above him.

Tye turned his attention back to Dan.

"I was going to let you live, Mr. Brighton. I was going to show you mercy. But my queen has other plans, I see." Tye looked up at the bats again, the overwhelming glee so evident on his monstrous face. "They do look hungry, don't they? They look like they're preparing for a feast."

And Dan was certain he knew who the main course was going to be.

So he ran.

He pulled himself up from the edge of the pool and ran.

But Tye only laughed.

"There's no where to go, silly man. You'll never escape their senses."

And Tye was right. Dan zigzagged his way through the maze of plants, but as soon as Dan made his way for the door the bats swooped down and blocked his way with a mass of leathery wings and rat-like faces that made him shutter with fear.

"I'll make sure that your son is told how brave you were to the end," Tye said as he smiled.

The bats were everywhere, so many that Dan wondered how there was even enough air in the room for him to breath.

He lowered himself and held his hands tightly around his head, watching from across the room as Tye stood tall, his wings opening to their fullest.

"And now you get to see just how different I have become!" he screamed aloud.

Dan closed his eyes. This was not what he wanted at all. But Tye's unnatural screeching caused him to open his eyes once more.

It was hard for Dan to see exactly what was going on the other side of the greenhouse with all the bats that flew, but as he watched he began to see Tye shake and quiver like had seen him do earlier.

But this time it was different. It was like watching the old scary movies where the werewolf begins to change.

As Dan watched, Tye's right leg shifted slightly and it began to rotate to the rear—then fell off.

That can't be possible!

And then Tye's other leg fell to the ground as well.

That's when Dan could see—truly see.

Dan was horrified as he watched Tye making his way towards him. Tye was worse than before—if there ever was a before. Any part of him that once had been recognizable as human was now gone.

He now looked more like a dragon.

Tye's massive wings held him aloft as he glided across the room bringing him closer and closer to Dan, a giant serpent's tail flowing from underneath.

Dan could feel the bats as they nipped at him with their fangs, their wings scraping his body as they pounded against him.

"When I am done with your son, father, I will then go for my masters. I have some unfinished business with them and the respect that I am due. In this form they will be quite amazed at how I can bring them around to my way of thinking."

Tye inched his way closer and closer, the fiendishness flowing from him.

And then, like someone had flipped a switch, the screaming of the bats stopped.

Oh, they flew with the same energy and thorough wickedness that they had brought from the beginning, but as they circled through the building it seemed that their focus had changed, now shifting to something else that called for their attention.

Dan watched as Tye's face dropped a degree from the shear enjoyment he was experiencing just a few moments ago, his gleeful smile now turning downward to a look of dour concern.

Tye held his position, no more than a few feet from where Dan knelt on the floor, his attention focused to following the bats as they made their way around.

It was at that instant that Dan became aware. It was as if he had been given an extra sense or understanding. Far off words, words that Dan could hear but not understand were being spoken, words that came at Tye like a knife to his heart. It was obvious to Dan that whatever someone was saying was something that Tye was not happy to hear in the least.

"But . . . but I have him!"

Tye's arms wailed at the bats as they flew around him, their agitating ways infuriating him even further.

"Don't do this, my queen! I have not forsaken you!"

And that's when Dan knew that something—somewhere off in the distance—had made a decision that was now shifting the course of the conflict. Tye had a look of dread on his face, something that Dan had not seen before.

Dan watched, amazed as the bats flew up and out of the hole that they had come through in the roof, leaving only Dan and Tye in the room.

Tye slowly turned, his gaze now cast down to where Dan was kneeling.

"Now you will see what my master will do," he said with a voice that was at once both threatening and sorrowful.

"What do you mean? What's going to happen?" Dan asked cautiously, still not moving from his spot.

The bats then reentered the greenhouse, streaming through with a ferociousness that was startling.

Dan pulled his hands over his head again, even tighter than before as he waited for the bats to make their assault at him.

But the attack on him never came.

As he peered out through his arms he was amazed and alarmed as the bats flew up to their highest point in the greenhouse and then made their way down, their attention now zeroed in on Tye.

The great monster just stood, unmoving, as the bats came at him in force. They tore at him and pelted him with a thrust that slammed Tye back into the far back wall, cracking and splintering the building's structure.

Dan watched as still more bats came through the hole in the roof, all directing their fury at Tye.

The monsters' great wings were being ripped and shredded as Tye gave one last retort.

"Now you see!" he screamed. "Now you see what power she has! And no one . . . no one is beyond her wrath!"

Dan could take no more and closed his eyes tightly.

The screaming of the bats drowned out Tye's last words, but Dan understood their meaning.

The noise seemed to go on forever, Dan never moving from his position.

But then it finally ended, the last of the screaming bats flying above him.

Dan finally opened his eyes slowly, not sure if he really wanted to see what was left in the place. Not sure if he wanted to see what remained of Tye.

As he stood and surveyed the area he found that not only were the bats no longer there, but neither was Tye.

Dan walked to the area where he had last seen the monster, expecting to see blood or bones or at least something that gave an indication that Tye had even been here—but he found nothing.

He turned and looked back up at the hole in the roof.

What had they done to him?

Dan turned and looked at the destruction that had rendered the once beautiful greenhouse to a state of ruin and waste.

And it was then that he felt something that he hadn't felt in what seemed like an eternity.

Sorrow.

True and absolute sorrow.

As he looked about the room he felt as though he had lost something, but as to what it was he didn't know.

And then it came to him. The greenhouse was like his world, his home. Once beautiful and tranquil, it now laid in ruin having been ripped asunder by forces that were at the same time awe inspiring and repulsive.

How could they do this? And why?

It was too much to take in, and he began to cry.

Dan staggered back to the door that led outside, finding his way as he stumbled down the solitary step as he exited. He landed on the ground with a thud, but it didn't matter.

"Why is this happening?!" he screamed to the heavens. "All I want is to get my son back! Do you hear me! All that I want is my son!"

Dan sat on the ground, crying and wondering what he was going to have to go through next, wondering what ordeal he was going to have to surrender himself to after this, when the horse reentered the clearing and came walking slowly up to him. It paused beside him, and then began licking the salt stained tears from the side of Dan's face.

"Some help you are," Dan said low. "You could have at least told me to get the hell out of there, you know."

Dan made his way to his feet, his hands finding their way to rub the horse's nose as he took several deeps breaths to regain his composure.

"If I could only understand you," he said, wondering what it must be like inside the horse's mind. "Maybe then you could tell me what is going on."

Dan stared into the cold black eyes of the horse, looking away as he felt a peculiar awareness coming from inside the beast.

"We've still got a ways to go, don't we?" Dan ask, his eyes moving to the horse's back, know that he was going to have a long ride again. "And I'm not sure if it's going to get any easier, is it?"

But the horse didn't show any acknowledgement to the question, not that Dan had expected it to.

Dan turned and looked back to the greenhouse, standing in his spot for what seemed like forever, his mind replaying over and over what he had just witnessed. He did not want to move. His confusion of what was now real and what was imagination was making him feel like he was drowning.

Dan took a deep breath and looked to the far off skyline, the silent moon's glow casting shadows on the wall of clouds to the west.

"Well, it looks like we're going to have to ride in bad weather," he said finally. "I hope you're up to it, because I'm definitely not."

The horse whinnied slightly, its head bobbing up and down.

And then Dan remembered what he had promised when they had first arrived—the water.

Dan didn't want to reenter the greenhouse. The evilness and disgust that was still so prominent in there were too fresh in his mind. But he knew that the horse needed this. And just as if Pat needed water or shelter in his time of need, Dan realized (and hoped) that whoever was taking care of Patrick was doing a better job of taking care of things than he was at this moment.

If this was what was being thrown in his direction for even trying to save his son, he couldn't even imagine what Patrick must have coming his way.

And that made Dan mad. Mad at himself for even hesitating at the task in front of him because of his own fear. The horse needed water and Dan was determined that he was going to go get it no matter what he had to go through to accomplish the deed.

As Dan made his way towards the greenhouse he looked to the sky again and knew that a lot worse would be coming his way. He knew now that whatever (or whoever) had sent the bats to dispatch Tye was ahead of him, and was probably waiting for his approach. What it was that was out there he couldn't be sure. But whatever it was, Dan knew that it was going to be the worst thing he had ever encountered in his life.

Of that, he knew he was sure.

CHAPTER 25

Lions, and Tigers, and Bears . . .

"So how's our boy doing?" Kirsdona asked as she walked up quietly, the heavy shadows of the neighboring mountains giving a deep darkness to the area as she passed.

Since his return with Syrian, Patrick had been unconscious, his long frame tossing and turning in exhaustive and fitful trials of sleep.

"I really can't tell," Bing replied. The penguin had sat beside the boy since his return, not accepting any offers of relief as he watched over their friend. "He's been talking in his sleep, but what he has to say is totally unintelligible. How's Syrian?"

Kirsdona looked back over her shoulder at the baboon who was huddled next to Sin for warmth.

"Well, except for the fact that his hair is now a lot whiter than it was before, his temperament seems about the same. But he won't talk about what went on in there. Whenever Melanbach or I ask him about it he only shakes his head and lowers his eyes."

Bing leaned back, peering around Kirsdona in the direction of the great baboon.

"Something horrendous must have occurred in there for someone of Syrian's stature to allow it to bother him so. I can't even imagine."

Kirsdona settled back on her haunches.

"I don't want to imagine. If he doesn't want to tell us, then I say let's just leave it alone."

Bing nodded in agreement. "Yes. Some things are best left alone."

Large, featherlike snowflakes began to fall silently around them. Kirsdona lifted her head, greeting their arrival.

"But there is something else that's been bothering me," Kirsdona continued. "How come the boy is the only one that's going through this? I mean, we went through that place the same as the he did. How come those creatures didn't steal any of our life as well?"

Bing smiled.

"That's just what I was sitting here thinking about. I don't have any real idea. Going with the thought that a place like that only existed in my nightmares; going through something of that nature is still bewildering.

"The only thing that I can come up with is that those creatures must look at Patrick as some sort of "beacon"—like a moth to a flame—and that the rest of us must seem barely lit from their perspective."

Kirsdona peered down at Patrick.

"So who is he, Bing?" her words barely above a hush as she posed her question.

"I don't know," Bing sighed. "I would think that by now we would have some kind of an answer, some clue, but I am at a loss to come up with an adequate one. The sad part is that we may be truly at the mercy of the witch queen. I am quite sure she knows exactly who he is. But if it will somehow give us the upper hand in all of this, then she will never let on that she has any idea."

"So, where are we anyhow?" the tiger asked as she looked around. "Do you have any clue?"

"I believe we are located near the southern mountains of the great north. Near the place the humans call Alaska. The boy never got a chance to really tell us. I'm imagining that it's somewhere close to where the witch is holed up. But as far as how close she may be, I have no idea."

"You know, for someone that's supposed to know so much, you aren't giving me much of an answer to any of my questions."

Bing smiled as he watched as Melanbach made his way back through the heavy brush returning to their circle.

"I wish I could do better, but unfortunately the questions you ask are impossible to answer at the moment. And I'm just so tired. I wish I could sleep, but I dare not for the consequences that it might bring."

The three of them sat quiet for a moment, staring at the boy as he slept, the silence finally broken by a sound of something (or someone) running across the snow a short distance from where they were at. Kirsdona lifted her head, trying to locate from which the direction the sound was coming.

"Do you hear that?" Bing asked.

"Who couldn't? Whoever it is, they're definitely not trying to go unnoticed."

"And they're in a hurry," Melanbach responded.

"Can you see them?"

The three of them turned to watch as Sin awoke, his large snout sniffing the air. The now much larger boar growled low, but then silenced as he seemed to recognize whatever it was in the distance.

"There they are," Kirsdona spoke. "There are three of them running just to our north."

"They seem to be in a hurry," Melanbach added as he made his way next to Bing.

"What should we do?" the tiger asked.

"Do you recognize their shapes?"

"Not in this dark from this distance."

"Well, then give them a shout. They're easily within the sound of our voices. If we welcome them over then perhaps they can tell us what they're doing out here. And if we get lucky, maybe they can tell us where we're at, as well."

But Melanbach only shook his head at their discussion.

"That is strange," Melanbach replied. "I wouldn't have thought any animal—besides the fools that we are—would still be in this area. Especially if what has been told is true."

"What's that?"

"That this is close to where the Great War took place."

"You mean to tell me that this is where we're located?"

"Well, if my scouting of the immediate area holds true. Then yes, this is indeed that spot."

"How do you know?"

"Yes, what did you find?"

Melanbach lowered his eyes.

"Just a few dead animals. Nothing more."

"Then how can you be so sure that we're that close."

"Because the animals I found were hyenas and giraffe. I don't believe that creatures of that ilk call this territory home."

The three turned their attention back to the animals that were running just ahead of their position.

"Kirsdona, I've changed my mind. I don't think a shout would be the best course of action. I think that we need to talk to these animals face to face."

Kirsdona turned and in three bounds was gone from sight following the unspoken directions from Bing.

The tiger ran hard through the soft under footing that the snow provided, trying to reach the three animals that were now moving north to south in front of her. The snowfall was getting heavier, but she could see their outlines as she drew nearer. Two were large in shape with the third somewhat smaller.

But there was no question that the three ran hard. Kirsdona lowered her head and extended her stride so that she could cut them off before they disappeared in the forest just ahead.

"Hey!" she called out. "Wait a minute!"

But the largest of the three animals in front of Kirsdona only turned briefly, barely acknowledging her calls, and continued running.

Kirsdona ran harder. She now circled wide so that she could arrive at the forest opening ahead before the animals she tracked. But when the animals she was chasing saw what she was attempting to do, they changed direction and veered off to the west.

"Oh, so that's how you want to play it," Kirsdona muttered under her breath as she ran, realizing what they were trying to do. "Fine by me."

The great tiger ran harder still, this time heading directly for the lead animal of the three. As she drew nearer the three shapes finally took on definitive personas. The largest of the three was an enormous brown bear. The bear was followed by a male lion and a mountain goat.

Kirsdona increased her stride to such a degree that she finally caught up with, and kept pace with, the bear who was charging hard at her side.

"Hey," she said between deep breaths and long strides. "You're not making this any easier. Hold on a minute. I just want to talk to you guys."

But the three continue their hard run, barely making eye contact with Kirsdona.

Finally Kirsdona had enough. She changed her direction and forcibly ran herself into the bear causing the animal to stumble and collide with the lion that ran at his side, each tumbling to a skidding stop in the heavy snow. The goat behind them tried to avoid the scene in front of her, but only succeeded in skidding into the backside of the bear as she tried to come to a stop.

The goat quickly righted herself, her attention and fury immediately directed at Kirsdona.

"Well that was about stupid! Why'd you have to do that, you dumb cat?"

The bear got to his feet at once and growled fiercely, ignoring the words of the goat.

"Out of our way, Kirsdona! We don't want any trouble, but we're prepared to provide some if you do not respect our request!"

Kirsdona was instantly puzzled—how does he know who I am?

Kirsdona stood silent, watching as the lion picked himself up and shook the snow from his mane. She expected him to come over and give her an equal amount of tongue lashing as the bear had just done, but instead the lion looked skittish, quickly placing himself on the other side of the bear as if he needed to use the bear as a buffer.

Kirsdona was beside herself with anger, her silence holding no longer.

"'What's the matter with me?' What's the matter with you guys! Why wouldn't you stop when I first ask? I'm not here to cause you any problems! We just wanted to ask you some questions, that's all."

The bear took a menacing step towards Kirsdona "We don't have time for your questions. We're trying to leave this land as fast as our legs will carry us. And I suggest you do the same. Now get out of our way."

"Leave? But we just got here. Why should we leave? What's wrong?"

"'We?' What do you mean by that? I only see the one of you."

Kirsdona thought for a moment on how much she should divulge, then spoke, "There are more than just myself."

The three animals that Kirsdona confronted looked back and forth to each other; their expressions carried the weight of worry and concern.

"Don't you have any idea where you're at?" the goat asked as she rolled her eyes.

Kirsdona shook her head. "No, should I?"

The goat frowned. "You know, for a cat your size, you sure must have a pea sized brain rattling around in that head of yours."

The bear reached out one of his paws and splashed some snow in the face of the goat.

"Pucket, that's enough. You can deal yourself a death wish by antagonizing the tiger if you want, but do it when I'm not around, alright? Even if you may not know who she is, I certainly do. And I know that she would just as soon slice you into several little pieces and serve you up for dinner, as to look at you. She's the great cat from the east that we've heard so much about."

The goat, Pucket, looked back at Kirsdona and smiled mischievously. "So, you're the one we've heard about. Ok, that makes sense," and she nodded. "Pretty impressive, if I must say so."

Kirsdona wrinkled her nose and shook her head. "What do you mean? What have you heard?"

"Word travels fast, tiger. We know who you are and what you're doing here. I just didn't expect you to get here so soon."

"Who? Who told you?" Kirsdona asked, perplexed that someone had spread the word of their travels.

"Word on a bird's tongue moves faster than that on the wind."

The goat began to look in a direction behind the cat.

"So where's the human?"

Kirsdona lowered her head, casually looking back in the direction that she had just come from and ignored the question.

"Who are you guys?" she asked. "And where did you come from?"

The lion then stepped from behind the bear.

"Gremm, we do not have time for this," the lion said, his voice filled with concern. "You promised."

Kirsdona, in a sign of respect and acknowledgement, gently bowed her head in the direction of lion acknowledging his designation as one of the kings of the beasts.

But the lion deflected his gaze, stepping back behind the bear, Kirsdona noticing that the lion was acting nervous and uncomfortable standing out in the snow as they were.

"I know, Tyrillia," the bear said as his shoulders slumped, "and we will. But first I want to take a moment and hear what the tiger has to say." The bear turned his attention back to Kirsdona. "So, do you have the boy?"

But Kirsdona only shook her head at the question, still trying to put together what was going on with the three mysterious travelers in front of her. "You haven't answered my question yet. There shouldn't be anyone else out here if I am to understand exactly where 'here' is. Who are you guys? And what are you doing out here? The only animals I thought I was going to encounter in this place were dead ones, and the three of you look very much alive."

The goat and lion looked visibly upset at Kirsdona's pressing questions and attitude.

"Let's go Gremm," the goat said as it moved in front of the bear. "She said we only had until morning before she would set out after us."

The bear's grim expression was the giveaway that Kirsdona picked up on instantly, and she nodded slyly.

"Oh, and let me guess who the 'she' is in all of this—the witch?"

The bear closed his eyes in resignation and nodded.

"Yes. We ran into a bad way with her," the bear sighed, "and she made us prisoners. We've only just recently been set free. That's how you came upon us, fleeing as best we could to leave this forsaken land and not look back."

Kirsdona sat back on her haunches, the cool snow chilling her underside. She turned and looked out to the dark, snow covered mountains that were now only visible with the early morning light.

"Is that where she's at, over there? Is that where you came from?"

The goat turned and pointed with her snout, "She's just past the second mountain, straight on through the fields of death till it brings you to the mount at the base."

"The base? The base of what?"

"Belial's Reach. It's what the area is referred to—it's what the humans call it."

"That's an odd name."

"It means 'the devil's hand.' And if you care to venture to that land then you'll see exactly what I mean. Have fun, for it's not a place that I would ever want to return."

The lion jumped at the final words of the goat.

"Can we please go now," he pleaded in a childlike voice, almost in tears. "Gremm, you promised. You promised."

The bear nodded silently.

"What's his problem?" Kirsdona asked, quite perplexed at the mental state in which the lion seemed to be in. "Isn't he supposed to be the one in charge? Or do I have my animal chain of command slightly askew?"

The goat lowered her head and began to walk around to comfort the lion.

The bear moved in closer to Kirsdona, his voice dropping to a hush.

"The witch queen did something to him. We're not really sure what, but somehow she got in his mind and messed him up. He hasn't been the same ever since.

"He was once what you are correct in believing him to be, the mighty king that we all know the male lion is, but as we tried to make our way through this land after the war his boldness got us captured. As we were confined and awaited our sentence, he was resolute on the single purpose that he would have to find a way to end the witch queen's life. He tried repeatedly to get at her, but at every instance he was rebuffed. When she had finally had enough of his arrogance she drew him into her inner chamber for discussion. When he came out he was as he is now."

The bear turned and looked on in pity at the once proud lion.

"His mind is gone, and he doesn't even remember who he was."

"We've been helping him to try and remember," the goat added. "But he struggles with it greatly. Every time he seems to be getting a bit closer to remembering, something happens to him and he goes all . . . funny."

"Funny?" Kirsdona asked.

"Like he's seeing something coming at him that isn't there," the bear replied. "He says that it's like tiny spiders, or bugs that are attacking him, but for the life of either of us we can't seem to see what he's talking about."

Kirsdona looked on at the great lion with a feeling that she had never experienced much before—fear.

Not fear of the lion.

But in fear of someone she hadn't even dealt with yet. If the witch could do that to the great lion, then Kirsdona had to wonder, what could she do to her.

"After the witch had finished with him, she came to us and told us to leave, giving us only a hurried day in which to make our way. She told us that if we were ever recaptured by any of her forces she would bring us back and turn us into stone."

Kirsdona lowered her eyes and took a heavy breath. She looked down at the many tracks they had made in the snow, half expecting a resolution to be found there as to what she was supposed to do next. She turned and looked once again in the direction where Bing and the others were waiting.

"Look, I know what I'm about to say is not something you're going to want to hear, but I think that if you came back with me the boy could keep you safe."

With her final words the lion jumped backwards as if he had been swatted, startled at the suggestion Kirsdona had just posed.

"No! No! We can't!" the lion said as he began to make his way away from the others, his movements taking him towards the nearby woods.

"Tyrillia, stop!" Gremm barked at the lion. The ferocity in which the words came forward from the bear even gave Kirsdona a quick startle. "Calm yourself. The situation has changed for the moment." The bear moved slowly to the lion's side. "We can't just keep running away. You know that we only said that we were going to make our way till we came to point where we were sufficiently safe from the witch. You have to believe me when I tell you that we are going to find a way to get your thoughts back. To return yourself to the rightful being you once were. We were never going to stay away forever—you know that!"

But the lion only shook his head from side to side.

"No, no, Gremm. You promised."

Kirsdona looked on as the bear shuffled over to comfort the lion. It was a sight that she would never have believed if she hadn't seen it for herself.

What had the witch queen done to him?

The goat came closer to Kirsdona, her nose twitching just before she sneezed.

"So where is the boy?"

"Just back that way, down where you came past the point at the edge of the forest."

"Is he . . ." the goat looked as if she was having trouble forming the right words for the question she wanted to ask. "Is he all that they have made him out to be? Is he the one that's going to end this madness?"

Kirsdona paused for a moment, unsure of how to answer. It was a question that she now had to consider being that she really hadn't thought on the subject before.

She had just gone along with the assumption that they all brought forward—that the boy was going to be the answer to all of this.

But did she really know? Had she seen him do anything that could really hold up that would put an end to an evil that no one had even encountered yet?

And after seeing what was going on with the lion, Kirsdona decided that she would tell them what she knew and let them draw their own conclusions.

"I think you need to come to where the boy is," she said firmly. "After you meet with the rest in our group, and hear what they have to say—and possibly the boy, as well—then you can make up your minds."

"What do you mean 'possibly the boy?'" the bear asked as he made his way back over. "Is there something about him that would prevent speech? I was led to believe that he could communicate with us."

"Yeah. He can talk to us. But at the moment he is a bit under the weather. Look, I think it would be in everyone's best interest, being that the sun is going to come over the horizon in a short while, for all of you to follow me. Once you've seen and heard, then you can be on your way if you are not satisfied. But if you really believe that the witch is going to be sending anyone out to look for you guys, then I'd be making up my mind pretty quick."

The goat looked over at the bear.

"What do you think, Gremm? I'm with you on this, either way."

As Kirsdona looked on at the bear she felt compassion for the animal, for he was now the one making choices that would affect all three.

"I don't know. We've traveled this far as it is—and we could use some help. But I don't want to get any more tangled up in something that is going to bring about our deaths."

The bear looked like he was struggling hard with his decision. His tired eyes seemed to plead with Kirsdona.

"I have to know, for you can see that I am now responsible for more than just my life. Are you sure that the boy can protect us?"

Kirsdona looked at the lion and nodded.

"I have already placed my life with him. And believe me, I wouldn't even bother with you all if I didn't think it was so.

"In the last few moments I have come to realize that you guys have been through something especially nasty. That tells me something. But you have to understand that from my perspective I believe you can help us as well. Because if what you say is true about her threats, I don't want to see myself turned into stone, either."

The bear did not take his stare away from Kirsdona, his eyes seeming to penetrate her soul as if he was searching her for the truth before he spoke.

"We'll give you an hour to hear you out. If you haven't convinced us by then, we'll have to continue on our way. That's the best we can give you."

Kirsdona nodded, "That's good enough for now, then. Besides, if you can give us a more precise set of directions—or even a guide if you all are so inclined—to show us exactly how to get to the witch, then with any luck—and if the boy holds true—we will put an end to this nonsense."

Kirsdona then watched as the bear and goat turned to the lion and began to coax their dismayed friend into agreeing on the change. The lion begged them not to change their course, arguing long and loud on every opportunity that the two presented. It was not an easy struggle, but in the end the lion finally gave in to their wishes and followed reluctantly behind as they returned to Kirsdona's side.

"Lead on, great tiger," the bear spoke with respect. "I am eager to see this human, and see if he is really that special."

"Well, I think he is," Kirsdona nodded, and then looked towards the goat, Pucket. "But then what do I know? I'm just some stupid cat."

The sun was just coming up, the clouds that were so thick with snow during the long winters night now vanishing in the early morning rays as Kirsdona made her entrance back to the smallish graveyard where Bing and the others had waited.

After the initial introductions were made, Bing, Melanbach and Syrian (after some initial prodding from the tiger) recounted their travels to their guests the best they could, telling not only what dangers they had overcome, but also announcing with some regularity the abilities that Patrick had put on display.

Pucket and Gremm looked on in wonder as the stories built and built, their facial expressions changing with every new encounter that was relayed to them that the group had experienced, finally climaxing in their arrival of just a few hours ago. They continually looked over to where the boy was sleeping, amazed that such an innocent human could be charged with the instruction to take on a power such as the witch.

As the stories grew more intense, the bear and goat were indeed impressed that such a small group could overcome the many hazards that had engaged the boy and his friends, their respect growing with each passing word that was spoke.

After much discussion (and extreme argumentative displays put forth by the lion) it was decided that the goat, bear and reluctant lion would help—but only so much as to allow them to determine their own fates. Gremm was adamant that if they found themselves in a place where their discovery was imminent that they at least be allowed to dispatch the lion to safety. This, and the promise by Bing and the others that they would do every thing in their power to bring the lion back to his rightful state of mind, was the only way in which they could persuade the lion to go along with their plans.

It was quickly determined then that the three newcomers would guide them past the fields of death, hopefully allowing them to enter the base at Belial's Reach under a veil of secrecy.

As it was explained to Bing and the others, that upon their initial arrival to the area (and subsequent escape), Gremm and his companions had found several secret passages that most of the Queen's minions were not aware existed. Most lay through frozen tunnels and outer passage ways that took much longer than what it would by taking a direct path over the snow to the base of the witch's encampment. Some had been created by hand, the areas of passage existing next to frozen waters and high drifting snow. Other ways were found by way of a natural camouflage, allowing those at quite some distance to go unseen through trees and overgrown bushes.

The two groups and their discussions lasted well into the afternoon, with Patrick sleeping the entire time. By the time he began to stir later in the day, the sun was now heading in the other direction, bringing early evening shadows to fall across their frozen holdup.

"Mom?" Patrick asked slowly as if he was awakening from a dream, his eyes still trying to adjust to his surroundings as he rolled to one side.

Kirsdona, who had finally taken over for Bing in overseeing the boy until he awoke, smiled at his inquiry.

"Not quite, sunshine," she replied gruffly. "It's just your aunty Kirsdona."

Patrick smiled lazily as he heard her voice, his eyes not yet fully open.

"Aunty Kirsdona, I'm hungry, can you make me some pancakes?" he asked playfully.

"Pancakes? What are pancakes?" the tiger asked as she wrinkled her nose. "I have some nice goat for you, though, if you'd like," she said as she turned towards Pucket who was giving her an eyeful in return. "I know I could go for some."

Patrick leaned forward on his elbows, "Goat? Where'd you get goat?"

Syrian stepped forward and pushed the tiger away as he scolded Kirsdona for her foolishness.

"Nonsense! All that you do is bring nothing but nonsense," he said as he shook his head. He then turned towards the boy, "I'm glad to see you're awake, young one. How are you feeling?"

Patrick yawned loud and long.

"I don't know. I guess I'm fine, but my head feels like a balloon. How long have I been asleep?"

"Almost an entire day through."

Patrick's eyes widened. "I didn't realize I was hurting that bad." He then caught sight of the newcomers that had joined up with their little group. "Who are they?"

"They are the ones who are going to take us the rest of the way," Syrian said as he turned and looked towards the bear and lion. "But I wouldn't push the point any further than you need. The lion is a bit skittish on the matter."

"Where's Bing?"

"He's asleep. I know it had been decided that we weren't going to allow him to sleep anymore so that he wouldn't have the dreams, but he was getting to the point where he was pitiful. We took a vote while you were asleep and came to the conclusion that since we are now so close to finally confronting the witch that it wouldn't matter if Tye really knew what direction we're going to take or not."

Patrick pulled himself to a sitting position and slowly began brushing the snow from his arms, the expression on his face making it was quite clear that he was still in a good deal of pain.

"But aren't you worried that once they read his dreams that they could find us rather easily? Now that we're this close they could probably be on us in no time at all."

Before Syrian could answer, Patrick noticed that the others were having a silent conversation amongst themselves, their eyes motioning in his direction every few seconds.

"Well," Syrian began, "we thought about that. We're going to let him sleep until the very moment we are ready to break camp. Once we are on the move then hopefully it will be a battle of wills to see who can find who first. It's not the best plan of action, but hopefully we might be able to use Bing's dreams to our advantage as well."

Patrick was listening to all that Syrian was saying, but at the same time watching as Melanbach and Gremm exchanged curious glances.

"Ok, what's going on?" Patrick spoke loudly to the others as they watched him. "You guys keep looking at me like I'm a freak or something. What's the matter?"

Melanbach scampered over and placed himself on Patrick's knee. "It's nothing of the sort. We were only wondering why you aren't experiencing the cold? Haven't you noticed the climate that we are now located in? You should be shivering, to say the least."

Patrick began to look around, now realizing just where they were located, his eyes taking in the wondrous beauty of his present surroundings.

Melanbach lightly touched his skin. He then looked behind the boy, motioning to the place where he had slept that was now melted through.

"You should be freezing, but from the touch of your skin I see that you are just the opposite. Your skin is as warm as it was in the tunnels. It's like you are here, but then again, it's like you are not."

Patrick immediately felt his arms and then his face, instantly realizing that Melanbach was telling him the truth.

"What does that mean?"

"It's just another mystery," Kirsdona piped in. "You're just one giant human mystery, wrapped in a boney human shell."

"I'm not boney," Patrick replied with an inward, thoughtful expression. "I'm just thin."

Kirsdona and the others chuckled. "I could use you as a toothpick."

Patrick stood, his long frame stretching his exhaustion aside. He began rubbing his chest and then started to wheeze, a thick phlegm filled cough erupting from his lungs. It was an alarming sight to the animals.

"Are you ok?" Pucket asked quietly.

"Yeah, I think so."

Patrick respectfully turned towards the goat and bear and offered his greetings, with Gremm and Pucket returning the same. Tyrillia, who stood away from the rest of the animals, merely nodded in an uncomfortable way.

Patrick's face then took a grim posture, his eyes turning towards the mountains to the west.

Kirsdona and the others looked across to one another as they could feel the heat radiating out from Patrick's body, the faint yellow glow taking hold of his skin.

"Patrick, are you sure you're ok? You're starting to . . . glow . . . again."

Patrick briefly glanced at his arms, his ease at seeing this new transformation taking place gave the appearance that he had accepted whatever was happening to him easier than the animals had.

"Is that where she's at?" he asked directly, ignoring the concern for his health.

Gremm stepped forward and raised his great paw, pointing out their next point of travel.

"Yes. She is just past the two breach points that stand in the shadows to the west. Once you clear the valley . . . she sits at the base of the 'Reach.' It is not a difficult journey to overcome."

Patrick noticed immediately that when the bear had paused when he said "valley" that his eyes quickly darted to the ground. There was only one valley that could bring such a reaction, and that was the valley where all the animals had died weeks ago in their initial confrontation with the witch and her forces.

"You said 'Reach?'" Patrick asked, unsure. "What's 'the Reach?'"

The animals quickly gave their explanations with Patrick trying to understand all as it was explained to him. He nodded slowly. This time he was the one who now carried a new found respect for his companions after learning how they came to dwell in the land just under the very nose of the Queen.

"You've actually met her?" Patrick asked in awe.

The only response he received was a slight nodding from the three creatures. It became painstakingly obvious to Patrick that they didn't want to acknowledge, or even remember, that they had ever encountered the being.

"I am not sure if we are taking the correct course of action or not, but if we are going to do this," Gremm said directly, "then I think we should get on with this as soon as possible."

"The sooner the better," Syrian interjected.

"Then we'll have to wake our sleeping beauty," Kirsdona said as she turned to locate Bing.

"The tree line to our south will be our first point to make without attracting attention. After that . . . well . . . it gets a little trickier. If there is anything that anyone needs then they should gather it and stand ready. We'll move when the shadows reach the human death markers beyond the rocks."

Patrick looked behind and saw that the shadows that Gremm spoke of would reach the head stones in only a few minutes, and that it didn't leave him with much time. The pain that was stirring in his muscles and bones was still giving him fits no matter how hard he tried to ignore it. He had led on to the others that he was fine, but the way he felt right now was no where near where he needed to be to continue on with the journey. He staggered a few steps to his left before he found a bare stone to sit on while he tried to gather his thoughts and catch his breath.

He watched as the animals scurried about, their grim expressions telling the tale. They were finally here.

After all the talk, and all discussions on what they would encounter when they reached this point in time, it was now finally upon them.

The witch (at one point the thought of actually seeing her unimaginable) was now just a few miles journey away, and that is something he thought he'd never see.

Patrick looked over to the darkened mountains that they had to travel around just to get to Belial's Reach. They looked terribly cold and unwelcome.

But he had to laugh.

What did you expect? A summer vacation and a welcoming party?

As he sat, watching the others in minor discussions on what was taking place and what was ahead of them, Patrick began to hear what sounded like whispering coming from just behind him.

He turned and looked around, but saw nothing.

The spirits were off to his right, and there was so few of them that he didn't even bother to give them any sort of acknowledgement. They stood alone and unmoving, almost like ornamental statues in the park.

The voices continued on, almost like there was an argument taking place at some places in the conversation.

Patrick stood and took several steps towards the tall grass that was just beyond a cluster of rocks in the opposite direction.

The voices were now slightly more pronounced, but they still carried a hushed tone as he moved towards them.

Patrick took another few, quiet steps, looking back towards his friends as he saw that they were beginning to reluctantly form for their journey.

And that's when he heard the fluttering of wings.

At first he lost his breath, instantly sure that Tye was now standing just around a boulder ahead that seemed to separate him from whoever was speaking.

He stopped short wondering if he should call to his friends for support, or to continue and listen to what was taking shape around the corner from where he stood.

When an enormous vulture took off from behind the rock, flying low and keeping to the east, Patrick was as surprised as he could possibly be. And then, to see the lion casually making his way around the other side of the huge rock, well, that gave him another moment of great surprise.

The lion was just as startled to see Patrick standing there as Patrick was, his eyes instantly making contact with Patrick's, then shifting nervously from side to side and darting away.

"Uh . . . hello, human," the lion said anxiously as he made his way past Patrick. "Are we ready to go yet?"

But Patrick was cautious. The lion hadn't given him any reason not to trust him, but just the same Patrick felt a sense of uneasiness whenever he set eyes upon the great beast. And with what Syrian had said about the lion seeming skittish, Patrick now wondered if there wasn't a little more meaning to what his friend had said.

"Uh . . . yeah, I guess so," he answered without giving much thought.

The lion moved past him at an even pace, with Patrick continuing on to the point at which the lion had just come from. Patrick looked at the tracks in the snow and wondered exactly what he had stumbled upon. There, side by side, were unmistakable prints deep in the snow made by a bird and a lion.

Patrick hurried back around the rock cluster, running to catch up with the lion before he was to join with the others.

"Uh . . . lion . . . Tyrillia . . . can I ask you something?" Patrick asked as he moved in front of the lion, blocking his advancement. "Who were you talking to back there behind the rocks?"

And then what he saw happened so fast that if Patrick hadn't been looking directly at the lion he would have missed it in a blink. For the lion's face instantly turned dark with a look of malice and suspicion that made Patrick take an immediate step backward. But just as quickly as the ferocious look came upon the lion, the lion's facial expression slid away, quickly changing to one of genuine concern. It was as if it had never happened.

"Talking to? What do you mean? I wasn't talking to anyone."

"Back there," Patrick pointed, "just around those rocks. I heard voices so I went to see who it was. I saw you come around the side. Were you talking to that bird?"

"Bird? What are you talking about? There are no birds around these parts, except maybe for your flightless little friend over there. You must be seeing things."

Patrick looked to the ground and shook his head.

"I know I heard someone. And I know I saw a bird flying away. I'm sorry, I just thought it was you."

The lion looked up at Patrick for quite a few seconds, his unnerving stare giving Patrick a brief moment of panic and causing him to look away. But when Patrick looked back into the face of the lion, the lion's expression had quickly melted to a warm and friendly smile that seemed forced and unnatural, something that made Patrick even more suspicious of the creature.

"It's ok, friend," the lion said as the words slid off his tongue in an uncomfortable way. "In the short time that I've been out here I've learned that the wind can play tricks with your mind in the way it swirls and dances through the trees. You must have just imagined you heard voices. I was not talking to anyone, least of all to a bird."

"But I saw . . ."

"No," the lion said firmly, "it wasn't me."

And with that, the lion moved away.

Patrick knew that he had seen the tracks in the snow, but as to why the lion had lied he didn't have an answer.

The others were now assembled and were waiting for Patrick to join them to begin the final stages of their journey.

"You coming kid, or are you looking for someone to help you build a snowman?" Kirdsona's voice rang out to him, coming from just in front of the others.

Patrick nodded silently and then shuffled towards the rear of the group.

"Are you ok?" Bing asked, surprising Patrick with his words.

"Yeah. I'll be ok," he responded as he moved a hand across his chest.

"You still look a little pale."

But Patrick only shook his head. He knew that he should tell Bing how he was feeling. He knew that he should at least tell Bing about the strange thing he had witnessed with the vulture and the lion.

But he did neither.

He only turned briefly and looked to the trees that they were now leaving behind, wondering if something was up there watching them.

He knew that he was not wrong in what he had seen, especially with the tracks in the snow and the bird flying away. But with the way he was feeling he wondered if the lion had been right to some degree.

Wondering if it had only been his imagination.

CHAPTER 26

Into the Lion's Mouth

Like wind blown sand the hardened snow crystals bit and snapped, stinging the eyes and lessoning their resolve, delivering to them the message that they were not wanted in this land. Even though most of them were built for weather such as this, a few of the animals still shivered mightily as they moved forward.

Patrick felt guilty as he walked along, his arms uncovered, his skin as warm as a summer's day. The wind and snow were annoying to him, but his respect and compassion for the animals made him wish that there was something he could do to ease their burden.

"How much further do we have to go?" Bing shouted ahead to Gremm who was pushing ahead at a pace that was far quicker than the others had wanted.

The mighty bear merely grunted, his acknowledgement coming in his non-responsive answer.

"We've still got a good ways, yet," Pucket shouted above the howling wind. "But we should find shelter before nightfall."

Bing nodded and trudged on, his tiny feet barely keeping above the snow line.

Patrick was walking slightly behind Bing, watching as his friend struggled with the wind and snow. He reached down and scooped the penguin up, cradling him in his arms.

"You don't have to do this, Patrick. I am quite sure that I can keep up the pace."

But Patrick only smiled.

"Oh, I'm not going to carry you," he said as he moved next to Kirsdona, depositing the bird onto the tiger's back. "But she will."

Kirsdona turned back sharply as Bing grabbed a hold of the hair on her back with which to steady himself. The tiger growled low as she rolled her eyes and shook her head.

"So now I'm a camel. Wonderful."

"Quiet!" Gremm growled immediately. "The purpose of moving as we are is to instill a sense of secrecy. Your words will only increase the chance of discovery if you do not cease at once."

Patrick watched as Kirsdona opened her mouth to reply to Gremm's outburst, but closed it slowly when she realized that the bear was right for speaking as he did.

They had come too far to allow something as stupid as careless talk to ensnare them at this point in time.

The group continued on, each moving in step with the great bear, their footsteps following each others to give the appearance that there was not as many in their group in case they were being followed.

From time to time the bear would stop and turn back to Pucket to ensure that they were following the correct course that was needed, the snow that had fallen giving the appearance that the landscape had changed, adding confusion to their journey.

At times the snow blew so hard that Patrick could barely see the bear as he moved, everything in front of him becoming a wash of blinding whiteness. He turned to keep and eye on the others, watching as Sin and Syrian (with Melanbach firmly planted on Sin's back) moved in line with each other, the boar amazingly keeping in time with Syrian's steps.

As soon as they came to the foot of the first mountain they were to pass, Gremm turned and motioned to a cave that was barely noticeable to all except Pucket. Several drifting snow banks blocked the way, but Gremm smashed them aside without much effort.

Because the weather had taken such a nasty turn everyone was growing more tense and miserable with each passing step.

They made their way into the cave, spending only a few restless hours before Gremm signaled that it was time to once again be on the move. This upset many within the group, but nary a word was spoken in protest for fear of the reprisal that Gremm may deliver upon them.

The wind and the snow had increased dramatically from when they had first entered the cave, but it didn't matter much to Gremm, whose stubborn will pushed them forward at the same relentless pace they had moved earlier, never lessoning his resolve to see this chore finished to its end.

Patrick walked steadily forward, his head down, his hands buried deep in his pockets. He understood why Gremm marched them on as he did, the complete understanding that the bear wanted nothing to do with this journey, but still felt a responsibility not only to himself, but also to Tyrillia, and to the other animals as well.

Patrick wondered if the bear was a father and had little ones at home that were missing him now. He wondered what drove him to shoulder a responsibility such as this, something that he could easily have passed off to Pucket, or even to Bing. Nevertheless, the bear took the burden upon himself to deliver Patrick to the witch, and it seemed that nothing would deter him from that undertaking.

They circled wide, skirting the base of the first mountain, and were now approaching the second when Patrick looked around at the landscape, beginning to take notice that they seemed to be moving in a downward fashion. The snow that had been so prevalent for so much of the journey was now tapering off, and in front of them wide patches of dried grasses and weeds began to show from underneath. Trees of many shapes and sizes that had once been cast in the heavy snow now sat open and free from their wintry coat.

Patrick heard an audible gasp come from Syrian, and he quickly lifted his head to look in the direction to where the baboon's sight was now fixed. Patrick's mouth fell open, as did the others', as they all looked off in the distance to the great mountainous range to their left.

It was Belial's Reach.

"Whoa," was the only thing that escaped Patrick's mouth, with none of the others uttering a word in response.

Patrick had never seen anything like it before. Not on television or in books. It was an alarming sight to behold. Five perfect peaks rose from the ground forming a rocky hand that seemed to stretch from within the bowels of the earth, reaching its grasp towards the heavens. The crest at the tips of each 'finger' were hidden by heavy, black clouds that Patrick could sense held storms much more fierce than the few he'd traveled through so far.

Patrick turned and was about to say something to Bing, when he saw in front of them another sight that was just as devastating as the mountains. He recognized at once what it was, but the descriptions that had been passed along did not do justice to the scene that opened in front of them. As each creature made their way forward they found they were entering the land where the great animal war had taken place.

Each animal stopped abruptly, the sight before them overwhelming their senses. As far as the eye could see animals of every kind lay in some form of decay and waste. Small and large, every creature that had perished still held the spot where they last had gathered their final breath.

It was a land that only Death herself could love.

Patrick paused for a moment and then walked ahead, leaving the others rooted in their spots, most still in awe at what they were seeing. He moved alone, sometimes stumbling over the frozen remains of animals that were too small to be accounted for, trying his best to understand what had taken place.

From behind him Patrick could hear Gremm moving in his direction.

"It's not a pretty sight, is it?" the bear said as he came to a stop beside Patrick.

"I . . . I don't know what to say," Patrick said as his head absently moved from side to side, his mind trying to absorb all that was around him. "I've never seen anything like this." Patrick turned towards the bear. "All of these animals died trying to fight the witch?"

Gremm nodded without looking over at Patrick.

"The animals, for the most part, had no real idea what they were up against. In the early stages word had traveled down as to what the witches were trying to do. The animals knew that they had to do something to put a stop to the massacre that was taking place amongst the humans, so they assembled a great group of beasts, thinking that by their shear numbers alone they could overwhelm whatever evil they would come across on this field."

Patrick noticed a slight sigh come from the bear as if he was remembering something, and it surprised him.

"But the queen did not get to her position of power by practicing foolish ways. She probably knew before the animals ever did what she would need to secure her stronghold, so she retained the services of all the underlying creatures that inhabit the earth as her aids. The ones that most of us never give much attention."

"The serpents and the insects," Patrick added.

"I guess you already know, then," the bear said as he took several steps further into the field. "Somehow she had put together an army of such might that most of the animals were caught so completely off guard by what they saw before them, that in their haste to retreat they actually caused the deaths of a great many creatures that were there to help."

Gremm held his head high, but from the sorrow in his voice it was obvious to Patrick that the memory of it all was bothersome to the great bear.

"The ones that stayed to fight . . ." he began again.

"You and Tyrillia and Pucket," Patrick interrupted.

"Yes," Gremm nodded. "And a great many more. We all fought back with all that we had, but of course it was to no avail. The queen had perverted some creatures into monstrous half-human, half-serpent things that fought with unparalleled abilities. They were nasty, wicked beings that spit venom and produced a savage bite."

Patrick watched as Pucket found her way next to Gremm.

"The other part of the problem was the amount of insects that were sent down upon us," she added. "They were the worst."

"Yes," Gremm continued. "Most of insects were not familiar with the climate in this area and had a hard enough time moving about, but with the overwhelming number that supported their forces, that even when many of the bugs died due to the exposure from the weather, there were just so many that continued on stinging and biting and ambushing our vision that the fighting was over before it really ever started."

Patrick looked down at his feet which were just inches from some kind of animal that he didn't recognize. The remains were half covered in snow and frozen solid.

"Yeah, we've seen what the bugs can do," Patrick said solemnly.

"Yes, I remember. The stories your friends told us earlier."

"But to do all this . . ." Patrick said as his words drifted away, his head shaking as if he didn't want to understand. "And yet, now we're standing here and she's not doing anything about it."

The great bear merely shrugged.

"That's a very good point. Why would she cause all this destruction in such short order, yet allow us to make our way here without even sending out a patrol to let us know that she knows we're here."

Bing walked up to the three, his eyes never leaving the Reach's high peaks that sat far off in the distance.

"Perhaps she doesn't know. Perhaps, since we're such a small party, and slightly insignificant at that, that she has no idea that we're even this close."

"But how can that be? She's been aware of most every step we've made since we first started out."

"Yes, but most of that was because of Tye. If he has no idea as to where we are, then how can she know any different? The area we now travel in is free of serpents or bugs, so none of her spies can catch us unawares. No one except us knows how we arrived at this point."

"And she doesn't know of the power that Patrick possesses that brought us here," Syrian added.

"It seems Tye was her key," Melanbach continued. "And now that we have hopefully left him behind, she probably believes that we're still miles away."

The animals and Patrick all looked back and forth to one another, like they knew that the opportunity that was before them was far from perfect, but it was an opportunity nonetheless. They all realized that they needed to seize the moment and make the most of their seemingly invisible ways.

"I think we need to stop here for the moment," Gremm spoke. "We can rest for a short while and regain our strength before we make our final push. There is plenty to eat for those of us that wish to dine on the carcasses."

"You're kidding," Patrick said as he made a face. "That's gross!"

"No," Gremm responded, his face never changing from its somber expression. "That is the way of the animal. That is the way of survival."

"But . . ." Patrick started again, but was quickly silenced by Bing.

"I'll talk to the boy, great bear. Please continue on as you will. We'll be ready to continue when you think it's best."

Patrick watched as all except for Bing and Syrian moved out into the great field looking for anything with which to satisfy their hunger.

"How can they do that?" he asked, completely appalled by what was taking place. "Don't they have any respect for the dead?"

But Syrian only smiled and placed a hand on Patrick's shoulder.

"They do, young one. This is how they pay their respects. Our ways are not human ways. Kirsdona, Gremm, and the others know that if the animals that lay here could speak they would want this to take place. They have already given up their bodies. If they can now provide nourishment for others to continue on to complete their task, then these same animals would want this to take place so that they can rest knowing that they will not have died in vane."

The three stood silent as Syrian's last words drifted away on the wind.

Patrick was not comfortable with what was happening, but he now understood that it was a necessary step.

"So what are you two going to eat?" he asked of the remaining two, wondering what he was going to eat as well.

Syrian reached down and plucked the remains of a handful of frozen wasps from the ground.

"Well, I guess this will have to do," he said as he slid the insects into his mouth with a crunch.

Patrick turned and looked down at Bing, watching as the smallish penguin only shrugged.

"Don't look at me, this is not my kind of dining, either. I think I can wait until I can find something a little more suited to my tastes."

The animals rested in the field for several hours, with most that chose to dine eating everything they could till they could eat no further.

Patrick, Melanbach, and Bing made their way up to some shallow rocks that were warm from the afternoon sun, the rocks forming a low lying cliff wall that overlooked most of the great field below them.

Patrick was still quite sore from his undertaking through the land of the dead, and he continued to wonder why he hadn't shook off most of the pain by now. He rubbed his chest and lower back, trying to ease the torment that still traveled through most of his bones.

Kirsdona and Sin were resting in a sunny area closer to the far exit through the field at the northern end, Patrick watching as their sides rose and fell with each sleepy breathe. He looked across the field, locating all the animals as they either slept or moved about.

All of the rest of the group was below him—except one.

"Where's the lion?" Patrick asked after a few moments of observation, now surprised to find that the creature was nowhere in sight.

"Hmm?" Bing said as he lazily opened his eyes.

"The lion—Tyrillia—I don't see him anywhere," Patrick said as he pressed the point forward.

"He's probably off feeding somewhere," Bing said as he yawned. "He must be out there, you just can't see him. Look for Gremm. The lion definitely won't go anywhere without the bear." Bing closed his eyes again. "I've never seen such a thing as that poor, pitiful creature."

Patrick didn't answer; instead he stood and began looking back and forth across the great field in an attempt to locate the lion.

But the creature was no where to be found.

Patrick made his way back down to the grassy areas below, tripping and sliding over the loose stones and gravel, his attention now focused on finding where the lion had made off to.

His eyesight followed the field's natural direction as it bent and rose towards the mountains. He began walking, following the unexplored path for a few hundred yards, barely staying within eyesight of his friends behind him.

Patrick wanted to call out, to yell "Tyrillia!" over and over to see if he could get the lion's attention, but he held his words for fear that he might confuse the creature and send him off in another direction.

Patrick looked to the skies to the northwest, back to the point where Belial's Reach loomed. He was surprised when he found several large birds, black against the backdrop, swooping down to a point just another few hundred yards away.

Patrick looked back to where his friends remained, wondering if he should venture any further beyond the point of their sight. He remembered the last time he had ventured this far from his friends, thinking back to his encounter with Death.

He took a deep breath and walked further still, finally coming to a point where he no longer felt safe.

But that's when he heard the voices. The same voices he had heard earlier that day at the old gravesite.

This time as he listened, the conversation was louder, with not a hint of secrecy taking place.

Patrick couldn't make out the words, but he could hear the jumps in certain syllables as points were stressed within the conversation.

Patrick continued on, cutting the distance between himself and the voices step by step. He couldn't clearly make out any of the group that was having the discussion, but the one thing he was sure of—the lion was definitely one of the parties involved. He couldn't see him yet, but there was no mistaking that voice.

As he made his way closer, Patrick hunched over, trying to keep himself close to the ground and unseen. He moved from tree to tree, and bush to bush, trying to get close enough so that he could listen to what was being said.

And then, as he peered around a group of tall, splintered trees, Patrick saw what he had feared.

It was the lion, talking with not only the vulture he had seen from before, but with three other vultures, as well. And what was even worse was that there were now snakes and lizards talking to the lion, too.

As Patrick watched, agonizing that he couldn't make out what exactly was being said, and wondering if he should try and get any closer, another vulture drifted down and landed with a heavy thud on a branch to his left, just several feet above Patrick's head.

Patrick held his breath and did not move, unsure if the enormous bird was even aware that a human was standing right beneath it or not. He guessed that the dead, dried leaves that still remained on the lower branches of the tree shielded him from the vulture's view.

"Has our friend come around to our way of thinking?" the bird asked in a high pitched, fingernails-on-a-chalkboard kind of voice. "Or do we now start picking the flesh off of his bones?"

Because of the distance Patrick still couldn't hear the other creatures' response to the question that the vulture had asked, but with the way in which the bird continually nodded Patrick felt that it was receiving the answer it wanted to hear.

"Good. Good," it replied, quite pleased with the response.

Patrick wondered what "Our way of thinking" meant, but he surmised that it probably wasn't the way of thinking that would be good for him—or his friends.

"I'll deliver the news to her majesty," the bird said as it began to ruffle it's wings before it was about to fly. "She'll . . ."

But then the vulture abruptly stopped in mid sentence.

Patrick slowly turned his head up to see what had caused the bird to stop speaking, knowing that too quick a motion could cause him to be seen.

"Well, hello there," the bird said as it leaned down, acting as if it was going to pluck out one of Patrick's eyes.

It didn't take much thought. In a flash Patrick began to run, his legs pushing him forward with all his might back in the direction where his friends would be waiting. He ran hard skipping in between trees and ragged bushes that slowed his progress, but it also made anyone that might be following him have to slow down as well. He looked over his shoulder only once, the terror at seeing all four of the vultures coming after him shaking him to his very core.

"BING! KIRSDONA! HELP!" he screamed at the top of his lungs as he rounded the corner coming back into view of his friends.

He watched as Kirsdona immediately jumped up, her eyes following the birds behind him as they peeled away, arcing back and heading in the direction from which they came.

"What's the matter? What's going on?" she asked as Patrick ran to her side.

Patrick fell to one knee, his head swimming with exhaustion.

"They . . . they were going . . . there's a trap," his words coming through broken gasps of air. "The lion. They're going to lead us into a trap."

"What?!" Kirsdona said, her body tensing, assuming the posture for aggression.

"They're going to trap us, Kirsdona. Those other animals . . . they're planning to trap us for the witch queen. Or maybe kill us . . . I don't know. I didn't hear what they said, but the lion was talking with a bunch of vultures and snakes. Back beyond the trees."

"Snakes? In this climate?"

Kirsdona looked in the direction that Patrick pointed, the same direction from which the lion now entered. In a matter of seconds all of the others were now gathered around Patrick and Kirsdona.

Patrick was resolute in his purpose. He knew for certain that he was correct in what he had seen, and explained again what he had witnessed.

"So, that is your plan," Kirsdona said as she turned towards Gremm and Pucket. "I knew that there was something going on. No one is just 'set free' when the witch has you imprisoned."

"What are you talking about?" Gremm answered in anger. "There has been no betrayal on our part."

"Yeah, why would we do such a thing?" Pucket answered as well. "It doesn't make any sense for us to put our lives in jeopardy just for you to get captured or killed. We could have kept going, remember? You were the ones who invited us."

"How do we even know what you were doing?" Kirsdona said as she advanced a step in Pucket's direction. "And to think I was beginning to like you two. And now we find out that all this time you were just leading us to our deaths."

"You don't know that, Kirsdona," Syrian said from her left. "That has yet to be proven out."

"If the boy says that it's so, then I have no reason to doubt him. I believe him without question."

Kirsdona then leaned in close to the mountain goat.

Gremm pushed himself in front of Pucket, "That would not be a wise move on your part, friend tiger."

Patrick quickly stepped between the two.

"Well, then why was Tyrillia talking to those vultures?" Patrick asked again. "I know what I heard."

"I believe that is a fair enough question," Bing interjected. "Let's hear from the one accused." Bing and the others then turned to face the lion who had casually made his way over to rejoin the others. "So, what were you doing in those parts, Tyrillia?"

The lion looked to the ground, his expression drifting towards one of confusion. As he stood in complete silence, it was though he had been caught and didn't know what to say.

As he watched the lion Patrick was spooked by the unsettling way in which the lion's face would twitch, looking as though the beast was struggling with some kind of unheard words.

"Tyrillia, would you like to explain what was taking place beyond the north gate?" Bing asked again.

And finally, after a few anxious moments had passed, the lion lifted his head to look at the others, a sly grin sliding across his lips.

"I was only looking for fresh water. I don't know why the boy is making all this fuss and inventing all of these stories about me. I came across a few of the local fowl and asked them directions to the local watering hole. That is all. I don't understand how all these elaborate stories have come to find a place in the boy's head. Especially about me."

Patrick jumped forward, "No way! I saw you!"

"And what did you see?" the lion purred forward.

"I saw you talking to those birds. And to those snakes."

"And what was being said?"

Patrick hesitated for a moment, trying to remember exactly what he had heard, realizing that the lion's slick words were trying to turn the tables and make him out to be the troublesome one.

"Well, I don't know what you said exactly, but the bird that was right next to me was asking if you had finally come around to their way of thinking. Or something weird like that. What does that mean? It didn't sound to me like you were asking them where you could get a drink."

The lion stared blankly ahead. His eyes moved only once as they darted in Gremm's direction.

"Who are you going to believe, Gremm. Some stupid human, or me, the one who has saved your life more times than I can remember."

Syrian made his way next to Patrick's side, his attention drawn to the bear.

"The boy has no reason to lie, Gremm. Of that, you have my word. But as to what is happening with your friend, I have no answer."

The bear let out a great sigh and lowered his head in resignation.

Patrick could sense that the bear had now shifted his belief in his own direction. The disgust on his face was obvious.

"What have you done, Tyrillia?" he asked in a low, sad voice.

The lion jumped slightly at the bear's words.

"What do you mean? I . . . I haven't done anything. I wouldn't hurt you, Gremm. You know that, don't you?"

The bear turned slowly, his expression heavy with what he was now going to say.

"What did you do, Tyrillia? What kind of danger did you put us in?"

To Patrick it looked as though the lion was going to start to cry, his eyes wide and his lower lip quivering.

But then the lion did something that the others did not expect. He growled.

"You fools," he said in a venomous way. "You would allow yourself to be dragged around like a dog on a leash, carrying on and on about this ridiculous human."

Except for Kirsdona and Gremm, all the rest began to move away from the ferocious looking beast. Even Sin, who was now growling himself, steadily moved backwards forming a protective posture in front of Patrick.

"While you have been groveling at the feet of the weakest of all the animals, I have been bartering our freedom from this wretched land."

Patrick watched as Gremm lowered his eyes, no longer able to look on at his friend.

Syrian positioned himself in front of Patrick and Sin, expecting some kind of trouble to come that way.

"What are you?" Kirsdona asked of the lion, a look of repulsion on her face. "You're supposed to carry on like your ancestors, not act like some kind of lunatic. You're the 'king of the beasts', for crying out loud."

"I know what I am, tiger. It's just that . . . it's just . . . I . . ."

And then the lion began to cry. His teeth were still barred, but he continued to sob uncontrollably.

"It's his mind," Pucket said to no one. "Whatever she did to him . . ."

Bing quickly gathered the others and began moving them to the high off rocks that he and Patrick had occupied earlier. Pucket was the only who was resistant to the move, but then she too could see that this was going to come to a terrible end, and reluctantly followed. Patrick looked at her face as they began to move away, her strained expression speaking volumes as to the compassion she felt for her damaged friend. It was obvious it was breaking her heart.

"I ask you again, Tyrillia," Gremm said in a gentle voice. "What have you done?"

Kirsdona began advancing on the lion, but Gremm moved in front of her and merely shook his head to get her to stop.

"He is mine to deal with, Kirsdona. This is not a task I would have you take part in."

Kirsdona stared at the lion, her contempt for the creature flowed from every pore on her body. But in the end, she simply nodded to the great bear's request, and stayed where she was.

The lion, who was now alternating between fits of crying and seething anger, narrowed his eyes at Gremm.

"You would take sides against me?"

"You have a problem, my friend," the bear started slowly. "A problem that you did not bring about. A problem that was placed upon you by a being that does not deserve the right to live any longer. She has diseased your mind and corrupted your very soul. And for whatever the reason, I do not know. But I can no longer care for you while this situation exists. I can see now that the boy has a responsibility to complete this task. And we have a responsibility to ensure that he is allowed that opportunity. If you are to continue in this world, it will no longer be with us."

The lion, upon hearing the last words spoken by the bear, roared his disapproval.

"NO! You cannot do this!"

The bear remained motionless, his eyes fixated on the spectacle in front of him.

"You are no longer allowed to continue on with us. You may have placed all of our lives in jeopardy. Now I ask you for the final time, Tyrillia, what did you do? What have you bargained away from us? What does she know about us? What did you tell her?"

The lion began to move like he was drunk, staggering to his right as he began to cry again.

Even though the spectacle that the lion had become was disheartening, Gremm still pressed on.

"Tyrillia? I want an answer."

Patrick knew at that moment that Gremm was going to kill the lion. No matter what Tyrillia was or was not going to tell him, Gremm was giving all the signs that he was surely going to end the lion's life.

Gremm took two steps closer to the lion, the lion reacting in terror at the bear's advancement.

"I'm sorry, Gremm! I'm sorry! It's just that she promised that I could have my mind back! She said that I could be like I was."

The bear moved another two steps closer.

"Please, Gremm! You have to understand, I was just trying to help all of us! She doesn't want to hurt any of the animals, she only wants the boy! Don't you see, I was only trying to help make things move along quickly. She only wants the boy!"

Two more steps.

Patrick could hear Pucket utter a soft "No" under her breath.

"I'm your friend, Gremm," the lion said as he tried to muster any sense of confidence that he had remaining, his voice booming loud. "I am the king of the beasts! You can't do this!"

And as the great bear raised his paw to draw first blood, something happened that surprised everyone that was witnessing the event, the momentous situation coming to a heart wrenching stop.

Kirsdona reached out and stopped Gremm's arm.

"No," she said in a commanding tone, shaking her head. "Let him go, Gremm."

"Move aside, tiger!" the bear ordered as he tried to break free. "I know what has to be done!"

But Kirsdona would not be swayed.

"Gremm, this isn't the right way. Even though what he did is something that I can't understand, I know enough to know that he doesn't deserve this," Kirsdona said in a noble way, her eye's darting towards the lion's. "At least not now."

Gremm looked deep into the face of the tiger, his anger at being stopped was still evident on his face.

"Let him go, Gremm," she said again. "Save your anger for the true betrayer." Kirsdona motioned towards the mountains to their west. "She lives over there."

Patrick couldn't breathe as he watched the ordeal play out. He was shocked to see Kirsdona display such judgment as to allow the creature to live.

The bear lowered his arm and took in a deep breath. He nodded to Kirsdona with respect, and then turned away from the lion. He walked several steps towards the hillside before he stopped and sat down.

Kirsdona followed Gremm's movements before she turned her attention back to Tyrillia. She stood, staring at him for almost a minute without saying a word, the lion not able to meet her gaze out of shame.

Patrick was unnerved by the silence, his hands shaking uncontrollably at his side.

But then Kirsdona spoke.

"You are free to go, lion," she said simply, surprising all that were listening to her.

"But . . . I . . ." the lion responded, confused.

"I said, you are free to go. I give you your life back."

The lion stood speechless, his mouth hanging open as he listened to the tiger's stinging words.

But then Kirsdona leaned forward, following through with her lethal retort.

"And the only thing that I ask—the only thing that any of us asks—is that you never look back in our direction. You are no longer welcome with us. Do you understand?"

But the lion only shook his head.

"No! No! That's not what I want at all! Please don't make me leave. I'll do better! I'll do anything you want, just please don't make me leave."

Kirsdona closed her eyes.

"You will leave, and never look back on us. You are not welcome here."

"No. I'll never make it on my own."

"And if you do come back our way . . . ."

"No!"

"If you do come back our way, I will kill you."

"No."

"If you are seen following us, if you are found conspiring with the witches, if you ever try to bring harm to any one of us again, I will end your life."

The great lion cried in terrible fits of anger.

"Do you understand?" Kirsdona asked again.

"No!"

"Do you understand?"

"Nonononononono! Please! Don't do this!"

Patrick watched as Kirsdona turned around and walked away, her head lowered and her tail falling straight behind her. She stopped beside the bear and sat down. With the both of their backs facing the lion it was a sign that the great beast was now an outcast, banished from their group.

The lion stood silent for a few moments before the realization of what had taken place really meant. He stopped crying and stood erect like the regal being that he once was not so long ago.

Again several moments passed, the lion finally turning and slowly making his way back along the lower areas of the mountain side, back through the areas that they had initially came, his eyes never moving towards the others up on the hillside.

Patrick and the others watched in silence as the lion walked on, moving along the rocks and trees until Patrick could no longer make out his form in the shadows.

"That was weird," Patrick said under his breath.

"If I hadn't seen it with my own eyes," Melanbach said next.

"Do you think he'll be ok?" Pucket asked quietly, her feelings for the great beast unmistakable.

"I don't know," Melanbach replied.

The air that hung around them was thick with unspoken thoughts, the sadness of the episode filling the quiet void between them.

"But it had to be done," Syrian said as he sighed and turned away.

They began moving back down from the rocks, moving to join up again with Gremm and Kirsdona.

After several minutes the animals gathered behind the tiger and bear, each creature hoping that someone would speak up and break the noiseless gloom.

Patrick looked over at Gremm, the bear sitting quiet, his eyes never leaving the ground in front of him.

"Now what do we do?" Patrick asked solemnly.

"We get the heck out of here," Pucket said almost at once.

"Yes," Bing nodded. "I know that I'm probably stating the obvious, but I'm quite sure that the witch now knows that we're here."

"You think?" the goat asked sarcastically.

Gremm turned to Kirsdona, a grim look on his face.

"You are indeed a credit to your kind, and I am proud to know you. Thank you for stopping my hand. If I would have followed through with my actions I think I would have regretted it for the rest of my life."

Kirsdona snorted and smiled wryly.

"Don't go thinking so highly of this little kitty you're standing in front of, Gremm. If you knew how close I came to slitting that cat's throat you might have to rethink what you just said to me."

Patrick watched as Kirsdona's eyes narrowed, her ferocious nature getting the better of her.

"So, which way do we have to go to get out of this dead animal zoo," she said as she stretched her long body.

"Well, we can't go the way we were supposed to," Pucket said matter of factly. "Whatever is beyond that pass is set to bring about our deaths. I'd just as soon avoid that area if it's ok with you guys."

"It might be an interesting game," Kirsdona said with a smirk. "To turn the tables on our guests. Some fresh vulture might be just what I need."

Gremm took a deep breath and looked to the mountains.

"If we move past those rocks that you have been sitting upon, up there by the cliff, then we can start to move higher and perhaps find a bridge or something that will take us over and around whatever the witch may have in store for us. I hate to say it, but there's really no other way."

"That's a heck of a climb," Bing said as he looked up towards the area of which Gremm spoke. "If we don't have to climb much higher than to where the tops of the trees span, then perhaps we can do what you say. Any higher than that and we run the risk of hitting bad weather."

"Well, let's get started," Kirsdona said as she began to move without waiting for the others to give the ok. "If that dumb lion comes back crying, I don't want to have to cause a scene."

A heavy silence followed her words, the other creatures surprised by her statement.

"You know, Kirsdona, I think a little compassion would be in order here," Bing added sharply. "I'm sure this is hard on our friends."

But the giant cat did not hesitate in her response.

"Compassion," Kirsdona said with a salty laugh, "is something that none of us has the luxury of taking with us at this point in time."

Patrick and the other animals could only look around to one another, unsure of what to say to Kirsdona's words. Patrick somehow felt that of all that were in their group she was probably the only one that truly understood what was coming their way. Her words may sound harsh, but the truth that echoed there was something that none of them could turn away from.

They began to walk behind her, following her steps as they began their trek up the side of the first mountain.

They climbed higher and higher, the smooth slope of the mountain not giving them any trouble as they made their way away from where they imagined trouble might be waiting. The snow and cold began to increase as they reached different levels, and soon, just before dark, they were overlooking the place where they had just left.

After they had reached a point where they could now move in a somewhat straight line, a place where Pucket imagined that some of her kind had cleared for travel, Patrick turned and took one last look at the place where Tyrillia had made his escape. From the point of view that Patrick now held the place where Tyrillia disappeared almost looked like a giant, snow covered mouth that was wide and threatening, waiting to swallow anything that might venture into it.

Patrick shook his head, wondering what doom that they had just sent sentenced Tyrillia to become a party too. The image of what had just taken place still echoing in his mind, the harshness of their travels finally revealing its ugly head.

He turned and quickly caught up with his friends, their steady travel allowing for no one to straggle behind.

CHAPTER 27

The Gathering of Beasts II

The snow drifted down like a pillow being emptied from above, the large feather-like flakes dropping silently around them. There was no wind to drive the snow, and of that Dan was thankful. He only had a thin jacket to give him any warmth, and the air was cold enough as it was, nipping at him with every opportunity.

The area they traveled through was a muted blanket of white. The only sound that he could hear was the horse's steady trot as it sloshed through the wet snow.

As they found their way to the top of the next hill, the peak flattened out to a plateau that carried them for almost a mile. The horse moved slowly, Dan wondering if that was because the horse was unsure of it's footing, or if maybe the great beast was in no hurry in moving towards the threatening mountain range in front of them. He wanted to find his son in the most desperate of ways, but with the weather as it was he knew that Patrick could not be moving much faster than they were, if at all. And hopefully that gave them some time.

The end of the plateau came quickly, and the horse stopped as they overlooked the valley that sat between the mountains. It was a picturesque sight with each side divided from the other by an enormous, snow covered river.

To the right was an open plain that had a slit cut into the base of the mountains that seemed to form a pass, or go between, that might allow them to escape the treacherous route without having to travel up and over the great peak. The only problem with that was that they were going to have to cross the river to get there. Frozen though it might be, Dan knew that it was still going to be an extremely difficult task.

To the left the valley opened up further, the land falling away to the southern plains which were broader and seemed less perilous. But there, too, was a problem that caught Dan's eye. Something sat at the base of the mountain to his left, a strange black mass that stood beneath the shadow of the mountain. Looking at it made him feel . . . uncomfortable. The area was still a few miles away, and much too far away to see with the naked eye. But whatever it was, Dan didn't like the look of it—nor could he take his eyes away from it.

What is that?

He couldn't be sure if it was just a shadow, or just a trick of the light and his imagination. But if the unknown could be avoided, then that was the direction he wanted to take.

Before Dan could ponder anymore on the strange mass (or the direction he wanted to pursue) the horse began moving them off to the left. Dan was surprised for a moment, but with the trust that had developed between the two he figured that the horse must be taking them in the direction they needed to go. The horse had almost become an extension of his own thoughts, so if the animal was going to the left, then so was he.

The air was crisp as they moved down the hillside, the snow finally tapering off to a few remaining flakes that skittered and danced their way to the ground.

As they drew closer, Dan listened to the river's frozen top creaking and snapping, the ice shifting as the water flowed beneath. His attention was being drawn more and more to the strange mass that he had seen up on the hillside, but the horse did not seem threatened in the least as they approached. If it was ok with the horse, then Dan had to believe that whatever it was must not be anything that would bring them harm.

The trees that dotted the valley made it difficult to see across the plain once they reached the bottom. Dan could now make out that whatever was on the other side of the trees was moving, but as to whether it was plant or animal, alive or dead, he had no clue.

The horse continued on, moving away from the river's edge and now going straight on towards the trees.

"I hope you know what you're doing," Dan said low to the horse, unsure of what to expect. The horse gave a sharp whinny, which startled Dan, and then picked up its pace as Dan's apprehension built.

He shifted his body back and forth trying to see what was ahead of them, but with all the snow that had fallen his view through the trees was still obstructed.

He looked above the tree line to their left, down past where the valley curled back and away towards another group of smaller peaks, when he caught sight of something that took his breath away.

He could see animals. He blinked twice to be sure, but from his vantage point it appeared to be a great gathering of animals.

"What is going on?" he said as he pulled back on the horse's mane to stop their movement. "What are you getting me into?"

But the horse didn't bother to acknowledge his request, instead only increasing his trot as he brought Dan into the clearing on the other side of the trees.

Animals of every kind looked on as the two of them approached, each creature as silent as air around them. And as Dan looked to the far off fields he now saw that more and more animals were pouring into the valley from every direction. It was as if they had been hiding, only now coming forward to show themselves.

"What is this?" Dan asked, his suspicion and anxieties racing to a boil.

He was completely caught off guard by the sight before him. He trusted the horse as if he were a human (and a friend), but the sight of all the animals brought to mind a television shows he had recently watched—"When Animals Attack!"—and he could not be sure of what his "friend" had brought him into.

The horse stopped and lowered itself to the ground, this time allowing Dan to step off without falling.

Dan turned quickly, giving the horse a scolding look, "You mean you could have done that the entire time? Thanks a lot, pal."

The horse rose again and moved next to the other horses that were gathered, each nudging and touching the great black horse as he passed.

Dan was at a loss as he looked around at all the great beasts, and was none too surprised to see that they were all staring back at him.

What am I supposed to do? What do they expect?

Dan stood motionless for more than a minute, afraid that any sudden movement on his part would cause the animals to become agitated and possibly aggressive.

A small, black panther, no larger than a collie dog, was the first to breach the awkward situation. It came up to Dan and rubbed against his leg like a house cat, purring as it went. Dan thought briefly about reaching down and petting the cat, but thought better of the idea (and only smiled nervously) as the cat twisted its way between his legs.

Then a balding gorilla, shivering slightly at the climate, came over to Dan. Without hesitation the gorilla reached out and took a hold of Dan's hand and placed it in his own.

Dan watched the gorilla carefully, hesitant of what he should do in kind. The gorilla's face looked unsure, as if he was waiting for Dan to make the next move. Cautiously Dan reached out his other hand and placed it on the gorilla's, feeling the leathery skin of the creature between his grasp.

The enormous beast then smiled, his broken and discolored teeth gleaming out from his mug-like face.

"Uh . . . hello," Dan said nervously.

The gorilla then stepped away and bowed deeply, almost falling over as he did.

A slight giggle escaped from Dan. He didn't know what to do next, so he awkwardly bowed in return.

Then he watched as all the animals bowed to him, which completely threw Dan for a loop. He could feel his chest tightening with disbelief. This was something he never expected, and was totally unprepared for.

He instantly nodded to each and every grouping, smiling as he did. And then he had an idea.

If it worked for the horses, then perhaps it will work here.

He took a deep breath, and trusting his instincts spoke the words that he hoped would bring the reaction he expected.

"Patrick Brighton."

The explosion of noise that erupted from the animals was deafening.

Birds, antelope, zebras, rhinoceros, (and every other kind of beast) seemed to cheer (as only animals can) in an elated way upon hearing the words.

Dan couldn't help but smile. They all knew his son, but as to the how or why he still didn't know.

After the cheering had subsided an awkward moment of silence passed. Dan looked to the ground, his unease still in question, and then raised his eyes.

"If any of you can understand me," he spoke to all, "can you please help me find my son. I'll do whatever you want, but please, if you know where he is at can you just take me to him?"

The animals then did something that unnerved Dan even further. They all moved towards him at once, each wanting nothing more than to touch the father of the boy they so revered.

Dan laughed and laughed as each came up to him and either rubbed against him or hugged him outright. This took an unprecedented amount of time, but the process did not stop until each and every animal made their way forward.

The gorilla that had made the initial contact then approached Dan again, this time pointing crudely in the direction of the mountains. The gorilla's face began moving in an unnatural way, and it seemed like he was choking on something just before he did the miraculous.

"Bright-one," it said in a very broken, barely recognizable kind of speech that came out sounding like he was burping.

The animal had created speech—no matter how odd it sounded—and of that Dan could not believe. He took a step back as if seeing something he shouldn't, his eyes as big as saucers.

"You spoke," Dan said in a near whisper.

The gorilla smiled as he turned back to the rest of the animals, beating on his chest with joy.

The rest of the animals then screamed with delight.

Dan pointed in the direction the gorilla had just given, repeating the words the beast had spoken.

"Bright one," he said in affirmation.

The gorilla stopped, his brow forming a frown, but then he pushed his mouth into that awkward position again.

"Bright-one," it said again, and then smiled.

Dan nodded joyfully, once again repeating the words.

"Bright one!"

The gorilla was overjoyed as he bounded up and down and fell over backwards.

"Bright one," Dan said again.

And he knew. Another miracle had been granted to him, the reason behind it still unclear in his mind. But he had to take the good with the bad (and he'd had lots of that recently), so he accepted this gift without question.

He listened as the animals whooped and hollered, acting like they were celebrating something fantastic (and they were, given the effort the gorilla had just made), but Dan could only turn and look on at the looming mountains behind him. If Patrick was somewhere beyond that pass then he knew he needed to get started at once. He didn't know how much time he had left, but he had to believe that if the animals had known of anything that put Patrick in any kind of bad way then surely their reaction would have been different.

Dan moved away from the animals as they roared in celebration, his focus now drifting to finding a way to make it past the great peaks before him. He knew it was not going to be easy, but then nothing had been so far.

Dan started walking towards the base of the hill that led to the mountains, his steps taken absently with no real direction, only knowing that he needed to start moving.

He heard the animals go quiet at his impending departure, and he turned to give his immediate goodbyes.

"I have to go," he said with a faint smile, and he pointed. "My son is over there somewhere. I have to go get him."

The animals did not understand his words, but it did not seem to matter, for the black horse that had brought him all this way quickly galloped in his direction and found his way to Dan's side.

Dan eyed the magnificent creature and rubbed his hand along its nose.

"Are you sure you want to do this?" he asked. "I don't know what's over there, and I'm not too sure if I'm coming back or not."

The horse paused for only a moment and then knelt. Dan didn't hesitate, climbing aboard once more before the horse rose to its fullest.

Dan nudged the sides of the horse with his heels to start moving, and the horse obliged immediately.

But what Dan didn't expect was that the rest of the animals began to move with him as well. He could hear the enormous shuffling of feet and paws behind him as he began to move forward.

"Whoa! No. No," he said as he turned. "You guys don't have to come, too. I don't think this is about you. I don't want to see any of you get hurt."

But the animals continued on, ignoring his words and beginning the trek towards the lower regions of the mountain's base.

Dan and the horse stood still, a stationary island in a sea of moving animals, until he finally succumbed to their wishes and once again nudged the horse forward.

"Ok, then," he said as he took a deep breath. "You guys lead the way."

As Dan watched the animals moving together it amazed him to see creatures that were mortal enemies walking side by side, never giving a thought to attacking one another, nor even giving an improper glance in the others' direction. He reasoned that whatever was now going on in the world it must be of such immense proportions that even these creatures were willing to put aside their differences to ensure that the problem was made right.

The journey lasted through the night and continued on to the next morning, the animals never stopping for a rest. They had found another crevice between the mountains that allowed for easy passage for most, the only animals having a problem were the elephants. Their feet and size caused them to move slowly, their footing never as solid on some of the more slippery slopes as the others.

Dan was amazed at how quiet they were, as well. Surely some of the creatures would have to make some sort of noise from time to time, but it seemed that holding their tongue was the uppermost in priorities. He had to reckon that they must approaching an area that held a sense of danger. Probably a lair of Tye's, no less.

Dan got so caught up in the noiseless air that he even began to breathe in shallower gasps, hoping his wheezing nose didn't belay their present whereabouts.

The animals moved up and over yet another ridge, the sun now coming up over the eastern hills behind them, illuminating shadowy areas that had remained hidden throughout the night. It was then that the first of the animals stopped and looked back. Dan was a good hundred yards or so behind the first groups and was alarmed when he saw that all the animals were now stopping.

"What's going on?" he asked, forgetting yet again that the animals couldn't understand him. "Why are we stopping?"

The horse continued his way forward, the animals parting to each side to allow them to make their way through. As Dan and the horse moved higher and higher up the mountain it didn't take long for him to see what was causing the animals to hesitate.

Dan looked off in the distance directly in front of them, the eerie mountainous range that gathered his attention sat out of place amongst the stoic, painted mountains, and loomed larger than life on the horizon.

"It looks like a crippled hand," he said aloud.

Dan's attention was drawn back to the horse, noticing that it was also staring at the strange peaks that were settled amongst the mountains.

Now that's spooky. He's getting the same vibe that I am.

And then Dan noticed that all the animals were looking in that direction.

"I guess that's the place we're going, huh?"

Dan could see the dark storm clouds ahead of them, and he felt afraid. It came from somewhere deep inside him, an unexplainable feeling that his heart was moving him in a direction he knew he needed to go, but where an uneasy buzz rang through his mind that screamed to him that he needed to turn around.

"I told you it wasn't going to get any easier," he said to the horse.

It took a few minutes, but finally Dan nudged the sides of his friend to start moving, the horse reluctantly beginning its trot once more.

CHAPTER 28

Bewitched

Patrick and his friends had found their way up and around the side of the first mountain, along a trail that the snow hadn't entirely hidden yet, their movements cautious as they snaked along the edge of a precipice that overlooked the trek they would have taken had they stayed on their initial course.

The group continued to move as one, their stride never more than a few inches from the next. Patrick thought it was more the fear of getting lost along the snow covered trail more than anything else that drove them to being as cautious as they were. There didn't seem to be another creature within miles of where they now walked, and the witch was still a day's travel away. It appeared nothing could bring them harm in their present course of travel, but Patrick also knew that allowing that way of thinking would surely be setting them up for a trap.

They made their way closer and closer towards Belial's Reach, the mountain range sitting ahead of them like a darkened stain against the beautiful blue and grey backdrop the other mountains provided. The storms surrounding the Reach were mesmerizing to Patrick as he watched the lighting flash and lick the sky above the peaks.

Even though the weather had no effect on him, Patrick's muscles still ached as he trudged step after step with no end in sight. He was tired, and with the lack of food as of late, he found that he was not much help in navigating the mountain. The others seemed to be managing just fine, but Patrick knew that if any of them were as hungry or as tired as he was that their own pride would never allow them to utter a word about it.

Just before morning light they stopped for a quick break. Patrick knew that Bing was thoroughly exhausted, and one of the first to find a rock to perch against as he tried to grab a quick nap. The others collapsed at whatever point they stood, their exhaustion evident in the heavy gasps of the air that each of them took as they settled in.

Patrick was too fidgety to relax. His mind kept replaying small tidbits from the journey he had just undertaken, wondering more and more on exactly what the witch would be like.

Would she try to kill him on the spot? Would she question him? Would she give him any answers to all the questions that raged in his mind?

Would she finally tell him who he really was?

Patrick's mind teased him into picturing her as the stereotypical haggard looking, hooked nose, broomstick riding sort of witch. His mind laughed at him as he thought this, for he really had no idea what she would be like. And that's what bothered him the most.

After all this time, and all this walking, he still didn't know anymore that the day he had left the barn.

They rested quietly for almost an hour before Bing woke up screaming. It was surprising to say the least to hear the little penguin making such a fuss. Bing had always been the so calm, and no one had ever heard him scream before, so to see him now was indeed quite a shock.

"What happened?" Kirsdona shouted as she came running around the corner from where she had been resting.

"It seems your friend has had a nightmare," Gremm spoke calmly.

"It's nothing. It's nothing," Bing said as he tried to regain his composure.

"You mean all that commotion came from him?" Kirsdona said, surprised. "The way it sounded I thought the lion had returned."

Bing glanced over at the tiger, a small smile gracing his face.

"I appreciate your concern."

"What did you dream?" Patrick asked as he knelt next to his friend.

"Yeah?" Kirsona added. "What could have been that bad?"

The others gathered in close to Bing, each wanting to know what it was that so devastated the small bird.

Bing stood and moved away from his friends, his eyes trained on the mountains to their west.

"We should not go the way we are," he said. "If we continue on our present course we are going to be walking into a trap."

"Is this the dreams that you spoke of earlier?" Pucket asked with concern, her attention turning to Gremm. "Then he is truly able to see the future?"

Bing never moved, his attention still focused on places unseen.

Patrick watched as Syrian made his way next to Bing, the baboon offering silent words of comfort to his friend.

"But there isn't any other way to go," Gremm spoke from the rear. "We are on a one way path. Surely with the information that he now has we should be able to bypass the problem."

"It's never quite that easy, I'm afraid."

"But I thought you only saw where we were going?" Syrian asked. "Not a particular episode or event. Only the path ahead of us."

"Is it possible to change our path?" Melanbach inquired, as well. "I mean, are you seeing the future as it will be, or are you seeing just one possible path that we can go down?"

Bing sighed and turned to his friends. "It has always been that what I dream has eventually come to be. I don't see how this would be any different."

"Then you don't know for sure if we must continue as we are?"

"I have never really given the thought of trying to alter that path. Until now."

"What did you see, Bing?" Patrick asked again.

And that's when he told them of the chamber.

It was a silent hole cut into the side of the mountain that sat adjacent to the Reach. He had seen it as clearly as he saw them now standing in front of him. An enormous river ran across, and through, the bowels of this mountain. It was there that Bing's dream had begun.

He told them of a woman dressed in red that laughed as they approached. And he told them that some of them would perish at her hands. As for the particulars of the dream, he couldn't (or wouldn't) provide any details.

"Well, then we must find another way," Syrian said to all.

But Gremm was not convinced.

"How do we know that the alternate path we choose is not the path that his dream has foreseen? We could go three different ways and still not be sure that we're going the way that's not leading us into disaster.

"And I must add again that there really isn't another way. If we decide to abandon the current path we're on then we are taking a chance of getting lost in the wilderness. This is the only way I traveled, and the only way I know. I realize that we could follow the direction of the Reach and use it as a heading point, but the ground below is full of pitfalls and traps. And I'm not sure at what locations the queen will have her spies located."

The debate was pointless, Melanbach pointed out. Being that there really wasn't an alternate path that they were sure of, their conclusions finally pointed to the only logical thing, and that was to continue on as they were.

"Besides, since we already know that danger lies ahead then we should be sufficiently prepared when it approaches."

Patrick didn't feel very reassured with the decision that was reached. He was beginning to feel like a puppet on the end of a string, with decisions being made for them that seemed out of their control.

"Then let's get going," Kirsdona said finally. "I want this to be over as soon as possible."

So once again they set off in the direction that Gremm had chosen, the path leading them through and around the most dangerous parts of the mountains. They traveled this path for most of the afternoon, and before too long it was decided that they needed another moment for rest.

They had come to a large, deep cave that offered them a chance to escape the weather and to try and find their way underground. Gremm had no idea how far back the cave would lead, but given their position he believed that they might find a way through the bowels of the mountain that might save them some time.

"But couldn't we get lost?" Patrick asked as he peered down into a deep, dark path. If it was a choice of going in the light instead of moving in the dark, then he wanted to take the light.

"True," the bear explained, "but with the alternative being to continue up and over the mountain it might be worth the risk to take a moment to explore what is before us."

After a few moments of initial investigation they found that the cave had multiple paths that led from its rear, with each creature arguing about which path they should take.

The largest of all the paths was the one chosen, with the incline of the path initially taking them down and deeper into the bowels of the mountain. They continually bickered about the way they traveled, debating whether or not they should turn around and find another way. But soon, and to their surprise, the path began to take them on an upward course. Steeper and steeper the incline began to lay out in front of them. The dark of the tunnel was overwhelming even for the creatures that were adept at seeing in the dark. They stumbled and bumped into one another, the squeaks and squawks erupting at every outrage as one creature stumbled into another.

Eventually they came to a large lighted tunnel that forked away from their present course, leading them out onto a long bridge made of ice.

Patrick was overjoyed to be out of the dark.

"I know where we are now," Gremm said with ease. "This was where I was trying to bring us the entire time, but I wasn't completely sure of the direction."

"This doesn't seem right," Melanbach said as he looked around. "This seems all too easy. I can't believe that she is going to let us walk right up to her front doorstep."

"Yes," Syrian added. "I can't believe that she wouldn't have at least a hundred fold of whatever she deemed necessary to engage us."

"True," Bing said as he ran the end of his wing along the ice at their feet. "But what if she's so assured that nothing can bring her harm? Perhaps she doesn't believe she needs to have such things. What if her power is such that she doesn't need protecting?"

But Syrian only shook his head. "Then why would she feel the need to destroy the animals as she did? Why cause such a scene?"

Bing thought for a moment and then turned to the others. "Perhaps it was nothing more than a distraction. Perhaps she only did that to bring fear to all the neighboring creatures to keep them at bay. Have any of you seen any of the local creatures that call this place home? I haven't seen anything nearby that would interfere with her plans. Its as though she accomplished exactly what she wanted. She wanted to create a comfort zone that would give her the freedom to enact her bidding."

Gremm lowered his head and nodded. "Then that would make sense as to why she allowed us to leave. If we were the harbinger of deadly news then no one would dare to proceed in this direction. I believe what you say, little bird, makes a great deal of sense."

"Then we are going to have to expedite our effort. If my dreams hold true, then she knows that we, and we alone, are on the path to find her stronghold. We need to be more cautious than we ever have before."

They began to make their way across the bridge, all the while looking down at the churning water several hundred feet below them.

"I know this isn't the best time," Gremm said as they walked. "But before we go any further I suppose there is something that I should mention. Something that I should have mentioned a good deal earlier."

The others grew silent while Gremm walked several feet ahead, stopping to watch the water below them dance and spray against the rocks.

"As we approach the shadow of the queen if you should see any flies buzzing about, acting out of the ordinary, you should do your best not to allow them the knowledge of your presence."

Patrick watched as Gremm and Pucket exchanged quick and dangerous glances.

"Flies? Up here?" Syrian asked. "Why flies?"

Pucket shook her head as if remembering a nightmare.

"Because they are wicked little terrors," she said as her voice trailed away in sorrow. "They can do things that you cannot imagine."

"What things?" Patrick asked, alarmed.

"Let's just say that you don't want to be caught alone with them."

"Oh, and why is that?" Bing asked.

Gremm turned and faced the others; once again Patrick saw that whatever was troubling the great bear was weighing heavily on his brow.

"Because they come from the depths of other regions that are unspeakable. Places where true evil is the rule. They are bound to the witch by her request."

"That doesn't sound good," Syrian uttered.

Gremm offered up a small, sly grin at Syrian's remark.

"If you only knew. These flies are of a different nature than that of the common fly you may be acquainted with. These creatures are the servants of the most foul kind of evil. I have seen this for myself, and I have heard her speak the words that make this true."

"But flies?" Kirsdona added. "Surely she could do better than that?"

Gremm turned and faced the tiger.

"Then you do not know her as I do, or who she truly is. She is the witch queen, of that there is no question. But she goes by many other names. Names that are of a nature that bring dread to those that hear the words. But in this instance she is known by a simple little quip that takes on grave circumstances for us all. The flies are hers and hers alone, because she is . . ."

". . . the Lord of the flies," Bing said as he finished Gremm's sentence, the penguin's focus falling away to the ground.

"Bing?" Patrick asked. "How do you know that?"

Bing sighed and stepped away from the group. "I have heard the term before."

"This is not good," Melanbach began. "I was hoping against hope that this was not going to be the case. If she is truly who Gremm alludes to, and who I am beginning to believe she is, then we are not going to be able to deal with her with any sort of ease. In fact, we have probably underestimated her as it is."

"Well this is a wonderful time to be mentioning that, don't you think?" Kirsdona added with a scowl.

"What can the flies do?" Patrick asked again. If the way Gremm and Pucket (and now Bing) were acting was any indication of what this particular bunch of flies could do then he wanted to know exactly what it was.

"Let's just say that when a willing subject presents itself the flies can bring about certain changes to their person."

"Changes?"

Gremm and Pucket stood silent with the last question hanging on the air. Their faces grew sullen and forlorn in the remembrance of what they must have seen. Their expressions made Patrick realize that he really didn't want to know what they could do.

Gremm looked up to the mountain that the bridge was drawing them into. They were now so close to Belial's Reach that Patrick could practically smell it.

"We'll take you as far as that opening in the side of the cliff wall," said the bear as he pointed. "After that you'll be on your own."

Patrick tilted his head back and looked in the direction that Gremm indicated. It was a low dark spot on the side of the cliff wall above them. If the bear hadn't of pointed it out then Patrick guessed that no one would have even noticed the hole.

"Unless we are going to grow wings and fly up there," Syrian began, "I'm hoping you have another way you're going to take us."

"I am somewhat familiar with the tunnels and inner chambers of this place. If what I am to believe is correct, the chamber above us connects with a long narrow tunnel that will take you to the other side of this mountain. It can bring you to a place where you will be within a morning's walk to the shadow of the Reach. After that Pucket and I will say our farewells."

"You sure you won't go any further? Your help and your friendship has been a blessing."

Gremm turned towards Pucket and slowly shook his head.

"I don't want to put her in any more danger than I already have. She'd never admit it, but she wants nothing more to do with this place. She's only came this far because I asked her to."

"Well none of us wants to be here," Kirsdona said coldly.

"I realize that, great tiger. But the things we have seen in that place has left a scar on us that can never be erased. Just being this close . . ." the bear turned and looked in the direction of Belial's Reach, " . . . is bad enough. I do not want to relive any of what I have seen before."

Even though they had made fast friends with the bear and goat, out of respect it was agreed upon that Gremm and Pucket would part from the others once they reached the opening above them. Patrick felt sad that they were going to part so soon from the two newcomers to their little group. It made him remember how he felt about Dog. It made him wish he was home.

Crossing the ice bridge had brought them once more along a precipice that scaled the outer walls at the base of the mountain, but Gremm quickly pointed out a hidden walkway that took them deep into the belly of the mountain. They moved with caution as they once again traveled in darkness, climbing higher and higher.

They made their way past several connecting tunnels that the bear ignored, his urgency at moving them along through the mountain becoming more and more obvious as his pace increased.

They came to several points where their advancement was almost of a completely vertical nature, but without the benefit of steps to ease their climb.

Patrick was growing weak, and his stomach growled its disapproval at being empty for as long as it had. He had never been so tired in all his life, and he slowly drifted to the back of the pack once more, barely keeping up with the rear.

Finally (and much to Patrick's relief) the tunnel they were in widened to form a long hallway, the light from outside giving a faint glow to the path in front of them.

Gremm paused as the hallway split into two wide chambers. The one to their left seemed to be the chamber that they had seen from below, the opening in the side of the wall giving a fantastic view to all the areas around the mountain.

"Look at that," Patrick said as he oversaw the view that the room presented. "You can see for miles."

The chamber to their right was hidden beyond a rounded wall that curved and bent back to places unseen.

Gremm seemed particularly agitated by the hallway to the right.

"What is it, Gremm," Bing asked. "What's the matter?"

"I don't know. Something's not right. I remember this area only vaguely. It was a place that Tyrillia and I were brought to while we were briefly imprisoned. I was made to wait in the chamber to the left. Tyrillia was taken to the chamber on the right."

"You mean the witch is here?" Patrick asked, alarmed at the thought.

Gremm shook his head slowly, "No. This was a place where we were initially brought to before we were taken to see the witch."

"Then her servants could be close by?"

"No. I don't believe this was a place that was used for anything more than a holding station. A 'look out' post, if you will."

"Then you could have brought us right into a trap!" Kirsdona snapped. "You knew that there could have been guards here!"

Gremm turned and faced Kirsdona. "That couldn't have happened. Between my sense of smell, and the sense of smell that your friend the boar possesses, we would have been alerted to anything ahead of us long ago."

"How do you know what Sin can sense?" Syrian asked.

Gremm chuckled lightly. "Because I am well aware of what that creature is. If he could see he would be the best guide you would ever come across. And the most ferocious. At least as far as finding the wretches and wicked things that you really should avoid.

"We all think we know so much, but in actuality know so little," the bear said as he began his way forward again, his eyes darting from side to side. "We're like a bunch of misfits, up here, poking around. We each have been given such great strengths, but such overwhelming weaknesses. We think we know what we're getting into, but in fact, we really have no idea."

The bear stopped just outside of the chamber to the left. "I think it would be in our best interests if we split up for the moment. Half of us need to check out the chamber to our left, while the rest of us examines the chamber to our right."

Gremm turned around and began to give instructions, "Kirsona, you take who you want with you . . ."

But the tiger interrupted, "I don't need a nursemaid straggling behind me. I'll go alone. I can be in and out . . ."

"No!" Gremm growled with authority. "You will take someone with you. You are one of our strengths. If something should happen to you then we need to know immediately." He then turned to the others. "Bing, Pucket, take the boar and follow the tiger. Syrian, Melanbach, and I will take the boy and make our way. If you should see anything don't hesitate to yell. It's not like it's going to matter at this point if they hear us."

The animals nodded, each exchanging weak glances with one another as they divided up. Patrick watched as the others moved into the chamber to the right, listening as Kirsdona muttered something about the bear and "militaristic rule" before Bing told her to hush.

Gremm gave a quick, "Stay close," to Patrick, Melanbach and Syrian as they entered the chamber.

Patrick was in awe as they made their way inside. The room opened up like a cathedral, with large, ivory colored columns dotting the room, each reaching from floor to ceiling. The room held no color other than the different shades of polished white stone and blackened slate. Stone statues of animals and humans formed a circular array along the outer walls that Patrick absently fingered as he walked by. Each statue was created to form a pose of either attack or fear, with each of the poses alternating statue by statue. The lifelike figures gave Patrick a nervous shiver at how detailed each stood. It almost looked as if every statue was merely holding its breath as it held its position. Whoever the artist was had a very exact eye for detail.

From the other chamber, but what seemed was a great distance away, Patrick could hear someone yell, "Are you guys ok?" which gave him a start. "Yeah, we're ok," he yelled back in reply. Patrick followed the sound of his voice as it echoed down the hallway, sounding like a moaning ghost as it trailed away.

Patrick turned his attention back and watched as Melanbach scampered along the inner most wall, stopping every now and again as if he was listening to something off in the distance.

Gremm was making his way to a large stone table at the far end of the chamber, his movements slow and cautious.

"What's that?" Patrick turned and asked Syrian who was still keeping close tabs on Patrick from behind.

"I believe it's an altar," he said absently. "But as to why it is here, I have no idea."

Patrick walked towards the large opening at the side of the chamber and peered out to the wide open lands before him.

Is this how a king would look out over his people? he wondered as he gazed out over the valley and rivers below, imagining thousands of creatures below him.

He stood, mesmerized by the sheer beauty in front of him, forgetting where he was for the moment, when from behind he began to hear Gremm growl.

"What . . ." was all that he could say as he turned, watching as Syrian instantly brought his fingers up to his lips to get him to "shhh."

Patrick followed Melanbach's progress as he slowly and secretively began to move behind his two companions, circling back and to the right, following another hallway into a different chamber.

Patrick knew that something was wrong straight away, the overwhelming feeling that something bad was going to happen couldn't be any stronger. He began walking forward, moving past the statues with quiet steps, making his way just in front of the altar.

It was then that they all began to hear a laughter that seemed to be coming from behind the wall in front of them.

"Stay back, boy," Gremm said as he held his position. "I know that sound."

"It's the dream," Syrian whispered. "If she's wearing red . . ."

Patrick stopped instantly, allowing Gremm to move ahead of him. The bear moved cautiously, his large, long claws clicking on the slate floor as he went. He took two strides up the alter steps, stopping only when he saw the woman to his left. She emerged from behind a hidden wall, the texture and coloring of the stone blending together to conceal the passageway.

Patrick stood awestruck, his mouth open and his eyes unable to leave the woman before him.

A hood was draped over her head and shoulders, the only features exposed were the lower parts of her face. A long, red tunic covered the rest of her features hiding any chance for Patrick to see what she may have looked like.

"Gremm, how nice to see you again," the woman's purred to the bear. Patrick could see her lips moving, but nothing more from beneath the shadows of her hood.

Gremm turned back to Patrick and Syrian, "That isn't her. This is some kind of trick. It looks like her, but the witch I know of would never hide her face." The great bear turned and motioned to Patrick, "Get him out of here!"

Immediately Syrian came to Patrick's side. He grabbed him by the arm and began to pull him to the rear of the chamber. But to their surprise they found their exit blocked. Three black and orange Gila monsters, almost as large as Patrick, snapped and hissed as they advanced.

The woman laughed behind her hooded veil.

"Did you think that we were going to allow you to come all this way and not welcome you properly?"

As the woman reached her hands up to her hood, ready to pull it back and reveal herself to them all, Melanbach came running back into the room from the entranceway he had earlier exited.

"Don't look at her!" he screamed as he came forward. "Move away!"

Without hesitation all three did as instructed and turned away from the woman.

"I just saw some other animals and humans in the antechamber behind the wall. They had been turned to stone. And the only way that could have happened is by witchcraft."

Patrick could hear the rustling of material as the woman began pulling back her hood. He turned slightly and caught a shadow on the wall of something he thought he'd never see. It was a woman's form to be sure, but what caught Patrick's breath was the sight of several small shapes that looked like snakes on the top of her head. He could hear their unmistakable hissing as he watched the shadows dance.

"Or a Medusa," Patrick said aloud.

Melanbach made his way to Patrick's feet, his eyes never venturing in the direction of the creature at the altar.

"I have heard men speak of beings where just the mere sight of them can cause you to turn to stone. It was just a guess on my part."

"What in the Creators' name is that?" Syrian asked

"It's a creature from mythology. If you look at her you'll be turned to stone. I read about them in a book at school. But they're not real. Or at least I didn't think they were!"

"Well, whatever is up there is very real, whether you want to believe it or not. I think that the statues that surround us are a testimony to that."

They each listened as the woman made her approach, her naked feet moving her silently towards them, beckoning to each with her haunting words.

"Come now, my pretties. Surely you want to gaze upon my beauty. Don't be afraid. It doesn't hurt."

Patrick jerked his eyes away from the shadow, afraid that if he continued to even look in that direction then something bad would happen to him.

Syrian was still behind Patrick, and he slowly made his way to him. Patrick jumped as Syrian's soft hands grabbed his arm.

"It's just me," Syrian whispered. "We've got to get you out of here, ok?"

Patrick nodded, keeping his eyes fixed on the floor in front of him.

"Under no circumstances can you look in that creatures' direction."

Patrick surprised himself with a quick chuckle, "Don't worry, I won't."

"Are the others ok?" Gremm asked of Melanbach, the bear taking slow steps from the alter moving in the Gila monsters' direction.

"They know that there is a presence here, but that is all," Melanbach said as he backed away, his tiny feet moving him furiously from both the Medusa and the monsters.

Just then Patrick could hear as Kirsdona, Bing and the others came running from the other chamber, now just making their way into the outer hallway.

"Stay back! Do not come inside!" Gremm screamed in a booming voice. "There is death waiting around the corner from you!"

But Pucket, her concern so evident for her friend the bear, could not stop her progress and she continued into the chamber. Patrick listened as Bing and Kirsdona tried to stop her, but it was too late. As soon as she rounded the corner, shouting out Gremm's name as she went, she instantly turned to stone as soon as her eyes came in contact with the Medusa's poisonous form.

"No!" Gremm cried out in anguish, his arm reaching out to Pucket just before she fell silent.

Patrick's eyes darted in Pucket's direction, his shock at seeing her turned into a statue of stone overwhelming his thoughts of safety. He wanted to get mad. He wanted to bring his gifts to the forefront and combat the creature that was tormenting them. But everything was happening too fast. It was as if everyone and everything had been sped up to higher degree of motion. Patrick couldn't think fast enough, or move fast enough, his mind three steps behind what was taking place. It was hard to bring forward your anger when fear was playing such a strong role.

He watched as the Gila monsters circled wide and to his right, trying to cut off any chance of escape, and forcing him and Syrian to stay within several feet of the Medusa's circle.

"You have just made a mistake, you miserable hag," Gremm spit out in disgust. "That innocent creature deserved better. She was but a youth. I will ensure that she will be the last person you take down."

"I'm sure she's in a better place," the witch laughed aloud. "Now, who's next? Come now, you've never seen such beauty as mine before. Take a look and see for yourself. You know you want to, just a quick glance. I truly am the most beautiful creature on the planet! Take a look and see if what I say is true."

Patrick was beside himself with fear. The sounds and sights came at him so fast it was overwhelming. He could hear Sin growling with such ferocity that he thought that the creature was going to shatter the walls with his own anger.

"Let Sin come in, Bing" Patrick yelled. "He'll take care of her."

But when the boar came into the room Patrick and the others were bewildered to see their friend do something that surprised them all—the boar did nothing. Once he came around the corner Sin stopped at once. It looked to Patrick like he was confused, as if he couldn't focus on the evil in front of him. His head kept turning back and forth from the lizards to the Medusa, never really stopping on either.

"What's wrong with him?" Patrick asked, now looking at Syrian who was also aware of Sin's strange behavior.

"I don't know. He should have eaten this room clean by now."

"I'm not sure that he can," Melanbach said simply. "The lizards have yet to move in a threatening motion. Once they do I'm sure our friend will dine well. As far as our lady friend is concerned, I think that is a bit more complicated. She is not a natural consequence of this planet. I think Sin is having a hard time recognizing what is what. He knows something is wrong, that something is trying to bring harm to Patrick, but since she is not of this world, and again, not making any direct threat in bringing harm to Patrick, he doesn't know what to do."

"Is that the witch queen?" Patrick asked to anyone that could hear him. "If she is, then someone better tell me what I'm supposed to do, because I don't have any idea."

"No," Bing yelled from beyond the stone wall. "She can only be one of the followers who gave up her life to serve the queen. She's another pawn. Stay calm, boy."

"Isn't there anything we can do?" Kirsdona yelled over the wall.

"No!" Gremm ordered again. "Just stay back. I will handle this once and for all."

Gremm had stopped his movement towards the Gila monsters and was now moving backwards swinging his arms behind him. His arms, with their razor sharp nails at the ends of his paws, cut through the air like a machete. Patrick knew that his aim was to cut her in any which way that he could, even though he had no idea what direction she had placed herself.

"Come now, little bear, how can you catch something that you can't even see?" she teased. "Just turn for moment and have a look! I'm right over here!"

Patrick could see from the shadows that the Medusa was now an equal distance from Gremm and himself. He surprised himself by the way his mind pleaded with him to turn his head and look, the overpowering way in which the words from the woman wormed their way into your head. It was taking everything he had not to look. If only he had a knife or a sword he could then act in unison with Gremm in order to bring the Medusa down.

Syrian had moved away and was trying to get the hissing Gila monsters to move closer to the edge of the room and away from him.

"I'm coming to get you, my little friend," the Medusa said gleefully. "I'm right behind you."

And Patrick thought she was, her voice was so close that he imagined he could feel her breath on his neck. He had no idea if she was talking to him, Syrian, or Gremm, but just the same he didn't care.

"Patrick," he could hear Bing calling out to him from the hallway, "do not look. I know her voice is like honey, the way it beckons to you."

"I'm not," he responded meekly, shutting his eyes tightly. But the allure of her voice demanded his attention. It just would not go away.

"Do not make the mistake and give in to her charms. If you need something to think on to keep your wits, remember your mother and father. Just picture their faces in your mind and try not to listen to her words."

Patrick began to move backwards, moving in the only direction he could, when he stumbled on something on the floor as he began to move away from the altar. He opened his eyes and found a piece of broken slate as big as a window sitting at his feet. The broken and jagged piece of stone appeared to have fallen from the ceiling.

Patrick listened to Gremm grunt with every stroke of his paw, slashing through the air with every intention of striking down the witch. He looked over at Syrian who was trying to draw the lizards' attention away from Gremm and himself.

Patrick thought again about having a knife or sword, and then looked to the piece of slate on the floor. He took a step back and reached for the ragged piece of stone. It was far heavier than he imagined. His legs and arms quivered as he lifted the flat stone, grunting as he brought it up to his waist.

"You can't shield yourself from me, little man. Sooner or later you will have to look."

Patrick knew that the witch mistook his action of picking up the flat stone for one of protection.

Syrian turned in time to see what Patrick was up to and immediately shook his head for Patrick to stop, but then held his silence once he realized what Patrick was attempting to do.

The Gila monsters were watching as well, and began to realize what the boy had in mind, immediately withdrawing their attention from the baboon and beginning to again advance on Patrick.

Patrick could tell that Gremm was trying to drive the medusa witch closer and closer to the edge of the cliff wall. Patrick held the piece of slate with all his strength and moved behind a double set of stone columns and waited his chance. He watched the shadows on the floor as they moved closer and closer.

But the lizards were closing in as well. Patrick jabbed at the beasts with the stone, trying to hold them off, but the weight of stone caused him to lose his balance and almost topple over the edge of the precipice.

Patrick hoped that the shadows didn't belay what he thought was true. It seemed that as Gremm moved towards the Medusa, she slowly, but continually, moved backwards, just keeping out of reach of the razor like claws as she continued to taunt him.

Patrick knew that his moment was fast approaching, but his overwhelming exhaustion was taking its toll. His arms were shaking as the weight of the stone seemed to multiply with each passing second. The sweat ran down his arms, finding a line to his fingers as the rock began to slide from his grasp.

Syrian could see that Patrick was losing the battle with holding his line behind the pillars and trying to fend off the Gila's. He grabbed one of the monsters' by the tail and began to pull backwards, the creature squirming and fighting against his efforts.

"There you are, my little monkey," the Medusa said as she approached Syrian, the sound coming from just behind Patrick's ear.

Patrick watched as Melanbach made his way to the altar's stone platform, waiting for an opportunity as Gremm forced the Medusa his way. Once she was close enough Melanbach threw himself at her right ankle and bit down hard. The witch screamed in agony as the large rat broke through her skin and sank his teeth deep into her flesh.

But an instant later Melanbach was in agony as well.

He broke free from his bite and fell back spitting and gagging on the greenish fluid that erupted from her wound. He rolled over and over, his body in fits and throws of convulsions.

The woman's voice changed from the charming harpy that had tried to entrance anyone that would listen, to a shrilly shriek of hatred that pierced the room like a siren.

"You will pay for that deed, you miserable vermin! My blood is death as well! I hope you enjoyed your last drink."

As she ended her sentence, and was concentrating on her wound, Patrick closed his eyes and estimated at what point her neck would be—and he knew it was time.

He gave one tremendous heave on the rock, swinging it up and over in a chopping arc. He could feel the stone move through the air like he was swinging an axe, the stone moving in one solid motion towards the witch.

And then it was over. He could feel the stone cut through her like neck a machete, the momentum of the stone pulling him close to the edge of the cliff. He stumbled once, but caught himself just short of falling over.

The head of the witch had been cleanly cut, and bounced like a ball to the far corner of the room.

But then something happened that no one expected. As Patrick let go of the stone, allowing it to tumble to the water below, he turned just in time to see the Medusa witch's body falling towards him, the greenish juices pouring from the spot on her neck where her head should have been. He couldn't move fast enough as the weight of her body came crashing down upon him, pushing him backwards. He tried to catch his balance, but his left foot slipped on the edge of the precipice and he fell over the edge of the cliff wall like a lamp falling off of a table.

Syrian was the first to move as he ran to the edge, "Oh no!" he cried, with Gremm making his way immediately after. The Gila monsters were so surprised by the circumstances that took place that they too moved to the edge of the cliff and peered over.

They each watched as Patrick fell like a bag of dirt. He hit the water below with a 'crash!' the waves rolling and toppling over him again and again.

"Oh no!" was all that Syrian could say as he watched.

Gremm flew in a rage and took off after the Gila's, swatting the lizards over the edge as well. The monsters were not as fortunate as Patrick, hitting the rocks below instead of the water.

"What's happening?" Bing shouted from the hallway.

Gremm ran to chamber's entranceway and told both Bing and Kirsdona what had happened. In an instant they were both by Syrian's side.

Kirsdona immediately turned to see if she could go help Patrick, when Bing grabbed her by her tail for her to stop.

"Wait! Look!" he said to all as he pointed.

In the water below they could see two dolphins circling the area where Patrick had fallen.

"Dolphins?" Kirsdona asked aloud. "How can there be dolphins in these waters?"

Bing turned to her at once, "How can any of this be happening? I don't think now is the time to question such things."

They watched as Patrick's body bobbed up and down in the churning water, the dolphins making their way closer and closer to him. Once they reached his body they used their snouts and pushed him underneath.

"What the heck are they doing?" Kirsdona asked. "They're going to drown him!"

"No. Remember back at the pond. He can breathe like a fish. But as to where they are taking him, and what they intend on doing with him, is something we need to find out."

Bing turned and pointed to Gremm, "I know we made a deal with you, Gremm. And if you want to leave I can understand. But under the circumstances we could still use your help."

The great bear turned and looked at the frozen statue of Pucket.

Gremm didn't hesitate, "I'm not going anywhere."

"Well then get everyone out of here and make your way to the Reach."

Bing looked over at the remains of Melanbach.

"We owe it to our friends to see this through till the end. Since I'm the only one that can swim, I'm going find out what our friends the dolphins are doing with the boy."

The penguin then leapt over the edge falling through the air until he crashed into the water below.

The others watched from above as Bing bobbed in the icy water, and then turned upside down, pushing himself underneath.

"Come on," Gremm growled as he made his towards the exit with the rest of the group behind him. "I hope the penguin knows what he's doing. Because if this is what is going to happen when we face the queen, then this is not going to have a happy ending."

CHAPTER 29

The Final Way

The water felt good as it flowed around him. He had been away from its touch for far too long.

Bing came back to the surface to catch his breath. He was a bird after all, and not a fish.

He could still see the dolphins, their shapes barely visible ahead of him, their tails propelling them through the water at a much faster pace than he could travel. Bing couldn't tell from his distance whether Patrick was conscious or not, but he had an idea that the dolphins were being especially cautious with him either way.

He threw himself into the water again and used his wings as flippers to propel himself forward, the speed he managed to keep was even surprising to himself. It was more fear driven than anything else, being that he was so afraid of losing Patrick.

Bing had never seen a river before, let alone swim in one. The water felt the same, obviously, but it reeked of soil, plants, and fish heads. And it tasted funny, too.

He was only about a hundred or so yards behind the dolphins, much too far to yell to them from under the water. He knew the best moment would come when they would surface to catch their breath. Hopefully he could gain their attention then.

Bing felt that the alarming thing in all this was that Patrick never moved, his body completely limp as the dolphins pushed him along with their snouts. He hoped that the boy was alright, the fall that he had taken was a dangerous one to say the least. He also wondered if the dolphins had any idea of what kind of power they guided in front of them. With the cavalier way in which they moved him through the water, Bing knew that once Patrick regained consciousness and realized what was happening he would probably have something to say about it—and the dolphins had better be prepared for when that time came.

Before too long Bing began to notice that the sides of the river were widening and the current was becoming much stronger. He realized that the river must be opening up into the ocean, or at least into an outlying levy that would bridge them to a larger body of water. He also knew he had little time before the dolphins would be in open waters and could make their way with greater speed. Speed of which Bing didn't possess.

After swimming a few more moments he began to notice a large shadowy shape coming towards him out of the corner of his eye. At first Bing dismissed it as just random plant shadows in the water, or possibly a boat overhead. But his mind quickly altered that perception when he found that whatever it was had now changed direction and was running a parallel course beside him.

Bing kept an eye towards the shadow as he continued to swim, but over the next few moments he noticed that whatever it was, was ever so slightly beginning to slide closer and closer in his direction.

Bing did not hold much fear of many of the creatures of the sea. Oh, there were a few things that from time to time would give him a start when he saw that he had ventured too far from his home and came face to face with something unfamiliar. But for the most part he knew the creatures of the water fairly well.

There was one thing, though, that he never liked to see when he was alone in the water searching for fish. It was the one thing that bothered him more than any other creature of the sea. Unfortunately for Bing, that was now the same exact creature that was moving beside him.

A killer whale.

Bing swallowed hard upon seeing the enormous creature's shape come into focus. This was something that he did not need at this moment in time.

Orca's, or killer whales, were enormous creatures whose temperaments ranged from extremely polite to extremely ferocious. The problem Bing found was that you never knew what you were going to get from one beast to the next. And that was aside from the point that they greatly enjoyed eating penguins.

Bing's heart jumped when he saw the thing begin to move even closer in his direction. He rose quickly to take in a quick breath of air before settling back underneath the water's surface. He didn't want to act like he was nervous (even though he was), and he was way too far away to make a break for the safety of land. He was readily aware that there wasn't any chance that he could outrun the enormous black and white behemoth, knowing that the great hulk could overtake him in a second. So before he allowed things to become too unsettling, he did the only thing he could think of for the moment—he began to talk to it.

"Hello!" Bing said in a cheery voice, a slight quiver coming from inside him. Bing smiled mightily at the whale, but to his chagrin the whale did not respond. He turned and looked ahead, continuing to keep a constant eye on the dolphins in front of him.

"I was wondering," Bing tried again, "could you do me a favor?"

But again the whale seemed to pay him no attention.

"I know this seems strange, me asking you for a favor, but considering the circumstances you'll see that I am in dire straits and could use a hand."

The whale continued to swim silently only twenty or so yards away, never acknowledging whether he was listening to Bing or not.

"My friend, a human boy, has been taken by two dolphins—if you look directly ahead of us you'll see the two that I speak of—and I need to get them to stop. My small body will never be able to swim fast enough to catch the two, and I was wondering if you could give me a ride closer so that I might converse with them? I realize that I am asking a lot, but with the tremendous way in which you can swim I know that you could deliver me to their location in seconds."

The whale continued on as he was, the only indication that Bing was even sure the beast was alive was the lolling way in which his eyes would blink every now and again.

"I have no reason to believe that you should help me in any way," Bing continued, "but if you could see your way to help me with this, I would forever be indebted."

The whale let out a low, quaking bellow, the water around them shimmering with bubbles as the whale released the air from his mouth. That's when Bing knew that the whale had been listening. The humongous creature darted instantly in Bing's direction, startling the bird as the whale pulled within a mere yard separating the two.

Bing hesitated for a moment, unsure if the great creature was going to eat him or not. Then the whale moved even closer, bumping Bing slightly as if to relay to him that he wished for Bing to take hold.

Bing smiled nervously as he watched the whale's great black eye follow him as he grabbed onto the whale's wide flipper.

"If you could just get me close to them, I believe I can get them to stop and listen to what I have to say."

The whale moved at once, the speed at which he swam nearly caused Bing to lose his grasp. It seemed like only an instant before they were swimming beside the two dolphins.

The dolphins, completely surprised to see an orca pull up beside them (let alone with a penguin holding on to the whale's pectoral fin), veered away to their right and made for murkier waters.

The whale turned with them, holding his course so that he continued to swim beside them, but not moving any closer than he needed in their direction.

Bing noticed that the land had fallen away below them and that they had finally emerged in outer waters. He wasn't familiar with the area and had no idea in which body of water they were now in, but he knew that if the dolphins decided to go deep he was not prepared to go with them. He had to be quick with his tongue in convincing them to give back the boy.

"Hello!" he said to the dolphins, much in the same voice he had used with the whale. He didn't want to sound false in his speech, but he didn't want to scare them away either. His skills at diplomacy were being tested to be sure.

But the dolphins did not seem to be in a mood to listen. They only increased their speed, Bing watching as Patrick's arms and legs flailed beside him in his unconscious state as the dolphins swam harder.

The whale increased his speed as well, much to Bing's appreciation, easily keeping pace with the dolphins.

"Please stop! I must have a word with you concerning the human you are taking with you! He is my friend!"

Bing could see that the dolphins exchanged quick glances with each other and then dove deeper into the water.

"Great," Bing muttered under his breath. But the whale had somehow sensed what was taking place and immediately dove down deep as well, now trying to cut off their course.

"Uh . . . great whale, I'm not so sure how far I can go down. In fact, I think I'm deeper now than I have ever been."

But the whale did not hesitate. It continued on, chasing the dolphins as they moved away.

Bing debated whether or not he should let go. His fear at being taken so far down, plus the fact that he might lose consciousness, gave him pause in his decision. He knew the others were depending on him, and couldn't lose Patrick or all hope would be lost. But having a dead penguin show up beside the dolphins (once they finally stopped to listen) wouldn't be very good either.

The dolphins swam straight down for what seemed like an eternity before they finally pulled up short and stopped. The exasperation on their faces was evident. The whale positioned itself several yards away with Bing holding onto the great beast for dear life.

"What is it that you want, foolish bird?" the first dolphin screeched at Bing.

"Yes," the second one followed, "what is it that you need?"

Bing attempted to regain his composure, his fright at the depth the now held evident to all. He wanted to take a breath to calm himself, but in his present position that was obviously impossible.

"I merely wanted to know where you were going with my friend. I think you are making a mistake by taking him with you."

"And what business is that of yours?" the dolphin to the left asked.

"Yes," the second one followed again, "why are you interested in what we're doing?"

"Well, you see, I need him back. He is the only hope we have in putting an end to the madness that is taking place above us."

"And what madness is this?" the first dolphin asked slyly. "I don't believe we need to concern ourselves with what is going on up there."

"Exactly," the second dolphin followed. "We don't see the need to be concerned with the surface dweller's problems."

Bing was losing patience with the constant double talk, and worrying about the amount of air he had left in his lungs.

"Do you two always talk like this?" he asked, confused by their ridiculous banter. "Look, I don't have much time to plead my case, so can only one of you do the talking, or is that too much to ask?"

The dolphins looked at one another and smiled in a disturbing manner.

"Speak little bird," the first dolphin said at last.

"Well, there is just too much to tell to have to explain it all. Suffice to say there is a great force just to the north of here that means to end the reign of mankind. It is an evil force that can only be stopped by the being that you have at your side. I need him back to complete his task."

The dolphins once again looked to each other as if they knew a secret.

"Oh, and what is it about this creature that makes him so special?"

"Yes, why him?"

The killer whale let out another low bellow of air sending out millions of tiny air bubbles towards the surface.

"Because we think that he has a gift from the maker that can prevent this from happening."

"Think? You don't sound so sure."

"Yes, you don't sound so sure."

"Would you two please STOP IT!" Bing screamed at them so loud that he even startled the whale.

"I don't think you even know who the boy is," the first dolphin replied, completely disregarding Bing's perturbed state.

"He hasn't a clue," spoke the second, rolling his eyes.

"I know who he is," Bing said, trying to convince them.

Bing could only stare at the two dolphins, his contempt for the two building with every word that they uttered. It wasn't so much the very nature of the creatures that bothered Bing, but rather the snobbish way in which they were treating him.

"And?" the first dolphin put forward. "What is that you know?"

"Yes, please tell us if you know so much."

Even the whale turned in Bing's direction waiting to hear the answer. But Bing had no answer to give. He knew the boy was special, of course. But as to who he really was, well, Bing was at a loss for words.

"You see little penguin," the second dolphin began, "we do know who he is."

"Yes, we know exactly who he is."

"And since you have no idea on the matter, then we feel that he is not worthy to remain in your charge."

"Yes, you can't have him."

"He is ours now and we will make him feel more welcome than he has ever felt in all of his life. Our home will now be his home."

Bing was beside himself with worry. He was losing control of the conversation and rapidly losing hope that he could retrieve his friend.

"I think we'll be leaving now and we're taking the boy with us."

"Yes, he's going with us."

"And don't try to follow us."

"Or we might have to see how a penguin will pop at these kinds of depths."

"But you can't," Bing pleaded. "You can't do this! There are too many lives at stake. He's got to return with me!"

Bing didn't know what to do. The dolphins turned to leave, and he couldn't do anything to prevent them. He thought for an instant about asking the whale to intervene, but he knew that it would be too much to ask of the great beast. If the dolphins decided to separate it would be an enormous chore to chase them down.

And that's when hope intervened.

It took only a few seconds for Bing to realize what was happening, but in the midst of all their debating Patrick finally woke from his unconscious state.

"Going? Where am I going?" he finally spoke.

Patrick heard someone talking. Two people actually. No, make that three.

And one of them was Bing. That was obvious. But as to where they were located, he hadn't a clue.

He opened his eyes slowly and was surprised to find that he was surrounded by water. He turned his head from side to side to gain his bearings, finding that he was in a place that was terribly unfamiliar.

"Going? Where am I going?" he asked as he turned around to find the ones that were causing all the commotion.

"Oh, thank the Creator!" Bing said loudly.

Patrick was surprised to see the two dolphins sitting so close to him, but was even more astonished to see the enormous killer whale just a few yards away.

"Whoa," he said as he tried to back pedal away from the massive brute.

The dolphins immediately positioned themselves between Patrick and the penguin.

"He is still going with us."

"Yes, he's ours."

Patrick wrinkled his brow as he listened to their words, unsure of how their meaning was intended.

"Bing, what's going on? Where are we? And who are these two?"

Bing sighed, and shook his head.

"You fell from the cliff wall. You hit the water pretty hard and lost consciousness. The two fine fellows in front of you have decided that since you fell into their domain that you are now in their possession, and will not let you return with me."

The dolphins nervously turned around to face Patrick, not knowing what to expect from the boy.

Patrick reached his hand up to his head and felt the side of his face, "Oh yeah, now I remember. I killed the witch, right?"

"You certainly did," Bing replied, nodding. He leaned in close to the dolphins, "Chopped her head clean off," he said with a glint of satisfaction.

Patrick looked down at his shirt expecting to see the green blood from the Medusa splattered across it.

"And the dolphins want to take me where?" he asked without looking up, his mind still clouded from his fall.

"I don't know," Bing said casually. "Where is it that you want to take him?" he asked of the two (now obviously nervous) dolphins.

Patrick watched as the two creatures looked back and forth from one another, neither of them offering a response to Bing's question.

"And why won't you let me go back with Bing?" Patrick asked. "I need to go back."

"Uh . . . well, we were hoping that you might like to come with us," the first dolphin spoke, his voice raising an octave. "Instead of with those land dwellers."

"Uh . . . to explore other regions of the oceans," the second one added.

Patrick was surprised by their comment, and added, "But I am a 'land dweller.'"

The dolphins looked utterly confused by his response.

"Oh, no, your eminence, you are so much more than that!"

"Yes, so much more."

Eminence? What's an 'eminence?' he wondered to himself.

"You don't have to return to the overland with him," the first said as he pointed to Bing. "There is much, much more to oversee down here."

But Bing was beside himself with panic.

"Patrick we have to go! I don't know how much longer I can remain down here!"

Patrick nodded in kind, and pushed his way past the dolphins, dismissing their silly talk.

"I take it that he's a friend of yours?" Patrick asked as he eyed the great whale. "Is he the one that's going to give us a ride?"

"Well, I haven't asked him as of yet," Bing replied as he turned towards the eye of the beast. "Can I impose on you for one last burden?"

Again the whale bellowed out a great bassoon like sound, the bubbles rising away towards the surface.

Patrick turned in time to see the dolphins moving slowly away, acting as if they were unsure if they should leave or stay. And just before the whale began to take Patrick and Bing from the area, Patrick briefly overheard one of the dolphins say to the other, "They're going to be so mad if we don't come back with him," wondering for a second who the dolphin could be talking about, but then dismissed their talk straightaway due to the silly nature in which they were carrying on.

The whale began with a burst that caught Patrick off guard, his hand barely finding hold on the same fin that Bing held on to. They rose to the surface only once, trolling along the edge of the water before diving back down again.

Patrick watched as Bing gave instructions to the whale on the area they needed to make towards, with the whale never acknowledging one way or another that he even understood. But with the speed the whale was moving it was obvious that he was taking them to some place that he was familiar. The next time that they broke the surface they had been brought to what Patrick could only make out as a large lagoon.

As Patrick emerged from the water he viewed the large semi-circle of rock with apprehension. The mountains rose vertically from the shore, sheer cliff walls that extended straight up with not much of a way for them to exit by land.

Bing turned and thanked the whale for bringing them as far as he had, the great beast never acknowledging the greeting, only turning and making his way back out to sea.

"Bing, I have no idea where we're at," Patrick said with a bewildered look on his face as he gazed at the cliff walls before them.

"Don't worry," Bing replied. "If what I am led to believe is correct we are just a stones throw from the river that led to Belial's Reach. We're now on the other side of the mountains that we had in front of us only a brief while ago."

Patrick nodded as if he understood, and followed the little penguin as he began to make his way through a small, hidden division between the rocks that Patrick hadn't seen.

"If we are fortunate we should emerge at the river's edge before nightfall."

They traveled upward for almost two hours over a gulley that ran down the side of the mountain, the gravel below their feet causing them to slip and slide from time to time before they finally came to firm footing. Before long they found themselves walking amongst green, vibrant trees and other flourishing plants, things that had been missing for so long in their travels.

"Have you noticed how warm it is?" Patrick asked of his friend.

"Yes. I noticed it as soon as we emerged from the water. I'm surprised you're only noticing it now."

"What's going on?" Patrick asked as he looked around. "What happened to all the snow?"

"I believe our friend, the witch, has made herself more comfortable. I suppose the weather got to be a bit much for her to bear."

Patrick was stunned, "She can change the weather?"

But Bing only laughed, "She's a witch. I imagine she can do a good deal more than just this."

They continued further and further up the side of the large hill, pausing to rest when they were only a few hundred yards from the top. Patrick turned briefly and looked skyward. They were now in the very shadow of the Reach, the clouds above them crackling with great bursts of lightning. It startled both he and Bing for the moment, Patrick wondering about the power of the witch, wondering if she had the power to cause the storms to intensify as they were.

They moved this way for another hundred yards or so, the lightning storm flashing the sky with great cracks of energy, when to his left something caught Patrick's attention. Ahead of him, on the side of a great mossy mound perched high above where they were walking was what appeared to be the figure of a woman hanging over the edge.

At the same time both Patrick and Bing uttered a quick, "Oh, no!" at what they were seeing, neither realizing that they were each looking in a different direction.

Without a thought Patrick began to make for the side of the mound, the wet clay causing his footing to slip, and not allowing for much of a hold as he tried to dig in his fingers. He began pulling himself up the small hill by grabbing at the roots and vines to allow his advance.

As he moved higher, his head just above the upper part of the hill, Patrick found that what had caught his attention was indeed a woman. She had been bound to a large wooden post that was wedged in the ground. The post was the thickness of a telephone pole, the woman's hands bound above her head by rope. The few clothes that were on her body were slashed and bloodied, looking as if they had been picked apart by the birds.

It was a difficult climb to make his way up, the awkward position she had been placed required Patrick to traverse the muddy side of the hill like a mountain climber, but after a few minutes of effort he finally made his way to the top.

As Patrick drew nearer to the peculiar scene the strangeness of the situation took an even more bizarre turn. He could see that the woman's ankles were bound to the post as well, but what caused him to hesitate was the sight below the bindings. Like a tree or plant, her feet had thick, black, root-like growths extending from underneath her toenails that ran deep into the ground below her. The roots seemed to have grown under her toenails and worked their way into her skin, almost like they had become a part of her.

"Patrick," Bing said quietly.

But Patrick was so amazed at the sight before him that he didn't hear Bing calling to him.

"Patrick!" Bing shouted this time.

Patrick snapped from his amazed state, pulling his stare away from the woman and looked down at Bing. "What's the matter?"

But then Patrick saw what Bing was trying to point out to him. Humans of many different kinds lay dead all around the base of the small hill upon which Patrick now stood. Black and white, old and young, men and women—it didn't matter as the bodies lay in same desperate state. Some where in military uniforms, while others were dressed similarly to how he was. But the one thing that was common to them all was that they were all dead.

"What happened?" Patrick asked, his face contorting into a mask of bewilderment.

"I don't know," Bing said as he shook his head. "But look at their hands. Every one of them is holding a knife or weapon of some fashion." Bing turned and looked up at the woman that Patrick stood next to, "It looks like they were trying to get to her."

"Why haven't they been melted?" Patrick asked. "How come they're bodies are still together?"

Bing walked over and stood beside a young, dark skinned man. He knelt down and touched the man's forearm every so slightly.

"I don't know," he said, his eyes never leaving the human at his feet. "Perhaps these people where like a few of the others we have seen. Like the fire people. Maybe there are a few humans that realized that they weren't affected by the plague and sought a way to end it. I don't have any idea as to why they would be different from the others, but somehow they found a way to make it this far. And from the looks of it something ended their life just short of accomplishing their task."

Patrick looked at the bound woman beside him, trying to understand what had taken place.

But then Patrick saw something that made him jump, his reaction almost causing him to fall off the edge of the hill.

The woman breathed.

It was a small exhale to be sure, something that was barely noticeable, but it was a sign that she was still alive.

Patrick looked to her face and saw something else that gave him a start. The air that she was exhaling held the faintest color of red. As the tiny wisps of wind that flowed around him caught hold of that air as she exhaled, it carried her breath away to places far to the east.

"Pestilence," Bing said from below. "We have found the source of the plague."

Patrick could only stare at her small frame, feeling sorry and helpless at the same time for the woman. He walked over and began untying her bindings. He removed the rope at her ankles first, and then undid the thick cord at her wrists. She collapsed forward at once, almost falling over the edge of the hill. Patrick caught her at her waste, lowering her to the ground at his feet.

A faint, "No," came from the woman as Patrick gently set her head down on the ground. He moved around to her feet and saw that the roots were still attached to the tissue beneath her nails. He reached down and began to tear the blackened things from her body, the vines tearing away with crisp snaps like snapping beans off a vine, their oily juices flowing away to the grass at her feet.

"What do I do?" Patrick shouted down to Bing. "It looks like she's dying, but I don't know what to do for her."

"There's nothing you can do," Bing said coldly. "Let her die."

"But shouldn't I help her?" Patrick pleaded.

But Bing only shook his head and looked to the ground. "She was a vessel, nothing more, nothing less. She chose her path, and look what it gave her. Let her explain to the Creator why she did what she did. That's not for us to judge."

Patrick stood and watched as the last few breaths escaped her. Finally her chest stopped moving and she was gone. Patrick could only reason that the black roots must have been what were keeping her alive.

Heavy gusts of wind blew past his ears with a faint whistle as Patrick stood quietly overlooking the scene before him. He felt like he was losing his soul, and with things moving as they were he wasn't sure if he could handle any more scenes like the one he had just witnessed.

He began to lower himself for the climb back down when he heard a horse in the distance galloping in their direction. He stood again and looked to the path ahead, wondering what tribulation could be coming for them next. What he saw didn't surprise him, the horse and rider not an unexpected thing at this juncture in time. He turned and looked at Bing, the small penguin looking petrified as he gazed upon the dark figure that approached.

She stopped just below the hill and just in front of Bing, the penguin backing away from the horses' massive hooves.

"So, young one," she said from the shadows of her hood, "I see our paths have crossed once again."

As the animals approached the very shadow of the Reach, Dan began to feel the temperature change almost immediately. He held his hands in front of him like a blind man, amazed at how he could feel the heat radiating like an oven from the base of the mountain. The strange part, though, was when he turned behind him he found the air was as cold as it ever was.

A few yards ahead of them stood a definitive line where the snow ended. He wondered at how the mountains could hold such a warm spot while snow and ice towered all around them—but there he stood, the evidence at his feet.

Dan found that the animals would not go any further past that spot. Not even the horse. It knelt and allowed Dan to step off, quickly moving away once Dan had moved from its back.

He'd noticed earlier that most of the animals had grown uneasy as the distance was being erased. Some of the animals had even taken to slowing their pace and began to lag behind.

The gorilla that had spoken to him was the only creature that now would venture in his direction, the massive brute walking towards him with his eyes never leaving the mountain.

Dan half heartedly smiled as the creature approached, his intuition telling him that whatever was within the bowels of the mountain frightened the gorilla terribly.

"Bright one?" Dan asked of the gorilla, pointing towards the mountain.

The gorilla turned and looked directly into Dan's eyes and nodded, acting as if he wasn't sure if he wanted to tell him the truth. Dan wondered what else the gorilla actually knew, his sad expression speaking volumes as to what might lie ahead.

Dan reached out and touched the side of the gorilla's face, sensing the worry that the creature felt for him, and nodded, "It'll be ok. Once I get my son back you might be surprised to see me again."

But the gorilla didn't return Dan's forced smile; the creature relayed a sense of compassion towards Dan for the consequences that lay before him, his long face remaining motionless at the human's curious words.

Dan turned and viewed the menacing sight before him as he began the last steps to the great mountain. Its base was still almost a mile from where Dan stood, the obvious layout beckoning for him to come forward, the view as close to a tropical setting as you could have imagined this far north.

He could see from the distance that at its edge huge plants and trees not common to this area stood where snow and ice should have been, the lush greens and reds and golden hues seemed out of place and had a fake, plastic look about them that made him feel uneasy. To Dan, it felt like an abomination. Tye, or whoever Tye was working for, had created this mess and there was nothing that Dan could do about it.

He watched as lizards and snakes and various other reptiles moved about the grasses and rocks with such freedom and ease. Dan had only known those kinds of creatures to be things that hid in the dark, moving only when they were clear of preying, watchful eyes. But they didn't seem to be fearful of anything as they paraded around the grounds, almost acting like they owned the place—and that bothered him. He now understood why the animals behind him held their ground and would venture no further.

He wasn't quite sure why, but again it reminded him of Tye. And it reminded him of the spiders. But worst of all, it reminded him that getting back his son was not going to be as simple as finding him and taking him by the hand.

He scanned the horizon for any sign of Patrick, but his mind laughed at him because he knew that he wouldn't find him that easily.

Where could he be?

His legs felt heavy as he walked, the anticipation of finally finding his son could not overcome the fear of what lay before him. He forced his steps to move quicker, pushing his stride so that he could cover the distance without thinking. Before long he was jogging, and then finally running, as he hurried his approach.

As Dan drew nearer to the foot of the mountain something caught his eye that surprised him. Off in the distance, away from where the entrance to the mountain began, several animals were chained to a huge rock wall that extended from the mountain itself. Dan watched as the lizards and snakes would move in close enough to taunt and torment the animals as if they were playing a cruel game, but never getting close enough so that the animals could retaliate.

It was a collection of creatures like no other Dan had seen. An enormous tiger the size of a small horse stood next to a very large wild boar, the creature as white as any snow Dan could imagine. A growling grizzly bear and a ferocious looking baboon stood slightly behind them, but just out of reach of the others. They all sat along a long rock wall, each looking like they were being treated miserably.

Dan instantly remembered the scene from in front of the school in Chicago, seeing the tiger stuffed into the back end of the little car as it tried to fend off the mice.

That's when he knew that Patrick had to be somewhere close.

And then two things instantly came to Dan's mind:

Perhaps these animals were imprisoned for helping his son?

And why weren't the animals behind him coming to their aid?

He knew that the answers could only come from one place, and that was from the animals before him.

Before Dan could get any closer he began to hear a horse galloping towards him from his right. He turned to see a large woman, looking a good deal like the warrior princess from television, Xena. He blinked twice, thinking he was imagining what he was seeing. She charged at him upon a horse that was even larger than the black one he had been riding. She made her way towards him like a proud conqueror, her sword drawn in front of her, and her long raven hair extending from her helmet. She was dressed in browns and blacks, her helmet only allowing her eyes to be seen from behind a mask of gold.

Dan stopped as the horse made its way to him, the woman pointing the sword directly at his throat.

"I believe you have come a long way for nothing, Daniel Brighton," she said with suddenness. Her words had a stinging bite as they came forward. "Your son is dead, and as I see it, your world will follow shortly."

Dan lost his breath for a moment and couldn't think of anything to say. He had traveled all this way in search for his son, and now as this woman proclaimed the impossible, he just wouldn't (and couldn't) believe her words.

"You're lying," he said flatly. "You wouldn't even be bothering with me now if that were true. I know he's out there, somewhere, but he's not dead. Not yet, anyway."

The woman pushed the sword further, the point now resting against his Adam's apple.

"Don't be so quick with your tongue, human, or perhaps I will have to carve it out. Sometimes what you think you know can only cause you more pain in the end."

Dan reached up and tried to slowly push the sword from his throat, "Human? Why would you say that? You look like one yourself, or should I have paid more attention to all those science fiction movies I missed as a kid?" He turned and looked back towards the mountain. "Where's Tye?"

The woman smiled again, "Astertye, the two faced trickster? I'm sure you will see him in short order. But be careful for what you wish, I wouldn't go looking for monsters if I were you."

Dan laughed slightly, "Monster? Is that what they're calling him these days? Yeah, I suppose I'd go along with that description."

The woman smiled in kind, "You really have no idea with what you are toying. I realize the damage he has bought to you and your son, but you shouldn't cloud your mind with visions of vindication. The end is but moments from now, and beyond your reach.

"I am War, the second of the four, and although I wear the skin of another of your kind, it is true that I am not human." She cocked her head to one side as if something he said had surprised her, "But I believe you know who I am," she smiled again, and her eyes grew narrow. "I believe you have always known who I am."

The woman's shape instantly changed from that of a heavy set woman of war, to a more voluptuous form with scarlet hair dressed in the same fashion as before.

She lifted her mask to show her face, revealing a figure that he knew was long since dead.

It was his sister.

Dan's eyes grew wide and he instantly took two steps back, "Oh my god! What are you?" was all that Dan could say.

"I have told you, but I don't think that you want to listen. Or perhaps your mind won't allow you to do so. Either way, we have wasted enough time on such trivial matters. My queen awaits and wishes to have a word with you."

Dan's sanity was in a pot that had just been kicked over. He had seen monstrous, ridiculously bizarre things that no other man had ever seen before, and probably had no right to, but now, with what he was witnessing, he was teetering on the edge of losing his mind.

"Your queen?" he said as he barely got the words from his lips. "Who's that?"

The woman pulled on the reigns of the horse and turned in the direction of the mountain.

"The one that wishes you dead."

CHAPTER 30

The Witch's Words

As Patrick came into view around the far corner to the lands at the base of the mountain, everything and everyone grew silent. The animals and the reptiles stood in quiet awe as they watched Death escort Bing and the boy to the very doorstep of the queen witch. Even the wind itself seemed to stop.

Patrick felt an overwhelming sense of relief that it was finally going to be over. He was afraid of course, but with all that had taken place his resolve was at a breaking point, and in a way he felt at peace. He realized that he was probably going to be killed. He couldn't fathom any other outcome, really. But at least he was finally going to receive the answers to all the questions that had been presented again and again.

Bing reached up and took Patrick by the hand. It was a simple gesture meant to demonstrate to Patrick that he wasn't alone, but Patrick knew that it was a hollow gesture at best. Bing meant it to be true, of course, but Patrick couldn't help but feel that he was never more alone in his life than at this very moment. And no one, and no thing, could help him as he took his final steps to meet the one that held the answers.

"Would you get this thing off me!" Kirsdona bellowed to one of the serpent creatures that guarded the animals to Patrick's left. Patrick turned to look at her briefly, a faint smile sliding across his face, glad to see that she was unharmed. He was only mildly surprised to see the remainder of his friends chained and imprisoned. If Death had known the instant Patrick had taken away Pestilence's life, then surely the queen had known of the others' approach as well.

It seemed she knew everything. And for some strange reason that made Patrick at least take heart. He needed a sense of understanding as to why all of this was taking place. With all the death and destruction that twisted around him, he needed someone to bring him closer to the truth. Even if it was a witch.

Patrick was amazed as he looked at the serpent creatures. Pucket and Gremm had been correct in their descriptions. They were nasty looking creatures that seemed to be some sort of perverted cross between a human and a lizard. They were the same size as a human, but the heads and legs and tails were all lizard—slick and scaly. How that was possible, Patrick didn't have the answer. But then again, how was any of this possible?

As they made their way past Sin, Patrick was surprised to see the enormous white boar explode with anger as Death passed within an arms length of the creature, the chains that bound him stretched to their fullest.

"Now, now, my brother, please calm yourself," she said as she taunted him. "The last time we met you weren't exactly on your best behavior."

Patrick was stunned by her response. He turned to her and asked incredulously, "Brother? You know him?"

Sin was now so mad that it looked as though the chains were only moments from breaking. His snarling outbursts gave Patrick a start, the beast looking like he wanted nothing more than to rip out the woman's throat.

The dark mistress's lips curled up into a tight little smile as she looked away, "Yes, of course I know him. He's my brother. Is that something that surprises you?"

"I just never would have thought," Patrick said as he swallowed hard, "that you and him were related."

Patrick stared at Death for a few moments longer before he turned and looked at the snarling boar.

How can that be? Death and Sin?

Patrick could only think that he was being led to the center stage of a spectacle of which he had no control. It was like he was the guest performer at the Circus of the Bizarre. "Ladies and gentlemen, if you would please direct your attention to the center ring . . ."

They finally stopped at the base of the mountain. The large cavern that opened before them was staged like an auditorium. He noticed that there was a large, dark pond towards the center, probably from all the melting snow, but he couldn't gauge its depth. There were no places to sit, the smooth, sculpted rock rolling away in an upward fashion creating an illusion of depth towards a large stone platform at its peak.

Patrick turned and looked back when he heard the horse that Death was riding come to a stop. The silence that surrounded him was overwhelming. It gave Patrick an ill feeling that something very bad was about to take place.

"Well," he said trying to sound brave, unbelieving that the words were actually coming from him. "Where is she?"

But Death didn't answer. She pulled on the reigns of her horse and turned away, riding towards the outer edge of the arena.

Patrick turned back towards the cavern. He felt like he and Bing were standing there alone, waiting to be sacrificed to some horrific monster. Patrick didn't know what kind of monster was coming his way, but his twelve year old imagination was doing its best to fill his head with all sorts of imagery to frighten him.

He could still hear Kirsdona and Sin making all kinds of commotion behind him, and that made him smile.

At least some of us still have some fight left.

He knew that Syrian and Gremm were just as mad as the other two, but the baboon and bear were more inclined to bide their time, waiting for the moment when it would be best served to unleash their anger.

Patrick lifted his eyes and noticed that ahead of them, chained to the wall high above the far opening in the base of the mountain, was Tye. It looked as if he had been put on display, his limp body hanging above the stone platform.

"Patrick, look," Bing said, pointing in the creatures' direction.

With the wings, tail, and scaly skin Tye now looked more like a dragon from the story books Patrick read as a child than he did a human. He was surprised that he could even recognize the man.

"I see him," Patrick said quietly.

It was strange to see Tye bound with chains around his neck and torso, his seemingly lifeless body displayed in warning for all to see. Tye was a twisted, evil being, of that there was no question, but to leave him up there still gave Patrick an uneasy feeling, thinking that even Tye deserved better than that.

Patrick stood in silence for several moments until he heard a sound behind him that made him forget everything else. It was the one sound that made him break down. Through the long days and endless nights he had done his best to remain as brave as he could, but when he heard his name being called by the one person he thought he'd never see again, he began to cry.

"Pat?" his father said from just behind him, coming across the field. "Oh my God! Patrick!"

When he turned and saw his father he couldn't move. It was almost too unbelievable to be true. He watched as his father began running towards him, the horse and rider behind never making an attempt to stop him.

His father scooped him up in his arms and hugged him, and he began to cry.

"Dad," was all that Patrick could say. He wasn't sure what else to say. He wanted to tell him everything he that had happened over the last nine days, but the words just wouldn't come forward. Instead he just held onto his dad's neck, not wanting to let go. His dad's embrace never felt as good as it did right now.

"Did you find mom?" Patrick asked quietly as he looked into his father's eyes. "Is she ok? I think she was hurt pretty bad . . ."

"She's ok," his father assured him. "She's at a hospital. I saw the ambulance take her myself."

Patrick smiled hesitantly. He knew his father was telling him the truth, but it was almost like he was holding something back.

"How did you get here?" Patrick asked shaking his head, still bewildered to see his father.

"You'd never believe it. Most of it was spent on a horse."

"A horse?"

"Yeah, I know. Can you believe me on a horse?"

Patrick pulled away and looked into his dad's face again, his entire body filled with an overpowering joy. He turned quickly and looked to Bing who was standing a few steps away.

"Bing," Patrick said with excitement and emotion, "this is my dad." And then he turned back to his dad. "Dad, this is my friend, Bing. He's one of the ones who saved me. He's one of the one who's been helping me."

Patrick watched as his father nodded his thanks to the little penguin, his face sincere in his appreciation.

Bing smiled and nodded in return, "He looks like a nice man, Patrick."

"Yeah. He's pretty cool."

"You can talk to him?" his father asked, astounded as he watched the communication taking place between his son and the penguin. "He knows what you're saying?"

"Yeah. Sometimes I still can't believe it," Patrick said excitedly as he turned back to where the rest of his friends were being held prisoner. "I can talk to all of them. They're all my friends."

Dan shook his head, his shoulders hunched forward. "But how? How can you talk to them?"

"I don't know," he said as he shrugged. "It just sort of happened. And you're not going to believe what else I can do."

"What?" Dan said, a look of distress crossing his face, almost as if he didn't want to know.

Patrick explained to him as best he could the few abilities that had come forward, his father wide-eyed through it all.

"Amazing. I don't know what to say. Do you know why this is happening to you? Do you have any idea?"

Patrick could only shake his head. "None. But guess what else I can do. I can drive. I'm pretty good, too."

"Then that was you driving the car? Back at the school?"

"Yeah," Patrick said, nodding.

"You wouldn't believe how close I was to catching you. I was riding a giant black horse . . ."

"You were on that horse?!" Patrick asked as he rolled his eyes. He went silent for a moment as he remembered thinking that it was Tye, and then he shook his head in disbelief. "I thought it was someone else."

"Tye?"

"You know him?!" Patrick said with a look of surprise.

"Oh, yeah. I know him."

They both turned and looked at the creature chained to the wall above the cavern.

"What happened to him?" they both asked at the same time.

There was a long silence as the question that was asked hung on the air.

But then an answer came forth.

The words fell forward from the deepest most part of the cavern, covering both Patrick and his father with a warmth and a pleasantness that caught them off guard.

"He decided to go his own way," came a voice that echoed softly off the cavern walls. It was the voice of a dream, both seductive and sweet. "Unfortunately that is something that my father taught me never to tolerate."

Patrick and Dan turned their attention to the right. The woman glided down from the mountain like a majestic figure that Patrick imagined could only have come from someplace mythical. It was almost like she floated, Patrick trying hard to tell if her feet were even moving beneath her black tunic. She was the most beautiful person he had ever seen in his life.

"You should close your mouth," she said to Patrick with a glint of a smile. "There are a great many insects around. I'd hate for you to choke on one that was flying absently about." Her eyes arched lightly. "I suppose it's for their benefit as much as it is for yours."

Patrick, unaware that his mouth was even open, closed it with a snap.

The woman smiled a thin lipped vamp, seeming quite pleased to see the individuals before her.

Then Patrick heard a buzzing. It was faint at first, but then erupted like a blast from a volcano as the flies burst forward from a hole in the side of the mountain. Thousands of the tiny insects rocketed skyward forming a giant dark cloud that hung in the air like smoke above their heads. Patrick remembered the warning that Gremm and Pucket had issued as he watched the flies circle and then form a sinister black shape to the witch's side.

Do not let the little monsters anywhere near you!

The woman continued closer and closer, Patrick not sure what he was supposed to do, his heart beating high in his chest. His father put his arm around Patrick's chest and pulled him behind, placing himself between Patrick and the witch. But then Patrick did the same to his father and stepped back to the front.

"No, dad. I think she wants me. I'll be ok," he said, never taking his eyes off the woman.

"Patrick, what is going on?" Dan finally asked, his voice demanding answers. "What do they want from you? Why is all of this happening?"

"I don't know," he said as he turned to look at his dad. "But she's the reason why I'm here. She's the one that is supposed to give me the answers." He turned back to the woman who was now only several yards away. "And I think I'm the one that's supposed to stop her."

The woman made her way in front of Patrick, her eyes sparkling like sapphires. She was wonderful.

He blinked twice as he looked at her hair. It seemed to be many different colors at once, shimmering and reflecting the light like spun glass.

"Then you are the brave soul I've heard so much about," she said as she nodded lightly.

Patrick could only stare. He had to remind himself to breathe, his body frozen by the vision of the being in front of him. He wanted to be brave, but his mind was such a jumbled mix of emotions at this point that he was having a hard time finding his way to 'bravery's' door.

Without taking her eyes away from Patrick she gave a quick command to the serpent creatures, her voice soft and relaxed. "Release the animals. They are my guest's friends, and I don't think that he would feel entirely welcome with them situated as they are."

The serpent creatures immediately began undoing the chains that bound the animals.

"But not the boar," she said as she raised her hand ever so slightly. "I believe we shall need to keep him restrained for the time being."

In a matter of seconds Syrian, Kirsdona, and Gremm joined Bing by Patrick's side. Kirsdona moved closest to the boy, only inches from Patrick's hip. "So this is the queen?" she asked with a rudeness that was even surprising for her.

But the witch never altered her subtle smile. "I am the one of which you speak, my dear lady. But I would watch that tone of yours. I understand that it has gotten you into some trouble from time to time. It could easily be confused for something that sounds a little more menacing than may be intended. You see, I'm not a person that takes to threats very well." She then pointed absently in the direction above the stone platform.

Patrick and the others once again looked toward the haggard remains of Tye.

"You didn't have to kill him," Syrian said under his breath.

But the witch only smiled. "Oh, he's not dead. Not yet, anyway. I have put him there only for my amusement. He's there as a reminder to all not to take my wishes for granted."

"But he was a man," Dan interjected. "How could you turn him into something as monstrous as that? That's not amusement."

The witch looked over her shoulder at Dan, her face surprised. "A man? Whatever gave you the idea that he was a man?"

"What do you mean?" Dan said, his brow wrinkling, his eyes narrow. "I saw him. I saw him before you changed him." He pointed to the flies. "Until they changed him. He was a man."

The witch folded her arms in front of her chest, her hands hidden inside her robe.

"It amazes me the simple power of illusion that can cloud a man's mind. Do you really believe that I would send a simple human to accomplish the complexity of my instructions?" She gave them all a look of amusement.

"Tye's a snake," Bing said at last, a look of contempt on his face. "He always was. He's never been anything more."

Patrick looked to his friend, stunned by his revelation. "You knew that? All this time you knew that he was a snake?"

"No," Bing shook his head. "I have only just come to that realization. I think that most of us knew in the back of our minds that he wasn't human. What exactly he was, well, I don't think any of us could really be sure."

Everyone except the witch turned and looked up at the creature still hanging from the wall. Patrick thought he saw Tye's left eye open slowly and then close as if he was in pain.

"But how?" was all that Patrick could ask.

"How?" the witch responded lightly. "That is an easy question. When a willing subject presents itself to me I am able to perform all kinds of wondrous deeds. Astertye volunteered his services to me, and I accepted. Just as I accepted all the gracious acts of volunteerism that the humans you have seen provided."

Her response struck Patrick like a slap to the face. It was something that he never gave a thought to until she brought it to his attention.

Patrick turned and looked back at Death. He looked at War. He remembered Pestilence. His head swiveled in the direction of the serpent creatures.

"You used them all?" he said, bewildered. "They were all once human? They're the Wicca?"

"Of course," she said. "What did you expect? What else are humans good for?"

"But . . ."

"I only placed Astertye in a man's outer skin to give him the advantage of accomplishing my desires. What you see before you now is more closely related to what he actually is."

Patrick didn't know what to say. He turned and looked to his father for answers, but his own realization was beginning to take hold as he looked around. He knew that his father had no idea about the initial contact the Wicca had made. His father had no idea about the book. And he was probably only now starting to realize small, complicated parts of what was actually taking place.

"Who are you?" Patrick asked, not sure he wanted the answer.

The witch queen smiled, a slight laugh escaping from her. "'Who am I?' Now that's a strange question. I thought the question you traveled all this way to have answered was, 'Who are you?'"

Patrick stared up at this wondrous spectacle, unsure of how someone could seem so magnificent. So breathtakingly beautiful. It was like he was becoming hypnotized. He couldn't speak.

"Who am I?" she asked of no one, and then turned around and walked a short distance to her left. "That is a question that is not so easily answered. I am not so sure you could understand the truth if I were to even speak it."

"And why is that?" Bing asked sharply, his words mocking her to a certain degree. "If you know so much, surely you can find the words that can fill our ears with understanding."

The woman's eyes darkened and the smiled melted from her face. "I don't believe you were the one I was speaking to, wise little bird. If silence is not a virtue that you'd care to practice, then perhaps your voice can amuse us until you can learn to keep quiet."

And then Bing began to talk. Not coherent, cohesive sentences. But words, and only words. And he could not stop.

"Fish bird stop can water snow tree feet belly mountain reindeer bottle rock paper death more sea but ice great with doesn't often asked send reason it inclusive is we guide delay should sound please . . ."

A terribly unpleasant, frightened look overcame him. He behaved like he couldn't breathe, his face contorting into shock as he struggled with the spell that had been placed upon him.

"Miniscule into that cinder black block and long course yesterday frown have three pretend mountains . . . ," the gibberish coming from Bing was now pitching higher and higher, his constant speaking unable to allow any air to pass through to his lungs.

Patrick was outraged. He ran to the side of his friend and tried to see if he could help, all the while the witch stood quiet as she watched the spectacle.

"Stop it!" Patrick screamed at her. "Stop it now!"

With a snap of her fingers Bing finally stopped, the little penguin falling to his side as he gasp for every drop of air that would come his way.

"We're not your toys!" Patrick yelled at her. "You just can't play with us just to make yourself laugh. That's not right."

Kirsdona lowered herself for an attack, and growled, "I can see that you never learned how to play nice with others. I believe you're going to regret hurting our friend."

Syrian stepped in front of Patrick and Bing. "Patrick, if you are going to do something, then do it now. Otherwise, leave. Do not let this tormentor extend her grasp to you."

But the woman only glanced in his direction. "Oh Syrian," she said with a purr. "Please. I have not even extended a hand in young Patrick's direction. I have only bid him welcome.

"In fact, I will show you all that I am a being that is quite capable of working together with your kind." And then the woman looked in the direction of Gremm. "Brother Gremm, you are now free to leave," she said with a sugary smile. "I no longer require your services. I believe we have concluded our business."

Patrick and the remainder of his friends turned their attention back and forth between the bear and the witch, unsure of the meaning of the witch's words.

"Gremm?" Kirsdona was the first to speak, a confused expression crossing her face. "What is she talking about?"

"No, Gremm," Syrian said barely above a whisper, his face conveying a look of understanding that Patrick couldn't comprehend. "Tell me it isn't so."

But the bear would not meet any of their questioning faces.

"What is she talking about?" Patrick asked, the painful realization beginning to dawn on him. "Gremm?"

But again the bear would not answer. Instead the great beast began to back away, his head hanging low to the ground.

"What did you do to him?" Kirsdona growled as she turned back to the witch. "What did you do to his head?"

"I did nothing, I assure you. I only requested a volunteer."

"Oh, no," was all that Bing could utter. "Not you, Gremm."

"No!" Patrick screamed. "I saw him fight back! I saw him help us!"

But the witch merely arched her brow, the words she used felt like poison. "Did you? He must be a better actor than I thought."

"But what about Tyrillia and Pucket?"

"I only needed the one. What happened with the others was another set of circumstances altogether unrelated."

Syrian moved in front of the bear, his hand reaching out and touching Gremm's shoulder. But the bear pulled away as if he was in pain. "Do not do this, Syrian. You do not understand what you are dealing with. Leave me go in peace."

Bing turned towards the witch. "But how? Why?"

"Do you really think that I would allow you to go unescorted through my land? I needed you to come to me without the influence of others."

"The influence of others? What are you talking about?"

But the witch easily dismissed the question from Bing. "I'm sure your family is waiting for you, Gremm," she said giving her attention to the bear as he made its way to the south. "Be sure to send along to them my greetings. And remember—do not look back."

Patrick watched as Gremm hesitated ever so slightly at the mention of his family, but the bear continued on until he was out of sight beyond the mountain pass.

"All this time it was a trap?" Patrick asked, dumbfounded by the turn of events.

"What did you do to him?" Kirsdona asked again through gritted teeth. She launched herself at the witch in that instant, the fury she held going forward in a mix of claws and teeth, "I'll kill you!"

But the witch did not seem the least bit concerned. She merely raised her hand, the tiger's lunge instantly freezing in mid air. Patrick and the others immediately stepped back, shocked that she had the power to bewitch Kirsdona as she had. The witch then walked forward and lightly touched the face of the motionless tiger. "I warned you, my pet. I am not someone that makes statements without backing them up. Maybe next time you'll listen."

"But why use Gremm?" Syrian asked. "Why do this to him? We were coming to you anyhow!"

"I realize," the witch nodded slowly. "But I knew that your little group was so determined to make your way here. And since you had eluded all the other methods that were employed to place you out of the way, then I wanted you to come the way I needed for you to come. I did not want any outside interference."

"Interference? By who?"

Patrick's father knelt beside him, eyeing his son from his head to his feet as if he expected to see something that gave him a clue to what abilities Patrick possessed. "Patrick, is your friend ok? I don't know what's going on, but if there is anything . . . anything special that you can do, I think you better do it now."

The witch then began walking closer to the rest of the group. As she approached, they all began to slide backwards on the sandy soil below their feet. Every step she took in their direction pushed them back an equal distance away from her. It was like an invisible hand gently guiding them away.

Everyone, that is, except Patrick.

"Hey!" Bing said aloud as he reached for Patrick to hold him.

"What's going on?!" Syrian asked as he leaned forward to grab hold of something to keep from falling.

"Dad!" Patrick yelled as his father slid away with the animals.

"What the . . ." Dan said briefly as his head swung from side to side as his feet moved across the earth without his effort. Each of them mystified at what was taking place.

Patrick was still on his knees as he watched the others sliding away from him by the power of the witch's words.

"I can see that your emotions are getting the best of each of you," she spoke calmly. "Your travels have been harsh. I believe that in order for me to have any further conversation with the boy, I will require a fair amount of distance until you calm down."

The animals continued to slide backwards until they were almost thirty yards behind Patrick.

Kirsdona was still airborne when the witch relinquished her hold on the tiger. She immediately fell to the ground with a thud. But the tiger got to her feet at once, and growled, "She's so dead!" before she tried another advance. But Kirsdona, along with the others, found that there was an invisible barrier that had been placed between them and the witch. They could move no further in that direction. They could move back and forth and to the rear, but not anywhere in the direction of Patrick.

Patrick was helpless as he watched his friends and his dad deal with what had been handed to them. His emotions were starting to get the better of him, and his anger was building. This did not go unnoticed by the witch. She casually watched as his skin hue began to change as he turned his anger in her direction.

"Why are you doing all of this?" he said in a burst of rage. "Why are you tormenting these women? Why are you killing all these people?"

"Calm yourself, boy," she said as she looked to the ground. "I'd hate for something to happen that you didn't intend on happening."

But Patrick would not stop, his anger still brimming to the top. "They only asked for your help. Those women summoned you to help them and this is how you repay their request? How dare you."

The witch's eyes widened at the last outburst by Patrick, and she glared at him in a wicked and maniacal way.

"Summoned me? Is that what you have been told?" she said, her voice just below a screech. "My dear child I believe you have been misled."

Patrick was surprised as he began to notice that the woman's beauty was starting to fade. The shape of her elongated teeth, and the curl of her lips, made Patrick feel as though the woman may be nothing more than a wolf in sheep's clothing.

Patrick swallowed hard, "What do you mean? I know what took place. They used the book and called you forward to help them."

But the witch only burst into laughter and shook her head. "These wretched and intolerable humans summon me? I don't believe there is a book for such a thing," she said with disgust. She pointed a long and crooked finger in Patrick's direction. "They did not summon me, my dear child, they summoned you."

And there it was. Her words hit Patrick right between the eyes, and he didn't even see it coming.

It was the one thing that he had never expected to hear.

Patrick could only blink twice and step backward. He was staggered by her words. "Me?" he asked incredulously. "What?"

"How?!" came the response that rippled through most of the crowd behind him.

"That can't be true!" Bing said, unbelieving. "That's not possible."

"It's only a lie meant to deceive us, Patrick," Syrian said quickly. "Don't listen to her words. She'll tell you anything she can to confuse you."

The queen continued her smile, quite pleased with the confusion that was now raining down around her.

"Why should I lie? There is no reason for it. The women who at one time had control of the Book of Time summoned forth a spirit to aid them in their search for rediscovery for the planet." She arched her eyes and folded her arms in front of her, "Believe me, I am not such a spirit."

Patrick could only stare at her. He had wanted answers to all of the questions that swirled and danced around him for so long. But now that he was getting those answers his mind could not hold them in place.

The witch moved quietly in front of Patrick, her foul breath falling over him as she continued.

"I have watched the earth witches and their movements from afar, and at how they bargained and slithered their way into acquiring the Book. Do not be so easily fooled into believing that they are simple in their ways. They can be quite brutal when they need to be.

"Once they had acquired the faded pages and deciphered the words within, I saw my chance to enter into this world like a shadow under a veil." The witch tilted her head in the direction of War and Death, the two women still sitting at the edge of the arena. "It's a rather interesting little book, I'll give you that. Something that I'll need to keep close.

"At first, the witches had hoped that I was the one that was there to help them to achieve their goals. Upon my arrival they plotted and planned, hoping that I would be the one to aid them in rebirthing the planet as they wished. But they quickly discovered that I had ulterior motives. They had no idea that the true person for their calling was a twelve year old boy from some far off land. How could they? Once I was made aware of your presence I was somewhat surprised myself.

"From the beginning I led them to believe that you were an embodiment of some sort of evil that would be a threat to them. I just applied the same logic to you that should have been applied to me. I lured them into believing that you were sent by unseen forces that would do everything in their power to stop them. They thought that you were going to try and prevent them from accomplishing their initial goal of restoring the planet, and that allowed me to persuade them into believing that the only way in which to stop you was to grant me total control. It was simple, really. I just stepped into the shoes that you were supposed to fill. In time they gave themselves to me, body and soul."

Patrick could hear his father yelling to from behind. It was now obvious that he had reasoned his way as to what was taking place. "Patrick! Get out of there! She's not what you think she is!"

But Patrick was completely enchanted by the witch's words. He could not turn away from her voice. He wanted to hear more.

"Allegiances were made with lower forms of this world to secure a place where I could, shall you say, set up shop. I gave to them the same freedoms that are enjoyed by most of the other creatures of this world. To explore and live freely without the threat of repulsion by man or beast. It wasn't a hard deal to strike, really. If you were in their position, how would you feel?"

"oUr maSTer Is A gRaCiouS hOSt," the flies thing hissed forward.

Patrick was horrified as he watched the fly thing speak.

"I then had to reach out and play on man's other fears. Jealousy, vindictiveness, spite, greed. Once War was set into motion, it was only a matter of time before the downfall of man would be complete. Pestilence was brought in to ensure the final product was delivered."

A sickly, wheezing voice came from the witch's right, "And what about Famine?"

Patrick watched as a small, frail woman, no taller than four feet high, walked to the witch's side. She looked like the child of a barren and lost world. There was barely any hair left on her head, the woman's skin thin and deep set, nothing more than decoration over bone. She was beyond the description of thin. She was the child of hunger.

The witch put her arm around the woman and pulled her close. "Ah, yes. Famine. The most pleasant of all the evils. Please be patient, child. Your time is almost upon this land. I will need man's food supplies diseased and spoiled in short order. But not just yet."

Patrick was repulsed by the display in front of him. "Why are you here?" he asked with a whisper.

The woman smiled unpleasantly. "My father and I saw an opportunity in which to take advantage of a situation. It did not involve a book. It did not involve rebirth or rediscovery. But it did involve deception. A practice which has proven to be a well thought out point of involvement that my family has become very good at."

The witch brought her hands together in front of her. "You see, there once was a father, a great and plentiful man, who thought his only child should have the opportunity to walk amongst the humans. To teach them. To educate them. To bring them around to his way of thinking of supposed beauty, love, and tolerance. He walked this earth for only a short amount of time, but the damage he did to my father while he was here was beyond measure. He was a being that left a lasting impression on all those he came in contact with, much to my father's displeasure."

Patrick's breathing became shallow for he now knew who she was talking about.

The witch turned and looked back at the mountain, folding her arms behind her back. "As of late, my father thought that it should only be fair that his only child have the same opportunity. To walk the planet. To breathe the air that man breathes. To enjoy the luxuries and privileges that man partakes. Only my father does not wish to teach or educate. He only wishes to stop this unending joke and finally sever the ties of man's domination of this planet."

Patrick was amazed. "Then you're . . ."

"A faithful daughter," the witch finished as she smiled. "That is what you meant to say, is it not? I only wish to carry out my fathers' desires. Just like any child."

The witch paused a moment and looked long into the face of Patrick. Patrick thought that she now looked more like an animal. That she looked like she wanted to eat him.

"I'm sorry that the conversation has turned. We were talking about you, weren't we?" she casually pointed out. "About what the animals believe that you are. About what the Wicca hoped that you are."

Patrick tried to stand tall in the midst of her words, but his legs had that rubbery, sick feel about them, and he was barely able to stand.

"Do you have any idea who you truly are?" She asked of Patrick

"I . . . I don't know," he answered. For some reason Patrick couldn't speak. The words wouldn't form in his mind. He didn't want to ask the question anymore. He didn't want to know the answer to the questions that he had traveled so long to have answered. He was now fearful of what the answers might truly be.

With a slow, burning gasp of air he found the strength to finally speak the words. "What am I?" he asked slowly, unsure.

The woman walked past Patrick to his left, moving towards his friends, stopping just a hair's breath from their point of entrapment. She looked down at each of them, a glint of her superiority evident in her smile.

The woman held up her hand, "Let me quickly help to soothe both your mind and your fears. You are not the being that the animals had hoped for. You are not the being that the Wicca had prayed for," she said shaking her head. "In fact, you are really not anything special at all."

Patrick felt like he had been struck by something unseen, the words she spoke piercing him like an arrow. He felt small and alone, still confused as to all that had happened to him.

"But what about all the things that I can do? What about the way I can stay under water? How I can talk to the animals? What about when my skin turns color and the sky goes black? What about the way I can travel through the land of the undead?"

The woman held her smile, her arms never flinching from their position. "I realize that in the simple context of a twelve year old's mind that the few simple things that you have accomplished may seem quite daunting and important. But they are only simple parlor tricks, my dear child," she said as she shook her head again, still showing her complete disregard for his small triumphs. "Nothing more. A capable shaman, or holy man can deliver the same results."

The witch looked to the ground and walked towards the water, her voice echoing off the surrounding rock.

"Oh, your friends, and the others, had hoped that you were something more. They believe that you are a spirit long since gone from this world. A spirit that they called forth with the Book who they believed could perform miraculous acts. One who has the ability to raise the mountains, can roll forth the rushing waters, and controls the clay and the stone. A being who works hand in hand with both Life and Death in dealing with all living things on the planet." The witch began to laugh. "They believe that you are the planet's caretaker. It's sentinel. It's guardian. The one being who has providence over the planet itself."

Patrick felt uncomfortable, almost ashamed for his thoughts, a slight giggle pushing past his lips. "But that sounds like they think I'm 'Mother Nature' or something," his head darting from side to side. "How can that be? I'm only a kid. I've only been alive for twelve years."

The witch narrowed her eyes, "Exactly." The disdain the witch felt for all that was human evident on her face as she smiled a tiny little smirk of hatred. "How fitting that a child of man would belittle the magnitude that such a spirit would bring."

Patrick was beginning to get panicky, his voice and disbelief rising in his chest.

"But I can't be that! There's no way! Caretaker of the planet? Mother Nature? That's crazy!"

His mind was now a shattered piece of glass, his breath short. He turned to his friends. He turned to Death. To War.

The woman walked over and laid a hand on Patrick's shoulder. Her touch felt harsh and unclean. "But you and I both know that you are not such a being. If any of what they believe was true, don't you think you would have discovered this about yourself by now? If you are this person that they speak of, then why haven't you displayed these abilities before? You cannot tell me that after twelve years of living the life you know to be true, that these simple creatures have convinced you over nine days that you are something more? You are far more intelligent than that, aren't you?

"I believe that if you look deep into your heart you will find the person you have always known yourself to be. You will see that you are nothing more than a simple human child. A child of this planet. A child of your parents." The witch shook her head softly. "Not the being of hope that the humans have summoned forward with the words from the book. In fact, I don't believe that there is such a being."

"But what about the dreams they had of me," Patrick said, his voice falling with his own doubt. "What about how everyone seems to know me."

Patrick was dumbfounded for the moment. He had come all this way to be told that he was nothing more than a human? That can't be.

"I'm sorry to disappoint you, but you are only a little boy who is lost, and far, far from home. A simple youth who has been misguided by both animals and by men." The witch looked truly upset by the words she was speaking. "I'm sorry to say that you have been fooled. The animals have been mistaken in their beliefs." The witch smiled softly, her face falling to a simple state of kindness. "You are nothing more than a human, I'm afraid. Unfortunately, they believe you are something more than what you truly are."

The witch turned towards his friends and spoke with a soured voice, "You should be ashamed of yourselves."

Patrick had taken many steps, and laid many stones to build the foundation of belief that he placed beneath him as to what he really was. He had listened to those around him and taken their words to be the truth. Early on he doubted what was being said about him, but over time he had come to believe that what they were telling him about himself was true.

Now, with the words that the witch was speaking, the foundation of faith that he had built underneath him, with all his beliefs and securities, was beginning to crumble into ruin and despair.

"If you look deep inside you know the words I speak are true. What you need to do—what I am allowing you to do—is to return home with your father. To return to your family. There is nothing more here that you can do. Go home and live your human life, Patrick Brighton. Go home and live while you still can."

Patrick turned and looked at the animals, his friends, his face pleading for some sense of understanding as to why they had told him everything that they had.

"Bing?" he said, his voice quivering with doubt. "Syrian?"

But both of his friends were stunned by the speech that the witch had just given. Her words had even bewitched them, finding a way to overcome their steadfast beliefs. Now it seemed, they too began to doubt the abilities the Patrick possessed. Her words seeping into their reason of believability.

"Dad . . . help me," Patrick pleaded softly.

But his father stood dumbstruck, unable to form words to the witch's statements.

It was Kirsdona who stepped forward finally, pushing her way to the furthest point that the barrier would allow. She smiled slyly, an expression of someone who knew something dangerous.

"Wait a minute, Patrick. If Miss High and Mighty up there has all the answers, then I'd like to ask her one last question. One last thing I need to know, your highness, that still isn't sitting right with me."

The witch turned and faced the tiger. "Go on," she said low, her eyes narrowing.

Kirsdona cocked her head to one side. "Why isn't he dead yet? I mean, what are you waiting for?" she asked plainly. "If he's just a small human boy from some far off land that has no significance to any of the outcomes that this world has to face, then why is he still alive?"

The witch held her head high, allowing the question from the boy's friend to settle in her thoughts.

"That is simple, really. You have seen it for yourself. There are some humans that have the ability to stave off the plague. It must be that he has that ability."

But Kirsdona only smiled wider and shook her head. "That's not what I meant. What I mean is: Why have you been wasting so much time with him? Why don't you just kill him and be done with it? I mean, if everyone was so worried about what he might be able to do, then why didn't you just have Tye kill him? It would really make things move along a lot faster around here if you'd just knock off the banter and get on with it. Why not just kill him and we can all call it a day?"

The witch stood unmoving on the rock before the altar, her face glaring in the direction of Kirsdona like the stone that surrounded her. "Watch your words, tiger. I would hate to add your death to your friend's growing list of burdens."

Patrick, too, looked at Kirsdona, but not with the same expression as the witch. He looked at the tiger as if she had lost her mind.

"Or is it that you can't," Kirsdona pondered as she looked away. "That maybe this small little human boy just might be everything you said he wasn't, and probably a little more, eh? You can't kill him, can you? You only wanted him put aside so that he'd never find out who he really is. Because he's probably the only thing that can stop you. And I bet he scares you a little bit, too, doesn't he?"

Kirsdona smiled wide. She then shifted her focus from the witch to Patrick, her face gaining an all knowing look of satisfaction. "Patrick, the logic that she's using doesn't make any sense. If you push all the other garbage aside, boy, and look deep inside you'll find the answers you want. You've had them inside you the entire time. You know what you are, Patrick. You've always known, if you think about it. You really don't expect some fork-tongued, she devil to tell you what you want to hear, do you? Do what she said and look into your heart. Look deep, but be brave. 'Cause I think what you're about to find in there is going to scare the crap out of all of us."

CHAPTER 31

Patrick Unleashed

Patrick was mad. But it wasn't the same kind of anger that he had held when he witnessed the death of Dog. Nor was it an arbitrary anger. He was focused with what was before him and he knew where his anger should be placed.

The words that the tiger had spoken were not entirely earth shattering. Nor were they something that calmed all of his fears. But it was the wake up call that he needed to hear just the same. Kirsdona's words were the cold water splash that shook him from the paralyzing stupor he had been placed by the witch's foul words.

Patrick could see that the witch now realized that he was starting to doubt her. It was as obvious as the red on an apple. She could see that the entire gathering was pushing past the spell of enchantment she had tried to cast with her words. But she did not back down from the chaos she was trying to preach. She gave one last advance on the boy's spirit, hoping to turn the tide back in her favor.

"Man has made his final way in the world. It is now my place and my time. You and your human world have forfeited the right to go on. Do not let the blasphemous words of your friend place your life in my path. You would be wise to allow her chaotic beliefs to fall away. I am going to end the time of man."

Patrick's anger kept him calm this time. He shook his head and met her eyes with his own, his words coming out in perfect pitch, "But I won't let you."

And he smiled. It was not a smile of evilness or vanity, but the knowing smile that this was probably going to be the end of his life. And it was not an unwelcome thing. The animals of the world knew what needed to be done. They had known the entire time. But it had now finally fallen on his shoulders, and his alone. He was even sure that the reptiles and the insects realized it as well. He was the only thing that stood between this woman and the extinction of man.

The witch stood, unbelieving. "Then you are a fool. Do you really find any kind of significance to man's very existence? Your time has been spent in such miniscule moments that cannot even put a dent in the momentous time that the mountains have lived and risen. That the trees have grown. That the water has flowed. You are mere fertilizer to the rebirth of this world. Nothing more. How can you not realize that?" The witch walked closer to where Patrick stood, the disgust on her face spilling over into her speech. "Your existence is no longer needed. And will not longer be tolerated. You are nothing more than the clay beneath my feet. It is time for you to go back to whence you came. Back to the land. Back to the water. Ashes to ashes and dust to dust, my young friend. There is nothing within your human made hands that can stop me now."

The witch held up her hand and motioned slightly, her hand grasping something unseen. Patrick could feel a force fall around him like he was placed inside an invisible box. He pushed his hands in all directions but found no exit.

"I should have taken care of this myself at a much earlier point in time," she sneered at Patrick. "Let this be a lesson to you. Never entrust to others what you should accomplish yourself."

Patrick pushed with all his strength at the invisible barrier, but never changing his position in the least.

Then a calm came over him as he began to think through his problem. It was like a funny little itch in the back of his mind, something he couldn't reach to scratch, but rather it annoyed him enough that he started to pay attention to it.

The witch was afraid of him, that now seemed obvious. But what was she afraid of?

Patrick decided that he didn't need to fight anymore against the box. To push against the barrier with all his strength seemed useless. But then he had another idea. Instead he stood upright, his hands falling to his sides. If he couldn't go to the witch, then perhaps he would bring her to him.

His eyes went bright and he smiled as he looked in her direction. He then looked at the bottom of her robe, at the rock underneath her feet. He focused all his attention on the smooth, ashen stone beneath her.

It began like a small earth tremor, the ground rumbling low. Patrick imagined the rock sliding towards him, imagining the earth enveloping back underneath itself like a moving sidewalk he had seen at the airport, bringing her in his direction.

And then, amazingly, it happened. Just as he envisioned it in his mind.

The witch was as surprised as anyone. Her face told Patrick everything he needed to know, the shock and indignation that formed there almost made Patrick laugh at the sight.

"Do not attempt to play games with me, boy," she spit forward, small drops of spittle flying from her lips. "That would be making a mistake that will cost you your life."

But Patrick didn't care, and didn't stop, the witch moving towards Patrick inch by inch as the rock fell away underneath him, the stone grinding and groaning as it fell away.

The flies buzzed with hatred and came at Patrick like a missile, their movements swift as they tried to make their way into his form. But the barrier the witch had placed around him worked two fold. One, it kept him from moving from within it. And second, it kept anything from coming in as well. It kept the flies from making their way to him, their frustration evident as they continued to bounce away on the invisible box with every approach.

Patrick turned and looked back at his friends, his expression so confident that his friends actually were stunned by the look. "What is he doing?" he heard Bing say with a sense of bewilderment.

"You go, boy," Kirsdona said with a jump in her voice. He could see his father smiling beside her.

Then Patrick tried taking that first step again, thinking that if the witch was somewhat distracted by the slight turn of events then she might not be focusing her attention on him as well as she should have been.

This time, much to Patrick's delight, the invisible barrier moved. Patrick could feel it move almost six inches in the witch's direction. The witch looked at Patrick in shock. She raised her hand and pushed outward as if she was trying to hold Patrick at bay, but the boy still advanced. The witch grinned slightly and then raised her other hand, this time the boy hesitated. He was no longer advancing. Patrick pushed with all his might again, forcing the barrier to move forward. This time, as he did, a small trickle of blood fell from his nose. He reached his hand up and wiped it clean, surprised to see the red.

The witch smiled, "I warned you, young one. I told you that it would mean your life. Don't be so casual about what is taking place. It doesn't need to be this way. You still have your friends. You still have your parents. What more do you need?"

"That's not the point," Patrick said as he stared at the blood on his hand. It reminded him of the blood from his lips when he had the tooth knocked from his mouth. He reached down and absently felt the nugget still sitting in his pocket. It reminded him of the pain that had been inflicted on him from Tye. It reminded him of the pain that had been placed upon his mother. On his father and his friends. On everyone else in the world. "You have caused so much pain to so many people that did nothing to you."

And then Patrick took another step in the witch's direction. The woman tried to hold off the advancement, but merely slid backwards on the sandy stone beneath her feet. She slid farther and farther as Patrick's anger advanced him, finally coming to stop against a stone wall at the closest end of the arena. Her look was incredulous.

Patrick stopped only ten feet from her, the flies still swirling all around him, their black mass at times completely placing him in shadow.

"Let me go," he said slowly.

The witch stood straight, lowering her hands to her sides. "You do not know with whom you are dealing with. You are making a grave mistake, young one."

The woman did not smile this time, but her expression was smug as she moved but a finger on her right hand. The box that Patrick was in began to shrink, pushing down on him from every direction. He had to think quickly, the swiftness with which the box was collapsing was causing him to fall to his knees.

If this is how she wants to play it, then I don't have anything to lose.

Patrick looked above and saw that several large stones were sitting just at the edge of the overhang above the witch's head.

If I'm the person that they think I am, then I should have a lot of things around me that I can use.

He only thought about the rocks falling from their perch, and they did. But the witch stopped them inches from her head, the rock floating above her.

"I see that you have become dangerous," she said, her eyes narrowed.

The box that was compressing Patrick disappeared in that instant. Patrick was as surprised as anyone. He pulled himself up, astonished that she had released him so quickly. He began brushing the dirt from his hands, completely unprepared for her next command.

"Kill him," she said to her insects.

Patrick had forgotten about the flies. With the invisible box gone they were now free to attack him at will. Flies numbering in the tens of thousands settled over Patrick like a large black hand—and then engulfed him.

Bing screamed, "No!" as he pounded on the invisible barrier that still separated Patrick from the others. Patrick's father and the rest threw themselves against the barrier, each aghast at what was now taking place.

The flies stormed into every orifice on Patrick's body with all the suddenness of a train. They filled him with their wicked selves until every last one of them had found a place inside him. He shook like he was getting electrified, his eyes bugging wide, his body barely able to stand. It tickled and burned as they made their way into him, his body feeling like it was being inflated with a thick tar.

But then a surprising thing happened. As Patrick felt his body began to shake, expecting the flies to change him into something that was beyond recognition, he began to sense that the flies inside him were starting to panic, as if something was going wrong. Their screeching noise was reaching deafening levels just before they began to go quiet. After they caused a few more seconds of trembling his body began to slow down. And then it finally stopped shaking. Patrick turned back to his friends (looking like he was going to be sick) and then belched loud, still unsure of what'd just happened.

The others looked upon him with wide eyed wonder.

"Where did the flies go?" Syrian asked, concerned.

"I don't know," Bing said in awe.

Though the animals couldn't understand what Dan was saying, he still said aloud, "I think he just ate them."

Patrick turned and spit on the ground, trying to get the awful taste from his mouth.

He turned back to the witch who was standing quietly next to the wall, her form mostly in shadow. "Sorry about that," he said of the flies. "I didn't know that's what would happen."

Patrick could see that she was beyond anger. Beyond seething. He could almost hear her teeth gnashing, but she held her position just the same.

At this point Patrick didn't trust her reaction, especially after what had just happened. He began to back away before she tried anything else.

"I just want to get my friends free," he said cautiously, unsure what her next point of contest would be.

But then the witch began to walk towards him, Patrick watching as a black shadowy substance began flowing from underneath the witch's tunic. It flowed outward from her like oil, but it moved like it had it's own thought and purpose, like it was a being all its own. He took several steps backward as the blackness leaked from beneath her, trying to keep his distance from whatever the nasty looking stuff was. The witch then began to rise in front of him, her body expanding outward as she started to grow in size.

And then she came at him. She moved with a speed that was remarkable, her hands clutching Patrick's throat in a second. She picked him up off the ground and then moved towards the pond, Patrick's feet dangling below him. He tried to kick and fight her off, but she was incredibly strong.

"Patrick!" Dan screamed behind him. His father tried to go forward, but was stopped by the invisible wall in front of them. "Oh my god!" He turned to the animals. "We've got to do something!"

The animals did not understand him, of course, but they did understand his reaction. It was the same as their own.

"There is only one thing that I can see that can move this to our favor!" Bing screamed at them. "Kirsdona, Syrian, you have got to go free Sin!"

In a flash the two were moving towards the still chained boar. The serpent creatures saw what was beginning to take shape and came at the two, snapping and biting and spitting venom. Dan, once he saw what was taking place with the tiger and the baboon, ran behind them, hoping that he could aid them in any way possible.

The witch became aware, as well, to what was taking place. She screamed for the serpent creatures to attack the father.

Patrick, upon hearing the order that was given, began to kick and thrash even harder. The witch was still growing in size, and the black ooze that was flowing from her was like acid, beginning to sear and burn anything and everything that it came in contact with.

Patrick also noticed a sinister thing taking place with the witch—her appearance was now taking on a more demonic flavor. The once beautiful woman was now blackened and cruel, her face growing long and distorted, her features being replaced by a hideous mask that was bizarre and ghoulish.

A bolt of lightning then flashed the sky above them. Patrick and the witch locked eyes. "So you think you can frighten me with a little lightning? Oh, no, no, no! It's going to take a lot more than that to end this!"

Patrick could see that the witch was taking steps into the water. She waded in up to her waist and then slammed his body under the water's surface.

Bing watched as the witch was trying to kill Patrick, but at the same time aware that the serpent things were making movement towards Patrick's father. He knew that the man could not understand his speech, but he still knew that the man could understand dramatic expression. He began to scream louder than he ever did in his life, jumping up and down to get the man's attention. He could see the man hesitate and then turn, now aware of what was taking place. Bing watched as the man grabbed a branch off the ground and used it as a weapon, protecting himself from the wicked things.

Bing then began to hear a horse coming his way. He turned and saw that both War and Death were riding in his direction. War had her sword drawn and lowered to a cutting position. Death was the same, moving towards him with her scythe raised for a deadly blow.

Kirsdona, upon hearing Bing's constant yelling, turned and saw what was taking place. She immediately began running in the direction of the penguin, hoping to stop the onslaught that was about to take place.

The sky was cracking as large thunderheads moved into the area overhead. Blasts of lightning began dotting the landscape. And rain, with droplets the size of a quarter, began pelting everything around them.

Kirsdona, seeing that War was going to make her way to Bing first, ran straight for her. She yelled, "You're mine!" as she leapt at the warrior woman, catching her off guard as the tiger hit her broadside, knocking her from the horse.

But the warrior was quick in her recovery. She rolled to her left and came up standing, waiting for the tiger to attack. War smiled, "I can see it in your eyes that you think that you can best me. But be warned, you have no idea what you are up against. In fact, you're already dead and you don't even know it."

Kirsdona did not smile. "You may have one long blade with which to kill, warrior, but I've got several." And she raised her arm to show the two inch daggers that extended from her paw. Kirsdona then threw herself at the woman.

Syrian, after seeing that Kirsdona had pulled away to defend Bing, ran once again in Sin's direction. The boar smiled slightly as he sensed the baboon coming his way, but then began growling ferociously as he became aware that his sister, Death, was coming right behind him.

Syrian pulled with all his might on the chains that held his friend in place. He put his feet up on the wall, bracing himself for leverage, and pulled even harder. He could see faint traces of powder beginning to fall from where the chain was secured.

"Sin, if your sister gets any closer she is going to want to kill me. Pull harder on the chains!"

The boar surged his way forward with a more determined force, the chains creaking as he attempted to pull free.

Dan could see that the baboon needed help. He threw the branch he was holding at the serpent creatures and ran to the baboon's side, grabbing the thick chain and pulling with all his might to free the boar.

At last, with Death only thirty feet away (and closing) the chain broke free of the wall sending Syrian and Dan tumbling end over end away from the wall.

But now that Sin was free the great boar did not hesitate, running straight for his sister, the dark woman lowering the scythe for her defense.

Patrick was under the water the entire time, doing his best to fend off the wicked woman's powerful grasp.

"Let's just see how long you can stay under, shall we," she said with death in her voice.

But Patrick was confused. She had to know that he could stay under the water?

Or perhaps she had only been told? Maybe she didn't know as much as he thought she did.

And then he had to wonder, I know that I can stay under the water forever, but can she?

Patrick ceased his struggling to break free, instead grabbing the front of the witch's tunic and placing his feet into her stomach. The witch was now four times his size, but he turned and twisted his body with all his strength, pulling the witch under the water with him. He was now on top and holding her down below him.

But just barely.

He watched as the witch's eyes grew wide with fury, and he smiled.

Let's just see how long you can hold your breath, he thought.

But he knew now was the time to break free. In the back of his mind, almost like there was a little voice giving him instructions, he knew what he needed to do. He merely thought that he wished a great gust of wind would scoop him up from the water and move him backwards—and it happened. He felt himself rising away from the witch, watching as the woman pushed her way back to the surface of the pond, gasping for air as she broke the surface. Patrick then he lowered himself on the rocks on the side of the mountain.

It was like magic.

Was I flying?

But he didn't have time to wonder about that. The witch could fly, and she was now coming for him. Patrick threw up his hands in the witch's direction, and rocks the size of footballs began pelting the woman with such force that she screamed in surprise.

The witch threw up her own hands and the rocks popped like balloons, the powdery residue they left behind falling to the ground like sand.

"I see you learn quick, young one. But I'm not going to tempt fate and give you any more lessons in your craft. I have come to complete a task, and I will see it completed whether you are alive or not."

Patrick looked over the witch's shoulder, seeing in the distance thousands upon thousands of animals coming this way.

What?! Where did they come from?

The witch, seeing Patrick's expression, turned and looked over her shoulder as well, now seeing the same thing as Patrick.

She shook her head. "They think they are coming to help. When in reality they are only coming to their death."

She threw her hands above her head and spoke words that Patrick could not understand. It was a spell, Patrick guessed, one that he could not understand.

And then Patrick had to step back, for what he saw next was more terrifying than anything else that he had seen so far. From under the witch's robe insects of every size and shape began to flow outward. More insects than Patrick could even have believed was possible in the world. Ants numbering in the millions, mayflies, and bees stormed forward from her like a tidal wave. Locusts, flying beetles, grasshoppers, and cockroaches descended like an avalanche from beneath her being. It was like a dark hand of death as it flowed towards the animals.

Patrick screamed, "No!" only once, thinking he needed to do something as quick as he could to reign in the insects.

But the witch moved with speed. She threw herself at Patrick and pulled his arms down to his side, holding him tightly in place.

"No, my pretty," she whispered in his ear. "Now you will watch the death of your friends. Now you will witness the power that my father possesses."

The only thing that Bing could do was to duck. With War being handled by Kirdsona, Death was now left as the lone rider coming in his direction. Bing knew that he was about to be killed.

But at the last instant, before the black rider's blow could be delivered, Sin exploded in front of him and hit the side of Death's horse with such force that the collision shook the ground.

The wild boar was now roughly the size of a small horse, and a force to be reckoned with. It stood, snarling over Death's fallen horse, looking for his sister. The woman raised herself and swung her scythe in Sin's direction, the boar moving with a speed unlike any other, dodging the killing blow.

"I see that you've taken another shape this time, brother," the dark woman spoke, her voice strong. "After I disposed of the last form you covered your true self in, I'd have thought that you'd find something a little better suited for revenge."

But Bing could see that Sin was in no mood for conversation. The boar lunged for her again and again, the two locked in an awkward dance of death and respect.

Patrick watched as the insects moved towards his friends and towards the animals in the distance.

The witch held him tightly, but he didn't need his hands or arms to create his thoughts. He looked to the darkened sky and only thought that he needed to see a tornado—when one appeared. It funneled down from the rolling clouds, twisting and churning like a finger of God.

The witch, now seeing what Patrick was doing, tightened her grasp around him in such a way that made Patrick loose his breathe. He felt like she was going to squeeze him until he burst like a balloon.

"Are you having fun yet?" she growled in his ear.

The tornado was still moving towards the insects, arcing and dipping with a roar that outweighed all the other sounds.

It was then that a second tornado appeared.

And then a third.

An unnatural lightning flashed from inside of each, dancing to the sides as if the tornados now had arms with which to pluck the insects from the air and ground.

Patrick then wished the air to lift him again. With the witch's grasp almost causing him to black out, he knew that he needed to break free now or he might not recover. He rose higher and higher in the air, listening to the witch's shriek of alarm at his own blossoming strength, but the woman would not let go.

Patrick knew then what he needed to do. With the witch still holding on to him he headed directly for one of the tornados.

Kirsdona and War circled each other, neither one willing to give any ground. Kirsdona had made lunge after lunge at the warrior woman, but had only managed a few faint scratches across the woman's arm. But the woman had stayed calm, never giving any ground to the beast before her.

The woman was fast, faster than any human or animal that Kirsdona had ever come across. She continually taunted Kirsdona, begging her to throw herself at the warrior. But Kirsdona was just as adept at combat as the woman. She knew the games that needed to be played before the final assault would be made. And when that moment came it would be swift and merciless.

Kirsdona held her ground, hoping that the woman would finally be drawn into a slightly closer circle with which to operate. Kirsdona did not move any further in War's direction, only holding her position as the woman advanced.

Finally, as the woman drew within a few yards, Kirsdona leapt in her direction. The woman threw her sword high and then brought it down in a stabbing motion hoping to inflict the fatal blow.

To all that watched as the two fought it seemed obvious that War had won the contest. Kirsdona screamed as it appeared the sword raced through her, and she fell to the ground in what looked like was horrible pain. The great tiger remained motionless with the sword lodged between her front leg and her chest.

Bing and Syrian screamed, "NO!" as they watched what'd taken place. Dan could tell from the animal's reaction that what had happened was impossible. They were stunned.

But as War approached to withdraw the blade, Kirsdona lifted her head and smiled. She pulled her arm away showing that the blade had not pierced her body, but had only been cupped in her armpit giving the appearance that she had been slain.

Kirsdona snapped forward and snatched War by the throat, throwing her to the ground. She allowed her long claws to slowly pierce the surface of the woman's throat.

"How does it feel to know that I have your life at my disposal?"

It appeared that Kirsdona was going to end the torment and kill the warrior woman right then and there. But the horse that War had been riding was only a few feet away, and when the beast saw that it's rider was down it galloped over and kicked Kirsdona in the side, sending her tumbling over and over into the weeds several yards away.

War got up and mounted her horse again, a sly smile across her face.

"Remember, great tiger, that you should never turn your back on your adversary. Even if it is a horse."

And she laughed.

Kirsdona was now so mad that she could spit fire.

Patrick watched as the tornados tore into the insects, sending them up into the great funnels and them scattering them away in every direction.

The witch still hung onto him as Patrick contemplated what he needed to do. He allowed the winds that cradled him to move him into the fury of the closest tornado, hoping that the fierce winds would tear the witch from his back.

"Remember," she hissed into his ear, her speech barely recognizable as the wind howled around them, "that you can die, human boy. I am only wearing the shell of one of your kind. You can't kill me this easily."

Patrick closed his eyes and headed into the tornado. "We'll see."

Patrick let go of the wind that carried him as soon as he entered the tornado, allowing the great funnel cloud to batter him and the witch with an unbridled fury like nothing he could ever imagine. The witch let go of him immediately. Patrick only saw her briefly as she blew away from him with a screech. She tumbled from view in the dark winds, the dirt and rocks and other ground particles blasting at her as she went round and round.

The witch may have been caught up in the tornado, but Patrick was smarter than that. He knew that he could be killed by the tornado's fury, but he also knew that he was the one that was controlling it. So even though he allowed the witch to believe that he had put himself in danger as well, he had already set up precautions to prevent any harm to come at him. He merely created a cushion of air around him and rode out the tornado's fury like he was on an amusement park ride. In fact, he thought it was kind of fun.

Finally Patrick lifted himself from the tornado and allowed himself to be placed back on the ground on the other side of the barrier that had prevented his friends from coming to his side.

The animals in the distance had stopped their advancement, and could only watched in awe as the insects were being swallowed up in the three ferocious tornados.

Once Patrick was sure that all of the insects were totally destroyed (or at least sent so far away that it would take them half a day to return) he dismissed the tornados with a thought. He expected to see the witch come tumbling out of one of the tornados, but when the three wind tunnels finally dissolved, only dirt, rocks, and various other debris fell down to the ground.

The witch was gone.

Patrick looked around the sky for any sign of her, shocked that he couldn't locate her straightaway.

Finally the battered and bloodied woman descended from the clouds to the grounds in front of him, her demeanor calm. Too calm. Patrick was totally surprised to see her keeping her composure after what he had just done to her.

Patrick watched her closely. She stared in his direction for only a moment before she turned and looked over at the two smaller battles that were taking place. She lifted herself off the ground without a sound, and moved slowly in the direction of Death.

"It is time," she said in a frightening way, her words causing Patrick to go cold.

Sin and Death had been battling one another as the others looked on, their blows never seeming to inflict any damage to the other.

But then Death then did something that surprised everyone. Upon the slight communication from the witch, the dark mistress turned her attention away from Sin and remounted her horse. She pulled on the reigns, and without a word rode directly at Patrick's father. Sin could sense what was about to take place and tried desperately to stop her, but Death had gained the upper hand with her quick decision and was moving faster than Sin could keep up.

Patrick watched in horror as Death was closing ground on his father, the black mistress raising her scythe to deliver the fatal blow.

"NO!" Patrick screamed as the scythe moved down as his father tried to move away, but it was too late. The scythe caught him in the back and he fell without question, collapsing on the ground in heap.

All eyes turned to see what had taken place, the area awash in stunned silence.

Kirsdona was so outraged as she watched Patrick's father fall that she lunged at the horse that War had been riding, grabbing the beast by it's hind quarters and began climbing up it's back. The horse bucked and screamed as the enormous tiger dug her paws deep into the horse's hide as she clawed her way towards War.

Kirsdona could see the fear now evident in the warrior woman's expression, and Kirsdona growled as she sunk her teeth into War's back, the woman screaming and falling backwards as the horse and rider tumbled on top of the tiger. They landed with sound that was like no other. Bones snapped and twisted in directions that bones should never go, the three of them crashing to the ground in a freefall of death.

Patrick was in shock.

In an instant everything had gone so incredibly wrong. He couldn't believe how fast it had turned. His naïve thoughts had him believing that he was going to conquer the witch and her evil, but as he stood surveying the sights before him he knew that this was not going to be.

Patrick's legs could not support him any long and he collapsed to the ground. He closed his eyes and screamed to the heavens with a heart wrenching cry of anguish.

His father was dead. Kirsdona was down.

As Patrick knelt on the ground he watched as the tears that fell from him dotted the soft dirt below.

With his father dead, he was lost. He was finished. He could no longer go on.

"You have made a mistake, Patrick Brighton, and now it has caused you not only the lives of your friends, but your father as well." The woman shook her head in disgust. "You should have listened to me. You could have lived out your life in relative ease."

The witch then lifted her head and spoke to all within the sound of her voice that remained within her allegiance. "Kill them all. Even the animals. Let nothing live."

Patrick was in a daze. He heard the witch's words, but he knew he could do nothing.

He wanted to get mad. He wanted to kill the witch. But he didn't think it was in him anymore. He could only sob as he felt his heart break into a million pieces.

Patrick heard the words that the witch had spoke earlier now coming back to haunt him.

"Ashes to ashes, dust to dust."

"You are nothing but a human."

And she was right.

"Nothing more than the clay and dirt below my feet."

He was nothing. Nothing but a human. Nothing but a lost human boy.

Patrick felt the dirt at his fingers as he leaned forward.

His dad was dead. His friends were being beaten back. And the only thing that he wanted now was for all of this to end.

"Just a human."

He raised his arm and wiped the tears from his face.

I'm not just a human, am I?

Patrick began shaking his head without even realizing it.

I know that I'm something else. I have to be.

And then he heard the words again in his thoughts.

"Made from the same clay and dirt and water that created the very first man that stood upon this wide earth, many many miles from where you stand right now."

They were the same words that the witch had spoken, but they were also the same words that had been spoken to him by someone else. Spoken to him at another time and place.

"You are only a human."

It was the words that Death had spoken to him days ago in the clearing.

"Made from the same clay and dirt and water . . ."

Patrick looked at the ground in front of him.

This is what I'm made of? And he felt the dirt below his hands, bunching the wet soil in his fists.

"... clay and dirt and water ..."

Patrick then lifted his head.

Well, then if this is what I'm made of ...

"You are only a human."

That's when he felt the earth at his hands start to go soft, like clay. Soft like putty. In fact, as he began to recant the words over and over in his mind, his hands started to fall into the ground before him like he was falling into quicksand.

... I know that I can do more than just sit here and cry.

Bing was watching Patrick the entire time, unsure of what he should do to help his friend. The feelings of loss were almost too much to bear. Bing wanted to cry, wanted to console his friend in the worst way. The boy had endured too much. Much more than any of them had expected.

But then, just like the time when they were first at the graveyard and he saw Patrick disappear, he again saw Patrick fall forward into the earth. It was alarming at first, Bing wondering if Patrick was running away. But he knew that Patrick would never do that. With his dad laying on the ground, and with Kirsdona fallen as she was, Patrick would never leave them now.

But then Bing had to ask himself, "What is it that he could be doing?"

At first, as Patrick fell forward he thought that he was falling back into the land of the dead—and that made him afraid. He didn't want to go back there. But then he realized that this time it was different. This place wasn't the same as that land. He didn't fall forward in the same freefall type of way. It was as if he was in quicksand, ever so slowly drifting downward. He fell forward in an unending dark, but it was thick. It had a texture, sort of like wet sand. He tried to reach out and grab something with which to steady himself, but there wasn't anything to grab and take hold of. His eyes were open and he tried to see where he was going, but there wasn't anything to see.

And then he heard a sound.

Thump thump.

It was dull, almost inaudible. But it was the only sound in this place.

Thump thump.

It sounded like it was below him as he drifted down, but seemed terribly far away.

Thump thump.

And then he began to see a very faint light in the distance below him. It looked like the dying embers of a fire. A faint reddish orange glow surrounded by an immense blackness.

Thump thump.

As he looked down at the light it reminded him of looking through those windows where the glass wasn't clear, but still allowed the light to come through. You could see shapes on the other side, but couldn't make out anything specific.

Thump thump.

He was getting closer to the light, the color now growing to a more orange than red, with a slight pale yellow at the center.

Thump thump.

And he was getting warm. Not hot. Just a very warm feeling as if he had just stepped next to a small fire.

Thump thump.

Patrick held his hands out in front of him as drew closer and closer to the thing. He couldn't tell the definite shape of the glowing object, but he now saw where the 'thump thump' sounds were coming from. The thing was beating like a heart.

Thump Thump. Now loud and steady.

Patrick felt compelled to reach his hands out and touch it. It was large, about the size and shape of a hot air balloon. As he laid his hands on the thing it felt coarse like dried paper with sinewy threads running through it. It's texture almost like a dried husk of corn. And it was like the thing was talking to him, giving him silent, barely understandable instructions. It was like this thing somehow knew him, and knew what was needed. Almost like he had been here before.

Thump thump. This time louder.

Patrick soon discovered that the object had layers like an onion and he ran his fingers along its outer surface trying to find a way in. Once he had located a gap in the layers he began to slide in his fingers, prying back the edges as he slipped his arms in up to his elbows.

Thump thump. Still louder.

He wedged his arms to spread the layer open, and pulled his entire body in. It was cold and wet inside, feeling like he was climbing into a bowl of pudding. The light inside the thing was blinding. It was brighter than the sun. But Patrick didn't care and kept his eyes open the entire time. He could still hear the 'thump thump' of the beating heart-like object once he was inside, but it was now muffled and not as loud.

And then he knew.

It came at him in a wild rush of ideas and thoughts like something he had never experienced before in his life. Images and smells and sounds flew at him from every direction at speeds that were as quick as a thought. He could hear voices and cries in the dark. He could smell things cooking on a fire, and at the same time nasty things being flushed down the drain. He could see from the tops of the tallest mountains, and at the same time watch the fish swim at the bottoms of the deepest oceans.

Patrick just wasn't in the earth anymore, or under the earth. He was the earth.

He could sense the trees and plants. The water. The air.

Everything and everywhere.

The lakes in China. The forests in Russia. The birds in Spain. The glaciers of the Antarctic. The weather patterns as they encircled the planet.

He found himself seeing places and things that he had never known or imagined.

He was overwhelmed for he knew now where he was located.

He was inside the heart of the world. The Earth's heart. The manifestation of the living world.

It was incredible. Spectacular. Breathtaking.

As he reached out his hands he could feel every thought, every breath, every taste.

But he wasn't afraid. In fact, he was exhilarated. It was better than the best video game ever.

Then Patrick had another realization come over him, one that explained it all.

The Wicca had been correct. Patrick now saw that he was exactly what the witch said that he was not. He was the Earth's Sheppard. It's sentinel. His spirit was Mother Nature, if you will. And because his spirit was tied directly to the Earth and all its substance, the witch could not kill him. She couldn't lay a hand on him, really.

Patrick now saw as to how all the dots to the puzzle were connected, and he felt a calm come over him as he allowed the knowledge to settle to a place that brought him peace.

It was contentment. It was bliss.

He had finally found enough courage to reach his hand inside the magic hat, and when he did, he not only found a rabbit inside, he found himself.

He knew what he was—and it was ok. He wasn't afraid of the answers to his questions anymore.

But in a blink he found his tranquility disturbed.

It was then that he heard her voice. Its cackling nature drew him back to the land that he'd just left. And he knew in that instant that he needed to refocus his attention and get back to the problem at hand.

He was brought here for a reason. He was allowed to come to this place with a purpose in mind. And it was now obvious as to what he needed to do.

He searched for the instruments that he would need, finding them in the most logical of places. Seeds that were long forgotten, buried under years and years of ice and rock and sludge were Patrick's first point of interest. Oak and Birch, Pine and Redwood. He knew that these would be the instruments that he could use to bring this to an end.

Bing stood alone, and he was devastated.

They had failed.

This was something that none of them had ever talked about. It was something that none of them had ever wanted to believe would be a possibility.

But there it was before him, and he could not turn away. Not yet.

Kirsdona was moaning to his right, her legs surely crushed under the great horse that had fallen on her. War laid just a few feet away, the death wound that Kirsdona had inflicted still flowing red. Patrick's father lay in the throws of death, the only thing moving on his body was his chest as it rose in the shallow gasps of air that still gave him life. Syrian was still fighting the serpent creatures, doing his best to hold them away from the fallen victims. Bing could not see Death anymore. Or Sin. Their titanic battle must have taken them to places unseen. Famine was gone, too. The smallish woman must have faded into the shadows, biding her time for another day.

Bing looked to the horizon and watched as the other animals held their position just a few hundred yards away. It looked as though the animals wanted to help, but they looked confused, as if they didn't know what they should do.

Bing turned to look at the witch. Her bloodied, monstrous face glaring at him with her victory.

"The boy . . . should . . . have listened to me," she said with shallow gasps of air.

"He did what he had to do," Bing replied solemnly. "As would have I, or any one of us, had we been given the chance. He . . ."

But then Bing stopped abruptly, his words falling away. He turned suddenly and looked all around him, confused by a feeling that reminded him of the times when he would wake from one of his dreams. It was unexplainable. And there was a sound that came to him from a direction he couldn't quite place. It was like the air was speaking to him, calling to him, but he knew that was impossible.

"What are you doing foolish bird?" the witch asked, alarmed by his peculiar actions.

Bing heard something far off, like the first morning crow of a rooster. He wasn't sure at first, but then it slowly got louder.

Bing looked down at the ground below his feet. It sounded like the earth was beginning to split underneath them, somewhere far below the surface.

And then he smiled.

Bing raised his eyes to meet the witch. "You should not be so quick to claim your victory, demon. I believe our young friend has got one last trick up his sleeve."

And he stepped away.

The witch stood dumbfounded. "What are you . . ." And then she saw.

The first tree pushed its way up through the ground in several steps.

It became a seedling.

Then sapling.

Then pole.

The tree matured quickly, suddenly. The tree's rapid growth accomplished in seconds what would normally take hundreds of years to produce. Before long the tree towered above them, hundreds of feet high. It's leaves thick and plentiful. It's color the most luscious assemblage of green.

Then the next tree came, maturing in the same manner. It took several seconds for the tree to reach its fullest height. It was an amazing thing to watch. Crunching, crackling as it burst through the ground and growing with monstrous ferocity.

Then the next tree burst forward the same as the first two, only this time the tree took no more than fifteen seconds to reach its highest point. Then the forth. And then the fifth.

"That's impossible," Bing heard Syrian say behind him as he watched the trees grow.

The witch laughed as she saw the display. "I see the boy is adding some flavor to the planet. Simple decorations. Nothing more. You, my friend, are mistaken in his behavior."

But Bing never wavered in his conviction. He only glanced at the witch and continued his slow movement away from her.

The next tree came up. Then the next. One by one they burst forward from the ground, maturing in mere seconds to their fullest height.

Bing was surprised to see that the witch took no notice that the trees were slowly beginning to surround her. Encircling her as each burst came from the ground.

"What is this display supposed to mean?" she said aloud. "He's lost the fight. What is he trying to prove?"

The next group of trees were Sequoias. The largest of all the trees burst through the ground like nails being driven through a board. They quickly made their way towards her, tree after tree erupting from the ground with monstrous explosions.

And then it slowly began to dawn on the witch as to the measure that Patrick was trying to provide.

She squawked at her realization, staggering backwards as tree after tree burst just below her last place of rest.

Now trees came up through the ground two at a time. Some behind her, and some in front.

The woman darted from side to side trying to find any point of escape as tree after tree exploded around her.

Then the trees began growing into each other. Even though a tree may have been holding a particular spot, as the next tree grew forward it cracked and tore into the other, sending large ragged splinters and branches crashing to the ground.

Bing watched as some of the areas of ground could no longer support the weight of all the trees, the earth below them beginning to crumble and fall away leaving great, long cracks in the earth's crust.

The witch tried to fly away from the area, but in every direction she looked to go trees were growing faster than she could move. The branches were now so thick above her that they blocked out the sky and she had nowhere to fly.

Bing watched as the witch then waved her arms, trying to create a spell to cause the trees to bend and break in half. But again, Patrick pushed so many trees from the ground around her that even though she took down more than a hundred trees it still only took Patrick a few seconds to replenish what she had caused to fall. And it seemed to Bing that the woman was having a hard time creating spells that worked on anything other than man or beast.

The trees were now growing four and five at a time in rapid succession. Growing into and on and around each other. They twisted and split within each other, forming mutated, perverse looking growths.

As Bing watched from several yards away, the trees finally found their mark. A large Redwood tree grew so quickly that the witch didn't have time to move, and as the tree formed it caught her right leg in its astounding growth spurt and pulled her skyward. The witch screamed in agony as the tree formed over, and in, her very being. Bing could see a large branch had pushed through her thigh as it dragged her higher and higher in the air.

Three more trees grew in the same spot that the last had just grown, roaring upward with a sound as if they were growling. The trees splintered and cracked their way upward until their growth caught the witch at mid torso, pulling her and stretching her body in directions that her body couldn't go. Instantly five more trees grew where the other three had just grown, tearing asunder the previous three trees.

The witch was dangling from a hundred feet up, one branch running through her leg while another was still growing as it pushed through her mid section.

"No!" she screamed over and over as still more trees grew into her, barking and snarling like an animal. Finally a large Birch branch made its way into her mouth causing her voice to fall silent.

Bing turned away. He couldn't stand to see the final outcome. The witch was dead, of that there was no question. He listened as the trees continued to rip her into so many pieces that there wasn't much way that she could have survived. He decided that he didn't need to witness the final scene.

Patrick was gone, and that was enough burden to carry on his thin shoulders.

When the final tree had stopped growing, a heavy silence fell over the arena. When the realization spread to all the remaining reptiles and insects as to what had finally happened, it was like the wind was released from their sails. Insect and animals, friend and enemy, each stood apart from one another and ceased their fighting. Even the serpent creatures collapsed at the witch's death, their hideous forms melting away to reveal the remains of their true selves.

There were no words that needed to be spoken. No apologies were needed to be given. Each animal and reptile merely looked to the ground or to the heavens and sighed.

Bing immediately made his way to Kirsdona's side to see how badly she was injured. The great tiger was laying quiet, her breathing slow.

"Kirsdona, how are you doing?" the penguin asked low.

And for the first time that the penguin could remember the tiger did not give a sarcastic answer in reply. "Not so good," she said as she grimaced. "And I'm worried about the unborn thing I'm carrying inside me. I think I've broken my hip, Bing. I can't get up."

Bing called for Syrian to come to his side, the baboon arriving at once. Other animals came as well, each offering their condolences and support in order to help the tiger and the other wounded.

"What just happened?" Kirsdona asked, her voice weak.

"I think Patrick just delivered his final ability," Syrian said in wonder.

Kirsdona raised her head, and looked around the area. "Where is he?" she asked.

Bing and Syrian could only look at one another, unsure of what answer to give.

"Well?" Kirsdona asked again, this time with worry.

"He's gone," Bing said finally, his expression grim.

Kirsdona looked heartbroken. She gently laid her head back down on the ground and closed her eyes.

Bing then turned away from the tiger and gave the others the briefest of instructions to the others. They needed to leave this place, and they needed to leave now. No one was sure what other surprises might lay in wait for them, so Bing figured that it would be in their best interests to leave as soon as they could.

Bing then checked on Patrick's father. The man opened his eyes slowly at the touch of the penguin's wing.

"How are you doing?" Bing asked with concern, but then smiled when the man made a face because he didn't understand what the penguin was saying. Bing was not a doctor and could not possibly tell what kind of damage Death's blow had delivered to Patrick's father, but he did not like the pale color of the man's skin. More animals gathered around the man, each confused as to what they should do for him. Finally an older, bald gorilla came forward and cradled the man's head in his arms. Bing watched as the man smiled faintly at the sight of the gorilla, and then closed his eyes with a painful expression.

It was determined then that they needed to fashion a way for Kirsdona and Patrick's father to travel. With the tiger's hip in the state that it was in they knew that she would have to be carried. The decision to use a piece of wood as a make shift sled to pull her back to safety was quickly agreed upon. Another sled was then fashioned to transport Patrick's father. Some thick vines from the nearby areas were used as rope to pull the sleds along. It wasn't the most comfortable means of transportation, but it would have to do for the moment.

Before too long the instructions were given to all the animals as to what was expected, and within the hour they were ready to move. They gathered themselves along the point at where Patrick had been first delivered to the Reach, just inside of where the snow line had ended. Most of the animals would travel no further past that line, still wary as they looked towards the monstrous assortment of trees that stood as a monument of the evil that they believed still existed there.

Bing and Syrian were the last to leave the arena at the base of the Reach. They both stood overlooking the beauty and the destruction that remained, each hoping that Patrick would pop out from somewhere with a smile on his face, his body unharmed. But they both knew that it wasn't going to happen that way. Their friend was gone. No words were passed between the two, for no words could not do justice to the sight in front of them.

They both looked skyward, Bing pointing out what looked like an eyeball that was imbedded in the bark of a tree way above them. They both shook their heads and sighed, slowly beginning to make their way with the other animals.

It was a somber moment for all the animals.

Jeffrey N. Snyder

"Are we ready?" Bing asked to the large assemblage. Most turned and nodded, with the rest only hanging their heads in respect for the dead. "Then let's go. I do not wish to spend another moment in this unnatural place."

Bing looked up the mountains above him, to the hand as it reached towards the sky.

Belial's Reach.

It was not a place that he would ever want to remember, let alone ever come back to. Not for any reason.

Bing watched as the animals began to move, waiting his turn until the last to ensure that every creature made their way from this dreadful land. He watched as they traveled to the edge of the snow, and then beyond.

Bing lastly made his way to the shortened side of the last stone wall, still surveying the land and remembering their remarkable journey. How incredible it all had been. Bing shook his head and wished that it could have ended differently. It was a shame that Patrick had to give his life only after finally finding out who he truly was. Thinking that it was unfair.

Bing then began to make his way with the others. He was lost in his remembrance about the boy when he stopped abruptly, remembering something that he and the others had completely forgotten. Surprised that he had forgotten something so important.

He remembered the Book of Ages.

Bing instantly turned back, thinking that they had never found the book and had never really looked for it. It had to be around here somewhere.

A strong, cold wind began to blow in his direction. Bing looked to the heavy clouds that approached, thinking that snow would soon be here. This place would once again be covered in layers of ice and snow that no man or animal could dig through.

Let the book go, his mind whispered to him. No one else will even know of its existence. Let the book fall back to its place of secrecy.

Bing stood in silence for a moment before he nodded to himself and looked to the ground. He knew that his thoughts were correct, and that it was time to move on.

He looked back towards the arena one last time before he turned away, giving one last glance to the carved out stone at the base of the mount. But a funny thing caught his attention before he could turn away. Something above the stone platform that caught his eye and made him lose his breath for a moment.

As he looked above the platform he couldn't believe what he was seeing. Or what he wasn't.

High above the area were long chains secured to the stone wall, looping over and over unto themselves, but holding nothing.

They were empty.

Tye was gone.

Bing felt his heart go cold. He looked around the arena for any signs of the nasty creature, but saw nothing. He looked to the sky, but only saw the same.

Bing then looked to the animal caravan, watching as Syrian was making his way to the rear of the pack. Bing was now almost two hundred yards behind Syrian and the others, the distance growing with each passing moment.

He thought about what he should do, beginning to panic as he wondered at where the wicked creature could have gone. But he quickly decided that there was nothing he could do now. Bad weather was moving in, and with the state that the others were in Bing didn't want to jeopardize their chance to leave this place. Or to cause alarm amongst the others about something that he wasn't sure about.

Perhaps Tye was dead, his mind told him. Perhaps the trees had gotten him the same as the witch. Or perhaps he had withered like a dried up old plant, dying away in his own hatred and vile ways, his remains blowing away to the far winds.

Perhaps.

Bing smiled grimly and shook his head. There was nothing else he could do.

Not now.

He turned the corner, a cold, unwelcome shiver running through his body, and he began to make his way with the others.

CHAPTER 32

The Last Path

Patrick felt the brilliant light shining on his face and wondered briefly if he was dead.

He opened his eyes slowly, holding up his hand to block out the sun. He was in water, of that he was sure, feeling the gentle ebb and flow as the wet stuff lapped up against him, but how he'd gotten there he didn't have a clue. He blinked several times trying to clear the fog that was in his head as he tried to regain some sense of focus, but it was like he was on a ship that was fighting rough seas, his stomach was churning and his head pounded over and over as if a bass drum had kicked in somewhere close.

As he began to gather in his surroundings he twisted around and looked up, finding that eight strange looking, dark skinned men were standing over him. They had bones and beads and various other colorful ornaments dangling from their lips, noses, and ears, and with the peculiar way in which their hair was cut it looked like they each had a small, black turtle perched on the top of their heads.

And they smelled. Bad.

Patrick turned away from the harsh odor and tried to catch his breath, quickly realizing where the true source of the smell was coming—it was him. He smelled awful. Like dung.

And then Patrick noticed something else—he was naked.

He immediately placed his hands to cover the places on his body that needed covering the most, and smiled meekly.

"Uh . . . you don't happen to know where my clothes are at, do you?" he asked of the strangers. The eight dark skinned men looked from one another in a confused manner, and then began talking in a language that Patrick didn't understand.

The one closest to him extended a hand which Patrick readily accepted. They pulled him up from the sandy mud and weedy mire, and one nice gentleman removed the cloth from around his waste and presented it to Patrick.

"You don't have to do that," Patrick said, horrified as the man stood naked in front of him. "You can keep it."

But the smiling stranger would not take no for an answer, continuing to push the small piece of cloth in Patrick's direction.

Patrick took the piece of clothing with an uneasy, "Ok," and wrapped it around his waste with the one thin piece of string that was attached to the cloth. It only covered his front side (much to Patrick's displeasure) with his backside hanging out for all to see, but he knew that for the moment this would have to do.

The strangers then began talking amongst each other, pointing and waving their hands in different directions. It seemed to Patrick that they were giving instructions on what to do with him next.

While the men talked, Patrick turned and surveyed his surroundings. He found that he had been laying at the edge of a wide river, the water snaking and twisting away from him, its dark blue color flowing with barely a ripple.

It seems that he had emerged from an underground river that's exit point was a ravine at the base of several large, rounded mountains. Patrick thought that this must have been where the Earth had decided to flush him out. He was still groggy from his ordeal, his head swimming with nightmarish images that he couldn't tell whether were real or imagined. Images that were troubling and dark; of things he wished he could forget.

The Indians were now smiling (which Patrick took as a good sign) and they grabbed his arm and paraded him forward. Because Patrick was so tired he was in no mood to argue with the strangers and followed them without question. His overwhelming thankfulness at seeing another human was enough to give him peace for the moment.

Though Patrick had no idea where he was at in the world, it wasn't long before he realized that he was being led through a jungle. Large, broad leaf trees, plants, and bushes flourished in every direction, and in the distance he could hear a waterfall's full fury. The area actually resembled more of a rain forest, but being that he didn't have a clue as to his location he just went with the term 'jungle.'

Patrick walked for a long time that day, much longer than he had hoped. He eventually ended up at the Indians' encampment, noticing that the only things that resembled any sort of permanent structure to the place were a few crude tarps that were strung up against the trees forming make-shift tents. It was probably the only location that the Indians knew to call home, but to Patrick it was so sparse and dirty that he could only imagine that this was only a momentary place for them to stay.

Patrick was given strange food that he ate without question (even though it smelled like the inside of a wet sneaker), and was given a place to sleep for the night under a small overhang situated next to a tree. It wasn't much, but he fell asleep without speaking a word of protest.

Early the next morning the eight strangers woke him before first light, and with their persistent hand signals and awkward language communicated to him that it was time to leave. They traveled in and out of the hot sun for most of the second day before finally coming to a small, straw and bamboo hut that Patrick guessed was several miles upstream from where he was initially found. It was not much to look at, but it was a far cry from the place he had slept the night before.

Patrick watched as one of the Indians went inside the hut and began talking to someone inside. After a few moments of back and forth conversation another man came out, this one (thankfully) wearing clothes. He was a large, dark skinned man like the others, with blue suspenders that held up his sagging pants, and a white straw hat that rested on the back of his sweaty bald head. The man smiled broadly at Patrick, picking him up and hugging him as if he was a long lost relative. Patrick couldn't help but smile at the man's reaction. The sweaty man was the same complexion as the others around him, be he seemed different, almost like he was the civilized version of his friends. And he smelled different, too. Like tobacco.

After the man set Patrick back down he turned and disappeared around to the side of his hut, before long reappearing with a ragged bundle of clothes that he handed to Patrick, motioning for him to put them on. The clothes were much too big and smelled like his grandma's old luggage, but Patrick was glad nonetheless to have something covering his rear and he put them on without a word.

The tobacco man then went back around the other side of the hut. This time he emerged with a small donkey in tow. Patrick had noticed a small wooden cart that was leaning against a tree to his left, and in no time at all the tobacco man hitched the donkey to the cart, the other eight men beginning to load the cart with crates of fruits and vegetables that they pulled from inside the hut. Patrick could sense there was a long trip ahead of him considering the amount of food the men were loading, and he let out a deep sigh knowing that the trip wasn't going to be an easy one. The tobacco man then positioned himself on a little stoop at the forward most edge of the cart, directing Patrick to get into the back.

As Patrick walked past the donkey the animal gave a slight, "Buenas tardes, Senior Patrick," with Patrick responding with a friendly, "Hello," in return. Patrick knew that the others had seen this interesting communication take place, probably thinking it somewhat odd that the boy would talk to the burro. But Patrick watched their faces for any sense of unease, surprised to see that they seemed quite unfazed by the action. It was almost like it was nothing out of the ordinary to them.

Patrick knew that his parents would have a fit if they knew he was going along with these men even though he had no idea who they were, or where they were taking him. But it was weird how he felt such a sense of trust and understanding about them, that even though he couldn't understand a word they said, he knew that what he was doing was the right thing to do.

Patrick then waved goodbye to the Indians, still not quite sure what was happening or what they were saying. He didn't even have any idea where the tobacco man was now taking him, but he smiled just the same and got into the cart.

As time moved on Patrick began to receive more of a complete picture as to where he had ended up. He found out that after the Earth had pushed him from her bowels he had traveled through a series of underground rivers, finally ending up at a rain forest at the upper most part of South America, along the upper edge of a river that no one could ever tell him the name of. The tribe of Indians that had found him was the Xikrin, a group of men and women that for the most part civilization had left alone, and they in turn did the same with the rest of civilization.

Patrick didn't realize it, but he had just begun a journey that would last for a good part of the next three weeks. He would eventually be passed on from person to person, each one communicating to him little about where he was and where they were taking him, but he began to suspect over time that he was on his way home.

The modes of transportation stayed simple, most of the time it was a cart with either a donkey or horse pulling them along, with a couple of trucks coming into play towards the end.

Patrick thought it was strange, though, at how it all unfolded.

Patrick couldn't communicate with the first three travelers that accompanied him, each one coming from deep within the most remote places of their countries, and none of them had any sort of grasp of the English language. But Patrick didn't care. He slept most of the time anyway, his ease at being in the company of humans again made him feel thankful just for their presence.

Each escort carried him for almost four full days worth of travel. At first Patrick thought it was puzzling that when the cart that they traveled in began to run low on food it would only be another few hours before another person would be waiting for them just around the next bend with a fully stocked wagon to continue their trip.

After a while, though, he realized that it was the birds who were the overseers of the entire operation. As to how they were communicating with the humans, Patrick had no idea. But it soon became obvious as he watched them flying constantly above him that they were the ones who were making all the arrangements. In fact, on one occasion Patrick even spied an odd crow perched next to his next driver as he silently woke from a midday nap. As Patrick laid in the back of the cart he watched as the crow nodded back and forth to the driver, whispering ever so discreetly his intentions.

After what Patrick guessed was a little more than two and a half weeks of traveling by cart, he and the elderly Hispanic woman who was his present escort finally found their way into the United States, just making their way across the border into Arizona. Most of the roads were barricaded against anyone traveling into the country because of the fears that still existed about the plague. But the woman driving the horse and cart didn't hesitate as she crossed the border, ignoring the pleading signs to "STOP!! UNDER PENALTY OF DEATH! TRESPASSERS WILL BE SHOT ON SIGHT!!"

Patrick was slightly alarmed by the foreboding signs, but as he looked all around the existing border there didn't seem to be anyone in the area to enforce the daunting rules. And when the elderly woman turned and spoke in an assuring tone with a smile across her face about something that Patrick totally didn't understand, he could only guess that she was trying to calm his obvious fears.

Her soothing words helped a little, but not much.

It was a chilly, clear morning, just after sun up on the eighteenth day after he had been found by the Xikrin, when Patrick finally met up with someone who spoke English.

Patrick was laying in the back of the cart staring blankly at the clouds overhead, listening to the clippity-clop of the horse's hooves against the road, when he heard the old woman suddenly give a "Whoa!" to the horse to get it to stop. Patrick jumped up and looked forward, noticing a flatbed truck just a little further ahead of them and parked at an angle to the road. Patrick saw a man leaning up against the open truck door with an impatient expression. He appeared to be in his early thirties, tall and thin with a clean shaven face. He was wearing jeans and a Texas Rangers ball cap, and had a cigarette dangling from the corner of his mouth. Patrick thought the man looked mad, but when the man saw the two of them approach he broke out in a wide smile and welcomed them with a hearty, "Howdy!"

Patrick found out soon enough that the driver's name was Rabbit. That wasn't his given name (which turned out to be Joe Pendry), but it was a nickname that had stuck with him since birth due to the extremely fast way in which he talked. Patrick found out that the man also had an unusual habit of saying "ok" after each of his sentences. Like, "And then we went to the movies, ok. And there was this guy who just wouldn't shut up. Ok, now I can put up with some things, ok. But I'm not going to pay my eight bucks and sit there and listen to someone talking the entire time, ok?" At first it was driving Patrick crazy with all the "Ok's" that the Rabbit spit out, but after a while Patrick sort of got used to it. At this point he was just thankful to have anyone to talk to, even if it was a man with an annoying habit.

They drove for the remainder of the first hour in silence, Patrick leaning his head out of the open window and gathering in the scenery of the southwest. The man finally asking Patrick if he was hungry, with Patrick replying that he was fine.

It was almost another hour before Rabbit finally asked Patrick what his name was. Patrick hesitated for a moment, not sure if he should lie or not.

Could this man have heard my name before?

Patrick didn't think so, only replying, "Patrick," with a slight nonchalance that didn't preclude that he knew anything special.

Patrick sat in silence, still puzzled at how all of these people stopped to help him without even a question as to who he was or what he was doing.

And how did the birds communicate with all of them anyhow?

It was definitely strange.

"Rabbit, can I ask you a question?" Patrick asked, his hand pushing aside his unwashed hair.

"Sure. Go ahead, buddy."

"Why are you doing this?"

"Ok, what do you mean?" Rabbit asked without taking his eyes off the road.

"I mean, why are you driving me? Who told you to do this?"

Rabbit hesitated slightly. "My dad. He said that there was a boy that had gotten lost from his family, ok. He said that the boy needed a ride to Texas." Rabbit looked over at Patrick. "I guess that's you, huh?"

Patrick only nodded and looked straight ahead.

"So, how long have you been gone . . . er, lost?" Rabbit said with a strange hesitation.

Patrick wanted to tell the man the truth. Rabbit seemed like a decent enough fellow, but Patrick knew that there would be too many questions that would come up once he started. And he was just too tired to go through all that. Not that Rabbit would even believe him.

"I got separated from my tour in South America when the plague first hit. We were touring the ruins. I really don't know how long I've been gone."

Rabbit shook his head, "Ok, so you've been gone this entire time?"

Patrick nodded.

"Are your parents ok?" Rabbit asked, concerned.

"Yeah. I think so," Patrick said, trying to be vague.

"Boy, you've sure missed a lot of stuff, ok. I mean, ok, things have gone on that have just been crazy." And when Rabbit said the last three words his voice escalated to a high pitched screech.

Patrick played dumb, trying to sound like he didn't know anything more about the plague other than a lot of people had died. He allowed Rabbit to fill in the blanks for him for the most part. Rabbit liked to talk (which was obvious) and it also allowed Patrick to learn quite a few things about stuff that he had no idea that'd taken place.

As rabbit explained it, that after the plague was going full tilt and killing off a small portion of the world (and everyone thinking that this was going to be the end of all mankind) that it all ended rather suddenly, like someone had flipped a switch. Everything just sort of stopped.

As word traveled around the world no one was really sure who or what had started the plague. As each country became sure that they weren't the ones that started the plague, they in turn decided to blame their neighboring countries that they suspected of being the culprit. Every one was pointing fingers.

The northern hemisphere of the world had been decimated by the disease, with the central and southern areas relatively unharmed. It was weeks before the various health agencies around the world proclaimed that the atmosphere was free of any of the remaining evidence of the plague. They treated most areas as if a nuclear bomb had gone off and radiation still remained. Vaccination programs were set up to try and prevent any further outbreak of the plague, but that quickly fell apart due to the fact that no one even knew what they vaccinating against.

So they tested and tested, and tested again, at last finally proclaiming that the air was safe. But a lot of people weren't so sure. Soon the men that wore the uniforms, and the women and men that wore the gowns, pulled off their coverings and began to realize that the plague was entirely gone. So fast in fact that it seemed like it had never existed.

Word soon traveled forward as to the supposed real reason as to why the plague had been set forth, and who had unleashed it. But as with most things in the world, the word that traveled forward was met with skepticism and harsh denials. No one wanted to believe it. A witch? Please. That was only from fairy tales and nonsense.

It was only a matter of time before cooler heads began to think in a more orderly fashion again, allowing the fighting and the warring to end.

It took a long time for people to come from their houses and from their places of refuge to once again walk the streets. Baby steps. That's what everyone kept saying. Let's just take baby steps. They knew that the world needed to be put back together. But for most that was a daunting task. It was like someone had dropped an egg on the floor and was told to put it back together. It seemed hopeless. But it happened. Slowly, but surely, people were beginning to step forward who were adept at certain tasks. After two weeks the first power plant was put back on line for the upper Midwest. The upper parts of Nova Scotia and Europe also got power and water and other necessities back in working order at about the same time.

It wasn't great news, but it was a start.

As Rabbit finished giving his explanations he let out a low whistle and shook his head, telling Patrick that he was indeed lucky that he had missed all the bad stuff that had went on.

Patrick smiled faintly, and nodded.

Yeah, lucky. I sure was lucky.

Patrick fell asleep long before the truck made its way into New Mexico, but his sleep didn't come very easy this time. It was reckless and harsh, with wild monsters stalking his dreams at every opportunity. He awoke several times with a jump, Rabbit always asking him if he was ok.

When they finally entered Texas Patrick began to feel a sense of excitement build. It had been well over a month since he had been taken by Tye, and he hadn't been this close to his home since then. As he sat up in his seat he was still surprised to see that there wasn't anyone else out and about. He knew that the plague had killed a great many, but he still had an idea that he'd see someone, somewhere, at some time. But even though he peered back into the many side streets along the highway they traveled there wasn't a soul to be seen.

And that's when it hit Patrick.

. . . there wasn't a soul to be seen.

Oh no.

Patrick's eyes went wide, and he knew what he had to do.

Patrick couldn't go a moment further without knowing for sure. He turned to Rabbit and asked the man if he wouldn't mind doing Patrick a favor.

"A graveyard?!" Rabbit asked with a queer expression, his voice full of concern. "Why in the world would you want to go there?"

"I need to see something, if you don't mind. I know it sounds crazy, but it will only take a second, I promise."

Rabbit let out a long sigh and spoke, "Well I'm not very familiar with the area, but I'm sure there's got to be a graveyard around here somewhere. We just passed a couple of churches a little bit ago. Where there's churches, there's usually graveyards."

Rabbit slowed the truck and then turned around. It took longer than either of them had anticipated, but they finally came across a small cemetery on the outskirts of Snyder, Texas.

Patrick got out of the truck before Rabbit had even brought it to a stop. He ran towards the large metal gate, hoping beyond hope that he wasn't going to find anyone there. The gate was locked, but Patrick could see well enough into the ornamented grounds to tell that there weren't any spirits remaining.

And he smiled.

He didn't exactly know what had happened to all the spirits, but he imagined that once the witch had been killed then perhaps the spirits were free to continue their journey into the next life.

At least that's what he hoped.

When Patrick climbed back into the truck Rabbit asked him if he found what he was looking for. Patrick nodded and replied, "Yeah." He then let out a pleasant little sigh. "That's all that I needed to see. Thanks."

Rabbit looked at him a moment longer with a wrinkled brow, and then asked, "Any place else we need to go? Haunted houses? Mummy's tombs?"

"No," Patrick said as he laughed. "That was it."

Rabbit then put the truck back into gear and started back down the road.

And though Patrick wasn't sure, he could have sworn that just before he turned away from the man he thought that he saw a faint little smile creasing Rabbit's face. But when he turned back to look, the man's face was as stoic as it ever was.

Patrick sat upright the remainder of the ride, marking the time mile by mile with the markers along the highway. The fall foliage was still in full bloom as he looked to the mountains to the north. The golds and reds and oranges reminding him of when he traveled through the mountains of the upper Midwest. Reminding him of his time that he spent with his friends. It seemed like like such a long time ago. It almost seemed like it was a dream.

It began to rain when they finally hit Virginia, the dark low clouds delivering a storm that pelted the truck with tiny pea sized hail and winds that teetered the truck from side to side. But the storm passed quickly, and before too long the sun took over the sky as they continued the rest of the way.

Patrick was so exited now that he felt like Rabbit could drop him off at just about anywhere and he could run the rest of the way home.

And then when they hit Wytheville, Patrick started to get fidgety, his hands drumming along the dashboard, his feet tapping on the floor board.

When Rabbit finally pulled his truck onto Kimbletown Road, Patrick began muttering a silent "Hurry up, hurry up," with Rabbit telling Patrick to "take it easy."

And finally he saw his house. He didn't see his mom, but he hoped she was in there anyway.

The truck finally stopped along the curb in front.

Patrick turned to Rabbit and said thanks. Rabbit only nodded and smiled, and then told Patrick something that he never forgot.

"You did a good thing, young man. There aren't too many people that could do what you did."

Patrick was shocked by his statement.

"But . . . how'd you . . ." Patrick began to respond to the man's words.

"But don't worry about it anymore. Someone's going to be watching out for you from here on out."

And then the man winked.

Someone's going to be watching out for you from here on out.

Patrick stood, rooted to his spot on the street as he watched the large red truck move away down his street. Rabbit tooted the blaring horn twice before he turned at the corner, and then disappeared as if he'd never existed.

Patrick could barely move, speechless.

How did he know? How did any of them know?

Patrick heard the front door to his house open behind him and he turned to see who was there.

It was his dad.

Patrick stood with his mouth open, staring at his father in disbelief.

Patrick started running up the driveway at his fastest, with his dad meeting him halfway. They both started laughing as soon as they embraced.

Patrick was dumbstruck. "But I thought you were dead," Patrick said, his eyes wide.

His dad only laughed. "Nah. Not yet, anyhow. It's going to take a lot more than that to knock me off, kiddo."

"But how . . . ?" Patrick said, still shocked to see his father alive.

And then he knew. It was Death. She must have spared him even though the witch had ordered him killed.

But why?

His father then turned and yelled into the house. "Pam! Pam! He's here!" And then he turned back to Patrick. "I don't know how you pulled it off, kid, but you sure are something else."

Patrick looked up at his father and smiled. He then looked to the front of the house and saw that his mother was standing on the front porch crying. He let go of his father and ran to her. He could see that her arm was in a sling, and that she had several large bruises on her face still showing purple from her episode with Tye.

"Mom, are you ok?" Patrick asked as he got nearer.

She nodded and then hugged him.

Patrick held onto his mother for an eternity, never wanting to let go.

"I thought you were dead," she whispered.

"No, not yet," he replied. "I guess I'm just like dad."

And then his mother pulled away from him and looked into his face. "What happened to your tooth? You look like a hockey player!"

Patrick smiled and remembered the tiny nugget, now lost forever in the pocket of his old pants. "I did have it, but I lost it. I kept it because it reminded me of home."

His mother shook her head in bewilderment. "Your father says that you have some kind of special powers or something," her face contorting into panic. "How can that be? What can you do?"

But Patrick only smiled and hugged her again. "I'll tell you about it later."

Patrick heard his father moving up the walkway behind him. Even though he couldn't see him, Patrick knew that the man was smiling.

"Hey," his father said quietly, laying a hand on his shoulder. "I've got something to show you. Come with me."

His dad took him from the front porch and led him around the side of the house, walking through the gate to the back yard. When Patrick saw the little penguin shading himself under the twin oak trees near the back of their yard, he was amazed.

It was Syrian who saw Patrick first and ran up to his friend with several leaping bounds, the happiness on his face a welcome sight.

Patrick couldn't help but start laughing, his joy at seeing his friends beyond anything he could imagine. When he saw his parents it was with a vision of love, a bond that was brought by birth. But when he saw Syrian and Bing it was like he had just been handed his favorite toy from his youth. It was special. It was wonderful.

He hugged Syrian as hard as he had hugged his mom and dad, the baboon laughing a hearty laugh that Patrick had never heard come from the baboon before.

Syrian pulled back from Patrick and looked deep into Patrick's eyes, "I'd thought we'd lost you." Syrian then shook his head. "You are truly a remarkable human."

Bing was several steps away when Patrick saw him coming towards him. Patrick took two steps and knelt, scooping up the smiling penguin and holding him in front of him like a doll.

"You know, I can stand," Bing said with that same authoritarian way in which he always spoke.

"Shut up, you dumb bird," Patrick said, and smiled. He pulled the penguin to this shoulder and embraced his friend. "It sure is good to see you guys."

"And us, you. We didn't have any idea what happened to you. Where did you go?"

Patrick explained as best he could, telling them of his journey into the Earth's heart, and his way to Central America. Of all those that had helped him make his way back to his home.

"What are they saying, son?" his dad asked him.

Patrick turned and smiled at his father. "They're just happy to see me. They never thought they'd see me again."

Patrick's mother laughed. "Yeah, tell them we thought the same thing."

"There's someone else that I think you'll want to see, Patrick," his father said. "She's over by the trees," and he pointed.

Patrick followed his father's direction, looking past the shoulder of Syrian, seeing the orange and black tail as it curled beyond the shrubs.

"She's been hurt Patrick," Bing said cautiously. "She can't walk. But you're parents have made her as comfortable as can be. You'll see."

There was a soft breeze that blew Patrick's hair, tossing it back and forth in front of his face. He began walking slowly towards the rear of the yard, the others staying behind him. He wasn't sure what to expect. Of what he might see.

He rounded the tree that was closest, catching the tiger unawares. Kirsdona turned and looked up at him, her face instantly flashing full of surprise at seeing her friend. But just as quickly as the expression of joy spread across her face, it vanished in a second. It was replaced with a dour, uneventful look of scorn that more suited Kirsdona'a disposition.

"It's about time you showed up," she said matter of factly.

Patrick was surprised to see her positioned as she was. Her hind quarters were wrapped tightly with a white medical cloth, with both her legs suspended in the air by a low hanging hammock. She didn't look uncomfortable, but she didn't exactly look comfortable either.

Patrick began to cry and ran to her. He wrapped his arms around her neck and hugged her with all that he had.

"Hey, take it easy," the tiger said playfully.

"You won't break," Patrick said as he hung onto her neck.

"I already did," she said sharply, and closed her eyes.

Kirsdona then did something that surprised Patrick, showing him a side of her that she'd never displayed before. She wrapped her huge paw around him and pulled him close. And then the tiger did something that surprised Patrick even more so. As Patrick pulled away and looked at the face of the enormous creature, he saw a solitary tear drift down from her right eye.

"You do like me," Patrick said through tears. "You can try and pretend all that you want that you don't. But you do like me."

But the tiger never said a word, only pulling the boy close again and hugged him like no other.

Bing and Syrian, as well as Patrick's parents, made their way to the spot underneath the oaks and watched as the two friends embraced. Bing and Syrian then walked over and joined the embrace with their friends.

And as Patrick's parents stood, arm in arm, watching the strange spectacle as a penguin, a baboon, and a broken tiger hugged their son, they could only look on in wonder. Imagining that whatever had taken place between this small little group, it had created a bond that they would never, ever want to disturb.

THE LAST LITTLE BIT

In the initial days after his return Patrick was made aware of several things that both startled and saddened him.

The first thing his parents alerted him to was that the fact that he and his family were the only ones that were left alive in his subdivision. It was disheartening at first to hear the words come from his parents, but he had already known that the plague had taken most everyone in the immediate area. Death had told him that weeks ago. Still he hoped against hope that there might be someone, anyone, that could offer him and his parents some sort of companionship.

It was true that he still had Bing, Syrian, and Kirsdona to keep him company. And that was a great pleasure, indeed. But no matter how hard he tried, he knew that the animals could never fill the void that another human could bring to his life.

At first, Patrick's mom and dad, as well as Bing and the others, tried to fill the void of companionship that bothered Patrick from time to time, but it still never completely erased the loneliness of not having someone his own age to play with. It wasn't that the animals weren't great fun (in fact, Patrick thought they were awesome!) but it was just having another human around, especially someone his own age, would make it easier to share the points of interest that only a human could understand. And being that his three animal companions were already older than he was in terms of maturity and growth, it only made it harder for him to relate his feelings to them.

Patrick often thought that (at times) it was like he had five parents instead of two.

There were other things that came into play with Patrick's life that were going to be different as well.

They still had running water and plenty of food to get them through, and they had electricity from the generator their dad had found at the local Home Depot. With all the gasoline still left in the tanks of the remaining cars in the area they knew that the generator wouldn't go empty any time soon. But his parents insisted that they didn't burn any more gasoline than they had to, and that meant that they used candles at night to erase the darkness.

Patrick thought it was funny how some things worked while others did not. They didn't have access to phones or the internet, but they did have television. CNN Europe and one Latin American channel were the only two channels that came in clearly, and even though they didn't understand the language at times, at least it was something to give them hope.

Patrick's father had even gone to the local Radio Shack and picked up a small short wave radio to see if they could talk to anyone out beyond where they lived. But even though they could hear faint voices from time to time, they were never able to make complete contact with anyone.

Patrick likened it to the movie Castaway. It was like they were on a desert island and had no other contact with the outside world. It was kind of cool, but at the same time kind of scary.

It was weird.

It wasn't long before Kirsdona gave birth to her cub. They all had watched as the tiger grew fatter and fatter, and grumpier and grumpier as the cub grew inside her.

Sometimes Patrick would come out to the backyard and just sit and stare at Kirsdona during that time, watching as the pregnant tiger (with her rear end still sitting in a sling) would stew about her present condition.

"What are you looking at?" she would ask in a distasteful tone.

"Nothing," Patrick would reply absently, pulling his knees to his chest.

"You don't have anything better to do?"

"Nope."

"You know that I'm going to eat you when I'm able to walk again, don't you?" she would say in her most unkind way.

But it never fazed the boy.

"Um hmm," Patrick would only reply and smile.

But when the time finally came it was a rather easy and uncomplicated birth with Patrick's mother and father assisting with the delivery, the cub and mother both fine afterwards.

"What are you going to name it?" Syrian asked as he stroked the small cubs head.

Kirsdona paused for a moment and thought. She then turned up to Patrick and asked an unusual question.

"What type of breed was our friend, Dog?" she asked, her brow turning upward.

"He was a golden retriever," Patrick answered with a curious tone.

Kirsdona nodded and looked down at her cub, pausing for a moment of thought. "Then that is his name—Golden."

Bing looked up at Patrick in surprise.

Patrick bent down and touched the tiny tiger behind the ear, "Hey, Golden. That's a pretty cool name you got there. You've got a lot to live up to."

As the weeks moved along Patrick began to notice several other things that confused him and gave him great deal of concern about who he really was.

The first thing he noticed was that he could not stay under water like he thought he should be able.

When he first returned it was kind of a neat little trick. He had taken time every now and again to place his head under a bathtub full of water to see if there was any amount of time that he couldn't hold his breath. It was kind of cool, actually, being under the water and breathing just like he did when he breathed the air. He only wished that there was someone that he could show it to, being that it seemed that he could stay under forever if that's what he wished. His mother had even caught him doing it one time and scolded him severely. When he questioned her as to why he couldn't do it, and what harm he was creating, she really didn't have an answer. She only gritted her teeth and told him to stop abusing his special gifts and stormed away.

But today, as he tried to hold his face under the water as he stood in front of the bathroom sink, a remarkable thing happened—he had to come up for air.

He was shocked at first, immediately throwing his face back under the water to test his new discovery. But after another thirty or so odd seconds he had to jerk himself up and gasp for air.

Patrick was stunned.

No.

But then he thought that maybe he needed for his entire body to be under the water for his abilities to work. So he filled up the bathtub again and stripped off his clothes and dove under the water. But again, he could only stay under for no more than thirty seconds.

Patrick immediately dried off and dressed, running to find his mom and dad to tell them the news. There wasn't any easy explanations given, but his father told him that he probably was over doing it and that he needed to take a break.

"It's probably like when you eat too much ice cream and your stomach lets you know that you've had enough," he said with caution, his eyes arching slightly. "You need to relax and quit trying to do things you don't need to do."

Patrick listened, but didn't like the answer much.

The second incident was the blow that brought Patrick to tears. And it seemed to mean the beginning of the end to his recently acquired talents.

Patrick had always thought it peculiar that as he walked through the woods, that unlike most people who would hear the chirps and flitters that the different birds would make above him, that he could actually hear them carrying on conversations. It was annoying at first, trying to block out the constant jabber that went on in the trees. But after a while he began to treat it like it was background noise and learned to ignore it.

One day, while he and the animals were out in the backyard minding Golden while Kirdsona was asleep, Patrick sat quietly underneath a tree listening to the birds overhead. They seemed to be having a conversation about the impending snow and whether or not they should have moved south for the winter. The weather had turned cold (as it was prone to do in the late parts of fall) and Patrick looked forward to seeing the snow and the holiday season begin.

But as Patrick listened to their silly conversation a funny thing happened. He didn't notice it right off, but as soon as he became aware that it was happening he knew that he needed to find out what was going on.

It began as one bird began talking to another several trees away. In the middle of it's conversation it uttered a short, "chirp." Patrick thought it was odd that the bird would make such a noise. But then, as the next bird answered in reply, it too inserted several "chirps" as it talked to the other.

Patrick looked skyward, wondering what kind of joke the birds were playing on him. But after a few seconds he began to become aware that they weren't doing it on purpose. He got up from his seat and walked to the furthest part of his back yard, listening as other birds were talking farther back in the woods. It seemed that they were doing it as well. Going back and forth between using words that he could understand in their conversation, and then in other parts inserting that annoying chirping noise.

Patrick walked over to where Bing was sitting and casually asked how Golden was doing. When he heard Bing reply to him with a quick little "squawk" Patrick began to get nervous.

"What's that?" Patrick said with a edgy little laugh. "That was a funny little noise."

But Bing only looked at him curiously. "What do squawk mean?" he asked with a smile on his face, looking as if he didn't understand what Patrick had meant.

Patrick pulled away, "Right there. What you just said."

"What squawk I squawk?" Bing said with concern this time.

Patrick felt a fear rise up him that he hadn't felt since his journey had started many months ago. He quickly looked over at Syrian.

"Syrian, say something to me," he shouted.

Syrian wrinkled his brow and frowned. "What do you ooo?" he asked quickly.

Patrick felt the bottom of his heart fall open. He closed his eyes and staggered to one knee. Immediately Bing and Syrian rushed to his side.

"Eee ooo ok?" Syrian asked of him.

"Do squawk squawk me to get squawk?" Bing asked, his face full of worry.

But Patrick knew then what the others did not. Either there was something wrong with his hearing, or he was losing his ability to understand the animals.

Please no! Not that!

Patrick shook his head from side to side, not wanting to believe what he knew was true. He took a deep breath and sighed.

"I think I'm beginning to lose the ability to understand you guys," he said solemnly.

"What?!" they both said at once.

"That can't be," Bing said, his face full of disbelief. "When squawk did you squawk squawk."

But Patrick only lowered his eyes. "Right there. What you just said. I only could understand a small part of it. The rest of it sounded like penguin."

Syrian and Bing could only stare in Patrick's direction. His revelation hit them like a thunderbolt.

After a few days it was obvious that what Patrick had said was coming to pass. And, not only could Patrick not understand the animals any longer, but now they couldn't understand him as well.

Everyone was heartbroken.

Patrick's mother and father realizing that Patrick was so upset about what was taking place tried to make him understand that what he had accomplished over that last several months was an intervention from the highest kind. That he shouldn't be upset about something that no one else had ever had the chance to experience.

But their consoling words didn't help.

They also told him that perhaps it was time for his friends to find their way back to rejoin their families. That maybe this was a sign that they needed to get on with their lives, as well.

"You know, Patrick, I realize that they're great friends of yours, but maybe they have children waiting for them back home. They've only stayed here this long for your sake, not theirs. Maybe its time that you should let them go."

Patrick nodded slowly at their soothing voices and explanations, but it didn't make it any easier for him to swallow.

On the third day after this discovery, as Patrick was taking out the food to Kirdsona and her cub, he realized that the time he had with his friends was over.

Kirsdona's broken hip still prevented her from too much movement, even though Patrick's dad had hooked up an old skateboard with a wide platform and placed it under the tiger's backside. She could pull herself along pretty well if she needed to, but she was none to happy about it. She felt crippled. She felt helpless. She felt that she wasn't the same tiger that she had always been. Patrick didn't need to be able to hear the words come from her to explain how she felt. He could tell just by watching her face.

On that night as Patrick walked the food across the back yard he noticed that Bing and Syrian were standing next to Kirsdona and her cub. It looked like they all had sad expressions on their faces. It looked like they were saying their goodbye's.

But Patrick didn't want to believe it. Since he couldn't understand the animals any longer, nor they him, he couldn't tell them that he didn't want them to go. But when Patrick watched as Syrian and Bing hugged Kirsdona he knew that they were going to leave. Kirsdona couldn't go, of course, at least until her hip was healed.

Patrick stood in the moonlight watching what was taking place, when Syrian noticed him standing just off the back porch. The great baboon smiled a wide and toothy grin, and nudged the little penguin. Bing then turned and stared at Patrick as well.

Patrick moved across the yard at his fastest, lowering himself to the ground next to his friends. He hugged them both with all his might, not ever wanting to let go. But he knew that if they wanted to leave then he'd have to understand.

He wasn't the same person that had undertaken the great adventure that he had at the beginning, and now he knew his friends had returned to the same small creatures that God intended them to be.

Patrick and Kirdsona watched with sadness as Bing and Syrian made their way into the forest behind the house, the dark swallowing them up after only a few silent steps.

Time once again took a giant step forward, and it was now seven months since Patrick returned home from South America. Patrick never received any further word from Bing or Syrian. Not that he expected to either. And how could he since he'd lost all his abilities to communicate with them in the time since his encounter with the witch.

Even now, the most he could do with Kirsdona was to check on the healing of her hip, and to feed her and her cub from time to time. The tiger was finally off of the skateboard and could now move gingerly around the backyard, taking slow but steady steps. Her cub kept her active most days, and the great animal seemed to generally enjoy being a mother.

Most of the world had returned to as much of a normal situation as could be expected. There weren't any schools set up as of yet, but the local municipalities distributed school books for parents to home school the children as best they could. This wasn't the most pleasing thing to come Patrick's way, but he understood that it had to be done.

Most of the power was back on, and the telephone worked again, although there never seemed to be anyone that his family called, nor was there anyone that called them. Patrick had known that most of his distant family had been killed in the plague, but he still wondered why there wasn't someone that would call from time to time.

It was eerie.

Patrick's father didn't talk much about what had happened during that time when he came to find him, and the fight with the witch. It was still too unsettling for him to talk about. Patrick noticed that his dad was still having bad dreams about it, and didn't sleep much during the night. His father assured him that he would be alright in time, it's just he needed a longer amount of time than Patrick did to heal.

Before too long a new family moved into the neighborhood and took up residence just down the street from where the Brighton's lived. They were a nice middle aged couple, Tom and Becky Bowman from Atlanta, Georgia. They didn't have any children, and weren't too happy when they found out the Brighton's had two tigers sleeping in their backyard, but Patrick's parents seemed to enjoy their company, and as far as Patrick was concerned that was fine by him.

It was now eight months since his return from South America, and Patrick had just celebrated his thirteenth birthday.

He found himself on a hot August afternoon pulling weeds in the garden of their backyard. At that moment he worked on removing the unwanted plants that grew amongst the tomatoes and beans, working his way down to the rows of tall corn. Patrick had become a vegetarian of sorts since his journey last fall, his thoughts of eating something that he at one time could communicate with kind of gave him the creeps. He knew that he'd eat a hamburger again one day, or maybe a small piece of chicken, but he just couldn't bring himself to do it now. It was too soon.

Patrick turned and watched as Golden and Kirsdona tussled with each other in a playful act of fighting, much like Patrick and his father did from time to time. Patrick smiled as he watched the interaction, but his heart ached for the wish that he could once again talk to the two of them as they played.

"Patrick, do you want any lemonade?" his mother yelled to him from the back porch.

Patrick turned and looked over at her. His father had just gone back into the house, the door silently following closed behind him.

"Yeah," he said absently. "I guess. I've still got all these weeds to get out of the garden."

"Ok, but don't stay out there too long," she warned. "You'll get a wicked sunburn in this heat. Take a break."

Patrick only nodded and began pulling on the embedded weeds that were giving him fits.

He reached up and pulled a couple of cherry tomatoes off the vine to his left and dropped them into his mouth, the warm juices popping in his mouth as the tomatoes broke apart. He reached for another when he heard someone call his name.

"Yeah," he answered as he turned back, expecting to see his mom with his lemonade. "I'm coming."

But when he stood and faced the house he saw that his mother was still inside.

He looked around the yard and finally towards the forward part of the fence, expecting to see one of his new neighbors standing there waiting. But no one was there.

"Patrick?" the voice called him again.

Patrick looked around to all four corners of the yard and beyond, expecting someone to come into view at any moment. He looked into the forest, wondering if someone was calling him from back there. But again, he saw no one.

Patrick heard a rustling in the bushes behind him and he turned in time to see two small squirrels emerge from underneath the overgrown weeds to his right.

Patrick's heart leaped in his chest. He looked down at the two small creatures, not wanting to believe what he was seeing.

"You are Patrick Brighton, aren't you?" the first squirrel asked with a hesitant voice.

Patrick took two steps and knelt beside them.

"Yes," he said as he looked around to see if anyone was watching them.

The two squirrels quickly exchanged nervous glances, with the first one moving to within two feet of Patrick's knees.

"I wish I had better news," he said with a pained expression on his little face. "But Patrick Brighton, we need your help."